I0589507

Aristophanes, W. J. Hickie

The Comedies of Aristophanes
A New and Literal Translation From the Revised Text of Dindorf...

ISBN/EAN: 9783744784245

Printed in Europe, USA, Canada, Australia, Japan

Cover: Foto ©Andreas Hilbeck / pixelio.de

More available books at **www.hansebooks.com**

THE COMEDIES OF
ARISTOPHANES

LITERALLY TRANSLATED, WITH NOTES
AND EXTRACTS FROM METRICAL VERSIONS

BY

WILLIAM JAMES HICKIE, M.A.

VOL. II.

LYSISTRATA, THE THESMORPHORIAZUSÆ, FROGS,
ECCLESIAZUSÆ AND PLUTUS

LONDON
G. BELL & SONS, LTD.
1913

LYSISTRATA.

DRAMATIS PERSONÆ.

LYSISTRATA.
CALONICE.
MYRRHINA.
STRATYLLIS.
LAMPITO.
VARIOUS WOMEN.
CHORUS OF OLD MEN.
CHORUS OF OLD WOMEN.
COMMITTEE-MAN.
CINESIAS.
A CHILD.
HERALD OF THE LACEDÆMONIANS.
VARIOUS ATHENIANS.
AMBASSADORS OF THE LACEDÆMONIANS.
MARKET-LOUNGERS.
POLICE.
SERVANT.

THE ARGUMENT.

"*Aristophanis* Λυσιστράτη. Schol. Lysistr. 173, Καλλίου ἄρχοντος ἰφ' οὗ εἰσήχθη τὸ δρᾶμα. Arg. Lysistr., ἐδιδάχθη ἐπὶ Καλλίου ἄρχοντος τοῦ μετὰ Κλεόκριτον ἄρξαντος. εἰσῆκται δὲ διὰ Καλλιστράτου. Schol. Lysistr. 1096, ἐπὶ Σικελιας ἔμελλον πλεῖν πρὸ ἐτῶν τεσσάρων τῆς καθέσεως τούτου τοῦ δράματος. Four years were the actual interval, 'rom the sailing of the expedition, B. c. 415, θέρους μεσοῦντος, to the ᴅionysia of the Archon Callias, B. c. 411. Musgrave has neglected these testimonies, and has followed Petitus in the chronology of this Play, which he places in Ol. 92, 4, or three years below the true time." *Clinton*, *Fasti Hellenici*, p. 73. Droysen, (Introduction to the Lysistrata, p. 127,) "It has not been recorded whether this play was brought on the stage at the Lenæan festival, or at the Dionysia, i. e. in January or March of the year 411. According to the internal evidence of the time, the *latter* would appear the more probable." The plot is this:—Lysistrata, the wife of an Athenian magistrate, takes it into her head to attempt a pacification between the belligerents. She summons a council of women, who come to a determination to expel their husbands from their beds, until they conclude a peace. In the mean time the elder women are commissioned to seize the Acropolis, and make themselves masters of the money which had been stowed therein for the purposes of war. Their design succeeds; and the husbands are reduced to a terrible plight by the novel resolution of their wives. Ambassadors at length come from the belligerent parties, and peace is concluded with the greatest despatch, under the direction of the clever Lysistrata.

LYSISTRATA.

[SCENE—*the front of a house.*]

LYS. WELL! if one had summoned them to the temple of Bacchus,[1] or Pan, or Colias,[2] or Genetyllis, it would not even have been possible to pass through by reason of the kettle-drums: but now not a single woman is present here; saving that my neighbour here is coming forth. [*Enter Calonice.*] Welcome, Calonice!

CALON. And you too, Lysistrata! Why are you troubled? Be not of a sad countenance, child! for it does not beseem you to arch[3] your eyebrows.

LYS. I am inflamed in my heart, Calonice, and am greatly vexed on account of us women, because we are considered among men to be bad;——

CALON. For,[4] by Jove, we are so!

LYS. ——and when it was told[5] them to meet together here,

---

[1] "Bacchus was considered libidinous. Eur. Ph. 21, ὁ δ' ἡδονῇ δοὺς, εἴς τε Βαγχεῖον πεσὼν, ἔσπειρεν ἡμῖν παῖδα." *Enger.*

[2] "Colias and Genetyllis were by-names of Venus. At the orgies of the above-mentioned deities the *kettle-drum* (τυμπάνον) was indispensable." *Droysen.* "The difference in usage between εἰς and ἐς in the comic writers is this; εἰς is used before vowels, ἐς before consonants. The tragic writers so far recede from this rule, as to write ἐς before a vowel, when the metre requires it. Cf. Porson, Præf. Hec. p. lvi. On the other side, see Fritzsche ad Thesm. vs. 657 Elmsley's opinion, (ad Acharn. vs. 42,) who would expel ἐς from the comic writers altogether, is plainly false." *Enger.*

[3] "τοξοποιεῖν τὰς ὀφρῦς· συστρέφειν αὐτάς." *Hesychius.*

[4] See Krüger, Gr. Gr. § 69, 32, obs. 21.

[5] Hermann (Vig. n. 213), Matthiä (Gr. Gr. § 564), Kön (Greg. Cor. p. 159), and Enger (ad loc.) consider these forms to be *nominatives absolute.* On the contrary, Krüger (Gr. Gr. § 56, 2, obs. 5) and Jelf (Gr. Gr. § 700) consider them *accusatives absolute.* Philologers

to deliberate about no small matter, they sleep, and have not come.

CALON. But, my dearest, they will come. Of a truth women find it difficult to get out. For one of us goes poking[1] about her husband, another wakens the servant, another puts the child to bed, another washes *hers*, another feeds *hers* with morsels.

LYS. But indeed there were other matters more important for them than these.

CALON. What is the matter, dear Lysistrata, for which you summon us women? What is the affair? Of what size is it?

LYS. Great.

CALON. Is it also thick?[2]

LYS. And thick, by Jove.

CALON. Why, how then have we not come?[3]

LYS. This is not the fashion of it; for, *if it had been so*, we should have quickly assembled. But there is a certain affair which has been investigated by me, and revolved with much sleeplessness.

CALON. Doubtless the matter revolved is somewhat subtle.

LYS. Aye, so subtle, that the safety of all Greece depends upon[4] the women.

CALON. Upon the women? Why, it depended[5] on a slight thing then.

LYS. Since[6] the affairs of the state depend upon us, either that there should be no longer any[7] Peloponnesians——

would do well to reflect whether the list of accusatives absolute be not already fuller than can be maintained by fair argument. Cf. Vesp. 1288.

[1] The Scholiast quotes from Sophron,

ἐνϑάδε κυπτάζουσι πλεῖσται γυναῖκες.

For this use of the aorist, see Krüger, Gr. Gr. § 53, 6, obs. 3.

[2] " Quod dixit Lysistrata μέγα, accipit Calonice de virili membro. *Brunck.*

[3] See Krüger, Gr. Gr. § 53, 6, obs. 2, and note on Pax, 1077.

[4] See Hermann, Vig. n. 388.

Enger, objecting to ἔχεσϑαι ἐπί τινος, as an unstatuteable construction, reads ἐπ' ὀλίγου ὀχεῖτ' ἄρα, which is a slight modification of Dobree's emendation.

[5] See Elmsley's note on Acharn. vs. 335.

[6] "Lysistrata was going to add '*or any Athenians*,' but stops herself, lest she should utter any thing ill-omened for her own country.

CALON. Then, by Jove, 'tis best they should no longer exist.

LYS. ——and that all the Bœotians perish utterly.[1]

CALON. Not all, pray; exempt the eels.[2]

LYS. But about Athens I will utter no such ill language.[3] Do you conjecture something[4] else! If the women assemble here, both those from Bœotia, and those from the Peloponnese, and we *from Attica,* we shall save Greece in common.

CALON. What prudent or brilliant *action* could women accomplish? we, who sit decked[5] out, wearing saffron-coloured robes, and beautified, and *wearing* loose Cimmerian vests, and sandals?

LYS. For[6] in truth these are even the very things, which I expect will save us; the little saffron-coloured robes, and the unguents, and the sandals, and the alkanet root, and the transparent vests.

CALON. In what manner, pray?

LYS. So that none of the men of the present day lift a spear against each other——

CALON. Then, by the two goddesses, I'll get me a saffron robe dyed.

Brunck. "This passage has been misunderstood by Brunck, Dindorf, and Bothe, who think Βοιωτίους τε in vs. 35 corresponds to this μήτε. The Scholiast rightly explains, '*μὴ πεισθέντας ἡμῖν μήτε τοὺς Ἀθηναίους μήτε τοὺς Πελοποννησίους (μηκέτ' εἶναι). ὡς φιλόπατρις δὲ ἀπεσιώπησε τοὺς Ἀθηναίους.*' He might have added *ἢ πεισθέντας τὴν Ἑλλάδα σωθῆναι,*—although *πεισθέντας* is scarcely correct,—for the correlative to *ἢ* in vs. 33, is what is contained in 39—41." *Enger.*

[1] Comp. note on Av. 1597.

[2] Comp. Acharn. 880. Pax, 1005.

[3] "*ἐπιγλωττήσομαι, ominabor.* Cf. Æsch. Prom. 927. Schol. ad Choeph. 1045." *Enger.* "*ἐπιγλωσσῶ· ἐποιωνίζου διὰ γλώττης.*" *Hesychius.*

[4] "*Aliud te suspicari velim.* So Plut. 361, *σὺ μηδὲν εἰς ἔμ' ὑπονόει τοιοῦτο, hoc in melius accipe.*" *Brunck* "*ὅτι ἀπολοῦνται δηλονότι.*" *Scholiast.* "Have thou a different notion of me." *Wheelwright.* "Bessres denk von mir." *Droysen.*

[5] "Who sit dress'd out with flowers, and bearing robes
   Of saffron hue, and richly broider'd o'er
   With loose Cimmerian vests and circling sandals." *Wheelwright*
"*Ξανθίζεσθαι· κοσμεῖσθαι τὰς τρίχας, ἢ βάπτεσθαι αὐτάς.*" *Hesychius.* Menander, *τὴν γυναῖκα γὰρ τὴν σώφρον' οὐ δεῖ τὰς τρίχας ξανθὰ ποιεῖν.* Cf. Eustath. Il. A. p. 82.

[6] See Hermann Vig. n. 295.

Lys. ——nor take a shield——

Calon. I'll put on a Cimmerian vest.

Lys. ——nor little sword.

Calon. I'll get sandals.

Lys. Ought not, then, the women to have been present ?

Calon. No, by Jove, but to have come flying long ago.[1]

Lys. Nay, my dear,[2] you'll see them thorough Attic—doing every thing later than they ought. Yet not even from the people of the sea-coast[3] is any woman present, nor from Salamis.

Calon. But those, I well know, have crossed over at day-break in the swift boats.

Lys. Nor have the Acharnian women[4] come, whom I expected and counted on to come hither the first.

Calon. At any rate the *wife* of Theogenes[5] consulted the statue of Hecate, with the intention of coming hither. But see! here now are some coming!. and, again, some others are coming! Hah! hah! Whence are they ?

Lys. From Anagyrus.

Calon. Aye, by Jove ! In sooth methinks Anagyrus[6] has oeen set in motion. [*Enter Myrrhina.*]

Myrrh. Surely we have not come too late, Lysistrata? What do you say? Why are you silent?

Lys. I do not commend you, Myrrhina, who have only now come about so important a matter.

---

[1] " Nay, but, by Jove, they should have flown long since."
Wheelwright.

[2] " Althougb the feminine of μέλεος is μελέα (Vesp. 312), yet the vocative ὦ μέλε is applied to cither sex." *Brunck.*   Cf. Eccles. 245.

[3] " The *Parali* are those that dwell on the sea-coast." *Droysen.* See Herm. Pol. Ant. § 106.

[4] " The Acharnian women, the neighbours of the Athenian women, had, through their numerous losses, learnt to hate the war right heartily." *Voss.*   They were distant from Attica only lx. stadia. For the construction, see notes on Pax, 791. Thesm. 502.

[5] " Whether this Theogenes be the Theogenes mentioned in Av. 822, may be doubted. For the Hecateion, see Vesp. 804." *Droysen.* Θουκάτειον ἤρετο is Bentley's emendation (ad Callim. Fr. ccxxvii.) for τἀκάτιον ἀνῄρετο. Compare Lobeck, Aglaoph. p. 1337. " οὗτος δειλὸς ἦν· εἶχε δὲ Ἑκάτης ἄγαλμα, οὗ ἐπυνθάνετο πανταχοῦ ἀπιών." *Scholiast.*

[6] This was one of the Attic demi, so called from a hero of that name, who having overturned the houses belonging to it, gave rise to the proverb κινεῖς τὸν Ἀνάγυρον lt also dei oted a stinking plant.

MYRRH. I had great difficulty in finding my girdle in the dark. But if it be very pressing,[1] tell it to us now we are present.

LYS. No, by Jove; but let us wait for a little while for the women from Bœotia and from the Peloponnese to come.

MYRRH. You say far better. But see! here now's Lampito approaching! [*Enter Lampito.*]

LYS. O dearest Laconian! welcome, Lampito! How your beauty, dearest, shines forth! What[2] a fresh colour you have! how vigorous your body is! You could even throttle a bull.

LAMP. I fully believe so, by the two goddesses! I exercise myself and spring against my buttocks.

LYS. What beautiful breasts[3] you have!

LAMP. Upon my word you handle me like a victim.

LYS. But from what country is this other young woman?

LAMP. By the two goddesses, a Bœotian of rank is coming to you. [*Enter Bœotian.*]

LYS. Aye, by Jove, O Bœotian, with a beautiful bosom.[4]

CALON. And, by Jove, with the hair very neatly plucked out.

LYS. Who is the other girl? [*Enter Corinthian.*]

LAMP. A good one, by the two goddesses; but a Corinthian.

LYS. Aye, by Jove, she is evidently good,[5]—see here! in these parts!

LAMP. But who brought together this company of women?

LYS. I here!

LAMP. Then say[6] to us what you wish.

LYS. Yea, by Jove, my dear woman.

---

[1] "Doch wenn es so äusserst dringend ist." *Droysen*
[2] Comp. Eq. 269. Pax, 1045.
[3] Comp. Vesp. 933. Av. 826. Nuh. 2, and vs. 1085, *infra*.
[4] Supply ἰκνεῖ from the former line.
[5] Comp. vs. 1157, *infra*. There is a play on χαίνω, χανδός. The loose character of the Corinthian women was notorious.
      "Tüchtig, meiner Seelen, ist
Und recht Korinthisch ihr Doppelhafen hier und dort." *Droysen.*
ταυταγὶ is used δεικτικῶς. Bergler renders it, "*bonam profecto esse apparet hinc ex istis indiciis.*" Enger, who approves of Bergler's interpretation, adds, "i. q. κατά γε ταῦτα ἅ ἐστιν ἐντευθενί. ἐντεῦθεν is used in the same way again in vs. 802, καὶ Μυρωνίδης γὰρ *ἦν τραχὺς ἐντεῦθεν.*"
[6] "Μουσίδδει· λαλεῖ, ὁμιλεῖ." *Hesychius.*

Myrrh. Mention, then, the important business, whatever this is.

Lys. I will now mention it. But before I mention it, I will ask you this small question.

Myrrh. Whatever you please.

Lys. Do you not long for the fathers of your children, who are absent on military service? for I well know that the husband of each one of you is abroad.[1]

Calon. In truth my husband has been absent, O unhappy man, five months in Thrace, guarding Eucrates.[2]

Lys. And mine *has been absent* seven whole months in Pylos.

Lamp. And mine, even if he ever does depart from the ranks,[3] having taken up his shield, flies off and disappears.

Lys. But not even a spark of a paramour is left; for since the Milesians[4] betrayed us, I have not seen a thing of the kind, which might have consoled us in the absence of our husbands. Would you be willing, therefore, with me to put an end to the war, if I were to find a contrivance?

Myrrh. Yea, by the two goddesses, I would *be willing*, if I were obliged even to pawn this upper garment, and drink *the proceeds* this very day.[5]

Calon. Methinks I would even cut myself in half like a turbot and give [6] it away.

---

[1] See Krüger, Gr. Gr. § 56, 1, obs. 3. Cf. vs. 92.

[2] "This Eucrates is not the person mentioned in Equit. 129, and elsewhere; but probably a brother of the celebrated Nicias. After the battle of Ægospotami he was nominated general by the people, and offered resistance to the oligarchs, who sought to win him over to their intrigues. For this he was put to death as soon as the Thirty came into power. See Lysias' speech on the confiscation of the property left by Nicias' brother. We know nothing more accurately about the expedition alluded to in the text." *Droys.*

[3] "ταγᾶς, with the first syllable short. Hence ταγοῦχος with the same quantity, ap. Æsch. Eum. 296. But ταγὸς lengthens the first syllable." *Brunck.*

[4] "The Milesians, at the instigation of Alcibiades, had revolted in the summer of the year 412. Cf. Thuc. viii. 17. Hence the sarcastic proverb πάλαι ποτ' ἦσαν ἄλκιμοι Μιλήσιοι." *Droysen.*

[5]
        "So mir Gott,
Ich sicher, müsst' Ich auch sogleich mein Mäntelchen
Im Trödel versetzen und—vertrinken diesen Tag." *Droysen.*

[6] See note on Thesm. 526.

LAMP. And I would even go up to Taygetus, if there[1] 1 were about to get a sight of peace.

LYS. I will[2] mention it; for the matter must not remain concealed. We, O women, if we are to compel the men to be at peace, must abstain——

MYRRH. From what? tell us!

LYS. Will you do it then?

MYRRH. We will do it, even if we must die.

LYS. Then we must abstain[3] from the marriage-bed. Why do you turn away from me? Whither are you going? Ho you! why do you compress your lips and shake your heads at me? Why is your colour changed? Why is the tear let fall? Will you do it, or will you not do it? or what do you pur pose[4] to do?

MYRRH. I cannot do it; let the war go on!

CALON. Neither can I, by Jove! let the war go on.[5]

LYS. You say this, you turbot? And yet,[6] just now, you said you would even cut yourself in half.

CALON. Any thing else, any thing else, whatever you wish. I am willing to walk even through fire, if I must: this[7] rather than the loss of conjugal rights; for there's nothing like them, dear Lysistrata.

LYS. (*to Myrrhina*). What, then, do you *say?*

MYRRH. I also am willing *to walk* through fire.

LYS. Oh, our entire race, devoted to lewdness! No wonder tragedies[8] are made from us; for we are nothing but "Neptune and a boat."[9] But, my dear Laconian, vote

[1] ὅπα = εἰ ἐκεῖ. See Krüger, Gr. Gr. § 54, 15, obs. 1. For ἰδεῖν we must read ἰδῆν.

[2] Cf. vs. 97. Eq. 40. Ran. 1461. Soph. Aj. 88. Rex, 95. Æsch. Theb. 371.

[3] See Krüger, Gr. Gr. § 56, 18, and § 44, 4, obs. 2.

[4] "Was zögert ihr?" *Droysen.* "*Aut quid cogitatis?*" *Brunck.* Which is preferable. Soph. Col. 317, ἆρ' ἔστιν; ἆρ' οὐκ ἔστιν; ἡ γνώμῃ πλανῶ;

[5] Equit. 670, οὐ δεόμεθα σπονδῶν· ὁ πόλεμος ἑρπέτω. For this position of γὰρ, cf. Vesp. 217.

[6] Cf. vs. 355. Hermann, Vig. n. 332.

[7] τοῦτο refers to the *notion* contained in the preceding line, and not to any specific word. This is often the case also with ὃ and αὐτό. See Viger, p. 289. Krüger, Gr. Gr. § 58, 2, obs. 8. Eccles. 465, 887, 888. Plut. 236, 492, 524, 645, 778. Aves, 604, 758.

[8] Alluding to such characters as the Phædra of Euripides.

[9] "This singular allusion is to the Sophoclean tragedy of *Tyro*,

with me! for if only you side with me, we may yet restore the affair.

LAMP. By the two goddesses, women find it hard to sleep alone without a husband. Yet still[1] *we must do it*, for there is great need of peace.

LYS. O thou dearest, and the only woman out of these!

CALON. But if we were to abstain as much as possible from what[2] you now mention, (which may heaven forefend!) would peace be made aught the more for this?

LYS. Aye, much, by the two goddesses! For if we were to sit[3] at home painted, and approach them lightly clad in our vests of fine linen, having the hairs plucked off our bosoms, the men would become enamoured, and desire to lie with us; and if we were not to come nigh them, but abstain, they would quickly make peace, I well know.[4]

LAMP. Of a truth Menelaus, when he had taken a side glance at the breasts[5] of Helen when naked, threw away his sword, I believe.

MYRRH. But what, my friend, if our husbands leave us?

LYS. The saying of Pherecrates,[6] "to flay a skinned dog."

CALON. These similes are idle talk. If they should lay hold of us and drag us to the chamber by force?

LYS. Do you hold on by the doors.

---

where the beautiful girl appears with Neptune in the beginning, and at the close with two little boys, whom she exposes in a boat." *Droysen.*

[1] Brunck reads ὅμως γα μὰν δεῖ· δεῖ γάρ εἰράνας μάλ' αὖ, from the conjecture of Toup on Suid. ii. p. 164. Enger, ὅμως γα μάν· δεῖ τᾶς γάρ εἰράνας μάλ' αὖ, from the conjecture of Tyrwhitt on Suid. iv p. 420.

[2] See Krüger, Gr. Gr. § 51, 10, obs. 1.

[3] For this form, see Krüger, Gr. Gr. § 38, 6. Cf. Hermann, Vig. n. 280. Dawes M. C. p. 440.

[4] For this use of οἶδ' ὅτι at the end of a verse, cf. 59, 764. Plut. 183, 889. Pax, 365, 373, 1296. Nub. 1175. Aves, 1401.

[5] The allusion is to the *Andromache* of Euripides, where Peleus thus reproaches Menelaus, vs. 628,

οὐκ ἔκτανες γυναῖκα χειρίαν λαβὼν,
ἀλλ' ὡς ἐσεῖδες μαστὸν, ἐκβαλὼν ξίφος,
φίλημ' ἐδέξω, προδότιν αἰκάλλων κύνα,
ἥσσων πεφυκὼς Κύπριδος, ὦ κάκιστε σύ.

[6] "Pherecrates was one of the most distinguished comedians of the day." *Droysen.* "The proverb is used of those who labour in vain." *Brunck.*

CALON. But what if they beat us?

LYS. You must be niggardly of conjugal rights; for there is no pleasure in these acts which are accomplished by force. Besides, you must pain them; and be assured they will very soon give up. For a man[1] will never be delighted, unless it suits the woman.[2]

CALON. If in truth you two are decided about this, we also agree.[3]

LAMP. And so we will persuade our husbands every where justly to keep peace without deceit. In what way, however, *could*[4] any one, on the other hand, persuade the unstable crowd of the Athenians not to talk nonsense?

LYS. We of course will persuade our party.

LAMP. Not as long as the triremes are in readiness[5] and

[1] We should evidently read ἀνήρ, inasmuch as ἀνήρ and γυνή are here *opposed notions*.

[2] "Ξυμφέρῃ· ἀντὶ τοῦ ἁρμόζηται." *Scholiast.*

[3] This verse is also found in Av. 1630. Reisig (Conject. p. 133) would place the comma after σφῶν.

[4] For this emphatic use of καὶ, cf. vs. 836, *infra*. Nub. 785, 840. Ran. 737. Aves, 508, 1446. Pax, 1289. Krüger, Gr. Gr. § 69, 32, obs. 16. Enger reads πᾶ κά τις ἀμπείσειεν αὖ μὴ πλαδδιῆν; Dobree had conjectured πᾷ κά τις ἀναπείσειεν; For πλαδδιῆν, cf. vs. 990, and Kön on Greg. Cor. p. 229.

[5] A *somewhat* similar construction is Herod. ix. 66, ὅπως αὐτὸν ὁρέωσι σπουδῆς ἔχοντα. Compare also Soph. Rex, 709, μαντικῆς ἔχον τέχνης. Dindorf renders it, "*Non persuadebis, quamdiu saltem triremes instruantur;*" and Brunck, "*Nequicquam, quamdiu in triremes conferentur studia.*" The Ravenna MS. exhibits σπονδάς, Aldus οὐ λισπυπύγας. Bentley conjectured οὐκ ἀσπίδας. "The Athenians had bestowed their treasure in the inner cell of the temple of Minerva. At the beginning of the war it had consisted of 6000 talents of silver, of which sum 1000 talents were set aside for cases of extreme necessity. These were also touched in the course of the Archon-year in which the Lysistrata was brought upon the stage." *Droysen.* Cf. Plut. 1194. Bothe and Enger, rejecting in toto the construction of ἔχω with a genitive, adopt the emendation of Valckenär, Eur. Diatrib. p. 235. Enger reads οὐχ ἇς πόδας γ' ἔχωντι ταὶ τριήριες, and adds, "ἇς primus intellexit Koenius ad Greg. Cor. p. 188, qui Hesychium affert: ἇς· ἕως, ὅπως, μέχρις οὖ. Koenius ad Greg. Cor. p. 189, et Dobræus τριήριες, quod recepimus." But in such phrases as ὡς εἶχε ποδῶν, ποδῶν is not the genitive *governed* by εἶχε, but the *Genitivus Respectús = quod pedes attinet.* See Krüger, Gr. Gr. § 47, 21. Bernhardy, W. S. p. 172. Arnold, Greek Ex. § 146, s. And with this view only have the recent editors left the genitive in the text. Moreover, Enger's οὐχ is wrong, unless followed by a comma or longer stop.

the inexhaustible sum of money is in the temple of the goddess

Lys. But this also has been well provided for; for to-day
we shall seize upon the Acropolis. For orders have been
given to the oldest to do this,[1] while we arrange these mat
ters, to seize upon the Acropolis while pretending to sacrifice.

Lamp. It may be altogether well,[2] for so you represent it.

Lys. Why then, Lampito, do we not swear to these things
as soon as possible, that they may be inviolable?

Lamp. Produce the oath, that we may swear.

Lys. You say well. Where is the policewoman?[3] Whither
are you staring? Set the shield before us upside down; and
let some one give me the sacrificial parts.

Calon. Lysistrata, what oath in the world will you make
us swear?

Lys. What? Over a shield, slaying sheep, as they say
Æschylus[4] once *did.*

Calon. Nay, do not swear anything about peace, O Lysistrata, over a shield.

Lys. What, then, should the oath be?

Calon. If we were to get a white horse[5] from some
quarter and sacrifice it as a victim.

Lys. For what purpose a white horse?

Calon. How then[6] shall we swear?

Lys. I will tell you, by Jove, if you wish. Let us place a
large black cup upside down,[7] and slaughter a Thasian jar of
wine, and swear over the cup—to pour no water in.

[1] "Den ältesten Fraun ist's aufgetragen, das zu thun." *Droysen.*
Brunck wrongly makes τοῦτο the nominative to προστέτακται, which
is used *impersonally.* τοῦτο is the object of δρᾶν, and is afterwards
explained by the infinitive in vs. 179. Comp. note on Thesm. 520.
For δοκούσαις, see Hermann, Vig. n. 217. Kön, Greg. Cor. p. 79.

[2] "*Omnino bene se res habebit, nam isto modo,* i. e. bene, *se habent
ea quoque, quæ abs te dicta sunt.* παντᾶ must be joined with καλῶς.
So vs. 1013, κράτιστα γὰρ παντᾶ λέγεις. And 169, παντᾶ δικαίως."
Enger.

[3] A word formed in jest, like κηρύκαινα, *a woman-herald,* Eccles. 713.

[4] The allusion is to Æsch. Theb. 42, seq. Enger reads εἰς ἀσπίδ',
ὥσπερ φάσ' ἐν Αἰσχύλῳ ποτέ.

[5] "λευκὸς ἵππος is the woman's substitute for the *bull* in Æschylus." *Brunck.*

[6] Cf. Av. 98, 1016. Equit. 955. Eccles. 927. So ἀλλὰ τίς; *who
then?* Nub. 827; and ἀλλὰ ποῖ; *whither then?* Pax, 222 Cf. vs. 493.

[7] Cf. Æschyl. Sept. Theb. 42, foll.

LAMP. O earth! I commend the oath prodigiously.[1]

LYS. Let some one bring a cup from within and a jar.

CALON. O dearest women, what a vast jar![2] Any one would be immediately exhilarated if he got this.

LYS. Set this down and take hold of the boar.[3] Mistress Persuasion,[4] and Cup sacred to friendship, receive the victims, being friendly to the women.[5] [*Calonice here pours the wine into the cup.*]

CALON. The blood is of a good colour and bubbles out well.

LAMP. (*stooping and smelling at the wine*). Moreover it smells sweet too, by Castor!

LYS. Permit me, women, to swear the first. [*Tries to drink out of the jar.*]

CALON. No, by Venus, unless you obtain it by lot.

LYS. Lampito, do all of you lay hold[6] on the cup, and let one say in behalf of *the rest* of you whatever I say; and you shall swear to these things, and abide by them. "There is no one, either paramour or husband"—

CALON. "There is no one, either paramour or husband"—

" Lysistrata's *μέλαιναν μεγάλην κύλικα* is substituted for the *μελάνδετον σάκος* of Æschylus, and *ὑπτίαν*, because the shield was put in that position. Cf. vs. 185, *supra*, and Ach. 583." *Brunck*. For *ὕπτιος* in this passage, see Liddell's Lex. in voc. For the participles, see note on Plut. 69, and Krüger, Gr. Gr. § 56, 15, obs. 2.

[1] *ἄφατον ὡς* go together, after the analogy of *θαυμαστὸς ὅσος, θαυμαστῶς ὡς*, &c. Comp. Viger, viii. sect. ix. Hermann, ib. n. 87. Krüger, Gr. Gr. § 51, 10, obs. 12. Jelf, § 823, obs. 7. Schäfer, Greg. Cor. p. 25. Arist. Av. 427. Nub. 750. vs. 1148, *infra*. Plut. 750. Herod. iv. 194. Vesp. 1279. So Menander, Fragm. ccxxxviii., *ἔγημε θαυμαστὴν γυναῖχ' ὡς σώφρονα*. "For *φεῦ δᾶ*, see Dindorf in Steph. Thes. ii. p. 488, and for *ἐπαινίω*, Kön on Greg. Cor. p. 229." *Enger*.

[2] " Reiske, *ὁ κεραμὼν ὅσος*, '*urna, testa, seria*, in genitivo *κεραμῶνος*, ut *πιθὼν, πυλὼν, πορνὼν*, &c.' I have adopted this with Dindorf, who aptly remarks that *πρηγορὼν* in Av. 1113, Equit. 374, has been similarly corrupted into *πρηγορεών*." *Enger*.

[3] By the *κάπρος* (the usual victim in such sacrifices) she means the *στάμνιον* (vs. 196) which is now brought on the stage. The easy flowing of the *blood* (vs. 205) was reckoned a good omen. Here it is applied to the spurting of the *wine* from the jar. Cf. vs. 238, where *καθαγίσω* must be understood of *drinking at the jar*.

[4] Because she hopes to persuade the men to make peace.

[5] Enger construes *ταῖς γυναιξὶν* after *δέξαι*. For this construction, see Pors. Hec. 533.

[6] Comp. Acharn. 259. Av. 850, and vs. 649, *infra*. "*ἐμπεδώσει ἀσφαλίσετε*." *Scholiast*. For *ἄπερ καὶ*, see note on Pax, 363.

Lys. "Who shall approach me in an amorous mood."
Say it!

Calon. "Who shall approach me in an amorous mood."
Bless me! Lysistrata, my knees sink under me.

Lys. "But I will spend my life at home in[1] chastity"—

Calon. "But I will spend my life at home in chastity"—

Lys. "Wearing a saffron-coloured robe, and decked out"—

Calon. "Wearing a saffron-coloured robe, and decked
out"—

Lys. "So that my husband may be as much as possible
enamoured"—

Calon. "So that my husband may be as much as possible
enamoured"—

Lys. "And I will never willingly comply with my husband"—

Calon. "And I will never willingly comply with my
husband"—

Lys. "But if he force me by violence against my will"—

Calon. "But if he force me by violence against my will"—

Lys. "I will be niggardly of conjugal rights and will not
indulge him"—

Calon. "I will be niggardly of conjugal rights and will
not indulge him"—

Lys. "I will not raise my slippers towards the roof" —

Calon. "I will not raise my slippers towards the roof"—

Lys. "I will not stand like a lioness upon a cheese-scraper"—

Calon. "I will not stand like a lioness upon a cheese-
scraper"—

Lys. "If[2] I abide by these, may I drink from hence"—

Calon. "If I abide by these, may I drink from hence"—

Lys. "But if I violate them, may the cup be[3] filled with
water"—

---

[1] "For the feminine form ἀταυρώτη Dindorf refers to Porson,
Med. vs. 822. Cf. Eustathius, Od. p. 1554, 29. Il. p. 259, 8, and p.
581, 20." *Enger.*

[2] "The sense of the conjunction *if* is often expressed by a parti-
ciple." *Franz.* Cf. Krüger, Gr. Gr. § 56, 11. Bergler compares
Eur. Iph. Taur. vs. 790, τὸν δ' ὅρκον, ὃν κατώμασ', ἐμπεδώσομεν.
Ibid. 758, τὸν ὅρκον εἶναι τόνδε μηκέτ' ἔμπεδον.

[3] For this form of the optative, cf. Ach. 236. Plut. 991, and vs.
253. *infra.* Soph. Phil. 119. Krüger. Gr. Gr. § 31, 9, obs. 5, and
Pars ii. p. 138. On the other side, see Buttmann, Gr. Gr. ii. p. 274.

CALON. "But if I violate them, may the cup be filled with water"—

LYS. Do you all swear to these?

MYRRH. Yea, by Jove!

LYS. Come, let me dedicate this. [*Takes a drink.*]

CALON. Your share *only*, my dear, that from the first we may be friends[1] of each other. [*The goblet is passed round. A cry of women is heard behind the scene.*]

LAMP. What shout *is that?*

LYS. The very thing[2] I spoke of! for the women have already seized upon the Acropolis of the goddess. Come, Lampito, do you go and arrange well your affairs, and leave these here with us as[3] hostages; and let us, along with the other women who are in the citadel,[4] go in and help to put in the bolts.

CALON. Do you not think, then, that the men will immediately render joint aid against us?

LYS. I care little for them. For they will not come with either so great threats or so much fire as to open these gates, except upon the terms which we mentioned.

CALON. Never, by Venus! For we women should be called unconquerable and abominable to no purpose. [*Enter chorus of old men carrying billets of wood and pans of charcoal.*]

CHO. Advance, Draces, lead on slowly, although[5] you are pained in your shoulder with carrying so great a weight of a trunk of fresh olive. Of a truth there are many unexpected things in long life, alas! for who would ever have expected, O Strymodorus,[6] to hear that women whom we

---

[1] "With φίλος, ἐχθρὸς, and πολέμιος, the genitive also is found; for the most part, however, only where they are used as substantives. Comp. § 47, 10." *Krüger.*

[2] See Krüger, Gr. Gr. § 51, 7, obs. 11.

[3] See Krüger, Gr. Gr. § 57, 3, obs. 1. Kön, Greg. Cor. p. 331, and note on Plut. 314.

[4] "πόλις anciently meant a particular part of the city, viz. the *citadel.* Cf. vss. 266, 302, 317, 487, 754, 758, 912, 1183." *Brunck.* The dative (ταῖς ἄλλαισι) depends on ξυνεμβάλωμεν.

[5] See Krüger's Gr. Gr. § 65, 5, obs. 15. Hermann, Vig. n. 307. For this whole chorus, see Burgess, Class. J. xxx. p. 287.

[6] This name appears also in the Vespæ, vs. 233, as belonging to one of the Chorus. And in Acharn. 272, as the name of a countryman.

supported at home, a manifest pest, would get possession[1] of the
sacred image, and seize upon my Acropolis, and also make fast
the Propylæa[2] with bolts and bars? But let us hasten to the
citadel as soon as possible, O Philurgus, so that we may place
these trunks round about them, as many as began and prose-
cuted this business, and heap up one pyre, and with our own
hands set fire to them all with one vote ; and the wife[3] of
Lycon the first. For, by Ceres, she shall not laugh at us,
while I am alive! Since not even Cleomenes,[4] who was
the first that seized upon it, departed scot-free ;[5] but nevertheless, though breathing Laconian fury, he went off, having
delivered up his arms[6] to me, with a very small little cloak,
dirty, squalid, unkempt, unwashed for seven years. So
savagely did I besiege that noted[7] man, sleeping at the doors
seventeen[8] deep. And shall I not then being present restrain
from so great daring these enemies to Euripides and to all the
gods? No longer then may my trophy[9] be in Tetrapolis!

[1] Comp. Blomf. Gloss. Ag. 569. Schäfer, Appar. Demosth. i. p. 536.
Ran. 1047. Nub. 792, 1440. Aves, 1070.
[2] "The name given to the single entrance into the temple of
Minerva." *Droysen.* "Comp. Suidas voc. πακτοῦν. Pollux viii. 113 ;
x. 27. Pausan. i. 22, 4." *Enger.*
[3] "Meaning Rhodia, the notorious wife of the celebrated Lycon."
Droysen, after the Scholiast. "Lysistrata. Cf. Meineke, Com. Fragm.
i. p. 117 ; ii. p. 441, 444, 535." *Enger.*
[4] "Cf. Herod. v. 72. Bergler remarks that Aristophanes is in
the habit of assigning to the Chorus actions which have taken place
long before any of those then living were born." *Enger.* "At first
the Spartans had assisted the Alcmæonids in expelling the tyrant
Hippias; but when, instead of the oligarchy they wished for, a
democracy was established under the management of Cleisthenes
the Alcmæonid, they sent their king Cleomenes to procure the victory for the aristocratical party under Isocrates. The Spartans were
besieged and obliged to capitulate." *Droysen.*
[5] "οὐκ ἀκρότητος οὐδὲ ἀράπιστος." *Photius* Lex.
[6] "When the aspirate has passed over to the preceding tenuis,
the sign of the spiritus asper should not be affixed. Therefore
Θῶπλα, not Θῶπλα." *Brunck.*
[7] "Also belagert hab' Ich den, wahrhaftig einen braven." *Droysen.*
[8] ἐπ' ἀσπίδας πέντε καὶ εἴκοσι, *five and twenty deep,* Thuc. iv. 93.
Cf. Arist. *Babylonians,* Fragm. v. Herod. vii. 188, vi. 111, ix. 31 ; and
Krüger on Xen. Anab. i. 7, 10. " καθεύδων is παρὰ προσδοκίαν for
φρουρῶν." *Enger.*
[9] "Da würd' mich nicht mein Siegesmaal in Marathon schlafen
    lassen." *Droysen.*

But indeed the steep part itself of my road towards the citadel, whither[1] I am hastening, remains for me *to traverse.* And we must manage to draw this at length, without a pack ass. How the yoke[2] has heavily pressed my shoulder! But nevertheless we must go, and must blow up the fire, lest at the end of our journey it be extinguished without our perceiving it. [*Blows at the coals.*] Faugh! faugh! Oh! oh, what a smoke! O king Hercules, how dreadfully it bites my eyes, like a mad dog, having assailed me from the pan! and this fire is by all means Lemnian[3] too. For *otherwise* it would never thus have bitten my sore eyes with its teeth. Hasten forwards to the citadel, and assist the goddess; or when shall we aid her better than now, Laches? [*Blows at the coals.*] Faugh! faugh! Oh! oh, what[4] a smoke! By the favour of the gods, this fire is awake and alive. Should we not therefore, if we were first to deposit the yoke here, and stick the torch of vine-wood into the pan and kindle it, then burst in the door like a ram?[5] And if the women do not undo the bolts when we call, we must set fire to the doors and oppress them with the smoke. Now let us deposit our load. [*Blows at the coals.*] Oh, what a smoke! Bless my soul! Who of the generals at Samos[6] will help with the yoke? This has now ceased to gall my back. It is your business, O pan,[7]

---

[1] See Krüger's Gr. Gr. § 62, 3, obs. 2.

[2] τῷ ξύλω, according to Brunck, is the *yoke* or *beam* used by porters to carry heavy weights = ἀναφορεύς. Cf. vss. 307, 313. So also Enger. "Es klemmt die Trage mir die Schulter." *Droysen.*

[3] "*Est hic ignis vere Lemnius.*" *Enger.* "Das ist bei Gott ein Aetnafeuer." *Droysen.* Comp. Soph. Phil. 797, 814. Æsch. Choeph. 631.

[4] See Krüger's Gr. Gr. § 47, 3, obs. 2.

[5] "Nicht wahr, wir legen ab zuerst die Trag' an dieser Stelle?
Geschwind sodann, ins Feuerfass gesteckt die Zündestecken
Und angebrannt, so stürzen wir aufs Thor da los gleich
Böcken." *Droysen.*

[6] See Thuc. viii. 21, 51—92. "The democratic form of government had been restored at Samos a little before. When the chorus of old men invokes the aid of the popular leaders who had brought this about at Samos, to assist them against the *women*, it refers at the same time to the men of high rank at Athens, who were striving to overthrow the democracy." *Enger.*

[7] Nub. 1497, σὸν ἔργον, ὦ δᾷς, ἰέναι πολλὴν φλόγα. Brunck makes vs. 316 stand in the oratio recta: *fac tædam incensam quum primum mihi feras;* so that ὅπως προσοίσεις may be *a command, a* in Equit.

to kindle your cinders, so tbat you may first bring me the torch aligbt. Mistress Victory, assist us, and let us set up[1] a trophy over tbe now present audacity of tbe women in the citadel. [*Enter chorus of women coming out of the citadel.*]

Cho. of Wom. Women, methinks I perceive flame and smoke as of a fire burning. We must basten more quickly. Fly, fly, Nicodice, before that Calyce and Critylla, being blown upon from all sides,[2] be set on fire by grievous laws and mischievous old men! But I am afraid of this. Surely I am not coming[3] to the rescue too late? For now, baving filled my bucket at the fountain early in the morning, witb difficulty, by reason of the crowd and tumult and clatter of pitchers, jostling with women-servants and runaway slaves, having brought it eagerly, I come witb water to the rescue of my fellow tribes-women being on fire. For I heard that old dotards were coming, carrying logs, about three talents in weight, as if about to wait upon persons at the bath,[4] threatening most dreadful words, that it behoved them to burn tbe abominable women to a cinder with fire; whom, O goddess, may I never see set on fire. but to bave delivered Greece and the citizens from war and madness! for whicb purpose, O guardian of the city with golden crest, tbey occupied thy seat. And I invoke thec as our ally, O Tritogenia, if any[5] man burn tbem

222, 456, 497, 687, 760, 1011. Eccles. 295, 955. Aves, 131. Vesp. 1292. Nub. 490, 824, 888, 1177. Pax, 77, 562, 1117. Cf. Krüger, Gr. Gr. § 54, 8, obs. 7. Hermann, Vig. n. 255. Harper's "Powers of the Greek Tenses," p. 114. Enger reads ὅπως πρώτιστ᾽ ἐμοί. Dindorf, who has left πρώτως in his text, doubts if Aristophanes used the adverb πρώτως; in which opinion he is joined by Lobeck, Phryn. p. 312, and Bergk, Rhen. Mus. 1841, i. p. 80. Reisig (Conject. p. 125) proposed πρόφρων, Bothe πρώτῳ γ᾽.

[1] See note on Ran. 169. Here the scene changes to the front of the Acropolis.

[2] For the gender, see Krüger, Gr. Gr. § 44, 2, obs. 4. Hermann, Vig. n. 51, and for ὄλεθρος, ibid. § 57, 1, obs. 3.

[3] "Am I a tardy helper?" *Wheelwright.* "Werd' Ich zu spät nicht helfen?" *Droysen.*

[4] "*Tanquam balneum calefacturos.*" *Brunck.* "Als wären sie Bader, zu heizen ein Bad." *Droysen.* "ὥσπερ βαλανεῖον ὑποκαύσοντες.' *Scholiast.*

[5] Enger reads εἴ τις—ὑποπίμπρησιν, and adds, "Reisig (Conject. p. 305) made this correction, in order to expel ὑποπίμπρῃσιν, a form of the conjunctive unknown to the Attics, which Brunck had introduced in place of the indicative. Bothe follows Reisig."

from below, to bring water along with us ! Let be ! What's [1]
this ? O men laboriously wieked ! for never would good or
pious men have been for doing this.

Cho. of Men. This affair has eome unexpeeted for us to
see.[2] See! here again's a swarm of women eoming out of
doors to the rescue ! [*They make a retrograde movement.*]

Cho. of Wom. Why do you insult[3] us ? We don't[4] seem
to be many, I suppose? And yet you don't see as yet the
ten-thousandth part of us.

Cho. of Men. O Phædrias, shall we suffer these to prate
so mueh? Ought one not to have broken one's cudgel about
them with beating them ?

Cho. of Wom. Let us also now deposit our pitchers on the
ground ; so that, if any one lay his hand upon us, this may
not be a hinderanee. [*They lay down their pitchers.*]

Cho. of Men. If, by Jove, one had already struek their
jaws twiee or thriee, like those[5] of Bupalus, they would not
have a voiee.

Cho. of Wom. Well now, there ! let any one strike me!
I'll stand and offer[6] myself ; and no other biteh shall ever
lay hold of your nose.[7]

Cho. of Men. If you will not be silent, I'll beat and
drive away your[8] old age.

[1] Comp. Vesp. 183, 1509. Av. 859, 1495. For πόνῳ πονηροί, cf.
Vesp. 466.

[2] Cf. vs. 1207, *infra*. Av. 1710, 1713. Pax, 821.

[3] "*Quid nos formidatis?*" *Brunck.* "τί εὐτελίζετε, ἢ φοβεῖσθε καὶ
τρέμετε.*" Scholiast.* "Comp. Hesychius and Suidas." *Enger.*

[4] Cf. Nub. 1260. Pax, 1211. Elmsley, Acharn. vs. 122.

[5] See Hor. Epod. vi. 14. "See Suidas in voc. Βούπαλος. The
point of the allusion is that Bupalus seems after that to have been
silenced." *Enger.* ἂν εἶχον is not necessarily restricted to *past* time.
This form often denotes what is brought on from the past time *up
to the present.* See Harper, Powers of the Greek Tenses, pp. 79, 145.
Krüger, Gr. Gr. § 54, 10, obs. 3.

[6] "*Os præbebo.*" *Brunck.*

[7] Meaning that she would anticipate such a casualty by pulling it
off. Cf. vs. 694. "*Nam ego, ut canis, tibi prius eos evellam.*" *Bergler.*
"Doch sollte bei den Hoden dann kein Köter mehr dich packen."
Droysen.
For οὐ μή, see Krüger, Gr. Gr. § 53, 7, obs. 6. Bernhardy, W. S.
p. 402.

[8] "Comp. vs. 448. Thesm. 567. This passage has been rightly
understood by the Scholiast in the Ravenna MS., ὡς πρὸς τὰς γραίας
ὁ τῶν γερόντων χόρος." *Enger.*

Cho. of Wom. Come forward and only touch Stratyllis with your finger!

Cho. of Men. But what, if I thump her with my fists? what mischief[1] will you do to me?

Cho. of Wom. I'll bite and tear out your lungs and entrails.[2]

Cho. of Men. There's no poet wiser[3] than Euripides; for there's no creature so shameless[4] as women.

Cho. of Wom. Let us take up the pitcher of water, O Rhodippe.

Cho. of Men. Why, O thou hateful to the gods, hast thou come hither with water?

Cho. of Wom. Why then *have you come* with fire, you old man nigh to the grave?[5] With the intention of setting yourself on fire?

Cho. of Men. I *have come* in order that I may heap up a pyre and set fire to your friends underneath.

Cho. of Wom. And I, that I might extinguish[6] your pyre with this.

Cho. of Men. Will you extinguish my fire?

Cho. of Wom. The deed itself[7] will soon show.

Cho. of Men. I don't know but I'll scorch you with[8] this torch just as I am.

---

[1] Porson compares Eurip. Bacch. 492, εἴφ' ὅ τι παθεῖν δεῖ· τί με τὸ δεινὸν ἐργάσει;

[2] Eur. Cycl. 236, τὰ σπλάγχν' ἐφαττ-ν ἐξαμήσεσθαι βίᾳ.

[3] The real meaning is, "more addicted to the use of the word σοφὸς in his poetry." Comp. Nub. 1376,

οὔκουν δικαίως, ὅστις οὐκ Εὐριπίδην ἐπαινεῖς
σοφώτατον;

See also Ran. 1420. Athenæus, xiv. p. 665, A.

[4] Cf. Soph. Electr. 622. Æsch. Theb. 182. "Aristophanes seems to have had in his mind some particular line of Euripides." *Enger.*

[5] "Old men are called τύμβοι, who are nigh to the grave." *Bergler.* Cf. Eur. Med 1209. Heracl. 167. "Du Dürrholz." *Droysen.*

[6] "The women say they have come in order that they might extinguish the pyre (τὴν σὴν πύραν), if the old men should set it on fire. Now the old men had *decided* to set it on fire. This is denoted by the conjunctive, the former case by the optative." *Enger.*

[7] "*Res ipsa mox indicabit.*" *Brunck.* Soph. Lemn. Fragm. viii., ταχὺ δ' αὐτὸ δείξει τοὔργον. Cf. Ran. 1261. Eccles. 933, 936. Vesp. 994. Plato, Theæt. p. 200, E. Hipp. Maj. p. 288, B. Eurip. Bacch. 974. Phœn. 632. See Heindorf, Plato, Phileb. § 99.

[8] Cf. Vesp. 1372—1378. For similar examples of "Anticipation."

CHO. OF WOM. If you happen to have any soap,[1] I'll provide a bath.

CHO. OF MEN. You a bath for me, you filthy wretch?

CHO. OF WOM. And that, too,[2] a nuptial one.

CHÓ. OF MEN. Did you hear her audacity?

CHO. OF WOM. For I am free.

CHO. OF MEN. I'll stop you from your present clamour.

CHO. OF WOM. But you shall no longer sit in the Heliæa.[3]

CHO. OF MEN. Set fire to her hair!

CHO. OF Wom. Thy task,[4] O Achelöus! [*The women empty their buckets on the men's heads.*]

CHO. OF MEN. Ah me, miserable!

CHO. OF WOM. Was it hot? [*Another volley of buckets.*]

CHO. OF MEN. Why, hot? Will you not stop? What are you doing?

CHO. OF WOM. I am watering you, that you may grow.

CHO. OF MEN. But I am parched[5] up and shaking already.

CHO. OF WOM. Therefore, since you have fire, you shall warm yourself. [*Enter committee-man.*[6]]

COM. Has the wantonness of the women burst forth, and their drumming, and their frequent orgies,[7] and this mourning on the roofs for Adonis,[8] which I once[9] heard when I was in

Enger refers to vss. 754, 905. Thesm. 1134. Ran. 310. See notes on Nub. 1148. Eccles. 1126.

[1] See Liddell's Lex. in voc. ῥύμμα. "Hast du vielen Schmutz am Leib." *Droysen.*

[2] See Krüger, Gr. Gr. § 51, 7, obs. 14.

[3] There is a play on the word ἥλιος, as in Vesp. 772. "I'll *cool you down* a bit."

[4] Cf. Aves, 862. She invokes the aid of the celebrated Ætolian river Achelöus: "Then, water, to thy work!" For this use of Achelöus for *water* in general, Dindorf refers to Servius' note on Virgil, Georg. i. 9. Add Aristoph. *Cocalus*, Fragm. vii.

[5] "ἀπὸ τοῦ ὕδατος δηλονότι τρέμει ὁ γέρων." *Scholiast.* "Starr bin Ich, klappr' am ganzen Leib." *Droysen.* "He says he has no need of being drenched with cold water, because he trembles already with old age and on account of his spare frame." *Enger.*

[6] See Liddell's Lex. in voc. πρόβουλος. Comp. Thuc. viii. 1 and Wesseling on Her. vi. 7.

[7] Cicero, Legg. ii. 15, "Novos vero deos sic Aristophanes facetissimus poeta veteris comœdiæ vexat, ut apud eum Sabazius et quidam alii peregrini judicati e civitate ejiciantur."

[8] Ezekiel viii. 14, "Women weeping for Tammuz." i. e. *tou* Adonis. Comp. Becker, Charicles, i. p. 228.

[9] "Das Ich jüngst hab gehört." *Droysen.*

the Assembly.   Demostratus (a plague take [1] him!) was advising to sail to Sicily; but his wife, dancing, cries, "Ah! ah, for Adonis!"   And Demostratus was advising [2] to enlist Zacynthian hoplites; but his wife upon the roof, being rather tipsy, tells them to mourn for Adonis.   But he, Cholozyges, hateful to the gods and abominable, overpowered her.   Such are their acts of wantonness. [3]

CHO. OF MEN. What then would *you say*, [4] if you were also to hear of the insolence of these? who have both insulted us in other respects, and drenched us with their pitchers, so that we may wring our garments, as if we had made water in them.

COM. Justly, by the briny Neptune!   For when we ourselves join with the women in villany, and teach them to be icentious, such [5] counsels spring from them; we, who speak n this wise in the workmen's [6] shops, "Goldsmith, as my wife was dancing in the evening, the clasp of the necklace you [7] made dropped out of the hole.   For my part, I must sail to Salamis; but do you, if you have leisure, come by all [8]

[1] On this form of imprecation, see Casaub. Athen, ii. 14, p. 112; commentators on Lucian, i. p. 218; Valckenär, Adon. p. 370, and on Schol. N. T. vol. i. p. 438.   Poeta incert. ap. Athen. ii. p. 55, C.   The opposite is ὥραις καλαῖς.   See Dindorf.

[2] "Da rieth der Unglücksredner." *Droysen.*   The decree for the Sicilian expedition was passed on the day for the festival of Adonis, which was thought unlucky.   Cf. Plut. Nicias, xii. xiii.

[3] The true reading I am persuaded is ἀκολαστήματα, as proposed by Bentley.   See Bekk. Anecd. vol. i. 367, 21.

[4] Comp. Nub. 154, τί δῆτ' ἂν ἕτερον εἰ πύθοιο Σωκράτους σόφισμα; See Elmsley, Acharn. 1011.   Krüger, Gr. Gr. § 69, 7, obs. 2.   Harper's Powers of the Greek Tenses, p. 96.   Pax, 907.   Nub. 690.   Equit. 1252.   Aves, 356.

[5] "From Æsch. Theb. 600, ἀφ' ἧς τὰ κεδνὰ βλαστάνει βουλεύματα." *Enger.*

[6] Brunck compares vss. 622, 1064.   Eccles. 420.   Ran. 69, 118.

[7] A case of *inverted assimilation* (*umgekehrte Assimilation*).   See Krüger, Gr. Gr. § 51, 10, obs. 9, who quotes from Lysias, (p. 649,) τὴν οὐσίαν ἣν κατέλιπεν οὐ πλείονος ἀξία ἐστίν.   Cf. Plut. 200.   Soph. Rex, 449.   Trach. 283.   Eur. Orest. 1604.   Plato, Men. p. 96, A. Hom. Il. Σ. 192.   So Virgil, Æn. i. 577, *Urbem quam statuo vestra est.* Plaut. Epid. iii. 4, 12, *istum quem quæris ego sum.*   See Bremi, Dem. Cor. § 16.   Dorv. Char. 593, 609.   Schäfer ad Eur. Orest. 1645. Richter, Anacol. i. p. 24.   Hermann, Vig. Append. p. 713.

[8] "παντὶ τρόπῳ." *Scholiast.*   "It increases the force of the imperative.   Cf. Fritzsche ad Thesm. 65.   Nub. 1327.   Ran. 1235. Eccles. 366.   Thesm. 65." *Enger.*

means towards evening and fit in the clasp[1] for her." And
some other one speaks after this manner to the shoemaker,
a youth, but able to do a man's work, "Shoemaker, the cross-
straps pinch the little toe[2] of my wife's foot, since it is tender.
Come you, therefore, at noon and loosen this, so that it may
be wider." Such things concur in such[3] affairs, when I, who
am a Committee-man, who have provided spars for oars,[4] am
shut out[5] from the gates by the women, now when there's
need of the money. But it's no[6] use to stand. Bring the
levers, that I may restrain them from their insolence. Why do
you gape, you wretch? Whither, again, are you staring, who
do nothing but look after a tavern? Will you not place your
levers under the gates and force your way on that side? and I
will join in forcing this way. [*Enter Lysistrata.*]

Lys. Do not force[7] with your levers! for I am coming
forth of my own accord. What need is there of levers? For
there is not more need of levers, than of sense and judgment.

Com. What, really, you abominable creature? Where is
the policeman? Seize her, and tie her hands behind her!

Lys. By Diana, if in truth he shall lay the tip of his hand
upon me, he shall weep for it, policeman[8] as he is! [*Policemen draw back.*]

Com. Are you afraid, you fellow? Will you not seize her
by the waist, and you with him, and bind her quickly?

---

[1] "We must mentally supply τῷ τρήματι, wherein there is an
intentional equivoque, as in τὴν βάλανον. Similarly Macho, ap.
Athen. p. 577, plays upon the ambiguity of the word βάλανος." *Enger*
[2] See Porson ap. Dawes, Misc. Crit. p. 384, ed. Kidd.
[3] "εἰς τὰς νῦν ὕβρεις." *Scholiast.*

　　"Das alles ist denn endlich nun so weit gediehn,
　　Dass mir, dem Probulen, der Ich Ruderknechte noch
　　Zu schaffen hab', und gerade jetzt noch Geld bedarf,
　　Das Weibervolk die Thore vor der Nase schliesst!
　　Doch nützt es nichts herumzustehen." *Droysen.*

[4] "See Böckh, Publ. E. Athen. i. p. 75, 119. Elmsley, Acharn.
552. Hesychius: κωπεῖς· τὰ εἰς κώπας εὔθετα ξύλα. Cf. Valckenaer
on Herod. v. 23, and Theoph. i. p. 176, ed. Schneid." *Enger*.
[5] "See Lobeck, Aj. vs. 1274." *Enger*.
[6] See Liddell's Lex. in voc. ἔργον, iv. 2.
[7] See note on Ran. 434.
[8] "Translate, *quum sit publicus minister*," *Enger*, who, after disap-
proving of Brunck's interpretation and Bothe's explanation, add:
" Lysistrata is unwilling to be touched,—not because it is igno-
minious,—but because she won't have it done at all."

1st Wom. By Pandrosus,[1] if in truth you shall only lay your hand upon her, you shall be trampled on and ease your-self again!

Com. "Shall ease yourself again," quoth'a! Where is there another[2] policeman? Bind this one the first, because she also chatters!

2nd Wom. By Diana,[3] if in truth you shall lay the tip of your hand upon her, you shall soon ask for a[4] cupping-glass!

Com. What's this? Where is there a policeman?[5] Lay hold on her! I will stop some of you from this going out.

3rd Wom. By Diana, if in truth you shall approach her, I'll pluck out the hairs that will make you scream![6] [*Police-men run away.*]

Com. Ah me, unfortunate! The policeman has deserted[7] me. But we must never be conquered by[8] women. [*Police come back.*] Let us march against them, O policemen, in order of battle!

Lys. By the two goddesses, then you shall know that with us also there are four companies of warlike women within, fully armed!

Com. Twist back their hands, policemen! [*Policemen lay hands on the women.*]

[1] "Pandrosus was the daughter of Cecrops, whose chapel, the most attràctive gem of Athenian architecture, stood upon the Acro-polis, near the Erectheion." *Droysen.* "Comp. Schol. Ravenn. ad Thesm. 533, and Fritzsche, ad Thesm. 2, c." *Enger.*

[2] "ἕτερος in Aristophanes, when without an article, always = ἄλ-λος. Where the discourse is of *two*, and the sense of *alter* is required, then ἕτερος takes the article, ὁ ἕτερος or ἅτερος. Cf. Ran. 1415. Nub. 114. Equit. 174. Ach. 117. Thesm. 227." *Brunck.* "Both the words and the context show that another, i. e. a *third*, bowman is meant, and not a *second* one." *Enger.*

[3] "Diana is thus called ap. Eur. Iph. T. 21. In Arist. Thesm. 858, Hecate is so called, where the Scholiast remarks, 'ἡ αὐτὴ γὰρ τῇ 'Εκάτῃ.' Bothe thinks Hecate is meant here." *Enger.* "Bei Hekate." *Droysen.*

[4] Comp. Pax, 541.

[5] "Voss: '*wo der Trabant?*' incorrectly : for he uses these words to *call up* a bowman, not to express *surprise*. τοῦτο τί ἦν ex-press his surprise at the coming of another woman." *Enger.*

[6] "So mausr' Ich die Haare, dass du quaken sollst!" *Droysen.* "ἐκκοκιῶ· ἀνατιλῶ, ἀνασπάσω. στενοκωκύτους· ἐφ' αἷς στενάξεις." *Scholiast.*

[7] "*Defecit me lictor,* i. c. aufugit." *Enger.*

[8] Comp. Soph. Antig. 673. Elmsley, Ach. 127

Lys. O allied women, run out from within, ye green-grocery-market-women, ye garlic-bread-selling-hostesses! Will ye not drag?[1] Will ye not beat? Will ye not smite? Will ye not revile? Will ye not behave impudently? [*Women rush in and drive off the policemen.*]' Stop! Retire! Do not despoil them!

Com. Ah me, how miserably have my policemen[2] fared!

Lys. Nay, what did you expect? Did you think you had come against some women-slaves, or do you 'suppose anger is not in women?

Com. Aye, by Apollo, and very much too, if a tavern[3] be near!

Cho. of Men. O commissioner of this land, who have wasted many words, why do you hold a parley with these wild beasts? Do you not know with what a bath these just now drenched us in our garments, and that too[4] without lye?

Cho. of Wom. But, my good sir, you ought not rashly to lay your hand upon your neighbours. But if you do this, you must have swelled eyes. For I am willing to sit modestly, like a virgin, offending no one here, nor even stirring a chip, unless one take my comb, like a wasp's nest, and irritate me.

Cho. of Men. O Jupiter! what ever shall we make of these[5] monsters? For these things are no longer bearable But you must inquire into this casualty along with me, with whatever intent they seized upon the citadel, and for what purpose *they seized upon* the Acropolis on the mighty rock, not to be trodden, the sacred enclosure. But ask repeatedly, and do not be persuaded,[6] and apply all tests. For it is disgraceful to leave such[7] an affair as this untested, having given it up.

[1] See Krüger, Gr. Gr. § 53, 7, obs. 4.
[2] See Krüger, Gr. Gr. § 43, 4, obs. 17.
[3] "A satirical reflection on the vinolent propensity of the Athenian women." *Wheelwright.* Cf. Thesm. 735, 736.
[4] See Krüger, Gr. Gr. § 51, 7, obs. 14. For κονία, comp. vs. 377. "i. e. ἄνευ νίτρου, ut explicat Scholiasta." *Enger.*
[5] οὐκ ἔχω ὅ τι χρήσωμαι αὐτῷ, Plat. Theag. p. 126, D. Cf. Lys. p. 213, C. 222, D. Crit. p. 45, B. Herm. Vig. n. 209, 210. For κνώδαλον, cf. Hom. Od. xvii. 317.
[6] "Und glaube nicht gleich." *Droysen.* Bergk (Rhen. Mus. 1841, i. p. 95) proposes μὴ φείδου.
[7] See Franz's Deutsch-Griechisches Wörterbuch in voc. *Sokhon,* und Krüger, Gr. Gr. § 54, 4, obs. 6.

Com. Well now, by Jove, I wish to learn this first from them; with what intent you shut up our citadel with your bolts.

Lys. That we might make the money safe, and that you might not fight on account of it.

Com. Why, are[1] we fighting on account of the money?

Lys. Aye, and all the other matters, too, have been thrown into confusion. For in order that Pisander[2] might be able to steal, and those who aim at offices, they were always stirring up some commotion.[3] Therefore let them do whatever they please, for that matter! for they shall no longer take out this money.

Com. What will you do then?[4]

Lys. Ask me this? We will manage it.

Com. Will you manage the money?

Lys. Why[5] do you think this strange? Do we not wholly manage your domestic property also for you?

Com. But *the case* is not the same.

Lys. How[6] not the same?

Com. We must carry on the war out[7] of this *money*.

Lys. But in the first place there is no occasion for war.

Com. Why, how otherwise shall we be saved?

Lys. We will save you.

Com. You?

Lys. Aye, we to be sure.

Com. A sad case indeed!

[1] See note on Eccles. 984.

[2] For some of his intrigues about this (b. c. 411) period, see Thuc. viii. 49, 53, 54, 56, 64, 65, 67, 68, 73, 90. Further notices in the note on Av. 1556. Cf. Meineke, Com. Frag. i. p. 177, ii. p. 501, 502.

[3] "Quacksalbern so immer ein neu Vomitiv." *Droysen.*

[4] Comp. vs. 193.

[5] "What thinkest thou so marvellous in this?" *Wheelwright*
  "Was scheint dir dabei so bedenklich?" *Droysen.*
For this mode of construing, see Krüger, Gr. Gr. § 57, 3, obs. 6, and obs. 7. The cases, however, appear to be dissimilar. A more perspicuous arrangement would be, τί δέ; δεινὸν τοῦτο νομίζεις; See note on Av. 1604. So in Nub. 1261, I would arrange, τί δ'; ὅστις εἰμί, τοῦτο βούλεσθ' εἰδέναι; For the argument employed, comp. Eccles. 210.

[6] Cf. vs. 521.

[7] Cf. Xen. Anab. i. 1, 9; ii. 6, 5; v. 3, 9; v. 6, 15. Krüger, Gr Gr. § 68, 16, obs. 10,

Lys. Be assured¹ that you shall be saved, even if you do not wish.

Com. You mention a shameful ease.

Lys. You are indignant: but this must be done notwithstanding.

Com. By Ceres, 'tis unjust!

Lys. We must save² you, my friends.

Com. Even if I don't want?

Lys. Aye, so much the more, for that matter.

Com. But how came you to care about war and peace?

Lys. We will tell you.

Com. (*with a significant motion of his fist*).   Tell me now quickly, that you may not get a beating!

Lys. Hear now, and try to restrain your hands!

Com. But I am not able: for through my passion³ it is difficult to restrain them.

Lys. Then you shall suffer for it so much the more.

Com. Croak this⁴ at yourself, old woman; but tell me *your story*.

Lys. I will do so.   During the former war and *former* time, through our modesty, we bore with you⁵ men, whatever you did; for you did not allow us to mutter: and then you did not please us.   But we perceived⁶ you very well; and oftentimes when we were at home we used⁷ to hear that you had determined some important matter badly; and then being pained internally,⁸ we used to ask you with a smile, "What

---

¹ Cf. Ach. 335, 590.

² "σωστέον *actively*, as always.   Dindorf decides otherwise.   See his note on Soph. Rex, 628, and cf. Hermann on the same passage." *Enger.*

³ "We have ὑπ' ὀργῆς without the article in vs. 1023.   See Hermann, Nub. 834."   *Enger.*

⁴ See Krüger, Gr. Gr. § 54, 3, obs. 1.

⁵ For ἀνέχομαι with a genitive, comp. Æsch. Axioch. 15.   Eur. Troad. 101.   Plato, Rep. viii. p. 564, C.   Apol. p. 31, B.   The construction is an example of *anticipation*.

⁶ See Krüger's note on Thucyd. i. 57, and Gr. Gr. § 47, 10, obs. 12.   "Droysen strangely enough: '*doch beachteten wir gar wohl euer Thun.*'   It should have been *sondern wir sahen es euch wohl an, und hin ten wohl auch, dass ihr einen übeln Rath gefasst.*"   *Enger.*

⁷ Comp. vs. 361, and note on Av. 1592, and for ἀν with an indicative = *soleo*, see note on Plut. 982. Aves, 520.

⁸ "In der Seele betrübt." *Droysen.*   "*Interno dolore ægrø*

has been determined by you to-day amongst the people[1] to post up upon the pillar[2] about peace?" "What's that to you?" the man used to say; "will you not be silent?" And I used to be silent.

WOMAN. But I would never have been silent.

COM. Aye, and you'd have howled too, if you were not silent.

LYS. So then I kept silence at home. We used to hear[3] perhaps of some other more pernicious decree of yours; and then we used to ask, "How is it, husband, that you manage these matters so foolishly?" But he having looked askance at me used immediately to tell me that, "if I will not weave[4] my warp, I should wail loudly in my head; but war shall be a care to men."[5]

COM. Rightly said of him, by Jove!

LYS. How[6] rightly, you wretch? if not even when you were determining badly, it was permitted us to advise you. But[7] when now we plainly heard you now *saying* in the streets, "Is there not a man in the country?" *and* some other said, "Certainly not, by Jove!" after this it was immediately determined by us women, being assembled, to save Greece in

Brunck. "τὴν μὲν καρδίαν λυπούμεναι, γελῶσαι δέ." *Scholiast.* "The Scholiast explains it rightly." *Enger.*

[1] "In Ekklesie." *Droysen.*

[2] Cf. Acharn. 727. "According to Paulmier, Aristophanes alludes to an inscription engraven by the authority of Alcibiades upon a column, upon which was engraven the treaty between the Lacedæmonians and Athenians." *Enger.*

[3] "Hinc factum, ut præterita imperfecta vel plusquamperfecta vel aorista in hac re usurparentur. Nam perfecta præsentium naturam sequuntur." *Hermann*, Vig. n. 289. Cf. Append. p. 722. So ἂν εἱστήκεσαν, *they used to stand*, Xen. Anab. i. 5, 2.

[4] Brunck's text exhibits εἰ μὴ . νήσεις, ὀτοτύξει τοι μακρὰ τὴν κεφαλήν. For the remarkable construction in this verse, see Plut. 612, and the passages there cited.

[5] "Facetiously adopted from the words of Hector to Andromache, Hom. Il. vi. 490,

$$\text{ἀλλ' εἰς οἶκον ἰοῦσα τὰ σαυτῆς ἔργα κόμιζε}$$
$$\text{ἱστόν τ', ἠλακάτην τε, καὶ ἀμφιπόλοισι κέλευε}$$
$$\text{ἔργον ἐποίχεσθαι· πόλεμος δ' ἄνδρεσσι μελήσει.}$$

These last words Lysistrata parodies in vs. 538, πόλεμος δ' γύναιξι μελήσει." *Brunck.* For this abrupt transition from the oratio obliqua to the oratio recta, see Krüger, Gr. Gr. § 65, 11, obs. 8.

[6] Comp. vs. 496   [7] Comp. Vesp. 121. Eccles. 195, 315, 82l.

common. For why[1] ought we to wait? If therefore you be willing to hear us in turn giving good advice, and to be silent in turn, as we *were then*, we would restore you.

Com. You *restore* us? You mention a shameful case, and not to be endured by me.

Lys. Hold your tongue!

Com. Must I hold my tongue for[2] you, you abominable creature, and that too wearing a hood about your head? Then may I not live!

Lys. Well, if this be an obstacle to you, there! take this hood from me, and take and put it about your head, and then hold your tongue!—and this little basket! and then gird yourself up[3] and card wool, munching beans![4] " but war shall be a care to women."

Cho. of Wom. Retire,[5] O women, from your pitchers, in order that we also in turn may assist our friends. For I would never be tired with dancing, nor would exhausting[6] weariness seize my knees. I am willing to venture[7] everything with these in the cause of virtue, in whom is intellect, is beauty, is boldness, is wisdom, is prudent patriotism. Come, most courageous *offspring* of grandmothers, and of fruitful nettles, advance with vehemence,[8] and do not yield! for you are now still running before the wind.

Lys. But if delightful Eros and the Cyprus-born Venus breathe desire upon our bosoms and our breasts, and then create in the men a pleasing passion and voluptuousness, I think that we shall some time be called amongst the Greeks Lysimachæ.[9]

Com. By having done what?

---

[1] Comp. vss. 194, 383, and for καὶ, see note on vs. 171.

[2] " σοί γε σιωπῶ; *tibine taceam?* ut Ran. 1134, ἐγὼ σιωπῶ τῷδε;" *Brunck.*

[3] " In allusion to the proverb τὸν σικυὸν τρώγουσα, γύναι, τὴν χλαῖναν ὕφαινε ap. Athen. iii. p. 73, D." *Enger.*

[4] Equit. 41, κυαμοτρώξ, Δῆμος πυκνίτης.

[5] " ἀπαίρει· ἀναχωρεῖ." *Hesychius.* Cf. Eccles. 818.

[6] " The form καματήριος, which Hermann defends from Hesychius, consider with Reisig to be as corrupt as θανατήριος for θανατηρός." *Enger.*

[7] See Krüger on Xen. Anab. iii. 1, 18.

[8] Comp. Thuc. v. 70, init., and note on Aves, 366.

[9] i. e. as having put an end to the war. Cf. Pax, 991, 992.

Lys. If in the first place we put a stop to people lounging[1] in the market-place with arms and acting madly.

Woman. Aye, by the Paphian Venus!

Lys. For now in truth in the pottery-market,[2] and in the vegetable-market alike, they walk about throughout the market-place with arms, like Corybantes.

Com. Yes, by Jove! for it becomes the brave.

Lys. And yet the affair is ridiculous, when a fellow with a shield and a Gorgon then[3] purchases mackarel.

Woman. At all events, by Jove, I saw a man with long hair, a commander of cavalry, upon a horse putting pease-soup into his brazen helmet, *which he had bought* from an old woman.   And another, again, a Thracian, shaking a shield and javelin like Tereus, frightened the woman that dealt in figs and swallowed the ripe ones.[4]

Com. How then *will* you *be* able to allay many disturbed affairs in the country, and to put an end to them?

Lys. Very[5] easily.

Com. How?   Show us!

Lys. Like as, when our thread is tangled, we take it in this way and draw it out with our spindles hither and thither, thus also will we put an end to this war, if you let us, having brought it to an end by means of embassies hither and thither.

Com. Do[6] you think, pray, to allay a dreadful state of

---

[1] So θύοντας, *people sacrificing*, Av. 984. Cf. Equit. 1263. Pax, 1003. Ran. 146. τοὺς ἀγοράζοντας would be much different. See Krüger, Gr. Gr. § 50, 4, obs. 3.

[2] "So Equit. 1375, τὰν τῷ μύρῳ, *in the perfume-market*. Vesp. 789, ἐν τοῖς ἰχθύσι, *in the fish-market*.   Eupolis apud Polluc. ix. 47,

> περιῆλθον εἰς τὰ σκόροδα καὶ τὰ κρόμμυα,
> καὶ τὸν λιβανωτὸν, κεὐθὺ τῶν ἀρωμάτων,
> καὶ περὶ τὰ γέλγη." *Brunck*.

So Thesm. 448, αἱ μυῤῥίναι, *the myrtle-wreath-market*. Cf. Aves, 13. *Triphales*, Fragm. vii. Bernhardy, W. S. p. 56. Pierson, Mœr. p. 351.

[3] Cf. notes on Aves, 536, 1456.

[4] "On this word, see W. Dindorf in Steph. Thes. voc. δρυπετής, who considers δρυπετής the true orthography. Comp. also Lehrs, Quest. Epic. p. 162." *Enger*.

[5] Comp. Equit. 403, 509.   Ach. 215.

[6] "Mit der Wollpolitik und der Spinngarnsart und der Wickel-
    manier so gedenkt ihr
  Zu vollbringen der Staatskunst schwieriges Werk? Unkluge
    ihr?" *Droysen*.

affairs with your wool, and threads, and spindles, you silly
women?

Lys. Aye, and if there was any sense in you, you would
administer[1] all your affairs after the fashion of our wool.

Com. How, pray? Come, let me see!

Lys. In the first place it behoved you, as if washing away
the dirt of a fleece in a bath, to flog the knaves headlong out
of the city, and to pick out the briers; and to tear in pieces
these who combine together and those who press themselves
close together[2] for the magistracies, and to pluck their heads;[3]
and then all to card public good-feeling into a basket, having
mixed up[4] both the resident-aliens and whatever stranger or
friend there is with you, and whoever is indebted to the public, and to mix these up[5] in one body; and, by Jove, to mark[6]
the states, as many as are colonies of this city, that these lie
uncared for, like the pieces of wool, each apart by itself; and
then, having taken the wool from all these, to bring it together, and collect it into one mass; and then to make a large
ball; and then, out of this to weave a cloak for the people.

Com. Is it not, therefore, shameful that these should cudgel[7]
these things and wind them off into a ball, who had not even
any concern in the war at all?

Lys. And yet, O you utterly accursed, we bear more than
twice as[8] much of it *as you do;* who in the first instance bore
sons and sent them forth as hoplites.[9]

[1] Comp. note on vs. 361.
[2] "τοὺς θλίβοντας εἰς τὴν πολίτειαν ἑαυτούς." *Scholiast.*
[3] "ὡς τὰ ἄκρα τῶν ἐρίων." *Scholiast.*
[4] "Nobis eo hæc spectare videntur, quod lanæ admiscebant ἔρια
τὰ ἀπὸ τῶν ξύλων, quo vides quam apta existat comparatio." *Enger.*
I should greatly prefer κᾆτα μιγνύντας, κ. τ. λ., as it stands in the
Leyden MS., for the sense required is evidently, "and then, having
mingled the resident-aliens, and whatever stranger or friend there
be with you, or public debtor, to mix up these also in one mass."
[5] "Scholiast: ἐγκατάμιξαι· ἐπιτίμους ποιῆσαι. For those who were
in debt to the public were accounted ἄτιμοι." *Enger.*
[6] "Und die Städte zumal, die von hier aus je gen Morgen und
        Abend gesandt sind,
    Man schaue umher und mustre sie durch, da, wie Flocken von
        uns, sie verloren
    Jetzt liegen umher." *Droysen.*
[7] "ῥαβδίζειν is said in allusion to ἱκραβδίζειν in vs. 576." *Enger.*
[8] "Doch leiden wir mehr als doppelt von ihm." *Droysen.*
[9] "He alludes to the disastrous Sicilian expedition, where the
number of hoplites lost was very great. Cf. Thuc. viii. 1." *Enger.*

Com. Be silent, and do not remind [1] us of our woes!

Lys. And then, when we ought to be cheered and enjoy our youth, we sleep alone on account of the expeditions. [2] And our case I omit: but I am grieved for the maidens who grow old in their chambers.

Com. Do not men, therefore, grow old as well?

Lys. But, by Jove, you do not mention a like case. For he, when he has come back, even though he be gray-headed, soon marries a young girl; but the woman's time is short, and if she do not take advantage of it, no one is willing to marry her; but she sits looking for omens. [3]

Com. But whoever is still able to act a manly part—

Lys. Why then [4] do you not die? You shall have a little pig: [5] you shall purchase a coffin: I will now knead you a honey-cake. [6] Take this and crown yourself! [*Drenches him with water.*]

1st Wom. And receive these [7] from me! [*Drenches him.*]

2nd Wom. And take this crown! [*Drenches him.*]

Lys. What is wanting? What do you desire? Go to the ship! Charon calls you, [8] and you hinder him from setting sail.

Com. Then is it not shameful that I should suffer these things? But, by Jove, I will show myself to the Committee forthwith, going as [9] I am.

Lys. Will you lay a complaint [10] against us, that we did not lay you out? But on the third day at any rate the sacrifices

---

[1] "Weck' nicht trübe Gedanken." *Droysen.*

[2] "στρατιά is sometimes undoubtedly used = στρατεία, but σ-οαρεία is never = στρατιά, an army." *Liddell.* See vs. 100. Eq. 587. Acharn. 251. Vesp. 354, 557. Thesm. 828, 1169. Cf. Krüger, Thuc. i. 3. Meineke, Com. Frag. ii. p. 568. Harles, Diat. Philol. Darmstadt, 1842, p. 55. "Ἡμέτερον, *quod ad rem nostram spectat, illud quidem mittite.*" *Brunck.*

[3] "i. e. speculating upon the probabilities of her marriage." *Wheelwright.* "Dann sitzt sie und blättert im Traumbuch." *Droysen.*

[4] "*Tu vero senex, qui non es* στῦσαι δυνατὸς, *cur non moreris?*" *Bergler.*

[5] See Elmsley, Acharn. 788. Cf. Acharn. 691.

[6] "ἡ μελιττοῦττα ἐδίδοτο τοῖς νεκροῖς." *Scholiast.*

[7] "τὰς ταινίας, ἃς τοῖς νεκροῖς ἔπεμπον οἱ φίλοι." *Scholiast.*

[8] Eurip. Alc. 254, Χάρων μ' ἤδη καλεῖ. τί μέλλεις; ἐπείγου. Cf. Soph. Col. 1627.

[9] "βεβρεγμένος." *Scholiast.*

[10] ἐγκαλεῖς is *future,* and refers to the object of his visit to the Committee. "Doch nicht um zu klagen," &c. *Droysen.* ὅτι is never elided in Aristophanes. See note or Plut. 137.

to the dead will come from us very early[1] in the morning ready prepared. [*Exeunt Committee-man and attendants.*]

CHO. OF MEN. It is his business to sleep no longer, who is free. But, sirs, let us strip[2] and set to work at this affair! For already these matters appear to me to savour of more and greater deeds; and especially I scent the tyranny of Hippias;[3] and I fear greatly lest some men of the Spartans, having assembled here in the house of Clisthenes,[4] should by craft stir up the women hateful to the gods to seize upon our money, and our pay, whereby I lived. For surely it is shameful that these, women as they are, should now advise the citizens, and prate about a brazen shield, and besides[5] reconcile us to the Lacedæmonians, to whom there's no trusting,[6] unless *one can* a gaping wolf. But these things, sirs, they have contrived for a tyranny. But over me they shall not tyrannize; for I will be on my guard, and will henceforth wear my sword in a myrtle-bough,[7] and will lounge in the market-

[1] "πρωΐ as a dissyllable is unknown to the Attic dialect, neither is it once found in Aristophanes." *Brunck.* "τὰ τρίτα are the offerings usually made on the third day from the burial." *Enger.*

[2] "*Exuendo nos præparemus*, as the autistrophic verse 637 shows. So vs. 662, the old men say ἀλλὰ τὴν ἐξωμίδ' ἐκδυώμεθα, and vs. 686, the women say ἀλλὰ χἠμεῖς θᾶττον ἐκδυώμεθα. Cf. Fritzsche, Thesm. 616. Meineke, Com. Frag. iii. 491." *Enger.*

[3] "He plays upon the ambiguity of the expression. The Chorus fears lest the Lacedæmonians have made a league with the Athenian women τὴν Ἱππίου τυραννίδα καταστήσοντες." *Enger.* Cf. Thuc. vi. 54—58.

[4] Comp. 1092. Vesp. 1187.

[5] "καὶ πρὸς, *et insuper*. Cf. Plut. 1001. Ran. 415, 611. Equit. 578. Ordo est: καὶ πρὸς διαλλάττειν ἡμᾶς ἀνδράσιν Λακωνικοῖς." *Brunck.* Enger also approves of Brunck's remark. Nevertheless I am convinced they are both in error. διαλλάττειν is used *absolutely*, and πρὸς is a *vox solita in hac re.* So Thuc. viii. 17, καὶ ἡ πρὸς βασιλέα ξυμμαχία Λακεδαιμονίοις ἐγένετο ἥδε. Comp. also viii. 36. I would therefore translate, "*and make peace between us and the Lacedæmonians.*"

[6] Hom. Od. xi. 456, οὐκέτι πιστὰ γύναιξιν.
"Denen just so viel zu traun ist, als 'nem Wolf mit offnem Rachen." *Droysen.*

[7] Referring to the celebrated scolion ap. Athen. xv. p. 695, A.,

ἐν μύρτου κλαδὶ τὸ ξίφος φορήσω,
ὥσπερ Ἁρμόδιος κἀριστογείτων, κ. τ. λ.

Cf. *Pelargi*, Fragm. ii. Bergk, Poet. Lyr. p. 871. There is at the same time an equivoque. See vs. 1004, *infra.*

place in arms nigh the statue[1] of Aristogiton, and will stand beside him thus;[2] for that very destiny is mine,[3] to smite the jaw of this old woman hateful to the gods.

Cho. of Wom. Then your mother shall not recognise[4] you when you enter the house. But, O dear matrons, let us first place these on the ground. For we, O all ye citizens, begin words serviceable to the state; naturally, since it reared me splendidly in luxury. As soon as[5] I was seven years of age I carried the peplus; and then,[6] when I was ten years of age, I was meal-grinder to Diana;[7] and then I was Arctos[8] at the Brauronia, wearing the saffron-coloured robe; and at length, when I was a beautiful girl, I carried the basket, wearing a chain of figs. Do I not then owe[9] it to the state to give it some good advice? But if I am a woman, do not grudge me this,[10] if I introduce something better than the present part of affairs. For I have a part in the contribution; for I contribute men. But you miserable old men have no part; for after you have expended[11] your ancestral fund, as it is called, which you got from the Persians,[12] you do not

---

[1] "*Prope Aristogitonis statuam.* Droysen incorrectly: *unserm Aristogeiton gleich.*" *Enger.* "*Suitably to.*" *Liddell.*

[2] "*Et ita quidem apud eum stabo.*" *Enger.*

[3] "*Illud ipsum enim meum est, ut tanquam alter Aristogiton, hujus anus imperium affectantis—malas feriam.*" *Enger.*

 "Da auch mir das Schicksal hiess." *Droysen.*

[4] "ὑπὸ τῶν πληγῶν τῶν παρ' ἡμῶν ἀλλοῖος γενήσῃ." *Scholiast.*

[5] See Krüger, Gr. Gr. § 56, 10, obs. 3.

[6] "Ordo est, ἀλετρὶς ἢ δεκέτις οὖσα τῇ Ἀρχηγέτι, κᾆτ' ἔχουσα τὸν κροκωτὸν ἄρκτος ἢ Βραυρωνίοις." *Bentley.*

[7] "On the form of the dative, cf. Lob. Phryn. p. 429. Ἀρχηγέτις is *Diana*, who was worshipped at Brauron, and to whom virgins were dedicated when they were ten years of age. Vid. Harpocr. voc. δεκατεύειν. Bekk. Anecd. p. 235, 1; 444, 30." *Enger.*

[8] See Liddell's Lex. in voc. ἄρκτος. Cf. note on Thesm. 1013.

[9] For the construction, see Lidd. Lex. in voc. προοφείλω. For ἆρα = *nonne*, see note on Plut. 546. "*Ego ergo, quæ tot honores in patriâ gessi, nonne debeo in compensationem ipsi utilia suadere.*" *Reiske.*

[10] "Verarget mir es nicht." *Droysen.*

[11] "He has been obliged by the metre to place εἶτα before the participle, which ought to follow it; for the natural order is: ἐπεὶ τὸν ἔρανον ἀναλ., εἶτα οὐκ ἀντ." *Brunck.* The example Enger quotes from Nub. 860, is *nihil ad rem.* In the mean time I conjecture ἐξαναλώσαντες.

[12] "This was a subscription made by the wealthy at the time of the Persian war." *Droysen.* See note on vs. 273.

pay in turn your contributions. But moreover we are in danger of being ruined by you. Then ought you to grumble? But if you shall annoy me at all, I will strike your jaw with this untanned buskin.

CHO. OF MEN. Then are not these matters great insolence? and methinks the matter will increase still more. But whoever is a perfect man must repel the matter. Come, let us strip off our sleeveless coat, since it behoveth a man forthwith to savour of manhood; but it does not become him to be muffled up. But come, ye white-footed,[1] now it behoveth us, who went to Lipsydrium,[2] when as yet[3] we were *men*, now *it behoveth* us to grow young again, and to make our whole body active,[4] and to shake off this old age. For if any of us shall afford these if it were but a small handle,[5] they will in no wise fail of assiduous handicraft; but they will both build ships, and furthermore attempt to fight by sea, and to sail against us, like Artemisia.[6] But if they turn themselves to horsemanship, I strike the Knights off the list. For a woman is a creature most skilful in horsemanship and having a good seat.[7] And she would not slip off when it runs. See the Amazons whom Micon painted[8] on horseback fighting with the men! But we ought to take and fit this neck[9] into the perforated stocks of all these.

[1] "ὁ Ἀριστοφάνης ἔφη τοὺς νῦν λεγομένους Ἀλκμαιωνίδας. οὗτοι γὰρ πόλεμον ἀράμενοι πρὸς Ἱππίαν τὸν τύραννον καὶ τοὺς Πεισιστρατίδας ἐτείχισαν τὸ Λειψύδριον." *Scholiast.*

[2] "Lipsydrium was a stronghold in Mount Parnes, from which place the Alcmæonids made attacks upon the tyrant Hippias." *Droys.* The interpreters inform us that a scolion upon Lipsydrium and the Alcmæonids used to be sung at banquets. It is found in Athenæus xv. p. 695, E. It is well known that the chorus have acts attributed to them which have occurred long before their time. See note on vs. 273.

[3] "λείπει νεώτεροι." *Scholiast.*   [4] Comp. Av. 1437.

[5] Comp. Equit. 841, 847. Nub. 551.

[6] "Artemisia, the Carian queen, fought in the sea-fight at Salamis against the Grecian fleet." *Droysen.*

[7] "δυνάμενον ἐποχεῖσθαι." *Scholiast.*

[8] "The Battle of the Amazons" was a celebrated painting in the Poicile at Athens executed by Micon, son of Phanichus. See Meurs. Ath. p. 20. Pausan. i. 15. The same subject is represented on several bas-reliefs in the British Museum.

[9] "The neck also was put into that perforated wood. Anacreon ap. Athen. viii. p. 354, πολλὰ μὲν ἐν δουρὶ τιθεὶς αὐχένα." *Bergler.*

CHO. OF WOM. By the two goddesses, if you shall provoke me, I will now let loose my passion,[1] and will make you to-day call your fellow-tribesmen to your aid, being pommeled. But let us also,[2] O women, speedily strip, so that we may savour of women angered even to biting.[3] Now let any one come near me! in order that he may never eat garlic or black beans.[4] Since, if you shall even merely speak ill of me, —for I am exceedingly angry,—I the beetle will deliver you like[5] an eagle that is laying eggs. For I will not care for you, if my Lampito live, and the dear Theban girl, well-born[6] Ismenia. For you will have no power, not even if you make decrees seven times, who, O wretch, wast hateful even[7] to all your neighbours. Therefore also yesterday, when I was making a feast[8] to Hecate, I invited from my neighbours a good and amiable girl as the companion of my children—an eel[9] from Bœotia ; but they said they would not send it, on account of your decrees. And you will not cease[10] from these decrees, till some one, having taken you by the leg, take and break your neck. O thou[11] authoress of this deed and design, why hast thou come to me from the house with a sad countenance ?

"Rightly Voss, *'diesen langgestreckten Hals :'* provided that be rightly understood. Neither Droysen nor Bothe have understood it. Cf. Eccles. 624. Equit. 1045." *Enger.* See note on Thesm. 74.

[1] "τὴν φύσιν λέγει, τὴν ὀργήν." *Scholiast.*

[2] "μιμοῦνται τοὺς τῶν ἀνδρῶν λόγους." *Scholiast.*

[3] "*Pertinaciter.*" *Brunck.* "πάνυ." *Scholiast.* "Ipsis dentibus tenens est αὐτοδάξ, ut idem significet, quod ὀδάξ, cujus tamen significatio augetur: *pertinaciter.*" *Enger.*

[4] The first being part of their provisions for *war*, the second for the *law-courts*. Cf. Eq. 41.

[5] "λείπει ὡς." *Scholiast.* See note on Plut. 314. For the fable, see note on Pax, 133.

[6] For similar accumulations of the attributive adjective, cf. Aves, 896. Soph. Aj. 205.

[7] "Du verhasst selbst deinen Nächsten." *Droysen.*

[8] "ἑορτήν." *Scholiast.* Comp. Lidd. Lex. in voc. "Als zuı Hekatefeier Ich den Kindern gab ein Schmäuschen." *Droysen.* τοῖς παισὶ belongs to τὴν ἑταίραν. Enger and Brunck put commas after ἐγὼ and γειτόνων.

[9] πιρὰ προσδοκίαν.   [10] See Matthiä, Gr. Gr. § 517, obs. 1.

[11] "From the *Telephus* of Euripides." *Scholiast.* "The other verse Aristophanes seems to have made himself, or adopted from some other source." *Enger.*

Lys. Wicked women's proceedings and the female mind make me down-hearted, and to walk up[1] and down.

Cho. of Wom. What do you say? what do you say?

Lys. The truth! the truth!

Cho. of Wom. What is there alarming? Tell it to your own friends!

Lys. But it is disgraceful[2] to mention, and difficult to keep silent.

Cho. of Wom. Do not then conceal from me what ill we have suffered.

Lys. To speak in fewest words,[3] we long for the men.

Cho. of Wom. O Jupiter!

Lys. Why call on[4] Jupiter? In truth this is so. Consequently I am no longer able to keep them from their husbands; for they are escaping by stealth. The first I caught widening the hole where the cave of Pan[5] is; the other, again, creeping down by the pulley;[6] the other deserting; the other one upon a sparrow, purposing now to fly down to the house of Orsilochus,[7] I dragged down yesterday by the hair. And they keep making all sorts of excuses[8] so as to depart home. In sooth, one of them is now coming. Hollo you! whither are you running? [*A woman attempts to run past.*]

1st Wom. I wish to go home; for my Milesian fleeces are being destroyed by the moths at home.

Lys. What[9] moths? Will you not go back again?

1st Wom. But, by the two goddesses, I will return speedily, when I have only spread them out on the couch—

Lys. Don't spread them out, or depart any whither!

"*Mulierum facta earumque libido anxiam me reddunt, ut quid facidum sit nesciam.*" *Enger.*

[2] "From Euripides." *Scholiast.* "From Æsch. Prom. 197." *Brunck.*

[3] "ἵνα συντόμως εἴπω." *Scholiast.*

[4] "The whole of that ἰὼ Ζεῦ and τί Ζῆν' αὖτεῖς, appears to be taken om Euripides." *Enger.* "The Schol. Villois. on Il. B. 153, appears to have had this passage in his mind." *Reisig.*

[5] "The cave of Pan under the rocks called *Macræ*, on the northern side of the Acropolis. Cf. Eur. Creus. vs. 946, and vs. 11. Meurs. Ath. ii. 6." *Brunck.*

[6] "This belonged to the well in the temple of Neptune." *Droysen.*

[7] "πορνοβοσκὸς καὶ μοιχὸς, καὶ ἐπιθηλύτητι κωμῳδεῖται." *Scholiast.*

[8] Comp. Herod. vi. 66.

[9] See note on vs. 1178 *infra.*

1st Wom. Must I then suffer the fleeces to be destroyed?

Lys. *Yes*, if there be need of this.[1]   [*1st woman goes back again.*]

2nd Wom. Ah me, miserable! miserable for my flax which I have left at home unhackled!

Lys. See! here's another coming out for her unhackled flax![2]   Come back again hither!

2nd Wom. But, by Diana,[3] I will return instantly when I have barked it?[4]

Lys. Don't[5] bark it! for if you begin this, another woman will wish to do the same.   [*2nd woman goes back again.*]

3rd Wom. O mistress[6] Ilithyia, delay my parturition until I shall have gone to a place not hallowed!

Lys. Why do you talk this nonsense?

3rd Wom. I shall bring forth immediately.

Lys. But you were not pregnant yesterday.

3rd Wom. But to-day *I am*.   Come, Lysistrata, send me home as soon as possible to the midwife!

Lys. What tale are you telling? What is this hard thing[7] that you have?

3rd Wom. A male child.

Lys. Not you, by Venus! except that[8] you appear to have some hollow brazen vessel. I will know.   [*Feels her dress.*] O you ridiculous! said you you were pregnant, when you had the sacred[9] helmet?

3rd Wom. And I am pregnant too, by Jove!

Lys. Why then had you this?

3rd Wom. In order that, if my delivery should come upon

---

[1] "Ist 's nöthig, ja!" *Droysen.* For μὴ διαπετάννυ μηδ' ἀπέλθῃς, (vs. 733,) see Hermann, Vig. n. 268.

[2] "When the woman talks of her *flax*, Lysistrata, in order to give an *obscene* turn to her words, substitutes ἄμοργις for ἀμοργίς. For ἀμοργὶς has no obscenity about it; whereas ἄμοργις or ἀμόργη = amurca, which is here transferred to another kind of liquid." *Enger.*

[3] Comp. note on vs. 443.

[4] "ἀπολέψασα. Cf. vs. 953." *Enger.*

[5] See note on Vesp. 1418.

[6] "ὦ πότνι' Εἰλείθυια, belong to *Tragedy*, so that πότνια with the first syllable long is no way offensive. Vid. Reisig, p. 102." *Enger.*

[7] See Krüger, Gr. Gr. § 57, 3, obs. 6.

[8] See Krüger, Gr. Gr. § 69, 4, obs. 6.

[9] "She calls the helmet ἱερὰν, because the woman had taken it from the temple of Minerva." *Enger.*

me while still in the Acropolis, I might go into[1] this helmet
and bring forth, as the pigeons do.

Lys. What do you say? You are making excuses. The
matter is evident. Will you not wait here for the helmet's[2]
naming-day?

3rd Wom. But I am not even able to sleep in the Acropolis, since once I saw the serpent, the guardian[3] of the house.

4th Wom. And I, unhappy, am destroyed with want of
sleep through the owls, which are constantly crying, "to-
who."[4]

Lys. My good women, cease from your juggling tricks!
You long for your husbands perhaps: but do you not think
that we long for them? They spend uneasy nights, I well
know. But hold out, my good friends, and persevere still
further for a short time! for we have an oracle that we shall
prevail, unless we be distracted by seditions. Now this is[5]
the oracle.

Cho. of Wom. Tell us what it says.[6]

Lys. Be silent now! "But when the Swallows,[7] avoiding
the Hoopoes, cower into one place, and abstain from the
phallus, there shall be a rest from evils, and high-thundering
Jove shall make[8] the higher to be lower"——

Cho. of Wom. Shall we lie above them?

[1] "ἐσβᾶσα is not to be understood in its proper force, nor are we
to infer from that that the helmet was of a vast size, seeing that she
had been able to hide it under her dress." *Enger.*

[2] παρὰ προσδοκίαν, for παιδίου.

[3] "τὸν ἱερὸν δράκοντα τῆς Ἀθηνᾶς, τὸν φύλακα τοῦ ναοῦ." *Scholiast.*
Cf. Valckn. Herod. viii. 41.

[4] "*Tutubantium.* Vid. interpretes ad Plaut. Men. iv. 2, 90." *Brunck.*
Shakspeare, Love's Labour Lost, act v. sc. 2,

      "Then nightly sings the staring owl,
            To-who;
      Tu-whit, to-who, a merry note,
      While greasy Joan doth keel the pot."

Comp. Dodwell, Itin. vol. ii. p. 43.

[5] Cf. Aves, 1026, and for the construction, see notes on Vesp. 80.
Aves, 179.

[6] An example of "Anticipation." See note on Nub. 1148. Eccles. 1126.   [7] "αἱ γυναῖκες." *Scholiast.*

[8] "This signifies the same as ἄνω κάτω ποιήσει. In this passage
= shall change the state of things so much, that the safety of the
state shall depend on the women, and not on the men." *Enger.*
"τὰ ἐπικρατέστερα εὐτελέστερα ποιήσει· τοὺς ἄνδρας δηλονότι." *Schol.*

Lys. ——"but if the Swallows be at variance,[1] and fly away with their wings from the sacred temple, no longer shall any bird whatever appear to be more lewd."

Cho. of Wom. By Jove, the oracle is clear! Let us not then, O all ye gods, give up through suffering; but let us go in. For this *will be* disgraceful, my dearest women, if we shall betray the oracle.[2] [*Exit Lysistrata.*]

Cho. of Men. I wish to tell you a story, which I once heard myself when I was yet a boy; in this wise:[3]—There was once a youth, Melanion, who, avoiding marriage, went to a desert place and dwelt in the mountains. And then he hunted hares,[4] having made nets: and he had a dog. And he returned home again no more by reason of his hatred. So much[5] did he abominate the women: and we, who are chaste, abominate them no less than Melanion.[6]

Old Man. I wish, old woman, to kiss you——

Woman. Then you shall not eat an onion.[7]

Old Man. —— and to lift up *your leg* and tread on you.

Woman. You wear a large beard.

Old Man. For Myronides[8] also was rough in those parts, and black-bottomed to all his foes; and thus also was Phormio.[9]

---

[1] "Doch wenn sie nicht einträchtiglich sind." *Droysen.*

[2] "If we leave the oracle in the lurch." *Droysen.*

[3] Enger's edition connects οὕτως with ἦν νέος, and gives a full stop after ὤν. οὕτως is the regular word used *to introduce a story.* Plato, Phæd. § 29, ἦν οὕτω δὴ παῖς, μᾶλλον δὲ νεανίσκος. Vesp. 1182, οὕτω ποτ' ἦν μῦς καὶ γαλῆ. Cf. Meineke, Com. Fragm. iii. p. 82, who adds, "οὕτως is generally prefixed to stories which a person is going to relate." "For Melanion the son of Amphidamas, and his love for Atalanta, see Apollod. iii. 9." *Dindorf.*

[4] See Lobeck, Phryn. p. 627.

[5] "We must write οὕτως . . . ἐβδελύχθη τὰς γυναῖκας." *Enger.*

[6] "And them with no inferior hate
We, as Melanion wise, abominate." *Wheelwright.*

[7] "Women are accustomed to slap the faces of those who kiss them when they don't choose. Correctly therefore the Scholiast: 'υἱον κλαύσει καὶ χωρὶς κρομμύων.'" *Enger.*

[8] "δύο Μυρωνίδαι ἦσαν· ἐνθάδε μέμνηται τοῦ ἐν Οἰνοφύτοις νικήσαντος." *Scholiast.* See Thucyd. i. 108. For καὶ γάρ, see Krüger, Gr. Gr. § 69, 32, obs. 21.

[9] "De Phormione Scholiasta ad Pac. 347: 'αὐτοῦ μέμνηται ὁ κωμικὸς ἐν Ἱππεῦσι (vs. 562) καὶ Βαβυλωνίοις, Εὔπολις Ἀσ ρατεύτοις.'" *Enger.* He was the son of Asopus. See note on Pax, 347. Brunck reads ὡς δὲ καὶ, which seems much better. See notes on Pax, 150, 363.

CHO. OF WOM. I also wish to tell you a story in reply to your Melanion. There was a certain Timon,[1] unsettled, encompassed round as to his face with unapproachable thorns,[2] a scion of the Furies. This Timon, then, by reason of his hatred, went off having imprecated many *curses* against wicked men. So much did he always hate in return your[3] wicked men; but he was very dear to the women.

WOMAN. Would you that I strike your jaw?

OLD MAN. By no means! I am afraid of it.

WOMAN. But I will strike you with my leg.

OLD MAN. You will show your ancles.

WOMAN. Yet, however, you would not see them with long hair, though I am an old woman, but depillated with the lamp.[4]

[*Enter Lysistrata attended by several women.*]

LYS. Ho! ho, women! come hither to me quickly!

1ST WOM. What's the matter? tell me, what means the cry?

LYS. I see a man, a man approaching frantic, seized[5] with the transports of love. O mistress,[6] who rulest over Cyprus and Cytheræ and Paphos, proceed straight on the course you are going!

1ST WOM. Where is he, whoever he is?

LYS. Near the *temple* of Ceres.[7]

1ST WOM. Oh, by Jove, in truth there is! Who[8] in the world *is* he?

LYS. Look! Does any one of you know him?

MYRRH. Yes, by Jove, I do; and he is my husband Cinesias.[9]

---

[1] See note on Aves, 1549. For ἀΐδρυτος, see Lob. Phryn. p. 730; Meineke, Com. Frag. ii. p. 135, 136; Eur. Iph. T. 971.

[2] "Der Welt mit unzugänglichem Hasse dorn umzäunt." *Droysen.*

[3] "ὑμῶν vix verum est." *Enger.* See Krüger, Gr. Gr. § 47, 9. τοῖς Μακεδόσιν αὐτῶν, Thuc. iv. 126. τῶν ἡβώντων αὐτῶν, ibid. 132. τοῖσιν ἀπράγμοσιν ὑμῶν, Vesp. 1040. Cf. ibid. 1274. Nub. 527.

[4] Comp. Eccles. 12.   [5] See Krüger, Gr. Gr. § 28, 10, obs. 5.

[6] "This appears to be a verse of some tragedian, so that Κύπρου with the first syllable long is no offence. See Reisig, p. 102." *Enger.*

[7] "There was a temple of Ceres, called Χλόη, in the city near the Acropolis. See Meurs. Gr. Fer. in Χλόεια." *Brunck.* "Cerec' name *Chloe* is taken from the *verdure* of the corn-fields. See Athen. xiv. p. 618 D. So '*flava Ceres*' in Virgil." *Bergler.*

[8] Cf. note on vs. 171

[9] "We must not understand Cinesias son of Meles, the Dithyrambic poet. See Meineke, Com. Frag. i. p. 229." *Enger*

Lys. 'Tis your business [1] now to roast him, and torture him, and cheat him utterly, and to love him and not love him, and to afford him all things, except those of which [2] the cuo is conscious.

Myrrh. Don't trouble yourself: I'll do so.

Lys. Moreover I will remain [3] here and cheat him utterly and roast him thoroughly. But do you depart! [*Exit Myrrhina, and enter Cinesias, attended by a servant leading his child by the hand.*]

Cin. Ah me, miserable! What a spasm and what a tension possesses me, [4] as if I were racked upon a wheel!

Lys. Who is this who stands within the outposts? [5]

Cin. I!

Lys. A man?

Cin. Yes, a man.

Lys. Then will you not begone out of the way?

Cin. Who are you who drive me out?

Lys. A day-watcher.

Cin. By the gods, then, call me out Myrrhina!

Lys. Must I call [6] your Myrrhina, quoth'a? Who are you?

Cin. Her husband, Cinesias the Pæonian. [7]

Lys. Welcome, thou dearest! for thy name [8] is not withont

---

[1] "Sei 's deines Amtes, ihn zu spicken, am Spiess zu drehn,
Herumzunarren, zu lieben ja, zu lieben nein,
Dich ihm hinzugeben, so weit—der Kelch es dir erlaubt!"
Droysen.

[2] See Krüger, Gr. Gr. § 51, 10, obs. 1.

[3] Dobree proposed περιμένουσ', *eum opperiens.*

[4] Plaut. Cist. ii. 1, 4, jactor, crucior, agitor, stimulor, versor in amoris rotâ miser. Cf. Plut. 876. Nub. 1208.

[5] "Halt! wer da innerhalb der Postenreihe?" *Droysen.*

[6] "καλέσω is the aorist subjunctive, and by ἰδοῦ she mocks the previous words of Cinesias, ἐκκάλεσόν μοι Μυρρίνην. See Dobree, Plut. 965." *Enger.* Cf. Krüger, Gr. Gr. § 54, 2, obs. 3. Mus. Crit. ii. p. 39. Elmsley, Med. vs. 1242. Dawes, M. C. p. 123. Hom. Il. K. 62. Eur. Med. 1275. For ἰδοῦ, see note on Eccles. 133.

[7] "Gentile Attici pagi." *Dindorf's Index.* Enger reads Πεονίδης, from the conjecture of Bentley. "παίζει πρὸς τὸ πέος, ὡς ἀπὸ δήμου -νός." *Scholiast.*

[8] "διαπαίζει τὰς γυναῖκας ὡς ἐρώσας τοῦ κινεῖν." *Scholiast.*

"Willkommen, Liebster! denn bei Gott nicht unberühmt
Ist hier bei uns dein Name mehr noch ungenannt;
Dein liebes Weibchen führt dich immerfort im Mund.
Wenn sie 'nen Apfel oder ein Ei hat, sagt sie gleich:
'O könnt' Ich 's meinem Kinesias geben.' " *Droysen.*

fame among us, nor yet inglorious. For your wife constantly has you in her mouth ;[1] and if she get an egg or an apple, she says, "May Cinesias have this!"

CIN. Oh, by the gods!

LYS. Yes, by Venus; and if any conversation about husbands arise, straightway your wife says, that every thing else is nonsense in comparison with Cinesias.

CIN. Go then, call her!

LYS. What then? will you give me any thing?

CIN. Aye, by Jove, will I, if you wish it! I have this What, then, I have, I give you.

LYS. Come then, let me[2] descend and call her.

CIN. Very quickly then! [*Exit Lysistrata.*] For I have no pleasure in my life since she went away from the house; but I am grieved when I go in ; and every thing appears to me to be desolate ; and I find no pleasure in my victuals when I eat, for I am tortured.

MYRRH. (*talking with Lysistrata in the Acropolis above*). I love him, I love him ; but he is not willing to be loved by me. Do not call me to him !

CIN. My dearest little Myrrhina, why do you act thus ? Come down[3] hither !

MYRRH. By Jove, I will not *go down* thither !

CIN. Will you not come down when I call you, Myrrhina ?

MYRRH. *No;* for you call me when you don't want me at all.

CIN. I not in want of you ? Nay, rather, undone.

MYRRH. I will go away.

CIN. Nay don't, pray ! but at least hearken to your little child ! [*Turning to the child.*] Ho you ! will you not call[4] your mother?

CHILD. Mamma! mamma! mamma![5]

---

[1] Comp. Æsch. Theb. 51.

[2] Cf. vss. 890, 916. Plut. 768, 790, 964. Pax, 234, 252. Vesp. 148, 990, 1497. Eccles. 725, 869. Soph. Phil. 1452. Sometimes the *present* subjunctive is used in the same manner. See Vesp. 906, 990. Krüger, Gr. Gr. § 54, 2, obs. 1. Elmsl. Heracl. 559. Med. 1242.

[3] See Krüger, Gr. Gr. § 36, 4, obs. 4.

[4] See Krüger, Gr. Gr. § 53, 7, obs. 4.

[5] "Puerulum non ipse Cinesias, ut Droysenius arbitratur, sed Manes gestabat. Vid. vs. 908." *Enger.*

CIN. Ho you! what are[1] you about? Do you not even pity the little child, being unwashed and unsuckled six days past?

MYRRH. Of course I pity it; but its father[2] is negligent.

CIN. Come down, my good girl, to your little child!

MYRRH. What[3] a thing it is to be a mother! I must descend. For what shall I do?[4] [*Enter Myrrhina.*]

CIN. Why she seems to me to have become much younger, and more loving[5] to look at; and in that she is cross to me, and bears herself haughtily,[6] these are the very things now which kill me with desire.

MYRRH. O thou dearest little child[7] of a bad father! come, let me kiss you, most dear to your mother!

CIN. Why, O wretch, do you do this, and comply with other women, and cause me to be grieved, and[8] art grieved yourself?

MYRRH. Don't put your hand on me!

CIN. While you are ruining[9] my and your property, which is in the house.

MYRRH. I care little about them.

CIN. Care you little about your thread, which is tossed[10] about by the cocks and hens?

---

[1] Comp. Nub. 708, 816. Vesp. 1. Av. 1044. Nub. 662, 791. See Krüger, Gr. Gr. § 46, 3, obs. 1.

[2] An example of the *Ethical Dative* (der ethische Dativ); mostly in the case of personal pronouns. See Krüger, Gr. Gr. § 48, 6, and vss. 101, 1192. Pax. 269, 282, 893. Nub. 1313.

[3] Eurip. Iph. A. 917, δεινὸν τὸ τίκτειν, καὶ φέρει φίλτρον μέγα. Cf. Phœn. 358.

[4] "Formulam illustravit Valck. ad Phœn. p. 335." *Brunck.* Cf. vs. 954. Pl. 603. Av. 1432. Eccles. 860. Nub. 798. Æsch. Theb. 1060, ed. Blomf.

[5] See note on Aves, 451.

[6] "Correctly the Ravenna Scholiast, 'ἀλαζονικῶς θρύπτεται.' On the etymology, Schol. Venet. ad Pac. 25, 'οἱ μὲν ἀπὸ βρένθους τοῦ φυτοῦ, οἱ δὲ μύρου εἶδος, ᾧ χρίονται αἱ γυναῖκες καὶ ἐπ' αὐτῷ μέγα φρονοῦσι.' Brunck cites Hemst. ad Lucian. Dial. Mort. x. 8, p. 367." *Enger.* Cf. Equit. 512. Xenoph. Anab. i. 8, 11.

[7] Æsch. Prom. Solut., ἐχθροῦ πατρός μοι τοῦτο φίλτατον τέκνον. Comp. vs. 684.

[8] A parody on Eur. Med. 1361, καὐτή γε λυπεῖ, καὶ κακῶν κοινωνὸς εἶ.

[9] Cf. vs. 999. Plut. 996. Vesp. 939. Nub. 1427. Aves, 822. Equit. 75, 1323.

[10] "Von den Hühnern ganz zerrissen wird." *Droysen.* "διασπωκίνης." *Scholiast.*

MYRRH. Even so, by Jove![1]

CIN. The rites of Venus have been so long a time uncelebrated by you. Will you not go back?

MYRRH. Not I, by Jove! unless you make peace and cease from the war.

CIN. Therefore, if it seem good to you, we will e'en do so.

MYRRH. Therefore, if it seem good to you, I will e'en go thither; but now I have sworn not to do it.

CIN. At least lie down with me for[2] a while!

MYRRH. Certainly not! and yet I cannot say[3] that I do not love you.

CIN. Do you love me? Why then do you[4] not lie down, my little Myrrhina?

MYRRH. O you ridiculous man! in presence of the child?

CIN. No, by Jove! but, Manes, do you take it home! [*Servant leads the child off.*] There! the child is now out of the way: will you not lie down?

MYRRH. Why, where *could* one do this, you rogue?

CIN. Very well,[5] where the *temple* of Pan is.

MYRRH. Why, how, pray, any longer could I go to the Acropolis pure?

CIN. Very 'well, I ween, after you have washed in the Clepsydra.[6]

MYRRH. Shall I then, pray, break my oath, you rogue, after having sworn?

CIN. On my head be it![7] Don't be concerned at all for your oath!

MYRRH. Come then, let me bring a little bed for us.

CIN. By no means! It suffices us upon the ground.

---

[1] "Ist einerlei!" *Droysen.*

[2] See note on Plut. 1055, and for ἀλλά, see note on Thesm. 424.

[3] "*Etsi non possim negare.*" *Brunck.* Cf. Thes. 603, ποῖ τις τρέψεται; Krüger, Gr. Gr. § 53, 7, obs. 3, and note on Aves, 847.

[4] See Krüger, Gr. Gr. § 53, 6, obs. 2.

[5] Brunck compares Eccles. 321. Thesm. 292. "In this passage Reisig saw that we must write, ὅπου; τὸ τοῦ Πανὸς καλόν, as I have edited." *Enger.* For τάλαν, see note on Eccles. 90.

[6] "Clepsydra was a fountain at Athens flowing from the Acropolis." *Brunck.* "It was called Clepsydra, because it was an intermittent spring. Formerly it was called Empedo." *Scholiast.*

[7] Comp. Ach. 833.

MYRRH. By Apollo, I will not[1] make you lie down upon the ground, although being such! [*Runs off.*]

CIN. Of a truth it is right well evident that my wife loves me.[2]

MYRRH. (*returning with a bedstead*). There! lie down quickly; and I will undress myself. [*Cinesias lies down upon the bed.*] And yet, bless[3] my soul, I must bring out a mattress.

CIN. What mattress? Don't talk to me[4] of that!

MYRRH. Yea, by Diana! for it were shameful *to lie* upon the bed-cords.

CIN. Let me give you a kiss then!

MYRRH. There! [*Kisses him and runs off.*]

CIN. Ah! Return then very quickly!

MYRRH. (*returning with a mattress*). There's a mattress! Lie down! I'll now undress myself. And yet, bless my soul! you have not a pillow.

CIN. Neither do I want one.

MYRRH. But, by Jove, I do! [*Runs off.*]

CIN. Truly my carcase is entertained like Hercules.[5]

MYRRH. (*returning with a pillow*). Rise! jump up![6]

CIN. I have every thing now.[7]

MYRRH. All, pray?[8]

CIN. Come then, my little treasure![9]

[1] μὰ τὸν Ἀπ. μὴ κατακλινῶ = οὐ μὴ κατακλινῶ. See note on Eccles. 1000. For καίπερ, see note on Eccles. 159.

[2] See note on Pax, 913. "A comma is generally placed after δήλη 'στιν, so that καλῶς is joined with φιλεῖ. The recent editors have rightly followed Schäfer on Greg. Cor. p. 531. See also his note on Soph Rex, 1008, ὦ παῖ, καλῶς εἰ δῆλος οὐκ εἰδὼς τί δρᾷς. where the Augustan glossographer rightly explains καλῶς by πάνυ." *Enger.*

[3] See notes on Vesp. 524. Av. 648. Cf. vss. 921, 926.

[4] See Krüger, Gr. Gr. § 48, 6, obs. 2, and § 62, 3, obs. 12. Cf. Equit. 19. Nub. 84, 433. Vesp. 1179, 1400, and vs. 938, *infra.*

[5] Comp. Equit. 1162, and see note on Plut. 314. "παροιμία ἐπὶ τῶν βραδυνόντων. οἱ γὰρ ὑποδεχόμενοι τὸν Ἡρακλέα βραδύνουσιν. ἀδηφάγος γὰρ ὁ ἥρως." *Scholiast.*

[6] "That I may put the pillow under you." *Scholiast.*

[7] "*Hæc sufficiant, jam omnia habeo : accumbe igitur*" *Enger.*

[8] "Officiosa mulier, quam hic Myrrhina gerit, quasi meditans, num revera nihil jam possit desiderari, se ipsam interrogat ἅπαντα δῆτα;" *Enger.* I have followed Brunck.

[9] Comp. Ach. 1201.

MYRRH. Now I'll undo my girdle![1] Remember then; do not deceive me about the peace.

CIN. Then[2] may I perish, by Jove!

MYRRH. You have not a counterpane.[3]

CIN. Neither do I want one, by Jove; but I want something else.

MYRRH. Don't trouble yourself! You shall do so; for I will come speedily. [*Runs off.*]

CIN. The woman[4] will kill me with her bed-clothes.

MYRRH. (*returning with a counterpane*). Raise yourself up!

CIN. But I am raised up already.

MYRRH. Would you that I anoint you?

CIN. Nay, do not, by Apollo!

MYRRH. Yea, by Venus, whether you will or no! [*Runs off.*]

CIN. O Lord Jove, would the unguent were[5] poured out!

MYRRH. (*returning with a flask of ointment*). Reach forth your hand now, and take it and anoint yourself!

CIN. By Apollo, this ointment is not sweet! unless to be dilatory and not savouring of marriage be so.[6]

MYRRH. Ah me, miserable! I have brought the Rhodian[7] unguent.

[1] "Das Busenband." *Droysen.*
[2] See notes on Av. 161, 1308.   [3] "Schlafpelz." *Droysen.*
[4] "ἀντὶ τοῦ ἡ γυνή." *Scholiast.* Cf. Krüger, Gr. Gr. § 43, 1, obs. 1. Viger, p. 77.
[5] "Dass alle Salbe zum Henker wäre!" *Droysen.* "Ubicunque εἴθε vel αἴθε additur optativo, significatur optari *ut sit aliquid nunc, quod non est*, aut *ut futurum sit, quod non est futurum.*" *Hermann.* "εἴθε, *utinam*, stands with an optative, or with an historical tense of the indicative: εἴθε ἄπίοι *utinam abeat*, εἴθε ἄπελθοι *utinam abierit*, εἴθε ἀπύει *utinam abiret*, εἴθε ἀπῆλθεν *utinam abiisset.*" *Krüger.* See his Grammar, § 54, 3, obs. 3. Cf. vs. 973, *infra.* Equit. 404, 619. Thesm. 1050. Eccles. 938, 947.
[6] "Voss translates it rightly enough as to the sense: '*nicht lieblich, nein bei Apollon, ist die Salbe da; nur ledigen Aufschub duftet sie, nichts Hochzeitliches.*' εἰ μὴ—γε after a negation *fortius affirmat*, and signifies the same as ἀλλά—γε. Vide L. Dindorf, ap. Steph. Thes. iii. p. 190. Cf. Equit. 185, μῶν ἐκ καλῶν εἰ κἀγαθῶν; ΑΛ. μὰ τοὺς θεούς, εἰ μὴ 'κ πονηρῶν γε, *immo ex improbis.* Thesm. 898, αὕτη Θεονόη Πρωτέως. Γ. μὰ τὼ θεώ, εἰ μὴ Κρίτυλλά γ' Ἀντιθέου Γαργηττόθεν, *immo sum Critylla.* Fritzsche has not rightly understood this passage." *Enger.*
[7] Bergler remarks, that the Rhodian unguent was an inferior sort. Enger reads ῥόδιον.

Cin. 'Tis excellent! Never mind it,[1] my good girl!

Myrrh. Nonsense! [*Runs off.*]

Cin. May he perish most miserably, who first boiled un-guents!

Myrrh. (*returning with a fresh flask*). Take this casket!

Cin. But I have another. Come, you tiresome[2] thing, lie down and don't bring me any thing at all!

Myrrh. I will do so, by Diana! In sooth I am taking off my shoes. But, my dearest, see that you vote to make peace.

Cin. I will determine about it. [*Exit Myrrhina.*] My wife has undone me and killed me, both in all other respects, and because she has flayed me and gone. Ah me! what shall I do?[3] Whom shall I solicit, being disappointed of the prettiest of all? How shall I educate this? Where's the Dog-fox?[4] Let out[5] a nurse to me.

Cho. of Men. O thou unhappy, thou art afflicted in thy soul with dreadful suffering, having been deceived! And I pity you, alas! alas! For what kidneys could hold out, what soul,[6] and what bowels, and what loins? What rump could, being strained, and not having to do with any one in the morning?[7]

Cin. O Jove, what dreadful convulsions![8]

Cho. of Men. This, however, has your all-abominable and all-execrable *wife* now done to you.

Cin. No, by Jove, but dear and sweetest of all!

Cho. of Men. Don't talk to me[9] of sweet! Abominable,

---

[1] Comp. Equit. 1243. Reisig, Com. Crit. Soph. Col. p. 344.

[2] "οἰζυρὸς, which has the υ long according to analogy and the usage of the poets, always shortens it in Aristophanes. Cf. Nub. 655. Vesp. 1504, 1514. Av. 1641." *Enger.*

[3] See note on vs. 884.   [4] See note on Equit. 1069.

[5] "Schaff schnell ein Hürlein Amme!" *Droysen.* He should have said "verpachte schnell," &c.

[6] "Parodied from the *Andromeda* of Euripides, ποῖαι λιβάδες, ποία σειρήν." *Scholiast.*

[7] Comp. vs. 1089, *infra*, and Pax, 1313.

[8] "δεινῶν ἀντισπασμῶν, without an article, is suspected by Reisig: on this see Hermann, Nub. 817." *Enger.* For similar omissions of the article see Nub. 1476. Plut. 1126, 1128, 1132. Eur. Hipp. 527, 1444. Alc. 400. Soph. Aj. 908. Plato, Rep. vi. p. 509, C. Eur. Orest. 402, 1022. Androm. 1179. Herc. F. 899, 1374. Hec. 661. Æsch. Pers. 114, 728 924.

[9] See note on vs. 1178.

abominable certainly. [*Exit Cinesias.*] O Jove, Jove, would that you would whirl her away and turn her round,[1] and carry her off with a great whirlwind and hurricane, as *you do* the heaps of corn, and then let her go, and she might be borne back again to the earth, and then suddenly bestride the trident! [*Enter Lacedæmonian Herald and Committee-man.*]

HER. Where is the Senate of the Athenians, or the[2] Prytanes? I wish to make an announcement.

COM. Whether are you a man or Conisalus?[3]

HER. By the two gods, I have come from Sparta as a herald, young[4] man, about the peace!

COM. And then, pray, have you come with a spear under your arm?

HER. No, by Jove, not I!

COM. Whither are you turning yourself? Why, pray, do you put forward your cloak? or have you a swelling in the groin from your journey?

HER. The fellow's a fool,[5] by Castor!

COM. But you are excited, O you most abominable!

HER. No, by Jove, not I! Don't talk nonsense[6] again!

COM. But what's this here?

HER. A Spartan scytale.[7]

COM. Aye, if this too is a Spartan scytale.[8] But tell me the truth, as to one[9] that knows! How are your affairs at Sparta?

[1] Comp. Thesm. 61.
[2] "The nominative masc. and fem. of the article originally began with a τ. τός and τή, however, are not found. In the nom. plur. the Dorians said τοί. ταί, as did the Epic writers frequently. Sometimes in Herodotus, i. 186, vi. 68." *Krüger.* Comp. Rose's Greek Inscriptions, p. 59, and Class. ii. No. 6, p. 66. For μυσίξαι, comp. vs. 94.
[3] "δαίμων πριαπώδης." *Scholiast.*
[4] "κυρσάνιε· νεανία, ἔφηβε." *Suidas.* "The two gods," in the mouth of a Spartan, mean Castor and Pollux. See note on Ach. 905.
[5] "λῆρος καὶ μάταιος." *Scholiast.* "παλαιόρ· μῶρος." *Hesychius.* "παλεός· ὁ σκώπτης. τίθεται καὶ ἐπὶ τοῦ ἄφρονος." *Suidas.*
[6] Pres. imperat. of πλαδδιάω, *nugor.* Cf. vs. 171. "So πάδη, ἱρώτη, ἔμβη, ὄρη." *Brunck.*
[7] See note on Av. 1283.
[8] "*Scilicet si hæc quoque (ἡ πόσθη μου) est scytaïa Laconica.*" *Enger.*
[9] "For the common formula ὡς πρὸς εἰδότα or εἰδότας, see Schæfer ad Greg. Cor. p. 833." *Enger.*

HER. All Sparta is excited, and all the allies are excited There is need of Pellene.[1]

COM. From whom did this misfortune fall upon you? From Pan?[2]

HER. No; Lampito, I think, began it; then the other women throughout Sparta at once, as if *starting* from one starting-post, drove away their husbands from their beds.

COM. How are you then?

HER. We are distressed;[3] for we go bending through the city, as if carrying[4] lamps. For the women will not even suffer us to touch them, till we all with one accord make peace with Greece.

COM. This thing has been sworn to by the women from all parts: I have just now[5] ascertained it. But bid them as soon as possible send here ambassadors with full powers *to treat* about peace! and I will bid the senate choose other ambassadors from hence. having exhibited this.

HER. I will fly; for you speak altogether most excellently. [*Exeunt Herald and Committee-man.*]

CHO. OF MEN. There is no wild beast more unconquerable than a woman, nor fire, nor any panther so shameless.

CHO. OF WOM. Why, are you aware of this, and then make war upon me, when it is in your power, you wretch, to have me a firm friend?

CHO. OF MEN. "For I will[6] never cease to hate woman."

CHO. OF WOM. Well, when[7] you please: but now I will not suffer you to be thus naked. For see how ridiculous you are! Come, let me come to you and put on[8] your sleeveless coat!

CHO. OF MEN. This,[9] by Jove, which you have done is

---

[1] "A *courtesan*, according to the Scholiast. Supposing this to be merely a conjecture of the Scholiast's, as Dindorf suspects, still the conjecture is a very probable one. Otherwise the passage is unintelligible." *Enger.*

[2] "ἐπεὶ ἐρωτικὸς ὁ Πάν." *Scholiast.* Cf. Eccles. 1069.

[3] Hermann refers to Kön on Greg. Cor. p. 230.

[4] "For those who carry lamps in a high wind are accustomed to stoop as they go, to keep them from being extinguished." *Bergler*

[5] Cf. Aves, 922.　　　　　[6] A quotation from Eurip. Hippol. 664.

[7] "Ganz wie dir 's gefällt!" *Droysen.*

[8] I understand this to be an *aorist subjunctive,* as vss. 864. 890, 916.

[9] See note on Plut. 555. "The adverb τότε denotes past time, both that which has long passed by, and that which has passed by

not amiss! But, indeed, through evil anger I formerly stripped it off.[1]

CHO. OF WOM. In the first place, you appear[2] a man; in the next place, you are not ridiculous: and if you had not vexed me, I would have seized and taken out this little insect in your eye, which now is in it.

CHO. OF MEN. This, it seems, is the thing which was distressing me. See! there's[3] my ring! Pull it out! and then show it me, when you've taken it out! for, by Jove, it has been stinging my eye this long while.

CHO. OF WOM. Well, I'll do so; although you are a cross man. O Jove! in truth a monstrous gnat to look at is in your eye. Don't you see it? Is not this gnat a Tricorysian one?[4]

CHO. OF MEN. By Jove, you have eased[5] me; for it has been digging wells in me this long while; so that, after it has been taken out, my tears flow copiously.

CHO. OF WOM. But I will wipe you clean, although you are very bad, and will kiss you.

CHO. OF MEN. Do not kiss[6] me!

CHO. OF WOM. Whether[7] you will or no.

CHO. OF MEN. A plague[8] take you! since you are wheedling by nature; and that saying is rightly said, and not badly "Neither with[9] utterly-abandoned *women*, nor without utterly-

very recently. It is rendered by *olim, prius, modo*. See Thesm. 13 Soph. Elect. 278, 676." *Brunck.*

[1] Cf. vs. 888, *supra.* Ran. 935. Aves, 268. Pax, 234, 316, 326, 337 Thesm. 747. Equit. 180, 366, 437.

[2] "Wieder siehst du jetzt ein Mann aus." *Droysen.*

[3] "He offers her a ring with which to take the gnat out of his eye." *Scholiast.* "The interpretation of the Scholiast is correct, neither is the copula necessary, since he offers the ring, saying, '*En, annulum! accipe et eme id.*' We are to understand a δακτύλιος φαρμακίτης, such as the ancients used for bites of animals." *Enger.* Cf. Plut. 884.

[4] "Tricorythus was an Attic burgh, where, according to the Scholiast, there were many gnats, and of a great size, as we learn from this passage." *Enger.*

[5] "Du hast mich recht erleichtert." *Droysen.*

[6] See Porson, Hec. 1166. Schäfer, Greg. Cor. p. 17.

[7] See note on Eccles. 981.　　[8] See note on vs. 391.

[9] Susarion, κακὸν γυναῖκες· ἀλλ' ὅμως, ὦ δημόται,
　　οὐκ ἔστιν οἰκεῖν οἰκίαν ἄνευ κακοῦ.
Comp. Strabo xiv. p. 659. Metellus Numidicus ap. Aul. Gell. i. 6.

abandoned *women.*" But now I make peace with you, and henceforth I will neither do any thing bad any more,[1] nor suffer it from you. Come, let us be united and begin[2] our song together !

Cho. of Wom. We are not prepared,[3] sirs, to speak any ill at all[4] of any of the citizens ; but, quite the contrary, both to say and do every thing good ; for our present[5] sufferings even are sufficient. But let every man and woman make it known,[6] if any wishes to receive money, two or three minæ : we have[7] plenty within, and have purses. And if ever peace appear, whoever shall have now borrowed from us, shall never repay what he shall have received We are going to entertain some Carystian[8] strangers, honourable and good men ; and I have still some broth ; and I had a sucking-pig ; and this I have slaughtered, so that you shall eat tender and fine meat. Come therefore to my house to-day ! But you ought to do this early,[9] having bathed, both you and your children ; and then to go in, and ask no one any questions, but boldly to proceed straight forward, as if into your own houses, for the door shall be——shut.

Cho. of Men. Well now, see ! here are the ambassadors from Sparta coming, trailing beards ! as if with a bandage[10] about their thighs. [*Enter Spartan Ambassadors.*] Spartans, in the first place, welcome ! next, tell us in what state you are come !

Spart. What need to say many words to you ? for you may see in what state we have come.

---

[1] Eur. Andr. 732, οὔτ' οἶν τι δράσω φλαῦρον, οὔτε πείσομαι.

[2] "*Incipiamus una canticum.*" *Brunck.*

[3] "Nicht ist es unser Wunsch." *Droysen.*

[4] Comp. Ed. Rev. vol. xix. p. 76. Porson, Hec. Præf. p. xxxvi.

[5] The disasters in Sicily and at Eretria. Cf. Thuc. viii. 95.

[6] "λεγέτω τίνος δεῖται." *Scholiast.*

[7] Enger has adopted Mr. Burges' conjecture ὡς πλέω 'στιν ἄχομεν βαλάντια, which he justly calls '*egregia sane emendatio.*'

[8] "διαβάλλονται ὡς μοιχοὶ οἱ Καρύστιοι." *Scholiast.* "It may be remarked, that when the oligarchy took their last steps for the overthrow of the democracy, Carystians appeared among the armed men who assisted them. Cf. Thuc. viii. 69." *Droysen.*

[9] For these early potations, Enger refers to Av. 131. Athen. i. p. 17, D., iii. p. 103, C., vii. p. 279. Pherecrates ap. Bekk. Anecd. p. 838, 19. Meineke, Com. Frag. ii. p. 548.

[10] See Lidd. Lex. "*Suile vimineum.*" *Brunck.* So Droysen.

CHO. OF MEN. Bless me! This calamity is dreadfully excited! It seems to be worse inflamed.

SPART. Unspeakably! What *can* one say?[1] But let some one come by all means and make peace with us, as he pleases.

CHO. OF MEN. Well now, I see these here aborigines putting back their dress from their bellies, like wrestlers, so that the disease[2] appears to be one belonging to an athlete. [*Enter Athenians.*]

ATHEN. Who can tell us where Lysistrata is? for see! we men here[3] *have come*, of such rank!

CHO. OF MEN. Both this disease and the other agree in this way.[4] Does a tension seize you towards morning?

ATHEN. No, by Jove, but we are killed when we undergo[5] this: so that, if some one will not quickly make peace between us, we shall certainly commit a rape upon Clisthenes.[6]

CHO. OF MEN. If you are wise, you will take your clothes, so that none of the mutilaters of the Hermæ[7] shall see you.

ATHEN. By Jove, you certainly say well!

SPART. Yea, by the two gods, by all means! Come, let us put on our dress![8]

ATHEN. Welcome, Spartans! We have suffered shameful things.

SPART. O my dearest! of a truth we should have suffered dreadful things, if the men could have seen[9] us excited.

---

[1] See note on vs. 171, *supra.*

[2]   "Dass man meinen möcht'
Es sei ein recht gymnastisch Wesen von Krankheit das." *Droysen.*

[3] Comp. Aves, 311, 1123. Nub. 141. Equit. 1099.

[4] "Ja, deine Krankheit ist und deren Einer Art." *Droysen.*
"ταύτῃ is an adverb : *et hic Atheniensium et alter Lacedæmoniorum morbus consentiunt isto modo, vel, hac in re.*" *Enger.* Cf. Bernh. W. S. p. 428.

[5] "i. e. πάσχοντες." *Enger.* "So in vs. 1090, δρᾶν refers, not to *action,* but to *suffering.* See Heindorf on Plato Soph. p. 403." *Dindorf* (on vs. 1165).

[6] Always ridiculed as a woman or else as effeminate. See note on Equit. 1374.

[7] "εἰ μὴ περιβαλεῖσθε, ἀλλὰ φανερὰ ἕξετε τὰ αἰδοῖα, ἀκρωτηριάσει τις ὑμᾶς τῶν Ἑρμοκοπιδῶν." *Scholiast.* Herod. ii. 51, τοῦ δὲ Ἑρμέω τὰ ἀγάλματα ὀρθὰ ἔχειν τὰ αἰδοῖα κ. τ. λ. There is also an allusion to the mutilation of the Hermæ. See Thuc. vi. 27, 61.

[8] An example of the use of the Digamma, as Dindorf remarks.

[9] εἰ ἂν εἶδον is no solœcism, as Monk (Hippol. 697) imagined. See Jelf, Gr. Gr. § 854, obs. 2. Matthiä. § 508, obs. 1. Harper's

ATHEN. Come now, Spartans, you must mention each severally. For what are you come hither?

SPART. As ambassadors about peace.

ATHEN. In truth you say well: we also *are come* on account of this. Why then do we not summon Lysistrata, who alone can make peace between us!

SPART. Aye, by the two gods, and Lysistratus,[1] if you like.

CHO. OF MEN. But there's no occasion, as it seems, for us to call her; for see! here she[2] is herself coming out, when she heard it! [*Enter Lysistrata.*] Hail! O thou bravest of all *women;* now it behoveth thee to be clever,[3] good, easy, grave, mild, and shrewd; for the chiefs of the Grecians, caught by thy charm, have yielded to thee, and referred all their grievances to thee in common.

LYS. Well, the business is not difficult, if one were to find people eager *for peace,*[4] and not making trial of each other. But I'll soon know. Where is Peace?[5] First take and lead forward the Spartans, and not with a hand violent or self-willed, nor as our husbands[6] used unskilfully to do it, but very affectionately,[7] as is proper women should. If any do not give his hand, lead him by the nose. [*Enter Peace represented by a beautiful girl.*] Come! do you also lead these Athenians, and lead them forward, having caught hold of them by whatever part they present. You Spartans, stand close beside me, and you on this side, and hear my words! I am a woman, it is true; but sense is in me :[8] "and of myself

Powers of the Greek Tenses, p. 81. Hermann, Vig. n. 291, 280. Bremi, Demosth. Cor. § 101. Schäfer, Meletem. Crit. p. 50, 61.

[1] A mere play upon the name Lysistrata, (cf. 554,) more especially with respect to its termination. No express allusion to the Lysistratus mentioned in Acharn. 855. Equit. 1265. Vesp. 787.

[2] "Sie kommt da selbst ja, da sie es hörte, schon heraus." *Droysen.*

[3] "Umsichtig, beherzt, nachgiebig, gerecht, ehrwürdig, gelinde, verständig." *Droysen.*

[4] "A metaphor taken from lovers, as Bothe rightly remarks. 'It is not difficult, says Lysistrata, to reconcile those who are in love with each other and have not as yet lain with each other,' i. e. that she will easily reconcile the Lacedæmonians and Athenians to Peace, if they are really enamoured with her. The Ravenna Scholiast therefore rightly explains it, ὀργῶντας, πρὸς εἰρήνην." *Enger.*

[5] Comp. Equit. 1389. Acharn. 989.

[6] "Noch wie es so unklug unsre Männer sonst gemacht." *Droys.*

[7] "Sanft und liebevoll." *Droysen.*

[8] "Ich bin ein Weib zwar, aber habe doch Verstand." *Droysen.* "μὲν, freilich, zwar ' Krüger.*

I am not ill off in respect of[1] intellect." By having often heard the remarks of my father and my elders, I have been not ill educated. I wish to take and justly chide you[2] in common, who, although you besprinkle your altars with the same lustral-water,[3] as kindred people, at Olympia, Pylæ, and Delphi——how many others could I mention, if there were occasion for me to be prolix?——are destroying Grecian men and Grecian cities with your armies, when barbarians[4] are before you as enemies. One part of my speech[5] is thus far finished.

ATHEN. I am killed with desire.

LYS. In the next place, ye Spartans,——for I will turn to you,——do you not know, when formerly Periclides[6] the Spartan came hither as a suppliant of the Athenians, and sat upon the altars, pale, in a red cloak, begging an army? At that time Messena[7] was pressing upon you, and at the same

---

[1] For the Genitivus Respectûs, see note on vs. 173. According to the Scholiast it is a quotation from the *Melanippe* of Euripides.

[2] "So will Ich euch denn ernstlich schelten insgemein,
     Wie ihr 's verdient."   *Droysen.*

[3] "See Athen. ix. p. 409. Hesych. v. δαλίον." *Enger.* Vs. 1130 is supposed to be taken from the *Erectheus* of Euripides. For Πυθοῖ, see Krüger, Gr. Gr. § 46, 1, obs. 4, and compare Cantharus, ap. Athen. i. p. 11, c.

[4] "Da 's doch genug Barbaren giebt." *Droysen.* "Expressed in the same way as Hor. i. 2, 21, '*Audiet cives acuisse ferrum, quo graves Persæ melius perirent.*' Paulmier would also punctuate after στρατεύμασιν: '*cum exercitu ex barbaris collecto viros et urbes Græcas perditum itis.*' For since the 20th year of the war the Lacedæmonians had had Persian auxiliaries, and the Athenians had invited the Thracians and Macærophori, who had overthrown Mycallesus. I quote Paulmier's explanation on this account, because the Ravenna Scholiast has hit upon the same." *Enger.*

[5] "Der eine Theil der Rede sei hiemit zu End'!" *Droysen.* "δεῦρ' ἀεί = ἕως τοῦ δεῦρο, *hucusque*. See Porson, Orest. 1679. The whole of this verse has a colour of tragic diction, and is perhaps taken from some tragedian." *Enger.*

[6] Plutarch, Cimon, p. 489, πέμπουσιν οὖν οἱ Λακεδαιμόνιοι Περικλείδαν εἰς Ἀθήνας, δεόμενοι βοηθεῖν, ὅν φησι κωμῳδῶν Ἀριστοφάνης καθεζόμενον ἐπὶ τοῖς βωμοῖς ὠχρὸν ἐν φοινικίδι στρατίαν ἀπαιτεῖν. For φοινικίς, see Liddell's Lex.

[7] Alluding to the revolt of the Helots, who posted themselves in Ithome, and successfully resisted the utmost efforts of the Spartans to dislodge them. See Thucyd. i. 101

time the god[1] was shaking the earth. But Cimon went with four thousand hoplites and saved the whole of Sparta. After you have been benefited in this way by the Athenians, do you devastate a land, from which you have received benefits?

ATHEN. By Jove, Lysistrata, these are in the wrong!

SPART. We are in the wrong: but sin is unspeakably beautiful.[2]

LYS. Do you suppose I shall let you[3] Athenians off? Know you not when the Spartans in turn came in arms and slew many Thessalians,[4] and many confederates and allies of Hippias, alone on that day[5] marching out with you to battle, and freed you, who were wearing servile[6] dresses, and in place of the servile dress, clothed your people again with a mantle?

SPART. I have never seen a better[7] woman!

ATHEN. And I, never yet a fairer bosom!

LYS. Why, then, when many benefactions[8] exist *on both sides*, do you fight, and not cease from your wickedness? Why do you not make peaee? Come, what's the hinderance?

SPART. We are willing, if one be willing to restore *to* us this spencer.

ATHEN. Of what kind, good sir?

SPART. Pylos,[9] which we have been wishing for and desiring this long while.

ATHEN. By Neptune, this you shall[10] not do!

---

[1] See Thuc. i. 101. This is rather a Thucydidean construction. Cf. note on Nubes, 274.

[2] For the construction, see note on vs. 198, *supra.*

[3] "*Putasne me vos Athenienses sine reprehensione dimissuram?*" *Enger.*

[4] "The Scholiast observes that the Thessalians had assisted Hippias. Cf. Herod. v. 63." *Enger.*

[5] "πολλοὺς ξυμμάχους are opposed to μόνοι ξυνεκμαχοῦντες. While Hippias had many allies, the Lacedæmonians were the only persons who brought assistance to you. ξυνεκμαχεῖν appears to differ from ξυμμαχεῖν in this, that it involves at the same time the notion of *delivering from danger.*" *Enger.* See Liddell's Lex. in voc.

[6] "Bergler remarks, that this was a servile and less respectable dress, with skins sewed to the lower part of it; and that in Athenæus (vi. p. 271) slaves are called κατωνακοφόρους." *Enger.*

[7] Comp. vss. 90, 91.

[8] "Da beid' ihr euch einander wohlgethan." *Droysen.*

[9] "Pylos, which had been gained by Cleon, was still in the possession of the Athenians, vs. 104." *Droysen.*

[10] "Nimmer setzt ihr das mir durch!" *Droysen*

LYS. Give it up to them, good sir '

ATHEN. And whom then shall we solicit?

LYS. Do you demand another place instead of this!

ATHEN. Then do you deliver up to us the what d'ye call 'em—in the first place this Echinus, and the Melian Gulf behind it, and the legs[1] of Megara!

SPART. No, by the two gods, not all, my good sir![2]

LYS. Give them up! do not dispute about legs!

ATHEN. I am willing now to strip and cultivate the land naked.[3]

SPART. And I, by the two gods, to dung them[4] in the morning.

LYS. When[5] you shall have made peace, you shall do so. But if you think fit to do this, deliberate, and go and consult your allies!

ATHEN. What[6] allies, my friend? We are excited. Will not our allies be of the same opinion—all to enjoy themselves?

SPART. Ours[7] will, at any rate, by the two gods!

ATHEN. Aye, by Jove! for the Carystians also will.[8]

LYS. You say well. Now therefore see that you be pure, so that we women may entertain you in the Acropolis with what we have in our chests. And there give oaths and assurances to each other; and then each of you shall take his own wife and depart.

ATHEN. Well, let us go as soon as possible.

SPART. Lead whither you please.

ATHEN. Yes, by Jove, as quickly as possible! [*Exeunt Lysistrata, Athenians, and Spartans.*]

CHO. OF WOM. I do not grudge to offer[9] my variegated bed-

---

[1] "τὰ Μεγαρικὰ τείχη." *Scholiast.* Cf. Liddell's Lex. in voc. σκέλος.

[2] "λισσάνιος· ἀγαθός." *Hesychius.* Cf. Phot. Lex. p. 225, 9.

[3] " ἀντὶ τοῦ θέλω εἰρήνην." *Scholiast.*

[4] " Stercorare agros." *Reisig.*

[5] Dindorf remarks that the Attics use ἐπὴν, not ἐπάν. He refers to L. Dindorf's note on Xenoph. Cyrop. iii. 2, 6.

[6] ποῖος, in such interruptions, without the article, rejects the mention of the aforesaid thing with aversion. See Krüger, Gr. Gr. § 51, 17, obs. 12.

[7] "*Meis.*" *Brunck.* But this is the *Attic* signification of the word.

[8] " Ja selbst beim Himmel auch die Karystier!" *Droysen.* See Krüger, Gr. Gr. § 69, 32, obs. 21. Cf. Plut. 187. Equit. 338.

[9] " *Stragulas vestes, et lænas, et xystidas, ... sine invidia volo*

clothes, and little cloaks, and state-robes,[1] and golden orna-
ments, as many as I have, to all to carry to their children,
and whenever any one's daughter is Canephorus. I tell you
all now to take of my property out of the house; and that
nothing is so well sealed up, that[2] you may not break the
sealing-wax, and bear away whatever is in the house. But
he shall see nothing when he looks, unless some of you see
sharper than I do. But if any of you has no food, and
maintains domestics and many small ehildren, he may receive
from me husked wheat; but the ehœnix-loaf is very fresh
to look at. Whatever poor person therefore wishes, let him
come to my house with saeks and wallets; for he shall receive
wheat; and Manes my servant shall put it into them. I fore-
warn you, however, not to come to my door, but to beware
of the dog.[3] [*Enter Market-loungers, and knock clamorously
at the door of the Citadel.*]

MARK. Open the door!

SERVANT (*coming out with a torch in his hand*). Will you
get away? Why do you sit? Shall I burn you with the
toreh?[4] The post is a troublesome one.[5]

MARK. I'll not do so!

SERV. If we must by all means do so, we will endure, to
gratify you.

CHO. OF MEN. And we too will endure with you.

SERV. Will you not begone? You shall howl aloud in
your hairs.[6] Will you not begone, so that[7] the Spartans may

omnibus præbere." *Brunck.* These genitives, however, might be construed after φθόνος ἔνεστί μοι (= φθονέω), and παρέχειν be considered
as the *exegetical infinitive*; for the regular construction of φθονέω is
dative of person and genitive of thing. Moreover the partitive
genitive seems inconsistent with the unrestrictive words ὅσ᾽ ἐστί μοι.
But as this construction immediately follows, (vs. 1195,) I have
followed Brunck.

[1] See Nub. vs. 70.   [2] See Bernhardy, W. S. p. 365.

[3] "See the commentators on Plaut. Mostell. iii. 2, 162." *Brunck.*

[4] Cf. Vesp. 1339.

[5] "*Molesta statio*, exclaims the doorkeeper. But perhaps the passage is corrupt. At all events we should have expected φορτικὸς ὁ
ὄχλος." *Enger.* Droysen translates it strangely enough: "recht
ein pöbelhafter Platz!"

[6] The best comment is vs. 448, *supra*, ἐκκοκκιῶ σου τὰς στενοκωκύτους
τρίχας. Cf. note on Plut. 612.

[7] "At leugth the market-loungers go away; soon, however, to
return again." *Enger.*

depart from the house in quietness, after their entertainment?
[*Enter an Athenian returning from the entertainment.*]

ATHEN. I have never seen such an entertainment! Upon
my word, the Spartans were even entertaining; but we were
the cleverest boon-companions [1] over the wine.

CHO. OF MEN. Aye, rightly *said:* because we *Athenians*
are not in our right senses when we are sober. If I prevail
upon the Athenians by my words,[2] we shall always go on
embassies [3] to all places drunk. F at present, whenever
we go to Sparta sober, we immediately look to see what
we can disturb:[4] so that, what they say, we hear not; but
what they don't say, this we wrongly suspect.[5] And we do
not make the same report about the same things.[6] But now
every thing pleases; so that, if any one were to sing *the
scolion* of Telamon,[7] when he ought to sing that of Clitagora,
we would praise [8] him, and swear a false oath beside *that it*

---

[1] "He laughs at the Athenians as bad counsellors when sober, but
excellent conductors of business when drunk." *Scholiast.*

[2] "Wenn meine Rede bei euch Athenern was vermag." *Droysen.*

[3] The usage of Thucydides is somewhat different. See Krüger
on Thuc. i. 31. Cf. Bernhardy, W. S. p. 350.

[4] "Gleich spähn wir umher, ob's nichts da aufzustören giebt."
Droysen.

[5] "Und was sie gar nicht sagen, das argwöhnen wir." *Droysen.*
"*Hæc suspicamur perperam.*" *Brunck.* "This we get wind of." *Liddell*

[6] "Nor of the same things make the same report." *Wheelwright.*
"Und melden was sie sagen, nie, wie sie 's gesagt." *Droysen.*

[7] This scolion is preserved ap. Athen. xv. p. 695, C.,

παῖ Τελαμᾶνος, Αἶαν αἰχμητὰ, λέγουσί σε
ἐς Τροῖαν ἄριστον ἐλθεῖν Δαναῶν μετ' 'Αχιλλία.

It was composed by Pindar. See Athen. i. p. 23, E., xi. p. 503, E.
Being of a *warlike* cast, it would be unsuited for a festive entertainment, and would be a malapropos substitute for the *peaceful*
scolion of Clitagora. Comp. Pax, 1270—1272. Acharn. 980—988.
But, says the Chorus, *we would now praise any thing and every thing,
so peaceful have we become, and so willing to be pleased with every thing.*
A small fragment of this scolion of Clitagora will be found in
Vesp. 1245. Cf. Nub. 684. Bergk, Poet. Lyr. p. 877. The words
'scolion of Clitagora," must be understood of a scolion *on the subject of* Clitagora, and not a scolion *composed by* Clitagora. So we
have "The scolion of Admetus," "The scolion of Harmodius," &c.
Cf. Ran. 1302. Aves, 1416. Vesp. 1222. *Pelargi*, Fragm. ii. *Daitaleis.*
Fragm. ii. Bergk, Poet. Lyr. p. 871—878.

[8] See note on Av. 788. Cf. ibid. 1858. "*Pejerabamus, recte factum
esse.*" *Bothe.*

was quite the thing. [*Market-loungers again crowd about the door.*]

SERV. But see! here are these people coming together again! Will you not begone, you scoundrels?

MARK. Yes, by Jove! for now they are coming out of the house.[1] [*Enter Spartans returning from the entertainment.*]

SPART. Take your wind-instruments, my dearest, so that I may dance the Dipodia, and sing[2] a pleasing strain upon the Athenians and upon us at the same time.

ATHEN. Take, then, your pipes,[3] by the gods! for I am pleased to see you dancing.

CHORUS OF SPARTANS. Rouse, O Mnemosyne. the youths,[4] and my Muse, who is cognizant of us and of the Athenians, when they at Artemisium dashed against the ships,[5] like to the gods, and conquered the Persians. But us, on the contrary, did Leonidas lead, like boars, I ween, sharpening their tusks; and abundant foam[6] sprang up about our jaws, and abundant *foam* at the same time flowed down our legs:[7] for the men, the Persians, were[8] not less numerous than the sands. Huntress Diana, slayer of wild beasts, virgin goddess. come hither to our truce, so that you may keep us united for a long time! Now again may fruitful friendship ever subsist through our covenants, and may we cease from the flattering foxes![9] O come hither, hither, O virgin huntress!

---

[1] "He expresses himself willing to go away now that he sees the feast is at an end." *Enger.*

[2] ἀείσω is a first aorist subjunctive. See Hom. Od. Ξ. 464. Herod. i. 23. So also διποδιάξω. ἵνα is not construed with a *future.* See Krüger, Gr. Gr. § 69, 31. Harper's Powers of the Greek Tenses, p. 124. Cf. Nub. 823. Av. 848, 1507, 1647. Vesp. 1362, where the same caution is necessary. On the other side, see Bernhardy, W. S. p. 401.

[3] "φυσαλλίδες· φυσητήρια, αὐλοί." *Hesychius.*

[4] "Recte Schol. Rav. μέλλοντας ὀρχεῖσθαι." *Enger.* See Pausan. ix. 29, 2. Burges in Class. J. xxx. p. 289—291.

[5] "*In naves Persarum.*" *Brunck.*

[6] "After Archilochus, πολλὸς δ' ἀφρὸς ἦν περὶ στόμα. And Sophocles, El. 719. And Æschylus, ἀφρὸς βορᾶς βροτείας ἐρρύη κατὰ στόμα." *Scholiast.*

[7] According to the Scholiast, an unexpected jest, as though they had made good use of their *legs* as well.

[8] "Cf. Hermann ad Soph. Trach. 517." *Enger.* See Matthiä, Gr. Gr. § 303, 1. Bernhardy, W. S. p. 417　Vesp. 1301.

[9] "τῶν πανούργων ῥητόρων." *Scholiast*

Lys. Come now, since the other matters have been transacted well, do you, Spartans, lead away these,[1] and you,
Athenians, the others! and let husband stand beside wife,
and wife beside husband: and then, after having danced in
honour[2] of the gods for our prosperous fortune, let us be cau-
tious henceforth never to sin again!

Chorus of Athenians. Lead forward the chorus! offer
thanks! and invoke Artemis! and invoke her twin brother,
leader of the chorus, the gracious Apollo! and invoke Nysius!
Bacchus,[3] who sparkles with his eyes amongst the Mænads!
and Jove blazing with fire! and invoke his venerable, blessed
spouse! and then the deities, whom we shall use as no forgetful witnesses respecting the noble Peace, which the goddess
Venus made! Alalai! io pæan![4] Raise yourselves[5] aloft!
io! io! io! for the victory![6] Evoe, evoe! evæ, evæ![7]
Spartan,[8] do you now produce a new song after our new
song.

Chorus of Spartans. Come[9] again, Spartan Muse, having left the lovely Taygetus, celebrating Apollo, the god of
Amyclæ, revered by us; and Minerva dwelling in a brazen
house;[10] and the brave Tyndaridæ, who sport beside the
Eurotas. Come, advance rapidly! Oh, come, bounding
lightly! so that we may celebrate Sparta, to whom the
choruses of the gods are a care and the sound of feet; and
the damsels, like fillies, bound up frequently with their feet
beside the Eurotas, making haste; and their locks are agitated, like those of the Bacchanals brandishing the thyrsus

---

[1] "What the Scholiast on vs. 1277 says, that Lacedæmonian
women were present, is hardly credible. The Lacedæmonians lead
away the women who had occupied the Acropolis, the Athenians
those women who formed the chorus in the beginning." *Enger*.

[2] "*In honorem Deorum.*" *Brunck*. For this idiom, see Krüger, Gr.
Gr. § 48, 4, obs. 4. Bernhardy, W. S. p. 86.

[3] Enger has adopted the conjecture proposed by Bergk, (Rhen.
Mus. 1841, p. 95,) ὃς μετὰ Μαινάσι βαγχιοῖ εὐάσιν.

[4] Comp. Aves, 1763.   [5] Comp. Eccles. 1179—1182.

[6] See Krüger, on Thuc. vi. 45. Cf. ibid. vi. 76, vii. 73.

[7] See Lobeck, Aglaoph. p. 1043.

[8] "Lakoner, nun beginn' auch du Gesang,
      Neuen zu neuem Feste!" *Droysen*.
   "Exhibit thy new song to answer mine!" *Wheelwright*.

[9] See Burges, Class. J. xxx. p. 291, 292.

[10] See Krüger on Thuc. i. 128. Pausan. ii. 7. 3.

and sporting.‑ And the chaste daughter of Leda, the comely
leader of the chorus, leads them. But come, bind your hair
with a fillet, and dance with hand and foot, like a stag ! and
at the same time make a noise cheering the chorus ; and again
celebrate the most mighty, the all-conquering goddess dwelling in a brazen house ! [*Exeunt omnes.*]

See Valckn. Adoniaz p. 275.

END OF THE LYSISTRATA.

THE THESMOPHORIAZUSÆ.

DRAMATIS PERSONÆ.

MNESILOCHUS, father-in-law of Euripides.
EURIPIDES.
SERVANT OF AGATHON
AGATHON.
AGATHON'S CHORUS
FEMALE HERALD.
CHORUS OF WOMEN
CERTAIN WOMEN.
CLISTHENES.
PRYTANIS.
POLICEMAN.
DANCING-GIRL. } Mutes.
BOY.

THE ARGUMENT.

"THE *Thesmophoriazusæ* was acted Ol. 92, 1, in the archonship of Callias. Scholiast on vs. 841, ἐπαινεῖ τὸν Λάμαχον νῦν· ἤδη γὰρ ἐτεθνήκει ἐν Σικελίᾳ τετάρτῳ ἔτει πρότερον. Lamachus died in the beginning of Ol. 91, 2. See Thuc. vi. 101. Scholiast on vs. 190, γέρων γὰρ τότε Εὐριπίδης ἦν· ἕκτῳ γοῦν ἔτει ὕστερον τελευτᾷ. Euripides died about the close of Ol. 93, 2, or the beginning of 93, 3. Scholiast on Ran. 53, ἡ γὰρ Ἀνδρομέδα ὀγδόῳ ἔτει προεισῆκται, i. e. Ol. 91, 4. Now Aristophanes himself (Thesm. vs. 1060) testifies that the *Andromeda* was acted the *year before* the *Thesmophoriazusæ*." *Fuger*. Dindorf and Wachsmuth also refer it to this year ; on the contrary, Dobree and Fritzsche refer it to Ol. 92, 2.

The *Thesmophoriazusæ* has a proper intrigue, a knot which is not closed till the conclusion, and in this therefore possesses a great advantage. Euripides, on account of the well-known hatred of women displayed in his tragedies, is accused and condemned at the Thesmophoria, at which festival women only were admitted. After a fruitless attempt to induce the effeminate poet Agathon to undertake the hazardous experiment, Euripides prevails on his father-in-law, Mnesilochus, who was somewhat advanced in years, to disguise himself as a woman, that under this assumed appearance he may plead his cause. The manner in which he does this gives rise to suspicions, and he is discovered to be a man ; he flies to the altar for refuge, and to secure himself still more from the impending danger, he snatches a child from the arms of one of the women, and threatens to kill it if they do not let him alone. Upon examination, however, it turns out to be a wine-skin, wrapped up like a child. Euripides now appears in a number of different shapes to save his friend : at one time he is Menelaus, who finds Helen again in Egypt ; at another time he is Echo, helping the chained Andromeda to pour out her lamentations, and immediately after he appears as Perseus, about to release her from the rock. At length he succeeds in rescuing Mnesilochus, who is fastened to a sort of pillory, by assuming the character of a procuress, and enticing away the officer of justice who has charge of him, a simple barbarian, by the charms of a dancing-girl. These parodied scenes, composed almost entirely in the very words of Euripides' tragedies, are inimitable. Whenever Euripides is introduced, we may always, generally speaking, lay our account with having the most ingenious and apposite ridicule : it seems as if the mind of Aristophanes possessed a peculiar and specific power of giving a comic turn to the poetry of this tragedian. Whatever be the faults of the present play, it will be very generally admitted to be the drollest and most facetious of all the writings of Aristophanes.

THE THESMOPHORIAZUSÆ.

[SCENE—the front of Agathon's house.]

MNESILOCHUS, EURIPIDES.

MNES. O JUPITER! will the swallow ever[1] appear? The man will kill me with dragging me about[2] from early dawn. Is it possible, Euripides, before I lose my spleen entirely, to learn from you whither you are leading me?

EUR. (*with great seriousness*). Nay, you must[3] not hear all that you will soon see, being present.

MNES. How say you? Tell it me again! Must I not hear?

EUR. Not what you are to see.

MNES. Then must I not even see?

EUR. Not what you must hear.

MNES. How do you advise me? Upon my word, you speak cleverly! You say I must neither hear nor see.

EUR. *Not so;* for, be well assured, the nature of each of them is distinct, of not hearing, and of not seeing.

---

[1] " Erscheint denn nie die Frühlingsschwalbe meiner Müh?"
Droysen.
" It is more suitable that Mnesilochus should ask *num quando?* than *quando?*" *Wellaner.* " As the appearance of the swallow in spring puts an end to winter, so the simple Mnesilochus wishes for some kind of a swallow to terminate his painful situation." *Droysen.* See note on Aves, 161, 1308.

[2] See Liddell's Lex. in voc. " ἀλοῶν· ἔξωθεν ἐν κύκλῳ περιάγων ὡς οἱ ἐν ταῖς ἅλωσιν." *Suidas.*

[3] " Nein, hören nicht das Alles musst du, was du gleich
Mit Augen sehn wirst!" *Droysen.*
Comp. Lidd. Lex. voc. παρίστημι. " The rich jest of this exordium lies in the philosophical mannerism of Euripides, who is fond of using his odd figures and antitheses every where." *Droysen.*

MNES. How distinct?

EUR. Thus have these been distinguished formerly.[1] For Ether, when first it was separated,[2] and in itself bore moving animals, first contrived an eye for that which ought to see, modelled after the sun's disk, and bored ears like a funnel.

MNES. On account of the funnel, then, must I[3] neither hear nor see? By Jove, I am delighted at having learned this in addition! What a thing, I ween, are learned conversazioni!

EUR. Many such matters mayest thou learn from me.

MNES. Would,[4] then, that, in addition to these good things, I could find out how I might still learn in addition to be lame[5] in my legs.

EUR. Come hither, and give me your attention!

MNES. Well!

EUR. Do you see this little door?[6]

[1] "τότε here means *olim*." *Brunck.* See note on Lys. 1023.

[2] "For soon as æther took a separate form,
And in itself bore moving animals,
She fabricated first the visual orb,
In imitation of the solar wheel." *Wheelwright.*

It would seem to be a parody upon the *Melanippe* of Euripides, Frag. xxii. Comp. also Arist. Ran. 892.

[3] "So, wegen des Trichters soll Ich weder hören noch sehn!
So wahr mich Zeus, froh bin Ich, dass Ich das zugelernt!
Was einem doch ein gelehrter Umgang nützlich ist!" *Droysen.*

"*Quantum est cum sapientibus conversari!*" *Brunck.* For the construction, see note on Aves, 451. "The interpreters have taken μή in Arist. Thesm. 19, as put for οὐ : badly. For it refers to the preceding words of Euripides, in which he had ordered Mnesilochus neither to see nor hear. In reference to these words, then, which might have been briefly stated, μήτε ἄκουε μήτε ὅρα, he says, διὰ τὴν χοάνην οὖν μήτ' ἀκούω μήθ' ὁρῶ; *wegen des Trichters also soll Ich weder hören noch sehen?*" *Hermann.*

[4] "See Markl. Suppl. 796. Valckn. Hippol. 208." *Brunck.* Cf. Pax, 68. Equit. 16, 1324. Ach. 991. Soph. Aj. 389. Phil. 531, 794, 1214. "*Utinam aliquo modo*: a familiar phraseology in wishes whose attainment one dare hardly hope for." *Schneidewin.* "It is somewhat weaker than *utinam*." *Bernhardy.* See his Wiss. Synt. p. 411. Schäfer on Soph. Col. 1100. The *optativus optans* is never found with ἄν, except in the formula πῶς ἄν ; and τίς ἄν ;

[5] i. e. in order that he may be no longer led about, but have lameness as an excuse. an easy task for Euripides ὁ χωλοποιὸς (Ach. 411. Ran. 846) to accomplish

[6] Comp. Nub. 92.

MNES. Yes, by Hercules, I think so!

EUR. Be silent then![1]

MNES. Must I be silent about the little door?

EUR. Hear!

MNES. Must I hear and be silent about the little door?

EUR. Here dwells[2] the illustrious Agathon the tragic poet.

MNES. Of what sort[3] is this Agathon?

EUR. There is a certain Agathon——

MNES. Is it the black, the strong one?

EUR. No; another one. Have you never seen him?[4]

MNES. Is it the shaggy-bearded one?[5]

EUR. Have you never seen him?

MNES. Certainly not, by Jove, as far as I know![6]

EUR. And yet you have coquetted with him, but you don't know it[7] perhaps. Come, let us crouch out of the way! for a domestic of his is coming out with fire and myrtle-wreaths. He seems about to make a previous[8] sacrifice on behalf of his poetic composition. [*They retire to one side.*]

SERVANT OF AGATHON (*coming out of the house*). Let all the people abstain from ill-omened words, having closed their mouths; for the company of the Muses is sojourning within

---

[1] Cratinus, (ap. Bekk. Anecd. p. 372, 8,) ἄκουε, σίγα, πρόσεχε τὸν νοῦν, δεῦρ' ὅρα.

[2] Poeta incertus ap. Schol. Eur. Troad 822,
ὅρας; ἐν τῇδε μὲν
ὁ τῶν Φρυγῶν τύραννος οἰκῶν τυγχάνει
γέρων, ἀπ' ὀργῆς Λαομέδων καλούμενος.

[3] Comp. Aves, 1021. Acharn. 963.

[4] " Agathon had commenced his literary career only three years before." *Scholiast.* " Aristophanes depicts him as a male coquette." *Droysen.* See Dawes, M. C. p. 577, ed. Kidd.

[5] " Egregie Vossius, ' *Nun, der mit dem Buschbart?* ' " *Fritzsche.*

[6] See Hermann, Vig. n. 154. Cf. Nub. 1252. Eccles. 350. Pax, 852. Blomf. gloss. Pers. 720, and for οὗτοι γε, see Herm. Vig. n. 266.

[7] " Mit ihm gebuhlt schon hast du wohl, nur weisst du 's nicht."
Droysen.

" Euripides laughs at the effeminate poet, whom he is going to make use of as a woman, and at the same time discloses to Mnesilochus what sort of person this Agathon is. Accordingly Mnesilochus, as soon as he sees Agathon, (vs. 98,) says, ἐγὼ γὰρ οὐχ ὁρῶ ἄνδρ' οὐδέν' ἐνθάδ' ὄντα, Κυρήνην δ' ὁρῶ. This therefore is what Euripides says, *Quid? non vidisti eum? Scilicet mulierem esse putabas.*" *Enger.*

[8] " Der Poesie Voropfer, scheint es, bringt er dar!" *Droysen.*
" ὅτε γὰρ δρᾶμα ποιῆσαι ἤθελον, πρότερον θυσίας ἐποίουν.' *Scholiast*

my master's house, composing lyric poems. And let the breathless [1] Ether check its blasts, and the azure wave of the sea not roar—

Mnes. Oh my!

Eur. Be silent! What are you saying? [2]

Serv.—and let the race of birds be put to sleep, and the feet of savage wild beasts that roam the woods not be put in motion.

Mnes. Oh my gracious!

Serv. For the beautifully-speaking Agathon our chief [3] is about—

Mnes. To be debauched?

Serv. Who's he that spoke?

Mnes. Breathless Ether.

Serv. —to lay the stocks, [4] the beginning of a drama. And he is bending new felloes for verses: others he is turning [5] on the lathe, other verses he is patching together; and he is coining maxims, and speaking in tropes, [6] and is moulding as in wax, and is rounding, and is casting—

Mnes. And is wenching.

Serv. What rustic [7] approaches our eaves?

Mnes. One who is ready to turn and whirl round and cast this toe of mine in the eaves of [8] you and your beautifully-speaking poet.

---

[1] This use of the nominative may be compared with the similar use of the accusative mentioned in the note on Equit. 345.

[2] Fritzsche and Enger read τί λέγει; *what is he saying?* which seems more appropriate.

[3] "πρόμος is both an ancient word used by Homer, and a thoroughly tragic one. See Æsch. Ag. 193, 398. Eum. 377. Suppl. 882. Soph. Col. 884. Rex, 660." *Fritzsche.* Comp. Meineke, Com. Frag. ii. p. 16.

[4] "δρύοχοι are the upright timbers supporting the keel, upon which the keel is laid when the shipwrights commence building a ship." *Brunck.*

[5] Hor. Ars Poet. 441, *Et male tornatos incudi reddere versus.* Comp. Epigr. ap. Schol. Equit. 753,

Καλλιμάχου τὸ τορευτὸν ἔπος τόδε.

[6] "*Et autonomasiis ornat.*" *Kuster.*

[7] Eur. Orest. 1271, τίς δ' ἀμφὶ μέλαθρον πολεῖ
σὸν ἀγρότας ἀνήρ;

[8] "The genitives σοῦ and τοῦ ποιήτου depend on θριγκοῦ." *Fritzsche.* Cf. Lys. 975.

Serv Doubtless you were a rake, old man, when you were young.[1]

Eur. My good sir, let this man go; but do you by all means[2] call out Agathon hither to me!

Serv. Make no entreaty; for he himself will come out soon; for he is beginning to make lyric poems. In truth, when it is winter, it is not easy to bend[3] the strophes, unless one come forth to the door to the sun. [*Exit.*]

Mnes. What then shall I do?

Eur. Wait; for he is coming forth. O Jove, what do you purpose[4] to do to me to-day?

Mnes. By the gods, I wish to learn what this business is. Why do you groan? Why are you vexed? You ought[5] not to conceal it, being my son-in-law.

Eur. A great evil is ready kneaded for me.

Mnes. Of what kind?[6]

Eur. On this day will be decided whether Euripides still lives[7] or is undone.

Mnes. Why, how? For now neither the courts are about

---

[1] "*Mirum ni, juvenis quum esses, protervus homo fueris.*" *Fritzsche.* In Dindorf's, Enger's, and Fritzsche's edition this verse is given without an interrogation.

[2] Fritzsche compares Nub. 1323. Ran. 1325. Eccles. 366. Add Lys. 412.

[3]
"Im Winter ist
Des Strophenbaues Zimmerkunst nicht eben leicht,
Wenn vor die Thür man nicht in die warme Sonne geht."
Droysen.
Fritzsche and Enger read θύρασι, Dindorf θύραζε. "Wherever θύρασιν occurs, it always signifies *extra fores, before the door.*" *Fritzsche.* Cf. Nub. 971. See Bernhardy, W. S. p. 81. Mehlhorn, Gr. Gr. § 129, 1. And for the omission of τις, see note on Aves, 167.

[4] Cf. Pax, 62.

[5] "Kuster renders it *non oportebat :* wrongly. χρῆν is, indeed, an imperfect tense, but is used of *present* time by the Attic poets, just as χρή is. Thom. M. ' χρῆν' καὶ ἀντὶ τοῦ ἔπρεπε, καὶ ἀντὶ τοῦ πρέπει.' κηδεστής denotes a person allied to another by affinity, and is used both of a *father-in-law* and a *son-in-law*, as *affinis* iu Latin." *Brunck.* Cf. Dawes, M. C. p. 490, ed. Kidd.

[6] See Krüger, Gr. Gr. § 51, 16, obs. 3.

[7] "*Hoc die judicabitur utrum adhuc vivat Euripides, an perierit.*" *Fritzsche.* For ἔστιν ζῶν, see Krüger, Gr. Gr. § 56, 3, obs. 3, and for this use of ἀπόλωλε, see note on Plut. 421.

to judge causes, nor is there a sitting of the Senate; for it is the third [1] day, the middle of the Thesmophoria.

EUR. In truth, I expect this very thing [2] even will destroy me. For the women have plotted against me, and are going to hold an assembly to-day about me in the temple of [3] Demeter and Persephone for my destruction.

MNES. Wherefore? why, pray? [4]

EUR. Because I represent them in tragedy and speak ill of them.

MNES. And justly too would you suffer, [5] by Neptune! But, as this is the case, [6] what contrivance have you?

EUR. To persuade Agathon the tragic poet to go to the temple of Demeter and Persephone.

MNES. What to do? Tell me!

EUR. To sit in assembly among the women, and to speak whatever [7] is necessary in my defence.

MNES. Openly, [8] or secretly?

---

[1]   " For this
Is the third day and midst of Ceres' feasts." *Wheelwright.*
" Es ist heut ja der Dritte, der Thesmophorien Mitteltag."
                                         Droysen.
" Ita statuendum de hâc re, ut quum jam inde a decimo die cele-- brari Thesmophoria cœpta essent, νηστεία dicta sit ab Atheniensibus ἡ τρίτη, eadem tamen quum media esset inter dies festos tres, quorum prolusio tantum erat Thesmophoria, κατ' ἐξοχὴν ἡ μέση diceretur. Nostro igitur loco ἡ τρίτη 'στι Θεσμ. ἡ μέση verba idem significant quod ἡ τρίτη 'στι Θεσμοφορίων ἡ νηστεία. Denique interpungere possis et ante et post Θεσμοφορίων, quod ad utrumque et ad τρίτη et ad μέση refertur. Rectius igitur omnino non interpungitur." *Enger.*

[2] Comp. Lys. 46.   [3] Comp. vss. 89. 295.

[4] See note on Pax, 1018.

[5] "*Et quidem meritam sic pœnam dederis.*" *Fritzsche.*

[6] "*Postquam hæc ita sunt comparata.*" *Enger.* "ἐκ τούτου, *hereupon, after this, therefore;* but ἐκ τούτων regularly *in consequence of this, on these grounds, for these reasons;* yet also synonymous with μετὰ ταῦτα. Cf. Hipp. i. 7. Œcon. ii. 1, 4, 12. Mem. iii. 5, 4. Krüger on Anab. i. 3, 11. Gr. Gr. § 43, 4, obs. 7." *Krüger.* Cf. Bernhardy, W. S. p. 230.

[7] For χἂν, see note on Lys. 277.

[8] " Fritzsche remarks that the whole of this verse has a tragic air, not only on account of the numbers and tragic words, but also on account of the repetition of the word λάθρα. The same remark might have been made upon the words τί δράσοντ'; εἰπέ μοι." *Enger.*

Eur. Secretly, clothed in a woman's stole.[1]

Mnes. The device is a clever[2] one, and exceedingly in conformity with your disposition; for ours is the prize[3] for trickery. [*The creaking of machinery is heard.*]

Eur. Hush!

Mnes. What's the matter?

Eur. Agathon is coming out.

Mnes. Why, of what sort is he?

Eur. He who is being wheeled[4] out. [*The doors of the back scene are thrown open, and Agathon is wheeled in, fantastically dressed in women's clothes.*]

Mnes. Assuredly[5] I am blind; for I don't see any man here: I see Cyrene.[6]

Eur. Hush! He is preparing again to sing.[7]

Mnes. "The ant's[8] paths?" or what is he plaintively singing?

Agath.[9] Damsels, take the torch sacred to the infernal

---

[1] Comp. Dryden, *Palamon and Arcite,*

  "The solemn feast of Ceres now was near,
  When long white linen stoles the matrons wear."

[2] "κομψὸς is applied to a person, who, though acting deceitfully, yet devises with ingenuity." *Fritzsche.*

[3] "*Noster est,* says Mnesilochus, ὁ πυραμοῦς, *non quidem τοῦ παν- νυχίζειν, attamen τοῦ τεχνάζειν.*" *Fritzsche.* See Lidd. Lex. in voc. πυραμοῦς, and cf. Equit. 277.

[4] "ἐπὶ ἐκκυκλήματος γὰρ φαίνεται." *Scholiast.* Cf. Acharn. 470, 409, and Schlegel, Dram. Lit. p. 170.

[5] "*Profecto cæcus sum.*" *Fritzsche.* ἀλλ' ἢ, *profecto, sane,* Lys. 928. Equit. 1162. Acharn. 1111, 1112.

[6] The name of a notorious courtesan of the day. See Ran. 1328.

[7] Comp. Aves, 226.

[8] "Ameisenläufe oder was sonst fantasirt er uns?" *Droysen.*

  "Den Pfad der Ameis' oder so was singet er?" *Voss.*

"*Formicarum semitas, an aliud quid gracili et exili voce cantillabit?*" *Kuster.* Compare Liddell's Lex. in voc. μυρμηκιά. Plautus, Menæchm. v. 3, 12, "Move formicinum gradum." Pherecrates ap. Plutarch. de Musica,

  οὗτος ἅπαντας, οὓς λέγω,
 παρελήλυθ' ᾄδων ἐκτραπέλους μυρμηκιάς.

See Dawes, M. C. p. 584, ed. Kidd.

[9] "What Agathon is here composing is, probably, not a festal ode for the Thesmophoria, but for some tragedy on the subject of Troy, —a *Cassandra* perhaps. We must further imagine the whole to be accompanied by a thoroughly modern and effeminate style of voluptuous music." *Droysen.* "This song is merely a *prelude* (προοί

goddesses,[1] and, with a free country, raise[2] a shout in the dance!

CHO.[3] In honour of which of the gods[4] is the ode? Tell us then! I am readily induced to honour the gods.[5]

AGATH. Come, then, Muse, glorify Phœbus, the drawer of the golden bow, who founded the walls[6] of the city in the land of Simois!

CHO. Deign to accept our most noble strains, O Phœbus, who in musical honours bearest off the sacred prize!

AGATH. And chant the maiden *dwelling* in oak-grown mountains, the huntress Diana!

CHO. I follow, celebrating and glorifying the revered off-spring of Latona, the unwedded Diana.

AGATH. And Latona, and the notes of the lyre[7] accompanying the dances of the Phrygian graces in harmony with the foot.

CHO. I honour queen Latona, and the lyre, the mother of songs, with an approved masculine[8] voice; by which[9] light

μιον), by which Agathon is, as it were, initiated into the making of tragedy." *Enger.*

[1] "Demeter and Cora." *Scholiast.* The words ξὺν ἐλευθέρᾳ πατρίδι are bracketed by Dindorf as an interpolation. "*Sumite, puellæ, tædam inferis sacram deabus, et quando nunc patria est libera, cum clamoribus tripudiate.* It is very plainly seen from vss. 121, 122, that the measure and numbers of this verse are adapted to the Lydian harmony." *Fritzsche.* Bernhardy (W. S.) makes χθονίαις an example of the construction illustrated in the note on Lys. 1277.

[2] "*Saltando clamorem tollere:* a Dithyrambic expression, many of which kind are intentionally used in this song in derision of Agathon's μελοποία." *Brunck.*

[3] Agathon's chorus is composed of the *Muses,* mentioned vs. 41.

[4] Dindorf compares Lucian, Tragop. 75, τίνι δαιμόνων ἄγουσι κωμαστὴν χορόν; See note on Lys. 1277.

[5] "*Animo meo facile imperari et persuaderi potest, ut deòs colat.*" *Reiske.* For τοὐμὸν = ἐγὼ, see Jelf, § 436, obs. 1. Matthiä, § 269, 1, § 285, § 466, 3. Cf. Eccles. 623.

[6] "γύαλα χώρας, *urbis Trojæ mœnia,* which are called γῆς ὁρίσματα in Eur. Hec. 16. So Kuster interprets it, and so also the ancient grammarian, ὃς τὴν Ἴλιον ἐτείχισεν." *Enger.*

[7] "'Ασιάδος, sc. *citharæ.* Etymol. M. p. 153, 13, ''Ασιάδος κιθάσματα, τῆς κιθάρας. οὕτως 'Αριστοφάνης εἶπε, παρῳδῶν τὸ ἐξ 'Ερεχθ... Εὐριπίδου. ἡ τρίχορδος κιθάρα οὕτω καλεῖται.'" *Brunck.*

[8] Soph. Phil. 1455, κτύπος ἄρσην πόντου.

τᾷ does not refer to βοᾷ, as Brunck and Kuster interpret it, but to κίθαρις." *Fritzsche.* "δαιμονίοις ὄμμασιν may be rightly unis kindled in divinely-inspired eyes, and by our sudden voice. On which account glorify king Phœbus with honours! Hail, happy child of Latona!

Mnes. How sweet the song, O venerable Genetyllides,[1] and womanish, and wanton, and lascivious![2] So that, whilst I listened, a tickling passed under my very bottom. I wish, O youth, to ask you who you are,[3] in the words of Æschylus in his Lycurgeia:[4] of what land,[5] you weakling? What's your country? What means the dress? what the confusion of fashions? What does the harp prattle[6] to the saffron-coloured robe? what the lyre to the head-dress? What mean the oil-flask and the girdle? How unsuitable! What connexion then between a mirror and a sword? And you yourself, O youth, are you reared[7] as a man? Why, where are the tokens of a man? Where is your cloak? Where are your boots?[8] Or[9] as a woman then? Where then[10] are

derstood of divinely-shining eyes, i. e. of the divinely-inspired minds of poets." *Enger.* Hermann reads στόμασιν for ὄμμασιν, and in the next line δι' ἀμφιδίου ὀπὸς, and translates, "*By which* (sc. lyre) *light comes to the inspired mouth, and by our twofold voice.* The voice is called *twofold*, because the strophes and antistrophes are sung by the Hemichori."

[1] "Wie süss der Gesang, ihr himmlischen Hürlein allzumal."
Droysen.

[2] "ἐπιμανδαλωτὸν osculum, Acharn. 1201." *Enger.*

[3] Fritzsche and Enger have adopted Porson's emendation, νεᾶνις, ἥτις εἶ. Cf. Nub. 691, 692.

[4] "He means Æschylus' tetralogy, the Lycurgeia. It consisted of the Ἠδωνοὶ, Βασσαρίδες, Νεανίσκοι, and Λυκοῦργος, the latter a *satyric* drama. The words ποδαπὸς ὁ γύννις are from the Ἠδωνοὶ, and are addressed to the captive Bacchus." *Scholiast.*

[5] Comp. Æsch. Suppl. 231. For the article, see note on Ran. 40.

[6] Comp. Nub. 1008, ὁπόταν πλάτανος πτελίᾳ ψιθυρίζῃ. For a similar reason he inserts στωμόλλετε in a quotation from Euripides, ap. Ran. 1310.

"Woher, du Weibling? welche Heimath sandte dich?
Was will der Aufzug? welch Verwirren alles Brauchs?
Was sagt die Leir zum Safrankleid, was Kithara
Zu Busenband und Schleif' und Schminknapf? nimmer passt 's!
Was hat der Spiegel gar Gemeinschaft und das Schwert?" *Droys.*

Epicharmus ap. Stob. Serm. lxxxix., τίς γὰρ κατόπτρῳ καὶ τυφλῷ κοινωνία; Eur. Iph. T. 254, τίς θαλλάσσης βουκόλοις κοινωνια; ἰ ͚ Equit. vs. 1022.

[7] Comp. Aves, 335.   [8] Comp. Vesp. 1158.

[9] See Krüger, Gr. Gr. § 69, 4, obs. 4.

[10] Comp. Aves, 103. Eur. Phœn. 558. Æsch. Choeph. 887.

your breasts? What do you say? Why are you silent? Nay, then, I'll judge of you[1] from your song, since you are not willing to tell me yourself.

AGATH. Old man,[2] old man, I heard, indeed, the censure of your envy, but the pain I did not feel! I wear my attire in accordance with[3] my thoughts. For it behoveth a poet, conformably to the dramas which he must compose, to have his turn of mind in accordance with these. For example,[4] if one be composing female dramas, the body *of the poet* ought to have a participation in their manners.

MNES. Therefore do you mount on horseback when you compose a Phædra?[5]

AGATH. But if one be composing male *dramas*, this is subsisting in the body.[6] But what we do not possess, this now is found to be all imitation.[7]

MNES. When therefore you compose satyric dramas, call me,[8] in order that I may actively compose poetry along with you in your rear.

---

[1] "*Ex carmine conjecturam facit* Mnesilochus, since it was of such a character that there could be no doubt as to whether a man or a woman was the author." *Enger.*

[2] "O Greis, O Greis, von deiner Misgunst hab' Ich wohl
Gehört den Tadel, doch geäussert nicht den Schmerz.
Ja mein Gewand, es stimmt zu meinen Gedanken stets;
Der Dichter muss gemäss der Dichtung, die er schafft,
Je den Charakter selber haben, den er giebt." *Droysen.*

" The sense is, *malignum convicium audivi quidem, sed ita ut quem mihi studueris parare, dolore non affectus sim.* Therefore he added the article to ἄλγησιν." *Enger.* Fritzsche remarks that Agathon is purposely made to commence his defence with an *antithesis*, a figure he was particularly fond of. Cf. vss. 198, 199, 201.

[3] " ἅμα γνώμῃ is, ἁρμόττουσαν τῇ γνώμῃ." *Enger.*

[4] See note on Aves, 378.

[5] Five dramas only of Agathon's have been recorded, Θυέστης, Ἀερόπη, Τήλεφος, Ἀλκμαίων, Ἄνθος.

[6] " There's something in the body correspondent." *Wheelwright.* Comp. Krüger, Gr. Gr. § 56, 3, obs. 3.

[7] See Liddell's Lex. in voc. συνθηρεύω. Wheelwright has expressed the meaning proposed by all the other interpreters,

" We strive to make our own by imitation."

The whole sentence is a parody upon the *Æolus* of Euripides Fragm. vi.

[8] " Wenn ein Satyrspiel du zu machen hast, so rufe mich,
Damit Ich die Stanzen machen helfe hinter dir." *Droysen.*
See Bernhardy, W. S. p. 358, and note on Ran. 169.

AGATH. Besides, it is unpolished [1] to see a poet boorish and rough with hair. Consider that that well-known [2] Ibycus, and Anacreon of Teos, and Alcæus, who softened down our music, wore a head-band, and practised soft Ionian airs ; [3] and that Phrynichus,—for you have certainly [4] heard him,—was both handsome himself and dressed handsomely. On this account then his dramas also were handsome : for it is [5] unavoidable that one compose similarly to one's nature.

MNES. On this account then Philocles, [6] as he is ugly, composes uglily ; and Xenocles, [7] as he is vile, composes vilely ; and Theognis, [8] again, as he is frigid, composes frigidly.

AGATH. Most unavoidably ! For, assuredly, being aware of this, I paid attention to my person.

MNES. How, by the gods?

EUR. Cease to abuse ! for I also was such a one, when I was his age, when I began to compose.

MNES. By Jove, I do not envy you your training.

EUR. Yet suffer me to tell on what account I came.

AGATH. Say on !

EUR. Agathon, "it [9] suits a wise man, who is able briefly

[1] "Sehr unpoetisch." *Droysen.* ἄλλως τε, *prætereaque, et insuper und vollends.* Cf. vs. 290, *infra,* and Hermann, Vig. n. 232.

[2] See Krüger, Gr. Gr. § 51, 7, obs. 7.

[3] See Liddell's Lex. in voc. διακλάω. "*Molliter delicateque vivebant.*" *Enger.*

[4] γὰρ οὖν, *nam profecto, nam certe, certe enim.* Cf. Vesp. 726. Soph. Col. 980. Ant. 741, 77, 1255. Eur. Bacch. 922. Elmsley ad Soph. Col. 494. "*Nam hunc profecto audisti,* i. e. his plays. So Ach. 10, προσδοκῶν τὸν Αἰσχύλον. He might easily have heard Phrynichus, for he was an Athenian, ἐπεὶ Ἀθηναῖος ἦν, as the scholiast explains it." *Enger.*

[5] "Nothwendig gleicht ja, was man schafft dem, was man ist." *Droysen*

[6] He was the son of Polypithes and grandson of Æschylus' sister. He was nicknamed Χολή on account of the *bitterness* of his songs. A tetralogy of his, the *Pandionida,* is spoken of. According to Aristides, (vol. ii. p. 422,) he carried off the prize from Sophocles' *Rex Œdipus.* His *ugliness* is alluded to in Aves, 1275. Cf Schol. ad Aves, 284. Meineke, Com. Fragm. i. p. 521.

[7] The son of Carcinus. See Vesp. 1501. He was principally a play-actor, and devoted himself to Sophocles' characters. Cf. Meinek. Com. Fragm. i. p. 505.

[8] Nicknamed *snow.* See Acharn. 140, and Schol. on Acharn. 11. He was afterwards one of the thirty tyrants. See Xen. Hell. ii. 3, 2.

[9] Vss. 177, 178, are taken verbatim from the *Æolus* of Euripides, Fragm. v.

to abridge many words in a proper manner." But having been smitten [1] by a new calamity, I have come to you as a suppliant.

AGATH. In need of what?

EUR. The women purpose to destroy me to-day at the Thesmophoria, because I speak ill of them.

AGATH. What aid then can you have from me? [2]

EUR. All; for if you secretly take your seat amongst the women, so as to seem to be a woman, and defend me, you will assuredly save [3] me: for you alone can speak in a manner worthy of me. [4]

AGATH. How then do you not defend yourself in person?

EUR. I will tell you. In the first place, I am known; next, I am gray-headed and have a beard; while you are of a good countenance, fair, [5] shaven, with a woman's voice, [6] delicate, and comely to look at.

AGATH. Euripides——

EUR. What's the matter?

AGATH. Did you ever compose *this verse?* " You take [7] pleasure in beholding the light; and do you not think your father takes pleasure *in beholding it?*"

EUR. I did.

AGATH. Don't expect then that I will undergo your misfortune *for you:* for I should be mad. But bear yourself what is yours, as a private matter. For it is not right to bear [8] one's calamities with artifices, but with endurance.

MNES. And yet you, you lewd fellow, are loose-breeched, not through words, but through endurance.

---

[1] Eur. Alc. 856, καίπερ βαρείᾳ ξυμφορᾷ πεπληγμένος. Cf. ibid. vs. 405.

[2] " And what assistance canst thou have from us?" *Wheelwright.*

[3] " *Profecto me servabis.*" *Enger.* " Rettest du mich offenbar."
Droysen.

[4] " Denn meiner würdig sprechen würdest du allein." *Droysen.*
" Euripides facetiously praises Agathon as like himself." *Enger.*

[5] Comp. Eccles. 387, 428.

[6] Shakspeare, *Midsummer-Night's Dream,* act i. sc. 2,
"BOTTOM. An I may hide my face, let me play Thisby too: I'll speak in a monstrous little voice;—' Thisne, Thisne,—Ah, Pyramus, my lover dear; thy Thisby dear!—and lady dear!'"

[7] A quotation from Eurip. Alc. 691. Comp. Nub. 1415. Lys. 763. Acharn. 555. Eur. Hec. 1225.

[8] " The Ravenna Scholiast wished to mark a zeugma here, which he resolved in this way, τας συμφοράς γὰρ οὐχὶ τοῖς τεχνάσμαμιν ἐκφεύγειν δίκαιον, ἀλλὰ τοῖς παθήμασιν φέρειν, nor do I object." *Fritzsche.*

Eur. But what is it, for which you fear to go thither?

Agath. I should perish more miserably than you.

Eur. How?

Agath. How?—seeming to steal the nightly labours of the women, and to filch away the women's love.

Mnes. "Steal," quoth'a! Nay, rather, by Jove, to be ravished! But, by Jove, the pretext is plausible.

Eur. What then? Will you do this?

Agath. Don't imagine it![1]

Eur. Oh thrice-unlucky! how I am undone!

Mnes. Euripides, my dearest, my son-in-law,[2] do not abandon yourself!

Eur. How then, pray, shall I act?

Mnes. Bid a long farewell to this fellow, and take and use me as you please.

Eur. Come then, since you give yourself up to me, strip off this garment!

Mnes. Well now, *it is* on the ground. But what are you going to do to me?

Eur. To shave[3] these clean, but singe clear the parts below.

Mnes. Well, do whatever you think fit! or I ought[4] never to have given myself up to you.

Eur. Agathon, you, of course, always carry a razor,—now lend us a razor!

Agath. Take it from thence yourself out of the razor-case.

Eur. (*to Agathon*). You are very good! [*To Mnesilochus.*] Sit yourself down! Puff out your right cheek! [*Mnesilochus sits down and Euripides commences shaving.*]

---

[1] Eur. Med. 365, ἀλλ' οὔτι ταύτῃ ταῦτα, μὴ δοκεῖτέ πω.

[2] Euripides had married Chœrine, daughter of Mnesilochus. His marriage, however, was an unhappy one, and he repudiated her and gave her to his servant Cephisophon. "ἔγημε πρῶτον μὲν Χοιρίνην, θυγατέρα Μνησιλόχου· ἐξ ἧς ἔσχε Μνησίλοχον, κοὶ. Μνησαοχίδην καὶ Εὐριπίδην. ἀπωσάμενος δὲ ταύτην, ἔσχε καὶ δευτέραν, καὶ ταύτης ὁμοίως ἀκολάστου πειραθείς" *Suidas.*

[3] "This is taken from the Idæi of Cratinus." *Scholiast.* Clemens Alexand. Strom. vi. p. 751, "Ἀριστοφάνης δὲ ὁ Κωμικὸς ἐν ταῖς πρώταις Θεσμοφοριαζούσαις τὰ ἐκ τῶν Κρατίνου Ἐμπιπράμενων μετήνεγκεν ἔπη." Fritzsche thinks the title of the play may have been Ἰδαῖοι ἢ Ἐμπιπράμενοι. Comp. Meinek. Com. Frag. ii. p. 54.

[4] "Sonst hätt' Ich gar nicht mich dir übergeben gemusst." *Droysen.* Enger reads ἐπιδιδόναι γ' αὐτὸν ὤφελον, which is a gross solœcism. Dobree proposed ἐπιδοῦναι γ' αὐτός, which at all events is Greek. Cf. Dawes, M. C. p. 585, ed. Kidd.

MNES. Ah me!

EUR. Why do you cry out? I'll put a gag in your mouth,[1] if you don't be silent.

MNES. Alas! woe is me! [*Mnesilochus starts up and attempts to run away.*]

EUR. Hollo you! whither are you running?[2]

MNES. To the temple of the august[3] goddesses; for, by Ceres, I will not stay here any longer,[4] being gashed!

EUR. Will you not then be ridiculous, pray, with the one half[5] of your face shaved?

MNES. I little care.

EUR. By the gods, by no means abandon me! Come hither! [*Takes him by the arm and makes him sit down again.*]

MNES. Ah me, miserable!

EUR. Keep quiet,[6] and lift up your head! Whither are you turning?

MNES. Mu! mu![7]

EUR. Why do you mutter?[8] Every thing has been accomplished well.

MNES. Ah me, miserable! Then I shall serve as a light-armed[9] soldier!

EUR. Don't be concerned about it; for you shall appear very comely. Do you wish to see yourself?

MNES. If you think fit, give me *the looking-glass.*

EUR. Do you see yourself?

---

[1] Comp. Equit. 375. "Einen Knebel werd' Ich dir anlegen." *Droysen.* For γενναῖος, see Lidd. in voc.

[2] Comp. Vesp. 854.

[3] Comp. Equit. 1312. Krüger, Gr. Gr. § 43, 3, obs. 11.

[4] From the conjecture of Porson, Advers. p. 37, approved by Reisig and Dindorf. Cf. Nub. 812. Vesp. 1442.

[5] "*Alterâ tantum maxillâ rasâ.*" *Brunck.* Cf. Herod. ii. 121.

[6] σαυτὸν belongs to ἀνάκυπτε. For this position of καὶ, cf. Pax, 417. Nub. 745. ἔχε σαυτὸν ἀτρέμα I believe to be a construction unknown to Greek writers. See Aves, 1200, 1244, 1577. Ran. 339. Nub. 261, 743.

[7] Comp. Equit. 10.

[8] So ὤζω, Æsch. Eum. 124. φεύζω, Agam. 1308. οἰμώζω, Soph. El. 788. οἴζω, Æsch. Agam. 1316. αἰάζω, Theb. 829. Comp. Valckn. Diatrib. p. 20.

[9] "The joke turns upon the ambiguity of the word ψιλὸς, which signifies *a light-armed soldier,* as well as *clean-shaved.* There is the same ambiguity in the Latin word *levis.*" *Brunck.*

MNES. No, by Jove, but Clisthenes![1]

EUR. Stand up, that I may singe[2] you; and stoop forwards![3]

MNES. Ah me, miserable! I shall become a sucking pig.[4]

EUR. Let some one bring a torch or a lamp from within! [*To Mnesilochus.*] Bend yourself forwards! Take care now of your extremities! [*Euripides begins to singe him.*]

MNES. It shall be my care, by Jove! only that[5] I am burning. Ah me, miserable! Water, water,[6] neighbours, before the flame take hold of my rump!

EUR. Be of good courage!

MNES. How be of good[7] courage, when I'm quite burnt up?

EUR. But you've no further trouble now; for you have finished the greatest part.

MNES. Foh! oh, what[8] soot! I have become burnt all about my rump.

EUR. Don't be concerned! for another shall wipe it with a sponge.[9]

MNES. He shall weep then, whoever shall wash my breech.

EUR. Agathon, since you grudge to give yourself up to me, at any rate at least lend us a dress for this man,[10] and a girdle; for you will not say that you haven't them.

AGATH. Take and use them! I don't grudge them.[11]

MNES. What then shall I take?

AGATH. What? First take and put on the saffron-coloured robe.

MNES. (*sniffing at it*). By Venus, it smells sweetly of— lechery! Gird me up quickly! Now bring[12] me a girdle! [*Euripides brings a girdle.*]

EUR. There!

---

[1] See 574, *seq.* Aves, 831. Lys. 1092.
[2] See note on Lys. 1243.
[3] See Krüger, Gr. Gr. § 56, 2, obs. 6.   [4] Comp. Equit. 1236.
[5] "Nur brenn' Ich schon." *Droysen.* Cf. Nub. 1429.
[6] See Krüger, Gr. Gr. § 62, 3, obs. 3.
[7] Plaut. *Curcul.* iv. 3, 21, "Bellator, vale!
      TH. Quid valeam?"
[8] Comp. Lys. 295.   [9] See Elmsley, Acharn. 463.
[10] "*Quoniam ipse te mihi invides, at saltem commoda mihi vestem in hujus usum, non enim dices te eâ carere.*" *Enger.* "The scene represents the interior of Agathon's house." *Brunck.*
[11] Eur. Herc. F. 333, κοσμεῖσθ' ἴσω μολόντες· οὐ φθονῶ πέπλων.
[12] "Reich' das Busenband!" *Droysen.*

2 M

MNES. Come then, fit me out about the legs.

EUR. We want a head-dress and headband.[1]

AGATH. Nay, rather, see here's a woman's cap[2] to put round him, which I wear by night!

EUR. By Jove, but it's even very suitable![3]

MNES. Will it fit me? [*Puts it on.*]

AGATH. By Jove, but it's capital!

EUR. Bring an upper garment![4]

AGATH. Take it from the little couch.

EUR. We want shoes.

AGATH. Here, take mine!

MNES. Will they fit me? At all events you like to wear them loose.

AGATH. Do you see[5] to this! But indeed[6] you have what you want. Let some one wheel me in as quickly as possible. [*Exit Agathon.*]

EUR. (*surveying Mnesilochus' attire*). He, though a man,[7] is now a woman in appearance. If you speak, see that you talk like a woman in your voice, well and naturally.[8]

[1] "Stirnband und Haarnetz fehlen noch." *Droysen.*

[2] "Kuster and Brunck rightly translate it *galericum*, and Droysen *Schweinemagen.*" *Enger.* "*Schweinemagen* means a particular kind of *night-cap* used by women. Moreover, this funny toilet-scene is especially worthy of notice on that account, that it teaches that we are not to imagine the dress of the Athenian women to have been by any means so simple as it is represented, perhaps, in ancient sculptures." *Droysen.*

[3] "Beim Zeus, er ist auch überaus bequem!" *Droysen.*

[4] "ἔγκυκλον was the last garment of all, and was put over the others, *palla*; but the κροκωτὸν was an *inner* garment, ἔνδυμα." *Brunck.*

[5] "*Tu hoc ipse videas.*" *Brunck.* "Da siehe du zu!" *Droysen.*

[6] "ἀλλὰ—γὰρ, aber—ja." *Krüger.* See his Grammar, § 69, 14. obs. 4.

[7] "Der ist ein Mann geboren, aber völlig jetzt
Ein Weib zu schauen!" *Droysen.*

"*Hic, qui quidem vir est, jam prorsus femina est specie.*" *Enger.* "*Vir quidem hic nobis speciem mulieris utique præ se fert.*" *Brunck.* "There should be no stop in this verse. '*We have at length transformed this man into a woman.*'" *Seager.* "Brunck and Seager translate it rightly." *Fritzsche.* To make *their* versions correct, it would be necessary to write ἀνὴρ, as Fritzsche has done. Enger saw this, who remarks, "If the article were added, the force of the antithesis would be destroyed."

[8] "Recht natürlich." *Droysen* "γυναικιεῖς· ὡς γυνὴ λαλήσεις" *Scholiast.*

Mnes. I will try.

Eur. Go then!

Mnes. No, by Apollo! unless you swear to me—

Eur. What?

Mnes. —that you will help to deliver me with all your arts,[1] if any misfortune befall me.

Eur. "I swear then by Ether, the dwelling of Jove."[2]

Mnes. Why rather than by the lodging of Hippocrates?[3]

Eur. I swear then by all your gods in a lump.[4]

Mnes. Remember this then, that "your mind[5] swore, but your tongue has not sworn;" neither will I bind *it* by an oath.

Eur. Hasten quickly; for the signal[6] for the assembly in the temple of Ceres is exhibited; but I will be off.   [*Exit Euripides.*]

Mnes. Come on then, Thratta, follow me!   See, Thratta,

---

[1] "Mich retten zu helfen auch
Mit allem Fleisse, wenn mir ein Unglück widerfährt." *Droysen.*
"*Omnibus artibus.* πασῇ τέχνῃ, *quavis ratione*, has a far different force." *Fritzsche.*

[2] A parody on the following line of the *Melanippe* of Euripides, ὄμνυμι δ᾽ ἱρὸν αἰθέρ᾽, οἴκησιν Διός. Comp. Valckn. Diatrib. p. 49. It is parodied again ap. Ran. 100, 311.

[3] See Nub. 1001, and Fragm. 177, c. ed. Dindorf. "The sons of Hippocrates were frequently ridiculed by the comedians for their stupidity. Schol. on Nub. 1001, ' οὑτοί εἰσι Τελέσιππος, Δημοφῶν, Περικλῆς, διαβαλλόμενοι εἰς ὑωδίαν.' See the other passages ap. Meinek. Com. Fragm. ii. p. 477. Their lot appears to have resembled that of the Euripidean Jove, since the Æther was both their domicile and βόσκημα. Hippocrates himself had died many years before." *Enger.* "Bergler, Brunck, and Voss are very wrong in translating this *contubernium*. The meaning is the same as in Æsch. Suppl. 267. Eum. 916. Kuster has rightly translated it "*insula urbana.*" *Fritzsche.*

[4] "ἀθρόους πάντας. τὸ γὰρ ἄρδην ὅμοιον τῷ φοράδην ἐνέγκαι." *Scholiast.* "Bei allen Göttern allzumal." *Droysen.* It would seem to be a parody upon Eurip. Med. 746. Fritzsche discovers in the line an allusion to the contemptuous atheism so generally attributed to Euripides. Cf. Schlegel, Dram. Lit. p. 116.

[5] A parody on Eur. Hippol. 612, ἡ γλῶσσ᾽ ὀμώμοχ᾽, ἡ δὲ φρὴν ἀνώμοτος. It is parodied again ap. Ran. 1471, and ibid. vs. 101, 102. After this line the old MSS. present us with an ancient *stage-direction* (παρεπιγραφή), ὀλολύζουσι γυναῖκες. ἱερὸν ὠθεῖται, i. e. *shouts of women are heard. The scene is changed to a temple.* Comp. Schlegel, Dram. Lit. pp. 55, 161.

[6] See note on Vesp. 690.

what a quantity of smoke[1] ascends as the torches burn! Come, O very-beautiful Thesmophoræ,[2] receive me with good luck,[3] both on my entrance here, and on my return home again! Thratta, take down the box, and then take out a cake, that I may take and offer it to the two goddesses. O highly-honoured mistress, dear Demeter, and thou, Persephone, let me, possessing much, often[4] sacrifice to thee! but if not, now at least be undiscovered! and let my daughter, my pig,[5] meet with a husband who is rich, and besides, silly[6] and stupid! and let my little boy[7] have sense and understanding! Where, where shall I sit down in a good place, that I may hear the orators? Do you, Thratta, be off out of the way! for it is not permitted slaves to hear the words.

FEMALE HERALD.

HER. Let there be[8] solemn silence! Let there be solemn

---

[1] Comp. Pax, 1192. Equit. 1219. Acharn. 150. Plut. 394. Nub. 2. Ran. 1278. Bernhardy, W. S. p. 52.

[2] " Ihr gnädig holden Thesmophoren, mit gutem Glück
Bei meinem Eingang, meinem Heimgang segnet mich." *Droysen.*

[3] " Elsewhere (Aves, 435, Eccles. 131) he uses τύχἀγαθῷ, which I have restored to Aves, 675, from the Ravenna MS., in place of the common reading ἀγαθῇ τύχῃ. Helladius (ap. Phot. Bibl. p. 529, 34) observes that both ἀγαθὴ τύχη and τύχη ἀγαθὴ are used by the Attics." *Dindorf.* " We distinguish these in this way: τύχῃ αγαθῷ, *quod bene vertat*, is a popularly adopted formula of no particular emphasis, while ἀγαθῇ τύχῃ, *quod felix, faustum, fortunatumque sit*, is used by one who fears bad fortune." *Fritzsche.* Cf. note on Aves, 435.

[4] " Und Persephassa, lass mich vielfach vieles dir
Zu opfern haben——sonderlich jetzt mich verborgen sein. '
                                                        Droysen
For ἀλλὰ νῦν, see note on Aves, 1598. Soph. El. 411. Col. 1276. Antig. 552. " Mnesilochus prays to the gods as if he were a woman, that he may be rich and able to make these offerings frequently. Bergler aptly compares Eur. El. 805." *Fritzsche.* See note on Ran. 169.

[5] Dindorf compares Vesp. 573.

[6] Cf. Eupolis ap. Athen. vi. p 236, F. For ἄλλως τε, see note on vs. 159, *supra.*

[7] " Mnesilochus, as if he were a mother who had the welfare of her children at heart, prays that his daughter may get a rich and stupid husband, and his son have sense and spirit. Moreover χοιρίον and ποσθαλίσκος aptly correspond to each other." *Enger.*

[8] " So in *Aves* we find him using *prose;* first, vs. 864, in the speech of the priest, then vss. 1035 and 1040, in the decree, then 1046, in

silence! Pray to the[1] Thesmophoræ, Demeter, and Cora,[2] and to Plutus, and to Calligenia, and to Tellus, nurse of youths,[3] and to Mercury,[4] and to the Graces, to convene this assembly and the present meeting in the most becoming and most profitable[5] manner:—very beneficially for the state of the Athenians, and fortunately for ourselves ; and that she may get her opinion passed, who acts and speaks the best for the people[6] of the Athenians and that of the women.[7] Pray for these things, and for yourselves what is good. Io Pæan! io Pæan! Let us rejoice!

CHORUS OF WOMEN KEEPING THE THESMOPHORIA.

CHO. We accept *the omen*,[8] and supplicate the race of the gods to appear and take pleasure in these prayers. O Jove of great renown! and thou with golden lyre, who inhabitest sacred Delos! and thou, all powerful damsel, gray-eyed, with spear of gold, who inhabitest a desirable city, come hither! and thou of many names, damsel slaying wild beasts, offspring of golden-eyed Latona! and thou marine, august Neptune, lord of the sea, having left thy fishy, storm-vexed[9] recess! and ye daughters of marine Nereus! and ye moun-

the indictment, and lastly vs. 1049, in the law. The Ravenna Scholiast learnedly observes πεζῇ εὐφημίᾳ χρῶνται οἱ κωμικοί, ἐπειδὰν εὐχὴν ἢ ψήφισμα εἰσάγωσιν." *Fritzsche.* Droysen has consequently exhibited the whole of this proclamation in prose.

[1] Even in the genitive and dative the form τοῖν is the more usual one with the Attics. See Blomfield's Remarks on Matthiä's Greek Grammar, p. xlix. Dawes, M. C. p. 570. Krüger, Gr. Gr. § 14, 9, obs. 2, § 44, 2, obs. 4, § 58, 1, obs. 3. Mehlhorn, Gr. Gr. § 232, note 6. The above form is found vs. 285, *supra.* Vesp. 7, 378. Eccles 502, 1106. Pax, 1109.

[2] Comp. Ran. 337.

[3] Pausanias, i. 22, 3, ἔστι δὲ καὶ Γῆς Κουροτρόφου, κ τὶ Δήμητρος ἱερὸν Χλόης. See Dawes, M. C. p. 516, ed. Kidd.

[4] Comp. Pax, 456.

[5] Comp. Krüger, Gr. Gr. § 55, 3, obs. 7—9.

[6] See note on Equit. 831.

[7] " Pherecrates has jested in a similar manner in his Γρᾶες, p. 19, Ἀθηναίαις αὐταῖς τε καὶ ταῖς ξυμμάχοις." *Fritzsche.*

[8] This refers to the last word (χαίρωμεν) spoken by the herald. Cf. Aves, 645, 646. So Eupolis (Δῆμοι, p. 110,) καὶ προσαγήλωμεν ἐπελθόντες. Χαίρετε πάντες. Β. δεχόμεσθα. " Guten Abend!" *Droysen.*

[9] " τὸν ὑπὸ τῶν ἀνέμων κινούμενον. πᾶσαν κίνησιν καλοῦσιν οἶστρον " *Scholiast.*

tain-roaming nymphs! And let the golden lyre accompany our prayers; and may we well-born Athenian women bring our debates to an accomplishment.[1]

HER. Pray to the Olympic gods and to the Olympic goddesses,[2] and to the Pythian gods and to the Pythian goddesses, and to the Delian gods and to the Delian goddesses, and to the other deities; if any one plots any evil[3] against the people of the women, or makes proposals of peace to Euripides[4] and the Persians for the purpose of any injury to the women, or purposes to be a tyrant,[5] or to join in bringing back the tyrant, or has denounced *a woman* as substituting a child, or if any woman's female slave, being a go-between, has whispered the matter in her master's ear, or if any, when sent, brings lying messages, or if any paramour deceives by telling falsehoods, and does not give what he shall have formerly promised, or if any old woman[6] gives presents to a paramour, or even if a mistress receives *presents*, betraying her friend, and if any male or female publican[7] falsifies the legal measure of the gallon or the half-pint, pray that he may perish miserably, himself and family, but pray that the gods may give many blessings[9] to all the rest of you.

[1] " τελέως is explained by the Scholiast ἐκκλησιασαιμεν ἐπι το γενέσθαι τελεστικὰ τὰ πράγματα, i. e. ὥστε τελεστικὰ τὰ πρ. γεν." *Enger*. So also Fritzsche. εὐγενεῖς is added because *slaves* (vs. 294) were excluded.

[2] Comp. Aves, 865, 866.   [3] Comp. Tyrtæus, Fragm. ii. vs. 10.

[4] " *Aut si quis legatos de pace et amicitiá mittendos conseat ad Euripidem Medosque.*" *Fritzsche*. Cf. Isocr. Panegyr. c. 42. Plutarch, Vit. Arist. c. 10. For ἐπὶ βλάβῃ, cf. vss. 360, 366.

[5] " When the Pisistratidæ were ejected from Athens, the people decreed that in every assembly of the people the crier should imprecate curses on him who should aim at a tyranny. To this practice we must refer the words, *aut si quis regnare cogitat, aut tyrannum* (Hippias was originally meant) *quantum in ipso est, reducere.* See Solon's law ap. Andocides, Myster. p. 97, 7, B." *Fritzsche*.

[6] " Od'r wenn Geschenke 'ne alte Frau an den Liebsten giebt,
   Od'r wenn Geschenke die Liebste, den Freund zu verlassen,
     nimmt."   *Droysen.*

[7] Comp. Plut. 435, 436.

[8] " Fritzsche remarks that it was usual to proclaim in the Assembly, ἐξώλη τοῦτον εἶναι αὐτὸν καὶ γένος καὶ οἰκίαν." *Enger.* Cf. Demosth. Fals. Leg. p. 71, 5, B. in Aristocr. p. 67, 8. Dinarch. in Aristog. 16, 8. Andocid. Myster. p. 98, 7, B.

[9] " πολλὰ καὶ ἀγαθὰ is a formula very much used by the Attic

Cho. We offer our united prayers that these wishes may come to be accomplished for the state, and accomplished for the people ; and that those women who give[1] the best advice (as many as this befalls) may get their opinions passed. But as many as for the sake of gain deceive, and violate the established oaths for the purpose of injury, or seek to revolutionize decrees and law, and tell our secrets to our enemies, or bring in the Persians for the purpose of injury to the country, act wickedly and injure the state. But, O all-powerful Jove, mayest thou accomplish this, so that the gods stand by us, although[2] we are women.

Her. Hear, every one ! [*Unfolds a paper and begins to read the preliminary decree.*] " These things have been determined on by the Senate of the women : Timoclea was Epistates,[3] Lysilla was secretary, Sostrata moved the decree ; to convene an assembly in the morning[4] in the middle of the Thesmophoria, when we are most at leisure ; and to debate first about Euripides, what he ought to suffer ; for he has been adjudged[5] guilty by us all." Who[6] wishes to speak ?

1st Woman. I.

writers. Cf. Lys 1159. Pax, 8, 436, 538. Vesp. 1350. In the opposite meaning they say πολλα και κακά. See Equit. 1276, 1329. Eccles. 453. This has been imitated by the Latins. Plaut. Pseud. i. 3, 138, '*Multa malaque in me dicta dixistis mihi.*'" .*Brunck*. See Krüger, Gr. Gr. § 69, 32, obs. 3. Blomf. Pers. 249. Hermann, Vig n. 323. Dawes, M. C. 452. Porson, Advers. p. 176. Weiske, Pleon. Gr. p. 185, and add Plut. 218. Pax, 968. Nub. 1329. Vesp. 1304. Antiphanes ap. Athen. x. p. 446, C.

[1] Enger, who reads λεγούσαις, translates, " *Ut omnes vincant, quibus contingit, ut optima suadeant,*" referring to vs. 306, and censuring Dindorf's reading λεγούσας. See Krüger, Gr. Gr. § 55, 2, obs. 7.

[2] See note on Eccles. 159.

[3] Comp. Thuc. iv. 118. Lucian, Deor. Concil. c. 14. Andocid. Myster. p. 96, 2, B. Inscr. ap. Böckh, Corp. Inscr. i. p. 112, ii. Tab. ii. n. 3. Plutarch, Vit. Dec. Orat. ii. p. 833. Schömann, Comit. p. 131. Fritzsche discovers in the passage a reflection upon three notorious characters, Timocles, Lysicles, and Sostratus. See Equit. 678, 684.

[4] Demosth. Midias, p. 8, τοὺς πρυτάνεις ποιεῖν ἐκκλησίαν ἐν Διονύσου τῇ ὑστεραίᾳ, ἐκ Πανδίων. ἐν δὲ ταύτῃ χρηματίζειν, πρῶτον μὲν περι ἱερῶν, κ. τ. λ. Cf. Dawes, M. C. p. 433, ed. Kidd.

[5] Comp. Aves, 1585.

[6] Comp. Eccles. 130, 147. Acharn. 145. Lucian, Tragop. c. 16. Deor. Concil. c. 1

HER. Then first put on this *crown*[1] before you speak. [*To the meeting.*] Be silent! Be quiet! Give[2] attention! for she is now expectorating, as the orators do. She seems to be going to make a long speech.

1ST WOMAN. Through no[3] ostentatiousness, by the two goddesses, have I stood up to speak, O women; but indeed I have been vexed, unhappy woman, now for a long time, seeing you treated with contumely by Euripides the son of the herb-woman,[4] and abused with much abuse[5] of every kind. For what abuse does he not[6] smear upon us? And where has he not calumniated us, where, in short,[7] are spectators, and tragic actors, and choruses? calling us adulteresses in disposition, lovers of the men, wine-bibbers,[8] traitresses, gossips, masses of wickedness, great pests to men. So that, as soon as[9] they come in from the wooden-benches, they look askance at us, and straightway search, lest[10] any paramour be concealed in the house. And we are no longer able to do any of those things which we formerly did: such badness has he taught our husbands. So that, if even any woman weave a crown,[11] she is thought to be in love; and if she let fall any vessel while roaming about the house, her husband asks her, "In whose honour is the pot broken? It must be for the Corinthian[12] stranger."

---

[1] For this practice of wearing a crown while speaking in the assembly, Brunck refers to Eccles. 130, 147, 163, 171. Aves, 463.

[2] Cratinus, (ap. Meinek. Com. Fragm. p. 190,) ἄκουε, σίγα, πρόσεχε τὸν νοῦν, δεῦρ' ὅρα.

[3] "*Nulla me ambitio temere eo abripuit, ut ad dicendum surgerem, mulieres.*" *Fritzsche.*

[4] Cf. vss. 456, 910, *infra.* Acharn. 457, 478. Equit. 19. Ran. 840 Pliny, N. H. xxii. 38, "*Hæc est, quam Aristophanes Euripidi poetæ objicit joculariter matrem ejus ne olus quidem venditasse, sed scandicem.*" Cf. Aul. Gell. N. A. xv. 20. Val. Max. iii. 4. Mus. Rhen. ii. p. 236 237.

[5] See note on vs. 351.

[6] See Krüger, Gr. Gr. § 51, 17, obs. 5. Bernhardy, W. S. p. 153.

[7] Comp. Vesp. 1120. Ruhnk. Tim. Lex. in voc. ἐμβραχυ.

[8] Enger, Fritzsche, Bothe, Brunck, and Kuster read οἰνοπίπας. See note on Equit. 407.

[9] See Krüger, Gr. Gr. § 56, 10, obs. 3.

[10] See Krüger, Gr. Gr. § 54, 8, obs. 10.

[11] Comp. Sappho ap. Bergk, Poet. Lyr. p. 607.

[12] "In derision of a passage in the *Sthenobœa* of Euripides, which is preserved in Athenæus, x. p. 427, E.,

Is any girl[1] sick ; straightway her brother says, " This colour
in the girl does not please me."   Well ; does any woman,
lacking children, wish to substitute a child ; it is not possible
even for this to go undiscovered ; for now the husbands sit
down beside[2] them.   And he has calumniated us to the old
men, who heretofore used to marry girls ; so that no old man
is willing to marry a woman, on account of this verse, " For[3]
a woman is ruler over an old bridegroom."   In the next
place, through him they now put seals and bolts[4] upon the
women's apartments, guarding us ; and moreover they keep
Molossian[5] dogs, a terror[6] to paramours.   And this, indeed,
is pardonable ; but as for what was permitted us heretofore,
to be ourselves the housekeepers, and to draw forth and take
barley-meal, oil, and wine ; not even this is any longer permitted us.   For the husbands now themselves carry secret
little keys, most ill-natured, certain Spartan[7] ones with three

>   πεσὸν δέ νιν λέ\ηθεν οὐδὲν ἐκ χερός·
>   ἀλλ' εὐϑὺς αὐδᾷ· τῷ Κορινθίῳ ξένῳ." *Brunck.*

Cf. Lys. 856. Cratinus ap. Athen. ii. p. 1038, ed. Dindorf. Rhenisch.
Mus. ii. p. 238, 239. " According to a custom among the Greeks,
whatever fell accidentally from the hand was consecrated to lost
friends." *Droysen.*   Aristophanes reflects at the same time upon the
immorality of the Corinthians.

[1] Aves, 79, ἔτνους δ' ἐπιϑυμεῖ, δεῖ τορύνης καὶ χύτρας, τρέχω ἐπι
τορύνην.   But the best illustration is Timocles ap. Athen. vi. p
223, D,

>   Οφθαλμιᾷ τις, εἰσὶ Φινεῖδαι τυφλοί.
>   τέϑνηκέ τῳ παῖς, ἡ Νιόβη κεκούφικε.
>   χωλός τίς ἐστι, τὸν Φιλοκτήτην ὅρα.
>   γέρων τις ἀτυχεῖ, κατέμαθει τὸν Οἰνέα.

Cf. also vs. 407 of this play. Eccles. 179. Demosth. Coron. p. 27t, 2
Olynth. iii. 18, 1. Eur. Orest. vs. 631.
[2] " During their confinement." *Scholiast.*
[3] This verse is a quotation from the *Phœnix* of Euripides, Frag.
v   The same sentiment is repeated in his *Danae,*

>   γυναικί τ' ἐχθρὸν χρῆμα πρεσβύτης ἀνήρ.

Which is also parodied by Aristophanes, Fragm. 497, ed. Dindorf,

>   αἰσχρὸν νέα γυναικὶ πρεσβύτης ἀνήρ.

[4] Reflecting, as Fritzsche thinks, upon vs. 58 of the *Danae.* Comp
Hor. Od. iii. 16. Menand. Fragm. incert. i. p. 53, ed. Didot.
[5] Comp. Eur. Hipp. 644.
[6] " μορμολυκεῖον δηλοῖ καὶ φόβητρον ἁπλῶς ἐν Θεσμοφοριαζούσαις."
Etymol. M. p. 590, 52.
[7] Comp. Plautus, Most. ii. 1, 57. Liddell's Lex. in voc. βάλανος
Menander, Μισουμενος, Fragm 11, p. 35, ed. Didot. Dawes, M. C
p. 550.

teeth. Previously, indeed, it was possible at least [1] to secretly open the door, if we got a three-obol [2] seal-ring made. But now this home-born slave [3] Euripides has taught them to have rings of worm-eaten wood, having them suspended about them. Now therefore I move [4] that we mix up some destruction in some [5] way or other for him, either by poison, or by some one artifice, so that he shall perish. These I speak openly; but the rest I will draw up in the form of a motion in conjunction with the secretary. [6]

Cho. Never yet did I hear a woman more intriguing than this, nor one that spoke more ably. For she speaks all justly, and has well examined all appearances, and weighed [7] all things in her mind, and shrewdly discovered artful, well-invented w.. ·ls ; so that, if Xenocles the son of Carcinus were to speak immediately after [8] her, he would appear to us all, as I think, to say absolutely nothing to the purpose.

[1] " ἀλλά, saltem, as in vs. 250, supra. Nub. 1364, 1369." Brunck. Cf. Pax, 660. Ach. 191. Lys. 904.

[2] Cf. Equit. 682. Aves, 18. Acharn. 962. Plut. 884. Pax, 1201. Antiphanes ap. Athen. iii. p. 123, B. Krüger, Gr. Gr. § 47, 17. Bernhardy, W. S. p. 164. For the custom, cf. Lys. 1197.

[3] " No one knows better than a home-born slave how domestic matters ought to be managed; therefore Euripides is called οἰκοτρίψ, i. e. cellæ culinæque scrutator." Fritzsche. So also Enger. Cf. Ran. 976.

[4] Cf. Equit. 654, 1311. Aves, 337. Vesp. 270.

[5] " ἀμωσγέπως = ἐνί γέ τῳ τρόπῳ, which is different from the formula μιᾷ γε τέχνῃ. With these expressions compare Thuc. vi. 34. Plato, Men. p. 129, ed. Stallbaum. The Attics never say ἢ γε, but very often ἢ—γε with one or two words between. See Thuc. iii. 45; vi. 18; viii. 27. Demosth. Fals. Leg. p. 46, 2, B. Xenoph. Hellen. iv. 8, 12. Arist. Pax, 273." Fritzsche.

[6] " Das andre geb' Ich bei dem Schreiber zu Protokoll." Droysen. See Liddell's Lex. voc. συγγράφω. Schömann, Comit. p. 118. Pollux, iv. 19. " Ἀριστοφάνης δὲ παίζει ἐν Θεσμοφοριαζούσαις, λέγων ἡ γραμματεύς." Suidas. See note on Eccles. 713.

[7] Æsch. Prom. Vinct. 112,

ἢ σοφὸς, ἢ σοφὸς ἦν, ὃς
πρῶτος ἐν γνώμῃ τόδ' ἐβάστασε.

[8] παρά, confestim secutus. So Demosth. 229, 19, παρὰ αὐτὰ τὰ ἀδικήματα λέγειν, to speak immediately upon the commission of the misdeeds. Cf. ibid. Panæt. p. 966, 20. Bernhardy, W. S. p. 258. Monk ad Alc. 936. Enger and Fritzsche have treated this passage most unhappily, not knowing this common force of παρά, which they might have learnt from almost every page of Demosthenes. What Brunck means by "dicere juxta illam," or Droysen by " neben ihr zu sprechen,'

2ND WOM. For the purpose of a few words I also have
come forward. For the other matters she has laid to his charge
rightly: but what I have suffered *personally*, these I wish
to state. My husband died in Cyprus,[1] having left behind
him five little children, whom I used to maintain with difficulty by plaiting wreaths in the myrtle-wreath-market.[2] Before this[3] I supported myself, indeed, but miserably.[4] But
now this fellow by representing in his tragedies,[5] has persuaded
the people that there are no gods; so that we do not now earn
even to the amount of[6] one half. Now therefore I exhort
and charge all to punish this man for many reasons; for, O
women, he does savage deeds to us, as having been reared
himself among the potherbs[8] in their wild state. But I will
be off to the market-place; for I have twenty bespoken[9]
wreaths to plait for people.

is to me quite unintelligible. For Xenocles, see note on vs. 169,
supra, and on Nub. 1259. Cf. Vesp. 1501. Enger quotes from Athen.
iv. p. 134, D.,

  δεῖπνά μοι ἔννεπε Μοῦσα πολύτροφα καὶ μάλα πολλὰ,
  ἃ Ξενοκλῆς ῥήτωρ ἐν 'Αθήναις δείπνισεν ἡμᾶς.

[1] " The last expedition to Cyprus took place forty years before.
Droysen and Fritzsche think the woman's husband died in this expedition. Fritzsche adds that he may have been a sailor who died
at Cyprus." *Enger.* The allusion is more probably to the events
recorded in the famous *Inscriptio Nointeliana* ap. Rose, p. 105.

[2] Comp. note on Lys. 557.

[3] " The Ravenna Scholiast, and Suidas, (in voc. τέως,) and the
Scholiast on Plato, (p. 334,) explain it by πρότερον or πρὸ τοῦ. The
grammarians are right, as is shown by the words immediately preceding, ἀγὼ μόλις ἔβοσκον. Further, as the words ἀλλ' ἡμικάκως
and οὐδ' εἰς ἥμισυ are opposed, so also the conjunctions τέως and
νῦν, which couple these sentences, ought to be opposed to each
other. Cf. Herod. vi. 12." *Enger.* Cf. also vs. 422.

[4] See Pollux, vi. 661. Lobeck, Phryn. p. 336.

[5] Fritzsche refers to Hec. 484, 958—960, *Bellerophon*, p. 112, *Melanippe*, p. 213, *Sisyphus*, p. 323, 324, ed. Matthiä.

[6] See Hermann, Vig. n. 380. Xen. Anab. i. 1, 10. Krüger, Gr.
Gr. § 68, 21, obs. 9, § 60, 8, obs. 1.

[7] There is a play upon the ambiguity of the word ἄγρια, which is
joined both with κακά and with λαχάνοις. " Euripides is ridiculed,
who in his *Phœnix*, Fragm. xi., said, γυνή τε πάντων ἀγριώτατον κακόν." *Enger.* Cf. Menand. ap. Bekk. Anecd. p. 332, 28. Aul. Gell.
N. A. xv. 20.

[8] Comp. note on vs. 387.

[9] " στεφ. δυνθ. *coronas localilias.* Vid. præter Schol. Rav. et Sui-
dam, Athen. xv. p. 680, C. Pollux, vii. 200. Hesych." *Enger.*

CHO. This other disposition, again, appears still cleverer than the former one.   How [1] she talked! not what was ill-timed, nor yet what was void of understanding, but all per-suasive, being possessed of sense and a subtle mind.   The man must manifestly [2] give us satisfaction for this insolence.

MNES. It is not wonderful, O women, that you who are so abused [3] should be exceedingly exasperated at Euripides, nor yet that your bile should boil over; for I myself hate that man, if I be not mad,—so [4] may I be blessed in my children!   But nevertheless we must grant the privilege of speaking amongst each other; for we are by ourselves, and there is no blabbing [5] of our conversation.   Why thus do we accuse [6] him, and are vexed, if, being cognizant of two or three misdeeds of ours, he has said them of us [7] who perpetrate innumerable?   For I myself, in the first place,—not to speak of any one else,—am conscious with myself of many shameful [8] acts: at all events of that [9] most shameful one, when I was a bride of three days, and my husband was sleeping beside me. Now I had a friend, [10] who had debauched me when I was seven years of age.   He, through love of me, came and began scratching at the door; and then I immediately understood it; and then I was for going down [11] secretly, but my husband asked me, "Whither are you going down?"   "Whither?—A

[1] See notes on Pax, 350, 363.
[2] Comp. Av. 1290. Plut. 948. Soph. Aj. 81. Thuc. vi. 60, *sub fin.*
[3] See Liddell's Lex. voc. ἀκούω, iii. Cf. vs. 388, *supra.*
[4] Cf. Nub. 520. Eur. Med. 714. Lucian, Philops. § 27. Hom. Il. A. 18. Hor. Od. i. 3, 1. Krüger, Gr. Gr. § 54, 3, obs. 5.
[5] "*Nam solæ sumus, neque ulla sermonem nostrum effert.*" *Fritzsche.* Cf. Euphron, ap. Athen. ix. p. 380, A. Aristoph. Plut. 1138. Eccles 443. Æsch. Eum. 910. Plato, Parmen. p. 137, A.
[6] Nub. 131, τί ταῦτ' ἔχων στραγγεύομαι; Cf. Eccles. 853. Acharn. 514. "The participle ἔχων, where it is said to be completely redundant, is always connected with *some censure.*" *Fritzsche.*
[7] "The full form would be, εἰ δύ' ἡμῶν ἢ τρία κακὰ ξυνειδὼς εἶπεν (ἡμᾶς' δύ' ἢ τρία κακὰ) δρώσας μυρία." *Fritzsche.*
[8] See Dawes, M. C. p. 585, ed. Kidd.
[9] *ἐκεῖνος* not unfrequently refers to what immediately *follows.* See vs. 498. Pax, 146. Equit. 885, 1012. Ach. 1195. Vesp. 47. Eccles 422, 465. Soph. Ajax, 94. Plato, Rep. x. p. 606, B. Xenoph. Cyrop. iii. 1, 28.
[10] *Friend* (φίλος) is the Attic euphemism for *paramour.* See vs. 346.
[11] "Der kam und raschelte voller Begier an unsrer Thür;
Sogleich verstand Ich 's; heimlich wol!t' Ich hinab zu ihm."
Droysen

colic[1] and pain, husband, possesses me in my stomach; therefore I am going to the necessary." "Go then!" said he. And then he began pounding juniper berries, anise, and sage. But after I had poured some water on the hinge,[2] I went out to my paramour; and then I conversed with him beside the statue[3] of Apollo, holding by the bay-tree. These, you see,[4] Euripides never yet at any time spoke of. Nor does he mention how we give ourselves up to our slaves and to muleteers, if we have not any other.[5] Nor how, when we junket ever so much during the night, we chew up garlic[6] in the morning, in order that the husband having smelt it when he comes in from the wall,[7] may not suspect us of doing any thing bad. These things, you see, he has never at any time spoken of. And if he does abuse a Phædra, what is this to us?[8] Neither has he ever mentioned that, how that well-known woman,[9] while showing her husband at day-break[10] how beautiful her upper garment is, sent out her paramour hidden in it—*that* he has never yet mentioned.[11] And I know another woman, who[12] for ten days said she was in labour, till she purchased

[1] Comp. Plut. 1131. Pax, 175. *Proagon*, Fragm. vii. ed. Dindorf.
[2] Comp. Plautus, Curcul. i. 3, 1. Liddell's Lex. voc. στρόφιγξ.
[3] "οὕτω καλούμενος Ἀπόλλων τετραγώνιος." *Scholiast.*
[4] Comp. Nub. 355, and Dawes, M. C. p. 586, ed. Kidd.
[5] For a similar pleonastic use of the second negative, cf. vss. 498—501, 718. Plut. 410.
[6] Xenoph. Conviv. iv. 8, ὁ Νικήρατος κρομμύων ὄζων ἐπιθυμεῖ οἴκαδε ἐλθεῖν, ἵν' ἡ γυνὴ αὐτοῦ πιστεύῃ μὴ διανοηθῆναι μηδένα ἂν φιλῆσαι αὐτόν. Cf. Hor. Epod. iii. 19.
[7] "Thucyd. viii. 69, ἦσαν δ' Ἀθηναῖοι πάντες ἀεὶ οἱ μὲν ἐπὶ τείχει, οἱ δ' ἐν τάξει, τῶν ἐν Δεκελείᾳ πολεμίων ἕνεκα ἐφ' ὅπλοις, which events belong to the same year in which this play was acted." *Enger.* Cf. Ach. vs. 72, and Dawes, M. C. p. 588, ed. Kidd.
[8] Comp. Lys 514. Equit. 1198. Eccles. 520. Krüger, Gr. Gr. § 48, 3, obs. 8. Bernhardy, W. S. p. 90.
[9] "ἡ γυνὴ is not *mulier quædam*, but *nota illa mulier*." *Fritzsche.*
[10] ὑπ' ὄρθρον, Dindorf. "Videtur ita res esse cogitanda, ut mulier propterea illo prætextu usa sit, ut cum encyclo adulterum occultante ex thalamo in αὐλὴν egredi possit, unde facile effugere adulter poterat." *Enger.*
[11] Comp. the construction in vss. 491, 492, 461.
[12] Comp. Plut. 365, 933. Pax, 676. Ran. 889. Nub. 599, 863. Aves, 144. Lys. 96. Eur. Iph. T. 146. Phœn. 266. Hec. 759. Hippol. 100. Æsch. Theb. 555 Elmsley, Heracl. 601. Porson and Schäfer,

a little child; while her husband went about purchasing drugs to procure a quick delivery.[1] But the child[2] an old woman brought in a pot with its mouth stopped with honey-comb,[3] that it might not squall. Then, when she that carried it nodded, *the wife* immediately cried out, " Go away,[4] husband, go away, for methinks I shall be immediately delivered." For *the child* kicked against the bottom of the pot.[5] And he ran off delighted, while she drew out *the stoppage* from the mouth of the child, and it cried out. And then the abomin-able[6] old woman who brought the child, runs smiling to the husband, and says, " A lion has been born to you, a lion ! your very image, both in all other respects whatever, and its nose is like yours, bcing crooked like an acorn-cup."[7]   Do

Orest. 1645. Hermann, Vig. n. 35. Krüger, Gr. Gr. § 51, 12. Mus. Crit. i. 72. Bernhardy, W. S. p. 302. Blomf. Theb. 549.

[1] See Bekk. Anecd. p. 74, 1. Pollux, ii. 7; iv. 208. The imper-fect of ἔρχομαι is rarely used by the Attic writers. See Elms. Heracl. 210. Krüger, Gr. Gr. § 40, p. 163.

[2] " This use of the article is worthy of notice. So τὴν δ', vs. 717. [Eccles. 316. Pax, 644. Lys. 395. Equit. 652. Cf. note on Eccles. 275.] Infants were exposed in pots, as we are informed by the Scholiast on this passage and on Ran. 1288, and by Hesychius in voc. ἐγχυτριεῖς and ἐγχυτρίζειν. Mœris, Att. p. 102. Schol. on Plato, Min. p. 315." *Enger.*

[3] " Sic Schol. ad Acharn. 452, σπόγγος πεπληρωμένος μέλιτος, καὶ τιθέασι τῷ στόματι τῶν παιδίων, ὅπως σιωπήσωσι ζητοῦντες τροφήν." *Enger.*

[4] " Fort, Lieber, fort ! gleich kommt 's zur Welt, so drängt 's
     im Bauch !
Das arme Kind arbeitete nämlich in Topfes Bauch.
Da lief er herzensfroh hinweg ; sie nahmen schnell
Das Wachs dem Kindchen aus dem Mund, da quarrt cs hell."
                                                Droysen

[5] " The Scholiast observes that μήτρας was expected ; and so the passage is commonly understood. But Thiersch has rightly ob-servcd that these are the words of Mnesilochus, and not of the lying-in woman." *Enger.* " Observe the difference between an aorist and a perfect: for if we had λελάκτικεν in our text, it would be a con-tinuation of the speech of the woman, unconsciously betraying herself and mentioning the *pot* through forgetfulness of her part; but now ἐλάκτισεν, *ferierat*, informs us that thesc are the words of Mncsilochus wittily narrating the affair." *Fritzsche.*

[6] Mnesilochus is here forgetful of his assumed character.

[7] " Kraus wie ein Eichelpeserich." *Droysen.* The interprctation given in the text is that proposed by Lycophron ap. Schol. ad Pac

we not practise these wicked acts? Yea, by Diana,[1] do we! And then are we angry at Euripides, "who[2] have suffered nothing greater than we have committed?"

CHO. This[3] certainly is wonderful, where the creature was found, and what land reared this so audacious *woman*. For I did not think the villanous *woman* would[4] even ever have dared thus shamelessly to say this publicly amongst us. But now every thing may take place. I commend the old proverb, "For[5] we must look about under every stone, lest an orator bite us." But indeed there existeth not any thing

199, and adopted by Fritzsche and Liddell. For ἀπαξάπαντα, see note on Equit. 845, and for καὶ after τά τ' ἄλλα, comp. Lys. 953. Æsch. Pers. 676. Eum. 697. Prom. Vinct. 954.

[1] "A very appropriate oath. Mnesilochus means Diana the *midwife*, who of course knew these things very well, and the vile artifices of the women." *Fritzsche.*

[2] A parody on the *Telephus* of Euripides, p. 342, ed. Matthiä,

εἶτα δὴ θυμούμεθα
οὐδὲν παθόντες μᾶλλον ἢ δεδρακότες;

Comp. Hec. vs. 623, and Rhenisch. Mus. ii. p. 240.

[3] For this use of τοῦτο to introduce something afterwards explained more fully, see Krüger, Gr. Gr. § 51, 7, obs. 4, and cf. Nub. 215, 380, 1262, 1412. Plut. 259, 573, 594, 898, 921. Vesp. 47, 653 1536. Pax, 146, 1075. Ran. 1369, and vs. 556 of this play.

[4] ἄν belongs to the infinitive (τολμῆσαι), as in Thucyd. viii. 66 ἐνῆσαν γὰρ καὶ οὓς οὐκ ἄν ποτέ τις ᾤετο ἐς ὀλιγαρχίαν τραπέσθαι. Cf. Pax, 710. Krüger on Thucyd. i. 22, and the similar passages quoted in the note on Equit. 1175. Brunck translates it correctly enough: "*improbam non rebar ne ausuram quidem fuisse.*" I mention this, as Droysen's "*Ich hätte nie geglaubt*" is liable to mislead. ἄν is not *frequently* doubled with an infinitive; see, however, vs. 442, *supra* Lys. 116. Antiphanes ap. Athen. ii. p. 60, E. Plato, Rep. ix. p. 178, E. Thucyd. i. 76, and note on Ran. 34.

[5] A parody upon a popular scolion of the day, which is quoted ap. Athen. xv p. 695, D., (cf. Bergk, Poet. Lyr. p. 876,)

ὑπὸ παντὶ λίθῳ σκορπίος, ὦ 'ταῖρ', ὑποδύεται·
φράζευ μή σε βάλῃ· τῷ δ' ἀφανεῖ πᾶς ἕπεται δόλος.

Praxilla ap. Schol. Ravenn., (cf. Bergk, Poet. Lyr. p. 819,)

ὑπὸ παντὶ λίθῳ σκορπίον, ὦ 'ταῖρε, φυλάσσεο.

"ῥήτωρ is substituted by the poet, since by λίθον he means τὸ βῆμα τῆς Πνυκός. Cf. Ach. 653. Pax, 663. Eccles. 87." *Enger.* See note on Equit. 956. For the effect of a sycophant's *bite*, see Plut. 885 The preceding words ἀλλ' ἅπαν, &c., are a proverbial expression applied to any thing which happened unexpectedly. Comp. Macho Athen. vi. p. 246, C. Herod. iv. 37, 195; v. 9, 97. Xenoph. Anab. 6, 11. "Aber jetzt ist alles möglich." *Droysen.*

more wicked for all purposes[1] than women shameless by na·
ture,—unless perhaps it be women.[2]

3RD WOM. You are certainly not in your right senses,
women, by Aglaurus![3] But you have either been bewitched,
or have suffered some other great evil, who permit this pesti-
lent creature to wantonly insult us all in such a manner. If
indeed there be any one *who will do it, it is well;* but if not,[4]
we ourselves and our slaves, having got ashes from some
quarter, will depillate her rump, so that she may be taught,
woman as she is, henceforth[5] not to speak ill of women.

MNES. Nay not my rump, pray, O women. For if, when
there was freedom of speech and it was permitted *us all* to
speak, as many citizens as are present, I then spoke what

[1] Comp. Ach. 951. Vesp. 1101. Ran. 968, 731. Plut. 273. Theoc.
xxii. 58. Æsch. Pers. 332. Prom. Vinc. 761. Antiphanes ap. Athen.
iii. p. 108, E. Valck. Phœn. 622. For φύσει, see Krüger, Gr. Gr. §
46, 4, obs. 1.

[2] Menander, οὐκ ἂν γένοιτ' ἐρῶντος ἀθλιώτερον
οὐδὲν γέροντος, πλὴν ἕτερος γέρων ἐρῶν.

Comp. eund. Fragm. cx. ed. Didot. Phocylides ap. Bergk, Poet.
Lyr. p. 338,

καὶ τόδε Φωκυλίδεω· Λέριοι κακοί· οὐχ ὁ μὲν, ὃς δ' οὔ.
πάντες, πλὴν Προκλέους· καὶ Προκλέης Λέριος.

The reader will recollect Porson's famous parody upon this, beginning,

"The Germans in Greek
Are sadly to seek," &c. &c.

Fritzsche and Enger read πλὴν ἄρ' εἰ. Cf. Aves, 601. Eur. *Danae*,
Fr. vi. Metagenes ap. Schol. Vesp. 1216.

[3] One of the daughters of Cecrops and Agraulos, by whom, as
well as by her sister *Pandrosus*, (Lys. vs. 439,) Athenian women
were accustomed to swear. The third daughter was *Herse*. See
Ovid, Metam. ii. 77. Hermann, Opusc. vii. p. 269.

[4] "Thut 's ein andrer, gut; thut 's keiner, rasch, so holen
Wir selbst mit unsern Mägden uns die ersten besten Kohlen."
Droysen.

"When she ought to have said *quoniam nemo adest, nos ipsæ cum ser-
vis vindictam sumemus,* she says *si nemo adest.*" *Enger.* See note on
Plut. 470.

[5] "According to Hermann (Vig. n. 26) and Krüger, (Gr. Gr. § 46,
3, obs. 2,) τὸ λοιπὸν = *henceforward,* implying unbroken continuance
of time, while τοῦ λοιποῦ = *for the future, iterum,* implying *repetition.*
τοῦ λοιποῦ, *for the future;* a prose form : frequent in Herodotus,
Lysias, and Demosthenes; occasionally in Thucydides, Isocrates,
and others : of the old Attics, only in Arist. Pax, 1084. The later
writers preferred λοιπὸν or τολοιπόν." *Bernhardy.* Both forms are
frequent in Xenophon.

pleas·I knew in defence of Euripides, ought I on this account to suffer punishment by being depillated by you?

3RD WOM. Why, ought you not to suffer punishment? who[1] alone hast dared to reply in defence of a man, who has done us many injuries, purposely devising tragedies where a woman has been vile, writing plays on Melanippes and Phædras.[2] But he never at any time wrote a play on[3] Penelope, because she has been adjudged to be a chaste woman.

MNES. I know the reason. For you could not mention a single Penelope among the women of the present day, but Phædras every one.

3RD WOM. You hear, women, what things the villanous *woman* has again said of us all.

MNES. And, by Jove, too, I have not yet mentioned as many as I am cognizant of! For would you that I mention more?

3RD WOM. Nay, you cannot any further; for you have poured forth all that you knew.

MNES. No, by Jove, not yet the ten-thousandth[4] part of what we do! For, you see, I have not mentioned this, how we take strigils[5] and then draw off the wine with a siphon.

---

[1] ὅστις introduces a predicate which belongs *exclusively* to *its* antecedent. See Æsch. P. V. 362. Hom. Il. Ψ. 43. Arist. Nub. 42, 537, 927, 1377. Equit. 311, 316, 352. Vesp. 621, 649, 700, 739, 924, 1167. Pax, 671, 1035. Ach. 225, 290, 303, 497, 645. Ran. 427. Plut. 13, 121, 281. Eccles. 1104. Lys. 699. Pax, 865, 970. Ed. Rev. No. xxxiii. p. 231.

[2] Comp. Ran. 1043. Euripides never wrote a play and called it "Phædra." The allusion is to his first *Hippolytus*, (Ἱππόλυτος καλυπτόμενος,) which was more frequently called his *Phædra*, from the prominence of that character, as Shakspeare's "Julius Cæsar" might be as appropriately called "Brutus." "εὑρίσκων λόγους = *inveniens tragœdiam;* unless you understand it as said invidiously against Euripides, who often violated all the traditional features of the ancient myths." *Fritzsche.*

[3] See Liddell's Lex. voc. ποιέω, i. 9.   [4] Comp. Lys. 355.

[5] "Aristophanes makes the women use *both* a strigil and a siphon. For first they take a strigil *through want of a cup*, (στλεγ. λαβοῦσαι,) *and then* they draw off the wine *with a siphon* (ἔπειτα σιφωνίζομεν τὸν οἶνον). I have lately seen several strigils in the Berlin Museum, which, though utterly incapable of being used as *siphons*, could nevertheless hold a small quantity of liquid, for they were all hollow." *Fritzsche.* Enger, who derides this interpretation of Fritzsche's, says, "The interpreters rightly observe that the women make use of a strigil *through want of a cup.*"

3RD WOM. You be hanged![1]

MNES. And how, again, while we give the meats from the Apaturia[2] to our go-betweens, we then say that the cat[3]——

3RD WOM. Me miserable! you talk nonsense.

MNES. Nor have I mentioned how another struck down her husband with the axe;[4] nor how another drove[5] her husband mad with philtres; nor how the Acharnian woman[6] once buried——

3RD WOM. May you utterly perish!

MNES. ——her father under the kitchen boiler.

3RD WOM. Are these, pray, endurable to hear?[7]

MNES. Nor how you, when your woman-slave had borne a male child, then substituted this for yourself, and gave up your little daughter to her.

3RD WOM. By the two goddesses, you certainly shall not get off with impunity for saying this! but I will twitch out your hairs.[8]

MNES. You shall not touch me, by Jove!

3RD WOM. Well now, see!

MNES. Well now, see!

3RD WOM. Take my cloak, Philista! [*Strips off her cloak.*]

MNES. Only put *your hand* upon me, and, by Diana, I will——

3RD WOM. What will you do?

MNES. I'll make you evacuate this sesame-cake[9] which you have devoured!

CHO. Cease railing at one another; for some woman[10] is

---

[1] Comp. Aves, 1530.   [2] See Acharn. 146.
[3] Comp. Pax, 1151. Vesp. 363.   [4] Comp. Hor. Sat. i. 1, 99.
[5] See Liddell's Lex. in voc. μαίνομαι.
[6] See note on vs. 499, *supra*.
[7] For the construction, cf. Plut. 899.
[8] " Aristophanes says αἱ πoκάδες after the similitude of αἱ πλοκάδες." *Fritzsche.* Cf. Lys. 448.
[9] Eupolis ap. Athen. xiv. p. 646, F.,

ὃς χαρίτων μὲν ὄζει,
καλλαβίδας δὲ βαίνει,
σηταμίδας δὲ χέζει,
μῆλα δὲ χρέμπτεται.

χεσεῖν is the second aorist infinitive. The future would be χεσεῖσθαι Cf. Lys. 440.

[10] The *woman* turns out to be Clisthenes, who is so often ridiculed for his effeminacy.

running towards us in haste.　Therefore, before she is near,[1]
be ye silent, in order that we may hear decorously what[2] she
is going to say.　[*Enter Clisthenes.*]

CLISTH. O women dear, ye kindred[3] of my disposition, I
show[4] by my cheeks that I am a friend to you; for I am
woman-mad, and am always your patron.[5]　And now[6] having
heard an important matter about you, which was canvassed a
little before[7] in the market-place, I have come to tell it and
announce it to you, in order that you may see and take care,
lest a terrible and important affair come suddenly upon you
off your guard.

CHO. What is it, boy? for 'tis natural to call you boy,[8] as
long as you have your cheeks thus smooth.

CLISTH. They say that Euripides has sent[9] a man up hither
to-day his own father-in-law, an old man.

CHO. For what deed? for the purpose of what design?

CLISTH. In order that he might be a spy upon your words,
whatever you deliberated and purposed to do.

CHO. Why, how was a man among women without being
detected?

CLISTH. Euripides singed and depillated him, and dressed
him up like a woman in all other respects.

MNES. Do you believe him in this? What man is so foolish,

---

1 "ἀντὶ τοῦ ἐγγὺς παρὰ τοῖς Ἀττικοῖς." *Scholiast.* Cf. Aristophanes'
Triphales, Fragm. i.　Soph. Phil. 1218.

2 See notes on Nub. 1148. Eccles. 1126.

3 "Excellently Voss, *Seelenanverwandte mir.*"　*Fritzsche.*

4 Thuc. i. 93, *καὶ δήλη ἡ οἰκοδομία ἔτι καὶ νῦν ἐστιν ὅτι κατὰ σπουδὴν
ἐγένετο.* See Krüger, Gr. Gr. § 56, 4, obs. 8. Bernhardy, W. S. p.
467. Hermann, Vig. n. 69. Liddell's Lex. voc. *δίκαιος,* C.　Comp.
Eur. Andr. 59, seq.

5 For the construction, cf. Demosth. Cor. p. 82, *καὶ σὺ προὐξένεις
αὐτῶν.*

6 "The particles *καὶ νῦν* denote that a common occurrence, and
one that usually happens, now takes place again.　See Eur. Helen.
408, 736."　*Fritzsche.*

7 "Hermann makes no doubt but *ὀλίγῳ τι* may be correctly used
for *ὀλίγῳ τινί,* or *ὀλίγῳ τῳ.* The correctness of Hermann's judgment
is shown by Herod. viii. 95, *καὶ ὀλίγῳ τι πρότερον τουτέων.*"　*Fritzsche.*
μὴ καὶ = ne forte = dass nicht etwa.　Cf. Æsch. Suppl. 399.

8 Comp. Vesp. 1297. Eur. Androm. 56, 64.

9 The Θεσμοφόριον stood on an elevated situation near the Acropolis

as to bear[1] to have his hairs plucked out? I don't believe it,
O ye highly-honoured goddesses!

CLISTH. You talk foolishly; for I would not have come to
report it, if I had not heard this from those who clearly knew.

CHO. This affair is a dreadful one which is announced.[2]
Come, women, we ought not to be idle, but to look out for the
man, and search where he has secretly taken his seat unknown to us. And do you, [*turning to Clisthenes,*] our
patron, help to find him out! so that you may have thanks
for this as well as for that.[3]

CLISTH. Come, let me see! [*Turning to one of the
women.*] First, who are you?

MNES. (*aside*). Whither can one[4] turn?

CLISTH. For you must be examined.

MNES. (*aside*). Me miserable!

4TH WOMAN. Did you ask me,[5] who I am? The wife of
Cleonymus.

CLISTH. Do you know who this woman is?

CHO. Oh yes, we know her! But examine the others.

CLISTH. But who, pray, is this who has the child?

4TH WOM. My nurse, by Jupiter!

MNES. (*aside*). I am[6] undone . [*Attempts to slip away.*]

CLISTH. (*turning to Mnesilochus*). Hollo you! whither are
you turning? Stay here! What's your ailment?[7]

MNES. Permit me to make water.

[1] Fritzsche retains ἠνείχετο, the reading of the old copies, translating, "*qui sibi pilos evelli sinebat,* (ut quidem ait Clisthenes)."
"Fritzsche is mistaken, for in this case Mnesilochus would be asking who the person was, who, as Clisthenes said, suffered his hairs
to be pulled out; which does not suit this passage." *Enger.* Cf.
Krüger, Gr. Gr. § 51, 13, obs. 10. Bernhardy, W. S. p. 292.

[2] Acharn. 135, ἕτερος ἀλάζων οὗτος εἰσκηρύττεται. See Krüger,
Gr. Gr. § 57, 3, obs. 7. Cf. Plat. Protag. p. 318, B. Phædon, p. 61,
C. Æsch. Prom. V. 251. Eur. Ion, 1281. Xenoph. Mem. ii. 6, 34.
Hom. Il. λ'. 611. Od. *i.* 348, and vss. 700, 702, *infra.* Lys. 748, 1022
Vesp. 1377. Ach. 829. Hom. Il. xiii. 612, 650.

[3] "Du hilf ihn selbst mit suchen, dass du diesen Ruhm
    Zu jenem dir, du unser Beschützer, hinzu verdienst." *Droysen.*

[4] See Krüger, Gr. Gr. § 53, 7, obs. 3. Hermann, Vig. n. 114
Bernhardy, W. S. p. 440; and cf. note on Aves, 847.

[5] Eur. Helen. 414, ὄνομα δὲ χώρας, ἥτις ἥδε καὶ λεώς, οὐκ οἶδα. See
Krüger, Gr. Gr. § 61, 6, obs. 2.

"*Perii!* sive *interii!*" *Fritzsche.*

"*Quidnam tibi subito mali accidit?*" *Fritzsche.*

Clistn. You're a shameless[1] creature. Do you then[2] do so! for I will wait here.[3]

Cho. Pray do wait, and watch her carefully too! for her alone, sir, we don't know.

Clisth. You're a long time[4] making water.

Mnes. Yes, by Jove, my good friend; for I suffer from strangury: I ate some nasturtium yesterday.

Clisth. Why do you chatter[5] about nasturtium? Will you not come hither to me? [*Drags him away from the corner.*]

Mnes. Why, pray, do you drag me when I am ill?

Clisth. Tell me, who's your husband?

Mnes. Do you inquire about[6] my husband? Do you know What's his name, of the burgh of Cothocidæ?[7]

Clisth. What's his name! What sort of a person?

Mnes. There is a What's his name, who once — — What d'ye call 'em, the son of What's his name——

Clisth. You appear to me to be talking nonsense. Have you ever[8] come up hither before?

Mnes. Yes, by Jove, every[9] year!

Clisth. And who is your messmate?[10]

Mnes. Mine is What's her name. Ah me, miserable!

Clisth. You say nothing to the purpose.[11]

5th Wom. (*to Clisthenes*). Go away! for I will[12] examine her properly by the rites of last year. And do you stand

---

[1] See note on Aves, 924.

[2] "The words δ' οὖν joined to an imperative are concessive: 'Tu igitur fac *sane.*' Cf. Vesp. 6, 764. Ach. 186. Lys. 491. Æsch. Prom. 935. Eum. 226." *Fritzsche.* Comp. Krüger, Gr. Gr. § 69, 52, obs. 3.

[3] "Warten werd' Ich hier so lang." *Droysen.*

[4] Comp Vesp. 940.

[5] This is a comic word, formed in derision of the preceding κάρδαμα. Thus Vesp. 652, ἀτὰρ ὦ πάτερ ἡμέτερε Κρονίδη—— Phil. παῦσαι καὶ μὴ πατέριζε. Comp. note on Pax, 1072.

[6] "Accusativus de quo." See Mus. Crit. i. p. 532. Cf. vs. 1217, *infra.*

[7] Of the tribe Œneïs, to which the orator Æschines belonged. See Hermann, Vig. n. 24.

[8] See note on Aves, 869.

[9] See Krüger, Gr. Gr. § 51, 13, obs. 15.

[10] "Deine Zeltgenossin." *Droysen.* "It appears very evident that the Thesmophoriazusæ pitched tents in front of the temple, and that several women dwelt together in the same tent." *Fritzsche*

[11] See Hermann, Vig. n. 13, 189.   [12] Comp. Ach. 110.

away, that you may not hear, as you are a man. [*Clisthenes retires to one side.*] Do you tell me, what one of the rites[1] used to be first exhibited to us.

MNES. Come, let me see! Nay,[2] what *was* the first?—We drank.

5TH WOM. What was the next after this?

MNES. We drank each other's health.

5TH WOM. This you heard from some one. What, then, was the third?

MNES. Xenylla asked for a night-stool; for there was no chamber-pot.[3]

5TH WOM. You say nothing to the purpose. Come hither, hither, Clisthenes! This is the man whom you speak of.

CLISTH. What then shall I do?

5TH WOM. Strip him; for he says nothing that is right.

MNES. And will you then[4] strip the mother of nine children?

CLISTH. Unloose your girdle quickly, you shameless crea‑ ture!

5TH WOM. How very stout and strong she appears! and, by Jove, too, she has no breasts, as we have.

MNES. For I am barren, and have never been pregnant.

5TH WOM. Now; but you were the mother of nine chil‑ dren a while ago.[5]

CLISTH. Stand upright! Whither are you thrusting down your hand?

5TH WOM. See there, it peeped out! and very fresh-coloured it is, you rogue.

CLISTH. Why, where is it?

5TH WOM. It's gone again to the front. [*Clisthenes goes in front of Mnesilochus.*]

CLISTH. It is not here.[6]

---

[1] Comp. Vesp. 831. Lobeck, Aglaoph. i. p. 54.

[2] Cf. Nub. 787. Hermann, Vig. n. 339. "The Ravenna Scho‑ liast remarks that the women are again upbraided with *vinolence.*" *Fritzsche.*

[3] Eupolis, (ap. Athen. i. p. 17, E.,) εἶεν, τίς εἶπεν ἀμ.δα, παῖ, πρῶ‑ τος μεταξὺ πίνων; Epicrates, (ap. Athen. vi. p. 262, D.,) τί γὰρ ἰχθιον ἢ, παῖ, παῖ καλεῖσθαι παρὰ πότον, ἢ τὴν ἀμίδα φέρειν; Comp. Plaut. *Mostell.* ii. 1, 39.

[4] See Hermann, Vig. n. 239.　　[5] See note on Lys. 1023.

[6] So ἐνμεντευθενὶ and τγδεδὶ, Metagenes ap. Athen. v. p. 269. F

5TH WOM. Nay, but[1] it has come hither again.

CLISTH. You've a kind of an isthmus,[2] fellow; you're worse than the Corinthians.

5TH WOM. Oh the abominable fellow![3]   On this account[4] then he reviled us in defence of Euripides.

MNES. Me miserable! in what troubles have I involved myself!

5TH WOM. Come now, what shall we do?

CLISTH. Guard him properly, so that he shall not escape; and I'll report these to the Prytanes.   [*Exit Clisthenes.*]

CHO. Then we ought now after this[5] to kindle our torches and gird ourselves up well and manfully, and strip off[6] our garments and search, if perchance some other man too has entered, and to run round the whole Thesmophorium[7] and the tents, and to examine closely the passages.   Come then,[8] first of all we ought to rouse a nimble foot and look about in every direction in silence.   Only we must not[9] loiter, since the time admits no further delay,[10] but we ought now first[11]

τηνδεδί, Aves, 18. νυνμενί, ibid. 448. ταυτηνδί, ibid. 1364. τουτουμενί, Ran. 965. τουτοδί, Plut. 227. Cf. Aves, 644. Equit. 1357. Lys. 1274. Eccles. 989. Plut. 1033. Ran. 611, 745, 752. Lobeck, Phryn. p. 414. Krüger, Gr. Gr. § 25, 6, obs. 7. Bernhardy, W. S. p. 196.

[1] μάλλά = *minime, immo* ——.   Cf. Aves, 110. Ran. 103, 611, 751, 745. Ach. 458.

[2] See Herod. vii. 24.   "Du hast 'ne Art von Isthmos." *Droysen.*

[3] Cf. Vesp. 900.   [4] For ταῦτ' ἄρα, cf. Bernhardy, W. S. p. 130.

[5] "Reisig has well observed that μετὰ ταῦτα is said generally in reference to sequence of time, and not in reference to one specific event; while μετὰ τοῦτο designates that circumstance only which has just preceded.   μετὰ ταῦτα either simply = *postea*, or denotes that several items have preceded." *Fritzsche.*

[6] As was usual for the chorus before it commenced its dance and song.   Cf. Lys. 662, 686. Acharn. 627. Pax, 729. Vesp. 408. Plato, Menex. p. 381, εἴ με κελεύοις ἀποδύντα ὀρχήσασθαι.

[7] "The *Thesmophorium* might rightly be called the *Pnyx;* for in the temple, as though it were the Pnyx, was held the Assembly concerning Euripides.   Therefore the words τὴν πύκνα πᾶσαν, &c. will mean *Thesmophorium totum et tentoria huic templo vicina,* which the women used to pitch on those festival days." *Fritzsche.* So also Enger.   [8] Comp. Lys. 1303.

[9] "Doch insonderheit man muss zögern nicht." *Droysen.*

[10] In Plut. 255 the construction is somewhat different: ὡς ὁ καιρος οὐχὶ μέλλειν.   For the negative, see Krüger, Gr. Gr. § 67, 7, obs. 1.

[11] See Liddell's Lex. voc. πρῶτος, ii. 3.   Krüger, Gr. Gr. § 43, ?. obs. 9. § 46, 3, obs. 2.   Hermann, Vig. n. 10.   Matthiä, § 425, and p. 487. Jelf, § 558. 1   "But τὴν πρώτην τρέχειν = τὴν πρώτην

to run as quickly as possible round about   Come then, search,
and quickly investigate all parts, if any other, again, is secretly sitting in *these* places.[1]   Cast your eye round in every
direction, and properly examine all parts, in this direction,
and in that.   For if he be detected[2] after having done unholy
deeds, he shall suffer punishment, and in addition to this shall
be an example[3] to all the others of insolence and unjust deeds
and ungodly manners; and he shall say that there are evidently gods; and he shall be forthwith a witness to all[4] men
to honour the gods, and that they justly pursuing what is
pious, and devising what is lawful, should do what is right.
And if they do not do so, the following shall happen to them:
when any of them is detected acting profanely, burning with
madness, mad with frenzy, if he do any thing,[5] he shall be a
conspicuous warning to all women and mortals[6] to behold,
that the god punishes what is unlawful and unholy, and it is
done immediately.   But it seems that pretty nigh all parts
have been properly examined by us: at any rate we don't
now see any other man sitting among us.   [*Mnesilochus
snatches a child from the arms of one of the women.*]

ὁδὸν τρέχειν.   Sed primâ quâque viâ currere oportet, quam celerrimè cir-
cumcirca.''   *Fritzsche.*
   [1] " Ob ein andrer heimlich hier noch auf der Lauer möge sein."
Droysen.   For the construction, see vs. 600, *supra.*
   [2] " Denn ertappen wir ihn bei so frevelndem Thun."   *Droysen.*
" ἀνόσια δρᾶν, h. l. is nothing more than *in Thesmophorium pene-
trare.*"   *Enger.*
   [3] " Ein warnendes Beispiel."   *Droysen.*
   [4]   " Wird Zeugniss sein
         Dass der Gottheit Jeder Ehrfurcht zollen muss,
            Dass fromm jeglicher scheun muss,
         Was das Gesetz heiliget, sinnen nur muss zu thun,
               Wie es sich wohl geziemt."   *Droysen.*

' The antistrophe and grammatical construction show that the
words δικαίως τ' ἐφέποντας are corrupt."   *Enger.*   The translation
in the text is that proposed by Brunck, Portus, and Reisig; though,
as Fritzsche properly observes, ὅσια καὶ νόμιμα are *naturally* connected together.   See note on Plut. 287.
   [5]   " The words εἴ τι δρῴη are corrupt, as the metre and sense
show."   *Enger.*   For τι, *any thing bad*, see Bernhardy, W. S. p. 440.
   [6] " When there ought to have been πᾶσιν γύναικι καὶ ἀνδράσι.
Aristophanes, for the sake of a jest, makes a strange opposition, as
if women were not to be reckoned in the number of mortals."
Fritzsche.

6TH WOM. Ah! Whither are you flying? Ho you! Ho you! will you not stay? Me miserable! miserable! And he is gone, having snatched away my child from my breast.

MNES. Bawl[1] away; but this you shall never feed with morsels, unless you let me go; but here at the altars[2] being struck with this sword upon its bloody veins, it shall stain the altar with blood.

6TH WOM. Oh me miserable! Will you not succour me, women? Will you not raise a mighty and rout-causing[3] shout, but suffer me to be deprived of my only child?

CHO. Ha! ha! O venerable Fates, what new portent,[4] again, is this which I behold? How all then[5] are deeds of audacity and shamelessness! What a deed is this, again, which he has done! what a deed, again, my friends!

MNES. How I'll knock your excessive arrogance out of you!

CHO. Are not these, pray, shameful deeds and more[6] than that?

6TH WOM. Shameful certainly, if one[7] has snatched away my child.

CHO. What then can one say to this, when this man is shameless enough to do[8] such things?

[1] "The forms ἄνωχθι, κέκραχθι, are well known." *Fritzsche.* Cf Vesp. 198, 415.

[2] "τῶν βωμῶν, ἀπὸ τοῦ τὰ μηρία ἐπάνω ἀποκεῖσθαι." *Scholiast.* "The Ravenna Scholiast rightly explains it, ἐπὶ τῶν βωμῶν, which, however, would have been better expressed ἐπὶ τοῦ βωμοῦ." *Fritzsche.* Those who retain the old interpretation ought at least to be prepared with examples of πλήσσειν ἐπὶ μηρίων.

[3] "All the interpreters, except Bothe alone, ridiculously take ϱοπαῖον as a *substantive.* Whereas πολλὴν βοὴν καὶ τροπαῖον mean *magnum clamorem atque ejusmodi, qui alterum in fugam conjiciat.*" *Fritzsche.* Cf. Equit. 246. "Bothe rightly perceived that τροπαῖον was an adjective = *clamorem, quo in fugam convertatur Mnesilochus.*" *Enger.* I could have wished that one of these scholars had given us a similar example of τροπαῖος being used of *two* terminations.

[4] See note on vs. 597, *supra.*

[5] "Particula ἄρα crebro significat, communem esse sententiam et in proverbium abiisse." *Fritzsche.*

[6] Comp. Aves, 1500.

[7] See Aves, 1350. Lys. 118. Krüger, Gr. Gr. § 51, 13, obs. 11. Bernhardy, Wissenschaft. Synt. p. 291, 292, and for ἔχει ἐξαρπάσσς, see Krüger, Gr. Gr. § 56, 3, obs. 6, and cf. Eccles. 355, 957. Aves, 852.

[8] "Wenn der
So schaamlos ist, dergleichen zu thun." *Droysen.*
Comp. Plato, Crit. p. 53, C.

MNES. And, be assured, I have not done yet.

6TH WOM. But certainly[1] you have come whence you have come;[2] and you shall not say[3] after having easily escaped, what a deed you have done, and got off; but shall receive punishment.

MNES. May this, however, by no means take place, I pray God!

CHO. Who then, who of the immortal gods, would come as your helper,[4] with your unjust[5] deeds?

MNES. You talk in vain: her[6] I will not let go.

CHO. But, by the two goddesses, perhaps you will not[7] insult us with impunity, and speak unholy words. For we will requite you for these with ungodly deeds,[8] as is reasonable: and perhaps some fortune, having cast[9] you into an evil of a different kind, will restrain you. But [*turning to Mica*] you ought to take these[10] *women-slaves*, and bring out some wood,

---

[1] "*Doch gewiss.*" *Kruger.*

[2] "*Unde quidem veneris, nescio.*" *Bentley.* So Soph. Col. 273, ἱκόμην ἵν' ἱκόμην. Polycrates ap. Athen. viii. p. 835, D, ἔγραψεν, ἄσσ' ἔγραψ'· ἐγὼ γὰρ οὐκ οἶδα. Comp. Eur. Orest. 78. Hec. 873. Med. 894, 1018. Æsch. Agam. 67, 1297. Soph. Colon. 376. Rex, 1376. Arist. Equit. 333. Acharn. 560. Hermann, Vig. n. 30. Reisig, Com. Crit. in Soph. Colon. p. 235. The allusion may, however, be to the proverb ἁλῶν φόρτος ἔνθεν ἦλθεν, ἔνθ' ἔβη, said of persons who lose what they have acquired. "In this passage the sense requires ἀλλ' οὖν ἥκεις, οἷ γ' ἥκεις, *pervenies, quo pervenies,* i. e. *nolo tibi dicere, in quæ mala incides.* Æsch. Cho. 778, μέλει θεοῖσιν, ὥσπερ ἂν μέλῃ πέρι.*" Hermann.

[3] See note on Equit. 722. But the present example is not precisely similar.

[4] Comp. Eur. Hippol. 673.

[5] "*Cum tuis injustis factis,* i. e. *in tantâ facinorum tuorum injustitiâ.* Compare ξὺν ἐλευθέρᾳ πατρίδι, *supra,* vs. 102." *Fritzsche.*

[6] Comp. Eur. Hec. 400.

[7] See note on Plut. 551.

[8] "It is impious and wicked to violate him who has fled for refuge to the altar." *Bergler.* "καθῆται ἐπὶ βωμοῦ ὡς ἱκετεύων." *Scholiast.* Enger and Hermann read ἀνοσίους ἐπ' ἀθέοις ἔργοις. καὶ γὰρ ἀνταμειψόμεσθα κ. τ. λ.

[9] "*Aliqua te fortuna in contraria mala conjectum forsitan reprimet.*" *Fritzsche.* The usual interpretation is, "*Having changed to an evil,*" &c. But there are strong grammatical reasons in favour of the other method. See note on Nub. 689. For τάχα in the sense of *perhaps* with an indicative, see Plato, Phædr. p. 256, C.

[10] "It is evident that τάσδε means *servas,* and not *faces,* as Fritzsche thought. Vide nos in Mus Rhen. Philolog. ii p. 244." *Enger.*

and burn the villain to ashes, and destroy him with fire as
soon as possible

6TH WOM. Let us gc to fetch the brushwocd, Mania.[1] And
I'll make you [*addressing Mnesilochus*] to-day a hot coal.

MNES. Set on fire and burn! But do you [*addressing the
child*] quickly strip off your Cretan[2] garment; and blame
your mother alone of women for your death, child. [*Strips
the child, whereupon it turns out to be a wine-skin dressed up
like an infant.*] What's this? The girl has become a wine-
skin[3] full of wine, and that too with Persian slippers. O ye
most thirsty[4] women, O most bibacious,[5] and contriving by
every device to tipple, O great[6] blessing to publicans, but to
us, on the contrary, a pest; and a pest also to the furniture[7]
and to the woof![8]

6TH. WOM. (*returning with a bundle of brushwood*). Heap
up beside him abundant brushwood, Mania.

MNES. Yes, heap it up! But do you answer me this question: do you say you bore this child?

6TH WOM. Yes, and carried it ten[9] months.

MNES. Did you carry it?

---

[1] The common name for a woman-servant, as Manes was for a
man-servant. Cf. Ran. 1344. For ἐπὶ in this sense, see Krüger,
Gr. Gr. § 68, 42, obs. 2.

[2] "Κρητικόν: Hesychius ἱματίδιον λεπτὸν καὶ βραχύ. τὰ γὰρ τοιαῦτα Κρητικὰ ἔλεγον. Cf. Phot. p. 178, 17. Eadem fuisse vestis,
quâ apud Athenienses rex sacrorum utebatur teste Polluce vii. 77
Meinekio (Com. Frag. ii. p. 560) videtur; diversam fuisse Fritzschius
statuit." *Enger*.

[3] Compare Shakspeare, King Henry IV., part i. act v. sc. 3,
where Prince Henry, on drawing out of Falstaff's pistol-case what
he thinks is a pistol, finds it to be *a bottle of sack!* Compare also
Plautus, Aulul. ii. 66. This being the νηστεία, it ought to have been
a day of strict abstinence.

[4] "Ihr gurgelheissen Weiber." *Droysen*.

[5] A comic superlative, like κλεπτίστατον, Ach. 425. αὐτότατος,
Plut. 83. προτεραίτερος, Equit. 1165. So also Sophron (ap. Mus.
Crit. ii. p. 352) uses προβατώτερος, *more sheepish*. Cf. Pax, 662.

[6] "O ihr der Kneipen grosser Segen, grosser Fluch
 Für uns und Fluch für Hausgeräth und Webestuhl!" *Droysen*.

[7] "ἅπαντα γὰρ ἕνεκα τοῦ πιεῖν ἐνέχυρα τίθεται καὶ πιπράσκεται."
Scholiust

[8] "For drunken women don't weave." *Enger*.

[9] Menander, Πλόκιον, Frag. iii., γυνὴ κυεῖ δεκάμηνος. Cf. Terence,
Adelph. iii. 4, 30. Plautus, Cistell. i. 3, 16. For ἤνεγκον, see Krüger,
Gr. Gr. § 40, p. 185. Bekk. Anecdot. i. p. 98, 12.

6TH WOM. Yea, by Diana!

MNES. Holding three Cotylæ, or how? tell me! [*Exposes the wine-skin to view.*]

6TH WOM. What have you done to me? You have stripped my child, you shameless fellow, being so little.

MNES. So little?

6TH WOM. Yes, by Jove, little!

MNES. How many years old is it? three Choæ,[1] or four?

6TH WOM. About so much,[2] and as long as since the Dionysia. But restore it.

MNES. No, by this[3] Apollo!

6TH WOM. Then we'll set fire to you.

MNES. Set fire by all means; but this shall be slaughtered forthwith.

6TH WOM. Nay, do not, I beseech you; but do to me what you please instead[4] of it.

MNES. You are very fond of your children by nature:[5] but this shall be slaughtered none the less.[6]

9TH WOM. Alas, my child! Give me a bowl,[7] Mania; so that certainly I may at least catch the blood of my child.

MNES. Hold it under, for I will gratify you in this one thing. [*Drinks up the wine-skin himself.*]

6TH WOM. May you perish miserably! How grudging and malevolent you are!

[1] As if its age were reckoned by so many *Pitcher-feasts* instead of years, as the Romans dated their wine from such and such consulships. According to the Scholiast χόας is a comic substitute for *years*, as if he had asked, "How many *gallons* old is it?—Three, or four?" Certainly the former interpretation destroys all the jest of the passage.

[2] "Almost so, and as much time as hath passed
From the late Dionysiac festival." *Wheelwright.*

"So grad', und die Zeit von den Dionysien her dazu." *Droysen.*

[3] "He points to the statue of Apollo which stood upon the stage. See Meineke on Menander, p. 256. Lobeck, Aglaoph. p. 256." *Enger.* Comp. Vesp. 869. Menander, Frag. ccxii. ed. Didot.

[4] "Thue mir an, was du willst, statt dieser Kleinen." *Droysen.*

[5] See Krüger, Gr. Gr. § 46, 4, obs. 1, and for τίς, see note on Aves, 924.

[6] Comp. Thucyd. i. 8, i. 74, i. 82. Æsch. Cho. 708. Krüger, Gr Gr. § 67, i. obs. 3. The opposite is οὐδὲν μᾶλλον.

[7] "τὸ ἀγγεῖον, εἰς ὃ τὸ αἷμα τῶν σφαζομένων ἱερείων δέχονται." *Photius.*
"*Ut, quoniam vivam non possum recipere, certe quidem sanguinem ejus recipiam.*" *Enger.* Comp. Lys. 205.

MNES. (*holding up the empty wine-skin*). This hide[1] belongs to the priestess.

6TH WOM. What belongs to the priestess?

MNES. (*tossing her the empty wine-skin*). Take it!

7TH WOM. Most wretched Mica, who has robbed you of[2]
your daughter? who has taken away your beloved child?[3]

6TH WOM. This villain! But since you are present, guard
him, in order that I may take Clisthenes and tell to the Prytanes[4] what this man has done. [*Exit 6th woman.*]

MNES. Come now, what shall be my contrivance for safety?
what my attempt? what my device? For he who is the
author *of this*, and who has involved[5] me in such troubles,
does not yet appear. Come, what messenger can I send to
him? Now I know a contrivance out of his Palamedes:[6]
I'll write upon the oars and throw them out, as that well-
known[7] character did. But the[8] oars are not at hand.
Whence therefore can it be possible for me to get oars?

[1] "It is agreed on all hands that the remainders of the victims, I
mean the *skins* and *feet*, belonged to the priests." *Fritzsche.* "In
the next verse he throws the woman the wine-skin, as if she were
the priest." *Enger.*

[2] "Aristophanes plays upon the ambiguity of the word: *Quis te
devirginabit?* for *Quis tibi puellam tuam ademit?*" *Brunck.* So also
Fritzsche, Enger, and Hermann. See his Opusc. iii. p. 328.

[3] This verse is bracketed by Dindorf as spurious, more especially
on account of the non-Attic form ἐξηρήσατο. See Lobeck, Phryn.
p. 718.

[4] Of course she does not go to the Prytanes; but this is a mere
excuse for leaving the stage. In fact, the person who here person-
ates Mica, will shortly have to reappear as Euripides. So she takes
this opportunity of changing her dress.

[5] For similar constructions of the participle, cf. Equit. 310, 759,
823, 1188. Lys. 1142.

[6] "The Palamedes of Euripides belonged to the tetralogy of the
Troades, and was brought on the stage B. c. 414—not 415, as Ælian
would lead us to believe." *Droysen.* "It was brought on the stage
Ol. 91, 1. Sophocles and Æschylus also wrote plays under this
name." *Fritzsche.* This date is also given by Clinton.

[7] Œax, brother of Palamedes. See Krüger, Gr. Gr. § 51, 7, obs.
7. "Euripides in his *Palamedes* had represented Œax inscribing
the death of Palamedes on a great number of oars, expecting that
one at least out of so many oars would reach the shores of Euboœa
and inform Nauplius of the death of his son." *Fritzsche.*

[8] "Brunck wonders at the article. Mnesilochus means those
oars which were used in the *Palamedes* of Euripides, or such as
those." *Fritzsche.*

whence?[1] But what if[2] I were to write on these here images
instead of the oars, and throw them about?   Much better!
Certainly indeed[3] both these are wood and those were wood.
O hands of mine, you must take in hand a practicable[4] deed!
Come now, you plates of polished tablets, receive the traces
of the graver, messengers of my miseries.   Ah me, this Rho
is a miserable[5] one! through what a furrow it goes, it goes!
Go ye, hasten through all roads, that way, this way!   You
ought speedily.   [*Exit Mnesilochus.*][6]

PARABASIS.

Cho. Let us then praise ourselves in our parabasis.[7]   And
yet every one says many ill things of the race of women, that
we are an utter evil[8] to men, and that all evils spring from us,
strifes, quarrels, sedition, painful grief, and war.   Come now,
if[9] we are an evil, why do you marry us, if indeed we are really

[1] For this repetition of the interrogative, cf. vss. 292, 715, *supra.*
Ran. 120. 1399. Equit. 82. Nub. 79. Theocr. xxvii. 38. Bernhardy,
W. S. p. 443.

[2] Eupolis, *Autolyc.* p. 97, τί δῆτ' ἂν εἰ μὴ τὸ σκάφιον αὐτῇ παρῆν;
Cf. Nub. 154. Eur. Helen. 1043.   A similar act of impiety is related
of Diagoras the Melian.   Being in want of firewood, he broke up a
statue of Hercules for that purpose.   "Mnesilochus inscribes his
misfortune upon the busts and statues of the gods, of which there
were several in the Thesmophorium, and throws them forth, so that
he might send Euripides letters worthy of Euripides." *Fritzsche.*
"Aristophanes is here ridiculing some verse of Euripides." *Enger.*
"Wie, wenn Ich die Götterbilder an der Ruder Statt
Beschrieben über Bord mir würfe? ja es geht!
Sind Holz doch diese, und jene desgleichen waren Holz." *Droysen.*

[3] See Herm. Vig. n. 297.   Cf. Hor. A. P. 399. Herod. vii. 239.

[4] See Liddell's Lex. in voc.   "He means such a deed as may
show him a πόρος, i. e. a way of safety." *Fritzsche.*   Enger also recognises in this word a play upon πόρον, vs. 769.   The same may
be observed of χεῖρες and ἐγχειρεῖν.

[5] In μοχθηρὸν there is a play on the preceding μόχθων.   Fritzsche
thinks his writing consisted of these words, Εὐριπίδη, χώρει, χώρει.

[6] "Mnesilochus is removed from sight by the machine, and then
the parabasis begins." *Fritzsche.*

[7] "*Nos igitur nosmet ipsas in hac parabasi laudabimus.*" *Fritzsche.*

[8] A favourite epithet with Euripides.   See Hippol. 616, 625, 628.

[9] Cf. Equit. 1132. Plut. 586. Eccles. 95, 219. Krüger, Gr. Gr. §
54, 12, obs. 8.   Otto on Cicer. *De Finibus*, i. 3.   "But this is *not a*
double protasis, but a repetition of nearly the same words.   What
she says is this: '*Si malum sumus, cur ducitis nos, hoc malum, uxores
et interdicitis ne exeamus?*'" *Enger.*

an evil, and forbid *any of us* either to go out, or to be caught peeping out,[1] but wish to guard the evil with so great diligence? And if the wife should go out any whither, and you then should discover her to be out of doors, you rage with madness, who ought to offer libations and rejoice, if indeed you really find the evil to be gone away from the house, and do not find it at home. And if we sleep in other people's houses, when we play[2] and are tired, every one searches for this evil, going round about the beds. And if we peep out[3] of a window, he seeks to get a sight of the evil. And if she retire again, being ashamed, so much the more does every one desire to see[4] the evil peep out again. So manifestly are we much better than you. And a test is at hand to see.[5] Let us make trial, which of the two are worse. For we say that you are; but you say that we are. Let us consider now, and compare each with each, placing each name[6] side by side, both the woman's and the man's. Charminus[7] is inferior to Nausimache: his deeds are manifest. And in truth also Cleophon[8] is, I ween, by all means inferior to Salabaccho. And none of you even attempts to contend with Aristomache for a long time,[9] that notable one at Marathon, and with Stratonice.

[1] Comp. Eccles. 1052. For the negative after verbs of *forbidding* &c., see Krüger, Gr. Gr. § 67, 12, obs. 3.

[2] "παίζειν is commonly said of a festival, which is celebrated with dances and other sports. Therefore this is the meaning of the Chorus: *At si domi alienæ obdormiverimus diem agentes festum lusuque fatigatæ, unusquisque hoc malum* (uxorem) *quærit, lectos circumiens.*' *Fritzsche.*   [3] Comp. Pax, 982.

[4] Brunck translates this in a very strange manner, as if τὸ κακὸν depended on ἐπιθυμεῖ, and ἰδεῖν were an exegetical infinitive.

[5] Æsch. Pers. 419, θάλασσα δ' οὐκέτ' ἦν ἰδεῖν. Cf. Eupolis ap. Athen. xiv. p. 638, E. Plut. 489. Dobree and Boissonade on Plut. 48. Krüger, Gr. Gr. § 55, 3, obs. 8.

[6] Fritzsche and Hermann read τοὔνομ' ἑκάστου.

[7] He had been admiral Ol. 92, 1, and defeated by Astyochus with the loss of six triremes. See Thucyd. viii. 41, 42. He is mentioned again, ibid. viii. 73. Hence the women argue he is inferior to *Nausimache,* (ναῦς, μάχομαι,) a noted strumpet. Her name is selected on account of the notion expressed by it. Salabaccho (Equit. ˉ65) was of the same profession as Nausimache. The other names, *Aristomache,* (ἄριστος, μάχη,) *Stratonice,* (στρατὸς, νίκη,) *Eubule,* (εὖ, βουλὴ,) are comic fictions, and stand for the *ideas* they express, viz. *The battle of Marathon, The Victory of the Army, Good Counsel.*

[8] See Ran. 678.

[9] " χρον. πολλ. referendum ad 'Αριστομάχ̀αν. non ad ἐγχειρεῖ." *Enger*

But what senator of those of last year, who delivered up his senatorial office[1] to another, is superior to Eubule? Not even he himself[2] will say this. So much[3] better do we profess to be than the men. Neither would a woman who has stolen at the rate[4] of fifty talents of the public money come into the city in a chariot; but when she may have committed her greatest[5] peculations, when she has stolen a bushel of wheat from her husband, she restores them[6] the same day. But we could point out many of these present who do this, and who are, in addition to this, more gluttonous than we, and footpads, and parasites,[7] and kidnappers. And in truth also they are, I ween, inferior to us in preserving[8] their patrimony. For still even now our loom[9] is safe, our weaving-beam, our baskets, and our parasol; while the beam[10] of many of these our husbands has perished from the house together with the head, and the parasol of many others has been cast from their shoulders in their expeditions. We women[11] could justly and deservedly[12] bring many charges against the men:

I could have wished he had supported this use of πολλοῦ χρόνου by similar examples. "*Nemo vestrum a longo tempore conatur.*" *Brunck.*

[1] This refers to the expulsion of the Senate (Ol. 92, 1) by the 400. See Thucyd. viii. 69, 70. So all the commentators, except Enger, who says, "It is evident this is not the allusion. Müller (Hist. Greek Lit. ii. p. 246) is very probably right in referring it to the senators having been compelled to yield up the greater part of their powers to the Probuli, (Ol. 91, 4,) as Thucydides testifies, viii. 1."

[2] "Here some particular senator is pointed out with the finger." *Enger.*

[3] A parody on Hom. Il. iv. 405.

[4] Compare Vesp. 669, 716. The person alluded to is Pisander. See Aves, 1556. Lys. 490. *Babylonians*, Fr. viii.

[5] "But when her greatest theft has been committed,
A basketful of corn." *Wheelwright.*

[6] "αὖτ' is αὐτὰ, not αὐτὸ, and refers to τὰ μέγιστα." *Fritzsche.* So also Enger.

[7] "Schmarotzer." *Droysen.*   [8] Comp. Lys. 488.

[9] "*Jugum textorium* amongst the Greeks was ἀντίον." *Fritzsche.* Cf. Hom. Il. xxiii. 762.

[10] Meaning the *shaft of the spear.* So immediately after they say "parasol," meaning by that their *shield.* In this the Scholiast thinks he alludes more especially to Cleonymus ὁ ῥίψασπις.

[11] See Krüger, Gr. Gr. § 50, 8, obs. 3. Cf. Aves, 1581. Pax, 508, 849, 1341.

[12] "The poet himself teaches us that there is no difference between ἐν δίκῃ and δικαίως· Nub. 1379 1380. Ph. ι ὴ τὸν Δί' ἐν δίκω

but one most monstrous. For it were proper, if any of us
bore a man serviceable to the state, a taxiarch or general, that
she should receive some honour, and that precedence be given
her at the Stenia and Scirophoria, and at the other festivals
which[1] we have been accustomed to keep. But if any woman bore a cowardly and worthless man, either a worthless
trierarch or a bad pilot, that she should sit behind her who
has borne the brave man, with her hair cut bowl-fashion.[2]
For how[3] is it equitable, O city, that the mother of Hyperbolus[4] should sit near the mother of Lamachus,[5] clothed in
white, and with loose flowing hair, and lend out money on
usury? To whom, if she were to lend out to any one, and
exact usury, no man ought to give any interest, but they[6]
ought to take away her money by force, saying this, "In
sooth you're deserving of interest, having borne such[7] produce." [*Re-enter Mnesilochus.*]

MNES. I've got a squint with looking for[8] him; but he
does not yet[9] *appear.* What then can be the hinderance?
It must be that he is ashamed of his Palamedes[10] because it is

γ' ἄν. STR. καὶ πῶς δικαίως; These words when joined together
mean, *jure meritoque.* Comp. διὰ κενῆς ἄλλως, Vesp. 929; εἰκῇ ῥᾳδίως, Ran. 733, and many others, ap. Musgr. Hec. 489. Bergl.
Vesp. 929." *Fritzsche.* So also Enger.

[1] "*Assimilation;* usually, but very falsely and improperly, called
attraction." *Krüger.* See his Grammar, § 51, 10. Cf. Plut. 1044.

[2] "εἶδος κουρᾶς δουλικῆς." *Scholiast.* Hesychius gives it to courtesans.

[3] Comp. Acharn. 700. For ὦ πόλις, Fritzsche compares Acharn.
27. Eupolis ap. Athen. x. p. 425, B. Soph. Rex, 629.

[4] See note on Nub. 1065. Cf. Thuc. viii. 73.

[5] This is the general so much ridiculed in the *Acharnians.* As he
was now dead, Aristophanes could afford to do him justice. He was
killed in the Sicilian expedition. See Thuc. vi. 103.

[6] μηδένα — — εἰπόντας. See note on Eccles. 680.

[7] The play on the words τόκος and τίκτω is of course lost in the
translation.

[8] Plautus, *Menæchm.* v. 3, 6, "lumbi sedendo, oculi expectando
dolent." Lucian, Lexiph. c. 3, ἐγὼ δὲ σίλλος (= ἰλλὸς) γεγένημαι
σε περιορῶν. Cf. Ach. 15.

[9] "*Is vero nondum adest,* viz. Euripides." *Fritzsche.* Comp. Vesp.
118. Krüger, Gr. Gr. § 62, 3, obs. 1, and note on Eccles. 275.

[10] "He means Euripides' play *Palamedes.* The sense is : *Euripides
nondum adest, quod eum fabulâ arcessivi, cujus ipsum nunc pudet. Itaque
aliâ fabulâ mihi est arcessendus.*" *Enger.* For the date of this play,
see note on vs. 770. It formed part of a tetralogy consisting of the

frigid. With what drama then can I draw[1] him up? I know it! I'll imitate his new[2] Helen. At all events I have a woman's dress.

7TH WOM. What are you again plotting? or why do you look gaping about?[3] You shall soon see[4] a bitter Helen, if you will not be orderly, until some of the Prytanes come.

MNES. (*as Helen*). "These[5] are the streams of the Nile with beautiful nymphs, which, in place of rain[6] from heaven, moistens the plain of white[7] Egypt, a people using black draughts."[8]

7TH WOM. You're a knave, by the torch-bearing[9] Hecate!

MNES. "Not[10] inglorious is my native land, Sparta, and Tyndareus is my sire."

7TH WOM. Is he your father, you pest? Nay, rather, Phrynondas.[11]

Alexander, Palamedes, Troades, Sisyphus (satyric drama). According to Ælian (V. H. ii. 8) he was beaten on this occasion by Xenocles.

[1] This is the technical word for drawing up with *a windlass*.

[2] "The Scholiast and others understand this of the *recent* publication of his *Helen*, which was just out. Voss (who is followed by Fritzsche) refers it to the *innovations* made by Euripides upon the story of Helen. The poet intended it to be understood in *both* these senses." *Enger.*

[3] See note on vs. 473, *supra*.   [4] Cf. Aves, 1468.

[5] This and the two following verses are taken from Eur. Hel. *init.*

[6] See Bekker's Anecdot. i. p. 73, 24. Blomf. Agam. 1512.

[7] In Euripides this last verse stands thus, λευκῆς τακείσης χιόνος ὑδραίνει γύας. Besides altering the words, Aristophanes has also altered the construction, making λευκῆς, which in Euripides is an epithet of χιόνος, agree with Αἰγύπτου, for the purpose of making the whole ridiculous; for Egypt is proverbially μελάμβωλος.

[8] Das Schwarzklystiren-Volk." *Droysen.* "Herodotus (ii. 77) and innumerable other authorities teach us that the Egyptians made use of the *syrmæa*, a medical draught, as a *purge*. Herodotus states that the Egyptians purged themselves every month for three continuous days. Cf. Æsch. Suppl. 145, 700." *Fritzsche.* He ridicules the double interpretation given in Passow's Lexicon (copied into Liddell) most unmercifully, remarking upon the absurdity of dressing the Egyptians in the σύρμα, (he might as well have given them the Roman *toga*,) a people whose dress (the καλάσιρις) was notoriously *white*: ἄνδρες λευκῶν ἐκ πεπλωμάτων, Æsch. Suppl. 701. "It is evident that the epithet *black* is applied to those bad humours from which they purged their bodies." *Enger.* Cf. Pax, 1254.

[9] Eur. Helen. 569, ὦ φωσφόρ' Ἑκάτη, πέμπε φάσματ' εὐμενῆ. Cf. note on Nub. 366.   [10] From Eur. Helen. 16, 17.

[11] An infamous Athenian, whose name has passed into a synonym

MNES. "And[1] I am called Helen."

7TH WOM. Are you again becoming a woman, before you've suffered punishment for your former acting the woman?[2]

MNES. "And[3] many men died on my account at the streams of the Scamander."

7TH WOM. And would[4] that you *had died* too.

MNES. "And[5] I am here; but my unhappy husband, my Menelaus, does not yet come. Why then[6] do I still live?"

7TH WOMAN. Through the laziness[7] of the crows.

MNES. "But[8] something as it were cheers my heart. Do not cheat[9] me of my coming hope, O Jove!" [*Enter Euripides attired as Menelaus.*]

EUR. "Who has[10] the rule over these fortified mansions, who[11] would receive strangers distressed with storm[12] and shipwreck on the open sea?"

MNES. "This[13] is the house of Proteus."

EUR. "What Proteus?"

with every thing vile. See Bekk. Anecd. i. p. 314, 26, and p. 71, 25. Compare Taylor on Æsch. Ctes. p. 632, 633, and Liddell's Lex. in voc. φρυνώνδειος. He is mentioned again in the *Amphiaraus*, Fragm. x.

[1] From Eur. Helen. 22.

[2] "Bevor du deine erste Weibelei gebüsst." *Droysen.* "Rightly the Schol. Rav. and Suidas, τῆς γυναικείας μιμήσεως For γυναικίζειν (vs. 268) is *mulierem imitari atque mentiri.*" *Fritzsche.*

[3] From Eur. Helen. 52, 53. Cf. ibid. 608, and Liddell's Lex. voc. ψυχή, ii. 2.

[4] See note on Nub. 41.   [5] From Eur. Helen. 49.

[6] From Eur. Helen. 56. *f.* ib. 301.

[7] "*Tu quidem vivis corvorum inertium beneficio.* The crows are lazy, who have not already torn you in pieces." *Fritzsche.*

[8] He hears Euripides singing at a distance. For ὥσπερ τις, comp. Vesp. 395, 713. Aves, 181, and Elmsl. Acharn. 193.

[9] A notable construction. See Porson, Hec. 1174. Schäfer ad Greg. Cor. p. 15. For ἡ ἐπιοῦσα, see Porson, Phœn. 1651.

[10] From Eur. Helen. 68.

[11] "This and the following verse are not found in Euripides, but are taken from some lost play of his." *Enger.* "Brunck badly conjectures ὃς ἂν δέξαιτο, for an opinion and conjecture are put forward about an *altogether indefinite* person. Cf. Soph. Col. 1172." *Fritzsche.* See Bernhardy, W. S. p. 406. Reisig, Com. Crit. Colon. p. 320.

[12] Comp. Æsch. Theb. 210.

[13] Taken from Eur. Helen. 460:

ΓΡ. Πρωτεὺς τήδ' οἰκεῖ δώματ'· Αἴγυπτος δὲ γῆ.
ΜΕΝ. Αἴγυπτος; ὦ δύστηνος, οἷ πέπλευκ' ἄρα.

2 K 2

7TH WOMAN. Oh thrice-unlucky! [*Turning to Euripides.*] He is telling lies, by the two goddesses! for Proteus[1] has been dead these ten years.

EUR. "At what country have we landed with our ship?"

MNES. "Egypt."

EUR. "O wretched! whither have we sailed!"

7TH WOMAN. Do you believe this fellow at all—the devil take[2] him — talking nonsense? This is the Thesmophorium.

EUR. "Is Proteus himself[3] within, or out of sight?"

7TH WOMAN. It must be that you are[4] still sea-sick, stranger, who having heard that Proteus is dead, then[5] ask if he is within, or out of sight.

EUR. "Alas, he is dead! Where has he been buried i.: the tomb?"

MNES. "This is his tomb,[6] upon which I am sitting."

7TH WOMAN. Then[7] may you perish miserably! and certainly indeed you will perish, who have the impudence to call the altar a tomb.

EUR. "Why,[8] pray, do you sit in these sepulchral seats covered[9] with a veil, O female stranger?"

---

[1] An Athenian, son of Epicles. See Thuc. i. 45, ii. 23. "ἔτη δέκα *multos annos* significare recte adnotat Fritzschius." *Enger.* See Krüger, Gr. Gr. § 46, 3, obs. 1.

[2] See Krüger, Gr. Gr. § 53, 7, obs. 9. Comp. Ach. 778, 865, 924, 952. Pax, 2. Aves, 1467. Eccles. 1052, 1076. Plut. 456, 713. Vesp. 756, 1033.

[3] In Eur. Helen. 473, we have,

ἔστ' οὖν ἐν οἴκοις, ὄντιν' ὀνομάζεις, ἄναξ;
ποῦ δῆτ' ἂν εἴη; πότερον ἐκτὸς, ἢ 'ν δόμοις;

Aristophanes uses ἐξώπιος in derision of Euripides' fondness for that word. Cf. Alc. 546. Suppl. 1038. Med. 624.

[4] Comp. vs. 848. Equit. 238, 880, 951. Aves, 52. Plut. 871. Pax, 306.

[5] For this use of εἶτα following a participle, see Porson, Advers. p. 275. Blomf. gloss. Prom. V. 802.

[6] Eur. Helen. 466, τόδ' ἐστὶν αὐτοῦ μνῆμα, παῖς δ' ἄρχει χθονός.

[7] "Dich hole der Geier und dich holen wird er auch,
Der du den Altar ein Todtenmal zu nennen wagst." *Droysen.* Comp. Eur. Iph. Aul. 1445. Troad. 264. For γί τοι, see Herm. Vig. n. 297.

[8] "Neither this nor the next two verses are found in Euripides." *Enger.*

[9] "Aristophanes invents this, in order to give coherence to what follows after vs. 904." *Enger*

MNES. "I am [1] forced to mingle in wedlock with the son of Proteus."

7TH WOMAN. Wherefore, you wretch, are you again deceiving the stranger? [*To Euripides.*] This fellow, O stranger, acting the knave, came up hither to the women for the stealing of the gold.

MNES. "Bark away, assailing [2] me with censure."

EUR. "Female stranger, who is the old woman who reviles [3] you?"

MNES. "This is Theonoe, daughter of Proteus."

7TH WOMAN. No, by the two goddesses! unless [4] Critylla daughter of Antitheus of Gargettus *be so.* But you're a knave.

MNES. "Say whatever you please. For I will never marry [5] your brother, having abandoned [6] Menelaus, my husband, in Troy."

EUR. "What say you, woman? Turn your sparkling eyes [7] *towards mine.*"

MNES. "I am ashamed before you, having been mauled [8] in my cheeks."

EUR. "What's this? Speechlessness [9] possesses me. Ye gods, what sight [10] do I behold? Who art thou, woman?"

---

[1] Eur. Helen. 62, παῖς ὁ τεθνηκότος θηρᾷ γαμεῖν.

[2] Soph. Ajax, 1244, ἡμᾶς κακοῖς βαλεῖτέ που. Eur. El. 902, μή μέ τις φθόνῳ βάλῃ. For τοὐμὸν σῶμα = ἐγώ, cf. Eur. Alc. 647. Heracl. 91, 529. Soph. Rex, 643.

[3] Comp. Acharn. 577. Eur. Hipp. 340. Alc. 707. Soph. El. 597

[4] See note on Lys. 943, and cf. Equit. 186. I may here borrow the words of Enger: "Varias virorum doctorum emendationes afferre, ut in re apertâ, inutile est."

[5] Eur. Phœn. 1587, ἦ γὰρ γαμοῦμαι ζῶσα παιδὶ σῷ ποτέ;

[6] Eur. Helen. 54,

καὶ δοκῶ προδοῦσ' ἐμὸν πόσιν σύναψαι πόλεμον "Ελλησιν μέγαν.

[7] "Aug' in Auge wirf den Blick." *Droysen.*

[8] "The Scholiast rightly enough explains it ἐπειδὴ ξυρηθεὶς ἦν But the wit of the passage turns upon this, that not only had Mnesilochus been *mauled* by Euripides, but Helen also had been roughly handled by the same poet. See his *Helen,* vss. 1089—1091." *Enger* Cf. Hec. 968.

[9] Comp. Eur. Herc. F. 515, 556. Helen, 549. Bekk. Aneed. i. p. 83, 9.

[10] "This verse is taken, with slight change, from Eurip. Hel. 565.

τίς εἶ; τίν' ὄψιν σὴν, γύναι, προσδέρκομαι;

Comp. ibid. 72. The four following verses are taken from Euripide without any change." *Brunck.*

MNES. "And who are you? for the same[1] word holds you and me."

EUR. "Are you a Grecian woman, or a woman of this country?"

MNES. "A Grecian woman. But I also wish to learn[2] yours."

EUR. "I see you very like to Helen, woman."

MNES. "And I you to Menelaus,[3] as far as may be judged from the pot-herbs."

EUR. "Then[4] you rightly recognise a most unfortunate man."

MNES. "O thou who hast come late to the arms of thy wife! Take me, take me, husband! Throw thy arms[5] around me! Come, let me kiss you! Take and lead me away, lead me away. lead me away. lead me away[6] very quickly."

7TH WOM. Then, by the two goddesses, he shall weep,[7] whoever shall lead you away, being beaten with the torch.

EUR. "Do you hinder me from leading my wife, the daughter of Tyndareus, to Sparta?"

7TH WOM. Ah me, what[8] a knave you also appear to me to be, and this man's counsellor! No wonder you were acting the Egyptian[9] this long while. But he shall suffer punishment; for the Prytanis is approaching, and the Policeman. [*Goes towards them.*]

EUR. This is unlucky. Well, I must sneak away.[10]

"Wer du? dasselbe Wort ergreift so mich wie dich." *Droysen.* Eur. Med. 252, ἀλλ' οὐ γὰρ αὐτὸς πρὸς σὲ κἄμ' ἥκει λόγος.

[2] Eur. Troad. 63, μάλιστ'· ἀτὰρ δὴ καὶ τὸ σὸν θέλω μαθεῖν. Cf. Helen. 562.

[3] Eur. Helen. 572, ἐγὼ δὲ Μενελάῳ γέ σ'· οὐδ' ἔχω τί φῶ.

[4] Vss. 911, 912, are from Eur. Helen. 565, 566.

[5] A parody upon Eur. Helen. 627, 628.

[6] The repetitions are in derision of Eur. Helen. 650,

πόσιν ἐμὸν ἐμὸν ἔχομεν ἔχομεν, ὃν ἔμενον
ἔμενον ἐκ Τρυίας πολυετῆ μολεῖν.

[7] κλαύσετ' is κλαύσεται, not κλαύσετε. Brunck compares vss. 1012, 1178. Lys. 927. Nub. 523, 1140. See Dawes, M. C. p. 496.

[8] Cf. vs. 1212, *infra.* Plut. 899. Lys. 462. Pax, 173, 425. Nub. 773.

[9] "Αἰγυπτιάζειν is ambiguous in this passage, as it may mean as well *de Ægypto quædam garrire*, as *Ægyptiorum versutiam et fraudulentos mores imitari.*" *Kuster.* So also Fritzsche and Enger For οὐκ ἔτος, see note on Acharn. vs. 413

[10] Cf. Aves, 1011.

Mnes. But what shall I do, unhappy man?

Eur. Remain quiet; for I will never abandon you, if I live;[1] unless my innumerable artifices fail me. [*Exit Euripides.*]

Mnes. This line[2] has drawn up nothing. [*Enter Prytanis and Policeman.*]

Pryt. Is this the knave of whom Clisthenes spoke to us? Ho you, why do you hang down[3] your head? Lead him[4] within, Policeman, and bind him to the plank, and then place him here and guard him, and suffer no one to approach him; but beat them with your whip, if any approach.

7th Wom. Yes, by Jove! for now assuredly[5] a tricky fellow[6] almost took him away from me.

Mnes. O Prytanis, by your right hand, which you are accustomed to hold[7] out bent, if any one offer you money, grant me a small favour, although about to die.

Pryt. In what shall I oblige[8] you?

Mnes. Order the Policeman to strip me naked and fasten me to the plank; in order that, being an old man, I may not in saffron-coloured robes, and a woman's night-cap, afford laughter to the crows, while I feast them.[9]

---

[1] " Fritzsche rightly interprets it *si modo quidquam in me erit vitæ.*" *Enger.*

[2] A metaphorical expression, taken from fishermen who draw nothing up. Comp. Vesp. 175. Eur. Electr. 581. Lucian, Hermotim. c. 28.   [3] Comp. Equit. 1354.

[4] " Fritzsche rightly perceived that εἰσάγων = *introducens*, and that it must not be joined with ἐν τῇ σανίδι, as Brunck has do: The Scythian is ordered to bind him behind the scenes and then bring him out and guard him on the stage (ἐνθαδί). Fritzsche remarks that Herodotus (vii. 33, ix. 120) speaks of the same punishment." *Enger.*

[5] Dobree, Fritzsche, and Enger read νῦν δή, *just now.* " I grant that νῦν δῆτ' may be defended in this sense : *Plane tu flagello percute, si quis accesserit; nunc enim* PROFECTO," &c. *Fritzsche.*

[6] Fritzsche understands this as an allusion to Euripides' fondness for introducing his heroes in *rags.* See Ran. 842. But in this way the woman would be represented as recognising Euripides under his disguise. The Scholiast, Bergler, and Enger refer it to vs. 877, where he talks of having come in a *ship.* See Dawes, M. C. p. 592

[7] Comp. Pax, 905—908. Equit. 1083.

[8] See Porson, Phœn. 740.

[9]   " Damit Ich nicht
Im Krokosjäckchen und Schweinemagen, Ich alter Mann
Zum Gespötte werde den Raben, die Ich atzen soll." *Droysen*

PRYT. It has been determined by the Senate to bind you with them on, in order that you may be clearly seen by the passers-by[1] to be a knave. [*Exit Prytanis*]

MNES. Oh my! oh my! O saffron robe, what things you have done! No longer is there any hope of safety. [*Policeman leads Mnesilochus within.*]

CHO.[2] Come now, let us sport, as is here the custom with the women, whenever on holy seasons we celebrate the solemn orgies of the two goddesses, which Pauson[3] also honours, and fasts, oftentimes protesting to them from season to season that such are frequently a care to himself.[4] Put yourself in motion, each of you, advance, come on lightly with your feet in a circle,[5] join hand to hand, move to the time[6] of the dance; go with swift feet. It behoveth the choral order[7] to look about, turning round the eye in every direction. And at the same time also celebrate, each of you, and honour with your

"The Scholiast absurdly joins τοῖς κόραξιν ἑστιῶν. On this annotation, see what I have said in the Rhen. Mus. Philolog. ii. p. 246." *Enger.* So also Fritzsche. See note on Nub. 689.

[1] Comp. Vesp. 623.

[2] "While the chorus is singing this, Mnesilochus is within, getting bound to the plank." *Enger.*

[3] Comp. Ach. 854. Plut. 602. He was a well-known painter of the day, and chiefly devoted himself to *caricatures*. His poverty was so noted that it passed into a proverb, Παύσωνος πτωχότερος. In this place he is represented as strictly observing the *fast*, (νηστεία,) not from any religious motive, but because he had nothing to eat. See Erasmus, Adagia, p. 564. Aristot. Polit. viii. 5. Poet. ii. 2. Lucian, Encom. Demosth. c. 24.

[4] "συνεπευχόμενος—μέλειν is a short form of speech, with a pregnant construction in which this sense is involved, συνεπευχόμενος καὶ λέγων, τοιαῦτα μέλειν θάμ' ἑαυτῷ, simul precans deas ET DICENS sive QUERENS talia sibi frequenter curæ esse." *Fritzsche.* "Fritzsche is right with respect to the construction, but not right with respect to the sense. *Pauso precatur deas contestaturque, frequenter sibi esse jejunium cordi,* i. e. he celebrates the third day of the Thesmophoria in such a manner as to be quite an example to the women." *Enger.*

[5] "A description of the dance in a circle with linked hands." *Fritzsche.* So also Enger and Kuster. "Fritzsche observes that the usual way of construing this, ἄγ' ἐς κύκλον, is wrong." *Enger.* Cf. Eccles. 478.

[6] "Im Takt des Tanzes rege sich jede." *Droysen.* "*Secundum rhythmum choreæ quælibet incedat.*" *Brunck.* Cf. Lobeck, Ajax, p. 325. Æsch. Eum. 307.

[7] "Andreas Divus rightly interprets it *choreæ constitutionem et ordinem.* Cf. Æsch. Agam. vs. 22." *Fritzsche.*

voice, the race of the Olympic gods, with a mind mad for
dancing. But if any one expects that I, woman as I am, will
speak ill of men during the sacred rites,[1] he does not think
rightly. But it behoveth us immediately, as our duty is, first
to dispose the graceful step of the circling dance.[2] Advance
with your feet, celebrating Apollo with beautiful lyre, and the
bow-bearing Diana, chaste queen. Hail, thou far-darter, and
grant us the victory! And let us celebrate, as is fitting,
Juno who presides over marriage, who sports in all the
dances, and keeps the keys of marriage.[3] And I entreat the
pastoral Mercury, and Pan, and the dear Nymphs, benevo-
lently to smile upon and take pleasure in our dances.[4] Begin
now zealously the Diple,[5] the joy of the dance. Let us sport,
O women, as is the custom! Assuredly we keep[6] the fast. But
come! turn to another *measure* with foot keeping good time;
round off[7] the whole ode. And do thou thyself,[8] O ivy-
wreathed king Bacchus, lead us; and I will celebrate thee
with chorus-loving odes,[9] O Evius, O Bromius, child of

[1] "They feared to speak ill of men, not so much because they
were in the temple, as because they were celebrating the sacred
orgies in the temple." *Fritzsche.* "But ἐν ἱερῷ does not mean *in
templo,* but *in sacris obeundis.*" *Enger.*

[2] "Erst dem schön verschlungnen Rundtanz anzuordnen seinen
  Schritt."   *Droysen.*

[3] See Lobeck, Aglaoph. p. 650.

[4] "The construction is, ἐπιγέλασαι ταῖς ἡμετέραις χορείαις, χαρέντα
αὐταῖς. Cf. Nub. 274. Add Vesp. 389." *Fritzsche.* The construction is more singular than Fritzsche seems to have been aware of.
χαρέντα is referred to the more remote noun Πᾶνα.

[5] "Kuster rightly perceived that the διπλῆ is a species of *dance,*—
as Hesychius testifies, διπλῆ· ὀρχήσεως εἶδος ἢ κρούματος,—and that
this is by apposition called χάριν χορείας." *Enger.* So also Fritzsche.
This species of dance is also mentioned by Pollux, iv. 105.

[6] "*Certe (utique) autem jejunium agimus.*" *Fritzsche.*

[7] From the conjecture of Bentley on Hor. A. P. 441. Comp. vs.
54. "τόρνευε reponendum arbitror, ut loco convenientius: *Verum
age, alio te converte composito pede ; torna totam cantilenam.*" *Bentley.*

[8] "It is very well known that Bacchus acted as leader of the
dance in the orgies. Cf. Eur. Bacch. 141. Soph. Ant. 153." *Fritzsche.*

[9] Vs. 990—1000 is confessedly "corrupto corruptius." In Dindorf we have σὲ μέλψω Εὔιον, ὦ Διόνυσε, χοροῖς τερπόμενος Εὔιον
Εὔιον, εὐοῖ ἀναχορεύων. The participles τερπ. and ἀναχ. cannot be
referred to the *chorus.* See vs. 965. I have translated as if there
had been σὲ φιλοχόροισι μέλψω, Εὔιε, ὦ Διός τε Βρόμιε καὶ Σεμέλας παῖ,
and in 994, Εὔιε, Εὔιε, εὐοῖ. See Fritzsche's and Enger's editions
As Dindorf has left it, no translation is possible.

Jove and Semele, delighting in dances, in the mountains among the pleasing hymns of the Nymphs, O Evius, Evius, beginning a choral dance, evoe! And the echo of Cithæron resounds around thee, and the thick-shaded mountains dark with leaves and the rocky dells re-echo; while around thee the beautiful-leaved ivy flourishes with its tendrils round about. [*Mnesilochus is brought upon the stage again by the Policeman fast bound to the plank.*]

POLICEMAN. There now[1] you shall wail to the open sky.

MNES. O Policeman, I beseech you!

POL. Don't beseech me!

MNES. Loosen the nail.

POL. Well, I am[2] doing so. [*Hammers it in tighter.*]

MNES. Ah me, miserable! you are hammering it in the more.[3]

POL. Do you wish[4] it *to be hammered* still more?

MNES. Alas, alas! May you perish miserably.

POL. Be silent, miserable old man! Come, let me bring a mat,[5] in order that I may guard you. [*Goes out and returns again with a mat.*]

MNES. These are the blessed fruits which[6] I have enjoyed from Euripides. Ha, ye gods, preserver Jove, there are hopes! The man does not seem likely to abandon[7] me; but he ran forth as[8] Perseus, and secretly gave me a sign that I

[1] Comp. Æsch. Prom. 82. Aristoph. Plut. 1129, 724. Vesp. 149. Hom. Il. xxi. 122.

[2] "The Scythian understands Mnesilochus very well, but does the contrary." *Enger*

[3] "Weh mir, Ich Armer! mehr hinein noch hämmerst du!" *Voss.*

[4] "*Visne etiam amplius?*" *Enger.* "Er wollen noch fester? (= Wollen Sie noch fester?)" *Droysen.*

[5] "This phraseology of the Scythian is very strange. When he intended to say φέρ' ἐγὼ ἐξενέγκω φορμὸν, ἵνα φυλάξω σε, he expresses himself in infinitives, φέρ' ἐγὼ ἐξενέγκειν φορμὸς, ἵνα φυλάξειν σοι, which he pronounces in his own fashion. But Brunck rightly observes that the Scythian goes and fetches a mat to lie down upon, that he may not be fatigued with standing." *Enger.*

[6] See Krüger's Gr. Gr. § 57, 3, obs. 7. Eccles. 426, τοῦτ' ἀπέλαισαν Ναυσικύδους τάγαθόν. And this construction (τινός τι) is the regular one in the prose writers. The accusative of the *simple object* (Diphilus ap. Athen. vi. p. 227, F. Bekk. Anecd. i. p. 47) is very rare. See Bernhardy, W. S. p. 149.

[7] Comp. Æsch. Eum. 900. Krüger, Gr. Gr. § 67, 7, obs. 3.

[8] "Recte Schol. Ravenn. ἀντὶ τοῦ ὡς Περσεύς." *Fritzsche.* Cf

must become Andromeda. At all events I'm furnished with
the fetters.[1]   Therefore it is still[2] evident that he will come
to save me ; for *otherwise* he would not have flown near me.
[*Enter Euripides as Perseus.*]

    Eur. Dear,[3] dear virgins, would I could approach and
escape the observation of the Policeman ! [*Addressing the
Policeman.*]   Dost thou[4] hear ? O, *I beseech* thee, who
dwellest in caves, by reverence, assent, permit me to come to
the woman !

    Mnes. Pitiless[5] was he, who bound me, the most distressed
of mortals. When I had with difficulty escaped the anti-
quated[6] old woman, I perished notwithstanding.   For this
Policeman has been standing by me this long while as my
keeper: has hung me up, undone and friendless, as a dinner

Krüger, Gr. Gr. § 57, 3, and note on Plut. 314. According to
Droysen, Euripides flies through the air *a la* Perseus. "Aristophanes is ridiculing the *Andromeda* of Euripides, which was acted
at the same time with his Helena." *Enger.* See note on vs. 848.
" From this it is understood, that Euripides came on the stage habited as Perseus, and at first personated Perseus, as Mnesilochus did
Andromeda; but with great confusion of character." *Fritzsche.*

    [1] *The* fetters, (τὰ δίσμα,) i. e. the fetters needed for personating
Andromeda bound to a rock. See Krüger, Gr. Gr. § 50, 2, obs. 4,
and Lys. 645. Brunck's version (*equidem re ipsa vinctus sum*) utterly
extinguishes the sense. Droysen translates it rightly enough,

    "Auch hab' Ich ja die Banden wenigstens."

    [2] See Dawes, M. C. p. 514.
    [3] "Vs. 1115 is taken from Euripides, the two next are Aristo-
phanes' own." *Enger.* See note on vs. 23, *supra.*
    [4] This and the two following verses of Euripides' speech to the
Policeman are parodied from Andromeda's address to the *echo.*
Accordingly Euripides addresses the Policeman as, " *Thou echo that
dwellest in caves.*" Comp. Eur. Hec. 1110. Ovid. Met. iii. 395. The
passage of Euripides is this,

πρὸς Αἰδοῦς σι τὰν ἐν ἄντροις,
        ἀπόπαυσον, ἴασον
'Αχοῖ με σὺν φίλαις γόου πόθον λαβεῖν.

    [5] " In this song Mnesilochus, through perturbation of mind,
speaks sometimes in his own character, sometimes in the character
of Andromeda, which has a very comical effect." *Brunck.*
    [6] "They render σαπρὰν, *putidam*. But rightly Phrynichus (p.
377) and Photius, 'σαπρὸν οὐ τὸ μοχθηρὸν καὶ φαῦλον, ἀλλὰ τὸ πα-
λαιόν. Εὔπολις.' "   *Fritzsche*

for the crows.   Do you see? not among dai.ces, nor yet *accompanied* by the girls[1] of my own age, do I stand with the ballot-box of pebbles, but, entangled in strong fetters, I am exposed as food for the whale Glaucetes.[2]   Lament me, O women, not with a bridal song, but with a prison-song,[3] since I have suffered wretched things, wretched man, oh me unhappy, unhappy! and among my other impious sufferings from my relations, supplicating the man,[4] kindling the all-tearful lamentation of death,[5] alas! alas! who first shaved me clean, who clothed me in a saffron-coloured robe ; and, in addition to this, sent me up to this temple, where the women *were assembled.*   Ah me, thou unrelenting god of my fate!   Oh me, accursed! Who at the presence of my woes will not look[6] upon my unenviable suffering?   Would that the fire-bearing star[7] of Æther would utterly destroy me, ill-fated man. For no longer is it pleasing to me to behold the immortal

---

[1] Cf. Eur. Phœn. 1265. Here he is "dancing among the girls of his own age;" presently he forgets himself and relapses into the old Athenian "with ballot-box in hand." Throughout the whole there is a *studied* confusion of persons, genders, and constructions. Aristophanes, like Rabelais, often writes incoherent nonsense designedly. See Aves, 926—930, 950, 951, 1000—1009. Ran. 1264—1267, 1274—1277, 1285—1295. Pax, 1070, 1071.

[2] "A famous glutton mentioned in Pax, 1008." *Brunck.* The Scholiast on Aves 348, cites from the *Andromeda*, ἐκθεῖναι κήτει φορβάν. "Glaucetes is called a whale by apposition, because he was in the habit of devouring fish like a whale." *Fritzsche.*

[3] Cf. Æsch. Eum. 306, 331, 344.

[4] "He might have written φῶτα λιτομένα in the regular way But γοᾶσθέ με precedes, to which the participles are accommodated." *Fritzsche.* ἀλλ' in Dindorf's text is evidently a misprint for ἄλλ'.

[5] "By 'Αΐδα γόον I understand the lament of the dying, *the death-song.* Compare Eur. Elect. 143." *Fritzsche.* Virgil, Æn. ii. 500, "Incendentem luctus."

[6] "There is no difficulty in the passage. We must remember the words in vs. 944, ἵνα τοῖς παριοῦσι δῆλος ᾖς πανοῦργος ὤν. Mnesilochus takes the words of Andromeda (τίς ἐπόψεται) imploring the aid of the gods, and perverts them to the opposite meaning to suit his own case. *He* wanted to be seen by the passers-by as little as possible." *Enger.* Cf. Eur. Hec. 227, 193. Fritzsche strangely enough translates it, "*unenviable on account of the presence of my woes.*"

[7] Fritzsche and Liddell understand *the thunderbolt.*

flame ; since I am hung up, the cut-throat woes of the gods,[1] for a quick journey to the dead.[2]

EUR. (*as Echo*). "Hail, O dear child! but may the gods destroy thy father Cepheus, who exposed thee."

MNES. (*as Andromeda*). "But who are you, who have pitied my suffering?"

EUR. "Echo, responsive mocker of words,[3] who, last year in this very place, myself even shared in the contest[4] with Euripides. But, child, you must act your own part, to weep[5] piteously."

MNES. "And you must weep in answer after me."

EUR. "This shall be my care: but commence your words." [*Goes behind the scene.*]

MNES. "O sacred[6] night, how long a course you pursue,

[1] "A most notable kind of apposition is one expressed by an accusative and common to the whole sentence: ἐκρεμάσθην, λαιμότμητ' ἄχη δαιμόνων. Euripides especially favours this *accusative of apposition*. Androm. 292. Herc. F. 226. Hec. 1075. Orest. 842. Iph. A. 234. Alc. 7. Iph. T. 1459. Elect. 1080." *Fritzsche*. See Krüger, Gr. Gr. § 57, 10, obs. 10. Bernhardy, W. S. p. 127, and add Ach. 1201. Ran. 381.

[2] Enger and Fritzsche read ἔπι, and construe it with νέκυσιν.

[3] Compare Nero's famous line, (alluded to by Persius, i. 102, "*Enim ingeminat, reparabilis adsonat Echo.*" Comp. also Hor. i. 12. 4; i. 20, 8. Ovid, Met. iii. 381, 493. Soph. Phil. 189.

[4] "Mitgekämpfet habe für Euripides." *Droysen*. "As for the assertion that Echo had *assisted* Euripides in this very place (the theatre) the year before, it is said in ridicule of Euripides, who had not hesitated to introduce Echo's "jocosa imago" into his tragedy of *Andromeda*. *How* Echo was introduced is told us by the Ravenna Scholiast, 'ἐπεὶ εἰσήγαγε κακοστένακτον τὴν Ἠχὼ ὁ Εὐριπίδης ἐν τῇ Ἀνδρομέδᾳ. εἰς τοῦτο παίζει.' That is, Echo answered the lamentations and sobs of Andromeda. But *upon the stage* Euripides' Echo neither came nor could come." *Fritzsche*.

[5] The infinitive is here *exegetical* of the preceding sentence. See examples ap. Krüger, Gr. Gr. § 57, 10, obs. 6, § 51, 7, obs. 4. In these cases the inf. is usually in apposition to a pronoun (mostly a *demonstrative*) in the preceding sentence. See Ran. 610, 1369. Pax, 1076. Plut. 1163. Lys. 1180. Nub. 216, 1412.

[6] "This highly poetic invocation to night is taken verbatim from the prologue to the *Andromeda* of Euripides, Fragm. xxviii. These verses are thus rendered by Ennius, (ap. Varro *de Linguâ Latinâ*, v. 8,)

> Quæ cava cæli signi tenentibus
> Conficis bigis." *Wheelwright*.

The whole passage is thus rendered by Grotius, (Excerpt. p. 370,)

> O nox, sacra nox, quam tu longos

driving over the starry back of sacred Æther through the most august Olympus."

EUR. (*from behind*[1] *the scene as Echo*). "Through Olympus."

MNES. "Why ever have I, Andromeda, obtained a share of woes above[2] the rest?"

EUR. "Obtained a share."

MNES. "Wretched[3] for my death."

EUR. "Wretched for my death."

MNES. "You will destroy me, old woman,[4] with chatter-ing."

EUR. "With chattering."

MNES. "By Jove, you have got in very troublesome."[5]

EUR. "Very."

MNES. "Good sir,[6] permit me to sing a monody, and you will oblige me.   Cease."

EUR. "Cease."

MNES. Go to the devil.

EUR. "Go to the devil."

MNES. What's the pest ?

EUR. "What's the pest ?"

MNES. You talk foolishly.

EUR. "You talk foolishly."

MNES. Plague take you.

EUR. "Plague take you."

Agitas cursus super astrigerum
Vecta ætherii dorsum templi
Et per Olympi veneranda loca.

[1] "So also Euripides' Echo had answered from behind the scenes.' *Fritzsche.*

[2] See Porson, Med. 284.

[3] "Here also, as in vs. 857, Aristophanes joins the words differently than Euripides had done.   For, as the Scholiast records, Andromeda had added μέλλουσα τυχεῖν." *Enger.*   See Krüger, Gr. Gr. § 47, 3, obs. 2, and § 47, 21, and notes on vs. 1109. Lys. 967.

[4] "One may infer from this appellation that Echo was commonly considered a decrepit old woman." *Fritzsche.*

[5] Eur. Iph. T. 273, εἴτ' οὖν ἐπ' ἀκταῖς θάσσετον Διοσκόρω; "are you the Dioscuri who sit upon," &c.   Cf. Pind. Nem. ix. 97. Thuc. vii. 38.   Plato, Phædon, p. 107, C.   Soph. Trach. 648.   Xenoph Hellen. v. 1, 10.   Krüger, Gr. Gr. § 57, 3, obs. 5.   Hermann, Vig Append. p. 733.

[6] "He addresses Euripides." *Enger.*

MNES. Confound you.

EUR. " Confound you."

POL. (*awaking* [1] *and starting up from his mat*). Hollo you, what are you talking?

EUR. " Hollo you, what are you talking?"

POL. I'll summon the Prytanes.

EUR. " I'll summon the Prytanes."

POL. What's the pest?

EUR. " What's the pest?"

POL. Whence was the voice? [2]

EUR. " Whence was the voice?"

POL. (*turning to Mnesilochus*). Are you talking? [3]

EUR. " Are you talking?"

POL. You shall weep.

EUR. " You shall weep."

POL. Are you laughing at me? [4]

EUR. " Are you laughing at me?"

MNES. (*to the Policeman*). No, by Jove! but this woman near you. [5]

EUR. " This near you."

POL. Where is the abominable *woman?* Now she's flying. Whither, whither are you flying?

EUR. " Whither, whither are you flying?"

POL. You shall not get off [6] with impunity.

EUR. " You shall not get off with impunity."

POL. Why, are you still muttering?

EUR. " Why, are you still muttering?"

POL. Catch [7] the abominable *woman!*

EUR. " Catch the abominable woman."

POL. The chattering and accursed woman.

EUR. (*entering as Perseus*). " Ye [8] gods! to what land of

[1] So Bothe, Fritzsche, and Enger.

[2] " πωτετοπωνὴ, i. e. πόθεν ἡ φωνή." *Brunck.*

[3] " *Tunc loqueris?*" *Brunck.* " The Policeman addresses Mnesilochus, thinking it was he who spoke." *Enger.*

[4] " καταγελᾷς μου." *Scholiast.*

[5] " I am by no means mocking you, says Mnesilochus, but this woman near you (Euripides in the character of Echo)." *Fritzsche.*

[6] Cf. Plut. 64. Equit. 235, 828. Hermann, Vig. n. 207.

[7] " λαβὲ is not said to Mnesilochus, but to some one passing by." *Fritzsche.*

[8] " The Scholiast informs us that the three first verses are taken

barbarians have we come with swift sandals? for I, Perseus, place my winged foot, cutting my way through mid air,[1] travelling to Argos, carrying the head of the Gorgon."[2]

Pol. What are you saying about[3] the head of Gorgus the secretary?

Eur. "I say the *head* of the Gorgon."

Pol. I also mean Gorgus.[4]

Eur. "Ha![5] what cliff is this which[6] I see, and virgin like to the goddesses, moored like[7] a ship?"

Mnes. "O stranger, pity me all wretched: loose me from my fetters."

Pol. Don't you talk! Accursed[8] for your audacity: do you chatter when about to die?

from the *Andromeda,* and the rest put together from some other part of that play." *Enger.*

[1] "Many adjectives, placed as predicates, are to be translated by substantives. μέσος ὁ τόπος, (seldom ὁ τόπος μέσος, because μέσος is regularly the emphatic word,) *the middle of the place.* On the contrary, ὁ μέσος τόπος, or (ὁ) τόπος ὁ μέσος, *the middle place.* ἄκρα ἡ χείρ, or ἡ χ. ἄκρα, *the top of the hand.* ἐσχάτη ἡ γῆ, or ἡ γῆ ἐσχάτη, *the extremity of the land.* ἥμισυς ὁ βίος, or ὁ βίος ἥμισυς, *half of his life.*" *Krüger.* Comp. Eur. Phœn. vs. 1. Rhes. vs. 423. Ovid. Fast. v. 666, *Alato qui pede carpis iter.* "The disputes of the mythologists respecting the *talaria* of Mercury and of Perseus are well known." *Fritzsche.*

[2] Cf. Aves, 824. Lys. 619. Equit. 84, 279 Pind. Pyth. iv. 446. This usage of the article is poetic. See Krüger on Xenoph. Anab i. 2, 7. Gr. Gr. § 50, 7, obs. 7.

[3] Fritzsche and Enger read τί λέγι; τῇ Γόργος πέρι, &c. *What say you? are you bringing the head of Gorgus?* According to them πέρι = φέρεις. Cf. vs. 1007.

[4] "ὁ δὲ Γόργος γραμματεύς, ἀλλὰ καὶ βάρβαρος." *Scholiast.*

[5] In Euripides, ἔα, τίν' ὄχθον τόνδ' ὁρῶ περίῤῥυτον
ἀφρῷ θαλάσσης, παρθένου τ' εἰκὼ τίνα;
Comp. Ovid, Met. iv. 671.

[6] See Krüger, Gr. Gr. § 57, 3, obs. 6.

[7] Comp. Cicero's translation of Æschylus' *Prometheus Solutus,* Tusc. ii. 10,

> *Adspicite religatum asperis*
> *Vinctumque saxis. Navem ut horrisono freto*
> *Noctem paventes timidi adnectunt navitæ,*
> *Saturnius me sic infixit Jupiter.*

Eur. Herc. Fur. 1094, ἰδού, τί δεσμοῖς ναῦς ὅπως ὡρμισμένος
ἧμαι;

[8] "If a Greek had intended that κατάρατε τόλμης should signify *cœleste ob audaciam tuam* he would have said τῆς τόλμης." *Fritzsche*

Eur. "O virgin, I pity you, seeing you hung up."

Pol. It is not a virgin, but a sinful old man, and a thief, and a knave.

Eur. "You talk foolishly, Policeman; for this is Andromeda, daughter of Cephcus."

Pol. Look at his breasts! Do they look like a woman's?

Eur. "Give me here your[1] hand, in order that I may touch the damsel; give me it, Policeman: for all men have their weaknesses, and love of this damsel has seized myself."

Pol. I'm not at all jealous of you; but if his face had been turned this way, I would not have refused your going and kissing[2] him.

Eur. "But why, Policeman, do you not permit me to release her and recline upon[3] the couch and marriage-bed?"

Pol. If you strongly desire to kiss the old fellow, bore through the plank and go to him.

Eur. "No, by Jove, but I will loosen the fetters."

Pol. Then I'll whip you.

Eur. "And yet I'll do so."

Pol. Then I'll[4] cut off your head with this scimetar.

Eur. "Alas! what shall I do? To what words shall I turn? But his barbarous nature will not give ear to them.[5] For in truth, if you were to offer new inventions of wisdom to stupid[6] people, you would spend your labour to no purpose.

See vs. 1072, where we have θανάτου τλήμων. See also note on Lys. 967.

[1] "Reich deine Hand her, dass Ich der Maid mich nahen kann!
Reich her, o Scythe! haften doch Schwachheiten an
Den Menschen allen." *Droysen.*
" *Porrige huc mihi manum, ut adpropinquem ad puellam eamque adtingam; porrige, Scytha.* Euripides tries the temper of the Policeman cautiously, for he sees that he will have to fly again, if the Policeman does not show himself good-natured." *Fritzsche.*

[2] "He uses the indicative for the infinitive, as in vs. 1109, supra." *Enger.*

[3] For this construction, see Porson, Hec. 1010.

[4] "Fritzsche perceived that the sense was τὴν κεφαλήν σου ἄρα τῇ ξιφομαχαίρᾳ ταύτῃ ἀποκόψω, and that the crooked scimetar of Perseus was meant." *Enger.* Brunck and Droysen otherwise.

[5] Comp. Equit. 632. Eur. Phœn. 469. Androm. 1238. Suppl. 977. Heracl. 549. Ion, 1607. Thucyd. iii. 31; vii. 49. "This verse is perhaps from the *Andromeda.*" *Enger.*

[6] "Denn dummen Menschen neue Weisheit kund zu thun,
Ist eitel aufgewandte Müh." *Droysen*

2 L

But I must apply some other device[1] which is adapted to
him." [*Exit Euripides.*]

Pol. Abominable fox! how he was for deceiving[2] me.

Mnes. Remember, Perseus, that you are leaving me
miserable.

Pol. What, you're still wishing to get the whip! [*Lies
down again and falls asleep.*]

Cho. It is[3] my custom to invite hither to[4] the chorus
Pallas, friend of the chorus, virgin, unwedded damsel, who
guards our city, and alone possesses visible sovereignty, and
is called guardian. Appear,[5] O thou that hatest tyrants, as is
fitting! Of a truth the people of the women[6] invokes thee;
and mayest thou come to me with Peace the friend of festivals.[7] Come, ye[8] mistresses, benevolent and propitious, to
your hallowed place;[9] where in truth it is not lawful for men
to behold the solemn orgies of the two goddesses, where, by
torch-light,[10] ye show your immortal countenances. Come,
approach, we supplicate you, O much-revered Thesmophoræ!
If ever before ye came[11] in answer to our call, come now, we
beseech you, here to us. [*Enter Euripides as an old procuress, accompanied by a dancing-girl and a boy with a flute.*]

Comp. Eur. Med. 300. Bacch. 480. Herc. F. 298. Theognis, 625.
Sophocles ap. Athen. x. 433, F., and note on Lys. 233.

[1] Comp. Nub. 480. Plaut. Cistell. ii. 2, 5.   [2] Comp. Vesp. 1290.

[3] " Pallas, die Freundin des Chorgesangs,
　　　Her mir zu laden zum Chor, ist recht,
　　　　Pallas, die keusche, die Jungfrau
　　　Welche ja unsere Stadt beherrscht,
　　　Sichtbar einzig des Landes herrscht,
　　　　Schlüsselwaltende Göttin!"   *Droysen.*

[4] Comp. Nub. 564. Equit. 559. Fragm. 314.

[5] *Veni, Minerva, quæ tyrannos abominaris, sicuti jus fasque est : populus
te profecto mulierum invocat.*" *Fritzsche.*

[6] Cf. vss. 306, 335.

[7] " Peace is called *the friend of festivals*, because, during the Peloponnesian war, the rural Dionysia and other festivals could not
even be celebrated on account of the frequent incursions of the
enemy." *Fritzsche.*

[8] " Demeter and Cora." See Reisig, Enarr. Colon. 1045.

[9] See Böckh, Pind. Ol. iii. 19.

[10] " Wo im Fackellicht ihr ein unsterbliches Schaun gönnt." *Droys.*

[11] See Elmsley's note on Acharn. 733. Med. 1041. Cf. Aves, 144.
Mcnk, Alc. 281. Hermann, Eur. El. 938. Soph. Col. 1881. Krüger,
Gr Gr. § 30, obs. 1.

Eur. Women, if you are willing to make[1] peace with me for the future, it is now in your power; I make you these proposals of peace on the understanding[2] that you are to be in no wise abused by me at all henceforth.

Cho. On account[3] of what matter do you bring forward this proposal?

Eur. This man in the plank is my father-in-law. If therefore I recover him, you shall never[4] be abused at all. But if you do not comply, I will accuse you to your husbands when they come home from the army of those things which you do secretly.[5]

Cho. For our[6] parts, be assured that we are prevailed upon. But this barbarian you must[7] prevail upon yourself.

Eur. That is my business; and yours, [*turning to the dancing-girl*,] Elaphium, is to remember to do what I told you on the road. In the first place therefore walk past him,[8] and gird yourself up. And do you, [*turning to the boy*,] Teredon,[9] play an accompaniment to the Persian[10] dance.

---

[1] "Mit mir Vertrag zu schliessen, möglich ist es jetzt." *Droysen.* "σπονδὰς, συμμαχίαν, εἰρήνην ποιεῖσθαι is said of him who makes a league himself, *to make a covenant;* σπονδὰς ποιεῖν of him who is merely instrumental towards a league's being made, *to bring about a covenant.* Thucyd. v. 38, οἱ Βοιώταρχοι are related to have wished τὴν ξυμμαχίαν ποιεῖν, but οἱ Βοιωτοί (c. 39) ξυμμαχίαν ἰδίαν ποιήσασθαι. Cf. ibid. 43, 17—49; ii. 29. Pax, 212, 1199. Acharn. 267. Lys. 154, 951, 1006. Aves, 1599." *Fritzsche.* See Bernhardy, W. S. p. 344.

[2] Comp. Plut. 1000, 1141. Acharn. 722. Thuc. i. 113. Krüger, Gr. Gr. § 68, 41, obs. 8, and § 65, 3, obs. 3. Bernhardy, W. S. p. 251

[3] "Aus welchem Anlass anerbietest das du uns?" *Droysen.*

[4] See Bernhardy, W. S. p. 404.

[5] "ὑποιτουρεῖν τι is said of women who do any thing in their own houses secretly or deceitfully." *Fritzsche.*

[6] "So viel an uns liegt, sind wir herzlich gern bereit." *Droysen.* "*Quod quidem ad nos attinet, scito nos tibi obsecundare.*" *Fritzsche.*

[7] A common use of the imperative. So Æsch. Prom. 713, στεῖχε, *you must go.* See Hermann, Vig. n. 143. Markland, Iph. A. 734, and cf. Ran. 1024.

[8] "διέρχεσθαι in this passage means *transire*, for the dancing-girl was to walk past the policeman in order to attract his attention." *Fritzsche.* So also Enger.

[9] "The termination -ηδών belongs to *masculine* proper names, as Σαρπηδών, Τετθρηδών. Comp. also vs. 1203." *Enger.*

[10] Comp. Xen. Anab. vi. 1, 10.

Pol. (*waking up*). What's this humming?[1] What band of revellers awakens me?

Eur. The girl was about to practise beforehand, Policeman; for she is going to certain people to dance.

Pol. Let her dance and practise,[2] I will not hinder her. [*She begins to dance.*] How nimble! like a flea in a sheepskin.

Eur. Pull up this dress, child, and sit upon the Policeman's knee and hold out your feet. that I may take off your shoes.[3]

Pol. Yes, yes, sit down, sit down, yes, yes, my little daughter. [*Dancing-girl sits down upon the Policeman's knee.*] Ah, how firm[4] her breast is, like a turnip.

Eur. (*to the boy*). Play you quicker! Are you still afraid of the Policeman?

Pol. Beauteous she is behind! You shall repent, if you do not remain within. Well! beauteous she is before!

Eur. It is well. Take your dress: it is time for us now to go.

Pol. Will she not kiss me first?

Eur. Certainly. [*To the dancing-girl.*] Kiss him! [*She kisses him.*]

Pol. Oh, oh, oh! Oh my! How sweet her lips! like Attic honey. Why does she not remain with me?

Eur. Farewell, Policeman! for this cannot be.

Pol. Yes, yes, old woman, gratify me in this.

Eur. Then will you give me a drachma?

Pol. Yes, yes, I'll give it you.

Eur. Then bring the money.

Pol. But I have not any.[5] Come, take my quiver.

Eur. Then you'll bring her again.

Pol. (*to the dancing-girl*). Follow me, my child! And do you, old woman, guard the old man.—But what's your name?

Eur. Artemisia. Therefore remember my name.

---

[1] Comp. Acharn. 866.

[2] "The Scythian, when he ought to have said, ὀρχησάσθω καὶ τελετησάτω, uses infinitives, and inflects ὀρχεῖσθαι like an active verb." *Enger.*

[3] See note on Lys. 1243.   [4] Comp. Ach. 1199

[5] See Donaldson, New Cratyl. p. 190, foll.

Pol. Artamuxia. [*Exit Policeman with the dancing-girl.*]

Eur. O crafty Mercury, this you manage well as yet. Do you then [*addressing the boy*] run off with this *flute*, my boy; and I will set him at liberty. Mind that you fly manfully, as soon as ever[1] you are at liberty, and hasten[2] home to your wife and children.

Mnes. This shall be my[3] care, if once I be at liberty.

Eur. Be thou[4] free! Your business! fly! before the Policeman comes and catches you.

Mnes. I will do so now. [*Exeunt Euripides and Mnesilochus.*]

Pol. (*returning with the dancing girl*). How agreeable your daughter is, old woman, and not ill-natured, but gentle. Where's the old woman? [*Dancing-girl slips off.*] Ah me, how I am undone! Where is the old man *gone* from hence? O old woman, old woman. I don't commend you, old woman. Artamuxia. The old woman has deceived me. [*Picks up his quiver and throws it across the stage.*] Away with you as soon as possible! It is rightly called quiver, for it imposes upon me. Ah me, what shall I do? Whither is the old woman *gone?* Artamuxia.

Cho. Are you inquiring for[5] the old woman, who was carrying the harp?

Pol. Yes, yes. Did you see her?

Cho. Both she herself has gone this way, and an old man was following her.

Pol. The old man with the saffron-coloured robe?

Cho. Yes; you might still catch her, if you were to pursue her this way.

Pol. Oh the abominable old woman! Which way[6] shall I run? Artamuxia.

Cho. Run straight upwards. Whither are you running?

---

[1] "Brunck observes that τάχιστα is to be joined with ὅταν, and not with φεύξει, as the editors have done." *Enger.*

[2] Comp. Eurip. Suppl. 730.

Comp. vs. 1064, *supra*. Pax, 148, 1006, 1276. Plut. 229.

[4] "Whilst releasing him he says *esto solutus.*" *Enger.*

"Accusativus de quo." See Mus. Crit. i. p. 632.

[6] One woman had told him one way, the other woman another. Comp. note on vs. 1127, *supra.*

Will you not run back this way? you are running the contrary way.

Pol. Me miserable! But Artamuxia is running off. [*Exit
Policeman.*]

Cho. Run then, run then, with a fair wind to the Devil!
But we have sported sufficiently; so that in truth it is time
for each to go home. May the Thesmophoræ return us a
gracious kindness for this. [*Exeunt omnes.*]

END OF THE THESMOPHORIAZUSÆ.

THE FROGS.

DRAMATIS PERSONÆ.

BACCHUS.
XANTHIAS (servant of Bacchus).
HERCULES.
DEAD MAN.
CHARON.
FROGS (subordinate Chorus).
CHORUS OF MYSTÆ.
ÆACUS.
SERVANT OF PROSERPINE.
FEMALE INNKEEPERS.
EURIPIDES.
ÆSCHYLUS.
PLUTO.
VARIOUS MUTES.

THE ARGUMENT.

ACCORDING to the notice of the ancient Didascalia, this play was acted at the Lenæan festival, January, B. c. 405, in the Archonship of Callias. It was brought out in Philonides' name, who gained the first prize, Phrynichus the second with his "Muses," and Plato the third with his "Cleophon." The Frogs was so much admired on account of its parabasis, that it was acted a second time;—very probably in the March of the same year, at the Great Dionysia. The Frogs has for its subject the decline of the Tragic Art. Bacchus has a great longing for Euripides, and determines to bring him back from the infernal world. In this he imitates Hercules, but although furnished with that hero's lion-skin and club, in sentiments he is very unlike him, and as a dastardly voluptuary affords much matter for laughter. He rows himself over the Acherusian lake, where the frogs merrily greet him with their melodious croakings. The proper Chorus, however, consists of the shades of those initiated in the Eleusinian mysteries. Æschylus had hitherto occupied the tragic throne in the world below, but Euripides wants to eject him. Pluto presides, but appoints Bacchus to determine this great controversy. The two poets, the sublimely wrathful Æschylus, and the subtle and conceited Euripides, stand opposite each other, and deliver specimens of their poetical powers; they sing, they declaim against each other; and their peculiar traits are characterized in masterly style. At last a balance is brought, and separate verses of each poet are weighed against each other. Notwithstanding all the efforts of Euripides to produce ponderous lines, those of Æschylus always make the scale of his rival to kick the beam. Bacchus in the mean time has become a convert to the merits of Æschylus, and although he had sworn to Euripides to take him back with him to the upper world, he dismisses him with a parody of one of his own verses in the *Hippolytus*:

"My tongue hath sworn, I however make choice of Æschylus."

Consequently Æschylus returns to the living world, and resigns the tragic throne in his absence to Sophocles. The scene is first laid at Thebes; afterwards it changes to the nether shore of the Acherusian lake; and finally to the infernal world, with the palace of Pluto in the background.

THE FROGS.

[SCENE—*the front of Hercules' temple.*]

BACCHUS,[1] XANTHIAS—[*the former with the lion's skin of Hercules thrown over his usual effeminate attire, and armed with that hero's club; the latter mounted on an ass, and carrying their travelling baggage on the end of a pole*].

XAN. SHALL I say some of the usual *jokes*, master, at which the spectators always laugh.[2]

BAC. Yes, by Jove, whatever you please, except "I am burdened;"[3] but beware of this, for it is by this time utterly sickening to me.[4]

XAN. Nor any thing else facetious?

---

[1] Bacchus is introduced very properly as the person in quest of a poet, since at his festival so many Athenian dramas, and this among the rest, were performed. It served also, as Frischlinus observes, to avert indignation from the head of the comedian, should any arise in the populace at this unsparing ridicule of their favourite Euripides. Of the Lenæan festival more will be said hereafter.

[2] It appears from this scene, that a custom prevailed among the inferior dramatic poets at Athens, of introducing servants laden with baggage, whose sole business it was to complain, and whose ὡς θλίβομαι, and ὡς πιέζομαι, were catchwords similar in their effects to those so ably exposed by Mr. Gifford in his Baviad.

[3] It is but justice to observe, that Aristophanes has himself, in more places than one, been guilty of the very fault he here inveighs against. See Lysist. 255, 314. The Scholiast mentions another passage from the *Thesmophoriazusæ Secundæ*, Fragm. viii. (ed. Dindorf). ὡς διά γε τοῦτο τοὔπος οὐ δύναμαι φέρειν

σκεύη τοσαῦτα, καὶ τὸν ὦμον θλίβομαι.

[4] "Das ist verbraucht bis zum Ueberdruss." *Droysen.* Comp Liddell's Lex. in voc. χολή.

BAC. Except, "How I am afflicted!"

XAN. What then? shall I say what is very laughable?

BAC. Aye, by Jove, boldly: that thing only[1] take care you say not——

XAN. What?

BAC. That with shifting the yoke[2] *from one shoulder to the other*, you desire to ease yourself.

XAN. Nor that I shall break wind with carrying so great a load upon me, unless some one shall remove it?

BAC. Nay, do not, I beseech you, except when I am about to vomit.

XAN. Then what occasion[3] was there that I should carry this baggage, if I am to do none of those things which Phrynichus[4] is accustomed to do, and Lycis, and Amipsias? They are always carrying baggage in Comedy.[5]

BAC. Don't do so then; for whenever, being a spectator, I see any of these stage tricks, I come away older by more than a year.[6]

XAN. O this thrice-unlucky neck then! because it is distressed, but must not utter what is laughable.

[1] Comp. Eccles. 258. For this exhortative use of ὅπως, see note on Lys. 316.

[2] Cf. Eccles. 833. Phœnissæ, Fragm. iii., (ed. Dindorf,) and note on Lys. 312.

[3]   "What's the use, then,
Of my being burthen'd here with all these bundles,
If I 'm to be deprived of the common jokes
That Phrynichus, and Lycis, and Amipsias
Allow the servants always in their Comedies,
Without exception, when they carry bundles?" *Frere.*

[4] These were comic poets contemporary with Aristophanes. The first gained the second prize with his *Muses* when the present comedy was brought upon the stage. Amipsias had gained the first prize over our author's first edition of the *Clouds;* and, again, over his *Aves.*

[5] This line is bracketed by Dindorf as spurious. Brunck's method of construing it makes the construction solecistic; for ποιέω is not construed with *a dative* in Attic Greek. See Dawes, M. C. p. 334. Elmsl. Med. 1271. Bernhardy, W. S. p. 123. Wherever the dative is found with ποιέω, it is the "Dativus Commodi." See Krüger, Gr. Gr. § 46, 12, obs. 3.

[6] The Scholiast quotes the following line from Homer as an illustration of this:

Αἶψα γὰρ ἐν κακότητι βροτοὶ καταγηράσκουσιν. Cf. vs. 91, *infra.*

BAC. Then is not this insolence and much conceit, when I, who am Bacchus, son of—a wine-jar,[1] am walking myself, and toiling, while I let him ride, in order that he might not be[2] distressed or carry a burden?

XAN. Why, do I not carry?

BAC. Why, how do you carry, who are carried?

XAN. Because I carry these.[3]

BAC. In what way?

XAN. Very heavily.

BAC. Does not the ass then carry this weight which you carry?

XAN. Certainly not what I hold and carry; no, by Jove!

BAC. Why, how do you carry, who are yourself carried by another?

XAN. I know not; but this shoulder of mine is burdened.

BAC. Do you then, since you deny that the ass assists you, in your turn take up and carry the ass.

XAN. Ah me, miserable! Why was I not at the sea-fight?[4] Of a truth I would have bid a long farewell to you.[5]

[1] Where he should have said "son of Jove," contrary to expectation, he calls himself "son of a wine-jar." The vessel here mentioned occurs also in the *Lysistrata*, 196: and that in which the portion of manna was set apart by the children of Israel as a memorial is called by the Septuagint στάμνος, Exod. xxvi. 33.

[2] Matthiä (after Reisig) remarks, "The optative seems to express that Dionysus had this intention when first he let Xanthias mount." Krüger supposes that along with the principal tense a past tense also is present to the mind at the same time. Such cases ought rather to be explained in conformity with the proper nature of the optative, i. e. a mood *expressing the thoughts of some one different from the speaker.* Cf. note on Equit. vs. 135. Here I refer it to the scheming of the lazy Xanthias to bring this about. Cf. Aves, 45, 1524. Eccles. 347. Pax, 32. Soph. Col. 11. Elect. 760. Eur. Iph. T. 1218.

[3] i. e. τὰ στρώματα.

[4] At the sea-fight at Arginusæ the slaves (who had distinguished themselves by their bravery) were presented with their freedom. This practice of arming slaves was not peculiar to Athens, since we find from Plutarch that Cleomenes armed two thousand Helots to oppose the Macedonian Leucaspidæ, in his war with that people and the Achæans; and the Helots were also present at the battle of Marathon, according to Pausanias. In Rome also, though it was highly criminal, as Virgil, Æn. ix. 547, tells us, for slaves to enter the army of their masters, yet, after the battle of Cannæ, eight thousand of them were armed, and, by their valour in subsequent actions, earned themselves liberty.

[5] For this repetition of ἂν with an *indicative* cf. Aves, 1593. Lys.

Bac. Dismount, you scoundrel, for now I go[1] near the door, whither I was first to betake myself. [*Knocks violently at the door.*] Little boy, boy, I say,[2] boy! [*Xanthias dismounts from his ass.*]

Her. (*from within*). Who knocked at the door? How Centaur-like[3] he rushed at it, whoever he is. [*The door opens, and Hercules comes out.*] Tell me, what's this?[4]

Bac. (*addressing Xanthias*). Boy![5]

Xan. What's the matter?

Bac. Did you not observe?

Xan. What?

Bac. How exceedingly he was afraid of me.

Xan. Yes, by Jove, lest you should be mad.

Her. (*aside*). By Ceres, I certainly am not able[6] to refrain from laughing, though I bite my lips; nevertheless I laugh.

Bac. My good sir, come forward; for I have some need of you.

Her. (*trying to suppress his laughter*). I am not able to drive away my laughter, when I see a lion's skin lying upon a saffron-coloured robe.[7] What's your purpose? Why

361, 511; Thuc. viii. 96; Eur. Alc. 96; Hippol. 497; Soph. El. 441, 697; Antig. 468, 680, 884; Ajax, 1144. See Mus. Crit. ii. p. 276. Herm. Vig. n. 283.

[1] For εἰμὶ βαδίζων, see Krüger's Gr. Gr. § 56, 3, obs. 3.

[2] See Krüger's Gr. Gr. § 38, 4, obs. 5.

[3] The simile is well chosen for the character of Hercules, who had himself witnessed the insolence of which he speaks. According to the Scholiast, this is ironically spoken by Hercules, as if Bacchus had been unable, through weakness and effeminacy, to strike the door violently. Plaut. Trucul. ii. 2, 1, *Quis illic est, qui tam proterve nostras ædes arietat?* With ὅστις we ought, strictly speaking, to supply the requisite form of the preceding verb (ἐνήλατο). See Krüger's Gr. Gr. § 51, 15, 1.

[4] Comp. Vesp. 183, 1509; Aves, 859, 1030, 1495; Lys. 350, 445; Plut. 1097.

[5] Comp. vs. 271, 521, 608, *infra;* Aves, 665, 1581, 1628; Equit. 1389; Vesp. 935; Eccles. 128, 734, 737, 739, 833; Krüger's Gr. Gr. § 45, 2, obs. 6, and § 50, 8, obs. 3.

[6] See Krüger, Gr. Gr. § 67, 11.

[7] So also in the Thesmoph. 143, Agathon is described as wearing a saffron vest, which was a mark of effeminacy among the Romans also.

have the buskin and club[1] come together ? Whither in the world have you been abroad ?

BAC. I embarked on board the Clisthenes.[2]

HER. And fought at sea ?

BAC. And we sunk either twelve or thirteen ships of the enemy too.[3]

HER. You two ?

BAC. Yea, by Apollo !

HER. "And then I awoke."[4]

BAC. And indeed, as I was reading the Andromeda to my-self[5] on board the ship, suddenly a desire smote my heart, you can't think how vehemently.[6]

HER. Desire ? How great[7] a one ?

BAC. A little one : as big as Molon.[8]

HER. For a woman ?

[1] Comp. note on Thesm. 139.

[2] He speaks of the effeminate Clisthenes as if he were a ship of that name. He had probably fitted out and manned a ship as Trierarch for the expedition to Arginusæ. He is introduced in the *Thesmophoriazusæ*, vs. 574, as a very woman in manners and character, and warns the Athenian ladies of the knavery of Euripides and Mnesilochus. Cf. Lys. 1092; Thesm. 235; Nub. 355; Aves, 831.

[3] "Whenever καὶ—γέ is used in answers, it adds something new, and more important than the preceding; answering to the Latin *atque adeo.*" *Enger.*

[4] The battle of Arginusæ had but just taken place, and, as usual, the most worthless fellows, who had been compelled to engage in it, were making themselves out each the hero of the day. Hercules, who would put a stop to Bacchus's vaunts, replies to him with the usual conclusion of those who relate their dreams. In the *Cyclops* of Euripides, Silenus, the mythological attendant of Bacchus, is boasting of some exploit against a giant, and, at the end, asks himself, doubtingly, whether it be not a dream. "A polite way of telling people that they have been romancing. It is remarked by the German translators, Conz and Welcker, that their ancestors had a similar proverbial mode of expression, used for a similar purpose, *und mit dem erwacht Ich.*" *Mitchell.*

[5] Plato, (ap. Athen. i. p. 5, B.,) τουτὶ διελθεῖν βούλομαι τὸ βιβλίον πρὸς ἐμαυτόν. Cf. Eccles. 921.

[6] Comp. Acharn. 12, 24; Nub. 881; Eccles. 399; Plut. 742; Monk, Hippol. 448; Hermann, Nub. 878.

[7] See note on Equit. 1324. Cf. Blomf. Pers. 340. Krüger, Gr. Gr. § 51, 16, obs. 3.

[8] Didymus relates that there were two of this name at Athens, one an actor, the other a robber. "Molon was remarkable for his bulk and stature." *Frere.*

BAC. Certainly not.

HER. For a boy, then ?[1]

BAC. By no means.

HER. For a man, then ?

BAC. Faugh !

HER. Have you been with Clisthenes ?

BAC. Do not mock me, brother, for[2] I am distressed ; such a desire utterly undoes me.

HER. Of what sort, my little brother ?

BAC. I am not able to tell it ; yet certainly[3] will I declare it to you in a riddle.[4]   Did you ever[5] suddenly desire pea-soup ?

HER. Pea-soup ? bless me ! ten thousand times in my life.

BAC. Shall I teach you thoroughly the truth[6] of the matter, or shall I declare it in some other way ?

HER. Nay, do not about the pea-soup at least ; for I understand *that instance* very well.

BAC. Therefore such a longing for Euripides consumes me——

HER. And that too[7] when he is dead ?

BAC. And no man could persuade me, so as not to go to fetch him.[8]

HER. To Hades below ?

[1] For this use of ἀλλά, cf. note on Lys. 193.

[2] See note on Nub. 232.

[3] ὅμως γε μέντοι, *attamen certe*. See Hermann, Vig. n. 337.

[4] See Eurip. Rhesus, 754. Æsch. Agam. 1192. Choeph. 887.

[5] In the Peace, 841, Hercules is laughed at for his voracity, which the complaints of the hostesses in this play abundantly testify. Bacchus, therefore, when he would give his brother the strongest idea of his passion for Euripides, reminds him of his own for the ἔτνος, which was made of boiled pulse, and the proper diet of the brave in fight, according to the Scholium. For ἤδη, see note on Equit. 869.

[6]   "Shall I state the matter to you plainly at once,
        Or put it circumlocutorily ?"   *Frere*, who adds in his note, " A ridicule of the circuitous preambles to confidential communication in tragedy." ἐκδιδάσκω is the present subjunctive. The Greeks do not use a present indicative in this kind of construction. Comp. Soph. Trach. 972. Eur. Ion, 711.

[7] See Krüger, Gr. Gr. § 51, 7, obs. 14.

[8] See Krüger, Gr. Gr. § 67, 12, obs. 6 ; and for ἐπί, ibid. § 69, 42. obs. 2.

BAC. Aye, and, by Jove, *lower still*, if there be aught still ower.[1]

HER. With[2] what intent ?

BAC. I want a clever poet, "for[3] some are no longer alive. and others who are living, are bad."

HER. What then, is not[4] Iophon alive?

BAC. Why, to be[5] sure this is even the only good thing still remaining, if indeed even this be good ; for I don't know[6] for certain even how this is.

HER. Do you not mean, then, to bring up Sophocles,[7] who is before[8] Euripides, if you must bring one from thence ?

BAC. Not before I shall have taken Iophon alone by himself, and tried him, what he can do without Sophocles. And besides, Euripides, as he is roguish, would even attempt to run away hither along with me, while the other is easy here, and easy there.[9]

HER. But where's Agathon ?[10]

[1] Plut. 397, εἰ δ' ἐστιν ἕτερός τις Ποσειδῶν, τὸν ἕτερον.

[2] Comp. Lys. 480, 487.

[3] The Scholiast observes that this is a hemistich from Euripides. The seventy-second line is also from the *Œneus* of that tragedian.

[4] Iophon was the son of Sophocles and Nicostrate. The praises bestowed on him here, however, are considerably qualified by what follows after, whence it would appear that Sophocles' children were not content with their attempt to wrest his personal fortune from him, but extended their rapacity to his literary property after his death. The Scholiast mentions a play of that tragedian, in which this undutiful son is introduced as bringing the action against his father, which was refuted by the recital of the *Œdipus Coloneus*. Cic. *de Senectute.*

[5] See Hermann, Vig. n. 299.

[6] Anticipation. Cf. vs. 79 ; Krüger, Gr. Gr. § 61, 6, obs. 1 ; and note on Nub. vs. 1148.

[7] See Monk, Alc. 25. Hippol. 1148. Cf. vs. 863, *infra.*

[8] "There appears to be a studied ambiguity in the expression." *Mitchell.*

[9] ἐνθάδε, *the upper world,* ἐκεῖ, *the lower world.* Cf. Soph. Ant. 75 ; Aj. 1389. Plato, Apol. p. 41, C.

[10] Agathon was the contemporary of Euripides, &c., and is mentioned by Aristotle in terms of praise for his delineation of the character of Achilles, which Tyrwhitt supposes to have been introduced into his tragedy of *Telephus.* See Arist. de Poet. cap. xxviii. From the fragments which remain of this author, it appears that his style was replete with ornament, particularly antithesis. See Eth. Nich. vi. 5. Athen. v. p. 185, A. Thesm. 60. Thesm. Secund Fragm i. " He was not dead, as might be supposed, but had re-

Bac. He has left me and gone, a good[1] poet, and much regretted by his friends.[2]

Her. Whither in the world is the poor fellow[3] *gone?*

Bac. To the banquet of the blest.

Her. And Xenocles?[4]

Bac. By Jove, may he perish utterly.

Her. And Pythangelus?[5]

Xan. (*aside*). But no account[6] made of me, though I am so dreadfully galled in my shoulder.

Her. Are there not therefore here more than ten thousand other mere lads who compose tragedies, more loquacious[7] than Euripides by more than a stadium?[8]

Bac. These are small fry, and chatter-boxes, "twittering-places of the swallows,"[9] disgraces to the art, who vanish speedily, if only they receive a chorus, after having once piddled upon tragedy.[10] But a poet of creative powers you could no longer find,[11] if you searched, who uttered a noble expression.

tired to Macedonia, to the court of king Archelaus." *Droysen* See Athenæus, xv. p. 673, F.

[1] A pun upon his name.   [2] Eur. Phœn. 324, ἤ ποθεινὸς φίλοις

[3] Eur. El. 231, ποῦ γῆς ὁ τλήμων τλήμονας φυγὰς ἔχων.

[4] Xenocles was the son of Carcinus, and obtained the prize against the *Alexander, Palamedes, Troades,* and *Sisyphus* of Euripides. See note on Nub. 1272. Cf. Thesm. 169, 440. Vesp. 1501.

[5] This poet has sunk into the oblivion his poetry probably deserved.   [6] "But nobody thinks of me." *Frere.*

[7] This fault is again noticed in Euripides, vs. 1101, and is remarked by Plutarch also, De Aud. Poet. p. 45, (vi. 163. *Reisk.*)

[8] Comp. vs. 18, πλεῖν ἢ 'νιαυτῷ πρεσβύτερος. Nub. 430, τῶν Ἑλλήνων ἑκατὸν σταδίοισιν ἄριστος. Alexis ap. Athen. p. 638, C., ἡμέρας δρόμῳ κρείττων.

[9] This expression occurs in the *Alcmena* of Euripides, Fragm. ii., and points at once to the garrulity and barbarisms of the poets alluded to. Virgil mentions the first, Geor. iv. 307, as an attribute of the swallow; and the latter we may gather from the interpretation of the Dodonæan pigeon by Herodotus, ii. 57, where he says, "as long as she (the Egyptian) spoke in a foreign language, she appeared to them (the natives) to utter the sounds of a bird." Such was the opinion passed upon our own tongue by Charles V.

[10] "Necdum enim r.nt adeo validi, ut cum eâ rem habere possint eo successu, quo gaudere solent οἱ γόνιμοι. De Tragœdiâ, tanquam de *meretrice,* loquitur, quæ amatoribus poetis copiam sui facit. Sic Equit. 517." *Brunck.*

[11] ποιήτην ἂν οὐχ εὕροις ζητῶν ἄν. Matthiä (Gr. Gr. § 598, b,

HER. How creative ?

BAC. So creative as to utter[1] some such venturous phrase as "Æther, little mansion[2] of Jove," or "Foot of time," or "The mind which was not willing to swear by the victims, and the tongue which swore apart from the mind."

HER. Do these please you ?

BAC. Nay, but[3] *they please me* to more than madness.

HER. Of a surety[4] they are knavish tricks, as appears even to you.

BAC. Do not direct[5] my mind; for you have a house of your own.

HER. And yet absolutely they appear most villanous.

BAC. Teach me to dine.[6]

600, 5) and Mitchell imagine that in this kind of formulæ one ἂν belongs to the optative, the other to the participle, so that the participle is *thereby* = εἰ c. optativo. More accurate grammarians have very properly rejected this as a monstrosity, and recognise in such constructions merely the usual repetition of ἂν with an optative, as in Thesm. 196. Moreover a participle *alone by itself* is constantly used as a protasis = εἰ c. optativo, as may be seen ap. Krüger, Gr. § 56, 11; Matthiä, § 566, 4; Jelf, § 697, b. A good example is Eur. Ph. 514.

[1] See Krüger, Gr. Gr. § 51, 13, obs. 10. Bernhardy recognises in these constructions a sort of *climax*. Mitchell very aptly compares Longin. xxxii. 3, εἰ δεῖ παρακεκινδυνευτικώτερόν τι λέξαι.

[2] This line is from the *Melanippe* of Euripides, and quoted correctly in the Thesm. 272, although here the comedian's malice or forgetfulness has led him to render it more ridiculous by the substitution of δωμάτιον for οἴκησιν. The expression, "foot of time," is in the *Bacchæ*, 876. Cf. Alex. Fragm. xxi. The passage which follows is a paraphrase of the celebrated line in the *Hippolytus*, vs. 608; see Thesm. 275. Cicero both translates and applauds it in the Offices, iii. 29.

[3] See note on Thesm. vs. 646, C. Cf. vss. 745, 751, *infra*. Ach. 458.

[4] One would hardly have thought it necessary to assure the merest tyro, that ἢ μὴν never did, and never could under any circumstances, signify *nihilominus tamen*; ἀλλ' ἅπαν γένοιτ' ἂν ἤδη. Those who cannot judge for themselves may consult Hermann's note on Eur. Alc. 64. "*Profecto inepta sunt, vel te judice.*" *Brunck.*

[5] "Rule not my thoughts; thou'rt master of thine own." *Dunster.* A parody on the following line of the *Andromeda* of Euripides,

μὴ τὸν ἐμὸν οἴκει νοῦν· ἐγὼ γὰρ ἀρκέσω.

[6] "*Ne sutor ultra crepidam.*" Hercules was a great glutton, and might therefore be supposed to understand the art which Bacchus recommends him to teach. He therefore says, "confine your instructions to gastronomy; it's something that you understand."

XAN. (*aside*). But no account of me.

BAC. But *tell me these*, for the sake of which[1] I have come with this dress, in imitation of you, that you might tell me your entertainers, if I should want them, whom you made use of at that time when you went to fetch Cerberus, the harbours, bakers' shops, brothels, resting-places, lodging-houses, springs, roads, cities, rooms, hostesses, and where there are fewest bugs.

XAN. (*aside*). But no account of me.

HER. Oh rash! why, will you dare to go?

BAC. And do you too say nothing further to this, but tell me about the roads, how we may soonest arrive at Hades below; and tell me neither a hot nor a very cold *way*.

HER. Come now, which of them shall I tell you first? Which?[2] for there is one *way* by a rope and a bench, if you hang yourself.

BAC. Have done, you tell me a choking one.

HER. But there is a compendious and well-beaten[3] path, that through a mortar.

BAC. Do you mean hemlock?

HER. Certainly.

BAC. Aye, a cold and chilly one, for it immediately benumbs[4] the shins.

HER. Would you have me tell you a speedy and down-hill *road*?

BAC. Yes, by Jove, for I am not good at walking.

HER. Creep down then to the Ceramicus.[5]

---

[1] See Krüger, Gr. Gr. § 51, 11.   [2] Cf. Nub. 79.

[3] The reader will perceive the pun. Plato, Phæd. p. 116, "And let some one bring in the poison, if it has been pounded. if not, let him beat it up." And again, p. 117, "And after he had pounded it for a considerable time, he came with the person who was to give the poison to Socrates, bringing it beaten in a cup."

[4] This is Plato's account of the effects of hemlock: Phæd. p. 118, "And then having violently squeezed his foot, he asked him [Socrates] if he felt it; but he said, no: and after this again his shins; and then he came up to us and told us that Socrates was becoming chilled and benumbed."

[5] The Ceramici were two districts, one within the walls of Athens, the other without. The latter is here meant. The former was an insignificant part of the town, and the resort of the lowest and most profligate of its inhabitants; the latter, however, was famous on many accounts, especially as the burying-place of deceased war-

Bac. And what then?

Her. When you have mounted on the lofty tower—

Bac. What must I do?

Her. Look out thence for the torch to be thrown down and then, when the spectators call to fling it, do you, too, fling [1] yourself—

Bac. Whither?

Her. Down.

Bac. But I should destroy the two membranes [2] of my brain: I could not travel this way.

Her. What then?

Bac. That whereby you then descended. [3]

Her. But the voyage is long; for you will immediately come to a large lake, altogether bottomless.

Bac. How then shall I get across?

Her. An old sailor-man will carry you over in a little boat only so big, when he has received two obols [4] as his fare.

Bac. Ha! what a mighty power the two obols have every where! How came they thither, too? [5]

---

riors: see Thucyd. ii. Of the celebration of the torch-race, mentioned by Herod. 8, as consecrated to Vulcan, with whom other writers join Minerva and Prometheus, more will be found in the note on vs. 1087 of this play. Cf. Vesp. 1203. Kuster says that the torch thrown from the tower was a signal for starting: Meursius understands each of the competitors to receive a torch from thence. "Hercules speaks as one standing on a higher ground than the place alluded to." *Mitchell.*

[1] Cf. Ach. 1001. Nub. 1080. Equit. 1187. This usage must not be confounded with that noticed in the note on vs. 169.

[2] Θρίον is properly a fig-leaf, but applied to the membranes of the head, according to the Scholiast, from their resemblance to the foliage of the fig-tree.

[3] Eur. Electr. 1041, ἐτρίφθην ἥνπερ ἦν πορεύσιμον. Orest. 1251, στῆτε τήνδ' ἁμαξήρη τρίβον. Herod. viii. 121, ἰέναι τὴν μεσόγαιαν. See Krüger, Gr. Gr. § 46, 6, obs. 2. Bernhardy, W. S. p. 115.

[4] In other mythological authorities Charon is said to be contented with a single obol, but the comedian increases his fare to two, for the purpose of introducing a sneer at that part of Solon's legislation, which, in the words of Mr. Mitchell, "made the country a nation of judges, or, to use the original term, a nation of *dicasts.*"

"Auf einem nur so grossen Nachen setzet dich
Ein alter Fährmann über für zwei Obolen Lohn." *Droysen.*

[5] "Wie kamen sie auch dort?" *Droysen.*
πως καὶ ἠλθέτην; would be somewhat different

Her. Theseus brought them. After this you will see snakes, and innumerable wild beasts most dreadful.

Bac. Do not try[1] to astound, or put me in a fright, for you will not dissuade me.

Her. Then *you will see* abundant mud,[2] and ever-flowing ordure ; and[3] people lying in this, if any where any one has ever wronged his guest,[4] or appropriated the wages of prostitution, or beaten his mother, or struck his father's cheek, or sworn a false oath, or if any have transcribed a passage of Morsimus.[5]

Bac. Yea, by the gods, in addition to these also there ought to have been, if any one learnt the Pyrrhic dance of Cinesias.[6]

Her. After that the breath of flutes shall encompass you, and you shall see a most beautiful light, as here,[7] and myrtle groves, and happy bands of men and women,[8] and abundant clapping of hands.

[1] See Porson and Schäfer on Eur. Ph. 79 ; Hermann, Vig. ii. 161.
[2] Plato mentions this, Phædon, 81,—"That whoever comes to hell uninitiated in the mysteries, or unatoned for by sacrifice, shall lie in mud." See also Æsch. Eum. 269 ; Virg. Æn. vi. 608.
[3] See note on Lys. 556.
[4] Aristophanes had in his mind Æsch. Eum. 259.
[5] Morsimus was a rival of Aristophanes in the drama, and is mentioned by him in the *Knights*, vs. 401, where the chorus wishes, as the strongest and deepest curse that could visit them, if ever they forget their hatred to Cleon, that they may be compelled to "sing a part in a tragedy of Morsimus." Cf. Pax, 801 ; Aves, 281, where he is called "son of Philocles."
[6] A native of Thebes, son of Meles, a player on the cithara, and a dithyrambic poet. He was so thin and weak, as to be obliged to support himself by *stays* made of lime-tree wood. See Aves, 1378 ; Ran. 1437. His dirty habits are alluded to in Eccles. 330. In Aves, 1372, he appears in the character of a begging poet. Spanheim produces a passage from Athenæus, itself a fragment of a lost play called *Gerytades*, and written by Aristophanes, in which, among the persons who, for their leanness and ghost-like appearance, were to be sent to hell on an embassy, is enumerated Cinesias, —ἀπὸ κυκλικῶν. See Aristoph. Fragm. 198, ed. Dindorf. The Pyrrhic dance required the Orthian strain, according to Athenæus.
[7] See note on vs. 82. "A brilliant sun was probably shining at the time over the theatre when the words were uttered." *Mitchell*. See Schlegel Dram. Lit. p. 53, 57 ; Pindar Thren. Fragm. i., τοῖσι λάμπει μὲν μένος ἀελίου τὰν ἰνθάδε νύκτα κάτω. Virg. Æn vi. 610, "Largior hic campos æther et lumine vestit purpureo."
[8] As a similar instance of asyndeton, Kuster cites Soph. Antig

Bac. But who, pray, are these ?

Her. The initiated—[1]

Xan. (*aside*). By Jove, I am certainly the ass[2] that carries the mystic implements. But I will not hold these any[3] longer. [*Throws his baggage on the ground.*]

Her. —who will tell you every thing whatever you want. For they dwell[4] very near along the very road, by Pluto's gates. And now fare you well, brother.[5] [*Hercules goes in and shuts the door.*]

Bac. Yea, by Jove, and fare you well also ; but do you (*to Xanthius*) take up the baggage again.

Xan. Before I have laid them down even ?

Bac. Aye, and very quickly, let me tell you !

Xan. Nay, do not, I beseech you, but hire some one ot those who are being carried forth to burial, who is going on this errand.[6]

Bac. But if I should not be able ?

Xan. Then let me take[7] them. [*A funeral procession with a dead body on a bier crosses the stage.*]

1079, ἀνδρῶν, γυναικῶν κωκύματα. See Krüger, Gr. Gr. § 59, 1, obs. 1.

[1] Virg. Æn. vi. 638. This alludes to an idea prevalent throughout Greece, but especially in Athens, that the Mystæ were to enjoy their time in the Elysian fields after death, crowned with myrtles, and possessed of all possible happiness. Euripides, in his Herc. Fur. 612, mentions the initiation of Hercules as a preliminary step to his descent into hell. To those who have time and opportunity for its perusal, the ingenious attempt of Dr. Warburton to prove Virgil's sixth book a description of the Eleusinian mysteries will most probably afford a more copious account of that festival than can be here given. Div. Leg. 2.

[2] These animals, says the Scholium, were used for carrying the necessary adjuncts to the performance of the mysteries from Athens to Eleusis ; they were often over-laden, and from this circumstance arose the proverb used by Xanthias, as indicating any intolerable burden.

[3] Thuc. iv. 117, ἐς τὸν πλείω χρόνον. See Krüger, Gr. Gr. § 50, 2, obs. 8 ; § 50, 4, obs. 13. This is the only passage in Aristophanes where this phrase is found.

[4] " Denn ihre Wohnung haben sie dort zu allernächst
    Und dicht am Wege, der zu Plutons Pforte führt." *Droysen.*

[5] Eur. Hippol. 1451, χαῖρε πολλά μοι, πάτερ.

[6] Eur. Bacch. 965, ἐπὶ τόδ' ἔρχομαι.
    " Der in den Wurf dir grade kommt." *Droysen.*

[7] " The infinitive was also used *absolutely*—certainly without any

Bac. You say well; for they are carrying forth[1] some dead man here.[2] Hollo you! You, I say! you,[3] the dead man! Fellow, will you carry some small baggage to Hades?

Dead Man. About[4] how many?

Bac. These here.

D. M. Will you pay two drachmæ[5] as my pay?

Bac. No, by Jove, but less.

D. M. (*to the bearers*). Go you slowly on your way.[6]

Bac. Stay, my good sir, if I may possibly make[7] a bargain with you.

D. M. Unless you will pay two drachmæ, don't talk.

Bac. Take nine obols.

D. M. Then may I come to life again! [*Funeral procession moves on.*]

Xan. How[8] haughty the accursed fellow is! Won't he smart for it? I'll go myself. [*Takes up the baggage again.*]

Bac. You are a good and noble fellow. Let us go to the boat. [*Here the scene changes*[9] *to the banks of the Styx.*]

Charon. Avast![10] put to shore!

ellipsis—for the denoting of a wish, (*optatively*,) as a kind of invocation, which may also express merely a person's *liking*. The subject in this case stands in the *accusative*. Æschylus, θεοὶ πολῖται, μή με δουλείας τυχεῖν. Aristophanes, μίσθωσαί τινα. Δ. ἐὰν δὲ μὴ ἔχω; Ξ. τότε μ' ἄγειν." *Krüger*. See his Grammar, § 55, 1, obs. 4, and obs. 5. Of course we must not confound such as these with the infinitive = imperative. Cf. vss. 887, 894. Eccles. 1107. Pax, 551. Aves, 448.

[1] The following dialogue may remind us of the concluding scene in Bombastes Furioso, which subsequent productions of a similar nature have imitated.

[2] Comp. Vesp. 182, 205, 1415. Pax, 840. Aves, 287, 279.

[3] Comp. Æsch. Prom. 980. Eur. Bacch. 910; Med. 273. Soph. Ant. 270. Hermann, Vig. n. 341.

[4] See Krüger, Gr. Gr. § 51, 16, obs. 6.

[5] The Attic drachma was six obols. Bacchus, therefore, offers him three-fourths.

[6] "Bearers, move on." *Frere*.   [7] See note on vs. 1460.

[8] Plut. 275, ὡς σεμνὸς οὑπίτριπτος. Cf. Eur. Hippol. 92, 492, 961, 1067.

"A pompous rascal! Won't he pay for't? Well!
I'll e'en proceed and carry it myself." *Dunster*.

[9] See Schlegel, Dram. Lit. p 161.

Mr. Mitchell has observed that the nautical language of th

X**AN**. (*gazing at the Styx with astonishment*). What's this?

B**AC**. By Jove, this[1] is that lake of which he was telling us; and I see a boat too.

X**AN**. Aye, by Neptune, and see here's Charon too!

B**AC**. Hail, Charon! hail, Charon! hail, Charon!

C**HA**. Who *is bound* to the resting-place from miseries[2] and troubles? who to the plain of Lethe, or to an ass-shearing,[3] or to the Cerberians,[4] or to the crows, or to Tænarus?[5]

B**AC**. I.

C**HA**. Get on board quickly.

B**AC**. Where d'ye think you shall put[6] in? to the crows really?

C**HA**. Yes, by Jove, as far as you are concerned.[7] Now, get on board.

Athenians was not very musical, as neither our own formerly or at present.

[1] See Krüger's important remarks on this construction, Gr. Gr. § 61, 7, and note on Aves, 179.

[2] Mitchell compares Plato, Legg. ii. p. 653, D. Soph. Phil. 878. Eur. Fragm. inc. clv.

[3] "ἐς ὄνου πόκας = land of *no where*." *Mitchell*. It was a common proverb, signifying impossibility, or rather what does not exist. In Greece, when any one attempted aught impossible, it was usual to say to him, ὄνον κείρεις, "you are shearing an ass."

[4] "*People among whom Cerberus dwells*, not without allusion to the Homeric Cimmerii." *Mitchell*. There were two nations of this name, one on the Palus Mœotis, who in the time of Cyaxares invaded Asia Minor, Herod. i. 6; another that dwelt on the western coast of Italy, and from their habits, such as concealing themselves in caves, &c., were supposed by the ancients to be denizens of hell. Homer, Virgil, and Milton have all availed themselves of this idea.

[5] A dark place at the foot of Malea, a promontory of Laconia, the southern point of Europe. Neptune had a temple there, and for an offence against him, the earthquake which demolished Sparta was supposed to have happened. There was a cave at Tænarus whence issued a black and unwholesome vapour, and this gave rise to the poetical fable of its being the passage through which Hercules dragged Cerberus. Virgil, Geor. iv. 467, mentions it as the road of Orpheus also. Cf. Eur. Herc. F. 23; Cyclops, 292.

[6] For similar uses of the simple verb in this sense Mitchell cites Soph. Phil. 305; Solon, Fragm. V. vs. 65.

[7] Comp. Acharn. 386, 958. Nub. 422. Soph. Phil. 774. Eur. Helen. 1274. Krüger, Gr. Gr. § 68, 19, obs 2.

BAC. Here, boy ! [*Bacchus gets into the boat.*]

CHA. I carry no slave, unless he has been in the battle[1] of the Carcasses.

XAN. No, by Jove; for I happened to have sore[2] eyes.

CHA. Will you not then, pray, run round the lake, round about ?[3]

XAN. Where then shall I wait for you ?

CHA. Near the stone of Auænus,[4] at the resting-places.

BAC. D'ye understand ?

XAN. Yes, certainly, I understand. Ah me, miserable! what *omen*[5] did I meet with as I left home? [*Xanthias runs off.*]

CHA. (*to Bacchus*). Sit to your oar. [*Bacchus goes and seats himself* ON *the oar instead of* AT *the oar.*] If any one further is for sailing, let him make haste. [*To Bacchus.*] Hollo you ! what are you doing?

BAC. What am I doing? why, what else but sitting on the oar, where you bade me ?

CHA. Will you not then, pray, sit down here, you fat-guts ?

BAC. (*seating himself*). There.

CHA. Will you not then put forth your hands and stretch them out ?

BAC. There. [*Makes a silly motion with his hands.*]

---

[1] The allusion is to the battle of Arginusæ. "The sense is: *nisi pugnæ navali interfuit et eo sibi libertatem paravit:* περὶ τῶν κρεῶν is said for περὶ τῶν σωμάτων." *Thiersch.* According to Mitchell, Charon judges of the battle from his stand-point as *ferryman*, and therefore speaks of it only as the battle in which so many *carcasses* had to be recovered for the rites of sepulture. And this seems the most probable explanation. Herod. viii. 102, ἀγῶνας δρομέονται περὶ σφέων αὐτέων.

[2] Thiersch supposes the allusion is to some Athenian of the day, who had made this excuse. For οὐ γὰρ ἀλλά, see note on Nub. 232.

[3] "So lauf' und lauf' nur hurtig rings um den Teich herum !"
Droysen.

[4] One of Aristophanes' equivoques, as αὐαίνου is at the same time the imperative of αὐαίνομαι = *be thou withered.* Cf. Æsch. Eum. 333

[5] The superstition of the ancients respecting the objects that fell in their way on leaving their houses is well known. Potter has enumerated several, as an eunuch, a black, and an ape, or a snake lying in the road, so as to part the company. Of these Polis and Hippocrates (not the physician) are said to have written books.

CHA. Don't be playing the fool,[1] but row stoutly with your feet against the stretcher.[2]

BAC. Why, how then shall I be able to row, being inexperienced and unused to the sea, and no Salaminian ?

CHA. Very easily ; for you shall hear most delightful melodies, as soon as you once lay to your oar.

BAC. From whom ?

CHA. From swans, the frogs, wondrous ones.

BAC. Now give the time !

CHA. Yeo ho ! yeo ho !

FROGS. Brekekekex, coax, coax, brekekekex, coax, coax. Marshy offspring of the fountains, let us utter an harmonious strain of hymns, my sweet-sounding song, coax, coax, which we sung in Limnæ[3] around the Nysæan[4] Bacchus, son of Jove, when the crowd of people rambling about in drunken revelry on the sacred festival of the Chytræ, marched through my demesne. Brekekekex, coax, coax.

BAC. I begin to have a pain in my bottom, you coax, coax. But you, no doubt,[5] don't care.

FROGS. Brekekekex, coax, coax.

BAC. May you perish then together with your coax ;[6] for you are nothing else but coax.

FROGS. Aye, justly, you busybody, for the Muses with

---

[1] See note on vs. 299, *infra.* Krüger, Gr. Gr. § 53, 7, obs. 5, and for ἔχων, ibid. § 56, 8, obs. 4, and note on Aves, 341.

[2] "Pull stoutly against the oar, going well back." *Liddell.* This can scarcely be the meaning.

[3] A swampy district in the neighbourhood of the Acropolis, where was the temple of Bacchus, and where the Bacchic festival was celebrated. There is an allusion at the same time to the natural haunt of the Frogs.

[4] Nysa is placed by some authors in Arabia, by others in Æthiopia. It was, with another of the same name in India, consecrated to Bacchus, and here the god is said to have been educated by the nymphs of the place. His connexion with it appears from his name Dionysus. A probable derivation of this name is the *Indian* one, which deduces it from δεῦνος and Νύσα, *king of Nysa.* See Creuzer as cited ap. Mitchell, p. 413.

[5] "Not *fortasse,* but *videlicet* or *profecto,* as Schäfer ad Long. p. 357, teaches us. Cf. Plut. 358, 1058. Eur. Heracl. 262." *Thiersch.* "Freilich." *Droysen.* For οὐδὲν μέλει, cf. Vesp. 1411.

[6] "Hol' euch mit eurem kex koax!
Ihr seid ja nichts als kex koax." *Droysen.*

Comp Pax, 1288. Thesm. 826.

beautiful lyre, and horn-footed[1] Pan, who plays reed-sounded strains, have loved me, and the harper Apollo is still more delighted with me on account of the reed,[2] which, put under the lyre, living in the water, I nourish in marshes. Brekekekex, coax, coax.

BAC. I have blisters, and my hinder-end has been sweating this long while, and then presently it will stoop and say "brekekekex, coax, coax." Come, O song-loving race, have done!

FROGS. Nay, rather, we will sing the more, if ever on[3] sunny days we have leapt through galingal and sedge, delighting in strains of song with many a dive; or at the bottom, avoiding the rain of Jove, have chanted[4] our varied watery choral music amid the noise of bursting bubbles. Brekekekex, coax, coax.

BAC. (*striking at them and splashing with his oar*). I'll take[5] this from you.

FROGS. Then in truth we shall suffer dreadful things.

BAC. But I more dreadful things, if I shall burst with rowing.

FROGS. Brekekekex, coax, coax.

BAC. A plague take you! for I don't care.

---

[1] This well-known piece of mythology is found in Homer's hymn to Pan, vs. 2.   See Liddell's Lex. in voc. κεροβάτης.

[2] The Limnæ, or marshes in which the chorus resided, furnished this plant, for the use of which in making the φόρμιγξ we have Homer's testimony. Hymn to Mercury, 47.

[3] "The rather loudly will we chant, I ween,
   For often we've been singing,
Beneath the sunbeam's golden sheen,
   Through sedge and duckweed springing.
      With gladsome strain
      We plunge beneath,
      Safe from the rain,
   While the bubbles crack again,
With the watery music of our breath—
      Croak! croak! croak!" *Larken.*

[4] "χορείαν φθέγγεσθαι, a bold expression for *inter saltandum, subliendum, cantare.*" *Dindorf.*

[5] "Das werd' Ich euch benehmen schon!" *Droysen.*

[6] *I take this hint, learn this lesson from you,* i. e. you shall not have this *brekekekesh koash koash* entirely to yourselves. Bacchus here commences a counter-strain." *Mitchell.*

Frogs. Nay, assuredly, we will screech as loud as our throats can compass,[1] throughout the day, brekekekex, coax, coax.

Bac. In this you shall not conquer me.

Frogs. Nor, assuredly, shall you us by any means.[2]

Bac. Never *shall you conquer me*, for I will screech brekekekex, coax, coax, even if I must all the day, till I overcome your coax. [*The frogs suddenly cease croaking.*] I thought I should[3] make you cease from your coax at last.

Cha. Have done! have done! put the boat to land with the oar; step out; pay your fare.

Bac. Take[4] now the two obols. [*Bacchus steps out and Charon pushes off again.*]

Bac. Xanthias![5] where's Xanthias? ho, Xanthias![6]

Xan. (*from a distance*). Hollo![7]

Bac. Come hither. [*Enter Xanthias.*]

Xan. Welcome, master.[8]

Bac. What's the state of things there?[9]

[1] Hom. Il. xi. vs. 462, ἤϋσεν ὅσον κεφαλὴ χάδε φωτός.

[2] "One would scarcely believe, without the express declaration of the Scholiast, that the frogs remained invisible. Yet it appears to have been a constant practice that the chorus, whenever it was engaged otherwise than in its proper character—in the technical language of the theatre a *parachoregema*—should not be visible. A similar case occurs in Thesm. 100 foll." *Droysen.* The present chorus of frogs is not the *proper* chorus, but the *subordinate* chorus. The proper chorus consists of the shades of the initiated.

[3] Comp. Nub. 1301. Soph. Phil. 1083. Hom. Il. xxii. 356. Od. xiii. 293. For this construction of παύω, comp. Eur. Troad. 1025. Bacch. 280. Soph. El. 798.

[4] See note on Equit. 1384.   [5] Comp. note on vs. 40, *supra.*

[6] According to Schlegel, the scene in the beginning is at Thebes, whence it changes to the banks of Acheron, without Bacchus or Xanthias leaving the stage; the hollow of the orchestra then becomes the river he is to cross, he embarks at one end of the Logeum, (which was a platform comprehending the proscenium, and in fact all that part of the theatre occupied by the actors,) rows along the orchestra, and lands on the other end, coasting, as it were, the proscenium, &c.; meantime the scene has again changed, and we are now presented with the infernal regions, and the palace, of Pluto in the centre.

[7] The old stage direction makes this μίμημα τοῦ συριγμοῦ.

[8] "Schön willkommen, Herr!" *Droysen.*

[9] "*Quid, qualia sunt, quæ illic* (in those places where you've been or now are) *habentur?*" *Dindorf.*

          "Was gab's auf deinem wege?" *Droysen.*

XAN. Darkness and mud.

BAC. Then did you see any where there the parricides and the perjured, of whom he spoke to us?

XAN. And did not you?

BAC. Aye, by Neptune, did I; and now, too, I see them. [*Turns and looks towards the audience.*] Come now, what shall we do?

XAN. It is best for us to go forward, for this is the place where he was saying the dreadful wild beasts were.

BAC. How he shall smart for it![1] He was humbugging, so that I might be frightened, as he knew me to be valiant, out of jealousy; for there is nothing so self-conceited as Hercules. But I should wish to fall in with one, and meet with an encounter worthy of my journey.

XAN. Well now,[2] by Jove, I hear some noise.

BAC. (*in a great fright*). Where, where is it?

XAN. From behind.

BAC. Go behind.

XAN. But it is in front.

BAC. Then go in front.

XAN. Well now, by Jove, I see a huge wild beast.

BAC. What sort of a one?

XAN. Dreadful: at any rate it becomes of every shape; at one time an ox, and now a mule, and at another time, again, a most beautiful woman.

BAC. Where is she? come, let me go to her.

XAN. But, again, it is no longer a woman, but now it is a dog.

BAC. Then it is the Empusa.[3]

[1]　　　　　　　　"Oh confound him;
He vapour'd and talk'd at random to deter me
From venturing.—He's amazingly conceited
And jealous of other people is Hercules;
He reckon'd I should rival him, and in fact
(Since I've come here so far) I should rather like
To meet with an adventure in some shape." *Frere*.

[2] "For numerous examples of καὶ μήν, followed by ὅδε, or its cases, when a new personage approaches, see Quart. Rev. ix. p. 354." *Mitchell*.

[3] "The Empusa, who is also spoken of (Eccles. 1066) as covered with bloody pustules, was a spectre sent by Hecate, who came across travellers, assumed all sorts of shapes, loved human flesh,— a Lamia." *Welcker*. Others suppose it to be Hecate herself, from

XAN At any rate her whole face blazes with fire.

BAC. And she has a brazen leg.

XAN. Aye, by Neptune, and the other, be well assured, is that of an ass.[1]

BAC. Whither then can I betake myself?

XAN. And whither I?

BAC. (*runs to the front of the stage*). O priest,[2] preserve me, that I may be your boon companion.

XAN. We shall perish, O king Hercules.

BAC. Don't call me,[3] fellow, I beseech you, or pronounce my[4] name.

XAN. O Bacchus, then.

BAC. This *name* still less than the other.

XAN. Go where you are going.   Hither, hither, master!

BAC. What's the matter?

XAN. Be of good courage: we are altogether prosperous,[5] and we may say, like Hegelochus,[6] "for after the billows again I see a calm."   The Empusa is gone.

a passage in the "Tagenistæ," a lost play of Aristophanes, where they are mentioned in apposition. Harpocration, however, corrects the Scholium, and changes δυστυχοῦσιν στοιχοῦσιν, making it thus one of the ἐνόδια σύμβολα, or omens of the way, before mentioned in these notes.

[1] See, however, Liddell's Lex. in voc.

    "Das andre von Eselsmist."   *Droysen.*

Cf. Athen. xiii. p. 566, F.

[2] This is addressed to the priest of Bacchus himself, who was mounted on a conspicuous seat in the theatre, from his share in the solemnities of the day. The conclusion alludes to the practice of drinking plentifully at the feasts of this god, and in which probably the priests' zeal was shown by their potations. "Among the entertainments given on occasion of the Dionysiac festivals, one of the most splendid was that furnished by the high-priest of the god." *Mitchell.*

[3] Vs. 202, *supra*, οὐ μὴ φλυαρήσεις, ἀλλ' ἀντιβὰς ἐλᾷς. Cf. vs. 462, 524, *infra*. Nub. 505. Eur. Hippol. 601, οὐ μὴ προσοίσεις χεῖρα, μήδ' ἅψει πέπλων. Nub. 296, οὐ μὴ σκώψει μηδὲ ποιήσεις. Cf. Vesp. 394. See Donalds. N. C. 583. Krüger, Gr. Gr. § 53, 7, obs. 5. The following are somewhat different: Soph. Trach. 1183, οὐ Θᾶσσον οἴσεις, μήδ' ἀπιστήσεις ἐμοί; Here μὴ is to be supplied to the first member from the following μήδε. So also Eur. Hippol. 498. Soph. Rex, 637. Ajax, 75. Æsch. Theb. 236. Plat. Sympos. p. 175, A. Hermann, Vig. n. 269. Schneidewin on Soph. Ajax, 75.

[4] Comp. Aves, 1505.   [5] Comp. 1706. Plut. 341.

[6] Hegelochus was an actor, who in performing the part of Orestes

Bac. Swear it.

Xan. By Jove.

Bac. And swear again.

Xan. By Jove.

Bac. Swear.

Xan. By Jove.

Bac. Ah me, miserable! how pale I grew at the sight of her!

Xan. But this fellow in his fright turned redder than I.

Bac. Ah me! Whence have these evils befallen me? Whom of the gods shall I accuse of ruining me? "Æther, little mansion of Jove," or, "Foot of time?" [*A distant sound of flute-music is heard from behind the scenes.*]

Xan. Hollo!

Bac. What's the matter?

Xan. Did you not hear?

Bac. What?

Xan. The breath of flutes.

Bac. I did; and a very mystical[1] odour of torches too breathed upon me. Come, let us crouch down softly and listen. [*Bacchus and Xanthias retire to one side.*]

Cho. of the Initiated (*behind the scenes*). Iacchus, O Iacchus, Iacchus, O Iacchus.[2]

in Euripides' play of that name, when he came to vs. 273, ἐκ κυμάτων γὰρ αὖθις αὖ γαλήν' ὁρῶ, being out of breath and not able to render the elision audible, converted the last words into γαλῆν ὁρῶ, i. e. "I see a weasel," instead of, "I see a calm," which would be small matter of rejoicing to the unfortunate son of Agamemnon, since the sight of those animals was accounted unlucky, and one of them crossing the way was sufficient to put a stop to a public assembly. *Pot. Ant.* vol. i. p. 341. Cf. Göttling, Gr. Accents, § 43. Mehlhorn, Gr. Gr. § 88, note 1. The Scholiast says that Plato (the comedian) ridiculed Hegelochus also, and produces two passages, one from Strattis, the other from Sannyrion, in which this pronunciation of his is noticed. For the construction, see Krüger, Gr. Gr. § 62, 3, obs. 12. Porson, Misc. Crit. p. 210.

[1] "Ein mystisch Rauchwoklüftchen hat mich angehaucht." *Droys.* "*Qualis in mysteriis esse solet.*" *Thiersch.*

[2] This was a name appropriated to Bacchus in the Eleusinian mysteries, and under which he appears in the Orphic hymns as son of Ceres; hence also the hymn sung in his honour had the same title, and this was originally derived from *the shouting* (ἰαχή) of the women. See Eur. Cycl. 69, and Æsch. S. C. Theb. 141. "The following scene is a humorous representation of the concluding cere-

XAN. There we have it,[1] master; the initiated, of whom he was telling us, are dancing some where here. At any rate they are chanting Iacchus, like Diagoras.[2]

BAC. To me also they appear so. Therefore it is best to keep quiet, so that we may know it for certain. [*Enter Chorus.*]

CHO. Iacchus, O highly-honoured, who dwellest here in your abodes, Iacchus, O Iacchus, come to thy pious votaries, to dance through this meadow;[3] shaking the full-fruited chaplet about your head abounding in myrtle,[4] and with bold foot treading a measure among the pious Mystæ, possessing the largest share of the Graces,[5] holy and sacred, the un-restrained, mirth-loving act of worship.

XAN. O venerable, highly-honoured daughter of Ceres, how sweetly the swine's flesh breathed[6] upon me!

mony of the Eleusinian mysteries, on the last day of which the worship of Bacchus, under the invocation of Iacchus, was united with that of Ceres. Iacchus seems to have been the last Avatar of the worship of Bacchus, as Pan was the first. For an account of the character of this worship, and its extreme discrepancy from that of Ceres, see the learned work of Mr. Ouvaroff, as translated by Mr. Christie." *Frere.*

[1] Comp. Ach. 41, 820. Lys. 241. Pax, 289, 516. Aves, 354, 507, and vs. 1342 of this play. Eur. Orest. 804. Helen. 630. Med. 98. Demosth. Mid. p. 583, 19. Plato, Phædr. p. 241, D.; Symp. p. 223, A. Krüger, Gr. Gr. § 51, 7, obs. 11, and § 61, 3, obs. 10. Bern-hardy, W. S. p. 279.

[2] The Scholia mention two persons of this name, the first, Dia-goras of Melos, an impious philosopher, accused of the crime for which Socrates suffered, against whom the Athenians were so in-flamed, that the Areopagites offered a talent to any who would bring his head before them, and two to him who should take him alive. Cic. de Nat. De. i. 23. The other Diagoras was a lyric poet, said to be ever introducing " Iacchus, Iacchus." The latter is meant here. See Bergk, Poet. Lyr. p. 846. The word Ἴακχος is used in three significations: first, the *deity;* secondly, *the sixth day of the mysteries;* thirdly, *the hymn* sung in his praise, as in this passage.

[3] " The Eleusinian dances were of two kinds, public and private. The former were executed in a beautiful meadow, near the well of Callichorus." *St. Croix,* as cited by Mitchell. The locality was the Ῥάριον πεδίον in the meadows of the Cephissus.

[4] Soph. Col. 16, βρύων δάφνης. Cf. Elmsl. ad loc. and Blomf. gloss. Agam. 163.

[5] Plutarch, in M. Ant. 926, mentions that Bacchus had the name Charitodotes, and his altar was united with that of the Graces at Olympia, according to Herodotus as cited by the Schol. Ol. v. 8.

[6] Swine were sacrificed to Ceres and Bacchus on account of the

BAC. Will you not then be quiet, if you *do* get a smell of sausage?

CHO. Brandish in your hand and wake up the flaming torches,[1] Iacchus, O Iacchus, thou Hesperus of the nocturnal orgies. The meadow gleams with flame; the knee of the old men moves swiftly;[2] and they shake off griefs and long cycles of aged years at the sacred act of worship.[3] But do thou, blessed deity, gleaming with thy torch, lead[4] straight forward to the flowery, meadowy plain the youths forming[5] the chorus.

It behoveth him to abstain[6] from ill-omened words, and make way for[7] our choirs, whoever is unskilled in such words, or is not pure in mind, or has neither seen nor celebrated with dances the orgies of the high-born Muses,[8] and has not been

injuries they commit in corn-fields and vineyards. Herodotus describes the Egyptian mode of sacrifice, ii. 47. προσέπνευσε is *impersonal*, and takes the *genitive of the origin of the smell*, (χοιρείων ερεῶν,) as ὄζω in Plut. 1020. Therefore it does not admit of a verbal translation in English. See Bernhardy, W. S. p. 142.

[1] The festival of Ceres was celebrated with torches, in commemoration of those which Ceres was said to have lighted at the fires of Etna in her search for Proserpine.

[2] There is a remarkable instance of this in Euripides, where Cadmus and Tiresias are seized with a desire of dancing, and the former says, "Whither ought we to lead the Chorus? whither set our foot, and shake the hoary head? Lead thou me, Tiresias, thou an old man, me an old man." *Bacch.* 114.

"Und den Greisen wird das Knie leicht." *Droysen.*

[3] "In der heiligen Festlust." *Droysen.*

[4] "Bacchum quasi præsentem faciunt sibi ducem, quia ipsius imago choro præibat." *Thiersch.*

[5] Soph. Aj. 697, ὦ θεῶν χοροποί ἄναξ.

[6] "Keep silence—keep peace—and let all the profane
From our holy solemnity duly refrain;
Whose souls, unenlightened by taste, are obscure;
Whose poetical notions are dark and impure;
    Whose theatrical conscience
    Is sullied by nonsense;
Who never were trained by the mighty Cratinus
In mystical orgies poetic and vinous;
Who delight in buffooning and jests out of season;
Who promote the designs of oppression and treason;
Who foster sedition and strife and debate;
All traitors, in short, to the stage and the state." *Frere*

[7] Virg. Æn. vi. 258, "O procul, O procul este."

[8] Μουσῶν is παρὰ προσδοκίαν for μυστῶν, and Κρατίνου fc · Διονύσου.

initiated in the Bacchanalian orgies of the tongue of Cratinus[1]
the bull-eater; or takes pleasure in buffoonish verses which
excite this *buffoonery* unseasonably;[2] or does not put down
hateful sedition, and is not good-natured to the citizens, but,
eager for his private gain, rouses it and blows it up; or when
the state is tempest-tossed, being a magistrate, receives bribes;
or betrays a garrison or ships, or exports from Ægina[3] forbidden exports, being another Thorycion, a vile collector of
tolls,[4] who used to send across to Epidaurus oar-paddings,
and sail-cloth, and pitch; or who persuades any one to supply
money for the ships of the enemy; or befouls the statues of
Hecate,[5] while he is accompanying with his voice the Cyclic
choruses; or, being an orator, then nibbles off the salaries of
the poets,[6] because he has been lampooned in the national
festivals of Bacchus.   These I order, and again I command
and again[8] the third time I command to make way for the

---

[1] "Cratinus is the great comic writer of the times of Pericles,
whom Aristophanes had in his younger days often and bitterly
assailed. See Equit. 400, 526. He had now been dead for a long
time, but still lived in people's memories as the hero of the comic
art." *Droysen*. The epithet *Taurophagus* belonged originally to
Bacchus, but Aristophanes introduced Cratinus in this place in
allusion to his *Bacchanalian* habits of drunkenness; on which see
Hor. Ep. I. xix. 1. It *may* be derived from the circumstance of a
bull being given to the dithyrambic conqueror. See Simonides,
Ep. 57. For the construction, see Bernhardy, W. S. p. 190, and
comp. Plut. 845.

[2] "Wer gemein witzreissender Worte sich freut, die zur Unzeit
　　　hören sich lassen."　　　　　　　　　　　　　　　　*Droysen.*

[3] Ægina, from its situation, would be chosen as the place for
exportation of illegal stores, and the Thorycion here mentioned
probably derived from his office numerous facilities in that line
of trade.

[4] Nothing further is known of this person than what may be
collected from this passage and from the brief notice of the Scholiast, who says he was a taxiarch during the Peloponnesian war.

[5] "The allusion is to a scandalous anecdote of Cinesias, the
dithyrambic poet. Cf. Eccles. vs. 330." *Droysen*. Compare also
Aves, 1054.

[6] "The person here put to the ban, as diminishing the poetic
honorarium, appears to have been the orator Agyrrhius. See the
Scholiast on Eccles. 102. Schömann de Com. p. 65." *Mitchell.*

[7] See note on Acharn. 1000.

[8] See Hermann, Vig. n. 235.

choruses of the Mystæ;[1] but do ye wake the song, and our night-festivals,[2] which become this festival.

Advance then manfully, each of you, to the flowery bosoms of the meadows, dancing, and joking, and sporting, and scoffing. We have breakfasted[3] sufficiently. Come, advance, and see that you[4] nobly extol the Preserver,[5] singing of her with your voice, who promises to save the country for ever, even if Thorycion be not willing. Come now, praise with divine songs and celebrate the goddess Ceres,[6] the fruit-bringing queen, with another species of hymns.

Ceres, queen[7] of holy orgies, assist us, and preserve thy own chorus, and let me securely throughout the day sport

[1] "Zu entfernen sich gleich vor dem mystischen Chor." *Droysen*.
[2] Cf. Herod. iv. 76. Soph. El. 92. Eur. Troad. 1080. Helen. 1385.
[3] " All have had a belly full
      Of breakfast brave and plentiful." *Frere*.
" Zum Imbiss heut' war sattsam da." *Droysen*.

Against this meaning, notwithstanding Brunck's note, there appears no very strong objection, if it be understood of the sacred banquet. " The expression *may* be metaphorical : *satis superque prælusum est, veniendum tandem ad rem.*" *Thiersch*. A possible reading would be ἠρίστευται, but I know of no authority for the use of it

[4] See note on Lys. vs. 316.
[5] Spanheim quotes Aristotle, (Rhet. iii. 11,) to support his opinion that Demeter is here meant, and mentions an inscription on a coin which attributes the same epithet to that goddess; but at the same time acknowledges that her daughter Persephone shares the title with her on the coins of the Cyzicenes. Droysen and Thiersch suppose it to belong to Minerva, because Ceres is celebrated below, and we know the appellation was bestowed on various deities, in different places, or at different times; whence it afterwards descended to kings, as Ptolemy Soter, &c. Liddell understands it to mean Demeter, Mitchell, Persephone.
[6] For the construction, see Bernhardy, W. S. p. 121, and comp. vs. 458. *infra*. Lys. 469. Ach. 1201.
[7] " Du keuscher Orgien Königin,
      Demeter, sei in Gnaden nah
      Und schirme selber deinen Chor :
      Lass sonder Fehl' den Tag hindurch
          Mich spielen, tanzen, singen,
      Mich sagen auch viel Spassiges,
      Mich sagen auch viel Ernstliches,
      Und, wenn Ich würdig deines Fest's
      Gespielet hab', gespottet hab',
          Den Siegeskranz mich schmücken." *Droysen*.

and dance, and let me say much that is laughable, and much[1] that is serious, and after having sported and jested[2] in a manner worthy of thy festival, let me wear the head-band as conqueror.[3]

But come on now, and invite hither with songs the blooming god, our partner in this choral dance.

O highly-honoured Iacchus, who invented the very sweet melody of the festival, follow along with us hither to the goddess, and show how long a journey[4] you accomplish without toil.

Iacchus, friend of the choral dance, escort me; for thou hast torn in pieces my sandals and my ragged garment for laughter and for economy,[5] and hast devised, so that we may sport and dance without punishment.[6]

Iacchus, friend of the choral dance, escort me; for, having glanced a little aside, I just now spied the bosom of a young and very pretty girl, our playmate, as it peeped out from her vest rent at the side. Iacchus, friend of the choral dance, escort me.

[1] For this *anaphora*, see Krüger, Gr. Gr. § 59, 1, obs. 4. For the infinitives, see Bernhardy, W. S. p. 357, and note on vs. 169, *supra*.

[2] Jests were introduced into the Eleusinia, because Ceres had been amused and made to smile by them during her search for her daughter.

[3] The allusion is to the prize of a triumphant headband ($\tau\alpha\iota\nu\iota\alpha$) given to the victor in the contest of wit and raillery, which took place as the procession was crossing the bridge of the Cephissus. See Mus. Crit. ii. p. 88. Aristophanes, however, means the victory over his fellow comedians.

[4] Eurip. Bacc. 194. Bergler and Thiersch suppose it to allude to the travels of Bacchus in India; Conz and Mitchell, to the procession of Iacchus from the Ceramicus to Eleusis; when, by the aid of the god, whose statue and mystic banners accompanied them, the votaries accomplished a long journey. " *Quam longam viam sine labore conficias.*" *Brunck.*

[5] " That many would wear this sacred robe till it fell into shreds, is natural enough; and it is at this *economical*, as well as reverential practice, and not, as Thiersch supposes, at the *thrifty* expenses of the choregus in the appointments of the drama, that the laugh in the text appears to be directed." *Mitchell.*

[6] " Und schaffst es auch, dass ungestraft
Wir spielen, tanzen, singen." *Droysen.*

XAN. Somehow I am always[1] inclined to follow; and I wish to sport and dance with her.

BAC. And I too.

CHO. Will ye then that we jointly mock at Archedemus?[2] who when seven years old had no clansmen; but now he is a demagogue among the dead above, and is chief[3] of the scoundrelism there. But I hear that Clisthenes[4] among the tombs depillates his[5] hinder parts, and lacerates his cheeks. And stooping forward he mourned for, and bewailed, and called upon Sebinus, who[6] is the Anaphlystian. And they say that Callias[7] too, this son of Hippobinus, was at the sea-

---

[1] Plut. 246, ἐγὼ δὲ τούτου τοῦ τρόπου πώς εἰμ' ἀεί. Eur. Hipp. 662, ἀεὶ γὰρ οὖν πως εἰσὶ κἀκεῖναι κακαί. Cf. Pax, 425. Bast ad Greg. Cor. p. 169. Porson, Med. 288. Elmsley, Med. p. 131.

[2] Archedemus at this time was powerful at Athens, and had the care of Deceleia. Xen. Hell. i. c. 7. The expression ἔφυσε φράτερας is a comic construction formed in jest, after the analogy of φύειν ὀδόντας, &c. The word expected was φραστῆρας, "*teeth that indicate the age;*" but he substitutes φράτερας, to ridicule him as an alien. See Donaldson, New Crat. p. 297. The custom is explained by Potter as follows:—"All fathers were obliged to enrol their sons in the register of their peculiar φρατρία, (or ward,) at which time they made oath that every son so registered was either born to them in lawful matrimony, or lawfully adopted. Notwithstanding which, the φράτερες, or members of that ward, had the liberty of rejecting any person against whom sufficient evidence appeared, concerning which they voted by private suffrage." And again, on this very passage, "Whereby they (the chorus) seem to intimate that he (Archedemus) had fraudulently insinuated himself into the number of the citizens, it being usual for those who were free-born to be registered before that age." Ant. i. 47. Cf. note on Aves, 1669.

[3] Comp. Herod. ix. 77, Λάμπων ὁ Πύθεω, Αἰγινητέων τὰ πρῶτα. See Blomf. gl. Pers. vs. 1. Hermann, Vig. n. 97. Krüger, Gr. Gr. § 43, 4, obs. 14. Bernhardy, W. S. p. 336.

[4] "The well-known effeminate fop Clisthenes had lost his dear friend, and was bewailing him among the graves in the Ceramicus. His friend is nominally called Sebiuus, and an Anaphlystian; his true name is unknown. Yet I believe I may venture to transplant him into the deme of *Cinædus.*" *Droysen.*

[5] See note on Pax, 880, and for the transition from the infinitive to the indicative, see Bernhardy, W. S. p. 388.

[6] See note on Thesm. 544, and Porson, Orest. 1645.

[7] He means Callias the son of *Hipponicus*, who is known to have squandered large sums upon sophists and courtesans. See Aves,

fight, dressed in a woman's lion-skin. [*Bacchus and Xanthias leave their hiding-place and come forward.*]

BAC. Could you peradventure tell us whereabouts in this place Pluto dwells?[1] for we are strangers newly come.

CHO. Do not go away far,[2] nor ask me again and again, but know that you are come to his very door.

BAC. Take them[3] up again, boy!

XAN. What is this thing but "Jove's[4] Corinth" in the baggage?

CHO. Now advance ye in the sacred circle[5] of the goddess, sporting through the flowery grove, who have a participation in the festival dear to the gods.

BAC. I will go with the damsels and women, where they celebrate the night-festival in honour[6] of the goddess, to carry the sacred torch.

283—286. He was Cybele's δᾳδοῦχος: hence Iphicrates nicknamed him μητραγύρτης.

[1] " Ihr könnt vielleicht uns sagen,
  Wo wohnt allhier denn Pluto?
Denn Fremde sind wir, eben hier erst angelangt." *Droysen.*
Cf. *Senectus,* Fragm. x., and see notes on Nub. 1148. Eccles. 1126.

[2] For similar examples of μηδὲν = μὴ, Mitchell cites Elmsley's Medea, vs. 152. Andr. vs. 88. Add Vesp. 1003, 1478. Lys. 431. Plut. 498. Comp. Plut. 962.

[3] Soph. Phil. 674, χωροῖς ἂν εἴσω. Cf. Elect. 1491. Antig. 444. Krüger, Gr. Gr. § 54, 3, obs. 8. Vs. 1467, *infra.* Pax, 958. Equit. 1161. Bernhardy, W. S., p. 410. Hermann on Soph. Antig. 215. Harper's Powers of the Greek Tenses, p. 93. Dorville Char. p. 238. The omission of ἂν converts the expression into a *wish, a modest proposal,* or *suggestion.* Cf. Vesp. 572. Xenoph. Anab. iii. 2, 37. Hermann, Vig. Append. p. 726. Bernhardy, W. S. p. 405. A question naturally arises; if χωροῖς ἂν εἴσω be good Greek to express a softened command, is οὐκ ἂν χωροῖς good Greek to express a softened *prohibition?* This may be safely answered in the affirmative. See Vesp. 726. Bernhardy, W. S. p. 410, and comp. Inscr. El. ap. Rose, p. 29, 30.

[4] Applied to any pestering *reiteration.* The proverb is here used by Xanthias with reference to line 165, where he receives a similar command. Cf. Eccles. 828. Pind. Nem. vii. 155. The origin of the saying is supposed to have been as follows: Once an ambassador came from Corinth to Megara, (their colony,) and threatened them, as rebels from the mother city, with vengeance human and divine, reiterating the words δικαίως ἂν στενάζοι ὁ Διὸς Κόρινθος, εἰ μὴ λάβοι δίκην, whereupon the Megarians, in a rage, took and beat him, crying παῖε, παῖε τὸν Διὸς Κόρινθον. Cf. Eccles. 828.

[5] i. e. the circular dance. See Thesm. 954.

[6] See Krüger, Gr. Gr. § 48, 4, obs. 4. Cf. Lys. 1277 Thesm. 104.

Cho. Let us proceed to the flowery meadows abounding in roses, sporting in our manner, the most beautiful in the dance,[1] which[2] the blessed Fates institute. For to us alone, as many as have been initiated, and conducted ourselves in a pious manner towards the foreigners and the citizens, are the sun and the light joyous.[3]

Bac. Come now, in what way shall I knock at the door? in what?[4] How then do the people of the country here knock?

Xan. Don't loiter,[5] but try the door, as you have your dress and your spirit after the manner of Hercules.

Bac. (*knocking at the door*). Boy! boy!

Æacus (*from within*). Who's there?[6]

Bac. Hercules the brave. [*Æacus comes out.*]

Æac. O you impure, and shameless, and audacious fellow, and abominable, and all-abominable, and most abominable! who dragged out our dog Cerberus,[7] which I had the care of, and darted away holding him by the throat, and ran clear off with him. But now you are held by the middle; such a black-hearted rock of Styx, and blood-dripping cliff of Acheron, environ you, and the roaming dogs[8] of Cocytus, and the hundred-headed Echidna,[9] which shall rend in sunder your viscera; and a Tartessian[10] serpent shall fasten on your lungs,

The allusion is to the night-festival which terminated the sixth and great day of the Eleusinian mysteries.

[1] " *Quocum pulchræ choreæ conjunctæ esse solent.*" *Thiersch.*

[2] " *Quam* (choream) *felici fato instituimus.*" *Dindorf.*

[3] See note on Aves, 1066.   [4] See note on Thesm. 772.

[5] See note on vs. 298, *supra.*

[6] In one of Lucian's dialogues, Menippus says to Æacus, "I know this too of thee, thou art porter." The salutation with which he receives Bacchus, under the idea of his being Hercules, is very like that bestowed by Mercury on Trygæus, Pax, 182.

[7] See notes on Nub. 366. Plut. 69.

[8] The *Furies.* Cf. Æsch. Eum. 237. Cho. 911, 1041.

[9] The Echidna of the poets was commonly represented as a beautiful woman to the waist, and thence downwards a serpent. Cf. Eur. Herc. F. 1191.

[10] Tartessus was probably considered (as Sicily and all countries with which the Greeks had least acquaintance) the resort of monsters. The poets supposed it the place wherein Phœbus unharnessed his wearied steeds at sunset, and also the habitation of Geryon. It is better known by its modern name, Cadiz. Cf. Herod. iv. 192.

while Tithrasian[1] Gorgons shall tear in pieces your kidneys, together with your entrails, stained with blood ; to fetch which I will set in motion a swift foot.[2]   [*Exit Æacus, and Bacchus falls down in a fright.*]

XAN. Hollo you ! what have you done?

BAC. Eased myself : invoke the god.[3]

XAN. O you ridiculous fellow ! will you not then get up quickly, before some stranger sees you ?

BAC. But I am fainting.   Come, bring a sponge to put to my heart.

XAN. There, take it !   [*Offers him a sponge.*]

BAC. Put it to it.

XAN. Where is it ?   [*Bacchus presents his posteriors to him.*]   Oh ye golden[4] gods ! is it there you keep your heart ?

BAC. Why, it crept down through fright into the bottom of my belly.[5]

XAN. O thou most cowardly of gods and men !

BAC. I? how am I cowardly,[6] who asked you for a sponge ? No other man then would have done it.[7]

XAN. What then[8] *would he have done?*

BAC. He would have lain sniftering, if he was a coward ; but I got up, and moreover wiped myself clean.

---

[1] Tithras was a deme of the tribe Ægeïs, and derived its name from Tithras, son of Pandion.   The females of this district appear to have borne the character of vixens.

[2] "The Scholiast informs us, that the horrific part of Æacus' speech is an imitation of an attempt at the sublime in Euripides' tragedy of *Theseus*, which is now lost; but which probably related to his descent to the infernal regions." *Frere.*   See Krüger, Gr. Gr. § 68, 42, obs. 2.   Bernhardy, W. S. p. 252.

[3] A parody on the form observed in making libation.   As soon as the libation was poured, they cried, κάλει θεόν.   Mitchell therefore translates, " *The libation has been made : invoke the god.*"

[4] According to Thiersch, merely said in conformity with that opinion, which considered every thing amongst the gods as *golden* Thus χρυσῆ Ἀφροδίτη, Hom. Il. iii. 64.

[5] Ὀλκάδες, Fragm. vi., διαλείχοντά μου τὸν κάτω σπατάγγην.   Cf Vesp. 713.

[6] " A coward !   Did not I show my presence of mind, And call for a sponge and water in a moment?" *Frere.* See note on Plut. 1046.

[7] " Das hätte so leicht kein andrer Mann gethan." *Droysen* See notes on vs. 866, *infra.* Vesp. 983.

[8] See note on Lys. 193.

XAN. Bravely done,[1] by Neptune!

BAC. By Jove, I think so. But did you not fear the sound of his words and his threats?

XAN. No, by Jove! I did not even give them a thought.

BAC. Come then, since you are so spirited and brave, do you take this club and the lion's skin and become me, if[2] you are so fearless of heart; and I will be your baggage-carrier in turn.

XAN. Give them now quickly, for I must[3] comply with you; and look at the Hercules-Xanthias, if I shall be a coward, and with a spirit like you. [*Dresses himself in the lion's skin.*]

BAC. No, by Jove, but truly the worthless slave of Melite.[4] Come then, let me take up[5] this baggage. [*Enter a maid-servant of Proserpine.*]

SERVANT. O dearest Hercules,[6] have you come? Come in hither; for the goddess, when she heard that you[7] were come, immediately began baking loaves, boiled[8] two or three pots of soup of bruised *peas*, broiled a whole ox, baked cheese-cakes and rolls. But do come in.

[1] See Mus. Crit. ii. p. 291.   [2] See note on Thesm 789.

[3] See note on Nub. 232. Bernhardy, W. S. p. 352.

[4] Melite was a deme of Attica, so called from the nymph of that name, with whom Hercules was in love. There was a temple there to Hercules Averter of ill, (Ἀλεξίκακος,) which name Bacchus exchanges παρ' ὑπόνοιαν for *Mastigias*. In the village of Melite, Hercules was initiated in the lesser mysteries. Cf. Müller's Dorians, i. p. 445. "A sarcasm is also implied against Callias, who was likewise of Melite, and used a lion-skin as his military dress." *Frere.* See note on Aves, 13.

[5] See note on Lys. 864.

[6] The transformation of master into servant is no sooner effected, than the servant of Proserpine comes out and addresses Xanthias as Hercules, endeavouring to tempt him in by the description of a feast; wherein it will be observed the peculiar taste of the son of Alcmena is consulted by the introduction of the ἔτνος, while his voracity is more than hinted at by the quantity of viands prepared.

[7] "Only in this case did the Attic tone of conversation allow an *enclitic* to stand at the commencement of a member of a sentence, which was closely connected with the preceding, and imparted to the pronoun a moderate emphasis: Nicomachus, (ap. Athen. vii. p. 291, B.,) ὧν εἰδέναι σοι κρεῖττον ἦν μοι πρὶν λαλεῖν. Plat. Parm. p. 135, D., εἰ δὲ μή σε (not σὲ) διαφεύξεται ἡ ἀλήθεια, and in the inaccuate expression, παῦσαί, με μὴ κάκιζε, in the ethical speech in Eur. Iph. A. 1436." *Bernhardy.*

[8] See note on Aves, 365, and Bernhardy W S p. 110.

Xan. No, I thank you.[1]

Ser. By Apollo, I will not suffer you to go[2] away! for[3] in truth she has been boiling poultry,[4] and toasting[5] sweetmeats, and mixing up most delicious wine. But come in along with me.

Xan. No, I thank you.

Ser. You are talking nonsense: I will not let you go; for there is a[6] very pretty flute-girl too within, and two or three dancing-girls besides.[7]

Xan. How say you? dancing girls?

Ser. Youngish,[8] and newly depillated. But do come in, for the cook was just going to take up the slices of salt fish, and the table was being carried in.

Xan. Go then, first of all tell the dancing-girls who are within, that ourself is coming in. [*Addressing Bacchus.*] Boy,[9] follow this way with the baggage. [*Exit maid-servant.*]

Bac. Hollo you! stop! you are not for taking it in earnest, surely,[10] because I dressed you up as Hercules in jest? Don't be trifling, Xanthias, but take up the baggage again and carry them.

Xan. What's the matter? Surely you don't intend to take away from me what you gave me yourself?

Bac. Not soon, but instantly[11] I'll do it. Lay down the skin!

[1] A civil way of declining an invitation or gift, corresponding to the "benigne" of Horace, (Epist. I. vii. vss. 16, 62,) and the "Ich danke" of the Germans. So πάνυ καλῶς, vs. 512. See Bekker's Anecdot. i. p. 49. Bentley on Terence, Heaut. iii. 2, 7.

[2] Lys. 1019, οὔ σε περιόψομαι γυμνὸν ὄντα. Cf. vs. 1476, *infra*. Thesm. 699. Nub. 124. Vesp. 439. Eccles. 370, 1055, 1068. Pax, 10. Krüger, Gr. Gr. § 56, 6, obs. 2. Mus. Crit. i. p. 187.

[3] "Cf. Porson et Elmsley ad Med. 675, 660." *Mitchell.* See note on Ach. 933.

[4] Nub. 339, κρέα τ' ὀρνίθεια κιχηλᾶν.

[5] Eccles. 844, φρύγεται τραγήματα.

[6] See notes on Equit. 1128, 400. Cf. also Aves, 1292.

[7] See Krüger, Gr. Gr. § 50, 4, 11, and note on vs. 1164, *infra*.

[8] Pherecrates (ap. Athen. vi. p. 269), κόραι δ' ἀρτίως ἡβυλλιῶσαι καὶ τὰ ῥόδα κεκαρμέναι.

[9] See note on vs. 40, *supra*.

[10] Comp. Lys. 354. Nub. 1260. Pax, 1211. Eccles. 330. Soph Phil. 1233. For the next line, see note on vs. 299, *supra*.

[11] "Not soon, but instantly.—
Down with the skin." *Dunster.*

XAN. I call you to witness this,[1] and commit *my cause* to the gods.

BAC. What[2] gods? Is it not silly and vain, that you should expect that, slave and mortal as you are, you shall be the son of Alcmena?

XAN. (*sulkily*). Never mind ;—'tis well ;—take them.[3] For you will perhaps want me some time, please God.[4]

CHO. This is[5] agreeably to the character of a man who possesses prudence and understanding, and who has sailed about much, always to roll himself over to the snug side[6] *of the ship*, rather than to stand like[7] a painted image, having assumed one appearance : whereas, to turn oneself to the easier side is agreeably to the character of a clever man and a Theramenes[8] by nature.

---

[1] Comp. Nub. 1297. Plut. 932. Vesp. 1436. Without $\tau a \bar{v} \tau a$, Nub. 1223. Ach. 926. Pax, 1119. Aves, 1031.

[2] See note on Lys. 1178.

[3] Comp. vs. 270, *supra*. Equit. 51, 949, 1187, 1384. Aves, 936. Lys. 533.

[4] See note on Plut. 345.

[5] Comp. vs. 540, *infra*. Eur. Bacch. 641. Helen. 958. Soph. Aj. 319. Krüger, Gr. Gr. § 68, 37, obs. 1. Bernhardy, W. S. p. 264, 292.

[6] " Dass er sich immer klüglich hinrollt
Nach dem nicht gefährdeten Schiffsbord,
Statt wie eine Statue stets
Dazustehn in einer Stellung."   *Droysen.*

All the commentators follow the Scholiast in his application of this passage to sailors, who run to that side of the ship which, in a storm, is kept uppermost by the waves. It is not unlikely, therefore, that the mention of the painted figures is only a continuation of the same allusion, and relates to the signs borne by vessels on their prows and sterns, chiefly the latter, as Ovid mentions,—" Accipit et pictos puppis adunca Deos." See Liddell's Lex. in voc. $\tau o \hat{i} \chi o \varsigma$.

[7] See note on Plut. 314.

[8] Theramenes was son of Hagnon, and a general at Athens, in the time of the comedian. His political character was so proverbially fickle and changeable, that he got the nickname of $\kappa \acute{o}$-$\theta o \rho v o \varsigma$, i. e. a shoe that would serve either foot. See Mus. Crit. ii p. 212. Thucydides bears testimony both to his talents and his changeable temper. (Thuc. viii. 68, 89.) On the fall of Athens, he became one of the thirty tyrants, but was far from participating in their cruelties. His humanity rendered him a dangerous inmate at their councils, and being accused by his colleague Critias, he was condemned, and ordered to drink hemlock ; which sentence, and its execution, he bore with a constancy quite foreign to his former character.

BAC. Why, would it not have been ridiculous, if Xanthias, slave as he is, wallowed on Milesian[1] bed-clothes, and paid court to a dancing-girl, and then asked for a chamber-pot;[2] while I looked at him and employed myself otherwise, and he, inasmuch as he is a knave himself, saw it, and then struck me with his fist and knocked out my front row of teeth out of my jaw. [*Enter two female innkeepers.*]

1ST INNK. Plathane,[3] Plathane, come hither; this is the villain that came into our inn one day, and eat up sixteen of our loaves.

2ND INNK. Yes, by Jove, that's the very man certainly.[4]

XAN. (*aside*). Mischief has come for somebody.[5]

1ST INNK. And in addition to this too, twenty pieces of boiled meat, at half an obol apiece.[6]

XAN. (*aside*). Somebody will suffer punishment.

1ST INNK. And that vast quantity[7] of garlic.

BAC. (*with great dignity*). You are talking foolishly, woman, and you don't know what you say.

1ST INNK. Then did you expect I should not know you again, because you had buskins[8] on? What then?[9] I have not yet mentioned the vast quantity of dried fish.

[1] The wool of Miletus was much celebrated among the ancients, both for its fineness and the dyes with which it was tinged. Thus Virgil, Geor. iii. 306 :—

"——————— Quamvis Milesia magno
Vellera mutantur, Tyrios incocta rubores."

See also Lysist. 729, and Cic. *Verres*, i. 34.

[2] Pamphilus, (ap. Athen. i. p. 4, D.,) ἀμίδα δότω τις· ἢ πλακοῦντά τις δότω. Eupolis, (ib. p. 17, C.,) τίς εἶπεν ἀμίδα πάμπρωτος μεταξὺ πίνων;

[3] "As Bacchus was before made answerable for the offence which Hercules had committed in seizing Cerberus, he is now accused of other misdemeanours which Hercules (agreeably to the character of voracity and violence attributed to him by the comic writers) might be supposed to have committed in the course of the same expedition." *Frere.*

[4] "Aye, sure enough, that's he, the very man." *Frere.*

[5] "The meaning is not, *alicui malum. imminet*, but *nobis* or *mihi imminet*. Xanthias might have inferred this from the looks and voices of the women." *Dindorf.* Soph. Ajax, 1138, τοῦτ' εἰς ἀνίαι τοῦπος ἔρχεταί τινι. Æsch. Cho. 52, φοβεῖταί τις. Cf. Theb. 398 Krüger, Gr. Gr. § 51, 16, obs. 8. Hermann, Vig. n. 114.

[6] See Bernhardy, W. S. p. 234.   [7] Cf. Soph. Elect. 564.

[8] "Buskins were peculiar to Bacchus: the woman mistaking him for Hercules, considers them as an attempt at disguise." *Frere.*

[9] "τί δαὶ in Arist. Ran. 558, may indeed be translated *quid porro*)

2ND INNK. No, by Jove, nor the fresh cheese, you rogue,[1] which this fellow devoured together with[2] the cheese-baskets. And then, when I demanded the money, he looked sour at me, and began to bellow.

XAN. His conduct exactly! this is[3] his way every where.

2ND INNK. And he drew his sword too, pretending[4] to be mad.

1ST INNK. Yes, by Jupiter, unhappy woman!

2ND INNK. And we two, I ween, through fear, immediately sprang up into the upper story, while he rushed out and went off with the rush-mats.

XAN. This also is his way of acting. But you ought to do something.

1ST INNK. (*to the stage attendants*). Go now, call Cleon my patron!

2ND INNK. And you Hyperbolus[5] for me, if you meet with him, that we may destroy him.

but still the idea of *surprise* remains, as when one mentions something greater than the preceding : *was denn?" Hermann.*

[1] "Addressed to her female companion." *Mitchell.* Cf. Lys. 910, 914. Eccles. 124, 242. Thesm. 644.

[2] See Bernhardy, W. S. p. 99.

[3] "Just like him! that's the way wherever he goes." *Frere.* "Xanthias endeavours to instigate the two women against his master." *Mitchell.*

[4] See note on Plut. 837.

[5] The comedian's vengeance pursues Cleon, his great enemy, to the very recesses of Tartarus, where he gives him both clients and company worthy of him. Hyperbolus was an Athenian, banished from his country on account of the peculiar infamy of his character. He had retired to Samos, where the friends of the democratic party rose and slew him. Thuc. vii. 73. He is mentioned in terms of strong reprobation in Equit. 1304, 1363, where Mr. Mitchell has a note, giving an account of the cause of his banishment. It appears he had endeavoured to effect a quarrel between Nicias and Alcibiades, and bring on the latter the punishment of ostracism. They united their influence, and declared him a person dangerous to the state. The people were surprised, being well acquainted with the meanness of his character; they humoured the jest, however, and in his banishment by ostracism, the better citizens gained the double advantage of being at once rid of him, and shortly after, of that punishment itself, which had come into disrepute from being exercised on such a villain. See Pierson on Mœr. p. 2, and for ἵνα, see Harper's Powers of the Greek Tenses, p 125. Krüger Gr. Gr. § 54, 8, obs. 4, § 69, 31.

1st Innk. O abominable throat! how I should like[1] to smash your grinders with a stone, with which you devoured my wares.[2]

2nd Innk. And I should like to cast you into the pit.

1st Innk. And I should like to take a sickle and cut out your gullet, with which you swallowed down my tripe.[3] But I will go to fetch[4] Cleon, who shall summon him to-day, and wind these out[5] of him. [*Exeunt female innkeepers.*]

Bac. May I die most miserably, if I don't love Xanthias!

Xan. I know, I know your[6] purpose: have done, have done with your talk! I will not become[7] Hercules.

Bac. By no means *say*[8] *so*, my dear little Xanthias.

Xan. Why, how could I become the son of Alcmena, "who am at the same time[9] a slave and a mortal?"

Bac. I know, I know that you are angry, and that you act so justly; and even if you were to beat me,[10] I could not gain-say you. But if ever I take them away from[11] you henceforth, may I myself perish most miserably, root and branch, my wife, my children, and the blear-eyed Archedemus.[12]

[1] " How I should like to strike those ugly teeth out
With a good big stone, you ravenous greedy villain!
You gormandizing villain!—that I should,—
Yes, that I should,—your wicked ugly fangs
That have eaten up my substance, and devour'd me.'' *Frere.*

[2] Comp. Vesp. 1398, and note on Pax, 880.

[3] Shakspeare, Hen. IV. part ii. act ii. sc. 1, " He hath eaten me out of house and home; he hath put all my substance into that fat belly of his :—but I will have some of it out again, or I'll ride thee o' nights, like the mare."

[4] See Krüger, Gr. Gr. § 68, 42, obs. 2. She retires in order to change her dress, as she will presently have to appear again as Æacus.

[5] For the construction, see Bernhardy, W. S. p. 146, 147.

[6] Cf. Plut. 1080.

[7] Comp. Acharn. 403. Krüger, Gr. Gr. § 54, 3, obs. 7. Hermann, Vig. n. 283.

[8] See Krüger, Gr. Gr. § 62, 3, obs. 12.

[9] Xanthias retorts upon his master in his own words. See vs. 513.

[10] " Stallbaum observes (Plat. Phileb. § 137) that κάν εἰ is always joined with an indicative or an optative, never with a subjunctive. Phædon, p. 71, B. Lysid. p. 209, E. Rep. ii. p. 376, A. Theag. p. 130, D. Phileb. p. 58, E. Demosth. p. 530, 21." *Mitchell.* Comp. Viger, p. 527.

[11] Comp. Thuc. viii. 29. Demosth. p. 50, 42. Krüger, Gr. Gr. § 47, 2, obs. 3.

[12] The preceding formula of imprecation was the most solemn of

XAN. I accept the oath,[1] and take *the dress* on these terms. [*Xanthias reassumes the dress of Hercules.*]

CHO. (*to Xanthias*). Now it is your business, since you have taken the garb which you wore at first, to make yourself young again, and again to look terror, mindful of the god to whom you liken yourself: but if you shall be detected talking nonsense, or shall utter[2] any thing cowardly, it is necessary that you take up the baggage again.

XAN. You advise me not amiss, my friends; but I happen myself also to be just reflecting on these matters. That, however, if there be any good to be got, he will endeavour to take these away from me again, I well know.[3] But nevertheless I will show myself brave in spirit, and looking sour.[4] And it seems to be needful, for now I hear a noise of the door. [*Re-enter Æacus attended by three myrmidons.*]

ÆAC. Quickly bind this dog-stealer, that he may suffer punishment! Make haste!

BAC. (*aside*). "Mischief has come[5] for somebody."

XAN. (*to Æacus*). Go to the devil! Don't approach me![6]

ÆAC. Well! you'll fight, will you?[7] Ditylas, and Sce-

---

all in use among the Athenians, as the punishment imprecated (see Plutus, vs. 1103) was the most awful. See Bernhardy, p. 290. Archedemus has been before mentioned in terms of ridicule, vs. 417, and the Scholiast supposes him to be here introduced, from the disorder of his eyes having originated in his intemperate fondness for wine. But see vs. 192, *supra*.

[1] Mitchell cites Æsch. Eum. 407. Ag. 1643. Eur. Helen. 847. Plat. Leg. xii. p. 949, B.

[2] Cf. Vesp. 1289. Eur. Ion, 972. Æsch. Ag. 1653. Ch. 41. Eum. 794.

[3] See the passages cited in the note on Lys. 154.

[4] This method of indicating qualities is common to our author: in the Wasps (vs. 455) βλεπόντων κάρδαμα. In the Plutus, 328, βλέπειν Ἄρη. In the Knights, vs. 631, κάβλεψε νᾶπυ. The *origanum* is mentioned by Theophrastus, in his Hist. of Plants, i. 19, as yielding a sour juice. See also Plin. N. H. xx. 67. "Auszusehen wie Sauerkraut." *Droysen.*

[5] Bacchus retorts upon Xanthias in Xanthias' own words. See vs. 552.

[6] The present tense of εἶμι = *a future* in Attic Greek; hence it admits of the same construction as a future. See Elmsley, Med. 1120. Krüger, Gr. Gr. § 53, 7, obs. 5. Bernhardy, W. S. p. 403.

[7] "Oh, hoh! do you mean to fight for it?" *Frere.*

blyas, and Pardocas,[1] come hither and fight with this fellow !
[*A scuffle ensues, in which Xanthias makes the officers keep
their distance.*]

BAC. (*vexed at Xanthias' success*). Is not this[2] shameful
then, that this fellow should make an assault, who steals other
people's property besides ?

XAN. (*ironically*). Nay, but[3] monstrous.

ÆAC. Aye, indeed, 'tis shocking and shameful.

XAN. Well now, by Jupiter, I am willing to die, if I ever
came hither, or stole any of your property, even of a hair's
value. Come, I'll do a very noble thing for you : take and
torture this slave of mine ; and if ever you find me out guilty,
lead me away and put me to death.

ÆAC. Why, how am I to torture him ?[4]

XAN. In every way : by tying him to a ladder,[5] by sus-
pending him, by scourging[6] him with a whip, by cudgelling

---

[1] See note on vs. 40. "The persons employed in the forcible
and personal execution of the law, as arrests &c., in Athens, were
foreign slaves, Scytbians, purchased for that purpose by the state.
These barbarous names are supposed to indicate persons of this
description." *Frere.*

[2] "Well, is not this quite monstrous and outrageous,
  To steal the dog, and then to make an assault,
  In justification of it?" *Frere.*

I have noticed that tbe Greeks *prefer* to place the subject of the infinitive *after* the infinitive, and the object of tbe infinitive before it.
See vss. 530, 596. Plut. 401. Vesp. 1368. Aves, 1280. Theoc. iii.
21. Cf. Bernhardy, W. S. p. 460. Very often the right understanding of the wbole sentence depends upon this principle. See Plato,
Crit. p. 48, E. ; Thuc. viii. 66, where, moreover, the omission of the
article as well shows that ἐπιβουλεύσαντα is the *subject*. For this ad-
verbial use of πρὸς, see Krüger, Gr. Gr. § 68, 2, obs. 2.

[3] See note on Thesm. vs. 646.

[4] Mr. Frere is mistaken in supposing this to be said in the softened, obliging tone of one who consults another's pleasure. See
Porson, Phœn. 1373. Hermann, Alc. 498.

[5] This passage is quoted by Arcbbishop Potter in his Antiq. vol.
i. p. 60 ; to whicb punishments he adds grinding at the mill, and
burning marks on their flesh. Commentators express surprise at
the modes of torture here allowed, and to which the masters were
compelled, wben summoned by tbeir adversaries, to surrender their
domestics, when a law was existing, whereby the person who killed
a slave became liable to the same penalty as the murderer of a free
citizen.

[6] The change of tense is worthy of notice. The two first are

him, by racking[1] him, and further, by pouring vinegar into his nostrils, by heaping bricks upon him,[2] and every other way; only don't beat him with leek or young onion.[3]

ÆAC. Your proposition is just; and if I maim your slave at all by beating him, the money shall be deposited.[4]

XAN. Nay,[5] nought of that; so lead him away and torture him, as I said.

ÆAC. Nay, rather, here, in order that he may speak before your face:[6] do you [*to Bacchus*] put down the baggage quickly, and see that you tell us no lies here.

BAC. I advise somebody not to torture me, who am an immortal; otherwise, blame yourself.[7]

ÆAC. What do you say?

BAC. I assert that I am an immortal,[8] Bacchus, son of Jove, but that this fellow is a slave.

ÆAC. (*to Xanthias*). Hear you this?

single acts, the others *continued* acts. The ὑστριχίς has been mentioned in Pax, 746.

[1] Comp. Plut. 875. Lys. 846.

[2] "Mit Ziegeln den Bauch bepacken." *Droysen.*

[3] That is, "torture him every way but in sport;" for with these plants, says the Scholiast, the Athenian boys were wont to beat each other in play. Cf. Theocr. vii. 105—108.

[4] "Ein billiger Vorschlag! sollt' Ich vielleicht den Burschen dir
    Zum Krüppel schlagen, so liegt das Ersatzgeld schon bereit."
                                                        Droysen.

   "A fair proposal: but in striking him
    If chance we maim him, damages will lie." *Dunster.*

"Demosthenes illustrates this in his speech against Pantænetus, (vol. ii. p. 978, Reisk.) *Demanding the slave, whom he affirms to be privy to this, for torture; and, should it be true, I myself was to owe him the damages unvalued; but, if false, the inquisitor Mnesicles was to be umpire of the value of the slave.*" *Spanheim.*

[5] See Krüger, Gr. Gr. § 48, 6, obs. 2, § 62, 3, obs. 12. Bernhardy, W. S. p. 353.

[6] Mitchell compares Æsch. Choeph. 566. Eur. Rhes. 422. Orest. 282. Androm. 1066. Soph. Antig. 307, 760. Add Terence, Eun. act. iv. sc. vii. vs. 24. For this use of ὅπως, see note on Lys. 316.

[7] "I'll tell you what:
    I'd advise people not to torture me;
    I give you notice—I'm a deity.
    So mind now—you'll have nobody to blame
    But your own self." *Frere.*

For τινί, see note on vs. 552, *supra.*

[8] Cf. vss. 635, 742, 831, *infra*, and Class. Mus. No. xxv. p. 230

Xan. Yes, I did. And so much the more too is he deserving of a whipping; for if he be a god he will not feel it.

Bac. Why then, since you also say you are a god, are you
not also beaten with the same number of blows as I?[1]

Xan. The proposition is just; and which ever of us [*to
Æacus*] you see crying first, or caring at all because he is
beaten, consider him to be no god.

Æac. It must be that you are a noble fellow, for you come
to fair terms.[2] Now strip.

Xan. How then will you test us fairly?

Æac. Easily, blow for blow each party.[3]

Xan. You say well.

Æac. Well!

Xan. Observe then if you see me flinching. [*Puts himself
in an attitude for receiving the blows.*]

Æac. (*striking him*). Now I have struck you.

Xan. No, by Jove!

Æac. Neither do you seem[4] to me *to have felt it.* But I
will go to this fellow and strike him. [*Strikes Bacchus.*]

Bac. (*pretending not to feel it*). When?

Æac. Assuredly I struck you.[5]

Bac. Why, how then did I not sneeze?

Æac. I know not: but I will try this fellow again.

Xan. Will[6] you not then make haste? [*Æacus strikes
him.*] Oh dear!

[1] " Warum denn, so auch du behauptest Gott zu sein,
Bekommst du nicht dieselben Prügel auch wie Ich?" *Droysen.*

[2] " Das muss Ich sagen, du bist ein ganzer Ehrenmann;
Denn du giebst der Billigkeit ihr Recht." *Droysen.*

[3] " Oh, easily enough—
Conveniently enough—a lash apiece,
Each in your turn; you can have 'em one by one." *Frere.*
" Then with the substantive repeated, *by turns, alternately.* So often
ἡμέρα παρ' ἡμέραν, *alternis diebus;* and others formed after the same
analogy. πληγὴν παρὰ πληγὴν, Arist. Ran. 643. λόγον παρὰ λόγον,
Plato, Rep. p. 348, A. ἓν παρ' ἓν, *vicissim,* Plut. Consol. ad Apoll.
p. 106." *Bernhardy.* Cf. Lobeck, Ajax, p. 294. Schäfer, Bos, p. 139.

[4] See note on Plut. 409.

[5] " Æacus perseveres and applies his discipline alternately to
Bacchus and Xanthias, and extorts from them various involuntary
exclamations of pain, which they immediately account for, and
justify in some ridiculous way." *Frere.*

[6] See Krüger, Gr. Gr. § 53, 7, obs. 4.

Æac. What's the meaning of "oh dear?" were you in pain?

Xan. No, by Jove, but I thought *only* when the festival of Hercules among the Diomeians takes place.[1]

Æac. The pious man![2] I must go this way again. [*Strikes Bacchus.*]

Bac. Oh! oh!

Æac. What's the matter?

Bac. I see horsemen.

Æac. Why then do you weep?

Bac. I smell onions.

Æac. For you don't care at all about it.

Bac. No care have I.

Æac. Then I must go to this fellow again. [*Strikes Xanthias.*]

Xan. Ah me!

Æac. What's the matter?

Xan. (*holding up his foot*). Take out the thorn.

Æac. (*much perplexed*). What's this affair? I must gc this way again. [*Strikes Bacchus.*]

Bac. O Apollo![3]——"who, I ween, inhabitest Delos or Pytho."

Xan. (*to Æacus*). He was pained. Did you not hear him?

Bac. Not I; for I was recollecting[4] an iambic verse of Hipponax.

[1] Diomeia was a deme of the tribe Ægeis, so called from Diomus, son of Colyttus, the friend of Hercules, who had a temple there, and was worshipped there in great splendour. The Diomeians are reproved in the Acharnians for their boastful temper; and, in a note on that passage, Mr. Mitchell observes, that "The Diomeian tribe did not assume a more heroic character in times posterior to Aristophanes; for it was among them that the sixty wits, (γελωτοποιοί,) who registered the squibs, the sarcasms, the follies, and eccentric characters of Athens, held their sittings, which even the tumult of the Macedonian war did not disturb."

[2] See Krüger, Gr. Gr. § 45, 2, obs. 4.

[3] "O Apollo—nemlich 'der du Pytho und Delos schirmst.'" *Droy.* To this the Scholiast adds two other lines,—

Ἢ Νάξον ἢ Μίλητον ἢ θείην Κλάρον

Ἵκου καθ' ἱέρ', ἢ Σκύθας ἀφίξεαι,—

and observes, that in his pain and confusion, Bacchus ascribes them to the wrong author, Ananius having composed them. Bergk, however, classes them amongst the writings of Hipponax. See his Poet. Lyr. p. 525. "See Fabric. Bibl. Gr. ii. 104." *Mitchell.*

[4] See Bernhardy, W. S. p. 176.

XAN. (*to Æacus*). You effect nothing. Come, smite his flanks.

ÆAC. No, by Jove, *no more I do*. [*To Bacchus.*] But now present your belly.

BAC. O Neptune !——

XAN. Some one was pained.[1]

BAC. ——"who rulest the Ægean[2] headland, or, in the depths, the azure sea."

ÆAC. By Ceres, I certainly am not able to discover as yet which of you is the god. But go in; for my master himself and Proserpine will distinguish you, inasmuch as they also are gods.

BAC. You say rightly; but I should have wished that you had done this before I received the blows. [*Exeunt Bacchus, Xanthias, and Æacus.*]

CHO. Muse[3] of the sacred chorus, advance, and come for the enjoyment[4] of our song, about to see the vast multitude of people, where innumerable philosophic arts[5] are sitting, more ambitious than Cleophon,[6] on whose incessantly chattering lips a Thracian swallow[7] roars dreadfully, seated on a foreign leaf;

---

[1] See note on vs. 552.

[2] The headland alluded to is Sunium in Attica, whence in the Knights, vs. 560, Neptune is called Suniaratus. According to the Scholiast, it is a quotation from the *Laocoon* of Sophocles, Fragm. cccxli.

[3] "Muse of the sacred choirs, advance,
Delighting in our song and dance;
Survey the peopled crowds, where sit
Innumerable tribes of wit." *Wheelwright.*

[4] See Lidd. Lex. in voc. τέρψις.

[5] Comp. Antiphanes ap. Stob. S. 68, 37, and see note on vs 1017, *infra*.

[6] There were several of this name at Athens, of whom the most conspicuous was the well-known lyre-maker, a public character in the time of Erasinides and his colleagues, and whom Xenophon relates (Hell. i. 7) to have fallen in a popular tumult soon after the murder of those generals. The Scholiast says, that Plato the comedian wrote a drama on this Cleophon, in which he accuses him of foreign parentage. It is supposed that Euripides alludes to him in the Orestes, 901. See Thesm. 805, and vs. 1532, *infra*.

[7] It was common for the Greeks to compare the speech of barbarians to the notes of birds. Thus Herodotus, speaking of the oracle at Dodona. See note on vs. 93, *supra*.

"Dem auf geschwätziger Lippe
Widerlich zwitschert und schwirrt

and it whimpers a tearful nightingale's dirge, that he must perish, even if the votes be equal.[1]

It is fitting that the sacred chorus should jointly recommend and teach what is useful for the state. In the first place therefore we move[2] that you put the citizens on a level, and remove their fears. And if any one has erred, having been deceived somewhat by the artifices of Phrynichus,[3] I assert that it ought to be allowed those who made a false step at that time to do away with their former transgressions by pleading their cause.[4] In the next place I assert that no one in the city ought to be civilly disqualified;[5] for it is disgraceful that those who have fought one battle at sea, should straight-

Eine Thrakerschwalbe,
Die sich hüpferlich wiegt auf barbarischem Zweig;
Doch er wimmert ein weinerlich Nachtigallied."   *Droysen.*

Shakspeare, *Midsummer-Night's Dream*, act i. sc. 2, "But I will aggravate my voice so, that I will roar you as gently as any sucking dove; I will roar you an 't were any nightingale."

[1] "Then the urns were opened, and the suffrages numbered in presence of the magistrate, who stood with a rod in his hand, which he laid over the beans as they were numbered, lest any person should, through treachery or mistake, omit any of them, or count the same twice. If the number of the black beans were greatest, he pronounced the person guilty; and, as a mark to denote his condemnation, drew a long line, whence ἅπασι τιμᾶν μακρὰν, in the comedian, *signifies to condemn all*: on the contrary, he drew a short line in token of absolution, if the white beans exceeded, or only equalled, the number of the black; for such was the clemency of the Athenian laws, that when the case seemed equally disputable on both sides, the severe and rigorous commands of justice gave place to the milder laws of mercy and compassion. And this rule seems to have been constantly observed in all the courts of Athens." *Potter.* See Bernhardy, W. S. p. 188.

[2] See the passages referred to in the note on Thesm. 428.

[3] See Thuc. viii. 25, 27, 48, 50, 51, 54, 90, 92. εἴ τις . . τοῖς ὀλισθοῦσιν (vs. 690). Comp. note on Eccles. 688.

[4] "Muss es, mein Ich, ihm vergönnt sein, wenn er da gestrauchelt ist,
Durch Verantwortung zu lösen seine Schuld in jenem Zwist."
Droysen.

[5] It appears that there were three degrees of ἀτιμία at Athens: (1.) When the criminal kept his property, but was deprived of some other privilege. (2.) When he suffered for debt to the public a confiscation of property and temporal suspension of his rights; and, (3.) When he and his descendants were for ever deprived of citizenship. "See Schömann 72, 111, 275. Wachsmuth, iii. 183, *Mitchell*

way be both Platæans,[1] and masters, instead ci slaves. Neither can I assert that this is not[2] proper.—Nay, I commend it; for it is the only sensible thing that you have done.[3] | But in addition to this, it is reasonable that you forgive this one mishap of theirs when they entreat you, who, as well as their fathers, have oftentimes fought at sea along with you, and are related to you by birth.[4]　Come, O ye most wise by nature, let us remit our anger and willingly admit all men as relations, and as civilly qualified, and as citizens, whoever engages in a sea-fight along with us.[5]　But if thus we shall be puffed up and shall pride ourselves upon our[6] city, and that too when we are[7] in the arms of the billows,[8] sometime hereafter in subsequent time[9] we shall appear not to be in our right senses.

But if I am[10] correct in discerning the life or the manners

[1] "i. e. should be put on a footing with the 200 Platæans, to whom the freedom of the city was given, after their escape from the well-known siege recorded in Thucyd. iii. 20, *seq.* See also Wachsmuth, ii. 149." *Mitchell.* For μίαν, see Bernhardy, W. S. p. 190.

[2] See Krüger, Gr. Gr. § 67, 12, obs. 6.　Bernhardy, W. S. p. 356. Though κοὐδὲ is a combination of the commonest occurrence, the opposite (οὐδὲ καὶ) is, according to Porson, (Misc. Crit p. 221,) quite unstatuteable.

[3] See Krüger, Gr. Gr. § 57, 3, obs. 7.

[4] Eur. Med. 1301, οἱ προσήκοντες γένει. See Krüger, Gr. Gr. § 46, 4, obs. 1. ξυμφορὰν is a euphemism for ἁμαρτίαν.

[5] "Auf, ihr von Natur so klugen, werfet allen Hass von hinnen,
Lasset jeden, der mit uns zur See gekämpft, uns ohn' Besinnen
Als verwandt, als voll, als Bürger anerkennen und gewinnen.'
Droysen.

For similar uses of ὅστις, see Porson's Advers. p. 217.

[6] See Lid. Lex. in voc. ἀποσεμνύνω. On the other side, Thiersch, "*quod attinet jus civitatis,* i. e. *in jure civitatis donando.*"

[7] "ἔχοντες pro ὄντες. Eur. Bacch. 89, ἔχουσ' ἐν ὠδίνων λοχίαις ἀνάγκαισι." *Mitchell.* The constructions cited in the note on Thesm. 473, are different.

[8] Æsch. Fragm. Inc. 301, Ψυχὰς ἔχοντες κυμάτων ἐν ἀγκάλαις. Cf. Cho. 587. Eur. Orest. 1371. Helen. 1071.

[9] "Werden später wir erkennen, dass wir nicht verständig waren."
Droysen.

Cf. Soph. Col. 614. Herod. i. 130. For the negative, see Elmsley, Med. 487. Hermann, Opusc. iii. p. 200. Krüger, Gr. Gr. § 67, 7, obs. ƒ.

[10] "This verse is from the *Œneus* of Ion the tragedian." *Droysen.* For ὅστις, see note on Thesm. 544.

of a ma.., wh) will yet suffer for it, Cligenes[1] the little, this ape, who now troubles us, the vilest bath-man *of all*, as many as[2] are masters of soap made from adulterated soda mixed up with ashes, and of Cimolian[3] earth, will not abide for a long time. But though he sees this, he is not for peace, lest he should one day be stripped[4] when drunk, when walking without his cudgel.

The freedom[5] of the city has often appeared to us to be similarly circumstanced with regard to the good and honourable citizens, as to the old coin and the new gold.[6] For neither do we employ these at all, which are not adulterated,[7] but the most excellent, as it appears, of all coins, and alone correctly struck, and proved by ringing every where, both among the Greeks and the barbarians, but this vile copper coin, struck but yesterday and lately with the vilest stamp;[8] and[9] we insult those of the citizens whom we know to be well-born, and discreet, and just, and good, and honourable men, and who have been trained in palæstras, and choruses, and music;[10] while we use for every[11] purpose the brazen,

---

[1] " Of Cligenes we know little beyond what the text teaches us, except that he was engaged with Cleophon and others (B. c. 407) in the banishment of Alcibiades." *Droysen.*

[2] " ὀπόσοι depends upon the omitted πάντων, which is implied in πονηρότατος. κρατεῖν κονίας (*pulverem tenere, obtinere*) is said of those who handle, who use, employ it." *Dindorf.* See Bernhardy, W. S. p. 304.

[3] " Cimolus, now *Argentiera*, an island in the Cretan Sea, producing chalk and fuller's earth. This γῆ Κιμωλία is still used for soap in the Archipelago." *Mitchell.*

[4] See note on Lys. 1023, and Bernhardy, W. S. p. 334.

[5] See Liddell's Lex. in voc. πόλις.

[6] The new coinage here mentioned is said to have been made in the year 40⅖, during the archonship of Antigenes. Spanheim remarks, that the coins he had examined of that date were, to a surprising degree, inferior to the money coined in Sicily and Magna Græcia. " By τἀρχαῖον νόμισμα, we are to understand the old Attic *silver* coin, so remarkable for its purity and intrinsic worth, and which is here set in opposition to a recent issue of gold coin, so alloyed and debased, that the poet hesitates not to call it a copper coinage (vs. 730)." *Mitchell.*

[7] See Porson, Hec. 358. Krüger, § 56, 3, obs. 1. Bernhardy, W. S p. 277, 334. [8] Cf. Plut. 862, 957. Ach. 517.

[9] οὔτε (721) . . . τῶν πολιτῶν τε. See note on Aves, 1597.

[10] The Greek μουσικὴ comprised all the elements of a liberal education. [11] See note on Thesm. 532.

foreigners, and slaves, rascals, and sprung[1] from rascals, who are the latest come; whom the city before this would not heedlessly and readily have used even as scape-goats.[2] Yet even now, ye senseless, change[3] your ways and again employ the good. For if you succeed, it will be creditable[4] to you; and if you fail at all, at any rate you will seem to the wise to suffer, if you *do* suffer[5] aught, from a stick[6] which is worthy. [*Re-enter Xanthias and Æacus.*]

ÆAC. By Jupiter the Preserver, your master[7] is a gentleman.

XAN. Most assuredly a gentleman, inasmuch[8] as he knows only to drink and wench.

ÆAC. To think of his not beating you,[9] when openly convicted, that you said you were the master, when you were the slave.

XAN. He would certainly have suffered for it.

ÆAC. Upon my word this is a servant-like act[10] which you have openly done, which I take pleasure in doing.

[1] Comp. Equit. 185, 337. Soph. Phil. 388, 874. El. 589. Demosth. p. 228, 19; 613, 1; 614, 19; 1327, 2. Lysias, 118, 12; 135, 38.

[2] φαρμακοῖσιν = καθάρμασιν.

[3] Mitchell compares Plut. 36. Eur. Iph. A. 343. Eupolis ap. Stob. Serm. iv.

[4] "*Laudi vobis erit.*" *Thiersch.*   [5] See note on Lys. 171.

[6] "The Chorus with an arch look adverts to a common proverb, which recommends a man about to hang himself, to select a good piece of timber for the purpose, and such as will not fail him by breaking with his weight." *Mitchell.* The proverb in question is, ἐπ᾽ ἀξίου γοῦν τοῦ ξύλου κἂν ἀπάγξασθαι. The author wished to remove by a timely jest any irritation which might have been caused by the preceding tiresome dose of politics. With this position of the adjective, the thing spoken of is not distinguished from any thing else, but *from itself under different circumstances.* Here the emphasis falls upon the adjective. See Krüger, Gr. Gr. § 50, 11. Bernhardy, W. S. p. 325.

[7] "By Jupiter! but he's a gentleman,
That master of yours." *Frere.*

See note on Nub. 366.

[8] ὅστις γε = *quippe qui.* See Thesm. 883, 888. Eur. Hippol. 1064. Demosth. p. 631, 6. Porson, Præf. Hec. p. 51. Schäfer on Soph. Trach. 336. Hermann, Soph. Rex, 588. Krüger on Xenoph. Anab. i. 6, 5; Gr. Gr. § 69, 15, obs. 1. Cf. vs. 1184, *infra.* Plat. Euth. p. 4, A.

[9] See note on Nub. 268, and Hermann, Vig. n. 19.

[10] "Well! that's well spoken; like a true-bred slave.
It's just the sort of language I delight in." *Frere.*

For the construction, see Krüger, Gr. Gr. § 57, 3, obs. 7.

XAN. Take pleasure, I pray you ?

ÆAC. Nay, but methinks I am an Epoptes,[1] when I curse my master in private.

XAN. But what, when you go out muttering, after having received many blows?

ÆAC. Then, too, I am delighted.

XAN. But what, when you play the inquisitive busybody?[2]

ÆAC. By Jove, *I am delighted*[3] as never any thing in the world was.

XAN. O Jupiter, the Protector of families ! And when you overhear what your masters[4] talk about ?

ÆAC. Nay, but I am more than mad with joy !

XAN. But what, when you blab this to those outside ?

ÆAC. I? Nay, by Jove, but when I do this, I am even transported beyond measure.

XAN. O Phœbus Apollo ! give me your right hand, and let me kiss you, and do you kiss me yourself, and tell me, by Jove, who[5] is our fellow-slave, what is this tumult, and clamour, and wrangling, within ?

ÆAC. Between Æschylus and Euripides.

XAN. Ha !

ÆAC. An affair, a mighty, a mighty affair[6] has been set a going among the dead, and a very great commotion.

XAN. Wherefore ?[7]

The Epoptæ are said by Potter to mean all who were admitted (in the year following their initiation to the lesser mysteries) to behold the Arcana of Eleusinian worship. The commentators on this passage, however, rank them with the Hierophant and torch-bearer as peculiar ministers, who could not obtain their office until they had been one year Mystæ. As then the Mystæ were accounted happy, the Epoptæ were proportionably capable of more exalted happiness. For μάλλά, see note on Thesm. 646.

[2] See Valckn. Hippol. 785.

[3] " With ὡς μὰ Δί' we must repeat χαίρω [ἤδομαι?] : *ita lætor, ut nullâ aliâ re me lætari scio.* Reiske proposed οὐδὲν ἀλλ' ἐγὼ sc. ἤδομαι." *Dindorf.*

[4] An example of " Anticipation." See Krüger, Gr. Gr. § 61, 6, obs. 2.

[5]
" And now for Jupiter's sake !—
For he's the patron of our cuffs and beatings." *Frere.*
" Beim grossen Zeus, dem uns gemeinsamen Prügelpatron." *Droys.*

[6] Cf. vss. 580, 584. Plut. 1080. Aves, 726. Plut. 348.

[7] " ἐκ τοῦ ; *quare?* Markland, Eur. Suppl. 131." *Porson.* See also Bernhardy, W. S. p. 312.

Æac. There is a law established here, that out of[1] the professions, as many as are important and ingenious, he who is the best of his own fellow-artists should receive[2] a public maintenance in the Prytaneum,[3] and a seat next to Pluto's——

Xan. I understand.

Æac. ——until some other person, better skilled in the art than he, should come ;[4] then it was his duty to give place.

Xan. Why then has this disturbed Æschylus ?

Æac. He held the tragic seat,[5] as being the best in his art.

Xan. But who now ?

Æac. As soon as Euripides came down, he began to show off to the foot-pads, and cut-purses, and parricides, and house-breakers ; of which sort of men[6] there is a vast quantity in Hades, and they, hearing his objections, and twistings, and turnings, went stark mad, and thought him the cleverest. And then elated he laid claim to the throne where Æschylus was sitting.

Xan. And was he not pelted ?[7]

[1] Bernhardy translates ἀπὸ τῶν τεχνῶν, *de artibus*, comparing Thuc. iii. 13, ἀπό τε τῶν Ἑλλήνων, ἀπό τε τῶν Ἀθηναίων, *respectu*. See his Wissensch. Synt. p. 222.

[2] αὐτὸν is merely *epanaleptic*, (Krüger, Gr. Gr. § 51, 5, obs. 1,) and may be neglected in translating. For similar constructions in Latin, see Terence, Eun. act v. sc. 4, vs. 6. Adelph. act iii. sc. 3, vs. 4.

[3] The Prytaneum is placed by Meursius to the north-east of the Acropolis, and was so called from the Prytanes meeting there. In it were the statues of Vesta and Peace. A maintenance in this place, at the public expense, was only granted to such as had deserved nobly of their country, the posterity of Harmodius and Aristogiton, the conquerors at Olympia, &c. " The under world is a copy of the upper world. An Athenian law gave a public maintenance in the Prytaneum and precedence to such as excelled their fellow-artists." *Voss.* Cf. Wachsmuth, iv. 316.

[4] See notes on Equit. 134, and on vs. 24, *supra*. Æacus of course is *quoting* the provisions of the *law*.

[5] " The Professor's chair of our own days grew out of the provisions made by the Roman emperors, when the sophists of the age were to be stimulated by honours and rewards of every kind, n order to create an effective opposition to the progress of Christianity." *Mitchell.*

[6] See Porson and Schäfer ad Eur. Orest. 908. Hermann, Vig. n. 28. Bernhardy, W. S. p. 296.

[7] Comp. Vesp. 1254, 1422.

Æac. No, by Jove, but the mob clamoured[1] to institute a trial, which of the two was the cleverer in his art?

Xan. The *mob* of rascals?

Æac. Aye, by Jove, prodigiously.[2]

Xan. But were there not others on Æschylus' side as allies?

Æac. The good are few, as here.[3] [*Points to the audience.*]

Xan. What then is Pluto intending to do?

Æac. To institute a contest, and trial, and ordeal of their skill forthwith.[4]

Xan. Why, how then did not Sophocles also lay claim to the seat?

Æac. Not he, by Jove, but kissed Æschylus as soon as he came down,[5] and gave him his right hand; and he[6] had given up to him the seat. But now he was intending, as Clidemides[7] said, to sit down as third combatant, and if Æschylus conquer, to remain in his place; but if not, he declared he would contend against Euripides in skill.

Xan. Will the affair take place then?

Æac. Yes, by Jove, in a short time hence. And the

---

[1] Comp. Eccles. 399. Eur. Tro. 526.

[2] Comp. Eur. Tro. 519. Soph. Ajax, 196. Antig. 418. For the construction, see Krüger, Gr. Gr. § 51, 10, obs. 12. Cf. vs. 1135.

[3] The author has here forgotten himself: ἐνθάδε ought to signify "*in Hades.*"

[4] Mitchell cites Eccles. 20. Demosth. Mid. 521, 7; 522, 14; 576, 12; 585, 9.

[5] "Sophocles was noted for a mild, easy character." *Frere.*

[6] "And Æschylus edg'd a little from his seat,
To give him room." *Frere.*

"Und wieder ihm bot jener an den Meisterthron." *Droysen.*

It is indeed quite possible to refer κἀκεῖνος to Sophocles. See Krüger, Gr. Gr. § 51, 7, obs. 10. Matthiä, § 471, 10. Bernhardy, W. S. p. 277. Porson, Misc. Crit. p. 216. "The verse seems very much like an interpolation." *Mitchell.*

[7] "Of Clidemides even the ancient commentators knew nothing: they conjectured that he was an actor of Sophocles'." *Droysen.* "Sophocles being a quiet, unostentatious character, which shows itself rather in deeds than words, did not publicly make known his intention of taking up the contest with Euripides, but only mentioned it to Clidemides his confidant, through whom it had transpired." *Welcker.*

dreadful contest will be agitated in this very[1] place; for poetic skill will be measured[2] by the scales.

XAN. How then?[3] will they weigh[4] tragedy by butcher's weight?

ÆAC. And they will bring[5] out rulers and yard-wands for verses, and they will make close-fitted oblong squares too in the form of a brick, and rules for drawing the diameter, and wedges. For Euripides says he will examine the tragedies word by word.[6]

XAN. Of a truth, I suppose Æschylus takes it ill.

ÆAC. At any rate, he bent his head down and looked sternly.

XAN. But who, pray, will decide this?

ÆAC. This was difficult: for they found[7] a scarcity of clever men. For neither was Æschylus on friendly terms with the Athenians——

XAN. Perhaps[8] he thought them house-breakers for the most part.

ÆAC. ——and[9] in other respects considered them mere

[1] "κἀνταῦθα δὴ = et quidem illo ipso in loco (in Pluto's palace). τὰ δεινὰ = grave certamen." *Dindorf.*

[2] "On futures, such as σταθμήσεται, see Monk's Hipp. 1458.' *Mitchell.*

[3] See Bernhardy, W. S. p. 141. Heindorf, Plat. Charm. 33.

[4] This alludes to the festival of Apaturia, at Athens, on the third day of which the young citizens were presented to be registered, and at which ceremony it was customary to offer a lamb to Diana. It was to be of a certain weight, and because it once happened that the by-standers (or, as the Scholiast says, the sponsors, for fear they should not have their due share of meat) cried out μεῖον, μεῖον, "too little, too little," the sacrificial lamb was ever afterwards called μεῖον, and the person who brought it to be weighed, μειαγωγὸς, and the act itself, μειαγωγία. "In one of the later scenes of this play the two poets put single verses into the opposite scales of a balance." *Frere.*

[5] "Herbringen sie gleich Richtholz und Elle für Wort und Vers,
Und Ziegelformen, ihre Patzen zu streichen drin,
Und Zirkel, Kantel, Winkelmaass; denn Euripides
Verlangt die Tragödien durchzumessen Vers für Vers." *Droysen*

[6] Cf. vs. 1198, and see Bernhardy, W. S. p. 240.

[7] See note on Thesm. 1157.

[8] "Wohl weil er in Masse selbe für Diebsgesindel hielt?' *Droysen*
"Considering them as rogues and villains mostly." *Frere.*

[9] See note on vs. 726, *supra.*

triflers with regard to judging of the abilities of poets.[1] So then they committed it to your master, because he was experienced in the art.[2] But let us go in; for whenever our masters are seriously engaged,[3] blows[4] are prepared for us. [*Exeunt Æacus and Xanthias.*]

Cho. Doubtless the loud-thunderer[5] will cherish dreadful wrath within, when he sees[6] his glib-tongued rival in art sharpening his teeth: then will he roll[7] his eyes through dreadful frenzy. And there will be[8] a helmet-nodding strife of horse-hair-crested words, and the rapid whirling of splinters,[9] and parings[10] of works, as the man repels the horse-

[1] Brunck remarks on this passage that the comedian was still sore from the failure of his Clouds.

> "As being ignorant and empty generally;
> And in their judgment of the stage particularly." *Frere.*

> "Und den Rest für allzu dämisch, um über Dichtergeist
> Urtheilen zu können." *Droysen.*

See Bernhardy, W. S. p. 261.

[2] See Bernhardy, W. S. p. 375.

[3] "σπουδάζειν, *majori cum studio graves res agere.*" *Dindorf.* "*Be serious,* or *earnest.*" *Liddell.*

[4] "*Verbera* (effect for cause) *nobis parata sunt, nisi adsimus.*" *Dindorf.*

[5] This passage is intended throughout to imitate the grandiloquent pomp of Æschylus, as contrasted with the minute prettiness of Euripides.

> "The full-mouthed master of the Tragic choir,
> We shall behold him foam with rage and ire;
>   Confronting in the list
> His eager, shrewd, sharp-tooth'd antagonist.
> Then will his visual orbs be wildly whirl'd,
> And huge invectives will be hurl'd." *Frere.*

[6] The reader must not imagine from this that ἰδεῖν governs *a genitive,* though I have found it *convenient* so to translate it. Θήγοντος ἀντιτέχνου is a *genitive absolute.* So Soph. Trach. 394, ὡς ἕρποντος εἰσορᾷς ἐμοῦ. See Reisig, Com. Crit. Colon. p. 332. Krüger on Xenoph. Anab. iii. 1, 19, and Gr. Gr. § 47, 10, obs. 8. Matthiä, Gr. Gr. § 548, 1; § 348, obs. 3. Neue on Soph. Trach. 394. On the other side see Bernhardy, W. S. p. 151. Jelf, Gr. Gr. § 683, 1.

[7] "*Oculos suos distorquebit.*" *Dindorf.*

[8] "Sein wird mähnenumflatterter Kampf der geharnischten Worte,
> Kecklich gewitzeltes Spitzengeschwätz, Feilspähne der Werke,
>   Wenn sich der Mann vor des geniusflammenden Alten
>   Rosslich stampfigen Worten wehrt." *Droysen.*

[9] "παραξόνια σχινδαλάμων = *rotationes* (agitationes) *audaces scindularum tenuium* (argumentationum subtilium)." *Dindorf.*

[10] "Finely carved works." *Liddell.*

mounted words of the ingenious[1] hero: while he, having bristled up the shaggy locks of his naturally-haired mane, and contracting his brows dreadfully, and roaring, will send forth bolt-fastened words,[2] tearing them up like planks with gigantic breath. On the other side the word-making, polished tongue, examiner of words, twisting about, agitating envious jaws, dissecting the words *of his opponent*, will refine away to nothing vast labour of the lungs.[3] [*Enter Bacchus, Pluto, Æschylus, and Euripides.*]

Eur. I will not give up[4] the seat: cease your advisings; for I assert, that I am superior to him in the art.

Bac. Æschylus, why are you silent? for you hear his language.

Eur. He will act the dignitary at first, just as he was always accustomed to play the marvellous in his tragedies.[5]

Bac. My good fellow,[6] speak not so very loftily.

Eur. I know him, and have looked him through of old—a fellow that writes savage poetry,[7] stubborn of speech, with an unbridled, licentious, unchecked tongue, unskilled in talk,[8] pomp-bundle-worded.

[1] Spanheim observes on the constant use of words compounded with φρὴν in the plays of Æschylus, Prom. 884, S. C. Theb. 760, Eum. 326, and also in his own prayer shortly after (vs. 886). The word ἱπποβάμων occurs in the Prom. 811. Supp. 299.

[2] γόμφος and its compounds are favourite terms with Æschylus. Mitchell cites Suppl. 921. Theb. 537. Pers. 71. Suppl. 434, 825.

[3] Pers. Sat. i. 14, " Grande aliquid, quod pulmo animæ prælargus anhelet."

[4] " Aufgeben werd' Ich nicht den Thron ! spar' deinen Rath,
    Denn dessen Meister rühm' Ich mich in unsrer Kunst." *Droys.*
See note on Lys. 119. For the construction of μεθίεσθαι, see Liddell's Lex. in voc. iii.

[5] " He's mustering up a grand commanding visage
    ——A silent attitude—the common trick
    That he begins with in his tragedies." *Frere.*
He alludes to a fashion Æschylus had of bringing his characters on the stage and keeping them for a long time silent. See vs. 912.

[6] Cf. vs. 1227. Aves, 1638. Eccles. 564, 784. Eur. Hec. 707. Heracl. 568. Reisig, Com. Crit. Colon. p. 243. This use of μεγάλα is very rare, although μέγα λέγειν is of common occurrence. See Bernhardy, W. S. p. 129.

[7] The allusion is, as Mitchell observes, to his Salvator-Rosa-like fondness for wild and savage scenery.

[8] " Unüberredsar " *Droysen.* Cf Liddell's Lex. in voc. Pollux, ii 125.

ÆSCH. Indeed? you son of the market-goddess,[1] do you *say* this of me,[2] vou gossip-gleaner, and drawer of beggarly characters, and rag-stitcher? But by no means shall you say it with impunity.

BAC. Cease, Æschylus, and do not passionately inflame your heart with wrath!

ÆSCH. Certainly not; before I shall have shown up clearly this introducer of lame characters, what sort[3] of a person he is, who speaks so boldly.

BAC. Boys, bring out a lamb, a black lamb, for a storm[4] is ready to issue forth.

ÆSCH. O thou that collectest Cretan[5] monodies, and introducest unholy nuptials into the art——

BAC. Hollo! stop, O highly-honoured Æschylus! And do you, O unlucky Euripides, get yourself out of the way of the hail-storm, if you are wise, lest through passion he smite your temples with a head-breaking word and let out your Telephus.[6] And do you, O Æschylus, not angrily, but temperately refute, and be refuted.[7] It is not meet that poets should rail at each other, like bread-women. But you instantly roar like a holm oak on fire.

---

[1] "Wahrhaftig, Sprosse jener Gartengöttin du!" *Droysen.*
The allusion is to Euripides' mother, Clito, *the market-gardener.* The line itself is a parody upon Euripides' own line, Frag. Inc. 200,

$$\text{ἄληθες, ὦ παῖ τῆς θαλασσίας θεοῦ;}$$

[2] See Krüger, Gr. Gr. § 62, 3, obs. 12.　　　　[3] Cf. Vesp. 530.
[4] "Quick! quick! A sacrifice to the winds! Make ready;
　　The storm of rage is gathering. Bring a victim." *Frere.*
Virgil, Æn. iii. 120, *Nigram Hiemi pecudem, Zephyris felicibus albam.*
"Bacchus does not call for a sacrifice. It is his buffoonish way of saying that Æschylus is going to be in a *stormy* passion." *Frere.*
[5] "O der du Kretischen Hurgesang zusammenfeilschst,
　　Und widernatürliche Ehen einführst in die Kunst." *Droysen.*
See Nub. 1372. He alludes to the Hippolytus, in which Phædra (who was of Cretan origin) plays a prominent part. The monodies here mentioned are at vs. 197 of that play. The comedian adverts also to his story of Macareus and Canace, (Ovid. Met. xi. 563,) and to his Pasiphaë.
[6] "Or else with one of his big thumping phrases
　　Yc·'ll get your brains dash'd out, and all your notions
　　And sentiments and matter mash'd to pieces." *Frere.*
Τήλεφον is παρὰ προσδοκίαν for ἐγκέφαλον.
[7] Plato, Gorg. p. 462, A., ἐν τῷ μέρει ἐρωτῶν καὶ ἐρωτώμενος, ὥσπερ ἐγώ τε καὶ Γοργίας, ἔλεγχέ τε καὶ ἐλέγχου. Cf. Cicer. Tusc. ii. 2.

Eur. I am ready, and do not decline, to bite, or to be bitten first, if he thinks proper, in iambics, in choral songs, and in the nerves of tragedy; and, by Jove, in the Peleus, too, and the Æolus, and the Meleager, nay, even the Telephus.[1]

Bac. What, pray, do you mean to do? Tell me, Æschylus!

Æsch. I was wishing[2] not to contend here; for our contest is not on equal terms.

Bac. Why, pray?

Æsch. Because[3] my poetry has not died with me, but this man's has died with him, so that he will be able to recite it. But still, since you think proper, I must do so.

Bac. Come then, let some one give me here frankincense and fire, that I may pray,[4] prior to the learned compositions, so as to decide[5] this contest most skilfully. But do you [*to the Chorus*] sing some song to the Muses.

Cho. O you chaste Muses, the nine[6] virgins of Jove, who look down upon the subtle, sagacious minds of maxim-coining men,[7] whenever they enter into competition as opponents with keenly-studied tricks of wrestling, come to observe the power of mouths most skilful in furnishing for themselves words and poetic saw-dust.[8] For now the mighty contest of skill is coming to action[9] forthwith.

[1] Comp. Pax, 280.

[2] There is no omission of ἄν in this passage, for the wish is a real one and not limited by conditions. See Æschin. Ctes. § 2. Matthiä, Gr. Gr. § 509, 5, *a.* Bernhardy, W. S. p. 373. ἄν is never omitted with the indicative except in hypothetical propositions. For cases of *this* kind, see Krüger, Gr. Gr. § 54, 10, obs. 1, and § 53, 10, obs. 5. Cf. vs. 1195, *infra.* Vesp. 709.

[3]   "Because my poems live on earth above,
          And his died with him, and descended here,
          And are at hand as ready witnesses." *Frere.*

[4] "Bacchus imitates the agonothetæ and prize arbiters, who in like manner were accustomed to offer prayer and sacrifice before theatrical or other contests." *Mitchell.*

[5] "Den Streit zu entscheiden musenkunstverständiglichst."*Droys.*

[6] Mitchell compares Eur. Med. 827.

[7] Thus in the Clouds, vs. 952. Knights, vs. 1379. Thesm. 55.
          "So oft sie mit gründlich studirten,
          Künstlich geführten Finessen
          Bewehrt sich entgegen im Kampf stehn." *Droysen.*

[8] "The ῥήματα is applied to Æschylus, the 'saw-dust' to Euripides." *Scholiast.*

[9]   "Denn der erhabene Kampf
          Ueber die Meisterschaft, jetzt wird er losgehen." *Droysen.*

BAC. Now do you two also offer up some prayer, before you recite your verses.

ÆSCH. (*offering frankincense*). O Ceres, who nourished my mind, may I be[1] worthy of your mysteries!

BAC. Come then, now do you also [*to Euripides*] offer frankincense.[2]

EUR. Excuse me; for the gods[3] to whom I pray, are different.

BAC. Are they some of your own, a new[4] coinage?

EUR. Most assuredly.

BAC. Come then, pray to your peculiar[5] gods.

EUR. O Air, my food,[6] and thou well-hung tongue, and sagacity, and sharp-smelling nostrils, may I rightly refute whatever arguments I assail.[7]

CHO. Well now, we are desirous to hear from you two learned men what hostile course of argument you will enter upon.   For their tongue has been exasperated, and the spirit

[1] Æschylus was a native of Eleusis, and therefore offers up his prayer to the patron goddess of that town. The mysteries, however, which he mentions, he had during his life-time been accused of divulging, but escaped by pleading ignorance of the sacred nature of what he had revealed. *Arist. Eth.* 3. See Franz's " Des Æschylos Oresteia," Introduction, p. xxxi. It is probable, therefore, that he had before his death been initiated. "The poetry of Æschylus is pervaded by a most earnest tone of religious feeling. His reverential, pious prayer, stands in striking contrast to the ' enlightened ' blasphemy of Euripides." *Droysen.* For the infinitive, see note on vs. 169, and Bernhardy, W. S. p. 357.

[2] Comp. Nub. 426. Vesp. 96.

[3] " Pray excuse me :—
The gods I worship are of other kinds." *Dunster.*
For this use of καλῶς, see note on vs. 508, and for the relative, see notes on Thesm. 502. Nub. 863, and Bernhardy, W. S. p. 303.

[4] The reader will remember one of the articles of Socrates' impeachment, ὅτι καινὰ εἰσήγαγε δαιμόνια, which was brought against him five years subsequently.

[5] " Dindorf and Thiersch observe, that there is a certain comic ambiguity in this word, which implies at once *peculiar*, and also *vulgar*, plebeian." *Mitchell.*

[6] " Meine Weide." *Droysen.* Cf. Nub. 331, 424.

[7] " Thou foodful Air, the nurse of all my notions;
And ye, the organic powers of sense and speech,
And keen, refined, olfactory discernment,
Assist my present search for faults and errors." *Frere.*
Comp. note on vs. 169, and Bernhardy W. S. p. 357.

of both is not devoid of courage, nor their souls sluggish. Therefore 'tis reasonable to expect that one will say something clever and well-polished ; while the other, tearing them up,[1] will fall on him with words torn up from the very roots, and toss about many long rolling words.

Bac. Come, you ought to recite as soon as possible : but in such manner that you shall utter what is polite, and neither metaphors,[2] nor such as any one else might say.

Eur. Well now, I will speak of myself subsequently, what I am in poetry ; but first I will convict this fellow, that he was an impostor and a quack, and *will show* with what *tricks* he cajoled the spectators, having received them reared as fools in the school of Phrynichus.[3] For first of all he used to muffle up and seat some single character, an Achilles[4] or a Niobe, without showing the face, a piece of tragic quackery,[5] who did not even utter so much——

[1] Dindorf translates this, *alterum convellentem illum, radicitus evulsis verbis irruentem, multas dissipaturum esse verborum tricas.*

[2] The first sarcasm is directed at the transcendental metaphors of Æschylus, the second at Euripides' fondness for the language of common life.

[3] Phrynichus the tragedian having brought on the stage a play, the subject of which was the taking of Miletus by the Persians, so powerfully affected his audience, that, to use the words of Herodotus, "the theatre melted into tears ;" and he was fined a thousand drachmæ for recalling their misfortunes to the minds of his countrymen. This play was acted b. c. 497. See Bentley, Phal. p. 183, 184. Æschylus died b. c. 455, in the 69th year of his age. The author of the argument prefixed to the Persæ asserts, on the authority of Glaucus, that Æschylus copied that play from the *Phœnissæ* of Phrynichus.

[4] The former of these characters was introduced in a play of Æschylus, called the *Ransom of Hector*, where he exchanged only a few words with Mercury, and continued silent during the rest of the play. Niobe was represented sitting mute on the tomb of her children until the third act of a drama which bore her name. Of Telephus, however, (see Tyrwhitt's note on Arist. Poet. p. 153, where that able commentator's only point of doubt seems to be accounted for upon this practice of Æschylus,) Euripides says nothing, conscious perhaps of the probability of his sarcasms being turned on himself. Bergler observes that Euripides has given in to the very same fault in the Adrastus of his *Suppliants*, and in his Hecuba, in the tragedy of that name: Supp. 104. Hec. 485.

[5] Πρόσχημα is used by Josephus to express the shadow of power which Hyrcanus possessed, while the reality was enjoyed by Herod and Phaselus. Antiq. xiv. 12. "Trauerspiels Aushängeschild." *Droysen.*

BAC. No, by Jove,[1] they certainly did not.

EUR. His chorus, on the other hand, used to hurl four series of songs one after another without ceasing ; while they were silent.

BAC. But I used to like the silence, and this used to please me no less than those that chatter now-a-days.

EUR. For you were a simpleton, be well assured.

BAC. I also think so myself.[2] But why did What's his name do this ?

EUR. Out of quackery,[3] that the spectator might sit expecting, when his Niobe would[4] utter something ; while the play would be going on.

BAC. O the thorough rascal! How I was cheated, then, by him ! [_To Æschylus._] Why are you stretching and yawning, and showing impatience ?

EUR. Because I expose him. And then, when he had trifled in this way, and the drama was now half over, he used to speak some dozen words as big[5] as bulls, with brows and crests, some tremendous fellows of terrific aspect, unknown to the spectators.

ÆSCH. Ah me, miserable !

BAC. (_to Æschylus_). Be silent.

EUR. But not a single plain word would he utter.[6]

BAC. (_to Æschylus_). Don't grind your teeth.

EUR. But either " Scamanders, or trenches, or griffin-eagles[7] of beaten brass upon shields," and neck-breaking words,[8] which it was not easy to guess the meaning of.

---

[1] " No more they did : 'tis very true." _Frere._

[2] See Krüger, Gr. Gr. § 51, 2, obs. 1.

[3] " Dunstmacherei." _Droysen._

[4] See Krüger, Gr. Gr. § 53, 7, obs. 8.

[5] " Worte büffelmäss'ge." _Droysen._ Cf. Pax, 1278.

[6] " EUR. He never used a simple word——
 BACCH. (_to Æschylus_). Don't grind your teeth so strangely.
 EUR. But ' Bulwarks and Scamanders,' and ' Hippogriffs and
  Gorgons,
 On burnish'd shields of brass,'—bloody remorseless phrases
 That nobody could understand." _Frere._

[7] See the Agam. vs. 522, 1168. Choeph. 363. Eum. 395. The Gryphons (or Griffins) occur in the Prom. 810, and are mentioned by Herodotus, iii. 116; iv. 13.

[8] " Sturzjähes Wortgeschwindel." _Droysen._

Bac. Aye, by the gods! at any rate I have lain[1] awake before now during a *long* space[2] of the night, trying to find out his " yellow horse-cock," what bird it is.

Æsch. It had been painted[3] as a device on the ships, you ignoramus.

Bac. But I thought it was Eryxis,[4] the son of Philoxenus.

Eur. Ought you then to have introduced a *cock*[5] into tragedy ?

Æsch. And what sort,[6] you enemy of the gods, are the things which you introduced?

Eur. Not horse-cocks, by Jove, nor yet goat-stags, as you do, such as they depict on the Persian tapestry :[7] but immediately, as soon as ever I received the art from you, puffed out with pompous phrases and ponderous words, I first of all reduced it, and took off its ponderousness with versicles, and argumentations, and with white beet,[8] giving it chatter-juice, filtering it from books : and then I nursed it up with monodies, making an infusion of Cephisophon.[9] Then I did not

---

[1] Here a distich of Euripides (Hipp. 375) is parodied : see Eq. 1290. The Hippalectryon occurred in the *Myrmidons* of Æschylus. It is ridiculed again in Pax, 1177. Aves, 800. See notes on Nub. 1148. Eccles. 1126.

[2] Mitchell cites Æsch. Agam. 534, 592.

[3] " A figure on the head of ships, you goose ;
    You must have seen them." *Frere.*

[4] Philoxenus, whose son and father appear to have had the same name, is mentioned by Aristotle as a great glutton. Eth. iii. c. 10. " Who Eryxis, the son of Philoxenus, was, we know not. The Scholiast says he was ridiculed for being deformed and of a perverse temper. His father, a pupil of Anaxagoras, has been occasionally mentioned by Aristophanes." *Droysen.* See Vesp. 84. Nub. 686.

[5] See note on Lys. 171.

[6] See Krüger, Gr. Gr. § 57, 16, obs. 3. Cratinus, (ap. Athen. iv. p. 164, E.,) εἶδες τὴν Θασίαν ἅλμην οἷ' ἄττα βαΰζει.

[7] The custom of painting monstrous figures of animals on eastern tapestry is commented on by Vossius, in his notes to Catullus, p. 197. The architecture of the temples in Hindostan at this day w 'ld furnish some curious patterns for a work of this sort. This tapestry is mentioned also by Aristotle, Mir. Ausc. c. 119. Plautus, Stich. act ii. sc. 1, vs. 54, calls them Babylonian.

[8] He means that he reduced the swelling with a *poultice of white beet.*

[9] It was in consequence of an intrigue between Cephisophon and the wife of Euripides, that the tragedian retired to the court of

trifle with whatever I met with, nor rashly[1] jumbled things together; but he who came forward first used straightway to tell the pedigree of the piece.[2]

BAC. For, by Jove, 'twas better than *to tell* your own.[3]

EUR. Then[4] from the first verse I used to leave nothing idle; but a woman[5] would speak for me, or a slave all the same, or a master, or a virgin, or an old woman.

ÆSCH. Then ought you not, pray, to have been put to death for daring to do this?

EUR. No, by Apollo; for I did it as a popular act.

BAC. No more of this, my good friend; for upon this subject your argumentation does not appear to the best advantage.[6]

Archelaus, king of Macedon. The sophist who forged the letters of Euripides was so little aware of this circumstance, that he has made the poet address one of his longest and most friendly epistles to the very person who had thus dishonoured him. See Bentley, Phal. p. 419, ed. Lond. 1777.

"Mit Säftchen feinster Schwätzelei, aus Büchern wohl erlesen;
Monodien bekam sie dann, vermengt mit Kephisophon, zu es-
sen." *Droysen.*

[1] "*In quæ incidit, quæ ipse occupat, excogitando.*" *Dindorf.*

[2] "I kept my plots distinct and clear, and to prevent confusion,
My leading characters rehearsed their pedigrees for prologues."
Frere

See Schlegel, Dram. Lit. p. 119.

[3] This witticism depends on the double meaning of the word γένος

[4] "Sodann von den ersten Versen an, nichts liess Ich müssig
dastehn,
Nein nein, es sprach, mir da die Frau, desgleichen sprach der
Sklave,
Es sprach der Mann, das Töchterlein, das alte Weib." *Droysen.*
See Bernhardy, W. S. p. 222.

[5] Aristotle, in his Poetics, (28,) has blamed the tragedian for introducing Melanippe discussing the philosophy of the Anaxagoræan
school, to prove to her father that the children she had herself
borne and concealed were the offspring of his cows! See Mus.
Crit. i. p. 531.

[6] "Denn diese Sachen sind fürwahr nicht deine starke Seite."
Droysen.

As if he had said, "the less you talk of your love of democracy the better." Socrates, Euripides, Plato, Xenophon, and Critias are known to have entertained a thorough contempt for democracy in any shape. Whatever Euripides may have said in his tragedies in favour of it, his real sentiments were opposed to it. "The phi-losophic sect to which Euripides belonged, were known to be hostile

EUR. Then I taught these[1] to speechify.——

ÆSCH. I grant you. Would that you had burst[2] asunder in the middle before you taught them.

EUR. And the introduction of subtle rules, and the cornering-off of verses, to notice, to see, to understand, to twist, to love, to use stratagems,[3] to suspect mischief,[4] to contrive all things cunningly[5]——

ÆSCH. I grant you.

EUR. Introducing domestic affairs, with which we are conversant, in which we are engaged, by which[6] I might be tested; for these,[7] being acquainted with the subjects, might criticise my art. But I used not to talk big, taking them away from their understandings, nor did I astound[8] them by introducing Cycni and Memnons with bells on their horses' trappings. And you will recognise[9] the pupils of each, his and mine. His are Phormisius[10] and Megænetus[11] the Mag-

to the democracy." *Frere.* Mr. Mitchell professes to understand the passage very differently.

[1] "i. e. the spectators." *Mitchell.*

[2] See note on Nub. 41.   [3] Comp. Ach. 385.

[4] Comp. Thesm. 396, 496.

[5] "Nach Regeln der Kunst zu Werke gehn, abzirkeln Zeil' um
    Zeile,
Bemerken, denken, sehen, verstehn, belisten, lieben, schleichen,
Argwöhnen, läugnen, her und hin erwägen." *Droysen.*

[6] "So that the audience, one and all, from personal experience,
Were competent to judge the piece, and form a fair opinion,
Whether my scenes and sentiments agreed with truth and na
    ture."   *Frere.*

"Und gab mich so dem Urtheil Preis, da jeder, dessen Kenner,
Urtheilte über meine Kunst."   *Droysen.*

Comp. Harper's Powers of the Greek Tenses, p. 79, 83.

[7] The audience.

[8] See Schlegel, Dram. Lit. p. 523.

[9] "Auch wird man seine Schüler leicht von meinen unterschei-
    den."   *Droysen.*

[10] Phormisius is mentioned in the Eccl. vs. 97, as hairy in his person; and the Scholiast says his rough aspect was Euripides' chief inducement to place him in the school of Æschylus the ἀγριοποιός. "A few years later he was in the notorious embassy to the king of Persia, which Plato the comic poet cut up in his 'Ambassadors.'" *Droysen.* For τουτουμενὶ, see note on Thesm. 646.

[11] "Magænetus, according to the Scholiast, was one of those who strove to be appointed a general." *Droysen.*

nesian, whiskered-lance[1]-trumpeters, sneering-pine-benders while mine are Clitophon,[2] and Theramenes the elegant.

BAC. Theramenes? a clever man and skilful in all things,[3] who, if he any where fall into troubles, and stand nigh unto them, escapes out of[4] his troubles, no Chian, but a Ceian.[5]

EUR. I certainly instructed[6] them to be prudent in such matters, by introducing into the art calculation and consideration; so that now they understand[7] and discern all things, and regulate both other matters and their households better than heretofore,[8] and look at things narrowly,—"How is this? Where is this? Who took this?"[9]

BAC. Yes, by the gods; at any rate every Athenian[10] now

[1] "Trompetengrimbartslanzenvolk, zähnknirschesichtenbeuger."
Droysen.
In the latter word there is an allusion to Sinis, a famous robber in Attica, who, from his prodigious strength, was able to bend the boughs of trees together, to which he then tied his prisoners, and afterwards, unloosing the bands that held together the branches, he suffered them to recoil, and his victims were torn limb from limb. He was put to death by Theseus. Ovid. Met. vii. vs. 440.

[2] "Clitophon, the son of Aristonymus, is the same person as he after whom one of Plato's Dialogues is named. He was a pupil and admirer of the sophist Thrasymachus, as Theramenes was of Prodicus: both therefore were educated after the 'new' mode." *Droysen.* For Theramenes, see note on 540, and for κομψὸς, see note on Thesm. 93.

[3] See note on Thesm. 646.   [4] Comp. Æsch. Eum. 142, ed. Franz.

[5] "Apparently a proverbial expression, implying one who can say *Sibboleth,* or *Shibboleth,* as will best serve his purpose. No allusion, say Brunck and Dindorf, to the game of dice is here to be understood. The expression is applicable to a man of versatile genius, who, like the bat in the fable, can be bird or mouse, as will best answer his end, being always found on the prosperous side." *Mitchell.* "The proverb is, however, said to refer not to this [game of dice], but to the contrast between the dishonest Chians and the honest Ceians." *Liddell.*

[6] See Schlegel, Dram. Lit. p. 176.

[7] Hesiod, Op. 291, οὗτος μὲν πανάριστος, ὃς αὐτὸς πάντῃ νοήσει.

[8] See Krüger, Gr. Gr. § 50, 1, obs. 19.

[9] "Marking every thing amiss—
  'Where is that?' and—'What is this?'
  'This is broken—That is gone.'
  'Tis the modern style and tone." *Frere.*

[10] "General distress had produced a stricter economy, which is here humorously attributed to the precepts of Euripides." *Frere.* For ἅπαξ τις, see Mus. Crit. ii. p. 20.

when he comes in, bawls to his domestics and inquires,—
" Where's the pitcher? Who has eaten off the sprat's head ?[1]
My last year's bowl is gone. Where is the garlic of yesterday? Who has nibbled at my olives?" But before this they
used to sit most stupid, gaping boobies[2] and blockheads.

CHO. " Thou seest this, O illustrious Achilles."[3] Come,
what wilt thou say to this? Only see that thine anger seize
thee not, and carry thee out of[4] the course; for he has laid
grievous things to your charge.[5] But, O noble man, see that
you do not reply with anger, but shorten sail, using the extremity[6] of your sails, and then gradually bear up, and watch
when you catch the wind gentle and steady. But, O thou
first[7] of the Greeks that built the lofty rhyme, and gave dignity to tragic nonsense,[8] boldly send forth thy torrent of
words.

ÆSCH. I am angry at the encounter, and my heart is indignant that[9] I must reply to this man. Yet, that he may
not say I am at a loss, [*to Euripides,*] answer[10] me, for what
ought we to admire a poet?

EUR. For cleverness and instruction, and because we make ✓
the people in the cities better.

ÆSCH. If then you have not done this, but from good and

---

[1] Anaxilas, (ap. Athen. vii. 313,) τοῦ κεστρέως κατεδήδοκεν τὸ κρά-
νιον.

[2] See Mus. Crit. i. p. 127.

[3] Harpocration has added to this verse (which is a quotation
from the *Myrmidons* of Æschylus) the two following:

Δοριλυμάντους Δαναῶν μόχθους,
Οὓς προπέπωκας εἴσω κλισίας.

It appears they were the words of some embassy to Achilles, en-
treating his assistance. See Bernhardy, W. S. p. 280.

[4] An allusion to the Hippodrome, at the terminus of which were
planted olives, to mark the limits of the course. See note on
Lys. 316.

[5] " Cf. Dobree's Advers. i. p. 247." *Mitchell.*

[6] For the construction of ἄκρος, see note on Thesm. 1099.

[7] " Zuerst aufthürmtest erhabene Phrasen." *Droysen.*

[8] " Und dem tragischen Spiel Pomp gabst und Kothurn." *Droys*
Aristophanes means to say, that he found tragedy a mass of ab-
surdities, and elevated it to tragic dignity. Mr. Mitchell very
aptly cites the testimony of Prof. Scholefield on this point, (Præf
'n Æschyl.,) " *Lateritiam invenit, marmoream reliquit.*"

[9] See Krüger, Gr. Gr. § 65, 5. obs. 7.

[10] Cf. Lys. 486, 487, and Bernhardy, W. S. 424.

noble characters have rendered[1] them most knavish, what will you say you are deserving[2] to suffer?

BAC. To be put to death; don't ask him.[3]

ÆSCH. Observe then what sort of men he originally received them from me, if noble and tall fellows,[4] and not citizens that shirk all state burdens,[5] nor loungers in the market, nor rogues, as they are now, nor villains; but breathing[6] of spears, and lances, and white-crested helmets, and casques and greaves, and seven-fold[7] courage.

EUR. This mischief now is spreading.[8] He will kill me with his repeated helmet-making.

BAC. And by having done what did you teach them to be so noble-minded? [*Æschylus is silent.*] Speak, Æschylus, and do not be churlishly haughty and angry.

ÆSCH. By having composed a drama full of martial spirit.

BAC. Of what kind?

ÆSCH. The "Seven against Thebes." Every man that saw it would long to be a warrior.[9]

BAC. Indeed this has been ill done of you; for you have made the Thebans[10] more courageous for the war; and for this you must be beaten.[11]

---

[1] "ἀπέδειξας = ἐποίησας, ἀπέφηνας, as often elsewhere. Cf. Plut. 127, 210." *Thiersch.*   [2] See Class. Mus. No. xxv. p. 230.

[3] "Death, to be sure! Take that answer from me." *Frere.* Cf. Plut. 499. Aves, 492.

[4] Comp. Vesp. 553.   [5] Comp. Ach. 601.

[6] As examples of this Æschylean construction, Mr. Mitchell refers to Agam. 366, 1280. Cho. 30. Eum. 835. Prom. V. 367.

[7] Comp. Hom. Il. vii. 223. Bernhardy translates θυμοὺς, *passionate ebullitions of rage.* So also vs. 676, *supra,* σοφίαι, *philosophic arts.* Plato, Legg. ii. p. 665, D., φρονήσεις, *judgments.* ibid. xi. p. 922, A., ἀνδρίαι, *brave deeds.* Plato, Theæt. p. 172, C., φιλοσοφίαι, *systems of philosophy.* Isocr. Areop. p. 147, παιδεῖαι, *stages in education.* Hom. Od. M. 341, θάνατοι, *kinds of death.* So also μανίαι, *cases of madness;* κάλλη, *beautiful forms;* βίοι, *means of living, modes of life;* ἀλήθειαι, *the true circumstances.* The plural denotes the various kinds of the thing mentioned. See Krüger, Gr. Gr. § 44, 3, obs. 2.

[8] Comp. Nub. 906. Vesp. 1483.

[9] For the construction, see Krüger, Gr. Gr. § 51, 9, obs. 2, and for ἂν ἠράσθη, see note on Aves, 788.

[10] i. e. "the Thebans of the comic poet's day, who at the commencement of the Peloponnesian War had united themselves with the Spartans, not the Thebans described in the drama of Æschylus." *Mitchell.* See Bernhardy, W. S. p. 335.

[11] Comp. note on Thesm. 1171.

Æsch. It was in your power to practise it ; but you did not turn yourselves to this. Then I published the "Persæ" after this[1] and taught them to desire always to conquer their adversaries, having embellished a most noble achievement.

Bac. Of a truth I was delighted, when report was made about the defunct Darius, and the chorus immediately struck its hands together thus and exclaimed " Alas !"[2]

Æsch. This it behoves poets to practise. For observe how useful the[3] noble poets have been from of old. Orpheus[4] made known to us mystic rites, and to abstain[5] from slaughter ; Musæus, thorough cures[6] of diseases, and oracles ; Hesiod, the cultivation of the earth, the season for fruits, and tillage ; and by what did the divine Homer obtain honour and glory, except this, that he taught what was useful, the marshalling of an army, brave deeds, and the equipment of heroes ?[7]

Bac. And yet, nevertheless, he did not teach the most

[1] Comp. note on Plut. 504.
[2] There is no passage in the *Persæ*, as handed down to us, in which the word ἰαυοῖ occurs ; but so inconsiderable an expression, in fact, little better than a direction to the chorus, might easily have been altered or omitted. Aristophanes appears to allude to their praise of the deceased monarch.
[3] See Krüger, Gr. Gr. § 47, 9.
[4] From this poet, the orgies of Bacchus, said to have been brought from Egypt to Greece by him, were called Orphica.
[5] Horace, A. P. 391,

  " Silvestres homines . . . .
  Cædibus ac victu fœdo deterruit Orpheus."

For this use of καὶ, see Krüger, Gr. Gr. § 59, 2, obs. 3.
[6] Spanheim observes that this is claimed by Prometheus in Æschylus. Musæus is supposed to have been son or scholar of Linus or Orpheus. Virgil assigns him a distinguished place in Elysium, Æn. vi. 677. The Scholiast mentions his tomb in Phalerum.

[7] " Orpheus instructed mankind in religion,
  Reclaimed them from bloodshed and barbarous rites ;
  Musæus delivered the doctrine of medicine,
  And warnings prophetic for ages to come ;
  Next came old Hesiod, teaching us husbandry,
  Ploughing and sowing, and rural affairs,
  Rural economy, rural astronomy,
  Homely morality, labour, and thrift.
  Homer himself, our adorable Homer,
  What was his title to praise and renown?
  What but the worth of the lessons he taught us,
  Discipline, arms, and equipment of war." *Frere.*

stupid Pautacles.[1] At any rate, lately, when he was for leading the procession, he tied on his helmet first and was going to fasten his crest on it.[2]

ÆSCH. But in truth many other brave men, of whose number also was the hero Lamachus: from whom my mind[3] copied and represented the many brave deeds of Patrocluses[4] and lion-hearted Teucers, that I might rouse the citizen to raise himself to these, whenever he should hear the trumpet. But, by Jupiter, I did not introduce harlot Phædras or Sthenobœas;[5] nor does any one know any[6] woman whom I ever represented in love.[7]

EUR. No, by Jove; for neither was there aught of Venus in you.

ÆSCH. Nor may there be; but over you and yours she presided very mightily;[8] so that she even cast you down yourself.[9]

[1] "Pantacles, whom Eupolis also called 'The awkward,' probably committed that comical awkwardness at the Panathenaia. He is said to have been Hipparch; therefore a person of some consequence.' *Droysen.*

[2] "Doch den Pantakles wenigstens hat er
Nichts grosses gelehrt, den verschrobenen!
Letzt, als führen er sollte den Festzug,
Band fest er zuerst sich den Helm,
Um sodann sich den Helmbusch drüber zu stecken." *Droysen.*

[3] "Ὅθεν = ἀφ' οὖ, viz. Ὁμήρου." *Dindorf.* In Athenæus (viii. 348) Æschylus calls his dramas τεμάχη μεγάλων δείπνων Ὁμήρου.

[4] For this use of the plural of proper names, see Krüger, Gr. Gr. § 44, 3, obs. 7. Bernhardy, W. S. p. 61. Longin. Sublim. xxiii. 3 and 4.

[5] The wife of Prœtus, king of Argos. Being unable to induce Bellerophon to listen to her, she accused him to her husband falsely, which occasioned his expedition against the Chimæra. Homer calls her Antæa. Il. vi. 152, &c. Comp. note on Thesm. 404, and for the second negative, see note on Plut. 551.

[6] Philetærus (ap. Athen. xiii. p. 587, E.), Θεολύτην δ' οὐκ οἶδεν οὐδεὶς, ὅτε τὸ πρῶτον ἐγένετο. See Krüger, Gr. Gr. § 51, 10, obs. 11.

[7] Spanheim observes that Æschylus' recollection must have totally failed him, when the whole plot of the Agamemnon (by many considered the best of his compositions remaining) turns on the adulterous passion of Clytæmnestra.

[8] Mitchell compares Eur. Hippol. 1, 445. Add Iph. Aul. 529, ed. Hartung, and Bernhardy, W. S. p. 334, and for πολλοῦ, cf. Nub. 915. Equit. 822. Bernhardy, W. S. p. 138.

[9] This alludes to Cephisophon's intrigue (see the note on that name). Euripides was unfortunate in his matrimonial connexions

BAC. Yea, by Jupiter, this is assuredly the case; for you have been yourself afflicted with those things, which you composed upon other men's wives.

EUR. Why, what harm, you wretched fellow, do my Sthenobœas do to the city?

ÆSCH. Because you have moved women, well-born, and the wives of well-born men, to drink hemlock, shamed on account of your Bellerophons.

EUR. But is this story which[1] I composed about Phædra, an unreal one?

ÆSCH. No, by Jove, but a real[2] one. Yet it becomes a poet to hide wickedness, and not to bring it forward, or represent it; for he who directs them is teacher to the little children, but poets to those[3] who are grown up. In truth, it greatly behoves us to speak what is useful.

EUR. If then you talk to us of Lycabettuses,[4] and the heights of Mount Parnes,[5] is this teaching what is useful, who ought to speak in the language of men?

having been twice married, and twice divorced; which, some think, accounts for the antipathy to women exhibited in his plays; to which, in justice, it must be added, his Alcestis forms an illustrious exception. Cf. note on Nub. 765. For the tmesis, cf. Nub. 792, 1440. Aves, 1070, 1506. Lys. 262. Plut. 65. Kön, Greg. Cor. p. 447. Blomf. Gloss. Agam. 569. Schäfer, Melet. Crit. p. 68. Bernhardy, W. S. p. 197. In Attic *prose* this usage is more doubtful. See, however, Schäfer, Demosth. vol. iv. p. 536.

[1] " But at least you 'll allow that I never invented it,
  Phædra's affair was a matter of fact." *Frere.*
" *An vero historiam de Phædrá composui aliter atque extabat?*" Brunck. Cf. Krüger, Gr. Gr. § 57, 3, obs. 7, and note on Thesm. 597.

[2] " A fact, with a vengeance! but horrible facts
  Should be buried in silence, not bruited abroad,
  Nor brought forth on the stage, nor emblazoned in poetry.
  Children and boys have a teacher assigned them—
  The bard is a master for manhood and youth,
  Bound to instruct them in virtue and truth." *Frere.*

[3] See Mus. Crit. ii. p. 120.

[4] Lycabettus, a mountain of Attica, situated near the confines of Bœotia, anciently abounding in wolves, (whence it derived its name,) and afterwards fruitful in olives. For similar examples of " Accusativus de quo," see Mus. Crit. i. p. 532. Bast, Greg. Cor. p. 128.

[5] Parnes, in Attica, must not be confounded with Parnassus in Phocis. For this use of the relative, see note on Plut. 1046.

Æsch. But, you wretch, it is necessary also to produce words which are equal[1] to the great thoughts and sentiments. And besides, it is natural that the demi-gods[2] have their words mightier *than ours*, for they also have their dresses grander than ours.[3] When I had beneficially established this, you utterly spoiled it.

Eur. By doing what?

Æsch. First by dressing royal personages in rags,[4] that they might appear to men to be piteous.

Eur. By doing what then have I injured in this?

Æsch. Therefore on account of this no one who is wealthy is willing to be trierarch,[5] but wraps himself in rags[6] and weeps, and declares he is poor.

Bac. Aye, by Ceres, with a tunic of fine wool underneath; and if he impose upon them by saying this, he emerges again in the fish-market.[7]

Æsch. Then, again, you taught them to practise loquacity and wordiness, which has emptied the palæstræ,[8] and worn the buttocks of the youths who chatter, and induced the crew of the Paralus[9] to contradict their commanders. And yet, at that time when I was living, they did not understand any thing else, but to call for barley cake and shout "Yo heave ho!"

Bac. Yes, by Apollo, did he, and to break wind too in the

---

[1] We find ὅμοιος also similarly construed : Pax, 527, ὅμοιον γυλίου στρατιωτικοῦ. See Bernhardy, W. S. p. 140.

[2] It will be observed that, in the *Prometheus*, Io is the only mortal character; and she is approximated to immortals by her singular fortunes and subsequent deification. In the *Eumenides*, Orestes and the Pythoness.

[3] See note on Eccles. 701.

[4] See the scene between Dicæopolis and Euripides, in the *Acharnians*, vs. 405, foll. The allusion is to his characters of Œneus and Telephus.

[5] The triremes at Athens were built and equipped by the wealthier citizens, no particular number of men being nominated to this office; but their number being increased or diminished according to the value of their estates, and the exigences of the commonwealth.

[6] See Bernhardy, W. S. p. 209.

[7] The Circus, a part of the Athenian agora, was principally occupied by these, where the wealthy and luxurious constantly resorted; fish, and particularly the Copaic eel, being considered among their chief delicacies. See the Acharnians, vs. 880. For ἰχθῦς, see note on Lys. 557.

[8] Comp. Nub. 1054.

[9] See Thuc. viii. 73, 74, 86

face of the rowers on the lowest bench,[1] and to befoul his messmate, and when on shore,[2] to rob people : but now to contradict, and no longer to row, and to sail this way, and, again,
that way.

ÆSCH. Of what evils is he not the cause? Has he not
represented pimps, and women[3] bringing forth in the temples,
and having connexion with their brothers, and saying, "to
live is not to live?" And then, in consequence of this,[4] our
city has been filled full of under-clerks, and of buffoonish
charlatans, who are always deceiving the people. But no
one is able any longer[5] now to carry a torch[6] through want of
exercise.

[1] Mention is made here of the θαλάμακες, the lowest tier of rowers
in a trireme, the middle being called zeugitæ, and the uppermost
thranitæ. It is rather remarkable that Athenæus (vol. i. 17) accuses Æschylus of introducing on the stage some drunken Greeks
playing pranks far beneath the dignity of tragedy, and not unlike
these.
[2] "On this transition from a plural number to a singular, see
Reisig's Conject. p. 151, seq., and Elmsley ad Eur. Med. 552."
Mitchell. Add Eccles. 207, 508, 618, 672. Vesp. 554. Thesm. 798.
Plut. 256. Nub. 975, 989. Pax, 640, 833. Equit. 1275. Krüger,
Gr. Gr. § 61, 4, obs. 1. Stallbaum on Plato, Rep. p. 389, D.
[3] The second of these charges is, according to the Scholiast, an
allusion to his Auge; the third to Canace. For a passage somewhat
similar to the ζῆν οὐ ζῆν, see the Hippolytus, 191. The Scholiast
quotes a passage from the Phrixus to the same purport. Compare
also Plato, Gorgias, p. 492, E., and vs. 1477, *infra.*
[4] See note on Thesm. 87.
[5] *ἔτι νυνὶ* belong of course to οἷός τέ ἐστι, and not to ἀγυμνασίας.
Adverbs require the *article* to admit of being used as attributive
adjectives.
[6] The Panathenaia were divided into Greater and Lesser, the
former being celebrated on the twenty-second of the month Heca-
tombæon, once in five years; the latter was observed every year, on
the twentieth of Thargelion. In this last there were three games,
managed by ten presidents elected out of all the tribes of Athens,
who continued in office four years. On the first day at even there
was a race with torches, wherein first footmen, and afterwards horsemen, contended : the same custom was likewise observed in the
greater festival. The second contention was εὐανδρίας ἀγών : i. e. a
gymnical exercise, so called because the combatants therein gave a
proof of their *strength* or *manhood.* The place of these games was
near the river, and called Panathenaïcum. The last was a musical
contention, first instituted by Pericles. In the songs used at this
time, they rehearsed the generous undertakings of Harmodius and
Aristogiton Meursius observes that the race began from the pe-

Bac. No, by Jove, certainly not; so that I was quite spent with laughing at the Panathenaia, when a fellow, slow, pale, and fat, was running with his head down,[1] being left behind, and acting strangely.[2] And then the people of the Ceramicus at the gates fall to beating his belly, sides, flanks, and buttocks; and he, being beaten with the flat of the hand,[3] fizzled a little and blew out the torch and ran away.

, Cho. Mighty is the affair, great is the strife, and mighty comes the war.[4] Therefore *it will be* a difficult task to decide, when the one strains[5] powerfully, and the other is able to rally and resist actively. But do not encamp in the same place[6] *always;* for there are many other approaches of captious arguments. Whatever therefore you have to dispute withal, state it, attack, rip up both what is old and what is new; and make a bold attempt to say something subtle and clever. But if you fear this, lest[7] ignorance be in the spectators, so as not to understand the subtleties, while you two speak; do not dread this; since this is no[8] longer so.\ For they have been soldiers, and each of them with a book[9] learns

destal of a statue of Prometheus, that the competitors were three in number, and the prize was his who could carry his torch first to the goal without extinguishing it. From the practice here mentioned by Aristophanes, " Plagæ Ceramicæ " came into use as a proverb, to signify blows struck with the open hand, and in jest. Cf. vs. 131, *supra.*

[1] Lys. 1002, ἂν γὰρ τὰν πόλιν ᾇπερ λυχνοφορίοντες ἐπικεκύφαμες.

[2] " Und macht da Grimassen wie toll ! " *Droysen.* According to Thiersch = δεινὰ πάσχων.

[3] See *Plutus Prior,* Fragm. i.

[4] " Hitziger Kampf ist aufgeregt." *Droysen.*

[5] See similar examples in Liddell, voc. τείνω, iii.

[6] " Auf und bleibt bei Einem Gang nicht ;
    Mancher Angriffspunkt noch beut sich für des Disputes Zwiegefecht." *Droysen.*

" *Quum multi alii etiam aditus* (opportunitates) *callide excogitatorum argumentorum, argutiarum, pateant, quum variis et rationibus aggredi se possint." Dindorf.* Cf. note on Thesm. 351.

[7] See Krüger, Gr. Gr. § 51, 7, obs. 4, and notes on Nub. 380. Thesm. 520.

[8] " That defect has been removed;
    They're prodigiously improved,
    Disciplined, alert, and smart
    Drilled, and exercised in a   *Frere.*

[9] *Philosophical* books are meant.

the rules of art: and besides, their intellects[1] are first rate; and now also they have been sharpened besides. Then don't fear but go through all, as far as the spectators are concerned, since they are clever.

Eur. Well now, I will[2] turn to your prologues themselves, so that I shall first of all scrutinize the first part of the tragedy of the clever man himself; for he was obscure in the enunciation of his plots.

Bac. And which of his will you examine?

Eur. Very many. But first recite me that from the Oresteia.[3]

Bac. Come now, be silent, every man ! Recite, Æschylus !

Æsch. " Terrestrial[4] Mercury, who watchest over thy paternal powers, be thou my preserver and ally, who supplicate thee. For I have come to this land and am returning."

Bac. (to Euripides). Are you able to censure any part of these ?

Eur. More than a dozen.

Bac. Why, they are but three lines altogether.

Eur. But each of them has twenty blunders. [Æschylus exhibits signs of great impatience, and a desire to interrupt Euripides.]

Bac. Æschylus, I recommend you to be silent ; otherwise, you will appear obnoxious to more, in addition to your three iambics.

---

[1] " Cf. Herod. i. 60. Demosth. Ep. iii. 1047, 11, seq." *Mitchell.* See Schlegel, Dram. Lit. p. 158.

[2] "So werd' Ich also gleich an deine Prologe gehn,
　　Um dergestalt den ersten Theil der Eragödie
　　Zuerst ihm zu kritisiren, diesem grossen Geist!
　　Verworren ist er, wenn er den Thatbestand bespricht."
　　　　　　　　　　　　　　　　　　　　Droysen.

[3] The Oresteia, according to the Scholiast, was a tetralogy, comprising the Agamemnon, Choephoræ, (of which this is the opening,) Eumenides, and Proteus Satyricus. See Franz's " Oresteia," Introduction, p. xvi. and Mus. Crit. ii. p. 77.

[4] Terrestrial Mercury with supreme espial
　　Inspector of that old paternal realm,
　　Aid and assist me now, your suppliant,
　　Revisiting and returning to my country." *Frere.*

These three lines form the commencement of the *Choephoræ,* the second piece of the Oresteia. " In this tragedy Orestes is represented as having secretly returned to Argos, standing at the tomb

ÆSCH. Shall I be silent for this fellow?[1]

BAC. Yes; if you will take my advice.

EUR. For he has blundered prodigiously[2] at the very outset.

ÆSCH. (*to Bacchus*). Do you see that you are talking foolishly?

BAC. Well, I am little concerned.

ÆSCH. How say you that I blunder?

EUR. Recite it again from the beginning.

ÆSCH. "Terrestrial Mercury, who watchest over thy paternal powers."

EUR. Does not Orestes then say this over the tomb of his deceased father?

ÆSCH. I do not deny it.[3]

EUR. Did he then say that Mercury[4] watched over this, when his father perished violently by the hand of a woman, through secret stratagems?

ÆSCH. It certainly was not that one; but he addressed Mercury, the helper,[5] as "Terrestrial," and made it plain by saying that he has obtained this prerogative from his father.

EUR. You have made a still greater blunder than I wanted; for if he have obtained the Terrestrial prerogative from his father—

BAC. He would thus be a tomb-robber by his father's side.

ÆSCH. Bacchus, you drink wine not redolent of flowers.[6]

of his father, and invoking Mercury, (not the vulgar patron of thieves, pedlars, and spies,) but that more awful deity, the terrestrial Hermes, the guardian of the dead, and inspector-general of the infernal regions, the care of which had been delegated to him by the paternal authority of Jupiter." *Frere.*

[1] Lys. 530, σοί γ', ὦ κατάρατε, σιωπῶ 'γω; Livy, iii. 41, "Negant se privato reticere." Plutarch, Erot. p. 760, A., μόνῳ Μαικήνᾳ καθεύδω. Lucilius, Fragm. Incert. Sat. lxxxix., "Non omnibus dormio." See Bernhardy, W. S. p. 85. Dawes, M. C. p. 126.

[2] See on vs. 781.   [3] Cf. Eur. Hec. 302.

[4] "So meint er denn, dass Hermes, als der Vater fiel
Gewalt erleidend durch des eignen Weibes Hand
In geheimer Arglist, treu dabei geholfen hat?" *Droysen.*
Euripides means to insinuate, that the Hermes invoked at the tomb of Agamemnon must have been Hermes δόλιος, the patron of deceit and stratagem, and not Hermes χθόνιος.

[5] By this name he is called in Homer, Il. xx. 73; xxiv. 360: in the latter of which the Scholiast gives as its meaning μεγαλωφίλης

[6] Comp. Plut. 805.

Bac. Recite him another *line*, and do you ⌊*to Euripides*⌋ look out for the fault.[1]

Æsch. "Be thou my preserver and ally, who supplicate thee. For I have come to this land and am returning."

Eur. The sapient Æschylus has told us the same thing twice.[2]

Bac. How twice?

Eur. (*to Bacchus*). Observe the expression; I will point it out to you : "For I have come to *this* land," says he, " and am returning." But "I have come," is the same[3] with "I am returning."

Bac. Yes, by Jove, just as if one were to say to one's neighbour, "Lend[4] me a kneading-trough, or, if you will,[5] a trough to knead in."

Æsch. (*to Bacchus*). This is certainly not the same, you chattering fellow ; but it is[6] a most excellent verse.

Bac. How, pray? tell[7] me how you make that out.

Æsch. "To have come" to a land[8] is in any one's power who has his part in a country, for he has come to it without any calamity[9] besides ; but a man in exile "comes and returns from exile."[10]

---

[1] Comp. vs. 1171, *infra*.

[2] Spanheim here observes that Eubulus the comedian derides Chæremon on the same point, for making use of the terms " water," and " the body of a river," in the same line, to express a single stream. See Aul. Gell. Noct. Att. xiii. 24.

[3] " Heimkehren aber ist mit Kommen einerlei." *Droysen.*

[4] Comp. Thesm. 219, 250.   [5] See Bekker's Anecdot. i. p. 358, 9.

[6] Comp. Plut. 371; Nub. 522, 829 ; Pax, 334 ; Krüger, § 56, 3, obs. 3.

[7] " Lass mich hören, wie du das sagen kannst." *Droysen.* " $\kappa\alpha\theta$' ὅτι appears to be said as $\kappa\alpha\theta$' ὄντινα τρόπον." *Thiersch.*

[8] " Es kommt ins Land, wer seiner Heimath nicht entbehrt,
Wer ohne weitren Zwang des Schicksals ging und kommt;
Doch wer verbannt war, kommt und kehret heim ins Land."
Droysen.

[9] For this use of ἄλλος, see Krüger, Gr. Gr. § 50, 4, obs. 11. It is commonly, but very erroneously, said to be *pleonastic* in such formulæ. "In these cases ἄλλος and ἕτερος may often be translated by '*besides*,' '*moreover*.' " *Krüger.* Cf vs. 515, *supra*.

[10] Demosthenes (Ag. Aristocr. vol. i. p. 636) has these words,— "For it is evidently impossible for a man to return (κατελθεῖν) to a country whence he has not previously been banished." See the Eumenides, vs. 459; Soph. Antig. vs. 200 ; Porson add. ad Eur. Med. 1011. The preposition has precisely the same force in κατάγω

Bac. Good, by Apollo! What say you, Euripides?

Eur. I deny that Orestes "returned" home; for he came secretly, without having prevailed upon the rulers.[1]

Bac. Good,[2] by Mercury! but I do not understand what you mean.

Eur. Therefore repeat another.

Bac. Come, Æschylus, be quick and repeat it; and do you [*to Euripides*] look to what is faulty.

Æsch. "Upon this mound of his tomb I call upon my father to hearken to me and hear."

Eur. There again[3] he utters another *tautology*, "to hearken and hear;" which[4] is most evidently the same thing.

Bac. Why, he was calling to dead people,[5] you wretch, whom we can't reach even by calling thrice.[6]

Æsch. But how did you compose your prologues?

Eur. I will show you; and if any where I say the same thing twice,[7] or you see any expletive in it foreign to the subject, spit upon me.

[1] i. e. Ægisthus and Clytæmnestra. Euripides would have made a shining figure (at least, as he appears here) among the tragedians of Tom Thumb's day. See the preface to that valuable drama.

[2] "That's well remarked; but I don't comprehend it." *Frere.*

[3]   "Wieder sagt er da einmal
Vernehmen, hören, was doch durchaus dasselbe ist." *Droysen.*
Comp. Nub. 670.

[4] The participle (ὂν) agrees in number with the predicate (ταυτὸν), in preference to the subject. See note on Nub. 1182.

[5]   "Why, don't you see, you ruffian!
It's a dead man he's calling to.—Three times
We call to 'em, but they can't be made to hear." *Frere.*
See note on Lys. 556.

[6] This alludes to a well-known custom. Hom. Od. ix. 65,
       Πρίν τινα τῶν δειλῶν ἑτάρων τρὶς ἕκαστον ἀῦσαι.
So also Virgil, Æn. vi. 505,
       " Et magna manes ter voce vocavi."
In like manner Hercules, in Theocritus xxiii. 43, calls Hylas thrice. This was practised only in the case of those who died in a foreign land, and whose souls were supposed to be recalled thereby to their native country. For the construction, see note on Nub. 689.

[7]   " I'll show ye; and if you'll point out a tautology,
  Or a single word clapt in to botch a verse—
That's all!—I'll give you leave to spit upon me." *Frere.*
Commentators have produced two passages in Euripides, in which, they assert, useless repetitions are introduced. The first is in the

Bac. (*to Euripides*). Come now, recite ; for[1] I must listen to the correctness of the verses of your prologues.

Eur. "Œdipus[2] was at first a fortunate man,"—

Æsch. No, by Jove, certainly not ;[3] but unfortunate by nature, inasmuch as[4] Apollo, before he was begotten, before even he was born, said he should kill his father. How was he "at first a fortunate man ?"

Eur. "And then, on the other hand, became the most wretched of mortals."

Æsch. No, by Jove, certainly not; nay, rather, he did not cease to be :[5] assuredly not ; when they exposed him as soon as he was born, in the winter, in an earthen vessel,[6] that he might not be brought up and become his father's murderer ; and then he went to Polybus swollen in his feet ;[7] and then, being himself a young man, married an old woman, and in addition to this, his own mother ; and then he blinded himself.

Bac. Then he had been fortunate,[8] if he had also been general along with Erasinides.[9]

Phœnissæ, 1380, where, speaking of Eteocles and Polynices, he says, δισσὼ στρατηγὼ καὶ διπλὼ στρατηλάτα ; the other in the *Orestes*, vs. 640,—μὴ κτυπεῖτε, μηδ' ἴστω κτύπος. It is but justice, however, to Euripides to observe, that his best editors expunge the former of these lines as spurious.

[1] οὐ γὰρ ἀλλά = καὶ γάρ. See note on Nub. 232. For μούστιν, see note on Eccles. 410.

[2] The opening of Euripides' *Antigone*, a play now lost.

[3] It is a curious fact, that while Æschylus (S. C. Theb. vs. 774) and Sophocles (Œd. Tyr. 1189) both assert the happiness of Œdipus before his fall, Euripides himself (Phœn. 1611) contradicts the assertion he has here made, by causing his hero to exclaim, " O fate, how, from the beginning, hast thou engendered me to misery ! "

[4] See note on vs. 740, *supra*.

[5] " *Non desiit esse infortunatus.*" *Dindorf.* For the negatives, see note on Plut. 551.

[6] See Thesm. 505, where an old woman is mentioned as carrying a supposititious child in one of these vessels.

[7] For the construction, see note on Plut. 734.

[8] For this construction, see Krüger, Gr. Gr. § 54, 10, obs. 1. ἄν is thrown out in this way, when the speaker would represent the consequence as *infallible*.

[9] Erasinides was one of the unfortunate commanders condemned to death after the battle of Arginusæ. Xen. Hell. i. 7.

" To complete his happiness
He ought to have served at sea with Erasinides." *Frere.*

2 q 2

Eur. You talk foolishly: I compose my prologues excellently.

Æsch. Well now, by Jove, I will not carp at each sentence of yours word by word;[1] but, with God's help,[2] I will demolish your prologues with a little oil-flask.[3]

Eur. You *demolish* my *prologues* with a little oil-flask?

Æsch. With one only. For you compose them in such a way that every thing fits your iambics, a little sheep-skin, a little oil-flask, a little bag. I will show you directly.

Eur. " You will show me," quoth'a !

Æsch. Yes.

Bac. (*to Euripides*). You ought now to recite.

Eur. " Ægyptus,[4] as the very widely circulated report has been spread, with fifty sons, by ship,[5] having landed[6] at Argos "—

Æsch. Lost a little oil-flask.

Eur. What is this " little oil-flask ?" A plague upon it !

Bac. Recite him another prologue, so that he[7] may investigate again.

Eur. " Bacchus,[8] who, clothed with thyrsi[9] and skins of fawns, amid torches, bounds over Parnassus[10] in the choral dance "—

[1] Cf. vs. 802, 1407, and Bernhardy, W. S. p. 240.

[2] See Krüger, Gr. Gr. § 68, 13, obs. 2.

[3] " Æschylus attacks Euripides for the monotony of his metre, and the continued recurrence of a pause on the fifth syllable, which he ridicules by a burlesque addition subjoined to all the verses in which this cadence is detected. The point and humour of this supplementary phrase is not explained to us by the ancient Scholiasts, nor has the industry of modern commentators enabled them to detect it. Euripides repeats the first lines of several of his tragedies, but falls perpetually upon the same pause, and is met at every turn by the same absurd supplement." *Frere.* See Mus. Crit. ii. p. 122

[4] From the prologue to the *Archelaus* of Euripides. The story of Egyptus and Danaus, with their fifty sons and daughters, is well known, as the arrival at Argos forms the subject of the *Suppliants* of Æschylus.

[5] Cf. Soph. Phil. 220.

[6] Cf. Eur. Helen. 1206, 1222. Cycl. 223, 349. Soph. Phil. 244, 270.

[7] " Dass er ihn eben so versucht." *Droysen.*

[8] The opening of the *Hypsipyle.* Catull. Epithal. Thet. 391,

" Sæpè vagus Liber Parnassi vertice summo."

[9] Eur. Bacch. 176, θύρσους ἀνάπτει καὶ νεβρῶν δορὰς ἔχειν.

[10] " Of this celebrated two-forked hill, it was observed that the

ÆSCH. Lost a little oil-flask.

BAC. Ah me! we have been smitten again[1] by the oil-flask!

EUR. But it shall be no trouble to us; for to this prologue he will not be able to attach an oil-flask. "There[2] is not a man who is fortunate in all respects; for either, being noble, he has not subsistence, or being low-born "—

ÆSCH. Lost a little oil-flask.

BAC. Euripides—

EUR. What's the matter?

BAC. I propose that you lower[3] your sails, for this little oil-flask will blow[4] strongly.

EUR. By Ceres, I would not even give it a thought: for now shall this be struck from him.

BAC. Come now, recite another, and keep clear of the oil-flask.

EUR. "Cadmus[5] once, having left the Sidonian city, the son of Agenor "—

ÆSCH. Lost a little oil-flask.

BAC. My good fellow,[6] buy the oil-flask of him, that he may not destroy our prologues.[7]

one fork belonged to Apollo and the Muses, the other to the god of wine. When and how each came into possession of his fork, is explained by the Pythian priestess, who opens the *Eumenides* of Æschylus. See Eum. 24, seq." *Mitchell.*

[1] According to Mitchell, in mimicry of Agam. 1314.

[2] The prologue to the *Sthenobæa.* The Scholiast has subjoined the half line omitted:

$$\pi\lambda o\upsilon\sigma\dot{\iota}\alpha\nu\ \dot{\alpha}\rho o\tilde{\iota}\ \pi\lambda\acute{\alpha}\kappa\alpha.$$

[3] See note on Thesm. 428.

[4] See Krüger, Gr. Gr. § 31, 3, obs. 11.

[5] From the second *Phrixus* of Euripides, of which Lucian, in Macrob., (vol. iii. p. 226, Reisk.,) Plutarch, in his Life of Isocrates, (vol. ix. p. 331,) and Hesychius, on the expression Γλυκερῷ Σιδωνίῳ, make mention. The Scholiast subjoins the omitted half line,—ἵκετ' ἐς Θήβης πέδον. There is a passage very nearly resembling it in the Bacch. vs. 170,

$$\text{Κάδμον ἐκκαλεῖ δόμων,}$$
$$\text{Ἀγήνορος παῖδ', ὃς πόλιν Σιδωνίαν}$$
$$\text{Λιπών.}$$

[6] See note on vs. 835, *supra*, and cf. Aves, 1638.

[7] Strattis, (ap. Schol. ad Eur. Orest. 269,) Εὐριπίδου δὲ δρᾶμα ἐξιώτατον διέκναισε. Bernhardy (W. S. p. 147) construes ἡμῶν after διακναίσῃ, and compares Equit. 1149, ἅττ' ἂν κεκλόφωσί μου. Nub.

Eur. What? Shall I buy[1] of him?

Bac. Yes, if you will take my advice.

Eur. Certainly not; for I shall be able to recite many prologues, where he will not be able to attach an oil-flask. "Pelops,[2] son of Tantalus, having gone to Pisa with swift steeds "—

Æsch. Lost a little oil-flask.

Bac. You see,[3] he has again attached his oil-flask. Come, my good fellow,[4] [to Æschylus,] still even now sell him it by all means; for you will get a very gentlemanly[5] one for an obol.

Eur. No, by Jupiter, not yet at least; for I have many still. "Œneus[6] once from the earth"—

Æsch. Lost a little oil-flask.

Eur. Let me first say the whole[7] of the verse. "Œneus once having got an abundant crop from the earth, while offering the first-fruits"—

Æsch. Lost a little oil-flask.

Bac. In the middle of his sacrifice? Why, who stole it?

Eur. Let him alone, my good sir; for let him speak to this. "Jove,[8] as has been said by Truth"——

982, ἁρπάζειν τῶν πρεσβυτέρων. Æschin. c. Timarch. p. 15, ἔκλεπτον τῆς πόλεως. Ibid. p. 25, ὑφείλετο τῶν δικαστῶν. Arist. Pax, 1118, ἁρπάσομαι σφῶν αὐτά. Soph. Rex, 1522, μηδαμῶς ταύτας γ' ἔλῃ μου. Ibid. 580, πάντ' ἐμοῦ κομίζεται. Colon. 541, πόλεος ἐξελέσθαι. To me, most of these appear to be *Possessive Genitives.*

[1] Acharn. 812, πόσου πρίωμαί σοι τὰ χοιρίδια; Ibid. 815, ὠνήσομαι σοι. Comp. Pax, 1261, and Bernhardy, W. S. p. 77.

[2] From the prologue to the *Iphigenia in Tauris.* Pisa was the capital of Œnomaus, and the scene of his unfortunate contest in the chariot-race with Pelops. After many contests between it and Elis for the presidency at the Olympic games, it was destroyed by the Eleans.

[3] Mitchell compares Eur. Bacch. 379. Hippol. 313.

[4] " Auf, Freund, auch jetzt noch schaff' ihm eine geschwind; du kaufst
    Von den 'Fein-und Guten' eine für cinen Obolos." *Droysen.*

[5] " The καλοκάγαθοί are the "Good Society" of Athens, the friends of Socrates, the educated classes, attached in their political views to the Spartan form of constitution, and averse to the democracy dominant at Athens,—the aristocrats, who would gladly have back the 'good old times.'" *Droysen.* For the Genitive of Price, see Krüger, Gr. Gr. § 47, 17.

[6] From the prologue to the *Meleager.* The other hemistich was οὐκ ἔθυσεν Ἀρτεμίδι.

[7] See Krüger, Gr. Gr. § 50, 11 obs. 7.

[8] The *Melanippe Sapiens* begins thus, to which Brunck has added.

Bac. He will destroy you; for he will say, "Lost a little oil-flask." For this little oil-flask sticks to your prologues, like warts to the eyes. Come, by the gods, turn [1] to his melodies!

Eur. Well now, I am [2] able to prove him to be a bad composer of melodies, and to be always introducing the same.

Cho. What ever will be the event? For I am considering what ever censure he will bring against a man, who has composed by far the most and best melodies in comparison with [3] those still living at the present day. For I wonder how he will ever censure this inspired [4] chief; and I fear for him.

Eur. Aye, very wondrous [5] melodies: it will soon [6] show itself. For I will contract all his melodies into one.

Bac. Well now, I'll take some of the counters and count them. [7]   [*A symphony is played on the flute.*]

Eur. "O Phthian Achilles, [8] why ever, when you hear the

Ἕλλην' ἔτικτε. It would have been as well for Euripides, when he jokes Æschylus for his Scamanders, to have recollected his own fondness for genealogy, so amply shown in the Iphigenia in Tauris.

[1] "There! that's enough—now come to his music, can't ye?"
                                              Frere.

[2] "Wahrhaftig, darthun kann Ich, dass er im Chorgesang
Vollkommen schwach ist und sich immer wiederholt." *Droysen.*

[3] Thucyd. v. 63, στρατόπεδον κάλλιστον τῶν μέχρι τοῦδε.   Cf. ib. i. 1; vi. 31. Krüger, Gr. Gr. § 47, 28, obs. 10. Buttmann, Soph. Phil. 1171. Krüger, Dion. p. 83, and on Thuc. i. 1.

[4] Orph. Hym. 30, Διόνυσον, βακχεῖον ἄνακτα.

[5] "Mighty fine music, truly! I'll give ye a sample;
Its every inch cut out to the same pattern."   *Frere.*

Euripides alludes to the frequent recurrence of the *dactylic* metre in Æschylus' tragedies.

[6] See note on Lys. 375.

[7] "The entertainment which follows, consists of a musical burlesque, in which each of the rival candidates is represented as exhibiting a caricature of the style of his opponent. This caricature seems to have consisted of a series of musical phrases, selected from their works; but, as the *music* was the only object, while the words served only to indicate the music which was attached to them; the words, which now remain alone, (the music having shared the common fate of all the other music of the ancients,) present little more than a jumble of sentences, incapable of being connected by any continuous meaning." *Frere.* Euripides exemplifies this by producing passages marked by a recurrence of the same musical cadence. For the construction, see note on Pax, 960, and Bernhardy, W. S. p. 146.

[8] The first two lines of this medley are from the address of the

murderous toil,[1] alas! do you not come to their assistance?
We who inhabit[2] the marsh, honour Mercury our ancestral
progenitor.   Alas! the toil—do you not come to their assistance?"[3]

Bac. There are two "toils" for you, Æschylus.

Eur. "O most glorious of the Achaians, wide-ruling son
of Atreus,[4] learn from me.   Alas! the toil—do you not come
to their assistance?"

Bac. This is the third "toil" for you, Æschylus.

Eur. "Speak words of good[5] omen: the chief priestesses[6]
are near, to open the temple of Diana.   Alas! the toil—do
you not come to their assistance? I am authorized[7] to declare
the propitious road-omen of the heroes.   Alas! the toil—do
you not come to their assistance?"

Bac. O King Jove,[8] what a vast quantity of "toils!"
Therefore I wish *to go*[9] to the bath; for I have a swelling in
my kidneys from the "toils."

Eur. Nay, not before you have heard another sct[10] of songs
made up from his citharœdic nomes.[11]

deputation to Achilles, in the *Myrmidons* of Æschylus; the third,
from his *Psychagogi*.

[1] In Dindorf's earlier editions this is improperly arranged.

[2] Comp. Thesm. 830. Krüger, Gr. Gr. § 50, 8, obs. 3, and § 45,
2, obs. 6.

[3] This verse consists of words torn from their construction, and
consequently incapable of any just translation. It is quoted merely
as a specimen of rhythm.

[4] Timachidas says this is from the *Telephus*, Asclepiades, from the
Iphigenia.

[5] "From what drama of Æschylus this verse is taken, the commentators are uncertain." *Mitchell*.

[6] The Scholiast says, οἱ διανέμοντες τὰ τῆς πόλεως, ἢ οἰκοῦντες ἐν
τῇ πόλει. Brunck asserts that they were guardians of the Melissæ,
or priestesses of Diana. Cf. Liddell's Lex. in voc.

[7] From the *Agamemnon*, vs. 104.

"Fug zu verkündigen hab' Ich der Helden gesegnete Abfahrt."
Droysen.
The remark made on vs. 1267, applies here also.

[8] Nub. 1, τὸ χρῆμα τῶν νυκτῶν ὅσον ἀπέραντον. *Babylonians*,
Fragm. xv., τὸ χρῆμα τῆς νεολαίας ὡς καλόν. See Bernhardy, W. S.
p. 427.

[9] See Hermann, Append. Vig. p. 700. Krüger, Gr. Gr. § 62, 3,
obs. 2. Bernhardy, W. S. p. 349.

[10] See Liddell's Lex. voc. στάσιμος. Mus. Crit. ii. p. 484. Aristot.
Rhet. 24, and Harper's Powers of the Greek Tenses, p. 132.

[11] Plutarch (De Mus. sc. vol. x. v. 652, Reisk.) assigns the inven-

Bac. Come now, repeat it, and don't add a "toil" to it. [*An accompaniment played on the cithara.*]

Eur. "How[1] the impetuous bird sends the two-throned sovereignty of the Achaians, youth of Greece,—phlattothratto-phlattothrat,—the Sphinx, the bitch, the president of mis-chances,—phlattothrattophlattothrat,—with spear and aveng-ing hand, — phlattothrattophlattothrat, — having permitted them to meet with the eager dogs that roam the air,—phlat-tothrattophlattothrat,—and the party hanging upon Ajax,—phlattothrattophlattothrat."

Bac. What is this "phlattothrat?" is it from Marathon, or whence did[2] you gather together the songs of the water-drawer?[3]

Æsch. Yet certainly I transferred them from a good *place* to a good *place*, that I might not be seen cropping the same sacred meadow of the Muses with Phrynichus.[4] But this fellow borrows from all the prostitutes,[5] from the scolia of Melitus,[6] from the Carian[7] flute-music, from dirges, from

tion of this νόμος to Terpander, and places among measures of this kind the "Orthian." Timachides, according to the Scholiast, no-tices the use of these μέλη by Æschylus.

[1] This medley is compounded partly of verses from the Agamem-non, and partly from other plays. As the original is throughout what Carlyle would call "a heap of clotted nonsense," the reader must not expect much better from the translation. Vs. 1285 is from the *Agamemnon*, vs. 1287 from the *Sphinx*, vs. 1289 from the *Aga-memnon*, vs. 1291 from an unknown play, vs. 1294 from the *Thracian Women*. The lines are quoted merely for the sake of the music which should accompany them, without any regard for the meaning of the words or their grammatical coherence.

[2] See note on Nub. 893.

[3] The ropes alluded to, were used chiefly to suspend buckets in wells, and hence these strains were sung by slaves, when employed in winding up the well-rope for water. See Liddell's Lex. in voc. ἱμαῖος, and Athen. xiv. p. 618, C.

[4] See Aves, vs. 749, where Phrynichus is compared to a bee.

[5] On the quantity of this word, see Dobree, Advers. ii. 175. Dawes, M. C. p. 213.

[6] The same dithyrambic poet who subsequently became the ac-cuser of Socrates. See note on Lys. 1237.

[7] Some commentators interpret this, "barbaric strains," on the authority of Homer, Il. xv. 867; others as "servile," from the num-ber of Carian slaves at that time in Greece. Cicero, Orat. c. 8, "Itaque Caria, Phrygia, et Mysia, quod minimè politæ minimèque elegantes sunt, adsciverunt aptum suis auribus opimum quoddam et tanquam adipatæ dictionis genus."

dance-tunes. It shall soon be made manifest. Let some one bring me the lyre. And yet, what occasion for a lyre against him? Where is she that rattles[1] with the castanets? Come hither, Muse of Euripides, to whose accompaniment these songs[2] are adapted for singing. [*Enter a woman with the castanets, most ludicrously habited as the Muse of Euripides.*]

Bac. This Muse was never accustomed to act the Lesbian; no.[3]

Æsch.[4] (*with an accompaniment of the castanets*). "Ye halcyons that twitter beside[5] the ever-flowing waves of the sea, moistening your bodies with the humid drops of your wings, being besprinkled; and ye spiders, that, dwelling under the roof in corners, wh-wh-wh-wh-wh-whirl[6] with your fingers the threads stretched on the web-beam, the cares of the tuneful[7] shuttle, where[8] the dolphin fond of the flute was leaping around the dark-beaked prows—oracles and stadia. The exhilaration[9] of the shoot of the vine, the toil-assuaging[10]

[1] Athen. xiv. 636, D., Δίδυμος δέ φησιν, εἰωθέναι τινὰς ἀντὶ τῆς λύρας κογχύλια καὶ ὄστρακα συγκρούοντας, ἔνρυθμον ἦχον τινὰ ἀποτελεῖν τοῖς ὀρχουμένοις.

[2] For the construction, see note on Plut. 489, and Krüger, Gr Gr. § 55, 3, obs. 7.

[3] See note on Plut. 551.

[4] "Æschylus here brings forward a fricassee of Euripidean phrases and rhythms. In order to thoroughly understand their striking characteristics, we must be more deeply initiated into the versification and music of the Greeks than we are. Nevertheless, the general caricature is intelligible enough." *Droysen.*

[5] According to Eichstadt and Böckh, taken from Euripides' first edition of the *Iphigenia in Aulis.* Cf. also Iph. Taur. vs. 1096, and Hartung's note on Eur. Iph. A. 1477.

[6] "Perhaps Euripides had so changed the old measures, that whereas formerly every syllable had a separate sound given it by the musician, he allowed a single syllable to be inflected through various tones." *Thiersch.* This, however, cannot have been peculiar to Euripides alone. See Feussner, "De metrorum et melorum discrimine," p. 5, foll. Eur. Orest. 1429, λίνον ἠλακάτᾳ δακτύλοις ἕλισσε. Cf. vs. 1348, *infra.*

[7] "For these κερκίδες, it seems, were a very *vocal* sort of things, nothing like the shuttles of 'these degenerate days.' Every one recollects the 'arguto pectine' of Virgil." *Twining* on Arist. Poet. note 127. A quotation from the *Meleager* of Euripides, Frag. xviii.

[8] From the *Electra* of Euripides, vs. 438.

[9] Imitated from the following fragment of the *Hypsiple*, οἰνάνθα φέρει τὸν ἱερὸν βότρυν.

[10] Eur. Bacch. 771, τὴν παυσίλυπον ἄμπελον.

tendril of the grape. Throw your arms[1] arouud me, my child." [*To Bacchus.*] Do you see this foot?[2]

Bac. I see it.

Æsch. What then? do you see this?

Bac. I see it.

Æsch. (*to Euripides*). Yet, however, though you compose such stuff, do you dare to censure my melodies, who compose melodies after the twelve modes of Cyrene? These are your melodies. But I wish further to go through the manner of your monodies "Oh[3] dark-shining dusk of Night, what unfortunate dream do you send to me from the unseen world, a minister of hell, having a soulless soul, child[4] of black Night, a horrible, dreadful sight, clad in black shroud, murderously, murderously glaring, having huge claws? Come, ye attendants, light me a lamp, and bring me dew from the rivers in pitchers, and warm some water, that I may wash[5] away the divine dream. Ho, thou marine deity! there we have it! Ho, ye fellow-inmates, behold these portents! Glyce has carried away my cock and is gone. O ye moun-

[1] From the *Hypsipele* of Euripides.

[2] In the metrical sense.

[3] The lines which follow are a burlesque of the monodies in the *Hecuba*, (see vs. 68 of that play,) and of the Iph. Taur. 151.

> "O dreary shades of night!
> What phantoms of affright
> Have scared my troubled sense
> With saucer-eyes immense;
> And huge horrific paws
> With bloody claws!
> Ye maidens, haste, and bring
> From the fair spring,
> A bucket of fresh water, whose clear stream
> May purify me from this dreadful dream.
> But oh! my dream is out!
> Ye maidens, search about!
> O mighty powers of mercy, can it be,
> That Glyke, Glyke, she,
> My friend and civil neighbour heretofore,
> Has robbed my hen-roost of its feathered store?" *Frere*

[4] Eur. Hec. 70, ὦ πότνια χθὼν, μελανοπτερ γων μᾶτερ ὀνείρων. Cf. Æsch. Eum. 394.

[5] The custom of expiating dreams by ablution is mentioned in the *Persæ* of Æschylus, vs. 205, where Atossa, after relating a terrific vision, proceeds,—

tain-born [1] nymphs! O Mania,[2] seize her. But [3] I, unhappy woman, chanced to be intent on my labours, wh-wh-wh-wh-wh-whirling with my hands a spindle full of flax, making a clue, that I might take it to market early in the morning and sell it. But he flew up, flew up [4] to heaven with the very light extremities [5] of his wings; and left behind to me woes, woes; and tears, tears from mine eyes I shed, I shed, unhappy woman. Come, O ye Cretans,[6] children of Ida, take your bows and succour me, and put your limbs in motion, encircling [7] the house. And at the same time let the maid Dictynna, beautiful Diana,[8] with her bitch-puppies go through the house on every side. And do thou, Hecate,[9] daughter of

'Επεὶ δ' ἀνέστην καὶ χεροῖν καλλίῤῥόου
"Εψαυσα πηγῆς ξὺν θυηπόλῳ χερί.

So also Circe in Apollonius Rhodius, iv. 670. Persius, Sat. ii. 16,
" Et noctem flumine purgat."

[1] From the *Xantriæ* of Euripides, according to Asclepiades.
[2] See note on Thesm. 728.
[3] " With the dawn I was beginning
  Spinning, spinning, spinning, spinning,
  Unconscious of the meditated crime ;
  Meaning to sell my yarn at market-time.
  Now tears alone are left me,
  My neighbour hath bereft me
  Of all—of all—of all—all but a tear !
  Since he, my faithful trusty Chanticleer,
  Is flown—is flown ! is gone—is gone !
  But, O ye nymphs of sacred Ida, bring
  Torches and bows, with arrows on the string ;
    And search around
    All the suspected ground." *Frere.*

[4] For instances of these repetitions, see the *Helen* of Euripides, vs. 195, 208 ; Iph. Taur. 188. Mitchell adds Orest. 1367, 1375, 1379, 1387, 1392, 1413, 1414, 1425, 1426, 1454, 1457, 1465, 1473, 1488, 1513.
[5] Eur. Bacch. 1205, λευκοπήχεσιν χειρῶν ἀκμαῖσι. Soph. Rex. 1034, ποδοῖν ἀκμαί.
[6] This and the following verse are quotations from the *Cretans* of Euripides.
[7] Æsch. Theb. 114, 'Αργεῖοι γὰρ πόλισμα Κάδμου κυκλοῦνται.
[8] " And thou, fair huntress of the sky,
  Deign to attend, descending from on high ;
  While Hecate with her tremendous torch,
  Even from the topmost garret to the porch,
  Explores the premises with search exact,
  To find the thief and ascertain the fact." *Frere.*
[9] On old coins Hecate is represented with torches

Jove, holding up lamps with double lights with very rapid hands, light me along to Glyce's, that I may enter and search after the theft."

Bac. Have done now with your melodies.

Æsch. I too have had enough. For I wish to bring him to the scales, which alone will try our poetry ; for they will test the weight of our expressions.

Bac. Come hither then, if I *must* do this,[1] vend the art of poets like cheese.[2] [*A huge pair of scales is brought on the stage.*]

Cho. The clever *poets* are painstaking. For this, again, is another novel prodigy, full of strangeness, which no[3] other person would have thought of ! By the deity,[4] I would not have believed it, if even any one of the common[5] people had told me, but would have thought he was trifling therein.

Bac. Come then, stand by near the scale.[6]

Æsch. and Eur. Very well.

Bac. And take hold and each of you recite your sentence, and do not let go till I cry "cuckoo" to you.[7]

Æsch. and Eur. We are keeping hold.

Bac. Now recite your verse into the scales.

Eur. "Would that[8] the hull of the Argo had not flown through."

[1] Plato, Gorgias, § 102, ἢ τοῦτο μὲν οὐδὲν δεῖ, αὐτὸν ἑαυτοῦ ἄρχειν. For this use of the demonstrative, see notes on Thesm. 520 ; Nub. 380. For καὶ, see note on Lys. 171.

[2] Or, rather, *to appraise like a petit maître.* As similar instances of this quaintness of expression, we may compare Equit. 289, κυνο-κοπήσω σου τὸ νῶτον. Pax, 747, ἐδενδροτόμησε τὸ νῶτον. Ran. 798, μειαγωγήσουσι τὴν τραγωδίαν. Empedocles, vs. 286, ὠοτοκεῖ μακρὰ δίνδρεα. Eupolis (ap. Bekk. Anecd. i. p. 84), βουκολεῖσθαι αἶγας.

[3] For this remarkable construction, cf. Lys. 259 ; Thuc. viii. 96 ; Plato, Apol. p 38, D. In the present passage it looks very like a *Latinism.* See Krüger, Gr. Gr. § 54, 14, obs. 2, and § 51, 17, obs. 7, and note on vs. 1456.

[4] For this elliptical expression, see Kön, Greg. Cor. p. 150. Bernhardy, W. S. p. 192.

[5] Mitchell cites Plato, Cratyl. p. 390, D. ; Theæt. p. 171, C. ; Demosth. p. 1370, 5 ; Soph. Rex, 393.

[6] In the Peace, vs. 1248, πλάστιγξ is used for the platter with which the game *Cottabus* was played. In the Choephoræ, 287, it occurs as a scourge ; and in the Rhesus of Euripides, 303, as part of a horse's trappings.

[7] "Und lasst sie nicht, bis dass Ich "kukuk " rufe, los." *Droysen*

[8] Opening of the *Medea.* For ὤφελεν, see note on Nub. 41. For σκάφος, see Blomf. gl. Pers. 425.

Æsch. ·O river[1] Sperchius, and ye cattle-feeding pastures."

Bac. "Cuckoo!" let go! Why, this man's side[2] sinks far lower.

Eur. Why, what ever is the reason?

Bac. Because he put in a river,[3] having like a wool-dealer made his verse wet as *they do* their fleeces; while the verse which you put in was furnished with wings.

Eur. Come, let him recite another and weigh it against *mine*.

Bac. Then take hold again.

Æsch. and Eur. See there!

Bac. Recite!

Eur. "There is no other temple of Persuasion,[4] save speech."—

Æsch. "For[5] Death alone of the gods loves not gifts."

Bac. Let go! let go! Why, this man's side declines again; for he put in Death, the weightiest of evils.

Eur. And I Persuasion,[6] a verse most admirably expressed.

Bac. But Persuasion is a light thing, and· has no sense. Come, search again for some other of your heavy ones, which shall draw down *the scale* for you, a mighty and huge one.

Eur. Come, where then have I such a one? where?

---

[1] From the *Philoctetes* of Æschylus. To the Sperchius, the "king of streams" in his father's land, Achilles offered his hair on the death of Patroclus. Homer, Il. xxiii. vs. 144.

[2] "Viel tiefer sinkt des Aischylos Seite." *Droysen.*

[3] "He slipped in a river, like the wool-jobbers,
To moisten his metre—but your line was light,
A thing with wings—ready to fly away." *Frere.*

Young readers would do well to remember that τοῦπος ἱπτερώμενον is not τὸ ἱπτερωμένον ἱπος. See vs. 1419, *infra.* Equit. 1106. Pax, 220, 1032. Eccles, 227, 721, 782. Schäfer on Theoc. xxvii. 37, and on Soph. Ajax, 573, and on Greg. Cor. p. 877. Krüger on Xenoph. Anab. i. 9, 18. Donaldson, New Crat. p. 382. So in Eur. Hippol. 681, we must read Ζεύς σε γεννήτωρ ἱμός. Cf. Bast, Greg. Cor. p. 170. Donaldson, Complete Greek Grammar, § 404.

[4] From the *Antigone* of Euripides. Pithu (worshipped under the name Suada, or Suadela, at Rome) was fabled to be the offspring of Venus and Mercury. Her symbols were a thunderbolt, chains of flowers, and the caduceus of her father.

[5] From the *Niobe* of Æschylus.

[6] "But I put in Persuasion finely expressed
In the best terms." *Frere*

Bac. I'll tell you: "Achilles has thrown [1] quatre-deux. Recite! for this is your last weighing.

Eur. "And in [2] his right hand he grasped a club heavy with iron."

Æsch. "For [3] chariot upon chariot, and corpse upon corpse."

Bac. He has foiled you again, even now.

Eur. In what way?

Bac. He put in two chariots and two corpses, which no; even a hundred Egyptians [4] could lift.

Æsch. And now let him no longer *dispute* with me word by word; but let him get into the scales and sit down, himself, his children, his wife, and Cephisophon, having taken his books [5] with him, while I will merely recite two verses of mine.

[1] Brunck observes that this is intended to ridicule the *Telephus* of Euripides, in which the principal characters are introduced playing at dice. "This line was ridiculed by Eupolis." *Frere.*

[2] From Euripides' *Meleager.*

[3] From the *Glaucus Potniensis* of Æschylus, to which Brunck subjoins this line,—

$$\text{ἵπποι δ' ἐφ' ἵπποις ἦσαν ἐμπεφυρμένοι.}$$

[4] Herodotus mentions the hard labour to which the Egyptians were compelled in building their pyramids. Cf. Aves, 1133. The optative in a relative clause requires the particle ἄν, in order to express *potentiality.* Cf. Krüger, Gr. Gr. § 54, 14, obs. 2, and vss. 906, 1377. Aves, 45, 163. On the contrary, when the relative in the sense of *soever* is construed with an optative, the particle ἄν is regularly omitted. See Harper, Powers of the Greek Tenses, p. 106. I have said "regularly;" because I have met indubitable instances of ἄν being used, even in *this* case. 'Inscriptio Teïa (ap. Chishul. Antiq. Asiat. p. 98), ὃς ἄν ἢ κιξαλλεύοι ἢ κιξάλλας ὑποδέχοιτο . . . . . ἀπόλλυσθαι αὐτὸν καὶ γένος τὸ ἐκείνου. Thuc. viii. 54, ἐψηφίσαντο πλεύσαντα τὸν Πεισάνδρον πράσσειν ὅπῃ ἄν αὐτοῖς δοκοίη ἄριστα. Ibid. 68, κράτιστος γενόμενος ἃ ἄν γνοίη εἰπεῖν. Add Xenoph. Anab. i. 3, 17; i. 5, 9; ii. 5, 11; iii. 2, 12; vii. 2, 6, and the passages cited by Bornemann on Xenoph. Anab. ii. 4, 26. In all these examples the particle refers the mind to a protasis with εἰ and an optative, which may be supplied from the context. See Krüger, Gr. Gr. § 54, 15, obs. 4, and Schömann on Isæus, p. 306. Elmsley (Ed. Rev. No. xvii. p. 238) has written inaccurately on this subject.

[5] "Athenæus (i. p. 3, A.), or his abridger, speaking of the books possessed by Larensius, observes, that as a collector, he surpassed those most admired for their collections, as Polycrates of Samos, Pisistratus of Athens, Euclid, Nicocrates of Cyprus; moreover, the kings of Pergamus *Euripides the poet*, Aristotle the philosopher," &c. *Mitchell.*

BAC. The men are friends of mine,[1] and I will not decide between them. For I will not become hostile to either of them; for the one[2] I consider clever, the other I am delighted with.

PLUTO. Then will you accomplish none of those things, for the sake of which you came?

BAC. But if I decide?

PLUT. You shall take one of the two, whichever you prefer, and depart, that you may not come in vain.

BAC. May you be prosperous! Come, hear this from me: I came down for a poet.[3]

EUR. On what account?

BAC. In order that the city may be saved and hold its choruses. Whichever therefore of you shall give some good advice to the state, him I purpose to take. In the first place, then, what opinion do you each entertain respecting Alcibiades?[4] For the state has difficult labour-pains.

EUR. But what opinion does it entertain respecting him?

BAC. What?[5] It longs for, yet detests him,[6] while it wishes to have him. But tell me what you think of him.

> [1] "Well, they 're both friends of mine—I shan't decide,
> To get myself ill-will from either party;
> One of them seems extraordinary clever,
> And the other suits my taste particularly." *Frere.*

" *Amici sunt isti.*" *Brunck.* To imagine that οἱ ἄνδρες φίλοι could be an *address*, may be excused in those who could translate τὸ ἔπος ἐπτερωμένον (vs. 1388) *a winged word.*

[2] "Bacchus expresses the judgment of the connoisseurs, and of the great mass of the people. The former praised Æschylus, the latter preferred Euripides." *Welcker.*

[3] See Krüger, Gr. Gr. § 68, 42, obs. 2.

[4] It appears that this was after the retreat of Alcibiades to the Chersonesus, on the unfortunate issue of the battle fought by his lieutenant, Antiochus, against Lysander. See Xenoph. Hell. i. 6, 16.

[5] It is very evident that the second τίνα ought to be given to Euripides, in conformity with a well-known idiom. See note on Thesm. 772. Otherwise it will be an inaccuracy of the kind noticed in the note on Aves, 1234. Since writing the above, I have seen my view fully confirmed by Bernhardy, W. S. p. 443.

[6] "Imitated from a verse in the Φρουροὶ of Ion, the Tragedian, in which Helen is reported to have said to Ulysses, σιγᾷ μὲν, ἐχθαίρω δὲ, βούλεταί γε μήν." *Mitchell.* Shakspeare, Othello, act iii. sc. ὀ,

"Who dotes, yet doubts; suspects, yet fondly loves."

See Class. Mus. No. xxv. p 249.

Eur. I hate a citizen, who shall show himself slow to benefit his country, but quick to greatly injure it; and *I hate* one who is full of resources for himself, but without resources for the state.

Bac. O Neptune, excellent! But [*to Æschylus*] what opinion do you hold?

Æsch. One must not rear a lion's whelp[1] within the city: above all not rear a lion in the city; but if one rear it, *one must* submit to its ways.

Bac. By Jupiter the Preserver, I am in doubt;[2] for the one has spoken cleverly, the other clearly.[3] But do each of you[4] deliver one opinion more about the state, what means of safety you have.

Eur. If any one were to wing Cleocritus[5] with Cinesias.

[1] It is worthy of note, that this sentiment is expressed by Euripides plainly, in his *Troades*, 718, respecting Astyanax, and under the same allegory in the *Heraclidæ*, 1005, where Eurystheus speaks to Alcmena of putting to death her grand-children. See Süvern, " Clouds," p. 61—75. According to him, the first line is a quotation from the Δῆμοι of Eupolis. He compares Æsch. Agam. 725, ed. Schütz.

[2] Eurip. Erecth. Fr. xii., αἰδοῦς δυσκρίτως ἔχω πέρι.

[3] There is the same jingle in the original.

[4] " So sagt mir also eure Meinung jeder noch
  In Betreff des Staates, wenn ihr zum Heil ihm eine habt."
Droysen.

[5] Cleocritus was a herald by profession. He is ridiculed in the Aves, 876. He appears afterwards as joined with Thrasybulus in the short civil war of the Piræus. Cleocritus was celebrated for his immense size, Cinesias for his extreme slenderness, (vs. 153, *supra*. Aves, 1377. Eccles. 330. Fr. 198,) and the poet means to hint that this would be a good way of getting rid of them both.

  " Beflügelte wer den Kleokritos mit Kinesias,
  Und hob' ein Windhauch über Meeres Gebreit ihn hin."
Droysen.

Vss. 1437—1441, were obelized by the Alexandrine critics. In Dindorf's edition, they are bracketed as doubtful. For the *nominative absolute* in vs. 1437, see Krüger, Gr. Gr. § 56, 9, obs. 3 and 4; § 45, 2, obs. 2 and 3, and cf. Plut. 277. Ach. 1182. Pax, 932, 1242, 1243. Vesp. 1288. Fragm. 509. Eur. Phœn. 294. Bernhardy, W. S. p. 68, and 479. Kün, Greg. Cor. p. 87. Elmsley, Soph. Rex, 60. Blomf. Gloss. Pers. 127. Gloss. Choeph. 513. Mus Crit. i. p. 213; ii. p. 292. " *Accusatives absolute of participles* are utterly without foundation, and ought to be banished from Greek educational books. See the very uncritical citations of Hemsterhuis l. c., and of Elmsley ad Eur. Iph. T. 930, p. 299." *Bernhardy.*

and the winds were to bear them over the plain[1] of the sea—

BAC. 'Twould look ridiculous: but what is the meaning of it?

EUR. If they were in a sea-fight, and then with vinegar cruets were to sprinkle *vinegar* in the enemy's eyes—[*Bacchus turns angrily away.*] I know, and am willing to speak.

BAC. Say on.

EUR. When we consider trustworthy what is now distrusted, and what is trusted, unworthy of trust—

BAC. How? I do[2] not understand you. Speak somehow less learnedly and more clearly.

EUR. If we were to distrust those citizens whom we now trust, and employ those whom we do not employ,[3] we might be saved. If we are now unsuccessful in these measures, how should we not be saved by doing the contrary?

BAC. Bravo, O Palamedes![4] O most clever intellect! Did you invent this yourself, or did Cephisophon?[5]

EUR. I only: but Cephisophon the vinegar-cruets.

BAC. (*to Æschylus*). What then do you say?

ÆSCH. Now tell me first about the city, what kind of persons it employs:[6] is it the good?

BAC. By no means.[7] It hates them most abominably.

ÆSCH. And does it take pleasure in the bad?

---

[1] Eur. Palam. Fragm. ii., πουτίας ὑπὲρ πλακός. Cf. Elect. 1349. Pind. Pyth. i. 24.

[2]
　　　　　　　　　　　"Wie? Ich versteh' es nicht!
　　Sprich etwas ungelehrter und verständlicher!" *Droysen.*

[3] Cf. Eur. Iph. A. 503. Hippol. 1000. Rhes. 859, and vs. 1455, *infra.*

[4] The name of one of Euripides' tragedies. See notes on Thesm. 770, 848. It is here used as synonymous with *trickster.* Athenæus, i. p. 17, has quoted this line of Eupolis:

　　　Παλαμηδικόν γε τοῦτο τοὐξεύρημα καὶ σοφόν.

[5] "It is well known that Euripides, in the details and execution of his pieces, availed himself of the assistance of a learned servant, Cephisophon; and he perhaps also consulted with him respecting his plots." *Schlegel.*

[6] See notes on Nub. 1148. Eccles. 1126.

[7] "Like the French *comment;* a civil interrogative, instead of a positive negative. Cf. Eccles. 976. Eur. Alc. 95. Androm. 84. Elect. 661." *Mitchell.* See Valck. Phœn. 1614. Wolf, Dem. Lept. p. 235. Classical Museum, No. xxv. p. 243, and add Eccles. 389 Vesp. 1145.

Bac. It certainly does not; but employs them of necessity.

Æsch. How[1] then could one save such a city, which nei-ther cloak nor goat-skin fits?

Bac. Devise *something*, by Jupiter! if *possibly* it may emerge again.[2]

Æsch. I will speak there;[3] but here I am not willing.

Bac. Nay, don't[4] say so; but send up your good counsel from here.

Æsch. When they consider the land[5] of their enemies to be theirs, and theirs their enemies', and their navy as their revenue, and their revenue as poverty.[6]

Bac. Good, but the judge[7] swallows them alone.

Plu. (*to Bacchus*). Decide![8]

Bac. This shall be your judgment; for I will choose him whom my soul desires.

Eur. Being mindful, then, of the gods by whom you swore, that you would assuredly take me away homewards, choose your friends.

Bac. "My[9] tongue has sworn," but I shall choose Æs-chylus.

---

[1] "The judgment which Æschylus pronounces on the city itself, by which a city, which hates the honest citizens, and yet does not give itself up altogether to the bad, is declared to have no chance of being saved, must, from the evident connexion of the thought with line 1425, be referred to Alcibiades alone." *Süvern.*

[2] For this tentative use of the hypothetical clause, see Krüger Gr. Gr. § 65, i. obs. 10. Hermann, Vig. n. 312. Cf. vs. 175, *supra.*

[3] i. e. in the world above. See vs. 82.

[4] See Krüger, Gr. Gr. § 62, 3, obs. 12.

[5] See Thucyd. i. 143, ii. 62.

[6] "When they the enemy's country shall invade,
    And leave their own for the enemy to ravage;
    When they shall think their ships their best resources,
    Their present revenues destructive." *Dunster*

[7] "That's well—but juries eat up every thing,
    And we shall lose our supper, if we stay." *Frere.*
The pay of the 6000 jurymen annually sworn in eats away so much of the revenue, that nothing is left for the navy." *Droysen.* Frere sees in it a double allusion; to the jurymen, and to the hurry of the actors and theatrical *judges* to get to the *supper*, which con-cluded the business of the day. Cf. Eccles. 1178. For this use of the neuter plural, see Bernhardy, W. S. p. 282.

[8] See note on vs. 437.

[9] Euripides' sophistry is here retorted on himself. See vs. 101 and Thesm. 275.

EUR. What have you done, O most abominable[1] of men?

BAC. I? I have adjudged Æschylus to be conqueror. For why not?

EUR. Do you look me in the face, after you have done a most shameful deed to me?

BAC. "Why shameful,[2] if the spectators do not think so?"

EUR. Wretch! will you allow me to be dead then?

BAC. "Who knows[3] but to live is to die, and to breathe, to feast, and to sleep, a sheep-skin."

PLU. Go[4] ye then within, Bacchus.

BAC. Why so?

PLU. That I may entertain you two, before you sail away.

BAC. You say well, by Jove; for I am not displeased with the matter. [*Exeunt Pluto, Bacchus, Æschylus, and Euripides.*]

CHO. Happy is the man who possesses perfect knowledge. And we may learn this by many instances. For this man, having been adjudged[5] to be wise, will depart home again, to the advantage of his citizens,[6] and to the advantage of his own relations and friends, by reason of his being intelligent.[7] 'Tis well then not to sit by Socrates[8] and chatter, having re-

---

[1] He forgets he is speaking to a god. So, Aves, 1638, Hercules addresses Neptune thus;

Ὦ δαιμόνι' ἀνθρώπων Πόσειδον.

[2] A parody on a line in the *Æolus* of Euripides; Brunck mentions a repartee of the courtesan Lais to the Tragedian, in which she twits him with the same line. See Athen. xiii. p. 582, C.

[3]   "Who knows but life is death,
   Breathing is supping, sleeping but a fleece?" *Wheelwright.*

Cf. vs. 1082. It is a parody on a notable line in the *Phrixus* of Euripides, which he has repeated in his *Hippolytus*, vs. 191, and in his *Polyidus.*

[4] Cf. Lys. 1166. Vesp. 975. Soph. Colon. 1102, 1104. Dorville, Char. p. 358. Bernhardy, W. S. p. 72. Schneidewin on Soph. Aj. 344. Terence, Adelph. act iv. sc. 4, vs. 27.

[5] Cf. Aves, 1585.   [6] Cf. Plut. 888.

[7] See this construction illustrated ap. Classical Museum, No. xxv p. 230.

[8] Speaking of his power of language, Mr. Mitchell says, "That a person possessed of so powerful a weapon should sometimes have been a little too much delighted with the use of it, is no subject of wonder." And again, "Much was affirmed by him, and little proved: both sides of the question were alternately taken, and the

jected music, and having neglected the most important parts of the tragic art. But to idly waste one's time on grand[1] words and petty quibbles, is the part of a madman. [*Re-enter Pluto, Bacchus, and Æschylus.*]

PLU. Come now, Æschylus, depart joyfully, and save our city by good advice, and instruct the senseless, for they are numerous; and take and give this [*offering a halter*] to Cleophon, and this [*offering a bowl of hemlock*] to the financiers Myrmex and Nicomachus[2] together, and this [*offering a scourge*] to Archenomus; and bid them come hither quickly to me, and not delay. And if they do not come quickly, by Apollo, I will brand them, and bind them hand and foot, and quickly despatch them under the earth along with Adimantus the son of Leucolophus.[3]

ÆSCH. I will do so; and do you give my seat to Sophocles to keep and preserve for me, if perchance I should ever return hither. For him I judge to be next in genius. But mind that the rascal, and liar, and buffoon, never sit upon my seat, even against his will.

PLU. (*to the Chorus*). Therefore do you light for him the sacred torches, and at the same time escort him, celebrating him with his own[4] melodies and songs.

CHO. Ye deities beneath the earth, in the first place[5] give a good journey to the poet departing and hastening to the

result left upon his hearers' minds was that he himself was in doubt, and only excited doubts in others," p. 100.

[1] Cf. Vesp. 1174. Soph. Aj. 1107. Eur. Hipp. 961.

[2] Nicomachus was a scribe, against whom Lysias spoke. He had been employed shortly after the overthrow of the Four Hundred in the Revision of the Laws of Solon. Of Myrmex and Archenomus nothing is known.

[3] The real name of his father was Leucolophides, which Aristophanes jestingly changes to Leucolophus. i. e. *White crest*. Eupolis, in his Πόλεις, says of him,

> οὐκ ἀργαλέον δῆτ' ἐστὶ πάσχειν τοῦτ' ἐμὲ
> τὸν Λευκολοφίδου παῖδα.

He was one of the generals at the battle of Ægos Potami, but was saved from the death inflicted on the rest of the prisoners. See Xenoph. Hell. i. 4, 21.

[4] For this singular construction of the pronoun, see Bernhardy, W. S. p. 277.

[5] This is partly from the *Glaucus Potniensis*, partly from the *Eumenides*, vs. 1010.

light, and to the city good thoughts of great blessings : for so we may cease altogether from great griefs and dreadful conflicts in arms. But let Cleophon[1] fight, and any other of these that pleases, in his native land. [*Exeunt omnes.*]

[1] See note on vs. 678, *supra*. Here allusion is made to his being a *foreigner*, and to his having caused the people to reject the offers of peace made by the Spartans after the battle of Arginusæ, when they proposed to evacuate Deceleia.

END OF THE FROGS.

THE ECCLESIAZUSÆ.

DRAMATIS PERSONÆ.

PRAXAGORA.
SEVERAL WOMEN.
CHORUS OF WOMEN.
BLEPYRUS (husband of Praxagora)
A NEIGHBOUR.
CHREMES.
TWO CITIZENS.
FEMALE CRIER.
A YOUNG WOMAN.
A YOUNG MAN.
THREE OLD WOMEN.
A MAID-SERVANT
A MASTER.

THE ARGUMENT.

O𝕽 the date of the *Ecclesiazusæ* we are not informed by any Didas-calia. We learn, however, from a note of the Scholiast on vs. 193, that it was brought on the stage two years after the league with the Bœotians; consequently, in the spring of the year 392, B. c.; and, (as may be inferred from the Scholiast on the *Frogs*, vs. 404,) at the Great Dionysia. The *Ecclesiazusæ* is, like the *Lysistrata*, a picture of woman's ascendency, but one much more depraved than the other. In the dress of men the women steal into the public assembly, and by means of the majority of voices which they have thus surreptitiously obtained, they decree a new constitution, in which there is to be a community of goods and of women. This is a satire on the ideal republics of the philosophers, with similar laws. Protagoras had projected such before Plato. This comedy appears to labour under the very same fault as the *Peace:* the introduction, the secret assembly of the women, their rehearsal of their parts as men, the description of the popular assembly, are all handled in the most masterly manner; but towards the middle the action stands still. Nothing remains but the representation of the perplexities and confusion which arise from the different communities, especially the community of women, and from the prescribed equality of rights in love both for the old and ugly, and for the young and beautiful. These perplexities are pleasant enough, but they turn too much on a repetition of the same joke.

THE ECCLESIAZUSÆ.

PRAXAGORA (*coming out of the house dressed in men's
clothes*). O bright eye of the wheel-formed lamp,[1] suspended
most commodiously in a situation commanding a wide view,
(for I will declare both your parentage[2] and your fortunes:[3]
for, having been driven with the wheel by[4] the force of the
potter, you possess in your nozzles[5] the bright honours of the
sun,) send forth the signal of flame agreed upon! For to
you alone we reveal it:—justly; for you also stand close by
us in our bed-chambers when we try the *various* modes of
Aphrodite; and no one excludes your eye from the house,
the witness of our bending bodies. And you alone cast light
into the secret recesses of our persons, when you singe[6] off
the hair which flourishes upon them. And you aid us when
secretly opening[7] the storehouses filled with fruits and the
Bacchic stream. And although you help to do this, you do
not babble of it to the neighbours. Wherefore you shall also
be privy to our present designs, as many as were determined

---

[1] This apostrophe to the lamp she has just hung up is a parody
on the pompous addresses to inanimate objects so frequent in the
prologues and monodies of Euripides. For the construction, see
Krüger, Gr. Gr. § 45, 3, obs. 5. Hermann, Vig. n. 260, d. Matthiä
p. 481. Jelf, § 479, 3.

[2] Ran. 946, ἀλλ᾽ οὐξιὼν πρώτιστα μέν μοι τὸ γένος εἴπ᾽ ἂν εὐθὺς
τοῦ δράματος.

[3] Comp. Æsch. Prom. 288. Pind. Pyth. viii. 103.

[4] For this construction, see Bernhardy, W. S. p. 225.

[5] The lamp would appear to have been one of those which were
furnished with double lights. Cf. Ran. 1361. ἐλαθεὶς is referred to
λύχνος, not to λαμπρὸν ὄμμα.

[6] Cf. Thesm. 216, 590. Lys. 825.   [7] Cf. Thesm. 424.

on by my friends at the Scira.[1] But none of them is present,
who ought to have come. And yet it is close upon day-
break; and the Assembly will take place immediately;[2] and
we must take possession of different[3] seats *from those* which
Phyromachus formerly ordered, if you still remember, and sit
down without being detected. What then can be the matter?
Have they their beards not sewed on, which they were ordered
to have? or has it been difficult for them to steal and take
their husbands' clothes? But I see a lamp there[4] approaching. Come, now let me[5] retire back, lest the person who
approaches should chance to be a man. [*Retires to one side.*]

1st WOMAN (*entering with a lamp*). It is time to go; for
the herald just now crowed[6] the second time, as we were
setting out.

PRAX. (*coming forward out of her hiding-place*). I was
lying awake the whole night expecting you. But come, let
me summon our neighbour here by tapping at her door: for
I must escape the notice of her husband. [*Taps at the
door.*]

2ND WOMAN (*coming out of the house*). I heard the tapping[7] of your fingers, as I was putting on my shoes, since I
was not asleep: for my husband, my dearest, (for he whom I
live with[8] is a Salaminian,) was occupying me the whole night

---

[1] "The Σκίρα or Σκιρροφορία was an anniversary solemnity at
Athens, in honour of Athena Σκιράς. The name is derived from
Sciras, a borough between Athens and Eleusis, where there was a
temple dedicated to that goddess." *Smith*. The principal ceremony
consisted in the carrying of a white parasol from the Acropolis to
Sciras. Cf. Thesm. 834. It was a woman's festival.

[2] Cf. Plut. 432, 942, 1191. Pax, 237. Equit. 284. Thesm. 750. Lys.
739, 744. Demosth. 354, 16; 398, 16; 569, 10; 586, 9. Æschin. 10, 32.

[3]   "Während statt der Plätze, die
Phyromachos für uns heantragt—wisst ihr noch?—
Wir uns der andern versichern müssten unversehns." *Droysen.*
"The allusion is to some decree proposed by Phyromachus." *Brunck.*

[4] "Doch 'ne Lampe seh' Ich da herkommen." *Droysen.*
See note on Aves, 992.   [5] See note on Lys. 864.

[6] "Es ist Zeit zu gehen; hat der Herold eben doch,
   Da aus dem Haus wir traten, zum zweiten Mal gekräht." *Droysen.*
The allusion is to the crowing of the cock. See Liddell's Lex. in
voc. κῆρυξ. Cf. Ran. 1380.

[7] Cf. Thesm. 481.   [8] "Dessen Frau Ich bin." *Droysen*

in the bed-clothes, so that it was only just now I could get this garment of his.

1st Wom. Well now I see Clinarete also, and Sostrate here now approaching, and Philænete. [*Enter Clinarete, Sostrate, and Philænete.*]

Prax. Will you not hasten then? for Glyce swore that that one of our[1] number who came last, should pay three choæ of wine, and a chœnix of chick-peas.

1st Wom. Don't you see Melistice, the wife of Smicythion, hastening in[2] her slippers? and she alone appears to me to have come forth from her husband undisturbed.[3]

2nd Wom. And don't you see Gusistrate, the wife of the innkeeper, with her lamp in her right hand, and the wife of Philodoretus, and the wife of Chæretades?

Prax. I see very many other women also approaching, all that are good for aught in the city.[4]

3rd Wom. (*entering, followed by many others*). And I, my dearest, escaped and stole away with very great difficulty; for my husband kept coughing the whole night, having been stuffed with anchovies over-night.[5]

Prax. Sit down then, since I see you are assembled, in order that I may ask you about this, if you have done all that was determined on at the Scira.

4th Wom. Yes. In the first place I have my armpits rougher[6] than a thicket, as was agreed upon. In the next place, whenever my husband went to the market, I anointed

---

[1] " The ordo is: τὴν ὑστάτην ἡμῶν ἤκουσαν ἀποτίσειν τρεῖς χόας οἴνου." *Brunck.*

[2] Wie flink in den Mannerschuhn sie heranklappt." *Droysen.*

[3]   " She alone of all
Seems to have passed the night without disturbance." *Smith.*
" κατὰ σχολὴν is *otiose,* in the same sense that Terence in the *Andrian* says, *aliam otiosus quæret,* ἑτέραν κατὰ σχολὴν ζητήσει, *a son aise.*" *Brunck.*

[4] " Die in der Stadt was Rechtes sind." *Droysen.* Xenoph. Hellen. v. 3, 6, ὅ τι ὄφελος στρατεύματος. Thuc. viii. 1, τοῖς πάνυ τῶν στρατιώτων. Cf. Theocr. vii. vs. 4. Epigr. xvi. 4. Apoll. R. iii. 347.

[5] " He supped on sprats, and got an indigestion;
So through the night 'twas nought but *cough, cough, cough!*"
           Smith.

[6] Juvenal, Sat. ii. 11,
" Hispida membra quidem et duræ per brachia setæ
Promittunt atrocem animum."——

my whole body, and basked the whole day standing in the sun-shine.[1]

5TH WOM. And I. I threw the razor out of the house the first thing, in order that I might be hairy all over, and no longer like a woman at all.

PRAX. Have you the beards, which we were all ordered to have, whenever we assembled?

4TH WOM. (*holding one up*). Yea, by Hecate! see! here's a fine one![2]

5TH WOM. (*holding one up*). And I one, not a little finer than *that* of Epicrates.[3]

PRAX. (*turning to the others*). But what do you say?

4TH WOM. They say yes; for they nod assent.

PRAX. Well now I perceive that you have done the other things. For you have Laconian shoes, and staffs, and your husbands' garments, as we ordered.

6TH WOM. I secretly brought away this club of[4] Lamia's as he was sleeping.

PRAX. This is one of those clubs, under whose[5] weight he fizzles.

[1] "It was the custom of the men to anoint the whole body with oil, and dry it in before the sun; and of the women, to shave themselves all over." *Gray.* For the preposition, see Bernhardy, W. S. p. 264.   [2] See note on Aves, 992.

[3] A brachylogy for τοῦ τοῦ Ἐπικράτους καλλίονα. When the subject of comparison and the object of comparison are the same word, instead of the latter being expressed in the genitive, along with the genitive governed by it, it is often omitted, and the possessive genitive alone expressed. Hom. Il. Φ. 191, κρείσσων Διὸς γενεὴ ποταμοῖο τέτυκται, i. e. γενεῆς ποταμοῖο. Herod. ii. 134, πυραμίδα καὶ οὗτος ἀπελίπετο πολλὸν ἐλάσσω τοῦ πατρός, i. e. τῆς πυραμίδος τοῦ πατρός. Cf. Hermann, Vig. ii. 55. Schäfer ad Schol. Apoll. R. p. 164. Richter on *Anacoluthon*, part i. p. 32, and note on vs. 701, *infra*, and on Plut. 368. Epicrates was remarkable for a bushy beard; hence Plato, the comic poet, nicknamed him σακεσφόρος. "Epicrates 'of the beard' had been a popular character since his participation in the expedition of Thrasybulus, for the liberation of the city. He understood how to make a right good use of this position. His and Phormisius' embassy to the court of Susa, gave occasion to a special comedy of Plato, the comic poet." *Droysen.*

[4] "Pherecrates, the comic poet, said of the hobgoblin Lamia, that it *puffs* with heaving its club. This is comically transferred to the sixth woman's husband." *Voss.* Cf. Vesp. 1177.

[5] "Wohl eine von denen, unter deren Last man—pupt."
                                                  Droysen.

6TH WOM. By Jupiter the Preserver,[1] he would be a fit person, if there ever was one, to cheat[2] the commonwealth, clothed in the leathern garment of Argus.

PRAX. But come! so that we may also transact what is next, whilst[3] the stars are still in the heavens; for the assembly, to which we are prepared to go, will take place with the dawn.[4]

1ST WOM. Yea, by Jove! wherefore you ought to take your seat under the Bema,[5] over against the Prytanes.

7TH WOM. (*holding up some wool*). By Jove, I brought these here, in order that I might card when the Assembly was[6] full.

PRAX. Full, you rogue?[7]

7TH WOM. Yes, by Diana! for how should I hear any worse, if I carded? My children are naked.

PRAX. "Carded," quoth 'a! you who ought to exhibit no part of your person to the meeting! [*Turning to the others.*] Therefore we should be finely off, if[8] the Assembly chanced to be full, and then some of us strode over and took up her dress[9] and exhibited her Phormisius.[10] Now if we take our seats first, we shall escape observation when we have wrapped our garments close round us: and when we let our beards hang down, which we will tie on there, who would not think us men on seeing us? At any rate Agyrrhius[11] has the

[1] To the examples cited on Nub. 366, add Eccles. 761, 1045, 1103. Plut. 877, 1186, 1189. Thesm. 858. Ran. 738, 1433. Aves, 15, 514.

[2] There is an allusion to the *Inachus* of Sophocles, in which Argus was introduced keeping watch over Io; but the whole passage is very obscure.

[3] See Equit. 111. Demosth. p. 15, 5. Blomf. gloss. Pers. 434. Harper, Powers of the Greek Tenses, p. 135. Hermann, Vig. n. 363. Append. p. 748. and for the preposition, see Bernhardy, W. S. p. 240.   [4] "Hebt mit frühem Morgen an." *Droyser.*

[5] Cf. Ach. 683. Pax, 680.

[6] "Wenn das Volk versammelt ist." *Droysen.*

[7] Cf. vs. 124, 742. Lys. 910, 914.   [8] See note on Thesm. 789.

[9]   "Wenn das Volk
    Bei einander wär', und eine zum Uebersteigen sich
    Aufnähme den Rock und zeigte ihren Phormisios." *Droysen.*

[10] "Phormisius, who was joined in the embassy with Epicrates (vs. 71), was remarkable for his hairy person." *Droysen.*

[11] "Agyrrhius, the upstart, had been an influential man in the state for more than twelve years past, and, as we may infer from Demosthenes' speech against Timocrates, a respectable character. He

beard of Pronomus, without being noticed.   And yet, before this, he was a woman.   But now, you see, he has the chief power in the state.   On this account, by the coming day,[1] let us venture on so great an enterprise, if by[2] any means we be able to seize upon the administration of the state, so as to do the state some good.   For now we neither sail[3] nor row.

7TH WOM. Why, how can[4] an effeminate conclave of women harangue the people ?

PRAX. Nay, rather, by far the best, I ween. For they say, that as many of the youths also as most resemble women, are the most skilful in speaking.   Now we have this by chance.[5]

7TH WOM. I know not: the want of experience is a sad thing.[6]

PRAX. Therefore we have assembled here on purpose,[7] so that we might practise beforehand what we must say there. You cannot be too quick[8] in tying on your beard ; and the others, as many as have practised speaking.

8TH WOM. But who of us, my friend, does not know how to speak ?

---

had been the author of the diminution of the comic *honorarium* (Ran. 367), and, later, of the increase of the Heliastic fee (Plut. 176, and vs. 184, *infra*).   How Agyrrhius, who did not resemble women merely in beardlessness, comes by the great beard of the flute-player Pronomus, I know not." *Droysen.* Plato, the comic poet, says of him,

$$\lambda\alpha\beta o\tilde{u}, \ \lambda\alpha\beta o\tilde{u} \ \tau\tilde{\eta}\varsigma \ \chi\epsilon\iota\rho\grave{o}\varsigma \ \dot{\omega}\varsigma \ \tau\acute{\alpha}\chi\iota\sigma\tau\acute{\alpha} \ \mu o\upsilon\cdot$$
$$\mu\acute{\epsilon}\lambda\lambda\omega \ \sigma\tau\rho\alpha\tau\eta\gamma\grave{o}\nu \ \chi\epsilon\iota\rho o\tau o\nu\epsilon\tilde{\iota}\nu \ \text{'}A\gamma\acute{\upsilon}\rho\rho\iota o\nu.$$

[1] See note on Thesm. 870.   [2] See note on Ran. 1460.

[3] "A Greek proverb runs, 'Money makes the rudder act and the wind blow.'" *Droysen.*

[4] "Wie kann der Frauen 'Schaamverhüllte Weiblichkeit' Zum Volke reden." *Droysen.* Cf. Krüger, Gr. Gr. § 53, 7, 3.

[5] "Und eben das ist uns der Schickung nach Beruf." *Droysen.* See note on Aves, 451.

[7] "And for this very reason are we met, To rehearse before we speak in downright earnest." *Smith.*

"The formula $o\dot{\upsilon}\kappa \ \dot{\alpha}\nu \ \phi\theta\acute{\alpha}\nu o\iota\varsigma$ is peculiar, e. gr. $\pi\epsilon\rho\alpha\acute{\iota}\nu\omega\nu$, Plato (Phæd. 100), $\lambda\acute{\epsilon}\gamma\omega\nu$ (Symp. 185), "*Say forthwith.*" Perhaps originally a question, '*Will you not sooner say?*' (than do something else); but afterwards so much obliterated by usage, that, unmindful of its origin, they said after the external analogy of this formula also $o\dot{\upsilon}\kappa \ \dot{\alpha}\nu \ \phi\theta\acute{\alpha}\nu o\iota\mu\iota, \ o\dot{\upsilon}\kappa \ \dot{\alpha}\nu \ \phi\theta\acute{\alpha}\nu o\iota$, in the sense, '*I will, he will certainly,*' &c., therefore synonymous with $\phi\theta\acute{\alpha}\nu o\iota\mu\iota \ \dot{\alpha}\nu, \ \phi\theta\acute{\alpha}\nu o\iota \ \dot{\alpha}\nu$." *Krüger.* Cf. Plut. 485, 874, 1133. Eur. Heracl. 721. Iph. T. 244.

PRAX. Come now, do you tie yours on, and quickly become
a man: and I myself also, when I have placed the chaplets,[1]
will tie on *my beard* along with you, if it should seem proper
to me to make any speech.[2]

2ND WOM. Come hither, dearest Praxagora, see, you rogue
how laughable even the affair seems.

PRAX. How laughable?

2ND WOM. Just as if one were to tie a beard on fried
cuttle-fish.[3]

PRAX. Purifier,[4] you must carry round—the cat.[5] Come
forward to the front![6] Ariphrades,[7] cease talking! Come forward and sit down! [*Here the women mimic the ceremonies of
the lustration.*] Who wishes to speak?[8]

8TH WOM. I do.

PRAX. Now put on the chaplet, and success to you![9]

8TH WOM. (*putting it on*). Very well.

PRAX. Speak away!

[1] " When speaking in the Assembly, it was customary to wear a
chaplet. See Thesm. 380." *Smith*.

[2] "Hier leg' Ich auch die Kränze her; Ich will mich selbst
      Nun auch bebarten, falls Ich etwa sprechen muss." *Droysen*.

[3] "We find as curious a simile in Shakspeare, *Merry Wives of
Windsor*, act i. sc. 4:
QUICKLY. Does he not wear a great round beard, like a glover's
paring-knife?
SIMPLE. No, forsooth: he hath but a little wee face, with a little
yellow beard; a cane-coloured beard." *Smith*.

[4] For this use of the article, see note on Ran. 40.   "The person
who made the lustration in the Assembly was called περιστίαρχος.
Pollux viii. 104, περὶ περιστιάρχων. ἐκάθαιρον χοιριδίοις μικροῖς οὗτοι
τὴν ἐκκλησίαν καὶ τὸ Θέατρον. καθάρσιον δὲ ἐκαλεῖτο τοῦτο τὸ χοιρίδιον."
Brunck.

[5] "A comic licence for τὸ χοιρίδιον." *Brunck*. "The place of
assembly was properly purified by a *young pig!* In default of the
pig, the women take a *cat* for that purpose. The three lines spoken
by Praxagora contain in short the essential forms observed on opening an Assembly. Cf. Acharn. 44." *Droysen*.

[6] "Come all within the circle." *Smith*. Cf. Ach. 43.

[7] "The character of Ariphrades, whom the poet ridicules by supposing him seated among the women, and *out-talking* even *them*, may
be seen in Equit. 1281, and Vesp. 1280." *Smith*. "Aristophanes
therefore had been rebuking the same man thirty years ago."
Droysen.

[8] "The usual question put by the κῆρυξ in the Assembly." *Smith*
Cf. Thesm 379   [9] See note on Thesm. 283.

8TH WOM. Then shall I speak before I drink?

PRAX. "Drink," quoth'a![1]

8TH WOM. Why have I crowned[2] myself *then*, my friend?

PRAX. Get out of the way! You would have done such things to us there also.

8TH WOM. How[3] then? don't they also drink in the Assembly?

PRAX. "Drink," quoth'a!

8TH WOM. Yes, by Diana! and that too unmixed *wine*. At any rate their decrees, as many as they make, are, to people considering well, mad ones, like drunken people's.[4] And, by Jove, they make libations too; or, on what account would they make so many prayers, if wine was not present? And they rail at one another too, like drunken men; and the policemen carry out him that plays drunken tricks.

PRAX. Go you and sit down; for you are a worthless thing.[5]

8TH WOM. By Jove, upon my word it were better for me not to have a beard; for, as it seems, I shall be parched with thirst. [*Goes and sits down.*]

PRAX. Is there any other who[6] wishes to speak?

9TH WOM. I do.

PRAX. Come now, crown yourself! for the business is going on.[7] Come now, see that[8] you speak after the manner of men, and properly, having leaned your body on your staff.

9TH WOM. I should have wished some other one of those accustomed *to speak* were giving the best advice. in order that[9]

---

[1] For this use of ἰδού, cf. vss. 93, 136, of this play. Equit. 87, 344, 703. Thesm. 206. Lys. 441. Nub. 818, 872, 1469. Pax, 198.

[2] " The ancients, as is well known, wore chaplets when carousing. See Hor. Odes, Book 1. xxxviii." *Smith.*

[3] See Matthiä, Gr. Gr. § 488, 9; Jelf, § 872, g.

[4] Cf. vss. 142, 310, and note on Lys. 556.

[5] Cf. Vesp. 997, 1504. Plut. 408. Equit. 1243. Aves, 577. Pax, 1222. Soph. Aj. 1231, 1275. Trach. 1107. Eur. Ion, 606. Rhes 821. Heracl. 168. Troad. 415. Orest. 717. Phœn. 417. Andr. 1080. Plato, Apol. p. 41, E. Rep. p. 341, C. 556, D. 562, D. Epigr. iii. Krüger, Gr. Gr. § 61, 8, obs. 3. Bernhardy, W. S. p. 336. Elmsley, Heracl. 168. Monk, Hippol. 634. Dorville, Char. p. 218. Lobeck, Aj. 1218. Elmsl. Her. 168.

[6] Xenoph. Mem. i. 4, 6, ἔστιν οὕστινας ἀνθρώπων τεθαύμακας ἐπι σοφίᾳ; Cf. Nub. 1290. Plato, Apol. p. 27, B. Krüger, Gr. Gr. § 51, 5, obs. 2. [7] " Unser Plan ist jetzt im Gang." *Droysen.*

[8] See note on Lys. 316. [9] See note on vs. 426, *infra.*

I might have been sitting quiet. But now,[1] according to my motion, I will not suffer a single *hostess* to make cisterns of water in the taverns.[2] I don't approve of it, by the two goddesses![3]

PRAX. "By the two goddesses!" Wretch, where have you your senses?

9TH WOM. What's the matter? for indeed I did not ask you for drink.

PRAX. No, by Jove; but you swore by the two goddesses, being a man. And yet you spoke[4] the rest most cleverly.

9TH WOM. (*correcting herself*). Oh!—by Apollo!

PRAX. (*snatching the chaplet from her*). Have done then! for I would[5] not put forward one foot to hold an assembly unless[6] this shall be arranged precisely.

9TH WOM. Give me the chaplet! I will speak again. For now I think I have gone over it properly in my mind. "To me, O women,[7] who are sitting *here*"——

PRAX. Again you are calling the men "women," you wretch.

---

[1] "So kann Ich's, falls ihr was auf meine Meinung gebt,
  Nicht leiden, dass sich die Frau in der Schenke Keller gräbt
  Zu Wasser; dagegen stimm' Ich bei den Göttinnen!" *Droysen.*
For κατά γε τὴν ἐμὴν, see Bernhardy, W. S. p. 186.

[2] "She means, perhaps, there shall be no water at all in the taverns." *Droysen.*

[3] "She swears by 'the two goddesses,' i. e. by Demeter and Persephone, an oath which only women use." *Droysen.*

[4] "The participle is made clear by καὶ, *also, even,* (negative, οὐδὲ, μηδὲ,) and καίπερ, which in Attic writers scarcely ever occurs otherwise than with *a participle* or a participial construction, whilst καίτοι is found only with an *independent clause* (with a finite verb). The later writers have been the first to use these vice versâ. Yet also in Plato, Symp. 219; Rep. 511; Lysias, 31, 34, if the text be not corrupt." *Krüger.* In the present instance the departure from the statutable construction is very remarkable.

[5] "Um keinen Preis
  Auch einen Schritt nur möcht' Ich zur Ekklesie thun,
  Bevor wir nicht mit diesen Dingen im Reinen sind." *Droysen.*

[6] "εἰ is rightly construed with a future indicative, although there be an optative with ἂν in the other member of the sentence. Eur. Hippol. 484,

  ἦ τἄρ' ἂν ὀψέ γ' ἄνδρες ἐξεύροιεν ἂν,
    εἰ μὴ γυναῖκες μηχανὰς εὑρήσομεν." *Brunck.*

Cf. Ran. 10. Æsch. Theb. 196. Eur. Hippol. 484. Tro. 736. See Krüger, Gr. Gr. § 45, 2, obs. 7. Cf. Pax, 466. Ach. 491.

9TH WOM. It's on account of Epigonus[1] yonder. For when I looked thither I thought I was speaking to women.

PRAX. Away with you also,[2] and sit down there.[3] Methinks I must take this *chaplet* myself and speak[4] for you. I pray to the gods that I may bring our plans to a successful issue. "I have an equal share in this country as you; but I am vexed and annoyed at all the transactions of the state. For I see it always employing bad leaders: and if any be good for one day, he is bad for ten. Have[5] you committed it to another; *he* will do still more mischief. Therefore it is difficult to advise men *so* hard to please *as you*, who are afraid of those who wish to love you, but those who are not willing you constantly supplicate. There was a time when we did not make use of Assemblies at all, but considered Agyrrhius[6] a villain. But now, when we do make use of them, he who has received money praises *the custom* above measure; but he who has not received, says that those who seek to receive pay in the Assembly are worthy of death."

1ST WOM. By Venus, you say this well.

PRAX. You have mentioned Venus,[7] you wretch. You would have done a pretty thing, if you had said this in the Assembly.

1ST WOM. But I would not have said it.

PRAX. (*to the first woman*). Neither accustom yourself now to say it. [*Returning to her subject.*] "Again, when we deliberated about this alliance,[8] they said the state would

---

[1] "Epigonus is otherwise unknown." *Droysen.*
[2] "*Et tu quoque, ut prior illa, facesse hinc.*" *Brunck.*
[3] "Hinweg mit dir auch! geh' und setz' dich dort bei Seit'."
Droysen.
In Brunck's version, *et posthac sede.*
[4] See Krüger, Gr. Gr. § 53, 7, 3.
[5] For this construction, see note on Thesm. 405.
[6] Cf. note on vs. 102, *supra.* "He had been lying a considerable time in prison for embezzling the public money." *Voss.*
[7] "*Venus!* thou silly wench! a pretty joke,
   I' faith, had this escaped thee in th' Assembly." *Smith.*
[8] "The alliance here meant is that concluded with the Thebans, Argives, and Corinthians, (Ol. 96, 2, in the Archonship of Diophantus,) through the mediation of Persia, which was followed by the Corinthian war (B. C. 394). Bloody factions arose in Corinth, which impeded the undertakings of the allies: on this account Athens was angry at Corinth. Their murdering those who were favour

perish, if it did not take place: and when now it did take
place, they were vexed; and the orator[1] who persuaded you
to it, immediately fled away. Is it necessary[2] to launch ships,
the poor man approves of it, but the wealthy[3] and the farmers
do not approve of it. You were vexed at the Corinthians, and
they at you.[4] But now they are good,—and do you now be
good *to them*. Argeus[5] is ignorant, but Hieronymus is
clever. A hope of safety peeped out, but it is banished
* * * * * * * * * * * Thrasybulus[6] himself not
being called to our aid."

able to Sparta, and their eager opposition to the Spartans who ap-
proached them, proved their fidelity to the common cause." *Droysen.*
  [1] "The Scholiast thinks Conon is meant. The bloody scenes at
Corinth took place about the time that he was hastening the re-
building of the walls at Athens (summer of 393); and the subsequent ill-humour of the Athenians and their disinclination to a
continuance of the war may be considered as the cause of Conon's
departure." *Droysen.* "I do not think this alludes to Conon.
The whole passage is obscure on account of the want of historical
records." *Brunck.*
  [2] See note on Thesm. 405.
  [3] See note on Plut. 89.
  [4] This is the most violent synchysis I have ever met with. See,
however, Pax, 558, 559. Plut. 280, 281. Krüger, Gr. Gr. § 61, 2,
obs. 1, and obs. 2.
  [5] I have followed Droysen in considering Ἀργεῖος a proper name.
Smith (after Brunck's note) translates it,

      " What though the Argives in the mass are dull,
        Hieronymus has skill, and he's an Argive."

In Dindorf's edition of Brunck's version it stands, "*Argeus rudis
est, Hieronymus autem sapiens. Salus leviter caput exseruit, at illam
respuitis: * * * * nec ipse Thrasybulus advocatus.*" "Of Argeus we
know nothing. Hieronymus, according to Diodorus (xiv. 81), was
one of Conon's associates. He was left in command of the fleet,
while Conon himself set out for the king of Persia, to obtain permission to make war upon the Spartans, with the assistance of the
Persian navy. Hieronymus' participation in the glorious sea-fight
at Cnidus may have obtained some importance for an otherwise
insignificant person." *Droysen.*
  [6] Dindorf's text exhibits marks of a *lacuna* between vs. 203 and
vs. 204. "This very difficult passage appears to refer to this, that
Thrasybulus, the well-known deliverer of the city from the domination of the Thirty, had set out in this year with forty ships to the
aid of the Rhodians without waiting for their invitation, in order
that they might free themselves from the domination of the Spartans.
The poet means, that the good prospects obtained by the victory at
Cnidus and the other events of the war would be lost through such

1st Wom. What a sagacious man !

Prax. (*to first woman*). Now you praise[1] rightly. [*Returning to her subject.*] "You, O people, are the cause of this. For you, receiving the public money as pay, watch, each of you, in private, what he shall gain ; while the state totters along like Æsimus.[2] If therefore you take my advice, you shall still be saved. I assert that we ought to intrust the state to the women. For in our houses we employ them as[3] stewards and managers."

2nd Wom. Well done ! well done ! by Jove ! well done ! say on, say on, O good sir !

Prax. "But that they are superior to us in their habits I will demonstrate. For, in the first place, they wash their wool in warm water, every one of them, after the ancient custom And you will not see them trying in a different way. But would not the city of the Athenians be saved, if it observed this properly,[4] unless it made itself[5] busy with some other new-fangled scheme ? They roast sitting, just as before. They carry *burdens* on their heads, just as before. They keep the Thesmophoria, just as before. They[6] bake their cheese-cakes, just as before. They torment their husbands,[7] just as before. They have paramours in the house, just as before. They buy dainties for themselves, just as before. They like their wine unmixed,[8] just as before. They delight[9] in being wantonly treated, just as before. Therefore, sirs, let us intrust the city

like undertakings as Thrasybulus recommended." *Droysen.* Few persons, I am persuaded, will approve of this view.
    "Him why not call then to the helm of the state ? " *Smith.*
  [1] See Harper's Powers of the Greek Tenses, p. 41 foll., and Bernhardy, W. S. p. 382. Krüger, Gr. Gr. § 53, 6, obs. 3.
  [2] "Indess der Staat gleich Aisimos so weiterhinkt." *Droysen.*
                    " Meantime
        The state, like Æsimus, gets lamely on." *Smith.*
" Æsimus, who is also mentioned by Lysias in his speech against Agoratus, was, according to the Scholiast, a lame, stupid man." *Droysen.*
  [3] See Krüger, Gr. Gr. § 57, 3, obs. 1, and note on Plut. 314.
  [4] " χρηστῶς· ἀντὶ τοῦ φυλακτικῶς· Ἀριστοφάνης. ἀντὶ τοῦ ἐφυλάττετο τὸν ἀρχαῖον νόμον, καὶ μὴ ἐπολυπραγμόνει, καὶ τὰς καινὰς εἰσέφερε πολιτείας." *Suidas.* Liddell (in voc. χρηστὸς) joins χρηστῶς εἶχε, so, as to = *recte se haberet.*   [5] See note on Thesm. 789.
  [6] This verse does not appear in Brunck's edition.
  [7] Brunck compares Plaut. Menæchm. iv. 1.
    [8] See note on Ran. 1388.   [9] Cf. Nub. 1070

to them, and not chatter exceedingly, nor inquire what in the world they will do; but let us fairly suffer them to govern, having considered this alone,[1] that, in the first place, being mothers, they will be desirous to save the soldiers; and in the next place, who could send provisions quicker than the parent? A woman is most ingenious[2] in providing money; and when governing, could never be deceived; for they themselves are accustomed to deceive. The rest I will omit: but if you take my advice in this, you will spend your lives happily."

1st Wom. Well done, O sweetest Praxagora, and cleverly! Whence, you rogue, did you learn this so prettily?

Prax. During the flight[3] I dwelt with my husband in the Pnyx; and then I learnt by hearing the orators.

1st Wom. No wonder then, my dear, you are[4] clever and wise: and we[5] women elect you as general on the spot, if you will effect these things, which you have in your mind. But if Cephalus[6] should be unlucky enough to meet[7] and insult you, how will you reply to him in the Assembly?

Prax. I will say he is crazed.

1st Wom. But this they all know.

Prax. But also that he is melancholy-mad.

1st Wom. This too they know.

Prax. But also that he tinkers[8] his pots badly, but the state well and prettily.

---

[1] "Voll Vertraun, wenn ihr nur bedenkt." *Droysen.*

[2] "Then for the *ways and means*, say who're more skilled
Than women? They too are such arch *deceivers*,
That, when in power, they ne'er will be *deceived*." *Smith.*
See note on Aves, 451.

[3] The long lapse of time will hardly allow us to refer this to the flight of the country people into the city in accordance with the policy of Pericles. "This difficult passage probably refers to the times of the Thirty Tyrants, wben *no* assemblies were held in the Pnyx, and the orators were *not allowed* to speak." *Droysen.*

[4] See note on Vesp. 451.

[5] See Krüger, Gr. Gr. § 50, 8, obs. 3.

[6] One of the demagogues of the day. His father was a *potter*.

[7] "προσφθαρείς, *accedens*. Φθείρεσθαι in Attic writers = *ire, venire*, but always in a bad sense, in reference to those who *go* or *wander* to their own or other people's injury or loss. Cf. Aves, 916. Pax, 72. Demostb. Mid. p. 660. Misc. Obs. vol. iv. p. 451." *Brunck.* Compare Liddell's Lex. in voc.

[8] A happy coincidence in the German language has enabled Droysen to translate tbis verbal play with singular felicity:

1st Wom. How then, if Neoclides[1] the blear-eyed insults you?

Prax. Him I bid count the hairs on a dog's tail.[2]

1st Wom. How then, if they knock you ?

Prax. I'll knock again; since I am not unused to many knocks.

1st Wom. That thing alone is unconsidered, what in the world you will do, if the Policemen try to drag you away.[3]

Prax. (*suiting the action to the word*). I'll nudge with the elbow in this way; for I will never be caught[4] by the middle.

1st Wom. And if they lift you up, we will bid them let you alone.

2nd Wom. This has been well considered by us. But that we have not thought of, how we shall remember then to hold up our hands; for we are accustomed to hold up our legs.

Prax. The thing is difficult: but nevertheless we must hold up our hands, having bared one arm up to the shoulder. Come then, gird up your tunics;[5] and put on your Laconian shoes as soon as possible, as you always see your husbands do, when they are about to go to the Assembly or out of doors. And then, when all these matters are well, tie on your beards. And when you shall have arranged them precisely, having them fitted on, put on also your husbands' garments, which[6] you stole; and then go, leaning on your staffs, singing

> "Dass er mache schlechte Kannen zwar,
> Auf 's Kannegiessern aber versteh' er trefflich sich."

[1] See vs. 398, *infra*, and Plut. 665.

[2] "*Huic ego dicam, ut in canis culum inspiciat.*" *Brunck.*
See Harper, Powers of the Greek Tenses, p. 41 foll., and Bernhardy, W. S. p. 382. Krüger, Gr. Gr. § 53, 6, obs. 3.

[3] "Ἕλκωσιν, *trahere velint.*" *Brunck.* Cf. Harper's Powers of the Greek Tenses, p. 50. Porson and Schäfer on Eur. Phœn. 79, 1231. Monk, Hippol. 592. Dorville, Char. p. 214. Hermann, Vig. n. 161. This usage is more especially frequent in διδόναι and πείθειν. See Krüger, Gr. Gr. § 53, 1, obs. 7.

[4] Cf. Acharn. 570. Equit. 387. Ran. 469.

[5] "τὰ χιτώνια is badly translated *vestes*. It ought to have been translated *tunicas succingite.*" *Brunck.* For the construction, see Schäfer, Melet. Crit. p. 88.

[6] "Aristophanes never uses the article for οὗτος or αὐτός.. This I have remarked on Plut. 44." *Brunck.* He should have added, *unless followed by δέ.* See Aves, 492, 530. Thesm. 505, 846. Eccles. 312, 316. Pax, 1182. Plut. 559, 691. Equit. 717. Blomfield on

some old man's[1] song, imitating the manner of the country people.

2ND WOM. You say well. But let us [*to those next her*] go before them; for I fancy other women also[2] will come forthwith[3] from the country to the Pnyx.

PRAX. Come, hasten! for it is the custom there for those who are not present at the Pnyx at day-break,[4] to skulk away, having not even a doit.[5] [*The women advance into the orchestra, and there form themselves into a chorus.*]

CHORUS. It is time for us to advance, O men,—for this[6] we ought mindfully to be always repeating, so that it may never escape[7] our memories. For the danger is not trifling, if we be caught entering upon so great an enterprise in secret. Let us go to the Assembly, O men; for the Thesmothetes threatened, that whoever should not come at dawn very early, in haste, looking sharp and sour, content[8] with garlic-pickle, he would not give him the three obols.

Theb. 81. Prom. V. 860. Bernhardy, W. S. p. 312. Mus. Crit. i. p. 488. Kön, Greg. Cor. p. 239.

[1] " Ein Lied aus alten Zeiten." *Droysen.* Cf. Vesp. 269.

[2] See Krüger, Gr. Gr. § 69, 32, obs. 21.

[3] " Grades Wegs." *Droysen.* " *Ex advorsum.*" *Brunck.* But Brunck's version would require ἀντικρύ. The adverbs in -υς generally refer to *time*, and their corresponding forms in -υ to *place*. Compare εὐθὺς and εὐθύ.

[4] See Porson, Hec. 979. Opusc. p. xciii.

[5] " By all means make good speed, remembering that
   Who gets not to the Pnyx at earliest dawn,
   Must home again return without a doit." *Smith.*
" It appears to have been a proverbial expression, or an allusion to the proverb παττάλου γυμνότερος, which occurs ap. Aristænet. Ep. xviii. lib. ii." *Bergler.*

[6] τοῦτο refers to the word ἄνδρες. They are to remember always to call themselves *men.* See note on Lys. 134.

[7] Elmsley (Mus. Crit. i. p. 483) alters this to καὶ μήποτ' ἐξολίσθῃ, i. e. ἐξολισθέτω, as Aristophanes does not join ὡς = *ita ut* with a conjunctive without ἄν. The usage in prose writers is just the reverse. See Harper, Powers of the Greek Tenses, p. 125. " The pronoun ἡμᾶς does not depend on ἐξολίσθῃ. The ordo is : τοῦτο γὰρ χρὴ μεμνημένας ἡμᾶς ἀεὶ λέγειν, ὡς μή ποτ' ἐξολίσθῃ." *Brunck.*
" Time now 'tis, my merry men, time now for us to start,
  That we are *men* repeating oft, lest we belie our part.
  Not slight would be the peril, if any prying eyes,
  In secret while we plot should pierce through our disguise.
  Then on, my merry men, for the council let us start." *Smith*

[8] See Bernhardy, W. S. p. 104.

Come, O Charitimides,[1] and Smicythus, and Draces, follow in haste, taking heed to yourself that you blunder in none of those things which you ought to effect. But see that, when we have received our ticket,[2] we then sit down[3] near each other, so that we may vote for all measures, as many as it behoves our sisterhood. And yet, what am I saying? for I ought to have called them "brotherhood."[4]

But see that we jostle those who have come from the city; as many as heretofore,[5] when a person had to receive only *one* obolus on his coming, used to sit and chatter, crowned with chaplets.[6] But now they are a great nuisance. But when the brave Myronides[7] held office, no one used to dare to conduct the affairs of the state for the receipt[8] of money; but each of them used[9] to come with drink in a little wine-skin, and bread at the same time, and two onions besides, and three olives.[10] But now, like people carrying clay, they seek to get three obols, whenever they transact any public business.

BLEPYRUS. (*coming out of his house attired in his wife's*

---

[1] The chorus addresses the leaders amongst the women by the names of *men.* Charitimides was commander of the Athenian navy. For Draces, see Lys. 254.

[2] See Liddell's Lex. in voc. σύμβολον, 3.

[3] The exhortative use of ὅπως is not confined to the *second* person. See vs. 300. Vesp. 1250. Nub. 882, 888. Ran. 8. Lys. 290. Pax, 562. Hermann, Vig. n. 255, and other examples ap. Krüger, Gr. Gr. § 54, 8, obs. 7.

[4] Φίλας—φίλους.

[5] They contrast the present eagerness to attend the Assemblies, now that the pay is *three* obols, with the unconcernedness of former times, when they only received *one* obol. *Then* they used to prefer to sit at home chattering, rather than attend the Assemblies.

> "Die sonst, wo der Lohn gering,
> Wo, wer zur Ekklesie ging,
> Nur einen Obol empfing,
> Heim sassen und schwatzten
> Gekränzet in Zierlichkeit." *Droysen.*

[6] Strattis ap. Athen. xv. p. 685, B.,

> λουσάμενοι δὲ πρὸ λαμπρᾶς
> ἡμέρας ἐν τοῖς στεφανώμασιν.

See Bernhardy, W. S. p. 209.

[7] A general in the times of Pericles,—not *Archon,* as Brunck makes him. See Thuc. i. 105, 108; iv. 95.

[8] "Staatesdienst zu brauchen als Geldverdienst." *Droysen*

[9] See note on Plut. 982.

[10] See note on Pax 647

petticoat and shoes). What's the matter? Whither in the world is my wife gone? for it is now near[1] morning, and she does not appear. I have been lying this long while wanting to ease myself, seeking to find my shoes and my garment in the dark. And when now,[2] on groping after it, I was not able to find it, but he, Sir-reverence, now continued to knock at the door,[3] I take this kerchief of my wife's, and I trail along her Persian slippers. But where, where could one ease himself in an unfrequented[4] place? or is every place a good place[5] by night? for now no one will see me easing myself. Ah me, miscrable! because I married a wife, being an old man.[6] How many stripes I deserve to get! For she never went out to do any good. But nevertheless I must certainly go aside to ease myself.

A NEIGHBOUR (*coming forward*). Who is it? Surely it is not Blepyrus[7] my neighbour? Yes, by Jove! 'tis he himself assuredly. [*Goes up to him.*] Tell me, what means this yellow[8] colour? Cinesias has not, I suppose, befouled you somehow?

BLEP. No; but I have come out with my wife's little saffron-coloured robe[9] on, which she is accustomed to put on.

NEIGH. But where is your garment?

BLEP. I can't tell. For when I looked for it, I did not find it in the bed-clothes.

NEIGH. Then did you not even bid[10] your wife tell you?

[1] Cf. vs. 20.

[2] Cf. vs. 195, *supra*. Lys. 523. Vesp. 121. Porson, Append. Toup. iv. p. 481. For ψηλαφῶν, compare Pax, 691.

[3] A Greek euphemism for πρωκτός.

[4] "ἐν καθαρῷ, *in a place free from people*. Hor. Epist. ii. 271, 'Puræ sunt plateæ, nihil ut meditantibus obstet.' Cf. Apoll. R. iii. 1201." *Brunck*.

[5] Cf. Thesm. 292. "It is the same as if he had said καλόν ἐστι." *Kuster*.

[6] Cf. Thesm. 412, 413.

[7] Terence, Andrian, iv. 5, 6, "Quem video? estne hic Crito sobrinus Chrysidis? is est." Eun. iii. 4, 7, "Sed quisnam a Thaide exit? is est, annon est? ipsus est."

[8] "There is an allusion to the πυῤῥίχη of Cinesias; for which see Ran. 153, and because the same person κατατετίληκε τῶν Ἑκαταίων, (Ran. 366)." *Bergler*.

[9] Plaut. Epid. ii. 2, 47, "caltulam aut crocotulam." Cf. Virg. Æn. ix. 614.

[10] See note on Equit. 1017.

BLEP. No, by Jove! for she does not happen to be within, but has slipped out[1] from the house without my knowledge. For which reason[2] also I fear lest she be doing some mischief.[3]

NEIGH. By Neptune, then you've suffered exactly the same as I;[4] for she I live with, is gone with the garment I used to wear. And this is not *the only thing*[5] which troubles me; but she *has* also *taken* my shoes. Therefore I was not able to find them any where.

BLEP. By Bacchus, neither could I my Laconian shoes! but as I wanted to ease myself, I put my feet into *my wife's* buskins and am hastening, in order that I might[6] not do it in the blanket, for it was clean-washed.[7]

NEIGH. What then can it be? Has some woman among her friends invited her to breakfast?

BLEP. In my[8] opinion *it is so*. She's certainly not an ill body, as far[9] as I know.

NEIGH. Come, you are as long about it as the rope of a draw-well.[10] It is time for me to go to the Assembly, if I find my garment, the only one I had.[11]

.

[1] Hesychius : ἐκτρυπῆσαι· ἐξελθεῖν λεληθότως.

[2] ὅ = δι' ὅ. See Porson and Pflugk on Hec. 13.

[3] Eurip. Med. 37, δέδοικα δ' αὐτὴν, μή τι βουλεύσῃ νέον. " νέον is often used in the same sense as κάκον. So Eur. Bacch. 360." *Brunck.* See Monk, Hipp. 860.

[4] Eur. Cycl. 634, ταὐτὸν πιπόνθατε ἄρ' ἐμοί. Bacch. 189, ταὐτά μοι πάσχεις ἄρα. Ion, 330, πέπονθέ σῇ μητρὶ ταὐτ' ἄλλη γυνή. Epicrates (ap. Athen. p. 570, B.), πεπονθέναι δὲ ταὐτά μοι δοκεῖ τοῖς ἀετοῖς. Add Plato, Polit. v. p. 468, D.

[5] " I wish that were all." *Droysen.* Cf. Eur. Hippol. 804. " μόνον is understood, of which there is a frequent ellipse. In vs. 358, we have the full form." *Brunck.* See Monk, Hippol. 359. Lobeck, Ajax, 747.

[6] For similar examples of what Brunck thinks is a solecism, see note on Ran. 24. In the present case, no other construction would be correct. To change ἐγχέσαιμι into a subjunctive, would make the danger *still future* to him; whereas that particular danger was over as soon as he left his bed. As he is *still hastening,* ἵεμαι, the reading of almost all the MSS. and editions has been very properly retained by Dindorf.

[7] Cf. Acharn. 845.

[8] Cf. Pax, 232. Bekk. Anecd. i. p. 32, 25. Bernhardy, W. S p 131.

[9] See notes on Thesm. 34. Nub. 1252.

[10] " At tu funem cacas." *Brunck.* [11] Comp. Plut. 36

BLEP. And I too, as soon as I shall have eased myself. But now a wild pear has shut up[1] my hinder end.

NEIGH. Is it *the wild pear* which Thrasybulus[2] spoke of to the Spartans? [*Exit.*]

BLEP. By Bacchus, at any rate it clings very tight to me But what shall I do? for not even is this the only thing which troubles me; but *to know*[3] where the dung will go to in future, when I eat. For now this Achradusian,[4] whoever in the world he is, has bolted the door. Who then will go for a doctor for me? and which one? Which of the breech-professors[5] is clever in his art? Does Amynon[6] know it? But perhaps he will deny it. Let some one summon Antisthenes[7] by all means. For this man, so far as groans[8] are concerned, knows what a breech wanting to ease itself means. O mistress Ilithyia,[9] do not suffer me to be burst or[10] shut up! lest I become a comic night-stool.[11] [*Enter Chremes.*]

[1] Soph. Antig. 180, γλῶσσαν ἐγκλείσας ἔχει. Cf. Krüger, Gr. Gr. § 56, 3, obs. 6. "ἐπέχει δὲ τὴν γαστέρα ἡ ἀχράς." *Scholiast.*

[2] "Was it of that same sort which gave the quinzy
    To Thrasybulus once?" *Smith.*
He had undertaken to speak against the Spartans, who had come with proposals for peace, (B. C. 393,) but afterwards excused himself, pretending to be labouring under a quinzy, brought on by eating *wild pears.* The Athenians suspected him of having been bribed by the Spartans. For a similar anecdote of Demosthenes, see Aul. Gell. xi. 9.

[3] For similar examples, see note on Nub. 1392.

[4] Of the deme of *Achras* (ἀχράς, vs. 355). For these comic demi, see note on Vesp. 151. "The ordo is: νῦν μὲν γὰρ οὗτος ὁ 'Α.χ., ὅστις ποτ' ἔστ' ἄνθρ., βεβ. τ. θύραν." *Brunck.* For θύραν, see note on vs. 316.

[5] "Read τῶν κατὰ πρωκτὸν, like Plato's διδάσκαλος τῶν κατὰ μουσικήν." *Bentley.*

[6] "Amynon, of course, is no physician, but an orator, who possessed a sufficient knowledge of the profession alluded to to qualify him, according to vs. 112, for state-affairs." *Droysen.* Cf. Nub. 1094.

[7] Thesm. 65, 'Αγάθωνά μοι δεῦρ' ἐκκάλεσον πάσῃ τέχνῃ. "Antisthenes, a miser, suffered from costiveness." *Voss.* See Quart. Rev. No. xiv. p. 453.

[8] "In στεναγματων, there is a comic allusion to τὸ στενὺν τοῦ πρωκτοῦ." *Toup.* See Bernhardy, W. S. p. 233.

[9] Terence, Andr. iii. 1, 15, "Juno Lucina fer opem, obsecro." "Aristophanes burlesques the language of tragedy, as Reisig has rightly observed." *Dindorf.* Cf. Pax, 10.

[10] "μηδὲ does not belong to βεβ., but to περιίδῃς, and, as the grammarians say, ἀπὸ κοινοῦ." *Faber.* Had it referred to βεβαλαιωμένον we should have had μήτε.

[11] "Dass Ich nicht ein Nachtstuhl werde für die Komödie." *Droys*

CHREM. Hollo you! what are you doing? You are not easing yourself, I suppose?

BLEP. I? Certainly not any longer, by Jove; but am rising up.

CHREM. Have you your wife's smock on?[1]

BLEP. Yes, for in the dark I chanced to find this in the house. But whence have you come, pray?

CHREM. From the Assembly.

BLEP. Why, is it dismissed already?

CHREM. Nay, rather, by Jove, at dawn. And indeed the vermilion,[2] O dearest Jove! which they threw about on all sides, afforded much laughter.

BLEP. Then did you get your three obols?

CHREM. Would[3] I had! But now I came too late; so that I am ashamed * * * * * * By Jove, *I have brought* nothing else but my pouch.[4]

BLEP. But what was the reason?

CHREM. A very great crowd of men, as never at any time[5] came all at once to the Pynx. And indeed, when we saw them, we compared them all to shoe-makers: for[6] the Assembly was marvellously[7] filled with white[8] to look at. So that neither I myself nor many others got *any thing*.

BLEP. Shouldn't I then get any thing, if I went now?

CHREM. By no[9] means: not even, by Jove, if you went then, when the cock[10] crowed the second time.

BLEP. Ah me, wretched! "O Antilochus,[11] loudly bewail me who live, more than the three obols:" for I[12] am undone.

---

[1] "The common reading is correct: Chremes asks this with astonishment." *Dindorf.*

[2] See Acharn. vs. 22.   [3] See note on Nub. 41.

[4] "I came too late, and to my shame have brought
  My wallet back as empty as I went." *Smith.*

Cf. Vesp. 315. Dindorf's edition here exhibits marks of a *lacuna.*

[5] See Dawes, M. C. p. 364. Pierson on Herodian, p. 461.

[6] See note on Nub. 232.

[7] See note on Lys. 198. Krüger, Gr. Gr. § 51, 10, obs. 12.

[8] On account of the fair complexions of the women who composed the greater part of the Assembly. Hence the comparison in vs. 385. For this use of the infinitive, see note on Plut. 489.

[9] See note on Ran. 1456.   [10] Cf. vs. 30, *supra.*

[11] A parody on the following lines of the *Myrmidons* of Æschylus,

  Ἀντίλοχ' ἀποίμωξόν με τοῦ τεθνηκότος
    τὸν ζῶντα μᾶλλον.

[12] See note on Thesm. 105.

But what was the cause, that so vast a crowd was assembled so early?[1]

CHREM. What else, but that the Prytanes determined to bring forward[2] a motion concerning the safety of the state? And then forthwith the blear-eyed Neoclides first crept forward.[3] And then you can't think[4] how the people bawled out, "Is it not shameful,[5] that this fellow should dare to harangue the people, and that too when the question is[6] concerning safety, who did not save his[7] own eye-lashes?" And he cried aloud and looked around and said, "What[8] then ought I to have done?"

BLEP. If I had happened to be present, I would have said, "Pound together garlic with fig-juice and put in Laconian[9] spurge, and anoint your eye-lids with it at night."

CHREM. After him the very clever Evæon[10] came forward, naked, as appeared to most,—he himself, however, said he had on[11] a tunic,—and then delivered a most democratic speech. "You see me, myself also, in want[12] of safety of the value of four staters. Yet, nevertheless, I will tell you how you shall

[1] Cf. Vesp. 242.   [2] Cf. Vesp. 174.
[3] A comic substitute for παρῄει.   [4] See note on Ran. 54.
[5] Cf. Vesp. 417.   [6] See Krüger, Gr. Gr. § 47, 4, obs. 3.
[7] "Der selbst nicht seine Wimpern heilen kann." *Droysen.*
Bergler compares Æschin. c. Timarch. p. 55, ed. Reiske.
[8] Eur. Orest. 550, τί χρῆν με δρᾶσαι;
[9] Eubulus ap. Athen. ii. p. 66,

κύκκον λαβοῦσα κνίδιον, ἢ τοῦ πεπέριος,
τρίψασ' ὁμοῦ σμύρνῃ διάπαττε τὴν ὁδόν.

See note on Pax, 1154, and Bernhardy, W. S. p. 144.
[10] "Evæon is otherwise unknown." *Droysen.*
[11] "T. Faber translates it, '*Ipse enim negabat se pallium habere.* Whence it is evident he read μέντ' οὐ 'φασκεν, as it is cited by Dawes, M. C. p. 214. But if the poet had meant this, he would have said οὐκ ἔφασκεν. For an initial vowel is never elided by a preceding οὐ. In the next place, that reading makes no sense. Therefore we must read μέντοι 'φασκεν. *Accessit nudus, ut plerisque videbatur, quamvis ipse contrarium affirmaret.*" *Porson.* This crasis, however, as Reisig (Synt. Crit. p. 26) and Dindorf (ad loc.) remark, is more correctly written μέντοὔφασκεν. So μοὔχρησεν, i. e. μοι ἔχρησεν Vesp. 159. Cf. vs. 1029. Ran. 1180, 1399. Pax, 334. Thesm. 624. Proagon, Frag. v. Elmsley, Præf. Rex, p. viii. ad Acharn. 611. Mus. Crit. i. p. 485. Class. Journ. No. iii. p. 508. Monthly Review, Sept. 1789, p. 249, Febr. 1796, p. 131. Krüger, Gr. Gr. Second Part, § 14, 6, obs. 4 (p. 28).
[12] Eur. Heracl. 11, σώζω τάδ', αὐτὸς δεόμενος σωτηρίας.

save the state and the citizens. For if the fullers furnish cloaks to those in want, as soon as ever the sun turns,[1] a pleurisy would never seize any of us. And as many as have no bed or bed-clothes, let them go[2] to the tanners' to sleep after they have been washed. But if he[3] shut them out with the door when it is winter, let him have to pay three goat-skins."

BLEP. By Bacchus, an excellent plan! But if he had added *that*, no one would have voted against it,—that the meal-hucksters should[4] furnish three chœnixes as[5] supper to all those in want, or suffer smartly for it; that they might have derived[6] this benefit from Nausicydes.

CHREM. After this then a handsome, fair-faced youth,[7] like to Nicias,[8] jumped up to harangue the people, and essayed to speak, to the intent that we ought to commit the state to the women. And then the mob of shoemakers cheered and cried out, that he spoke[9] well: but those from the country grumbled loudly.

BLEP. For, by Jove, they had sense.

CHREM. But they were the weaker[10] party; while he per-

---

[1] "To be understood of the *winter solstice*." *Kuster.* "Of the *autumnal solstice*." *Bergler.* "Read τραπῇ. The Greeks say ἥλιος τρέπεται, not τρέπει." *Faber.* For the construction, cf. Lys. 696.

[2] See note on Ran. 169.

[3] See note on Ran. 1075. Cf. Lys. 775.

[4] See notes on Thesm. 1063, 520. Nub. 380.

[5] See note on Plut. 314.

[6] ἵνα in this construction denotes that the proposition is not, or has not been realized, because the principal clause contains something merely desiderated. See Krüger, Gr. Gr. § 54, 8, obs. 8. Harper's "Powers of the Greek Tenses," p. 114. Bernhardy, W. S. p. 376. Hermann, Vig. n. 244, 350. Elmsl. Soph. Rex, 1389. Monk, Hippol. 643. Dorville, Char. p. 225. Dawes, M. C. p. 423. Bekker's Anecd. i. p. 149, 9. "Nausicydes was a rich meal-huckster at Athens, mentioned also by Xenophon Mem. 7, 16." *Droysen.* See note on Thesm. 1008.

[7] The speaker, of course, was Blepyrus' wife Praxagora.

[8] "The Nicias here mentioned is a different person from the celebrated leader of the Sicilian expedition: his nephew, probably, as Paulmier thinks." *Brunck.*

[9] Cf. Xenoph. Anab. v. 1, 3. The optative is used to denote the opinion of the σκυτοτομικὸν πλῆθος, not that of the narrator or author

[10]   "Sie waren aber die Minderzahl, indess er laut Fortfuhr."   *Droysen*

severed in his clamour, saying much good of the women, but much[1] ill of you.

BLEP. Why, what did he say?

CHREM. First he said you were a knave.

BLEP. And of you?

CHREM. Don't ask this yet And then a thief.

BLEP. I only?

CHREM. And, by Jove, an informer too.

BLEP. I only?

CHREM. And, by Jove, the greater part of these here.
[*Points to the audience.*]

BLEP. Who denies this?[2]

CHREM. A woman, on the other hand, he said was a clever and money-getting thing; and he said they did not constantly divulge the secrets of the Thesmophoria, while you and I always did so when we were senators.

BLEP. And, by Mercury, in this he did not lie!

CHREM. Then he said they lent to[3] each other garments, gold, silver, drinking-cups,[4] all alone,[5] not in the presence of witnesses: and that they returned all these, and did not keep them back;[6] while most of us, he said, did so.

BLEP. Yes, by Neptune, in the presence of witnesses!

CHREM. That they did not act the informer, did not bring actions, nor put down the democracy; but he praised the women for many good qualities, and for very many other reasons.

BLEP. What then was decreed?

CHREM. To commit the state to them. For[7] this plan alone appeared not to have been tried as yet in the state.

BLEP. And has it been decreed?

CHREM. Certainly.

[1] See Krüger, Gr. Gr. § 69, 32, obs. 3.
[2] "Wer bestreitet das?" *Droysen.*
[3] The more usual construction would be ἀλλήλαις.
[4] See Monthly Review, 1796, vol. xix. p. 125
[5] Cf. Soph. Ajax, 467. Eur. Med. 513. So οἰόθεν οἶος, Hom. Il vii. 39.
[6] Cf. Nub. 1464.

"For 'mong the many changes which our city
Has oft experienced, this alone, it seems,
Remained untried." *Smith.*
"Es schien, dass diess allein noch nicht zu Athen versucht sei
Droysen

BLEP. And have all matters been committed to them, which used to be a care to the citizens?

CHREM. So it is.

BLEP. Then shall I not go to Court, but my wife?

CHREM. No, nor any longer shall you rear *the children* you have, but your wife.

BLEP. Nor any longer is it my business to groan[1] at day-break?

CHREM. No; by Jove! but this now is the women's care; while you shall remain at home without groans.

BLEP. That thing is alarming for such as[2] us; lest, when they have received the government[3] of the state, they then compel us by force——

CHREM. What to do?

BLEP. ——to lie with them.

CHREM. But what if we be not able?

BLEP. They will not give us our breakfast.

CHREM. Do you, by Jove, manage this, that you may breakfast and amuse yourself at the same time.

BLEP. Compulsion is most dreadful.[4]

CHREM. But if this shall be profitable for the state, every man ought to do so. Certainly indeed[5] there is a saying of our elders,[6] "Whatever senseless or silly measures we determine on, that they all turn[7] out for our advantage." And

[1] "Auch nicht den Tag angähn' Ich künftig auf der Pnyx?"
Droysen.

"No more then need I sigh for break of day
    When the court meets!" *Smith.*

See notes on Aves, 161, 1308.

[2] "Für Leute unsers Alters." *Droysen.* See Krüger, Gr. Gr. § 51, 10, obs. 7. Bernhardy, W. S. p. 300.

[3] Cf. Equit. 1109.

[4] "Aye, but compulsion's odious." *Smith.*

[5] See Hermann, Vig. n. 297.

[6] "Auch giebt 's ein Sprichwort aus den alten Zeiten her:
Was unverständlich wir beschliessen und verkehrt,
Das wird zu unserm Besten doch zuletzt gedeihn." *Droysen.*

Nub. 587,   φασὶ γὰρ δυσβουλίαν
τῇδε τῇ πόλει προσεῖναι, ταῦτα μέντοι τʋὺς θεοὺς,
ἅττ' ἂν ὑμεῖς ἐξαμάρτητ', ἐπὶ τὸ βέλτιον τρέπειν.

Eupolis ap. Athen. x. p. 425,
                  ὦ πόλις, πόλις,
ὡς εὐτυχὴς εἶ μᾶλλον, ἢ καλῶς φρονεῖς.

[7] Nub. 594, ἐπὶ τὸ βέλτιον τὸ πρᾶγμα τῇ πόλει συνοίσεται. Cf. Nub 590 Bernhardy, W. S. p. 252.

may they turn out so, O mistress Pallas and ye gods ! But I
will depart: and fare-you-well! [*Exit Chremes.*]

BLEP. And you too *farewell*, O Chremes ! [*Goes into his
house.*]

CHORUS OF WOMEN. Advance, proceed! Is there any of
the men that is following us? Turn about! look! guard
yourself carefully,—for knaves are numerous,—lest perchance
some one being behind us, should espy[1] our dress. But step
along, stamping[2] with your feet as much as possible. This
affair would bring disgrace upon us all among[3] the men, if[4] it
were discovered. Wherefore gird yourself up, and look about[5]
in that direction and on the right, lest the affair shall become a mishap.[6] Come, let us hasten! for we are now near
the place, whence we set out to the Assembly, when we went[7]
there: and we may see the house, whence is our general, who
devised the measure which has now been decreed by the citizens. Wherefore it is fitting that we do not loiter waiting
longer, equipped with beards, lest some one shall see us,
and perhaps[8] denounce us. But come hither to the shade,[9]
having come to the wall,[10] glancing aside with one eye,[11] change
your dress again as you were *before*, and do not loiter: for.

---

[1] "Erspähe." *Droysen.* "*Habitum nostrum observet.*" *Brunck.*

[2] Cf. vs. 545, *infra*. The interchange of genders (σαυτὴν, vs. 481.
ἐπικτυπῶν, vs. 483. περισκοπουμένη, vs. 487) is at least remarkable.
"Sæpe chorus mulierum de se in genere masculino loquitur."
Reiske. Cf. vs. 589, *infra*. Lys. 1304. Eur. Hippol. 1107, ed. Monk.
Bernhardy, W. S. p. 429. Dawes, M. C. p. 572. Hermann, Vig. ii.
50. Dorville, Char. p. 292. Mus. Crit. i. p. 334; ii. p. 296.

[3]   "Denn würden wir noch jetzt entdeckt,
So brächt' es ewig Schimpf und Schand beim Männervolk uns
      allen.   *Droysen.*

It is wrongly translated in Brunck's version.

[4] A participle is often the representative of an *hypothetical* clause.
See Krüger, Gr. Gr. as cited in the note on Ran. 96.

[5] Cf. Aves, 1196, 424. Thesm. 666.

[6] "*Ne hæc res infortunio nobis sit.*" *Brunck.* See Bernhardy, W.
S. p. 402, and cf. vs. 495

[7] See Krüger, Gr. Gr. § 38, 3, obs. 1.

[8] In Brunck's edition ἴσω κατάπτῃ. "The comic writers never
use ἐς before a vowel, or ἴσω." *Dindorf.* For this remarkable interchange, see Bernhardy, W. S. p. 402.

[9]   "So retire we one and all,
      Within the friendly shade of yon projecting wall." *Smith.*

[10] See Liddell's Lex. in voc. τειχίον.   [11] Cf. Vesp. 197

see here! now we behold our general coming from the Assembly. Come, hasten every one, and hate to have a beard[1] on your jaws. For see! they have come with this dress on this long while. [*Enter Praxagora and other women from the Assembly, no longer disguised os men.*]

PRAX. (*addressing the chorus*). These measures, O women, which we deliberated on, have turned out successfully. But throw off your cloaks as soon as possible, before any of the men see you! let the men's shoes go far away! undo[2] the fastened Laconian shoe-strings! throw away your staffs! And do you now [*to a female servant*] put them in order. I wish to creep in secretly, before[3] my husband sees me, and deposit his garment again whence I took it, and the other things which I brought out.

CHO. Now all the things you spoke of are lying in order It is your business to instruct us in the rest, by doing what useful thing we shall seem rightly to obey you. For I know I have conversed with no woman cleverer than you.

PRAX. Wait then, in order that I may use you[4] all as advisers in the office to which I have been just now elected. For there, in the uproar and danger, you have been most courageous.

BLEP. (*suddenly coming out of his house*). Ho you! whence have you come, Praxagora?

PRAX. What's that to you,[5] my dear?

BLEP. "What's that to me?" How foolishly *you ask.*

PRAX. You certainly will not say, from a paramour.

BLEP. Perhaps not from *one.*[6]

PRAX. Well now you can put this to the test.

BLEP. How?

PRAX. If my head smells of perfume.[7]

[1] Hence the epithet σακεσφόρος applied to Epicrates, by Plato the comic writer. See note on vs. 71. So the philosophers are called σακκογενειοτρόφοι ap. Athen. iv. p. 162.

[2] See note on Ran. 1075.

[3] "Instead of any of the other moods the infinitive [with πρὶν] is also admissible." *Harper.* See Krüger, Gr. Gr. § 54, 17, obs. 6 Bernhardy, W. S. p. 400. Mus. Crit. ii. p. 13.

[4] In some MSS. χρήσομαι. See note on Lys. 1243. Cf. Porson Opusc. p. xciii. Præf. Hec. p. lix.

[5] See Krüger, Gr. Gr. § 48, 3, 8.

[6] "From *two,* belike, not *one.*" *Smith.*

[7] For this construction, see note on Pax, 525.

BLEP. How then? does not a woman intrigue even without perfume?

PRAX. I, unhappy, certainly not.[1]

BLEP. Why[2] then did you go off at day-break in silence with my garment?

PRAX. A woman my companion and friend sent for me in the night, being in the pains of labour.[3]

BLEP. And then was it not possible for you to go when you had told me?

PRAX. And not to care for the woman in child-bed,[4] being in such a condition, husband?

BLEP. Yes, if you had told me. But there is some mischief in this.

PRAX. Nay, by the two goddesses! but I went just as I was; for she who came in quest of[5] me, begged me to set out by all means.

BLEP. Then ought you not to have worn your own[6] garment? But after you had stripped me, and thrown your upper garment over me, you went off and left me as if I were laid out[7] for burial; only that you did not crown[8] me, nor yet place a vase[9] beside me.

PRAX. For it was cold; while I am thin and weak. So then I put it on, in order that I might be warm.[10] But I left you lying in the warmth, and in the bed-clothes, husband.

---

[1] "Such is the rule with *me*." *Smith.* "Ich wenigstens nic.' *Droysen.*

[2]   " Warum denn gingst du heute früh
    In aller Stille fort und nahmst mir den Mantel mit?" *Droysen.*

[3] Alciphron I. Epist. 28, ὠδίνουσά με ἀρτίως ἥκειν ὡς ἑαυτὴν ἡ τοῦ γείτονος μετέπεμψε γυνή.

[4] See Liddell Lex. in voc. λεχώ.

[5] Imperfect of μεθήκω. Cf. Equit. 937. Brunck has translated it as if his reading had been μετεπέμψατο.

[6] "Blepyrus had come upon the stage in his wife's dress." *Brunck.*

[7] Cf. Aves, 474. See note on Plut. 69.

[8] "It was customary to crown the dead. Cf. Meurs. ad Lycoph. 799." *Kuster.*

[9] The so-called *lachrymatory*. Cf. vs. 996, 1032, 1111, *infra.*
                    " Es fehlte nichts
Als dass du 'nen Kranz und ein Thränenfläschen daneben stellst."
                                        Droysen.

[10] "θερμαινοίμην." *Suidas.* Cf. Bekk. Anecdot. i. p. 14, 24; 381, 25. Mus. Crit. ii. p. 36.

BLEP. But with what view[1] went my Laconian shoes and my staff along with you?

PRAX. I changed shoes with you, in order that I might keep the garment safe,[2] imitating you, and stamping with my feet, and striking the stones with the staff.

BLEP. Do you know then that you have lost a sextary[3] of wheat, which I ought to have received from the Assembly?

PRAX. Don't be concerned; for she has borne a male child.

BLEP. The Assembly?

PRAX. No, by Jove! but the woman I went to. But has it been held?[4]

BLEP. Yes, by Jove! Did you not know that I told you yesterday?

PRAX. I just now recollect it.

BLEP. Then don't you know what has been decreed?

PRAX. No, by Jove! not I.

BLEP. Then sit down and chew cuttle-fish;[5] for they say the state has been committed to you.

PRAX. What to do? to weave?

BLEP. No, by Jove! but to rule.

PRAX. What?

BLEP. The affairs of the state, every one.

PRAX. By Venus, the state[6] will be happy henceforth!

BLEP. On what account?

PRAX. For many reasons. For no longer will it be permitted for the audacious to act shamefully towards it henceforth, and no where to give evidence, nor to act the informer——

BLEP. By the gods, by no means do this, nor take away[7] my livelihood.

[1] See Krüger, Gr. Gr. § 51, 17, obs. 8, § 62, 3, obs. 9, and Bernhardy, W. S. p. 240.

[2] She imitated her husband's gait and dress, in order that she might not be robbed by the λωποδύται.   [3] Cf. note on Nub. 645.

[4] "War heut' denn Ekklesie?" *Droysen.*

[5] "The sense is: *sede et in posterum laute et beate vivito; tibi enim magnum imperium paratum video.*" *Faber.* To *eat cuttle-fish* was synonymous with enjoying the highest felicity; hence Suidas translates it by τρυφᾶν. See Athen. viii. p. 324, C.

[6] In Brunck's edition γ' ἄρ'. "Very wrongly. See Hermann, Orphic. p. 216. Lobeck, Ajax, p. 302." *Dindorf.* For τὸ λοιπὸν, see note on Thesm. 539.

Soph. Phil. 933, πρὸς θεῶν ⸱ ατρώων ⸱ τὸν βίον με ἀϕείλες.

Cho. My good sir,[1] suffer your wife to speak.

Prax. ——nor to steal clothes, nor to envy one's neigh
bours, nor to be naked, nor that any one be poor,[2] nor to rail
at one another, nor to seize as a pledge[3] and carry off.

Cho. By Neptune, grand *promises,* if she shall not prove
false.

Prax. But I will[4] demonstrate this, so that you shall bear
me witness, and this man himself not gainsay me at all.[5]

Cho. Now it behoves you to rouse a prudent mind and
deep thought friendly to the commons, who know how to defend your friends. For your inventiveness of mind comes for
the public prosperity, delighting the commons[6] with innumerable aids[7] for life, showing what it is able to effect. It is
time:[8] for our state has need of some clever contrivance.
Come, do you only accomplish[9] what has never been done nor
mentioned before as yet. For they hate, if they see the old
things often. Come, you ought not to delay, but now to begin[10] your plans; for quickness enjoys the greatest share[11] of
favour with the spectators.

Prax. Well now, I am confident that I shall teach what is

[1] Cf. note on Ran. 1227.
[2] Cf. Shakspeare, Henry VI. part ii. act iv. sc. 2.
[3] " No defamation, no distraint for debt." *Smith.*

" Kein Zank der Partheien, kein Verhaft für fällige Schuld."
Droysen.

Cf. vs. 755, *infra.* Nub. 35, 241.

[4] " So klar beweis' Ich 's, dass du zeugen wirst für mich,
Und meinem Mann selbst nichts zu erwiedern möglich ist."
Droysen.

[5] Cf. Nub. 1343, and for the interchange of μοι and ἐμοί, cf.
Aves, 545.

[6] See Krüger, Gr. Gr. § 57, 1, obs. 1.
[7] " For this form Reisig cites Etymol. M. 462, 20. Alpheus, Epigr.
ii. vs. 6." *Dindorf.*
[8] " Denn Zeit ist 's." *Droysen.*
[9] Cf. Ran. 1170, 1383. Plut. 648. Plato, Protag. p. 354, B. Shilleto
on Demosth. Fals. Leg. § 272.
[10] " Read ἀλλὰ πέτεσθαι. See Lys. 55." *Bentley.* But see Bernhardy, W. S. p. 95.
[11] " πλείστων, Toup on Suidas, iii. p. 228, but needlessly. Thucyd.
i. 84, αἰδὼς σωφροσύνης πλεῖστον μετέχει. Ran. 335, χαρίτων πλεῖστον
ἔχουσαν μέρος. Which sufficiently confirm the common reading.
μέρος is understood." *Porson.* Cf. Plut. 226. Xenoph. Cyrop. vii.
2, 28. Porson, Append. Toup, iv. p. 477. Schäfer on Bos Ell. p
279 *seq.* Krüger, Gr. Gr. § 47, 15 obs. 1.

useful. But this is the thing I am most apprehensive about, whether the spectators[1] will be willing to make innovations, and not *rather* abide by the very-customary and ancient usages

BLEP. Now about making innovations,[2] don't be alarmed; for to do this and to neglect what is ancient, is with us equivalent to another constitution.

PRAX. Now let none of you reply[3] or interrupt me, before he understands the plan and has heard the speaker.[4] For I will declare that all ought to enjoy all things in common, and live upon[5] the same property ; and not for one to be rich, and another miserably poor ; nor one to cultivate much *land*, and another to have not even enough to be buried in ;[6] nor one to have[7] many slaves, and another not even a footman. But I will make one common subsistence for all, and that[8] too equal.

[1] Xenoph. Anab. ii. 4, 7, ἐγὼ μὲν οὖν τὸν βασιλέα, εἴπερ προθυμεῖται ἡμᾶς ἀπολέσαι, οὐκ οἶδα ὅ τι δεῖ αὐτὸν ὀμόσαι. Aves, 1269, δεινόν γε τὸν κήρυκα τὸν παρὰ τοὺς βροτοὺς οἰχόμενον, εἰ μηδέποτε νοστήσει πάλιν. Soph. Rex, 246, κατεύχομαι δὲ τὸν δεδρακότα, εἴτε τις εἷς ὢν λέληθεν, εἴτε πλειόνων μέτα, κακὸν κακῶς νιν ἄμοιρον ἐκτρίψαι βίον. Cf. Hom. Od. Π. 78 ; Δ. 652 ; Α. 275. Soph. Electr. 1364. Trach. 287. Krüger's note on Thuc. ii. 62, *init.* Bernhardy, W. S. p. 132. Porson Præf. Hec. p. vii. In the present passage, τοὺς θεατὰς depends on δέδοικα, and the construction is an example of " Anticipation." See examples cited in the note on Nub. 1148, and on vs. 1126, *infra.* For εἰ after verbs of *fearing*, see Krüger, Gr. Gr. § 65, 1, obs. 9.

[2] " Um den Fortschritt sei nicht weiter besorgt; denn es herrscht
    Fortschreiten und Neuern
    Und Verachten des Altherkömmlichen hier als wahrer und
    einziger Herrscher." *Droysen.*
Cf. Acts, xvii. 21. Bernhardy, W. S. p. 231. In this construction μὲν always stands between the preposition and the article. See Krüger, Gr. Gr. § 50, 1, obs. 13. Cf. note on vs. 625, *infra.*

[3] Acharn. 221, μὴ γὰρ ἐγχάνῃ ποτέ. Plato, Legg. ix. p. 861, E., μή τις οἴηται. Symp. p. 213, E., μή μοι μέμφηται. See Krüger, Gr. Gr. § 54, 2, obs. 2. Elmsley, Soph. Rex, Præf. p. xxxviii. and vss. 903, 49. Edinburgh Rev. No. xxxviii. p. 488. Porson, Orest. 776. Monk, Hippol. vs. 893. Hermann, Greg. Cor. p. 867. Vig. n. 267. Neue on Soph. Rex, 49.

[4] " Praxagora is delivering a *general* remark how people ought to listen to the speaker, therefore uses the *masculine* gender." *Bergler.*

[5] " Vom Gemeingut jeglicher leben." *Droysen.*

[6] " Cf. Plut. 556. Æschin. p. 14, 13, ed. Steph. Demosth. Mid. p 549, 12, ed. Reiske." *Porson.*

[7] χρῆσθαι, like *utor* in Latin, often = *habeo.*

[8] Instead of καὶ ταῦτα, *and that too*, the Greeks often use καὶ οὗτος,

BLEP. How then will it be common to all ?

PRAX. You shall eat dung before me.[1]

BLEP. And shall we have a community of dung ?

PRAX. No, by Jove! but you were the first to interrupt[2] me. For I was going to say this : I will first of all make the land common to[3] all, and the silver, and the other things, as many as each has. Then we will maintain you out of these, being common, husbanding, and sparing, and giving our attention to it.

BLEP. How then if any of us do not possess land, but silver and Darics,[4] personal[5] property ?

PRAX. He shall pay it in[6] for the public use ; and if he do not pay[7] it in, he shall be forsworn.

BLEP. Why, he acquired it by this ![8]

PRAX. But in truth it will be of no use to him at all.

BLEP. On what account, pray ?

PRAX. No one will do any *wickedness* through poverty : for all will be possessed of all things ; loaves, slices of salt fish, barley cakes, cloaks, wine, chaplets, chick-pease. So that what advantage will it be not to pay it in ? For do you find it out and make it known.

BLEP. Then do not these even now thieve more, who have these *worldly goods ?*[9]

---

in agreement with its proper noun. See Plut. 546. Pax, 744, 1278. Aves, 275. Xenoph. Anab. ii. 5, 21. Herod. i. 147 ; vi. 11. Donaldson, N. C. p. 264. Dobree on Plut. 546.

[1] "Seemingly a proverbial expression applied to unseasonable interruptions." *Brunck.*   [2] Cf. Plut. 1102.

[3] For the construction, cf. Æsch. Prom. 1092. Pind. Nem. i. 48. Bernhardy, W. S. p. 172. In vs. 595, *supra*, we had the dative.

[4] A *gold* coin. "See Pollux, iii. 87. Böckh, Publ. Ec. Athen. vol. i. p. 23." *Dindorf.* For ὅστις = εἴ τις, see Krüger, Gr. Gr. § 51, 13, obs. 12.

[5] See Liddell's Lex. voc. ἀφανὴς, 4. "See Harpocrat. voc. ἀφανὴς οὐσία." *Kuster.*

[6] "Der zahlt 's ein zum Gemeinschatze." *Droysen.* See note on Lys. 134.

[7] According to *Hotibius* (Bothe) = μὴ καταθήσει καὶ ψευδορκήσει, which is a singular exposition to come from a Greek scholar ;—as if μὴ καταθήσει = οὐ καταθήσει. See Elmsley, Med. vs. 204. Mus Crit. ii. p. 597. Neue ad Soph. Antig. 84 ; Aj. 573.

[8] i. e. διὰ τοῦτο τὸ ψευδορκεῖν. See note on Lys. 134.

[9] "Yet oft the greatest rogues are those, in wealth who most
     abound."   *Smith*

Prax. Yes ; formerly, my good sir, when we used the former laws. But now,—for substance shall be in common,—what[1] is the advantage of not paying in ?

Blep. If on seeing a girl any one should desire her and wish to lie with her, he will be able[2] to make presents by taking from these ; but he will enjoy a share of the common property by sleeping with her.

Prax. But he will be permitted to sleep with her for nothing ; for I will make[3] them in common for the men to lie with, and for any one that pleases to beget children.

Blep. How then, if all shall go to the most beautiful of them and seek to lie with her ?

Prax. The uglier and more flat-nosed women shall sit by the side of the beautiful ;[4] and then if any desire her,[5] he shall first lie with the ugly one.

Blep. Why, how shall our powers not[6] fail us old men, before we get there where you say, if we have to do with the ugly ones *first* ?

Prax. They will not fight.

Blep. What about ?

Prax. Be of good courage ! don't fear !—they will not fight

Blep. What about ?"

Prax. About your not sleeping with them.[8]   And such a law is provided for you.

Blep. Your plan[9] has some sense ; for it has been provided

---

[1] See Bernhardy, W. S. p. 444.

[2] "ἕξει (i. e. δυνήσεται) δοῦναι (sc: τῇ μείρακι) ἀφελων, *demens, detrahens, decerpens,* τούτων, *ex iis quæ ille sibi reservarit, nec in commune deposuerit.*" *Brunck.*

[3] The construction is somewhat ambiguous. In Brunck's version it is rendered, "*Namque faciam, ut illæ communes cum viris cubent, et cuilibet volenti liberos pariant.*" Similarly Droysen. But this construction will hardly suit vs. 615.

[4] "*Formosas, pulchras.*" *Kuster.*

[5] i. e. τῆς ὡραιοτάτης. "Und jemand nach der Schönen verlangt." *Droysen.* See note on Ran. 1075. For the omission of τὶς, see note on Aves, 167, and comp. vss. 611, 633, 642, 643, 662, 670, 672.

[6] Cf. vs. 640, *infra.*   [7] See Porson, Opusc. p. 23.

[8] "Those words τοῦ μὴ ξυγκαταδαρθεῖν ought to have been translated more closely · *si cum illis non concubueritis ;* or, *quia cum illis non concumbetis.*" *Brunck.* "Sie wehrt dir den Beischlaf nicht." *Droysen.*

[9] τὸ ὑμέτερον, strictly speaking, = υμεῖς. So τὸ σὸν = σὺ, τὸ ἐμὸν = ἐγὼ. See note on Thesm. 105. The corresponding clause to ↲

that no woman's arms be empty. But what will the men[1] do?
For *the women* will avoid the more ugly ones, and go to the
handsome.[2]

PRAX. But the uglier[3] men shall watch for the handsomer
ones as they are departing from dinner, and shall have an eye
upon them in the public places.   And the women shall not
be permitted to sleep with the handsome men, before they
gratify[4] the ugly and the little ones.

BLEP. Then the nose of Lysicrates[5] will now be as proud
as that of the handsome men.

PRAX. Yes, by Apollo! And the plan will be a democratic
one too, and a great mockery[6] of the more dignified and of
those who wear rings, when a person wearing slippers[7] shall

μὲν ὑμέτερον is τὸ δὲ τῶν ἀνδρῶν (vs. 624) = οἱ ἄνδρες. Many similar
examples will be found ap. Bernhardy, W. S. p. 327.

[1] "Jedoch, wie wird es den Männern ergehen?" *Droysen.*

[2] "Read ἐπὶ τοὺς δέ." *Porson.* So Brunck and Dindorf. But
this is a deflection from the regular rule; for whenever ὁ μὲν or ὁ
δὲ is construed with a preposition, the μὲν and δὲ stand *between* the
preposition and the governed case of the article. See Krüger, Gr.
Gr. § 50, 1, obs. 13. Bernhardy, W. S. p. 198. Hermann, Vig. n. 5,
and note on vs. 586, *supra.* See, however, Vesp. 94. Lys. 593. Plut.
559. Krüger, Gr. Gr. § 68, 5, obs. 1.   A prose writer would have
said ἐπὶ δὲ τούς.

[3] Dindorf's text here differs widely from that of Brunck, both in
reading and punctuation.

[4] Porson, (ap. Gaisford ad Eur. Suppl. p. 206,) Elmsley, (Heracl.
vs. 959. Med. p. 119,) and Reisig (i. p. 65) alter the reading to
πρὶν . . . χαρίσασθαι, on the pretence that Aristophanes never omits
ἂν in this construction; which is certainly a curious way of proving
their rule.   They ought to have shown that the omission is contrary
to the philosophy of the language.   " Many of these conjunctions
are found with the conjunctive also without ἂν, even in classical
prose, inasmuch as the thought is represented as not at all problem-
atical.   This is more frequently the case with πρὶν and μέχρι (οὗ),
especially in Thucydides and the poets." *Krüger.* Cf. Bernhardy,
W. S. p. 400. Hermann ap. Harper, " Powers of the Greek Tenses,"
p. 131. Jelf, Gr. Gr. § 842, 2. Lys. 1005. Praxagora has no doubt,
from the provisions of the law, but that the women will do so.   For
this use of χαρίζεσθαι, see Equit. 517. Ruhnk. Tim. p. 274

[5] Cf. vs. 736. Aves, 513. " He seems to have been remarkable
on the same account as Juvenal's barber of Beneventum, and
Shakspeare's Bardolph." *Smith.* For the construction, see note on
Plut. 368.   [6] Cf. Vesp. 575.

[7] i. e. an old man. See Plut. 759. " Probably proper names are
concealed under these words: ὅταν Ἐμβάδι γ᾽ εἴπῃ Πρότερος."
Bentley. Reiske thinks Ἐμβὰς may have been the nickname of some

say, "Give place first, and then watch when I have finished
and allow you to play the second part."

BLEP. How then, if we live in this manner, will each be
able to distinguish his own sons?

PRAX. But what occasion is there? for they will consider
all those who are older than themselves in age to be their
fathers.

BLEP. Therefore they will rightly and properly throttle
every old man[1] one after another through ignorance; for
even now, when they know their true father, they throttle
him.   What then? when he is unknown, how will they not
then even dung upon him?

PRAX. But he who is standing by will not permit it.
Formerly[2] they had no concern about other people's fathers,
if any one beat them; whereas now, if any hear *a father*
beaten, being alarmed lest any person should be beating his
father, he will oppose those[3] who do this.

BLEP. The rest you say not amiss.   But if Epicurus were
to come to me, or Leucolophas,[4] and call me father, this now
would be terrible to hear.

PRAX. A much more terrible thing, however, than this
thing is——

BLEP. What?

PRAX. If Aristyllus[5] were to kiss you, saying you were
his father.

BLEP. He would suffer for it and howl.

PRAX. And you would smell of mint.   But he was born
before the decree was made, so there is no fear lest he kiss you.

BLEP. I should indeed have suffered[6] a terrible thing.
But who is to cultivate the land?

man of rank, as Κόθορνος was of Theramenes. In this state of doubt
Dindorf has retained the reading of the Ravenna MS.

[1] "Mit Fug und mit Recht von den Alten den ersten den besten."
Droysen. Cf. Nub. 888. Aves, 1352.

[2] "Vordem liess keiner sich's kümmern, ob ein Anderer Prügel
vom Sohne bekam." *Droysen.*

[3] τύπτῃ . . τοῖς δρῶσιν. For this transition from the singular to
the plural, see note on vs. 688, *infra.*

[4] "Epicurus and Leucolophas are otherwise unknown." *Droysen.*

[5] See Plut. 314. He bore the same character as Ariphrades.

[6] For this Attic form of the first person, see Krüger, Gr. Gr. § 30,
6, obs. "In English it must be rendered, '*that would indeed have
been intolerable.*' δεινός has the same meaning in δεινὰ πάσχειν. δεινὸν

Prax. The slaves.   But it shall be your concern, when the shadow of the gnomon is ten feet long,[1] to go to a banquet, anointed with oil.[2]

Blep. But about garments, what will be your contrivance? For this also[3] must be asked.[4]

Prax. In the first place what you have at present will be at hand; and the rest we will weave.

Blep. One thing further I ask: if one be cast[5] in a suit before the magistrates at the suit of any one, from what source will he pay off this? For it is not right *to pay it* out of the common fund.

Prax. But in the first place there shall not even be any suits.

Blep. But how many this will ruin!

Prax. I also make[6] a decree for this. For on what account, you rogue, should there be any?

Blep. By Apollo, for many reasons! in the first place, for one reason, I ween, if any one, being in debt, denies it.

Prax. Whence[7] then did the lender lend *the money*, when all things are in common? He is, I ween, convicted of theft.

Blep. By Ceres, you instruct us well! Now let some one[8] tell me this: whence shall those who beat people pay off *an action*[9] for assault, when they insult people after a banquet? For I fancy you'll be at a loss about this.

Prax. Out of the barley-cake[10] which he eats. For when

ποιεῖσθαι, δεινὸν λέγεις. See examples ap. Elmsl. Acharn. 323." *Dobree.*

[1] "τῇ σκίᾳ δ' ἐτεκμαίροντο τὸν καιρὸν τῆς ἐπὶ τὸ δεῖπνον ὁδοῦ, ἣν καὶ στοιχεῖον ἐκάλουν. καὶ ἕδει σπεύδειν, εἰ δεκάπουν τὸ στοιχεῖον εἴη." *Pollux,* vi. 44.   [2] Cf. Plut. 616.

[3] See Krüger, Gr. Gr. § 69, 32, obs. 21. Bernhardy, W. S. p. 261.

[4] In Brunck's edition ἔρεσθαι. But such forms as ἔρομαι and ἔρεσθαι are very suspicious.

[5] "*Si quis multam alicui debeat, a magistratibus damnatus.*" *Brunck.*

[6] Herod. i. 120, ταύτῃ πλεῖστος γνώμην εἰμί. See Bernhardy, W. S. p. 381.

[7] "*Unde acceptam fœnori dedit pecuniam ille, qui dedit?* i. e. he must have stolen it from the common fund, as no one possesses any thing in private." *Bergler.*

[8] "Read τουτί τις νῦν φρασάτω μοι." *Porson.* See note on vs. 618, *supra.*

[9] "τὴν δίκην is understood." *Brunck.* Cf. Dorville, Charit. p. 478.

[10] "This mode of punishment was adopted at Lacedæmon, where

one diminishes this, he will not insult again so readily, after he has been punished in his belly.

BLEP. And, on the other hand, will there be no thief?

PRAX. Why, how shall he steal when he has[1] a share *of all things?*

BLEP. Then will they not even strip people by night?[2]

PRAX. Not, if you sleep—at home;[3] nor, if *you sleep* abroad, as they used before. For all shall have subsistence. And if any one tries[4] to strip a person, he shall give *them* of his own accord. For what occasion is there for him to resist? for he shall go and get another better than that from the common stock?

BLEP. Then will the men[5] not even play at dice?

PRAX. Why, for what *stake*[6] shall any one do this?

BLEP. What will you make our mode of life?

PRAX. Common to all. For I say I will make the city one house, having broken up[7] all into one; so that they may go into each other's houses.

BLEP. But where will you serve up the dinner?

PRAX. I will make the law-courts and the porticoes[8] wholly men's apartments.

BLEP. What use will the Bema be to you?

PRAX. I will set the mixers and the water-pots on it; and it shall be for the boys to sing of those who are brave in war, and *of him*, whoever[9] has been cowardly, so that they[10] may not dine, through shame.

it was customary to eat together in public." *Smith.* Cf. Nicocles ap. Athen. iv. p. 141, A.

[1] " *Qui omnium sit particeps.*" *Brunck.* "Wenn Alles gemeinsam ist." *Droysen.* Cf. note on Lys. vs. 13.

[2] Cf. vs. 796, *infra.* Nub. 721. Hom. Il. Θ. 470. But the regular form is νυκτός. See Bernhardy, W. S. p. 145.

[3] " παρὰ προσδοκίαν. For it is certain that, if he keep at home, he will be safe from footpads." *Faber.*

[4] See Porson, Phœn. 79.

[5] See Reisig Conject. i. p. 155, and notes on Aves, 161, 1308. Cf. also vs. 668, *supra.*

[6] "There'll be no stake for which to game." *Smith.*

[7] Cf. Terence, Adelph. v. 7, 10.

[8] See Elmsley, Acharn. 548. Heracl. 431.

[9] εἴ τις=ὅστις. See Krüger, Gr. Gr. § 65, 5, obs. 9.

[10] For the transition from the singular (εἴ τις) to the plural (δειπνῶσι), see note on Ran. 1075, and cf. vs. 688, *infra.* Thesm. 848, 844.

BLEP. By Apollo, a nice plan! But what will you make of[1]
the urns for the lots?

PRAX. I will deposit them in the market-place; and then
I will place all the people beside the statue of Harmodius and
choose them by lot, until he who has drawn the lot departs joyfully, knowing in what letter he is to dine.[2]　And *the crier*[3]
shall command those of Beta to follow to the royal[4] portioo
to dine; and Theta to the *portico* next this;[5] and those of
Kappa to go to the flour-market.[6]

BLEP. That they may gohhle up[7] *the flour?*

PRAX. No, hy Jove! hut that they may dine there.

BLEP. But whoever[8] has not the necessary[9] letter drawn,
according to which he is to dine, all will drive away.

PRAX. But it shall not he so with us. For we will supply
all things to all in abundance; so that every one when he is
drunk shall go home together with his chaplet,[10] having taken
his torch. And the women in the thoroughfares, meeting
with them coming from[11] dinner, will say as follows: " Come
hither[12] to me. There is a heautiful girl here." " And at my

---

[1] Nub. 858, τὰς δ' ἐμβάδας ποῖ τέτροφας; *but what have you made
of your shoes?* For this form of the perfect, see Krüger, Gr. Gr. § 31,
ū, obs. 4.　For κηλωτήριον, see Aristoph. Γῆρας, Fragm. xvii.

[2] " δέον εἰπεῖν δικάζει, εἶπε δειπνεῖ." *Scholiast.*　Plut. 972, ἀλλ' οὐ
λαχοῦσ' ἔπινες ἐν τῷ γράμματι; The ten law-courts at Athens were
marked with the first ten letters of the alphabet, and the jurymen
drew by lot each a small ticket marked with a letter which directed
him to the court he was to go to.

[3] For this omission, see Krüger, Gr. Gr. § 61, 4, obs. 3. Bernhardy, W. S. p. 191.

[4] " Βασίλειον.　Because it begins with Beta." *Bergler.*

[5] " In der Halle daneben." *Droysen.*　So Brunck.　" ἐς τὴν στοὰν
λεχθεῖσαν παρὰ τὸ γράμμα τοῦτο θῆτα, i. e. ἐς τὸ Θησεῖον." *Faber.* So
the Scholiast.

[6] " Hesychius: ἀλφίτων στοά, ἐν Ἀθήναις, ἐν ᾗ τὰ ἄλφιτα ἐπωλεῖτο.
Of this portico, the Scholiast also speaks on Acharn. 547, and
Eustathius on Il. Λ. p. 868, 37, ed Rom." *Kuster.*　" στοὰ μυρόπωλις
apud Megalopolitas Arcadiæ Pausan. viii. 50, p. 663, 14." *Porson.*

[7] ἵνα κάπτωσιν; a pun on the preceding κάππα.

[8] ὅτῳ—τούτους. Cf. vs. 680, *supra.* Ran. 689. Plato, Euthyph.
o. 8. Monk, Hippol. 78. Elmsley, Soph. Rex. 713. Quart. Rev
vol. viii. p. 220. Krüger, Gr. Gr. § 58, 4, obs. 5.

[9] For the article, see note on Thesm. vs. 1012.

[10] Cf. Plut. vs. 1041.　　[11] See Bernhardy, W. S. p. 221.

[12] " Seemingly an allusion to the words of the Syrens." *Faber.*

house," some other woman will say from the chamber above, "both very beautiful and very fair. You must sleep with me, however, before[1] her." And the uglier[2] men following the handsome[3] men and the youths will say as follows "Hollo, you! whither are you running? You will effect nothing at all by going : for it has been decreed for the flat-nosed and the ugly to take the first turn ; but that you in the mean time amuse yourself in the porch." Come now, tell me, do these please you?

BLEP. Very much.

PRAX. Then I must go to the market-place, that I may receive the public revenue,[4] having taken a clear-voiced female-crier.[5] For it is necessary that I do this, as I have been chosen to govern,[6] and that I arrange the messes, so that in the first place you may banquet to-day.

BLEP. Why, shall[7] we banquet forthwith?

PRAX. Certainly. In the next place, I wish to put a stop to the harlots every one.

BLEP. Wherefore?[8]

PRAX. This is plain: that these of ours[9] may enjoy the flower of the youth. And it is not proper that the women-slaves should deck themselves out and filch away the love of

---

[1] A harsh construction, instead of $\pi\rho\acute{o}\tau\epsilon\rho\nu$ $\mathring{\eta}$ $\pi\alpha\rho$ $\alpha\mathring{\upsilon}\tau\mathring{\eta}$. So Thuc. i. 85, $\mathring{\epsilon}\xi\epsilon\sigma\tau\iota$ δ' $\mathring{\eta}\mu\widetilde{\iota}\nu$ $\mu\widetilde{\alpha}\lambda\lambda\nu$ $\mathring{\epsilon}\tau\acute{\epsilon}\rho\omega\nu$, i. e. $\mathring{\eta}$ $\mathring{\epsilon}\tau\acute{\epsilon}\rho\iota\varsigma$. Plut. 558, $\tau\nu\widetilde{\nu}$ $\Pi\lambda\nu\widetilde{\tau}\nu$ $\pi\alpha\rho\acute{\epsilon}\chi\omega$ $\beta\epsilon\lambda\tau\acute{\iota}\nu\alpha\varsigma$ $\mathring{\alpha}\nu\delta\rho\alpha\varsigma$, i. e. $\mathring{\eta}$ $\Pi\lambda\nu\widetilde{\tau}\varsigma$ $\pi\alpha\rho\acute{\epsilon}\chi\epsilon\iota$. Cf. vs. 71, *supra*. Aves, 569. Ran. 1061. Thuc. ii. 60; ii. 15; vi. 1; vi. 16; vii. 63. Soph. Antig. 74. Hermann, Vig. n. 55. Krüger, Gr. Gr. § 47, 27, obs. 1. Bernhardy, W. S, p. 437, and p. 233.

[2] "Above, in vs. 702, notwithstanding Brunck's opinion, οἱ $\phi\alpha\nu\lambda\acute{o}\tau\epsilon\rho\iota$ appears to me the true reading : the ugly men check the handsome, and assert the right given them by the new laws, of going first." *Seager*.

[3] "Read $\tau\nu\widetilde{\iota}\varsigma$ $\epsilon\mathring{\upsilon}\pi\rho\epsilon\pi\acute{\epsilon}\sigma\iota\nu$ δ'." *Bentley*. Cf. Porson ap. Mus. Crit. ii. p. 121. Opusc. p. xciii. For the article, cf. note on Aves, 590.

[4] Liddell compares Lysias, 185, 3. Vesp. vs. 664.

[5] So Plut. 970, $\sigma\nu\kappa\phi\acute{\alpha}\nu\tau\rho\iota\alpha$. Lys. 184, $\mathring{\eta}$ $\Sigma\kappa\acute{\nu}\theta\alpha\iota\nu\alpha$. Thesm. 432, $\mathring{\eta}$ $\gamma\rho\alpha\mu\mu\alpha\tau\epsilon\acute{\nu}\varsigma$. Ibid. 541, $\mathring{\alpha}\nu\tau\alpha\acute{\iota}$. Aristoph. Fragm. 399, $\sigma\nu\nu\theta\epsilon\acute{\alpha}\tau\rho\iota\alpha$. Plat. Euthyd. p. 297, C., $\sigma\phi\acute{\iota}\sigma\tau\rho\iota\alpha$. Cf. vss. 491, 500, 727, 835, 870.

[6] "Da Ich erwählt bin als Archontin." *Droysen*.

[7]   "What will
    To-day behold us banqueting in public?" *Smith*.

[8] Cf. Pax, 409. Hermann, Vig. n. 349.

[9] I should prefer $\mu\mathring{\eta}$ $'\chi\omega\sigma\iota\nu$ $\alpha\mathring{\upsilon}\tau\alpha\acute{\iota}$. i. e. $\pi\acute{o}\rho\nu\alpha\iota$.

the free women, but should sleep only with the men-slaves, with their persons depillated like [2] a slave.

BLEP. Come now, let me follow [3] you close by, that I may be gazed at, [4] and that people may say [5] as follows: "Do you not admire this *husband* [6] of our general?" [*Exeunt Praxagora and Blepyrus.*]

1ST CITIZEN. [7] I will make ready and overhaul my substance, in order that I may carry my chattels to the market-place. Do you, O Meal-sieve, [8] pretty as you are, come hither prettily out of the house the first of my goods, so that you may be a Basket-bearer, [9] being powdered with meal, [10] who hast overturned [11] many bags of mine.

Where is the Stool-carrier? [12] Pot, [13] come forth hither! By Jove, you are black! nor [14] *could you have been blacker,*

[1] Thesm. 204, δοκῶν γυναικῶν ἔργα νυκτερήσια
κλέπτειν ὑφαρπάζειν τε θήλειαν Κύπριν.

[2] See Krüger, Gr. Gr. § 57, 3, obs. 1. Bernhardy, W. S. p. 57, and note on Plut. 314.

[3] See note on Lys. 864.

[4] "*Ut obviorum convertam in me oculos.*" *Brunck.*

[5] See Bernhardy, W. S. p. 79.   [6] See Bernhardy, W. S. p. 160

[7] Here the scene changes to the front of a townsman's house in Athens. The first citizen, assisted by his servants, is seen bringing out of the house his goods and chattels. These he addresses by name, as if they were human beings, assigning to each its proper place, title, and duties, as if to take part in the Panathenaian festival. The whole speech is a parody on the ordering of a public procession.

[8] "Komm' du hervor, Mehlschwinge, schön im schönen Putz."
Droysen.

Pax, 1330, χὦπως μετ' ἐμοῦ καλὴ καλῶς κατακείσει. Acharn. 253, ἄγ', ὦ θύγατερ, ὅπως τὸ κανοῦν καλὴ καλῶς οἴσεις. Antiphanes ap. Athen. ii. p. 60, D., ἃ δὴ δίδωσιν ἡμῖν ὁ τόπος ἄθλι' ἀθλίοις. Plaut. Asin. iii. 3, "I sane bella belle." Curcul. iv. 2, "Sequere istum bella belle." Cf. Plut. 418, 879. Thesm. 168—170. Equit. 189, 190. Eur. Hippol. 645.

[9] See Liddell Lex. voc. κανηφορος.

[10] "Bemehlstäubt." *Droysen.* "σμηχθεῖσα." *Scholiast.* "*Fucata.*" *Faber* and *Kuster.* "*Painted.*" *Liddell.* "*Cerussata.*" *Brunck.*

[11] "*Evertisti.*" *Brunck.* "*In quam tot mei sacci inversi sunt purgandæ farinæ.*" *Faber.* "Fein gesiebt hast." *Droysen.* So also *Smith.*

[12] Female μέτοικοι were obliged to attend upon the κανηφόροι with a parasol and a camp-stool. Cf. Aves, 1551.

[13] For the article, see note on Ran. 40, and Bernhardy, W. S. p. 67

[14] "Wie schwarz! du könntest schwärzer nicht sein, wär' in dir
Die Pommade gekocht, mit der sich das Haar Lysikrates färbt."
Droysen.

if you had boiled the dye with which Lysicrates blackens
his hair. Come hither, Tire-woman,[1] stand next her!
Water-bearer,[2] here! bring hither this water-pot! And do
you, Harper,[3] come forth hither! who have often wakened me
in the dead of the night[4] for the Assembly with your early[5]
strain. Let him with the hive[6] come forth! Bring the honey-
combs! Place the olive-wreaths[7] near! and bring out the two
tripods, and the oil-flask. Now leave the little pots and the
lumber."[8]

2ND CIT. (*grumbling to himself*). Shall I pay in[9] my property? Then I shall be a wretched man and possessed of little
sense. No, by Neptune, never![10] but will first scrutinize
and examine them[11] frequently. For I will not so foolishly
throw away my earnings and savings for nothing,[12] before I
learn[13] the whole matter, how it is. Hollo you! what mean
these chattels? Have you brought them out because you are
flitting, or are you carrying them to put them in pawn?[14]

1ST CIT. By no means.

2ND CIT. Why then are they thus in a row? Surely you
are not leading a procession in honour[15] of Hiero the auctioneer?

---

[1] Cf. vs. 734, 739, and note on Ran. 40. "Κομμώτρια, ἐμπλέκτρια,
ἡ κοσμοῦσα τὰς γυναῖκας." *Suidas.*

[2] According to Faber, the utensil addressed is *a stand for a water
vessel.*

[3] The *cock* is meant. Cf. vs. 30, *supra.* Vesp. 100. Aves, 489.

[4] See Liddell Lex. voc. ἀωρί.   [5] A pun on τὸν ὄρθιον νόμον.

[6] "Ho! there within, the skeps and honey-combs
     Bring forth." *Smith.*

"A *hive*." *Faber.* "A *bowl* or *basin*." *Liddell.* "Der Muldenträger
trete vor!" *Droysen.*

[7] "Read κόμιζε, καὶ θάλλους καθίστη." *Bentley.*

[8] "The pipkins and such small fry you may leave.' *Smith.*
"Das Gerümpel." *Droysen.*

[9] See Bernhardy, W. S. p. 377.

[10] In Brunck μὰ τὸν Ποσειδῶ γ'. Porson (Advers. p. 36) corrects
μὰ τὸν Ποσειδῶ οὐδέποτέ γ', because γὲ cannot be immediately subjoined to an oath. To this reading Dindorf assents.

[11] The new decrees of Praxagora.

[12] "*Temere, nullius rei causâ.*" *Faber.*

[13] πρὶν ἐκπύθωμαι, the reading of the MSS. is changed by Porson,
Elmsley, and Dindorf to πρὶν ἂν ἐκπ. See note on vs. 620. In this
place the alteration is for the better. For the "Anticipation," see
note on Nub. 1148, and on vs. 1126, *infra.*

[14] Cf. Plut. 451.

[15] "Hiero was a celebrated auctioneer of the day." *Smith.* Cf

1st Cit. No, by Jove ! but I am about to deliver them into the market-place for the good of the state, conformably to the laws enacted.

2nd Cit. Art going to deliver them in?'

1st Cit. Certainly.

2nd Cit. Then you are an unhappy man, by Jove the Preserver !

1st Cit. How?

2nd Cit. How ? Easily.[1]

1st Cit. How then ? ought I not to obey the laws ?

2nd Cit. What laws,[2] you unhappy man?

1st Cit. Those enacted.

2nd Cit. Enacted? How silly you are[3] then !

1st Cit. Silly ?

2nd Cit. Certainly.—Nay, rather, the most foolish of all together.

1st Cit. Because I do what is ordered ?[4]

2nd Cit. Why, ought a sensible man to do what is ordered ?

1st Cit. Most assuredly.

2nd Cit. Nay, rather, a stupid man.

1st Cit. And do you not intend to pay them in ?

2nd Cit. I'll take care[5] not, till[6] I see what the people determine on.

Lys. 1277. Thesm. 104. Ran. 445. I do not remember to have met with any other instance of οὔ τι μὴ with interrogation.

[1] *"Facile dictu est."* *Brunck.* See note on Aves, 1234, and on Ran. 1424.

[2] Cf. note on Lys. 1178.

[3] See note on Vesp. 451, and cf. Vesp. 821. Pherecrates ap. Athen. x. p. 415, C.

[4] Bergler compares Eurip. Phœn. 1640.

[5] Cf. Herod. i. 65 ; i. 108.

[6] "πρὶν ἀν with a conjunctive is regularly found only after *negative* clauses or *a question containing a negation.* The same rule also holds for the optative with πρίν." *Krüger.* Cf. Elmsley, Med. vs. 77, 215. Harper's "Powers of the Greek Tenses," p. 136. In the present passage the negation is contained in the preceding φυλάξουαι, as in the very similar passage, ap. Eur. Med. 1218. Cf. Soph. Antig. 175. See also notes on Nub. 1148, and vs. 1126, *infra.*

"Bevor Ich sehe, was der Mehrzahl Willen ist." *Droysen.*

"Before I learn what says the general voice." *Smith.*

1st Cit. Why, what else but that they are[1] ready to carry their property?

2nd Cit. Well, I'd believe,[2] if I saw.

1st Cit. At any rate they talk of it in the streets.

2nd Cit. Why, they *will* talk of it.

1st Cit. And they say[3] they will take them up and carry them.

2nd Cit. Why, they *will* say so.

1st Cit. You will kill me with disbelieving every thing.

2nd Cit. Why, they *will* disbelieve you.

1st Cit. May Jove destroy you!

2nd Cit. Why, they *will* destroy you. Do you think any of them who has sense will carry *his property?* For this is not a national[4] custom; but, by Jove, we ought only to receive. For the gods[5] also *do so.* But you will perceive *that* from the hands of the statues: for when we pray to them to give us blessings, they stand extending the hand with the hollow uppermost,[6] not as about to give any thing, but that they may receive something.

1st Cit. You wretch,[7] let me do something useful;[8] for these must be bound together. Where is my thong?

2nd Cit. Why, will you really carry them?

1st Cit. Yes, by Jove! and now indeed I am binding together these two tripods.

---

[1] Cf. Pax, 923. Nub. 1287. Ran. 198.

[2] For the omission of ἀν, see Krüger, Gr. Gr. § 54, 10, obs. 1. Bernhardy, W. S. p. 374, and notes on Vesp. 983. Ran. 866.

[3] Φημὶ, properly, = *express ono's thoughts;* λέγω, in reference to *the purport* of what is uttered; εἰπεῖν, in reference to the *form* of the speech.

[4] See note on Acharn. 1000.

[5] "The ordo is: λαμβάνειν ἡμᾶς μόνον δεῖ. καὶ γὰρ οἱ θεοὶ (μόνον λαμβάνουσι)· γνώσει δὲ (τοῦτο) ἀπὸ τῶν χειρῶν τῶν ἀγαλμάτων. καὶ γὰρ ὅταν εὐχώμεθα (αὐτοῖς) διδόναι (ἡμῖν) τἀγαθὰ, (τὰ ἀγάλματα) ἕστηκεν ἐκτείνοντα τὴν χεῖρα ὑπτίαν." *Brunck.* For ἕστηκεν, see note on Aves, 515.

"At Athens 'tis the mode to *take,* not give." *Smith.*

[6] "The same as τὴν χεῖρα κοίλην, Thesm. 937." *Brunck.* See note on Ran. 1388.

[7] "Gottloser Mensch du! lass mich thun, was nöthig ist."
                                                        Droysen.

[8] Cf. Plut. 623.

2ND CIT. What[1] folly! To think of your[2] not waiting for the others *to see* what[3] they will do, and then at this point at length——

1ST CIT. Do what?

2ND CIT. Continue waiting; and then to tarry yet longer.

1ST CIT. For what purpose, pray?[4]

2ND CIT. If perchance[5] an earthquake were to take place, or a horrible meteor, or a weasel[6] were to dart across *the market-place*, they would stop carrying, you gaping fool.

1ST CIT. At any rate I should be nicely off, if I did not know where to pay these in.

2ND CIT. See lest *you do* not *know* where you could take them to.[7] Be of good courage! you shall pay them in,[8] even if you go on the last day of the month.

1ST CIT. Why?

2ND CIT. I know that they[9] vote for a thing quickly, and again deny whatever they have decreed.

1ST CIT. They will carry them, my friend.

2ND CIT. But what if they do not bring them?

1ST CIT. Never mind, they'll bring them.

2ND CIT. But what if they do not bring them?

1ST CIT. I'll battle with them.

2ND CIT. But what if they get the better of you?

---

[1] Cf. Nubes, 818. Vesp. 161. Eur. Med. 1051. Alc. 842. Krüger, Gr. Gr. § 47, 3, obs. 1. Kön, Greg. Cor. p. 137. The article is rarely omitted in this phrase. See note on Lys. 967.

[2] See Nub. 819. Bernhardy, W. S. p. 355, and note on Nub. 268.

[3] See similar examples in the note on Nub. 1392, and add vs. 560, *supra*.

[4] Cf. Nub. 1192.

[5] "πολλακις = *fortasse*." *Hotibius* (*Bothe*). See Liddell Lex. voc. πολλάκις, iii., and Krüger's note on Thuc. ii. 13, *init*.

[6] Cf. Theoph. Charact. cap. xvi. Hor. Od. iii. 27, 5.

[7] Of this truly difficult passage I can only say, that I have not met with any satisfactory explanation in any of the commentators. Heindorf (ad Plat. Phæd. p. 36) conjectures λάβῃς. Brunck's method (ἀλλὰ δέδοικα μὴ οὐκ ἔχῃς ὅποι λάβοις) is solœcistic. The same may be said of εἰ μὴ οὐκ ἔχοις ὅποι λάβοις.

[8]   "Fear not,
They'll take them gladly, e'en at the month's end." *Smith*.

[9] "*Ego nostros homines novi, qui in decernendo præproperi sunt, ac rursum negant facturos se, quæ decreta fuerint*." *Brunck*.

1st Cit. I'll leave the things and go away.

2nd Cit. But what if they sell them?

1st Cit. Split you![1]

2nd Cit. But what if I split?

1st Cit. You'll do right.[2]

2nd Cit. And will you be eager to carry them?

1st Cit. I shall; for I see my own neighbours carrying *theirs.*

2nd Cit. Antisthenes[3] to be sure will certainly bring them in. It would be[4] much more agreeable to him to ease himself first for more than thirty days.[5]

1st Cit. Plague take you!

2nd Cit. And what will Callimachus the chorus-master contribute to them?

1st Cit. More than Callias.[6]

2nd Cit. This man will throw away his property.

1st Cit. You say strange things.

2nd Cit. What is there strange? as if I was not always seeing such decrees taking place. Don't you know that *decree*[7] which was determined on about the salt?

1st Cit. I do.

---

[1] Cf. note on Aves, vs. 2.

[2] i. e. *you'll be rightly served.* See Krüger, Gr. Gr. § 56, 8, obs. 2. Bernhardy, W. S. p. 476, and note on Plut. 863.

[3] Mentioned above, vs. 366.

[4] "Understand ἔσται or δόξει αὐτῷ." *Brunck.* "Aristophanes means to say: *Hunc Antisthenem, quamvis alias ægre possit cacare, tamen libentius vel triginta dies cacaturum, quam bona sua in commune allaturum.*" *Bergler.*

[5] So Acharn. vs. 857, ῥιγῶν τε καὶ πεινῶν ἀεὶ πλεῖν ἢ τριάκονθ' ἡμέρας τοῦ μηνὸς ἑκάστου. Cf. ib. vs. 82.

[6] "This is Callias the son of Hipponicus, of the most noble family in Athens, at one time the richest of the citizens, but now, through his profligacy and keeping open table for the Sophists, (Aves, 283—286,) so much reduced, that even the poor chorus-master Callimachus is richer than he." *Droysen.* He afterwards committed suicide, in order to avoid beggary. See Ælian, Var. Hist. iv. 23. Andoc. π. μυστ. p. 55. Aristot. Rhetor. iii. 2. For the construction, see note on vs. 701, *supra.*

[7] "Attica did not produce sufficient salt for their own use. (Acharn. 760.) A decree which had been lately made to lower the price, was found to be impracticable; therefore it was immediately repealed." *Droysen.* "Cf. Böckh, Pub. Econ. Ath. i. p. 65, 110." *Dindorf*

2ND CIT. Don't you know when we voted for those copper[1] coins?

1ST CIT. Aye, and that coinage was a loss to me. For I sold some bunches of grapes and went away with my mouth full of copper coins. And then I went to the market-place for some barley-meal. Then, just as I was holding my bag under *for the meal*, the crier proclaimed that " henceforth no one take copper; for we use silver."

2ND CIT. And were we not[3] all lately swearing that the state would have five hundred talents from the tax of one fortieth, which Euripides[4] devised? and immediately every man was for plastering Euripides with gold.[5] But as soon as on our examining[6] it, it appeared to be " Jove's[7] Corinth," and the measure did not suffice, every man again was for plastering Euripides with pitch.[8]

1ST CIT. The case is not the same, my good sir. At that time we were rulers, but now the women.

2ND CIT. Whom I'll be on my guard against, by Neptune lest they make water upon me.

1ST CIT. I don't know what you're babbling about. [*To his servant.*] Boy,[9] carry the yoke!

In the Archonship of Callias. See note on Ran. 725.

[*] For this custom of carrying money in the mouth, see Vesp. 791. Aves, 503. Pollux, ix. 63. Theoph. Charact. cap. vi.

[3] " Beschwuren neulich nicht wir alle, dass die Stadt
Fünfhundert Talente Steuer durch den Vierzigsten
Bekommen solle, den Euripides angesetzt?
Sogleich vergoldete jedermann den Euripides." *Droysen.*

For τὸ ἔναγχος, see Bernhardy, W. S. p. 328.

[4] " Böckh (Publ. Econ. Athen. ii. p. 27) understands the *son of* the tragedian." *Dindorf.* " The decree of Euripides,—probably a son of Adimantus,—directed that every Athenian should pay into the state $2\frac{1}{2}$ per cent. upon his taxable property; a decree which naturally pressed heaviest upon the rich, and therefore was never carried." *Droysen.*

[5] " *Laudibus magnifice ornabat.*" *Kuster.* Cf. Nub. 912 Diphilus ap. Athen. x. p. 422, B.

[6] Cf. Longin. Subl. i. § 1.   [7] See note on Ran. 439.

[8] " *Maledictis quasi pice nigrâ deformabant.*" *Bergler.*

[9] See note on Ran. 40. For ἀνάφορον, cf. Ran. 8. Lys. 290. " ξύλον ἀμφίκοιλον, ἐν ᾧ τὰ φορτία ἐξαρτήσαντες οἱ ἐργάται βαστάζουσιν." *Suidas.*

[*Enter a Female-crier.*]

CRIER. O all ye citizens,[1]—for so this is now,—come, hasten straight[2] to our Princess-President, in order that chance may point out to you, drawing lots man by man,[3] where you shall dine; for the tables are piled up[4] and furnished with all good things, and the couches are heaped with goatskins and carpets. They are mixing[5] goblets; the female-perfumers are standing in order; the slices of salt-fish are boiling; they are spitting the hare's flesh; cakes[6] are baking; chaplets are plaiting; sweetmeats[7] are toasting; the youngest women are boiling pots[8] of pea-soup; and Smoius amongst them with a Knight's uniform on is cleansing thoroughly the women's cups. And Geron[9] comes with a cloak on and light sandals, laughing loudly with another youth; and his shoes lie uncared for, and his threadbare coat is thrown off.[10] Wherefore come! for he who carries the barley-cake[11] is standing. Come, open your mouths! [*Exit.*]

2ND CIT. Therefore I will certainly go. For why do I keep standing here, when these things have been decreed by the state?

1ST CIT. Why, whither will you go, if you have not paid in your property?

2ND CIT. To dinner.

1ST CIT. Certainly not, if there be any sense in them, until you deliver in[12] *your property.*

---

[1] "Ihr Bürgerinnensöhne—denn so heisst ihr jetzt." *Droysen.*

[2] Cf. Equit. 254. Aves, 1421. Pax, 68, 77, 301, 819. Eur. Hippol. 1197. Gerytad. Fragm. xix. Fragm. Incert. 527.

[3] See Bernhardy, W. S. p. 240.

[4] Cf. Nub. 1203. Bekk. Anecd. i. 13, 24. Zonar. Lex. i. p. 840. Athen. i. sect. 20, p. 20. For the *genitive* with this verb, see Equit. 100. Alcman, Fragm. xvii., and Bernhardy, W. S. p. 168.

[5] See Dawes, M. C. p. 481. Porson, Orest. 1645. Misc. Cr. p. 93.

[6] See Athen. iii. p. 110, B., who cites this clause. but with the change of λάγανα for πόπανα.

[7] Cf. Ran. 510.　　[8] Cf. Ran. 505. Bernhardy, W. S. p. 163.

[9] Krüger (Gr. Gr. § 50, 4, obs. 11) cites this passage as an example of the so-called pleonastic use of ἕτερος, (see note on Ran. 1164,) evidently taking Γέρων for an *old man*, instead of a proper name. But the true reading is undoubtedly Γέρης. See vs. 932.

[10] Comp. Ran. 455.

[11] "Speed ye, since dish in hand the sewer waits." *Smith.*

[12] In the early editions and some of the MSS. ἄν is omitted. See

2ND CIT. Well, I will deliver it in.

1ST CIT. When?

2ND CIT. I shall not be a hinderance,[1] my good sir.

1ST CIT. How, pray?[2]

2ND CIT. I assert that others will deliver in *their property* still later than I.

1ST CIT. But will you go to dinner notwithstanding?

2ND CIT. Why, what[3] must I do? for it behoves those who have right understanding to assist the state to the best of their ability.

1ST CIT. But what if they hinder you?

2ND CIT. I'll join[4] battle with them with my head bent forward.[5]

1ST CIT. But what if they whip you?

2ND CIT. I'll summon them.

1ST CIT. But what if they laugh at you?

2ND CIT. Standing at the doors—

1ST CIT. What will you do? Tell me!

2ND CIT. I'll snatch away[6] the victuals from those who are carrying them in.

1ST CIT. Then go too late! Do you, Sicon and Parmeno, take up my entire property.[7]

2ND CIT. Come then, let me[8] help you to carry them.

1ST CIT. No, by no[9] means! For I am afraid lest you lay claim to my property even before the Princess-President, when I pay[10] it in.   [*Exit with his servants.*]

note on vs. 629, and Harper, Powers of the Greek Tenses, p. 132. Bentley and Brunck read πρίν γ' ἂν ἀπενέγκῃς, Porson (ap. Kidd ad Dawes, M. C. p. 525) reads πρὶν ἄν γ' ἀπ. "Both forms are in use. See Elmsl. Acharn. 176. Reisig, i. p. 66." *Dindorf.* Who reads πρὶν ἂν ἀπ.

[1] "They shall not have to wait for me." *Smith.* See note on vs. 623, *supra.*

[2] See Liddell's Lex. voc. τίς, viii. 4.

[3] See note on Lys. 884.   [4] Cf. Lys. 45.

[5] "*Contra ibo submisso capite.*" *Hotibius.* "The Latins have no word to express κύψας in this passage. The French say: *Aller tête baissée vers les ennemis.*" *Faber.*
            "I'll force my way ram-fashion." *Smith.*

[6] See note on Ran. 1228.

[7] Brunck compares Æsch. Theb. 819. Eur. Ion, 1316.

[8] See note on Lys. 864.   [9] See note on Vesp. 1418.

[10] "*Quando deposuero.*" *Brunck.* But this would require καταθῶ. See Matthiä, Gr. Gr. p. 894, note.

2ND CIT. By Jove, of a truth I have need of some con-trivance, so that I may retain the property I have, and may somehow partake in common with these of the things which are kneading. It seems to me to be just. I must go to the same place to dine,[1] and must not delay. [*Exit.*][2]

1ST OLD WOMAN. Why in the world are the men not come? it has been time this long while : for I am standing idle, painted over with white lead,[3] and clad in a saffron-coloured robe, and humming a tune[4] to myself, playing amorously, in order that I may catch[5] some of them as he is passing by. Ye Muses, come hither to my mouth, having devised some Ionian[6] ditty.

YOUNG WOMAN (*looking out from an opposite window*). Now you've been beforehand[7] with me in peeping out, you[8] ugly old woman ; and you thought you would strip unwatched vines,[9] as I was not present here, and allure some one by singing. But I'll sing against you, if you do this.[10] For even if this be tiresome[11] to the spectators, nevertheless it has something amusing in it and belonging to comedy.

[*An ugly old Man crosses the stage.*]

1ST OLD WOMAN (*pointing to the old man*). Converse

---

[1] For the accusative, see Krüger, Gr. Gr. § 56, 18, obs. 3.

[2] Here the scene changes to a public street in Athens : an old woman, painted, and attired in a saffron-coloured robe, appears at a window.

[3] Bergler compares Lucil. Epigr. Anthol. ii. c. 9,

$$\mu\grave{\eta} \ \tau o\acute{\iota}\nu\nu\nu \ \tau\grave{o} \ \pi\rho\acute{o}\sigma\omega\pi o\nu \ \H{a}\pi a\nu \ \psi\iota\mu\acute{\nu}\theta\wp \ \kappa a\tau\acute{a}\pi\lambda a\tau\tau\epsilon,$$
$$\H{\omega}\sigma\tau\epsilon \ \pi\rho o\sigma\omega\pi\epsilon\~{\iota}o\nu, \ \kappa o\grave{\upsilon}\chi\grave{\iota} \ \pi\rho\acute{o}\sigma\omega\pi o\nu \ \H{\epsilon}\chi\epsilon\iota\nu.$$

It was used as a cosmetic to whiten the face. See Athen. xiii. p. 557, F.

[4] Cf. vs. 931. Vesp. 219. Ran. 53. Dawes, M. C. p. 584, ed. Kidd.

[5] ὅπως ἂν περιλάβοιμι. A noted violation of Attic syntax. See note on Aves, 1338.

[6] For the construction, see the examples cited in the note on Pax, 1154. The voluptuous character of the Ionians was notorious. See vs. 918, *infra.* Thesm. 163. Horat. Od. iii. 6, 21. Athen. xii. p. 524—526. Their μοιχικα ἄσματα also, like those of the Locrians, en-joyed a very unenviable notoriety. See Athen. xiv. p. 620.

[7] Cf. vs. 596, *supra.* [8] See note on Thesm. 1025.

[9] Cf. Vesp. 634.

[10] i. e. *sing.* So vs. 888, τοῦτο = a *singing match.* See note on Lys. 134.

[11] "Und ist der Spass alltäglich unserm Publikum auch ;
So ist es doch was Lustiges und Komödienbrauch." *Droysen.*
"The young woman speaks this *ex personâ poetæ.*" *Bergler.*

with this old man, and retire with him! But do you, my little darling of a flute-player,[1] take your flute and accompany me with a tune worthy of me and of you. [*Sings to the flute.*] "If any one wishes to experience some good, he should sleep with me. For knowledge is not in young women,[2] but in the ripe[3] ones: nor would any of them be willing to love more than I the friend with whom I had to do; but she would fly off to another."

YOUNG WOM. Do not envy the young women. For pleasure[4] is in their tender limbs, and blossoms on their bosoms: while you, old woman, have had[5] your eyebrows polled, and have been painted, an object[6] of love for Orcus.

1ST OLD WOM. May your teeth drop out, and may you lose your couch when wishing to be caressed, and may you find a serpent in the bed, and draw it towards you, wishing to kiss it.

YOUNG WOM. (*sings*). "Alas! alas! what ever shall I do?[7] my friend[8] is not come, and I am left here alone: for my mother has gone elsewhere; and as for the rest, these I must make of no account. Come, O nurse, I beseech you, summon Orthagoras,[9] that you may enjoy yourself, I entreat you."

1ST OLD WOM. (*sings*). "Already, you wretch, you are prurient in the Ionian manner,[10] and you appear to me also

[1] "Herzensflötenbläserchen." *Droysen.*
[2] A parody on Eur. Phœn. 529.

> "Nicht verstehn es die jungen Kätzchen,
> Sondern wir, die reifen Schätzchen." *Droysen.*

[3] Cf. Xenarchus ap. Athen. xiii. p. 569, B.
[4] Eur. Hippol. 967, τὸ μωρὸν γυναιξὶν ἐμπέφυκε.
[5] See Liddell's Lex. in voc. παραλέγω.
[6] Cf. vs. 973, *infra.*
[7] Cf. Vesp. 1000. Nub. 791, 461. Pax, 276. Blomf. gloss. Theb 144. Dorville, Charit. p. 361.
[8] ἑταῖρος = φίλος, vs. 898. "No doubt taken from Euripides." *Reiske.*
[9] A mock proper name with an obscene allusion. Readers of Rabelais will be at no loss for similar fictions. "*Mentula arrecta*, from ὀρθὸς and ἐγείρω." *Faber.* "τὸ αἰδοῖον." *Scholiast.* "Isaac Vossius on Pompon. Mel. ii. 2, thinks Bacchus is invoked by this name." *Porson.* For this use of the optative, see Bernhardy, W. S. p. 400.
[10] "See Toup Suid. iii. p. 134." *Porson.* See also Ran. 450. Pax.

a Labda[1] after the fashion of the Lesbians. But you will never filch away my darling; and you shall not spoil or intercept my hour."[2]

YOUNG WOM. Sing as much as you please, and peep out like a weasel; for no one will sooner come in unto you than[3] me.

1ST OLD WOM. Then is it not for your burial?[4]

YOUNG WOM. It would be a strange thing, you old woman.

1ST OLD WOM. Certainly not.

YOUNG WOM. Why, how could one tell any thing new to an old woman?

1ST OLD WOM. My old age won't distress you.

YOUNG WOM. What then? your alkanet,[5] rather, and your white lead?

1ST OLD WOM. Why do you talk to me?[6]

YOUNG WOM. And why do you peep out?

1ST OLD WOM. I? I am singing to myself[7] in honour of my friend Epigenes..

YOUNG WOM. Why, have you any other friend than Gcres?[8]

1ST OLD WOM. He'll show you; for he will come to me presently. For see! there he is himself! [*A young man is seen at a distance.*]

639. Neue ad Sapph. Fragment. p. 51, 52. Bernhardy, W. S. p. 223.

[1] "λ was called λάβδα amongst the Attics." *Krüger.* "δοκεῖς δ' ἐμοὶ καὶ τοὺς ἄνδρας λεσβίσουσα. See Vesp. 1346. Ran. 1308." *Brunck.* "See Toup, Suid. ii. p. 168, seq." *Dindorf.*

[2] "Du sollst mein Stündchen mir nicht stören noch stehlen."

Droysen.

[3] See Krüger, Gr. Gr. § 49, 2, obs. 7. Bernhardy, W. S. p. 140. Soph. Ant. 182. Trach. 577. So after ἄλλος. See Krüger, Gr. Gr. § 68, 14, obs. 2. Nubes, 653. Soph. Ajax, 444. Æsch. Prom. 467. "See the elegant note of Jer. Markland, Eur. Suppl. 419." *Porson.* Cf. Class. J. No. iii. p. 509.

[4] In Brunck's and Dindorf's texts *without* interrogation, but in the versions which accompany their texts *with* interrogation. I should prefer οὐκοῦν, from which Droysen seems to have made his translation, "Ja dich auszuziehn!"

[5] The Athenian substitute for *rouge.*

[6] Cf. Ran. 176. Pax, 161. Acharn. 1113.

[7] Cf. Ran. 53.

[8] "φαλακρὸς οὗτος καὶ πένης." *Scholiast.* See note on vs. 848, supra.

YOUNG WOM. He is not wanting any thing with you, you pest.

1ST OLD WOM. Yes, by Jove, you skinny jade!

YOUNG WOM. He himself will soon show;[1] for I will go away. [*Retires from the window.*]

1ST OLD WOM. And I too, that you may know that I am much wiser than you. [*Retires from the window.*]

[*Enter a young Man crowned with flowers, and bearing a torch.*]

YOUNG MAN. Would[2] it were permitted to sleep with the young girl, and one was not obliged[3] first to have to do with a snub-nosed or elderly one. For this is intolerable to a free man.

1ST OLD WOM. (*peeping out and talking aside*). Then, by Jove, you'll wench to your cost! For these are not the times of Charixene.[4] You are bound[5] to do this in conformity with the law, if we are under a democratic government. But I'll withdraw to watch what in the world he will do. [*Retires again.*]

YOUNG MAN. O ye gods, may I find[6] my beautiful one alone, to whom I am coming drunk, desiring her this long while.

YOUNG WOM. (*cautiously peeping out*). I have deceived the accursed old woman; for she is gone, thinking that I would remain within.

1ST OLD WOM. (*peeping out*). Nay, this is he himself,[7] of whom I made mention. [*Sings.*] "Come hither, pray! Come hither, pray, my beloved! come hither to me! and see that you be my bedfellow during the night.[8] For love of these

---

[1] Cf. note on Lys. 375.   [2] See note on Lys. 940.

[3] καὶ μηδὲν πρότερον, Brunck. Dindorf has introduced Elmsley's conjecture (Mus. Crit. ii. p. 44, ad Med. p. 74) μὴ 'δει. But this was not necessary. See note on Ran. 434.

[4] "ἐπὶ Χαριξένης. ἐπὶ μωρίᾳ ἡ Χαριξένη διεβεβόητο, ἀρχαία οὖσα. ἔνιοι δὲ καὶ ποιήτριαν αὐτὴν ἐρωτικῶν λέγουσιν. ἔστι δὲ καὶ παροιμία· οἷα τὰ ἐπὶ Χαριξένης." *Hesychius.* "ἐπὶ Χαριξένης. αὐλητρὶς ἡ Χαριξένη ἀρχαία, καὶ ποιήτρια κρουμάτων· οἱ δὲ, μελοποιόν. Θεόπομπος Σειρῆσιν, αὐλεῖ γὰρ σαπρὰ αὕτη γε κρουμάτια τὰ ἐπὶ Χαριξένης." *Etymol. Mag.* Cf. vs. 985, *infra*, and Bernhardy, W. S. p. 279, and p. 246.

[5] Cf. Herod. ix. 60; viii. 137.

[6] See note on Lys. 940.   [7] Cf. Nub. 1403. Vesp. 820.

[8] See Dawes, M. C. p. 553. Toup on Suid. iii. p. 187, and note on Lys. 316.

curls of yours agitates me exceedingly; and marvellous desire
assails me, which has worn[1] me away. Permit me, Love, I
beseech thee, and make him come to my bed."

YOUNG MAN (*standing under the young woman's window
and singing*). "Come[2] hither, pray! come hither, pray! and
do thou run down and open this door; otherwise I will fall
down and lie here. My beloved, come, I wish to rest in thy
bosom.[3] O Venus, wherefore dost thou make me mad after
her? Permit me, Love, I beseech thee, and make her come
to my bed. And this has been mentioned sufficiently for[4]
my anguish. But do thou, my dearest, oh, I beseech thee,
open to me, embrace me! Through thee I suffer pains. O my
beloved[5] object decked with gold,[6] child of Venus, the Muse's
honey-bee, nurseling[7] of the Graces, Beauty's face,[8] open to
me, embrace me! Through thee I suffer pains."

[1] See note on Thesm. 706.

[2] This is remarkable as being a specimen of the *serenades* (παρα-
κλαυσίθυρα) of the Greeks. Other examples are Theocr. iii. 23.
Plautus, Curcul. i. 2, 60. Propert. i. 16, 17. Horat. Od. iii. 10.
Tibull. i. 2, 9. Ovid, Amor. El. vi.

> " Hither, hither, quick repair,
> Ope the door to me, my fair;
> Cruel! if thou dost deny,
> On these rugged stones I'll lie,
> Till at length shall ruthless death
> Claim thy hapless lover's breath.
> Then, sweetest, deign to ease my pain,
> And pillowed on thy breast,
> O let me sink to rest!
> Eros! blooming and fair,
> List thou to my prayer,
> That this maid all-divine
> At length may be mine." *Smith.*

[3] See Bernhardy, W. S. p. 99.

[4] "*Hactenus quidem pro meâ necessitate satis dictum fuit.*" *Brunck.*

[5] "Julianus Epist. 18, ἵνα σὲ, τὸ μέλημα τοὐμὸν, ὡς φησὶν Σαπφὼ,
περιπτύξωμαι." *Bentley.*

[6] Cf. Eur. Iph. A. 219.

[7] Ibycus, (ap. Athen. xiii. p. 564. F.,)

> Εὐρύαλε, γλυκερῶν Χαρίτων θάλος
> καλλικόμων μελέδημα, σὲ μὲν Κύπρις
> ἅ τ' ἀγανοβλέφαρος Πειθὼ ῥοδέοισιν ἐν ἄνθεσι θρέψαν.

[8] "Du goldner Hort meiner Gedanken, Biene du des Liedes,
Du Kypris Kind, Pflegling der Huldgöttin, du Wonnenantlitz
Droysen.

A parody on Eur. Phœn. 1498, στολίδα κροκόεσσαν τρυφᾶς.

1st old Wom. (*suddenly coming out*).   Ho you! why do you knock?   Do you seek me?

Young Man. By no means.[1]

1st old Wom. And[2] yet you knocked furiously at the door.

Young Man. Then may I die, *if I did*.

1st old Wom. In want of whom, then, have you come with a torch?

Young Man. In search of a certain Anaphlystian.[3]

1st old Wom. What man?

Young Man. Not your Sebinus,[4] whom you perhaps expect.

1st old Wom. (*seizing him by the arm*).   Yes, by Venus! whether[5] you wish it or no.

Young Man. But we are not now bringing[6] into court those above sixty years old; but have adjourned[7] them to another time.   For[8] we are judging those under twenty *years*.

1st old Wom. This was in the time of the former government, my sweet.[9]   But now it is decreed to bring in us first.

Young Man. Yes, for him that pleases to do so,[10] after the manner of the law at draughts.

[1] See note on Ran. 1456.

[2] Comp. Aves, 86, 1011. Equit. 495.

[3] Ran. 427, Σεβῖνον, ὅστις ἐστὶν ἀναφλύστιος.   In Σεβῖνος there is an allusion to the word βινεῖν in this passage.   And so the old woman (vs. 981) evidently understands it.

[4] αὐτήν σε κινοῦνϑ᾽, *Brunck*.   "Reisig, (i. p. xiii.,) by comparing the verse in the *Ranæ*, appears to have restored the true reading, οὐ τὸν Σεβῖνον." *Dindorf*. "Read Σεβῖνον: *illum Sebinum*, qui τῷ δήμῳ Ἀναφλύστιος *erat*.   See Ran. 427." *Bentley*.

[5] Cf. vs. 1097, *infra*. Lys. 939, 1036. Nub. 295. Æsch. Theb. 423. Eur. Ion, 871.

[6] "An allusion to the manner of introducing causes into the courts of justice, according to the age of the plaintiffs; first, those (as I imagine) above 60 years of age, and so downwards.   After which, if there were several, they cast lots, whose should be heard first." *Gray*.   See Bernhardy, W. S. p. 346.

[7] See Bernhardy, W. S. p. 346.

[8] For this position of γὰρ, cf. vs. 375, *supra*. Vesp. 217. Plut. 146 Lys. 130, 489.   Eubulus ap. Athen. ii. p. 69, C. Philemon ap. Stob Serm. lxii. 2. Eur. Hippol. 470, 698, 703.

[9] "ὑποκοριστικὸν, as ὦ μαλακίων, vs. 1058, *infra*." *Bergler*.   See Ruhnken, Tim. Lex. p. 132.

[10] "Provided we're *inclined*; for as in playing chess, We're at liberty to *take*,—or *pass* you by, I guess." *Smith*

1st OLD WOM. But not even do you dine[1] according to the law at draughts.

YOUNG MAN. I don't know what you mean. I must knock at this[2] door.

1st OLD WOM. Yes, when you shall have first knocked at my door.[3]

YOUNG MAN. But I am not now asking for a bolting-sieve.[4]

1st OLD WOM. I know that I am loved: but now you are astonished that you found me out of doors. Come, put forward your lips.

YOUNG MAN. Nay, my dear, I am afraid of your lover.

1st OLD WOM. Whom?

YOUNG MAN. The best of painters.

1st OLD WOM. But who is he?

YOUNG MAN. He that paints the vases for the dead.[5] But go away! that he may not see you at the door.

1st OLD WOM. I know, I know what[6] you wish.

YOUNG MAN. For I also, by Jove, *know*[7] you!

1st OLD WOM. By Venus, who obtained me by lot,[8] I will not let you go.[9]

YOUNG MAN. You are mad, old woman.

---

[1] "Read οὐδ' ἐδείπνεις." *Bentley.*

[2] See note on Thesm. 646.   [3] Cf. Lys. 1212, and vs. 257, *supra.*

[4] There is an allusion to the preceding κρούειν.

[5] "Der, Liebste, der für die Leichenkammer die Vasen mahlt."
                                                Droysen.
He means that she was a τυμβογρᾴδινν. Painters of this class corresponded to our *sign-painters.* Cf. vs. 538, *supra.*

[6] See Elmsley, Med. vs. 1086. Iph. T. 766. Hermann, Soph. Ajax, 1238.

[7] "*Etenim hercle ego te quoque novi.*" *Brunck.* "Ich gleichfalls, was du." *Droysen.* "*And I know what you want:*" an example of Anticipation. Elmsley (Ach. 127) proposed καί σ' ἔγωγε. But see Krüger, Gr. Gr. § 69, 32, obs. 21.

[8] "Der Ich eigen bin." *Droysen.* Cf. Hom. Il. xxiii. 79. Eur. Hec. 102.

[9] This is the same as οὐ μὴ ἀφήσω, the οὐ being contained in the preceding μὰ τὴν 'Αφρ. "Instead of the former negative οὐ, the negative μὰ used in an oath is found with the accusative. *Arist. Lys.* 918, μὰ τὸν 'Απόλλω μή σ' ἐγώ, καίπερ τοιοῦτον ὄντα, κατακλινῶ χαμαί. Comp. *Eccl.* 1000. *Aves*, 195; according to which in *Ran.* 508, οὐ after 'Απόλλω should be struck out." *Matthiä.* See Elmsley, Soph. Col. 177, and cf. vss. 1075, 1085, of this play.

1st OLD WOM. You talk foolishly; for I will lead you to my bed.

YOUNG MAN. Why then[1] should we purchase hooks for our buckets, when it is in one's power, by letting down such an old woman as this, to draw up the buckets from the wells ?[2]

1st OLD WOM. Do not jeer me, you wretch,[3] but follow this way to my house.

YOUNG MAN. But there is no necessity for me, unless you have paid in to the state the five-hundredth of your—years.[4]

1st OLD WOM. By Venus, yet you must! for I delight in sleeping with men so young as you.

YOUNG MAN. But I abominate *sleeping with* women so old as you; and I will never comply.

1st OLD WOM. (*producing a paper*).   But, by Jove, this, shall compel you !

YOUNG MAN. And what is this?

1st OLD WOM.   A decree, according to which you must come to me.

YOUNG MAN. Read[5] whatever in the world it *is*.

1st OLD WOM.   Well now, I read it.   [*Reads.*]   "It has been decreed by the women that, if a young man desire a young woman, he shall not have to do with her before he shall

---

[1] "Henceforth to draw our buckets up, that we shall never need
  Or pulley, hook, or rope, by all will be agreed;
  By the heels we 'll let this harpy down, and in a trice our pails,
  From the well will safe be lifted, clutched in her crooked nails."
                                                                Smith.

[2] φρεάτων. "Cf. Strattis ap. Athen. iii. p. 124, D. Alexis, p. 123, F. Apollodorus, p. 125, A." *Porson.*   "See Porson, Advers. p. 68. Maltby, Thes. p. lxxx. 1051." *Dobree.*

[3] "Read ὦ τάν." *Bentley.*

[4] All MSS. and editions before Brunck's read τῶν ἱμῶν, i. e. οὐσιῶν, where there is an allusion to the law of exchange of property on declining any of the public liturgies.   Brunck adopts Tyrwhitt's emendation τῶν ἐτῶν, which, he says, "lepidam et facetam comico sententiam reddit."   "Imo absurdam. Vide Böckh, Staatsh. der Athen. T. ii. p. 56." *Dindorf.*   Nevertheless, in Dindorf's last edition we find τῶν ἐτῶν.

[5] An example of "Anticipation," for λέγε τί ποτε αὐτὸ κᾶστι. See note on Nub. 1148, and on vs. 1126, *infra.*   For this use of καὶ see note on Lys. 171.

have first[1] lain with the old[2] woman. But if he be not willing first to lie with *the old woman*, but desire the young woman, be it permitted for the elderly women to drag the young man with impunity, having laid hold of him[3] by the middle."

YOUNG MAN. Ah me! to-day I shall become a Procrustes.[4]

1ST OLD WOM. Yes; for you must obey our laws.

YOUNG MAN. But how, if a tribesman[5] of mine, or one of my friends, comes and rescues me?

1ST OLD WOM. But no man is any longer authorized beyond a medimnus *of corn*.[6]

YOUNG MAN. But is there no swearing off?[7]

1ST OLD WOM. No; for there is no occasion for shuffling.[8]

YOUNG MAN. But I 'll pretend to be a merchant.[9]

1ST OLD WOM. Aye, to your cost.[10]

YOUNG MAN. What then must I do?

1ST OLD WOM. Follow this way to my house.

YOUNG MAN. Why, is there a necessity for me *to do* this?

1ST OLD WOM. Aye, a Diomedean[11] *necessity*.

YOUNG MAN. Then first strew me some origanum[12] under-

---

[1] " By this Thucydides' προέγραψα πρῶτον (i. 23) may be defended, which ought to have been admitted into the text." *Porson.* The accumulation, πρὶν, πρῶτον, προκρ. is no doubt intentional. See Krüger's note on Xen. Anab. i. 4, 14.

[2] For the article, see Bernhardy, W. S. p. 315.

[3] Cf. Lys. vs. 119. For *ἀνατί*, see Ruhnken, Tim. Lex. p. 81.

[4] A play on the preceding προκρούειν, in sense as well as sound.

[5] See Krüger, Gr. Gr. § 47, 9.

[6] A woman could not on her own authority contract a debt, with any person, for more than the value of a medimnus of corn. See Isæus *de Hæred. Arist.* p. 259. This, of course, is now applied to the *men*, the women being at the head of the state.

[7] ἐξωμοσία corresponds to our *essoine*.

> " From every work he challenged *essoin*
> For contemplation's sake; yet otherwise
> His life he led in lawless riotise." *Chaucer.*

[8] Plut. 1154, ἀλλ' οὐκ ἔργον ἔστ' οὐδὲν στροφῶν.

[9] Cf. Plut. 904. These enjoyed several immunities. See Demosth Apatur. init. Elmsley, Acharn. 592.

[10] Cf. Ach. 827. Aves, 1391. *Amphiaraus*, Fragm. iv.

[11] Plato, Rep. vi. p. 493, D., ἡ Διομηδεία λεγομένη ἀνάγκη ποιεῖν αὐτῷ πάντα. Translated by Catullus, " *Ututa necessitas*." Diomedes the Thracian compelled strangers to lie with his daughters.

[12] " Apparently yielding, he bids her prepare a couch, not however a *nuptial*, but a *funeral* one, as best suited to her who was θανάτου μέλημα." *Smith.*

neath, and break off and place under four vine-twigs, and wear a tænia, and place beside you the vases, and set down the earthen vessel[1] of water before your door.

1ST OLD WOM. (*sarcastically*). Assuredly you will moreover buy me a chaplet[2] too!

YOUNG MAN. Yes, by Jove! if it be of the waxen[3] sort; for I fancy you will immediately fall in pieces[4] within.

YOUNG WOM. (*suddenly coming out of her house*). Whither are you dragging this man?

1ST OLD WOM. I am leading in mine own.

YOUNG WOM. Not discreetly: for he is not of the age for sleeping with you, being so young; since you might more fitly be his mother than his wife.—Wherefore, if you shall establish this law, you will fill the whole earth with Œdipuses.

1ST OLD WOM. O you all-abominable, you devised this argument through envy. But I'll be revenged on you. [*Exit.*]

YOUNG MAN. By Jove the preserver, you have obliged me, my darling, by having removed the old woman from me. Wherefore, in return for these good deeds, I will at night return you a kindness great and thick.[5] [*Young woman takes him by the arm.*]

2ND OLD WOM. (*suddenly coming up*). Hollo you! whither are you dragging this man in violation of the law, when the written law orders him first to sleep with me?

YOUNG MAN. Ah me, miserable! Whence did you pop out,—the devil take[6] you! For this pest is more abominable than that.

2ND OLD WOM. (*trying to drag him away*). Come this way!

YOUNG MAN (*to the young woman*). By no means suffer me to be dragged away by this *old woman*, I beseech you!

[1] To purify those who were engaged about the corpse. They washed themselves with it on leaving the house. See Bernhardy, W. S. p. 163.

[2] See vs. 538, *supra*.

[3] Alluding to the *wax-tapers* used at funerals. See note on Pax. 1154.

[4] Shakspeare, Pericles, act iv. sc. 3, "What else, man? The stuff we have, a strong wind will blow it to pieces, they are so pitifully sodden."

[5] Cf. Pax, 907. Acharn. 787. Lys. 23. Plaut. Casin. v. 2, 28; v. 2, 36. For εἰς ἑσπέραν, see Bernhardy, W. S p. 216, and note on Vesp. 1085.

[6] See note on Thesm. 879.

2ND OLD WOM. Nay, I do not *drag you*, but the law drags you. [*Exit young woman.*]

YOUNG MAN. It does not *drag* me, but an Empusa clothed in a bloody blister.[1]

2ND OLD WOM. Follow this way quickly, my darling,[2] and don't chatter!

YOUNG MAN. Come then, permit me first to go to the necessary and recover my spirits, otherwise you 'll see me presently making something yellow[3] on the spot through fear.

2ND OLD WOM. Be of good courage! come! you shall ease yourself in the house.

YOUNG MAN. I fear lest *I do* even[4] more than I wish. But I will put in two sufficient sureties.

2ND OLD WOM. Put me in no sureties!

3RD OLD WOM. (*running up*). Whither, whither are you going with her?

YOUNG MAN. I *am* not *going*, but am dragged. But many blessings on you, whoever you are,[5] because you did not suffer me to be destroyed. [*Catches sight of her for the first time.*] O Hercules! O ye Pans![6] O ye Corybantes! O ye Dioscuri! this pest, again, is much more abominable than the other. But what in the world is this thing, I beseech you? Are you an ape covered over with white lead,[7] or an old woman sent up from the dead?[8]

---

[1] He alludes to the *flame-coloured* κροκωτὸν which the old woman had on. For the Empusa, see note on Ran. 293.

[2] Cf. vs. 985, *supra*.

[3] Vs. 329, τί τοῦτό σοι τὸ πυῤῥόν ἐστιν; οὔ τι που
       Κινησίας σου κατατετίληκέν που;

[4] Cf. vs. 658. Plut. 764. Aves, 1349. Vesp. 906.

[5] One would rather have expected ἥτις γε εἶ.

[6] *This* use of the plural is peculiar to the comic and the later writers. See Krüger, Gr. Gr. § 44, 3, obs. 7. Bernhardy, W. S p. 61. Lobeck on Soph. Ajax, 190. Cf. Acharn. 267.

[7] Cf. Eubulus ap. Athen. xiii. p. 557, F.

"Art some ape daub'd with paint, and trick'd out for a show,
Or a beldame sent up from the regions below?"   *Smith.*

[8] "So in Suidas: πλειόνων, τῶν νεκρῶν. Eustathius ad Odyss. p. 1382, l. 18, ὡς δὲ καὶ νεκροῖς προσφυὲς τὸ, οἱ πολλοί, καὶ τὲ, πλείους, δηλοῖ ὁ εἰπὼν τὸ, ἀπελεύσομαι παρὰ τοὺς πλείονας, ὅ ἐστι, θανοῦμαι πλείονας γὰρ, τοὺς τεθνεῶτας ἐκεῖνος ἔφη." *Brunck.* So in an oracle ap. Pausan. i. 43, Μεγαρέας εὖ πράξειν, ἢν μετὰ τῶν πλειόνων βουλεύσωνται. See Bernhardy, W. S. p. 433.

3RD OLD WOM. Do not jeer me, but follow this way.

2ND OLD WOM. Nay, rather, this way.

3RD OLD WOM. *Be assured* that I will never let you go.

2ND OLD WOM. Neither, indeed, will I.

YOUNG MAN. You will tear me in pieces, the devil take
you ![1]

2ND OLD WOM. For you ought to follow me in conformity
with the law.

3RD OLD WOM. Not if another old woman still uglier
appear.

YOUNG MAN. Come, if I first perish miserably through you,
how shall I come to that beautiful one ?

3RD OLD WOM. Do you look to *that* yourself : but this you
must do.

YOUNG MAN. Then by lying with which of you first shall I
be set free ?

2ND OLD WOM. Don't you know? you must come this
way.

YOUNG MAN. Then let this one let me go.

3RD OLD WOM. Nay, rather, come this way to my house.

YOUNG MAN. Yes, if she will let me go.

2ND OLD WOM. But, by Jove, I will not let you go.

3RD OLD WOM. Neither, indeed, will I.

YOUNG MAN. You would be dangerous, if you were ferry-
men.

2ND OLD WOM. Why so ?

YOUNG MAN. You would wear out those on board by dragging them.

2ND OLD WOM. Follow this way in silence !

3RD OLD WOM. No, by Jove, but to my house.

YOUNG MAN. This affair is plainly according to the decree[2]

---

[1] See note on Thesm. 879.

[2] " Hesychius: εἰσήνεγκε γὰρ οὗτος ψήφισμα, ὥστε διειλημμένους
τοὺς κρινομένους ἑκατέρωθεν ἀπολογεῖσθαι. Mention is made of the
same decree of Cannonus ap. Xenoph. Hellen. i. 7, 21, ταῦτ᾽ εἰπὼν
Εὐρυπτόλεμος, ἔγραψε γνώμην, κατὰ τοῦ Καννώνου ψήφισμα, κρίνεσθαι
τοὺς ἄνδρας δίχα ἕκαστον· ἡ δὲ τῆς βουλῆς ἦν, μιᾷ ψήφῳ ἅπαντας
κρίνειν. It was provided by the decree of Cannonus, that where
there were many criminals charged with the same offence, each
should be tried separately. The young man says the necessity is
imposed upon him according to the decree of Cannonus,—not κρίνειν
δίχα ἕκαστον, but βινεῖν, *permolere.*" *Brunck.*

of Cannonus; I must lie with you divided into two.[1] How then shall I be able to row[2] both double-handed?

2ND OLD WOM. Very well, when you shall have eaten a pot of onions.[3]

YOUNG MAN. Ah me, miserable! I am now dragged close to the door. [*The 2nd old woman here attempts to drag him into her house and exclude the 3rd old woman.*]

3RD OLD WOM. (*to the 2nd old woman*). But it shall be no[4] advantage to you; for I will rush in along with you.[5]

YOUNG MAN. Nay, do not, by the gods![6] for it is better to be afflicted with one than two evils.

3RD OLD WOM. Yea, by Hecate! whether you wish it or no.[7]

YOUNG MAN (*to the audience*). O thrice-unlucky, if I must lie with an ugly old woman the whole night and the whole day; and then, again, as soon as I am freed from her, with a Phryne,[8] who has a flask[9] on her jaws. Am I not wretched? Nay, rather, by Jove[10] the Preserver, a most wretched man, and unfortunate, who[11] must swim with such wild beasts.

---

[1] Aristophanes evidently distorts the sense of this word from the sense it bears in the above decree. " Whereas in the decree it ran, that the defendants should διειλημμένους ἀπολογεῖσθαι, the young man says that he διαλελημμένον, *in diversa diductum*, as it were, must serve the two old women *at the same time.*" *Brunck.* This is confirmed by the δικωπεῖν ἀμφοτέρας of the next line, for ἀμφοτέρας can only signify *binas simul;* though vs. 1092 seems to oppose this view Shakspeare, *Merry Wives of Windsor*, act v. sc. 5, " Divide me like a bribe-buck, to each a haunch."

[2] See Plato ap. Athen. x. p. 456, A.

[3] See Athen. ii. p. 64, B. seq.

[4] " *Nihil plus efficies.*" *Faber.* Cf. Isocr. p. 41, B. Plato, Symp. p. 217, C. Plut. 531. Soph. Rex, 919. Eur. Phœn. 563. Hippol. 284. Iph. A. 1383. Helen. 329. Lobeck, Ajax, p. 224. Bernhardy, W. S. p. 90.

[5] " *Una tecum irrumpam in ædes.*" *Bergler.*

[6] See Krüger, Gr. Gr. § 68, 37, obs. 2.

[7] Cf. note on vs. 981, *supra.*

[8] The name of several noted courtesans of antiquity. See Athen. xiii. p. 591, C. 583, B. 590, D. Here with a play on its other meaning, *a toad.* " Understand *a nasty old woman.*" *Faber.*

[9] " Die einen Scheffel Schminke auf ihren Kiefern hat." *Droysen* Kuster, the Scholiast, and Suidas understand it of her cheeks puffed out like the sides of a flask.

[10] See note on Nub. 366, and on vs. 79, *supra*, and Hermann, Vig. n. 342.

[11] See note on Thesm. 377, and comp. vs. 1117, *infra.*

But nevertheless, if I suffer[1] aught from these strumpets[2] by oftentimes[3] sailing in hither, let them bury[4] me at the very mouth of the entrance ; and the surviving one,[5] having covered alive with pitch, and then having armed her two feet with lead all round about the ancles, let them place above, on the top of the mound, as a substitute[6] for a funeral vase.   [*Exit with the two old women.*][7]

MAID-SERVANT (*entering from the banquet*).   O happy people, and happy me, and my[8] mistress herself most happy, and you, as many as stand at the doors, and all our neighbours, and our tribesmen, and I the servant in addition to these, who have my head anointed with excellent unguents, O Jove !   But the Thasian[9] jars, again, far surpass all these ; for they abide in the head a long time ; whereas all the rest lose their bloom and fly off.[10]   Wherefore they are far the best,—far, certainly, ye gods !   Fill out pure wine : it will cheer *the women* the whole night, who select whatever has the most fragrance.   Come, O ye women, point out to me my master, the husband of my mistress,[11] where he is.[12]

[1] " A well-known euphemism for *die*. Cf. Theocr. viii. 10. Meleager, Epigr. xvi. Aristoph. Vesp. 385." *Brunck.*

[2] Hesychius : κασαλβάς· πόρνη αἰσχροποιός.

[3] " πολλὰ πολλάκις are two adverbs placed ἐκ παραλλήλου, like αὖθις αὖ." *Brunck.*   " πολλάκις = *fortasse*, as in vs. 791." *Hotibius* (*Bothe*).

[4] See note on Ran. 169.

[5] I have translated this passage agreeably to the opinions of the commentators, but with great doubts as to the correctness of this view.   I know of no passage where μολυβδόω takes an accusative, with the sense of *plumbo munire*. τὼ πόδε seems rather to depend on ἐπιθεῖναι, and μολυβδ. to belong to περὶ τὰ σφυρά.

[6] See Bernhardy, W. S. p. 130.

[7] Here the scene changes to an open place in Athens.

[8] An example of the *Schema Colophonium*. Cf. vss. 915, 1040. Pax, 76, 269, 282, 893.   Lys. 101, 1192. Aves, 273, 277. Krüger, Gr. Gr. § 48, 6. Bernhardy, W. S. p. 88, 89.

[9] See Plut. 1021. Lys. 196. Athen. i. p. 28 foll. p. 32, A.

[10] " Doch all das andre, schnell verblüht, verfliegt im Nu." *Droysen.*

[11] " *Heræ meæ.* So Pl. 4, τῷ κεκτημένῳ, *hero.*" *Brunck.* Cf. Soph. Phil. 573, 778.   Bernhardy, W. S. p. 316.

[12] An example of " Anticipation." See note on Nub. 1148. Brunck refers to Hom. Il. B. 409 ; N. 310.   Od. A. 115.   Taylor's Index Attic. ad Lysiam, p. 917.   Add vs. 752, 770, 788, *supra.* Pax, 604. Bernhardy, W. S. p. 466,

CHO. We think you will find[1] him if you remain here.

MAID-SER. Most certainly; for see![2] here he comes to the dinner! [*Enter Master.*] O master, O happy, O thrice fortunate!

MASTER. I?

MAID-SER. Yes you, by Jove, as never man was![3] For who could be happier[4] *than you*, who alone of the citizens, being more than thirty thousand[5] in number, have not dined?

CHO. You have certainly mentioned a happy man.[6]

MAID-SER Whither, whither are you going?

MAST. I am going to the dinner.

MAID-SER. By Venus, you are far the latest of all! Nevertheless, your wife bade[7] me take you with me and bring you, and these young women along with you. Some Chian wine is left, and the rest of the good things. Wherefore do not loiter! And whoever of the spectators is favourable[8] to us, and whoever of the judges[9] is not inclined to the other

---

[1] See the examples cited in the note on Aves, 1653.

[2] See note on Aves, 992.

[3] Cf. Vesp. 150, 889, 1223. Plut. 247, 901.

[4] Shakspeare, Hamlet, act v. sc. 2, "Why do we wrap the gentleman in our *more rawer* breath?" Hen. VIII. act i. sc. 1, "There is no English soul *more stronger* to direct you." Tempest, act i. sc. 2, "The duke of Milan, and his *more braver* daughter." Plautus, Menæchm. Prol. 55, "Magis majores nugas egerit." See Krüger, Gr. Gr. § 49, 7, obs. 5. Thom. M. p. 596. Hermann, Vig. n. 60. Blomf. ad Theb. 670. Monk, Hipp. 487.

[5] See Athen. vi. p. 272, C. Mus. Crit. i. p. 541. Dawes, M. C. p. 180, ed. Kidd, and note on Vesp. 662. "See Böckh *Staatsh. der Athener*, i. p. 36." *Dindorf*.

[6] "Das Glück des Mannes hast du deutlichst dargethan." *Droysen*.

[7] See note on Equit. 1017.

[8] "Porson (Hec. 788) corrects κεἰ τῶν θεατῶν ὧν τις εὔνους τυγχάνει, for that τυγχάνω is not used without a participle of the substantive-verb. This has been sufficiently refuted by Erfurdt, ibid. p. 570. Schäfer, Bos Ell. p. 785. Heindorf, Plato Gorg. p. 190, and others." *Dindorf*. We learn from Dobree's note on this passage, that Porson afterwards so far retracted this opinion, as to allow the omission of the participle in the Tragedians. With respect to the prose writers and comedians, he does not seem to have changed his opinion. The verbals in -τος, (such as ἀνώμοτος, Med. 733,) Dobree considers as *participles*.

[9] The *critical* judges of the competing plays are meant.

side,[1] let him come with us; for we will provide all things.
Will you not, then, kindly tell all, and omit[2] nobody, but
freely invite old man,[3] youth, and boy? for dinner is provided
for them every one,—if they go away home.[4] [*Exeunt Master and Maid-servant.*]

Cho. I will now hasten to the dinner. And see! I also have
this torch opportunely! Why then do you keep loitering,[5]
and don't take these and lead them away? And while you
are descending I will sing you a song for the beginning of
dinner.[6] [*To the spectators.*] I wish to make a slight suggestion to the judges: to the clever, to prefer[7] me, remembering my clever parts; to those who laugh merrily, to prefer
me on account of my jokes. Therefore of course I bid almost
all to prefer me; and that my lot should not be[8] any cause
of detriment to me, because I obtained[9] it first; but they
ought to remember all these things and not violate their oaths,
but always judge the choruses justly; and not to resemble
in their manners the vile harlots, who remember only whoever happen to be[10] the last comers.

[1] "*Favorem suum alicui accommodet, alio respiciens quam quo deceat.*"
Faber.
[2] The οὐ of the preceding οὔκουν belongs also to the μή of the following line, so as to = οὐ μὴ παραλείψεις. See note on vs. 1000, *supra*.
Invernizius reads παραλείψῃς. But the Attics appear never to have
used the 1st aor. act. of this verb. See Schäfer ad Gnomic. p. 148.
Schol. Apoll. R. p. 407. Matthiä (Gr. Gr. p. 862) has written very
crudely on this passage, as though it were an example of μή with
a future. See note on vs. 603, *supra*.
[3] See Bernhardy, W. S. p. 58.   [4] A jest παρὰ προσδοκίαν.
[5] Cf. vs. 853. Nub. 509. For ἀλλά, see note on Thesm. 230.
[6] Cf. Aves, 639
[7] "Für mich zu sein." *Droysen.* Cf. Liddell's Lex. in voc. κρίνω, ii.
[8] The infinitive depends on ὑποθέσθαι (vs. 1154). "*Nec sortem
esse causam nobis cujusquam mali, quod nempe ante ceteros sorte ductus in
scenam prodii.*" *Bergler.* As many plays had to be exhibited on the
same day, the several competitors had to decide by lot in what
order their pieces should be exhibited. We learn from this passage
that Aristophanes' chorus drew the first lot.
[9] ἡμῖν——προσείληχα. So Eur. Hippol. 244, αἰδούμεθα τὰ λελεγμένα
μοι. Cf. Ran. 213. Aves, 1262, 1263. Plut. 280. Pax, 558, 559. Eur.
Helen. 657. El. 608. Hippol. 1055. Hec. 794, 795. Krüger, Gr. Gr.
§ 61, 2, obs. 1, and obs. 2. Bernhardy, W. S. p. 415. Lobeck, Ajax,
vs. 191. Monk, Hippol. 268. Porson, Præf. Hec. p. xxvi. and ad
Hec. 968. Hermann, Vig. n. 138. For this form of the perfect, see
Kruger, Gr. Gr. § 28, 10, obs. 5.
[10] See Bernhardy, W. S. p. 323, and note on Vesp. 1318.

1st Semichorus. Oh! oh![1] 'tis time now, O dear women, to retire to the dinner, if we are to finish the business.[2]   Therefore do you also move your feet in the Cretan[3] fashion.

2nd Semichorus. I am doing so.

1st Semichorus. And these hollow flanks now with your legs to the rhythm! for presently there will come an oyster-saltfish-skate-shark-remainder-of-heads-dressed-with-vinegar-laserpitium-leek-mixed-with-honey-thrush-blackbird-pigeon-dove-roasted-cock's-brains-wagtail-cushat-hare-stewed-in-new-wine-and-seasoned-with-green-corn-with-its-shoulders-fricassee.[4]   So do you, having heard this, quickly and speedily take a bowl.   And then make haste and take pea-soup, that you may feast upon it.

2nd Semichorus. But perhaps they are greedy.

Cho. Raise yourselves aloft! io! evæ!   We will dine, evoe! evæ! evæ! for the victory:[5] evæ! evæ! evæ! evæ![6]

[1] See Bernhardy, W. S. p. 74.   [2] Comp. vs. 148, *supra.*
[3] Cf. Athen. i. p. 22, B. v. p. 181, B. "*Cretico rhythmo.*" *Brunck.* So Droysen.
[4] The above monstrous word in the original consists of seventy-seven syllables.   For similar long comic compounds, cf. Lys. 457, 458. Vesp. 505, 520.   So Philoxenus (ap. Athen. xiv. p. 643), πυρο-βρομολευκερεβινθοακανθουμικριτοαδυβρωματοπαντανάμικτον.   Pratinas (ap. Athen. xiv. p. 617, E.), λαλοβαρυπαραμελορυθμοβάταν. Shakspeare, Love's Labour Lost, act v. sc. 1, "I marvel thy master hath not eaten thee for a word; for thou art not so long by the head as *honorificabilitudinitatibus.*"   This is outdone by Rabelais' "*Antipericatametaanaparbeugedamphicribrationes.*" See Mehlhorn, Gr. Gr. p. 32, *note.*
[5] See Porson ap. Kidd on Dawes, M. C. p. 584.
[6] Cf. Lys. 1292.

END OF THE ECCLESIAZUSÆ.

PLUTUS.

DRAMATIS PERSONÆ

CHREMYLUS.
CARIO (servant of Chremylus).
CHORUS OF COUNTRY-PEOPLE
PLUTUS (the god of riches).
BLEPSIDEMUS.
POVERTY.
WIFE OF CHREMYLUS
JUST MAN.
INFORMER.
OLD WOMAN.
YOUNG MAN.
MERCURY.
PRIEST OF JUPITER.

THE ARGUMENT

"THE Plutus, according to an indubitable tradition, was twice brought upon the stage; first, in the year 408, B. C., in the Archonship of Diocles, and then, in the year 388, B. C., in the Archonship of Antipater. In its second representation, the Plutus contended successfully against the "Lacedæmonians" of Nicochares, the "Admetus" of Aristomenes, the "Adonis" of Nicophon, and the "Pasiphaë" of Alcæus. The Greek Scholiasts frequently assert that our present text is the *first* Plutus. This view is in decided contradiction to the play itself, which contains numerous allusions to the times of the Archon Antipater. The opinion of later philologers, which has been sanctioned by the great authority of Hemsterhuis, represents our present text as a riffaccimento of the two editions. But recent investigations have completely refuted this position. We therefore may confidently assume that the Plutus we have before us is just in the state in which Aristophanes in the latter years of his life brought it on the stage." *Droysen.* See the Scholiast on vs. 173. The argument is simply this:—Chremylus, a poor, but just man, consults the Delphic oracle about his son, whether he ought not to be instructed in injustice and knavery, and the other arts whereby worldly men acquired riches. The god answered him nothing plainly, but merely told him he was to follow whomsoever he should first light upon on leaving the temple. The first person he meets with is a blind old man. This turns out to be Plutus, the god of riches, whom Jupiter had deprived of his eyesight in order that he might no longer distinguish between the just and the unjust. By the help of Æsculapius, Plutus is restored to the use of his eyes. Whereupon all the just are made rich, and the unjust reduced to indigence. In an artistic point of view, the Plutus must rank as by far the lowest of the existing works of Aristophanes. In its absence of personal interest, and its sparingness of personal satire, it approximates more nearly to a whimsical allegory than a proper comedy.

PLUTUS.

SCENE--*The front of a farm-house with a road leading to it.
A blind old man is seen followed at some distance by*
CHREMYLUS *and his servant* CARIO.

CARIO. How troublesome[1] a thing it is, O Jupiter and ye
gods, to be the slave of a crazy master! For if the servant
should happen to have given the best advice, and it should
seem fit to his master not to do this, it must be that the servant share the evils;[2] for fortune suffers not the *natural*
owner to be master of his person, but the purchaser. And so
much for this.[3] But Loxias[4] who prophesies from his tripod
of beaten gold I censure with this just censure, because being
a physician and a clever soothsayer, as they say, he has sent
away my master melancholy-mad,[5] who is following behind[6]
a blind man, acting contrary to what it became him to do ; for
we who see lead the blind ; whereas he follows him, and compels
me besides ; and that too without even[7] answering a syllable[8]
at all. Therefore it is not possible for me to hold my

[1] Theogn. 335, ἀργαλέον φρονέοντα παρ ἄφροσι πόλλ' ἀγορεύειν.
[2] Philemon ap. Stob. Serm. lxii. 2,

> κακόν ἐστι δούλῳ δεσπότης πράττων κακῶς·
> μετέχειν ἀνάγκη τῶν κακῶν γὰρ γίγνεται.

[3] " *Et haec quidem sic se habent.* Lat. *et haec quidem hactenus.*"
Fischer. Cf. Aves, 800. Æsch. Prom. V. 500.

[4] Called by Cicero (Divin. ii. 56) " Flexiloqua."

[5] " Ganz von Sinnen." *Droysen.* "So voll schwarzer Galle." *Voss.*

[6] See Mœris, Lex. p. 240, ed. Pierson. For ὅστις, see note on
Thesm. 544. Herod. i. 45, ὄπισθε δὲ εἵπετό οἱ ὁ φονεύς. ibid. i. 84,
ἑπουτό οἱ ὄπισθε. See Bernhardy, W. S. p. 98.

[7] Most MSS. and editions read ἀποκρινομένου. The Ravenna MS.
ἀποκρινομένῳ. Dindorf's reading is from the conjecture of Bentley.

[8] Cf. Antiphanes ap. Athen. viii. p. 343, A.

tongue, unless you tell me, master, for what in the world we are following this man, but I 'll give you trouble; for you will not beat[1] me while I wear the chaplet.

CHR. No, by Jove, but if you trouble me in any way, *I 'll do it* when I have taken away your chaplet, that you may grieve the more.

CA. Nonsense! for I will not cease until you tell me who in the world this is; for I ask it, being exceedingly well[2] dis-posed to you.

CHR. Well then, I will not hide it from you, for I do believe you to be the most faithful of my domestics, and—the arrantest thief.[3] I, though a religious and just man, was unprosperous and poor.

CA. In truth I know it.

CHR. While others, sacrilegious persons, demagogues, and informers, and villains, were rich.

CA. I believe[4] you.

CHR. So I went to the god to consult him, thinking that my own life,[5] unhappy man, had now nearly been wasted away, but to ask about my son,[6] who is my only one,[7] if he

---

[1] This is the Attic form. See Mœr. Lex. p. 373,' ed. Pierson. Thom. M. p. 860. Lobeck, Phryn. p. 764. ἔτυψα is Homeric, though found also in Æsch. Eum. 151. Aristotle (Pol. ii. 9, 9) has even ἐτύπτησα, but this is un-Attic. "The chaplet which he is wearing from his visit to Delphi makes his person sacred, and secures him from blows." *Droysen.*

[2] Porson cites τυχὸν ἴσως, Timocles ap. Athen. viii. p. 339. Forte temere, Liv. x. 43. Una simul, Terent. Heaut. vi. 30. Rursus denuo, Plaut. Pænul. Prolog. 79. Cf. also Pax, 1302.

[3] παρὰ προσδοκίαν. For this irregular form of the adjective, see Krüger, Gr. Gr. § 12, 5, obs. "Vide J. Taylor, ad Æsch. c. Ctesi-phont. p. 652, et J. Upton, Observ. in Shaksp. p. 161." *Porson.* " Den verschwiegensten." *Droysen.*

[4] "πιστεύω." *Scholiast.* Cf. vs. 251, *infra.*

[5] Cf. Nub. 1202. Ach. 910. So Hor. Sat. i. 4, 22, " mea scripta timentis." " *Concluding indeed the quiver of my miserable days to be al-most shot out.*" *Fielding.*

[6] The construction is precisely the same as in Nub. 1148, καί μοι τὸν υἱὸν, εἰ μεμάθηκε τὸν λόγον ἐκεῖνον, εἰπέ. In both υἱὸν is an ex-ample of "Accusativus de quo," as in Eur. Iph. A. 739, (ed. Har-tung,) ἐξιστορήσων εἰμι μόχθον Ἑλλάδος. See Eccles. 356. Ran. 1454. Mus. Crit. i. p. 532. Bast, Greg. Cor. p. 127, 128; and is transferred to the former member of the sentence by "Anticipation." See note on Nub. 1158. Eccles. 1126. " 33-38, from Hesiod, Op. et D. 268." *Porson.*　　　　　　　　　　　[7] Comp. Eccles. 353.

ought to change his habits and be knavish, unjust, nothing good;[1] since I thought this very thing to be advantageous for life.

CA. What then did Phœbus proclaim from amongst his chaplets ?[2]

CHR. You shall hear: for the god told me this plainly; whomsoever I should first meet with[3] on going out,[4] him he bid me[5] never let go, but prevail on him to accompany me home.

CA. And whom then did you first meet with?

CHR. With this man.

CA. Then did you not understand the meaning of the god, when it directed you, O most stupid, in the plainest terms, to educate[6] your son after the fashion of the country?

CHR. By what[7] do you judge of this?

CA. It is evident that even a blind man fancies he knows this,[8] that it is very advantageous to practise no virtue in these times.

CHR. It is not possible that the oracle inclines to this,[9] but to something else of greater moment. But if this fellow tell us who in the world he is, and on account of what, and in want of what he came hither with us, we might understand what our oracle[10] means.

[1] See Porson, Præf. Hec. p. xxiv. Krüger, Gr. Gr. § 61, 8, obs. 3, and cf. Thesm. 394.

[2] An allusion to the chaplets worn by the Pythoness.

[3] See Krüger, Gr. Gr. § 54, 14, obs. 4.

[4] "*E templo egressus.*" *Fischer.*

[5] See note on Equit. 1017, and on Vesp. 416.

[6] "*That your son should pursue the manners of his country.*" *Fielding.* So Kuster, Bergler, Fischer, and Droysen. It would have been as well if some one of these writers had quoted a similar instance of φράζειν σοι τὸν υἱὸν ἀσκεῖν, κ. τ. λ.

[7] See Bernhardy, W. S. p. 103.

[8] "Es ist klar, ein Blinder selbst muss das ja einsehn." *Droysen.* Mr. Seager's interpretation (Class. J. No. iii. p. 505) is simply an impossible one. Eccles. 1127, ἡμῖν ἂν ἐξευρεῖν δοκεῖς.

[9] Antiphanes (ap. Athen. x. p. 449, A.), ἦν θ' ὁ γρῖφος ἐνταῦθα ῥίπων.

[10] A common case of "Anticipation," as in vss. 35, 56, 72. See notes on Nub. 1148. Eccles. 1126. Of course it has no resemblance whatever to Virgil's "Urbem quam statuo vestra est;" which is a case of *Inverted Assimilation,* as in vs. 200, *infra.* See note on Lys. 408. Eccles. 415, ἦν γὰρ παρίνωσ οἱ κναφῆς χλαίνας, πλευρῖτις οὐδὲν' ἂν λάβοι.

Ca. (*to Plutus*).　Come now, do you declare yourself, who you are, before I do what comes next.[1]　You must be very quick about speaking.

Plu. A plague take you![2]

Ca. (*to Chrem.*).　Do you understand whom he professes himself to be?

Chr. He says this to you, not to me; for you inquire of him uncouthly and roughly.　But [*to Plutus*] if you take any pleasure in the manners of a man of honour, tell me!

Plu. Go, hang yourself!

Ca. Take[3] the man, and omen of the god.

Chr. By Ceres, you certainly shall not any longer escape[4] unpunished!

Ca. For unless you will tell us, I will kill you, you wretch in a wretched way.[5]

Plu. Good sirs, depart from me.

Chr. Not a whit.[6]

Ca. Well now, what I say, is best, master: I'll kill this fellow in a most wretched way; for I will set him up on[7] some precipice and leave him and go away, that he may fall and break his neck.

Chr. Well, up with him quickly.

Plu. By no means.

Chr. Will you not tell us then?

> [1] "Come on, thou first declare thyself, or I
>   Do what shall follow."　　　　　　*Wheelwright.*
> "Bevor Ich weiter mit dir verfahre." *Droysen.*

Kuster refers to Eur. Phœn. 1204. Ion, 256, for similar phrases.

[2] Cf. vs. 62, *infra.* Vesp. 584.　On the contrary, the regular use in the Tragic writers is λέγειν τινὰ χαίρειν, εἰπεῖν τινὰ κλάειν, with the *accusative.*　See Bernhardy, W. S. p. 124.

[3] An intentional ambiguity, δέχου as applied to ὄρνιν means *accept.* See Krüger on Xenoph. Anab. i. 8, 17.　"It is a bad omen that the man promised by Apollo speaks of nothing but *plagues* and *hanging.*" *Droysen.*

[4] See note on Thesm. 1094. Cf. Equit. 235, 828.

[5] See note on Eccles. 730.　For ἀπό σ' ὀλῶ, see note on Ran. 1047

[6] See Arist. *Cocalus*, Fragm. iii., and note on Ran. 1456.

[7] For this accumulation of participles, cf. vs. 318—321, *infra* Eccles. 536—538. Aves, 759, 1086, 1364, 1521, 1609, 1613, 1624. Ran 467, 468, 543, 773, 775, 1097. Pax, 1020. Acharn. 275. Lys. 106, 308. Thesm. 655. Equit. 856. Plato, Euthyph. p. 9, **A.**; Menex. p 243, C.; Rep. ii. p. 366, A. Antiph. p. 115, 7. Thuc. iv. 38. Krüger Gr. Gr. § 56, 15. obs. 2

Plu. But if you learn who I am, I well know that you will do me some mischief, and not let me go.[1]

Chr. By the gods will we, if you wish it.

Plu. Then first let me go.

Chr. Lo! we let you go.

Plu. Hear now; for, as it seems, I must speak what I was[2] prepared to conceal: I am Plutus.

Chr. O most abominable of all men! did you hold your tongue then, you Plutus?[3]

Ca. You Plutus, so wretchedly circumstanced?

Chr. O Phœbus Apollo, and ye gods and dæmons, and Jove, what do you say? Are you really he?

Plu. Yes.

Chr. He himself?

Plu. His very self.[4]

Chr. Whence then, tell us, come you *so* squalid?

Plu. I come from the house of Patrocles,[5] who has not washed himself since he was born.

Chr. But how did you suffer this mishap?[6] Declare it to me.

Plu. Jupiter treated me in this manner through envy towards mankind. For when I was a boy,[7] I threatened that I

---

[1] ἐργάσεσθε ... ἀφήσετον. So Eccles. 1087, ἕλκοντε ἂν ἀπεκναίετε.

[2] This was the old Attic form. See Elmsley, Præf. Soph. Rex, p. xii. Krüger, Gr. Gr. § 38, 2, obs. 1. But not invariably ἦ. See Hermann, Eur. Alc. 665. Præf. Soph. Rex, p. xiii.

[3] Acharn. 558, ταυτὶ σὺ τολμᾷς πτωχὸς ὢν ἡμᾶς λέγειν; *you beggar.* Cf. ib. 578, 593. Nub. 929, 1249. Aves, 911, 1431. Eur. Hippol. 1084. Iph. A. 304, ed. Hartung.

[4] Plaut. Trinum, iv. 2, 144. Syc. "Ipsus es?" Ch. "Ipsus, inquam, Charmides sum." Syc. "Ergo ipsusne es?" Ch. "Ipsisimus." So vs. 182, μονώτατος. See Thom. M. p. 128, and note on Thesm. 735.

[5] According to the Scholiast, a wealthy Athenian, who, from parsimony, "affected a Spartan mode of living," being too miserly to attend the public baths. Πατροκλέους φειδωλότερος afterwards became a proverb to express the utmost meanness and avarice. "Probably son of Charidemus and half-brother of Socrates, whom Aristophanes ridicules in his Πελαργοί (Frag. 386, ed. Dindorf) as a dirty niggard. The public baths were too dear for such people. See Nub. 837." *Droysen.* Cf. Aves, 1554, 790.

[6] His blindness.

[7] See Krüger, Gr. Gr. § 58, 1, obs. 2, and note on vs. 292, *infra*

would go to the just, and[2] wise, and well-behaved alone. So he made me blind, that I might not distinguish any of these. So much does he envy the good.

CHR. And yet he is honoured by the good and the just alone.

PLU. I grant you.

CHR. Come, what then? if you were to recover your sight again, just as formerly,[3] would you now shun the wicked?

PLU. Certainly.

CHR. But would you go to the just?

PLU. Most assuredly; for I have not seen[4] them for a long time.[5]

CHR. And no wonder too; for neither have I, who see.

PLU. Now let me go; for now you know all about me.[6]

CHR. No, by Jove! but so much the more will we keep hold of you.

PLU. Did I not say that you would[7] cause me trouble?

CHR. And do you, I beseech you, comply, and do not abandon me; for you will never[8] find a man better in his morals than I, if you search. No, by Jove! for there is no other[9] save me.

[1] In the *oratio obliqua* the Attics use the future optative where the future indicative would be used in the *oratio recta*. See Harper's Powers of the Greek Tenses, p. 150. Mus. Crit. i. p. 523. Kruger, Gr. Gr. § 54, 8, obs. 6.

[2] A violation of Sharp's canon : for he evidently intends to make *three* classes. Cf. vs. 387, *infra*. So Aves, 590, οἱ κνῖπις καὶ ψῆνες. Add Pax, 556. Thesm. 491. Ran. 444. Eccles. 198, 703, 750. *Triphales*, Fragm. vii. The Attics neglect it wherever the neglect is not likely to cause any mistake or obscurity.

[3] See note on Pax, 350.

[4] "See Porson on Dawes, M. C. p. 369, ed. Kidd." *Dobree.*

[5] Thesm. 806, πρὸς Ἀριστομάχην δὲ χρόνου πολλοῦ. Plato, Phæd. init. συχνοῦ χρόνου. See Bernhardy, W. S. p. 139. In Plut. 1041, and Vesp. 1476, Aristophanes uses διὰ πολλοῦ χρόνου. In the present passage Porson proposed πολλοῦ ἀπὸ χρόνου. But this phrase is no where found in Aristophanes, neither is it suitable for the passage. He is telling *for* how long, not how long *ago*, this was the case.

[6] "Denn ihr wisset meine Geschichte nun." *Droysen.* See Bernhardy, W. S. p. 221.

[7] "μέλλω mostly has the force of our *werden, sollen, mussen.*' *Hermann* regards it as merely an auxiliary verb. "Würdet mir Umstände machen." *Droysen.*

[8] Of course ἔτι belongs to εὑρήσεις.   [9] i.e. no other *honest man.*

Plu. They all say this: but when they actually get possession of me, and become wealthy, they absolutely exceed all bounds in their wickedness.

Chr. So it is: yet all are not wicked.

Plu. No, by Jove, *not all*, but all without exception.[1]

Ca. You shall suffer[2] for it severely.

Chr. And that you may know how many blessings you will have, if you stay with us, give your attention, that you may hear. For I think, I think,—with god's permission[3] it shall be spoken,—that I shall free you from this[4] blindness, having made you see.

Plu. By no means do this; for I do not wish to recover my sight again.

Chr. What do you say?

Ca. This fellow is a born[5] miserable.

Plu. I know indeed that Jupiter would destroy me, if he were to hear of the follies of these men.[6]

Chr. But does he not do this now, who suffers you to go about stumbling ?[7]

Plu. I know not; but I dread him exceedingly.

---

[1] "Not all, but one and all." *Wheelwright.* "*Non hercle omnes modo, sed ad unum omnes simul.*" *Brunck.*

[2] The future οἰμώξω is never found in Attic writers. See Monk, Alc. 645. Krüger, Gr. Gr. § 40.

[3] From Eur. Med. 625. See Viger, p. 641. "Synes. Epist. 131, σὺν θεῷ εἰρήσθω." *Bergler.* Cf. Ran. 553. Pax, 1187. So Theoc. vii. 12, σὺν Μοίσαισι, *by the favour of the Muses.* Id. ii. 28, σὺν δαίμονι, *auxiliante deo.*

[4] This belongs to the *first* edition of the *Plutus.* "Instead of this verse, according to the Scholiast, his second edition had τῆς ξυμφορᾶς ταύτης σε παύσειν, ἥ σ' ἔχει." *Porson.*

[5] "Geboren ist zum Elend dieser Mensch." *Droysen.*

[6] This harsh and disordered construction can scarcely have proceeded from Aristophanes. The passage would seem to be made up from the various readings of the two editions. "The Aldine Scholiast informs us that this passage was altered in the *second* edition of the *Plutus.* But whether he himself had before his eyes ἐπεὶ or ἔμ' εἰ, is uncertain." *Porson.* For similar instances of disordered construction, cf. vs. 369, 492, *infra.* Aves, 99, 144. Vesp. 1179. Nub. 379, 1061. Equit. 744, 745, 1080, 1081. Ran. 31, 32. Eccles. 170, 1049.

[7] "The sense is: *nonne vero hoc Jupiter fecit, qui te ita oberrare sinit, ut corpus, aut pedes, offendas, impingas?*" *Beck.* Lucian in his *Timon* has borrowed a great deal from Aristophanes. In c. 24, he says ἄνω κάτω πλανῶμαι περινοστῶν. For ὅστις, see note on Thesm. 544.

CHR. What really, O you most cowardly of all deities ?[1] For do you suppose the sovereignty[2] of Jove and his thunder-bolts would be worth a three-obol piece,[3] if you should reco-ver your sight, if it were but for a short time ?

PLU. Ah ! say not so, you wretch !

CHR. Be quiet ;[4] for I will demonstrate you to be far more powerful than Jupiter.

PLU. Me ?[5]

CHR. Aye, by heaven. For, for example,[6] through whom does Jupiter rule the gods ?

CA. Through money, for he has most of it.

CHR. Come, who then is it that supplies[7] him with this ?

CA. This person here.

CHR. And through whom do men sacrifice to him? is it not through him ?.

CA. And, by Jupiter, they pray openly[8] to be rich.

CHR. Is not he then the cause, and might he not easily put an end to this, if he wished ?

PLU. Why so ?[9] why pray ?

CHR. Because[10] no man would any longer sacrifice, either ox or barley-cake, or any thing else whatever, if you were not willing.

[1] “Wahrhaftig ? O furchtsamster aller Dämonen du !
Was? glaubst du es würde Zeus Regiment und Donnerkeil
Noch einen Obolus gelten, wenn du je einmal
Noch sehend würdest, wär's auch nur auf kurze Zeit.” *Droysen.*
For ἄληθες, see Thom. M. p. 311.

[2] “Parodied from Æsch. P. V. 10.” *Spanheim.*

[3] Plautus, Pœn. i. 2, 168, “ Nam ego sum homo trioboli.”

[4] See note on Thesm. 230.

[5] “Sc. σὺ ἀποδείξεις ἐμὲ τοῦ Διὸς πολὺ μεῖζον δύνασθαι;” *Fischer.*

[6] “Zum Exempel.” *Droysen.* See Viger, p. 393. “This cate-chising is completely in the manner of the sophistical teaching of the times, and has its parallels in other comedies and in the Dia-logues of Plato.” *Droysen.* For this use of διὰ, see Bernhardy, W. S. p. 237.

[7] Comp. vss. 519, 824, 1097. Aves, 60, 95. Nub. 1260.

[8] “ ἄντικρυς, palam.” *Fischer.* Cf. Thesm. 296. Pax, 1320 Juvenal, Sat. x. 23.

[9] Cf. Nub. 755.

[10] According to Porson (Hec. 112) ὅτι is never elided by the *comic* writers. Krüger (Gr. Gr. 2nd Part, § 12, 2, obs. 10) says ὅτι is never elided by the *Attics*, though occasionally in Homer and Theo-critus. Cf. ibid. § 11, 3, obs. 3. See Ach. 516. Equit. 101. Nub. 1223. Lvs 611. Thesm. 275. Ran. 1386.

PLU. How?

CHR. How? it is not possible for him to purchase it. I ween, unless you yourself be present [1] and give him the money; so that you alone will put down the power of Jove, if he annoy you in any way.

PLU. What do you say? do they sacrifice to him through me?

CHR. Certainly. And, by Jupiter, if there be any thing magnificent and beautiful or agreeable to men,[2] it is through you: for all things are subservient [3] to riches.

CA. I, in truth, have become a slave on account of a trifling sum of money,[4] because I was not equally rich as *others*.

CHR. And they say that the Corinthian courtesans, when any poor man tries them, do not even pay any attention to him, but if a rich man *try*, that they immediately turn any thing to [5] him.

CA. And they say that the boys do this very thing, not for their lovers', but the money's sake.

CHR. Not the better sort, but the catamites; for the better sort do not ask for money.

CA. What then?[6]

CHR. One *asks for* a good horse, another hunting dogs.[7]

CA. For, perhaps, being ashamed to ask for money, they gloss over[8] their wickedness by a false name.

[1] Horace, Sat. ii. 3, 68, " Rejectâ prædâ, quam præsens Mercurius fert."

[2] Cf. Pindar, Olymp. xiv. 6.

[3] Thus Euripides in the *Phœnissæ*, l. 442,

$$Τὰ \ χρήματ' \ ἀνθρώποισι \ τιμιώτατα,$$
$$Δυναμίν \ τε \ πλείστην \ τῶν \ ἐν \ ἀνθρώποις \ ἔχε.$$

Horace, Sat. ii. 3, 94,

" Omnis res,
Virtus, fama, decus, divina, humanaque pulchris
Divitiis parent."

Elmsley (Heracl. 287) proposed τοῦ πλουτεῖν, since ὑπήκοος mostly governs a *genitive*.

[4] See Xenoph. Mem. ii. 5, 2.

[5] See Bernhardy, W. S. p. 215.

[6] " τί δαί; *was sonst? was denn?* Arist. Plut. 156, αἰτοῦσιν οἱα ἀργύριον οἱ χρηστοί. CH. τί δαί; *quid igitur aliud?* Cf. vs. 905. Aves, 1451, 1640. Nub. 491. Vesp. 1212. Ach. 764." *Hermann.*

[7] " Einen Zug Jagdhunde." *Droysen.*

[8] " Under a specious name they veil their guilt." *Wheelwright.* Cicero, Orat. iii. 39, " Quandoquidem iste circumvestit dictis."

CHR. And all arts and clever contrivances among men have been invented through you. For one of them sits and makes shoes; and some other one is a smith,[1] and another a carpenter; another is a goldsmith, having received gold from you; another, by Jove, steals clothes; another is a housebreaker; another is a fuller;[2] another washes fleeces; another is a tanner; another sells onions; another, having been detected as an adulterer, is depillated through you.

PLU. Ah me, miserable! this has been unknown to me this long while.

CA. And does not the Great King pride himself through him? And is not the Assembly held through him? But how? —do you not man the triremes? tell me. And does not he support the mercenaries in Corinth?[3] And will not Pamphilus[4] suffer through him? And will not the "Needle-seller"[5] along with Pamphilus? And does not Agyrrhius[6] fart through

[1] "Under pretence of running through the different trades and occupations of men, he points with his finger at certain persons amongst the spectators, whom he taxes with theft," &c. *Madam Dacier.* For ἕτερός τις, see note on Pax, 831.

[2] γναφεύει is Dawes' correction for κναφεύει, as Aristophanes does not lengthen short syllables before κν. Moreover, κναφεύει belongs to the old Attic, while γναφεύει is the later Attic in vogue in the time of the *Plutus.* But see Dobree's note on this passage.

[3] An allusion to the war with Sparta, maintained by Athens Thebes, Argos, and Corinth, under Iphicrates, Chabrias, Polystratus, and Callias. It broke out Ol. 96, 2, after the return of Agesilaus from Asia, and was carried on for six years, chiefly in the Corinthian territory. See Pausan. Lacon. iii. 9, 6; iv. 17, 3. Xenoph. Hellen. iv. 2. It was terminated by the peace of Antalcidas, Ol. 98, 2.

[4] "Pamphilus, a distinguished Athenian, (Lysias, c. Alcib. p. 294, ed. Bekker,) had, according to the statement of the Scholiast, appropriated some of the public money, and been punished on that account by banishment and confiscation: an anachronism, probably, of twenty years. Pamphilus had been sent at this time to Ægina as general. Being closely hemmed in by the Spartans, he prayed for assistance. The expense of such an expedition hindered the carrying out of the decree which had been made for his relief, and it was not till five months afterwards that assistance came to him." *Droysen.*

[5] The nickname of a person well known to the audience. He was a parasite of Pamphilus.

[6] See note on Eccles. 102. "An upstart, through the favour of the people admiral in the year 389 after Thrasybulus, enriched through some rather equivocal state employments, and insolent on

him? And [*to Plutus*] does not Philepsius[1] relate fables on account of you? And is not the alliance[2] with the Egyptians through you. And does not Lais, through you, love Philonides?[3] And the tower of Timotheus[4]——

CHR. ——May it fall upon you. And [*to Plutus*] are not all our affairs transacted through you? For you alone[5] are the cause of all, both of our miseries and our blessings, be well assured.

CA. At any rate, in wars also, they always conquer, upon whom he only sits down.[6]

PLU. Am I able, single as I am, to effect so many things?

CHR. And, by Jupiter, far more than these; so that no one[7]

account of his riches, 'as a well-fed ass.' Demosthenes, however, in his speech against Timocrates, speaks of him as an honourable man, well inclined to the people, and very solicitous for the public weal." *Droysen.*

[1] "Philepsius, like Agyrrhius, was one of the statesmen of that period, and not, as the Scholiasts relate, a buffoon. According to the speech of Demosthenes referred to above, he was condemned for embezzling the public money. In his defence he may have invented some stories, in order to account for the disappearance of the money out of the treasury." *Droysen.*

[2] "This alliance was sought by the Egyptians for that insurrection of theirs against the Persians, of which Isocrates (in Panegyr.) makes mention, and in consequence of which a protracted war arose, in which three years later Cyprus also took part." *Droysen.*

[3] Of Philonides little is known, except that he was a native of Melita, and a rich and profligate character. Athenæus (xiii. p. 592) says expressly that Ναῒς ought to be read in place of Λαῒς in this passage (γραπτέον Ναῒς, καὶ οὐ Λαῒς); and from Lysias (c. Philonidem, Fragm. 130, p. 33, ed. Reiske) we learn that Philonides' mistress *was* Nais, and not Lais, and that the relations of Nais employed Lysias to conduct a prosecution against him for using her ill. The commentators state that Lais would at this time be only fourteen years of age. But chronological arguments are of little avail with our present text of the *Plutus*, as what we now possess is merely a rifaccimento of the two editions.

[4] "The son of the celebrated Conon. He built himself a kind of a tower to dwell in, in the middle of the city, which might appear rather to be an aiming at a tyranny than in accordance with republican equality." *Droysen.*

[5] Cf. Equit. 352. Theocr. xv. 137. Thom. M. p. 620. Schneidewin, Præf. in Hyperid. Orat. p. xvii.

[6] "Auf deren Seite dieser die Schaale sinken macht." *Droysen.*
"*Into whose scale this gentleman throws himself.*" *Fielding.*

[7] Menander, γυνὴ γυναικὸς οὐδὲν πώποτε διαφέρει. The Greeks

has ever at any time been sated of you.   For of all the rest
there is[1] a satiety.   Of love,
   Cl. Of bread,
   Chr. Of music,
   Ca. Of sweetmeats,
   Chr. Of honour,
   Ca. Of cheesecakes,
   Chr. Of manly virtue,
   Ca. Of dried figs,
   Chr. Of ambition,
   Ca. Of barley-cake,
   Chr. Of military command,
   Ca. Of lentil-broth.[2]

Chr. But of you[3] no one has ever at any time been sated.
But if any one get thirteen talents, so much the more does he
desire to get sixteen.   And if he accomplish this, he wishes
for forty, or he says his life is not worth[4] living.

Plu. In truth you appear to me to speak exceedingly well;
but one thing only I fear.

Chr. Tell us, what about.

Plu. How I shall become master of this power which[5] you
say I have.

---

say either οὐδεὶς πώποτε (which is much more frequent) or οὐδεὶς
οὐεπώποτε (as in vs. 193, 420), never οὐδεὶς οὔποτε. Cf. vs. 236, 241,
245. Vesp. 1226. Nub. 637. Equit. 569. Thuc. i. 70. Xenoph. Anab.
i. 3,5; i. 7, 11; i. 9, 19. Cyrop. iii. 2, 15. Mem. i. 1, 10. Œcon. ii.
11. Plato, Tim. p. 29, E. Demosth. (ed. Bremi), § 107, § 203, § 219,
§ 244, § 246, § 251, § 271, § 279.

[1] Parodied from Homer, Il. N. 636,
     πάντων μὲν κόρος ἐστὶ, καὶ ὕπνου καὶ φιλότητος.

[2] Chremylus rises in a regular climax from love and music to
military glory; the slave, in as direct an anticlimax, comes from
bread, sweetmeats, &c., down to lentil-broth.

[3] Juvenal, xiv. 139, "Crescit amor nummi quantum ipsa pecunia
crescit."

[4] "Sonst sei ihm das Leben, sagt er, nicht mehr lebenswerth."
                                  Droysen.
Cf. vs. 969, *infra*. Eur. Hippol. 821, 867. Ion, 670. Ennius ap.
Ciceron. Lael. 6. Æsch. Fals. Leg. p. 191, ed. Reiske. Cicero,
Orat. ii. 6, "Vita non vitalis." Similarly οὐ βιώσιμον, Eur. Heracl.
600. Soph. Antig. 566. Cf. Mus. Crit. ii. p. 122.

[5] For this construction, see note on Lys. 408, and Bernhard, W.
S. p. 303.

CHR. Yes, by Jove, you shall! But even all say[1] that wealth is a most[2] timid thing.

PLU. By no means; but some housebreaker has calumniated me. For having once crept into the[3] house, he was not able to get any thing, having found every thing locked up; so then he called my forethought cowardice.

CHR. Let nothing trouble you[4] now; for if you be a zealous man yourself in the business, I'll make you more sharp-sighted than Lynceus.

PLU. How then will you be able to do this, mortal as you are?

CHR. I have some good hope from what Phœbus himself told me, having shaken the Pythian laurel.

PLU. And was he then privy to this?

CHR. Certainly.

PLU. Take care!

CHR. Do not be at all concerned, my good sir; for I, be well assured of this, will accomplish this myself, even if I must die for it.

CA. And I too, if you wish it.

CHR. And many others[5] will be our allies, as many as had no bread, though they were just.

PLU. Deary me! you tell us of miserable allies.

CHR. Not so, if they become rich again as before. But do you [*to Cario*] go and run quickly——

CA. What am I to do? Tell me.

CHR. Call my fellow-labourers,—and you will probably find them working hard in the fields,—that each, being present here, may share an equal portion with us of this Plutus.

CA. Well now, I am going. But let some one *of the servants* from within take and carry in this small bit of meat.[6]

CHR. (*taking the meat*). This shall be my care: but run

---

[1] So Beck. The method proposed by the other commentators would require ἀλλὰ καὶ to be preceded by a *negative*.

[2] "In ridicule of Euripides, Phœn. 606, δειλὸν δ' ὁ πλοῦτος καὶ φιλόψυχον κακόν." *Porson.* Cf. Eur. *Archelaus*, Fragm. 23, ὁ πλοῦτος δ' ἀμαθία δειλόν 9' ἄμα. For the construction, see Matthiä, Gr. Gr. § 437, 4.

[3] For the article, see Bernhardy, W. S. p. 315.

[4] Hom. Il. Σ. 463, μή τοι ταῦτα μελόντων.

[5] See note on Thesm. 350.

[6] Cario's share of the sacrifice. When Chremylus sacrificed to Apollo, the remnants of the victim were distributed among the spectators.

quickly.[1] [*Exit Cario.*] And do you, O Plutus, most excellent of all gods, go in this way with me; for this is [2] the house which you must to-day fill with riches, by fair means or by foul.[3]

PLU. But, by the gods, I am exceedingly loth to be always going into other people's houses. For I never at any time got any good from it.[4] For if I chance to go into the house of a miser, he immediately buries [5] me deep in the earth: and if any good man, his friend, come to him asking to get some small sum of money, he denies that he has ever at any time even seen me. But if I chance to go into the house of a mad fellow, I am exposed to harlots and dice and driven out of doors naked in a moment of time.[6]

CHR. Yes; for you never at any time met with [7] a moderate man. But I am somehow always of this character.[8] For I both take pleasure in saving, as never man did, and again in spending,[9] whenever there is occasion for it. But let us go in; for I wish both my wife to see you [10] and my only son, whom I love most of all—next to you.

PLU. I believe you.

---

[1] Cf. vs. 349, 648, 974. Nub. 181, 506, 635, 1253. Ran. 1171. Equit. 71, 119. Ach. 571. Vesp. 30, 202, 398, 847, 1158, 1210. Pax, 275, 872. Eccles. 1058. Thesm. 255. Lys. 438, 920. Bernhardy, W. S. p. 383. Viger, p. 350. "Cf. Alberti ad Hesych. i. p. 409." *Fischer.*

[2] See note on Vesp. 80.

[3] Cf. Equit. 256. Acharn. 373. Nub. 99. Terence, Andr. i 3, 9, "Quo jure quâque injuriâ."

[4] i. e. from going in. "εἰσέρχεσθαι." *Scholiast.* "*Nihil inde boni mihi obtigit unquam.*" *Brunck.* See note on Lys. 134, and cf. Nub. 1231, and note on Thesm. 1008.

[5] So vs. 244. See Krüger, Gr. Gr. § 53, 6, obs. 3. Bernhardy, W. S. p. 382. "Herod. viii. 53, ἐρρίπτεον ἑωϋτοὺς κατὰ τοῦ τείχεος κάτω. See Acharn. 97." *Dobree.*

[6] "Alciphron, iii. 56, ἀνάγκη σε γυμνὸν τῆς οἰκίας θύραζε ἐν ἀκαρεῖ χρόνου ἐκβληθέντα ἐκπεσεῖν." *Dobree.* Cf. Lucian, Tim. 2, 23.

[7] See Bernhardy, W. S. p. 95.

[8] "Ich aber bin von diesem Charakter aller Zeit." *Droysen.*

[9] For examples of the present ἀναλόω, Liddell refers to Æsch. Theb. 813. Eur. Med. 325. Thuc. iii. 81. Xenoph. Hier. 11, 1. See Krüger, Gr. Gr. § 40, in voc. ἀναλίσκω.

[10] So Brunck. "For I would have you see my wife and only son." *Wheelwright.* And so Droysen and Fielding, forgetting that Plutus was *blind.* The syntax, however, is wholly in their favour. See note on Ran. 616.

CHR. For why should one not tell the truth to you?
[*Exeunt Chremylus and Plutus.*]

CA. Oh you who have often eaten of the same thyme[2] with
my master, his friends, and fellow-tribesmen, and lovers of
labour, come, make haste, hurry, since the time does not admit delay, but it is at the very crisis at which you ought
be present[3] and lend your aid.

CHORUS OF COUNTRY-PEOPLE.[4] Don't you see then that
we have been actively hastening this long while, as is reasonable those should who are now feeble old men? But you,
perhaps, expect that I should run, before you even tell me
this,[5] on what account your master has called me hither.

CA. Have I not then, I ween, been telling you this long
while? It is you yourself that don't hear. For my master
says that you shall all of you live pleasantly, freed from your
dreary and unpleasant mode of life.

CHO. But what, pray, and whence, is this thing which he
speaks of?

CA. He has come hither with a certain old man, ye wretches,
who is filthy, crooked, miserable, wrinkled, bald, and tooth-
less; and, by heaven, I think he is circumcised,[6] too.

CHO. O you who have announced golden tidings,[7] how say

---

[1] Here the scene changes to the open country. Bergler compares
Eur. Iph. Aul. 1395, τί γὰρ τἀληθὲς οὐκ εἴποι τις ἄν;

[2] See Liddell's Lex. in voc. θύμος. Porson compares Antiphanes
ap. Athen. iii. p. 108, F.

[3] A transition from plural to singular. See notes on Vesp 554.
Ran. 1075.

[4] The Chorus here make their first appearance; with the morose-
ness of old age, they grant no more indulgence to the elated feel-
ings of the insolent slave, than he to their years and infirmities.

[5] ταῦτα ... ὅτου χάριν. ταῦτα is *very often* referred to a *single* object.
See vs. 898. Aves, 482. Nub. 1339. Eccles. 422. Eur. Hippol. 468,
478. Phœn. 780. Andr. 370. Soph. Colon. 787. Sappho, Fragm.
xxviii. Plato, Phæd. p. 62, D. p. 68, B. Xenoph. Anab. i. 7, 4; i.
9, 24. Krüger, Gr. Gr. § 44, 4, obs. 3. Bernhardy, W. S. p. 282.
Bremi on Demosth. Cor. § 200. Neue on Soph. El. 1124. Wunder
on Soph. Phil. 1326. For this use of a demonstrative to introduce
something afterwards explained, see note on Thesm. 520.

[6] Eckard thinks this is an allusion to the Jews.

[7] Cf. vs. 530, *infra.* Pax, 135, and the examples cited ap. Class.
Mus. No. xxv. p. 246. So also Ovid, Fast. i. 700, " Pondere rastri,"
the heavy harrow. See Bernhardy, W. S. p. 54. Hermann, Vig.
Append. p. 703. 712. Schneidewin, Soph. Aj. 159. Porson cites

you? tell me again! For you plainly show that he is come
with a heap of money.

CA. Nay, rather, with[1] a heap of the ills of age.

CHO. Do you expect, after humbugging us, to get off unpunished, and that, too, when I have a staff?

CA. Why, do you consider me to be altogether such a man
by nature in all respects, and do you think that I would say[2]
nothing true?

CHO. How haughty the rascal[3] is! Your legs are crying
out, "Oh! Oh!" longing for the stocks and fetters.

CA. But are you not for going, when now your letter[4] has
assigned[5] you to administer justice in the tomb, and Charon[6]
gives you your ticket?[7]

CHO. Split you![8] What an impudent fellow you are, and
arrant knave by nature, who[9] humbug us, and have not yet
had the patience to tell us on what account your master has
called me hither, who,[10] after labouring much, have come
hither readily, though we had no leisure, passing over[11] many
roots of thyme.

CA. Well then, I will not conceal it any longer; for, sirs,
my master has come with Plutus, who will make you rich.

CHO. Why, is it really possible for us all to be rich?

CA. Nay, rather, by the gods, *all* Midases,[12] if you get
ass's cars.

Julian, Epist. xii. p. 381, A., ἐγὼ δὲ προσθείην ἐκ τῆς κωμῳδίας, ὦ
χρυσὸν ἀγγείλας ἐπῶν.

[1] sc. δηλῶ. Cf. Plautus, Merc. iii. 4, 53.

[2] See the examples cited in the note on Aves, 1653.

[3] Cf. Ran. 179.   [4] See note on Eccles. 683.

[5] A nominative absolute. See note on Ran. 1437. This transition
from a participle to a finite verb with δὲ is sufficiently defended by
the following passages: Thucyd. i. 36, τρία μὲν ὄντα λόγου ἄξια τοῖς
Ἕλλησι ναυτικά, τούτων δ' εἰ περιόψεσθε τὰ δύο εἰς ταὐτὸν ἐλθεῖν. Isocr.
π. Ἀντιδ. p. 26, δέον αὐτοὺς τὴν φρόνησιν ἀσκεῖν, οἱ δὲ χεῖρον πεπαι-
δεῦνται. See Bernhardy, W. S. p. 487, *note.*

[6] In this passage Cario, punning on the σωρός of the old men, tells
them their letter is Σ, namely, ἐν σορῷ.

[7] See Liddell's Lex. in voc. σύμβολον, i. 3.

[8] Cf. Aves, 2, 1257, and vs. 892, *infra,* and see Bernhardy, W.
S. p. 73.   [9] See note on Thesm. 544.

[10] Referred to the more remote ἡμῖν (vs. 280).

[11] "Boissonade thinks this is in ridicule of some tragedian."
Dobree.

[12] The accusative before the infinitive (εἶναι, vs. 286). "The au-

Cho. How I am delighted and gladdened, and wish to dance for joy, if you are really speaking [1] this truly.

Ca. Well now, I should like [2] to lead you, imitating [3] the Cyclops, threttanelo! and moving thus to and fro with my feet. But come, my children, crying out frequently, and bleating [4] the strains [5] of sheep and stinking goats, follow me lewdly, and you shall breakfast like [6] goats.

Cho. And we, on the other hand, bleating, when we have caught you, this Cyclops, threttanelo! dirty, with a wallet and dewy, wild potherbs, having a drunken head-ache, leading your sheep, and carelessly asleep some where, will take a great lighted, sharp stake and try to blind you.

---

cusative is right. Lysias, Funeb. p. 86, ed. Reisk., ἀποθανεῖν μὲν αὐτοῖς μετὰ πάντων προσηκεῖν, ἀγαθοὺς δ' εἶναι μετ' ὀλίγων. Cf. ibid. p. 129. Eurip. ap. Plutarch. ii. p. 166, E., δεινή τις ἀνδρὶ καὶ γυναικὶ συμφορὰ δουλοὺς γενέσθαι. See Hermann, Vig. n. 217. Blomf. Prom. 225. Agam. 1022. Priscian, xviii. p. 1173-4, ed. Putsch." *Dobree*. He might have added that it was not only *right*, but that the Greeks *preferred* the accusative in the second member. See vss. 531, 799. Pax, 128. Thesm. 675. Xenoph. Anab. i. 2, 1; ii. 1, 19; iii. 1, 5; v. 2, 12; vi. 4, 38; vii. 6, 16. Hom. Il. X. 109. Krüger on Xenoph. Anab. i. 2, 1, and Gr. Gr. § 55, 2, obs. 7. Bernhardy, W. S. p. 367, Class. Mus. No. xxv. p. 243. Hermann, Opusc. iii. p. 242. Dorville, Char. p. 269. Lobeck, Ajax, 1006.

[1] I have little doubt but that Aristophanes wrote τοῦτ'. See Schneidewin, Hyperid. Orat. p. 47, and Krüger, Gr. Gr. § 61, 8, obs. 3. Dobree compares Demosth. Onet. *init.*

[2] Cf. vs. 319, *infra.*

[3] The account of Polyphemus, as given in the Odyssey, is well known. In the time of Dionysius, the tyrant of Syracuse, there was living in that city a courtesan, named Galatea, of whom the king was enamoured; but being jealous of Philoxenus of Cythera, the dithyrambic poet, also an admirer of his mistress, he banished him to the stone quarries, whereupon Philoxenus revenged himself by a satirical poem, entitled, "The Loves of the Cyclops," which is mentioned by Aristotle, in his treatise on Poetry. In this he represented Dionysius under the character of Polyphemus. The word *threttanelo* has no meaning in itself, but was coined by Philoxenus to imitate the sound of the Cyclops' cithara.

[4] τέκεα .. ἐπαναβοῶντες. An example of what the graminarians call σχῆμα πρὸς τὸ σημαινόμενον. Cf. Vesp. 408. Ach. 872, and see Krüger, Gr. Gr. § 58, 4, obs. i. Bernhardy, W. S. p. 428. Porson, Phœn. 1730. Elmsley, Rex, 1167. Hermann, Vig. 49. Kün, Greg. Cor. p. 71, 93.

[5] Supposed to be an imitation of Eupolis

[6] See note on vs. 314.

CA. And I will imitate in all her ways Circe, who mixed up the drugs, who once in Corinth[1] persuaded the companions of Philonides, as if they were boars, to eat kneaded dung ; while she herself kneaded it for them. But do you, grunting for delight, follow, like swine, your mother.

CHO. Therefore we, having caught you, the Circe, who mixed up the drugs and bewitched and defiled our companions, imitating for delight the son of Laertes, will hang you up[2] by your testicles, and besmear your nostrils with dung, like a goat's ; while you, gaping like[3] Aristyllus, shall say, " Follow, like swine, your mother."

CA. But come now, do you now have done with your jests and turn yourselves into another shape ;[4] while I should like now to go unknown to my master and take some bread and meat and eat it, and so afterwards to join in the work. [*Exit Cario.*]

CHREMYLUS (*entering and addressing the Chorus*). To bid you " hail,"[5] my fellow-tribesmen, is now old-fashioned and obsolete ; so I " embrace you," because you have come readily and eagerly, and not[6] tardily. But see that you be[7] my

[1] " After the mention of the Cyclops, Cario is led to that of Circe, who, with her medicated potions, transformed the companions of Ulysses into swine. [Hom. Od. K. 280, seq.] Instead of *Philonides*, he ought to have named Ulysses, and the island of the Lestrygons in the room of *Corinth.*" *Wheelwright.*

[2] An allusion to the punishment inflicted upon Melanthius the goat-herd. See Hom. Od. xxii. 175.

[3] Very often a substantive is subjoined predicatively to another noun, where we translate it by *as, like, for.* So Eccles. 724, κατωνάκην τὸν χοῖρον ἀποτετιλμένας, *like a slave.* Thesm. 1011, σημεῖον ὑπεδήλωσε ἐκδραμὼν Περσεὺς, *a la Perseus.* Lys. 928, τὸ πέος τόδ' Ἡρακλῆς ξενίζεται, *like Hercules.* Plut. vs. 295, τράγοι δ' ἀκρατιεῖσθε, *like goats.* Menander (ap. Athen. iv. p. 172, A.), κρεάδι' ὀπτᾷ καὶ κίχλας τραγήματα, *as sweetmeats.* Kön (Greg. Cor. p. 331) cites from the Greek romance-writers νῦν δὲ φιλείτωσαν ἀλλήλους ἄδελφοι, *like brothers.* Cf. Demosth. p. 2, B. Xenoph Cyrop. v. 2, 14. Plato, Legg. x. p. 903, E. Eur. Orest. 545. Krüger, Gr. Gr. §57, 3. Bernhardy, W. S. p. 333. Kön, Greg. Cor. p. 331. Dorville, Charit. p. 219. Schäfer, Appar. Crit. Demosth. i. p. 868. Aristyllus was a poet of infamous character. He is also mentioned in the Eccles. 647.

[4] " This must be referred to those transformations into goats and hogs, which Cario humorously supposes to have actually happened.' *Fielding.* " *Ad aliud cantici genus.*" *Brunck.*

[5] Cf. Eur. Med. 661.   [6] See note on Aves, 1650.
[7] See note on Lys. 316.

co-adjutors in the rest as well, and truly preservers of the god.

Cho. Be of good courage! for you shall think I look downright martial.[1] For it would be absurd,[2] if we constantly jostle one another in the Assembly for the sake of three obols, while I were to yield up Plutus himself to any one to take away.[3]

Chr. Well now, I see also Blepsidemus here approaching: and 'tis plain[4] from his gait and haste that he has heard something of the affair. [*Enter Blepsidemus.*]

Bl. (*talking to himself*). What then can the affair be? whence and in what way has Chremylus suddenly become rich? I don't believe it: and yet, by Hercules, there was much talk among those who sat in the barbers' shops,[5] that the man has suddenly become wealthy. But this very thing is marvellous to me, that he, being well off, sends for his friends. In truth he does not[6] do a thing fashionable in the country.

Chr. (*aside*). Well then, by the gods, I'll tell him, without concealing any thing.[7] O Blepsidemus, we are better off than yesterday, so that it is permitted you to share; for you are of the number of my friends.[8]

---

[1] A parody on Æsch. Theb. 53, 483. Cf. Bernhardy, W. S. p. 111.

[2] δεινὸν γὰρ (ἂν εἴη), εἰ ὠστιζόμεσθα, παρείην δέ. ὠστιζόμεσθα is an objective actuality, whereas παρείην (the real protasis to δεινὸν ἂν εἴη) is a *merely supposed* case. See Krüger, Gr. Gr. § 54, 12, obs. 8. Porson (Phœn. vs. 91) thus notices this construction: "Diversos modos jungit Euripides, quoniam ad tempora diversa spectant. . . . Similiter modos variavit Aristophanes, Plut. 310, δεινὸν γὰρ— παρείην, ubi alterum (τὸ ὠστίζεσθαι) revera quotidie fiebat; alterum vero (τὸ παριέναι τὸν Πλοῦτον) ex futuri temporis eventu pendebat." Cf. Aves, 1225-7.

[3] For this use of the infinitive, see Krüger, Gr. Gr. § 55, 3, obs. 21. The accusative Πλοῦτον is generally made to depend on λαβεῖν, but Porson (l. c.) very properly construes it with παρείην.

[4] See notes on Thesm. 575. Pax, 913.

[5] "Lysias περὶ τοῦ ἀδυνάτου, p. 754, ed. Reisk. ἕκαστος γὰρ ὑμῶν εἴθισται προσφοιτᾶν, ὁ μὲν πρὸς μυροπώλιον, ὁ δὲ πρὸς κουρεῖον, ὁ δὲ πρὸς σκυτοτομεῖον, ὁ δ' ὅπη ἂν τύχῃ." Dobree. Cf. Terent. Phorm. i. 2, 38. This use of ἐπὶ is rare. See Bernhardy, W. S. p. 249.

[6] Cf. vs. 889, *infra*. "*Non sane facit hoc pro recepto hic more.*" Brunck.

[7] Eur. Phœn. 460, ἐγὼ γὰρ οὐδὲν, μᾶτερ, ἀποκρύψας ἐρῶ.

[8] Cf. vs. 869. Aves, 271. Nub. 104, 107. Eccles. 78, 349. Xenoph. Anab. i. 2. 3. Krüger, Gr. Gr. § 47, 9, obs. 2.

Bl. But have you really become[1] rich, as people say ?

Chr. Nay, but I shall be very soon, if God please ;[2] for there is—there is some hazard in the affair.

Bl. Of what sort ?[3]

Chr. Such as—

Bl. Tell me quickly[4] what in the world you mean.[5]

Chr.—that, if we succeed, we shall be always well off ;[6] but if we be foiled, we shall be utterly undone.

Bl. This load[7] looks bad, and does not please me. For your suddenly becoming so excessively rich, and, again, your fearing, is in character with a man[8] who has done nothing good.

Chr. How nothing good ?

Bl. If, by Jove, you have come from thence, having stolen any silver or gold from the god, and then, perhaps, repent.

Chr. O Apollo, averter of evil ! not I, by Jove !

Bl. Cease talking nonsense, my good sir ; for I know it for certain.

Chr. Do you suspect nothing of the kind[9] of me.

Bl. Alas ! how there is absolutely no good[10] in any one ! but all are slaves[11] of gain.

[1] In vs. 339, γεγένημαι. Plato almost confines himself to γέγονα, while Thucydides uses only γεγένημαι. Aristophanes uses both forms.

[2] "So Gott es will." *Droysen.* The same as σὺν Θεῷ, vs. 114, and ἢν θεοὶ θέλωσιν, vs. 405. Cf. Pax, 1187. Ran. 433.

[3] See note on Nub. 765. Equit. 1324.

[4] See note on vs. 229, *supra.*

[5] Schäfer compares Soph. Rex, 655, φράζε δὴ τί φῄς. Xenoph. Anab. ii. 1, 15, σὺ δ' ἡμῖν εἰπὲ τί λέγεις. Add Plato, Legg. p. 819, λέγ' ὅ τι καὶ φῄς. Cf. note on Eccles. 774.

[6] The infinitive πράττειν depends on οἷος (vs. 349). See Krüger, Gr. Gr. § 55, 3, obs. 5. Matthiä, § 479, *a.* Jelf, § 823, obs. 3. οἷος in these formulæ = τοιοῦτος ὥστε. See Hermann, Vig. n. 79.

[7] "Das scheint mir eine schlechte Ladung im Schiff des Glücks."
Droysen.

[8] See Krüger, Gr. Gr. § 68, 37, obs. 1, and for οὐδὲν ὑγιὲς, ibid. § 61, 8, obs. 3.

[9] See Elmsley, Soph. Rex, 734.

[10] Dobree compares vs. 870, *infra.* Plato, Phæd. p. 89, E. p. 90, C. Cratyl. sub fin. Eur. Bacch. 262. Helen. 752. Demosth. Pantæn. p. 969. Fals. Leg. p. 353.

[11] Nub. 1081, ἥττων ἔρωτός ἐστι καὶ γυναικῶν. Soph. Antig. 680, γυναικῶν ἥσσονες. Trach. 489, ἔρωτος. Plato, Protag. p. 353, C., ἡδονῶν. Xenoph. Mem. i. 5, 1, γαστρός. The opposite is Eur. Danaid. 85, κρείσσων χρημάτων.

CHR. By Ceres, you certainly do not appear to me to be in your right senses.

BL. (*aside*). How much he has altered[1] from the character[2] he formerly had!

CHR. By heaven, fellow, you are mad!

BL. (*aside*). But not even does his glance itself keep[3] in its place, but is like[4] to one who has committed some villany.

CHR. I know what you are croaking[5] about: you seek to get a share, as if I had stolen something.

BL. I seek to get a share? of what?

CHR. Whereas[6] it is not of such nature, but different.[7]

BL. Have you not stolen, but snatched it away?[8]

CHR. You are possessed.

BL. But have you, in truth, not even defrauded any one?

CHR. Not I, indeed![9]

BL. O Hercules, come, whither can[10] one turn himself? for you will not tell the truth.

[1] See Bekker's Anecd. i. p. 60. Cf. Vesp. 1451. Eur. Bacch. 944.

[2] See notes on Thesm. 502. Nub. 863.

[3] Xenoph. Econ. x. 10, ἐπισκοπουμένην εἰ κατὰ χώραν ἔχει ἕκαστα. Cf. Ran. 793. Herod. iv. 135; vi. 42. More frequently we have the synonymous phrase κατὰ χ. μένειν. See Equit. 1354. Thuc. i. 18; ii. 58; iii. 22; iv. 26; iv. 76.

[4] Arist. Acb. 789, συγγενὴς ὁ κύσθος αὐτῆς θατέρα, i. e. τῷ τῆς ἑτέρας. Aves, 31, νόσον νοσοῦμεν τὴν ἐναντίαν Σάκᾳ, i. e. ἢ ἦν νοσεῖ Σάκας. Hom. Il. P. 51, κόμαι Χαρίτεσσιν ὁμοῖαι, i. e. ταῖς τῶν Χαρίτων κόμαις ὁμοῖαι. Xenoph. Cyrop. vi. 1, 50, ἅρματα ὅμοια ἐκείνῳ, i. e. τοῖς ἐκείνου ἅρμασιν. Hom. Il. A. 163, οὐ μέν σοί ποτε ἴσον ἔχω γέρας, i. e. τῷ σῷ γέρα. So Eur. Iph. A. 262. See Bernhardy, W. S. p. 432. Schäfer, Meletem. Crit. p. 57, foll. 134.

[5] Cf. Lys. 506. Voss compares Hor. Sat. ii. 5, 56. Elmsley on Acharn. 255, proposes οὲ μέν. This would be an example of "Anticipation," so common in Aristophanes. See notes on Nub. 1148. Eccles. 1126. But the harshness of the present construction is little improved by this. Besides, σὲ stands *first* only when it is very *emphatic*. See Æsch. Prom. 944. Soph. Ajax, 1228. Antig. 441. Elect. 1445. For similar examples of disordered construction, see note on vs. 119, *supra*.

[6] τὸ δὲ, *whereas:* a usage very common in Plato. See Krüger, Gr. Gr. § 50, 1, obs. 14.

[7] ἑτέρως ἔχον (ἐστίν). See Krüger, Gr. Gr. § 56, 3, obs. 3, and cf. Ran. 1161.

[8] See Jelf, Gr. Gr. § 873, obs. 2. Hoogeveen, Gr. Part. p. 126, ed. Seager. "*Oh! then you have not stolen, you have taken it away by violence.*" *Fielding*. Bergler compares Plaut. Epid. i. 1, 10.

[9] Cf. Aves, 1391.   [10] See Hermann, Soph. Aj. 904. Vig. n. 108.

Chr. For you accuse me before you know my case.

Bl. My good friend, I will[1] settle this for you at a very trifling expense, before the city hear of it, by stopping the orators' mouths[2] with small coin.

Chr. And verily, by the gods, methinks you would[3] in a friendly way lay out three minæ and set down twelve.

Bl. I see a certain person[4] who will sit at the Bema, holding the suppliant's bough,[5] with his children and his wife; and who will not differ at all, not even in any way,[6] from the Heraclidæ of Pamphilus.[7]

Chr. Not so, you wretch, but on the contrary,[8] I will cause the good alone, and the clever and discreet, to become rich.

Bl. What do you say? have you stolen so very much?

Chr. Ah me, what miseries! you will destroy me.

Bl. Nay, rather, you *will destroy* yourself, as it seems to me.[9]

[1] "Hör', Lieber, Ich will die Gefahr dir für ein Weniges
Zu Ende bringen, eh' die Stadt davon erfährt;
Mit einigen Hellern stopfen den Rednern wir den Mund."
Droysen.

For ἐθέλω, cf. vs. 375, *supra.* Vesp. 536.

[2] Cf. Pax, 645.

[3] "Nay, by the gods,
To me thou hast th' appearance of a man
Who'd spend three minæ in this friendly turn,
And bring a bill for twelve." *Wheelwright.*

For the infinitive with ἄν, see examples cited in the note on Aves, 1653.

[4] Cf. Acharn. 1128—1131, and see note on Ran. 552.

[5] The "supplex oliva" of Statius, Theb. xii. 492.

[6] See Krüger, Gr. Gr. § 51, 15, obs. 3.

[7] On the death of Hercules, Eurystheus transferred his hatred from the father to the children, and the Heraclidæ, being compelled to quit the Peloponnesus, came with Alcmena in a suppliant train to Athens: this tradition was made the subject of a tragedy by Chærephon, and, according to one of the Scholiasts, supplied the celebrated painter, Pamphilus, with an exercise for his pencil on the walls of the Pœcile. "It is uncertain whether Pamphilus, a tragedian, be meant here, who, as Euripides and Æschylus, made the Heraclidæ the subject of a tragedy; or the painter of that name, so celebrated in later times, who painted that subject in the Pœcile." *Droysen.* See also Elmsley, Heraclid. vs. 11.

[8] Lexicon Sangermanicum (Bekk. Anecd. i. p. 418), ἀπαρτὶ παρὰ τοῖς κωμικοῖς, τὸ ἐκ τοῦ ἐναντίου. Cf. Liddell's Lex. in voc.

[9] Cf. vss. 409, 1035. Ran. 645, 918. Nub. 1271. Eubulus ap. Athen. 34, D.

Chr. Certainly not; for I have got Plutus, you sorry wretch.

Bl. You, Plutus? what[1] Plutus?

Chr. The god himself.

Bl. Why, where is he?

Chr. Within.

Bl. Where?

Chr. At my house.

Bl. At your house?

Chr. Certainly.

Bl. Go to the devil! Plutus at your house?

Chr. Yes, by the gods!

Bl. Are you speaking truth?

Chr. Yes.

Bl. By Vesta?

Chr. Yea, by Neptune!

Bl. Do you mean the sea Neptune?

Chr. Aye, and t'other Neptune, if there be any other.

Bl. Then are you not for sending him round to us also your friends?

Chr. The affair is not yet come to this point.[2]

Bl. What do you say? not to the sharing[3] point—eh?

Chr. No, by Jupiter! for we must first——

Bl. What?

Chr. Cause him to see.

Bl. Whom to see? tell me.

Chr. Plutus, as before, in some way or other.[4]

Bl. Why, is he really blind?

Chr. Yes, by heaven!

Bl No wonder,[5] then, he never at any time came to me.

Chr. But, if the gods please, he shall come now

---

[1] See Porson, Phœn. 892, and note on Lys. 1178.

[2] Cf. Equit. 843. Soph. Antig. 39.

[3] "*Non in eo, ut nos participes facias?*" *Brunck.* "*Res nondum eo rediit, ut nobis quoque Plutum tradas?*" *Fischer.* "Porson, Bentley, and Bothe conjecture οὐ τῷ, very badly. Cf. vs. 889." *Dobree.* For this singular construction, see Bernhardy, W. S. p. 204.

[4] Cf. Thesm. 430, and vs. 413, *infra*.

[5] "Kein Wunder ist's denn, dass er zu mir noch nimmer kam.
Droysen

BL. Ought[1] you not then to call in some physician?

CHR. What physician then is there now in the city? For neither is the fee of any value,[2] nor the profession.

BL. Let us see.

CHR. But there is none.

BL. Neither do I think so.

CHR. No, by Jupiter; but 'tis best to lay him on a couch in[3] the temple of Æsculapius,[4] as I was intending this long while.[5]

BL. Nay, rather, far *the best*, by the gods. Do not then delay, but make haste and do something or other.

CHR. Well now, I am going.

BL. Hasten then.

CHR. I am doing this very thing. [*Enter Poverty.*]

POV. O you pitiful mannikins, who dare to do[6] a hasty and unholy and unlawful deed! whither? whither? why do you fly? will you not remain?

BL. O Hercules!

POV. I will destroy you, you wretches, in a wretched[7] way; for you are venturing on a daring act not to be borne, but such as no other person even at any time, either[8] god or man, *has ventured on;* therefore you are undone.[9]

Aristoph. *Æolosicon*, Fragm. viii.,

οὐκ ἐτὸς, ὦ γυναῖκες,
πᾶσι κακοῖσιν ἡμᾶς
φλῶσιν ἑκάστοθ' ἄνδρες.

See note on Acharn. vs. 411, and cf. vs. 1166.

[1] See note on Thesm. 74.   [2] See note on Eccles. 444.

[3] See Jelf, Gr. Gr. § 646, *a.*

[4] In the way from the theatre to the citadel, near the tomb of Talos, stood the temple of Æsculapius, adorned with pictures of himself and his daughters: within its precincts was the fountain where Mars committed that murder which gave rise to the court of Areopagus. The temple was in great repute, as appears from the dedication of some Sarmatian shields in it.

[5] "Was Ich vorher mir schon gedacht." *Droysen.*

[6] Apparently a parody upon Eurip. Med. 1118, ὦ δεινὸν ἔργον παρανόμως εἰργασμένη.

[7] See note on Eccles. 730, and cf. vs. 95, *supra.*

[8] See Porson, Præf. Hec. p. 17. Elmsley, Suppl. vs. 158.

[9] Poverty speaks of the future as already past, to indicate that it will certainly happen." *Fischer.* See Thesm. 77. Pax, 250, 364, 367. Aves, 338. Krüger, Gr. Gr. § 53, 10, obs. 5. It may be referred to the Greek fondness for objectising subjective conceptions and con-

CHR. But who are you? for you appear to me to be ghastly pale.

BL. Perhaps 'tis some Fury from tragedy:[1] at least she certainly looks very mad and tragic.

CHR. But she has no torches.

BL. Then she shall suffer for it.

POV. Whom do you think me to be?

CHR. Some hostess[2] or pulse-porridge-seller: for otherwise you would not have[3] cried out so loud against us, having been wronged[4] in no way.

POV. What, really? for have you not acted most shamefully in seeking to banish me from every place?[5]

CHR. Is not then the Barathrum left you? But you ought to tell me immediately who you are.

POV. One who will make you to-day give satisfaction, because you seek to expel me from hence.

BL. Is it the tavern-keeper of our neighbourhood,[6] who is always cheating[7] me grossly with her half-pints?

POV. Nay,[8] but I am Poverty, who have been dwelling with you many years.

BL. (*running away*). O King Apollo, and ye gods! Whither must one fly?[9]

CHR. Hollo! what are you about? O you most cowardly[10] beast, will you not stay?

BL. By no means.

CHR. Will you not stay? What! shall we two men fly from one woman?

BL. Yes, for 'tis Poverty, you wretch, than whom there is no living being any where more ruinous.

CHR. Stand, I beseech you, stand!

sidering as an actuality what has not yet passed from thought into an external taking place. " Sterben müsst ihr drum." *Droysen*.

[1] Plutarch, Dion, p. 182, C., εἶδε γυναῖκα μεγάλην, στολῇ μὲν καὶ προσώπῳ μηδὲν ἐριννύος τραγικῆς παραλλάττουσαν, σαίρουσαν δὲ καλλύντρῳ τινὶ τὴν οἰκίαν. See note on Aves, 924.

[2] " Eine Hurenwirthin." *Droysen*.

[3] See Elmsley, Acharn. 351.   [4] Cf. vs. 457.

[5] " Von allem Ort." *Droysen*. " Χώρα, *place*, in this passage= *domus civium bonorum*." *Fischer*.

[6] Nicostratus ap. Athen. xv. p. 700, B., ὁ κάπηλος γὰρ οἷς ·ὁ γειτόνων. See note on Aves, 13.

[7] Cf. Thesm. 347.   [8] Cf. vs. 347, *supra*.

[9] See note on vs. 1027, *infra*.   [10] Cf Aves, 86

BL. No, by Jove, not I.

CHR. Well now, I tell you, we shall do a deed by far the most shameful of all deeds, if we shall leave the god unprotected and fly[1] any whither, through fear of her, and not fight it out.

BL. Relying on what sort of arms or strength? For what sort of breast-plate and what sort of shield does not the most abominable wretch put in pawn?[2]

CHR. Be of good courage; for this god alone, I well know, can set up a trophy over her ways.[3]

POV. And do you also dare to mutter, you scoundrels, when you have been detected in the very act of doing shameful things?

CHR. But why do you, the devil take you,[4] come against us and revile us, being wronged not[5] even in any way?

POV. For do you think, oh, by the gods![6] that you wrong me in no way, in endeavouring to make Plutus see again?

CHR. What wrong then do we do you in this, if we contrive good for all men?

POV. But what good could you devise?

CHR. What? by banishing you from Greece in the first place.

POV. By banishing me? and what greater evil do you suppose you could do to men?

CHR. What? if we were[7] to delay to do this and forget it.

POV. Well now, I wish first to render you an account of this very matter.[8] And if I prove that I am the sole cause

---

[1] See Elmsley, Iph. T. 777. Acharn. 733. Mus. Crit. ii. p. 294.

[2] Cf. Hermippus ap. Athen. xi. p. 478, C. " Poverty has made them violators of the law ; for it was rigorously forbidden to pawn arms or farming utensils." *Voss.* Thesm. 491; οὐδ' ὡς ὑπὸ τῶν δούλων σποδούμεθα, ἢν μὴ 'χωμεν ἕτερον, οὐ λέγει. Hom. Od. Γ. 27, οὐ γὰρ οἴω οὖ σε θεῶν ἀέκητι γενέσθαι. See Krüger, Gr. Gr. § 67, 11, obs. 3.

[3] " *This god alone, I am confident, will triumph over all the tricks of this woman.*" *Fielding.* Teles, Stob. p. 19, vs. 28, κὰν τάδε δρᾷς, ῥᾳδίως στήσεις τρόπαιον κατὰ πενίας. In τρόπων we have a comic substitute for τροπῆς. See Mus. Crit. i. p. 104.

[4] See note on Thesm. 879.   [5] Cf. vss. 385, 428.

[6] Cf. vs. 1176. Vesp. 484. Krüger, Gr. Gr. § 68, 37, obs. 2.

[7] " Wenn länger wir säumten und gar vergässen, es zu thun!"
Droysen.

Cf. Plautus, Aulul. iv. 4, 15.

[8] Wakefield (Silv. Crit. i. p. 75) takes αὐτοῦ for an adverb of place, *ipso in loco,* which seems very unsuitable.

of all blessings to you, and that you live through me, *it is well;*[1] but if not, now do this, whatever seems good to you.

Chr. Do you dare to say this, O most abominable ?

Pov. Aye, and do you suffer yourself to be taught.[2] For I think I shall very easily prove that you are altogether in the wrong, if you say you will make the just wealthy.

Chr. O cudgels and pillories,[3] will you not aid me ?

Pov. You ought not to complain angrily and cry out before you know.

Bl. Why, who would be able not to cry out " oh ! oh !" at hearing such things ?

Pov. He who is in his right senses.[4]

Chr. What penalty, then, shall I set down[5] in the title of the suit for you, if you be cast ?

Pov. Whatever seems good to you.

Chr. You say well.

Pov. For you also must suffer the same, if you lose your cause.

Bl. Do you think then twenty deaths[6] sufficient ?

Chr. Yes, for her ; but two only will suffice for us.

Pov. You cannot be too quick in doing[7] this : for what just plea could any one any longer bring[8] against me ?

[1] Kuster refers to Hom. Il. A. 185. Eustathius on Hom. l. c. Arist. Thesm. 536. Anonym. ap. Athen. viii. p. 360. See Krüger, Gr. Gr. § 54. 12. obs. 12. Stallbaum, Plat. Rep. p. 575, D. Kön. Greg. Cor. p. 48. Hermann, Vig. n. 308. So Menander, (Fragm cxli. ed. Didot,) εἰ μὲν δή τινα πόρον ἔχεις, εἰ δὲ μὴ, νενόηκ᾽ ἐγώ. It is usual to supply καλῶς ἔχει.

[2] Cf. Eur. Hec. 303.

[3] " Cratinus ap. Pollux, x. c. 40, ἐν τῷ κυφῶνι τὴν αὐχένα ἔχων. Athenæus, viii. p. 351, ἰδὼν δ᾽ ἐν τῷ κυφῶνι δεδεμένους δύο." *Spanheim.*

[4] See Krüger, Gr. Gr. § 56, 3, obs. 3.

[5] " Was für 'ne Busse dictir' Ich in diesem Handel dir, wenn du verlierest?"   *Droysen.*

[6] Shakspeare, *As you like it*, act v. sc. 1, " I will·kill thee a hundred and fifty ways; therefore tremble and depart." Cf. note on Ran. 1017.

[7] i. e. in dying. " ἀντὶ τοῦ ἀποθανόντες. οὐκ ἂν, φησὶν, ἀναβάλοισθε ἀποθανόντες." *Scholiast.* Eur. Orest. 925, οὐ φθάνοιτ᾽ ἔτ᾽ ἂν θνήσκοντες. Ibid. 930, κοὐ φθάνοι θνήσκων τις ἂν See note on Eccles. 118.

[8] " Denn wer noch hat was Rechtes zu erwiedern mir?" *Droysen.* " For what could any one in justice answer?"   *Wheelwright.*

Cho. Well, you ought now to say something clever, by which you shall conquer her, opposing her in argument, and not effeminately give in.[1]

Chr. I think that this is plain for all alike to understand,[2] that it is just that the good men should be prosperous, but the wicked and the ungodly, I ween, the contrary[3] of this. We therefore desiring that this[4] should take place, have with difficulty found out a plan, excellent, and noble, and useful for every[5] enterprise. For if Plutus now should have the use of his eyes, and not go about blind, he will go to the good men,[6] and not leave them, but will fly from the wicked and the ungodly; and then he will make all to be good and rich, I ween, and to reverence[7] things divine. And yet, who could ever devise a better thing than this[8] for men?

[1] Herod. iii. 104, ἐνδιδόναι μαλακὸν οὐδέν. Eur. Hel. 515, ἢν δ' ἐνδιδῷ τι μαλθακόν. Athen. xiv. p. 621, B., οὐδὲν φιλάνθρωπον οὐδὲ ἱλαρὸν ἐνδίδως. The future ἐνδώσετε takes μὴ because, grammatically, it is construed with the *relative* (ᾧ), quite as much as νικήσετε is (see Krüger, Gr. Gr. § 67, 4); and rather expresses what *should* or *ought* to be done, (Krüger, § 53, 7, obs. 3. Cf. Eur. Cycl. 131 Med. 605,) than what will positively happen. "For the construction of ἐνδώσετε, see Elmsley, Med. 804." *Dobree.*

[2] "The order is οἶμαι τουτὶ εἶναι φανερὸν πᾶσι γνῶναι." *Dobree.* See Pax, 821. Aves, 122. Lys. 1207. Thesm. 800. Æsch. Pers. 417. Xenoph. Anab. i. 5, 9. Thuc. vii. 71. Philippus ap. Athen. viii. p. 459, B. Demosth. Aphob. p. 855, 14. Hermann, Vig. n. 134. Krüger, Gr. Gr. § 55, 3, obs. 8. Bernhardy, W. S. p. 360. Elmsley, Heracl. 1011. Dawes, M. C. p. 159. Dorville, Char. p. 469, 526.

[3] Sc. πράττειν. For τούτων, see note on vs. 259, *supra.*

[4]   "We then desiring that it should be so,
        Have found, with much ado, a fine device,
        Generous and useful for all enterprise." *Wheelwright.*

Similarly Droysen. The construction is precisely the same as in Eur. Hippol. 1342, Κύπρις γὰρ ἤθελ' ὥστε γίγνεσθαι τάδε. See Eur. Hec. 842, and many similar examples ap. Matthiä, Gr. Gr. p. 915. For the neuter τοῦτο, see note on Lys. 134.

[5] See Blomf. Append. Pers. vs. 42.

[6] Cf. vs. 490, 597. Aves, 616, 1153, 1388. Vesp. 95, 199, 1040, 1262, 1274. Lys. 819. Ran. 1030, 1446. So Dinarch. c. Demosth. p. 97, τὰ μεγάλα τῶν ἀδικημάτων. Herod. ii. 17, ἡ ἰθέα τῶν ὁδῶν. Aristot. Ethic. x. 1, οἱ ἀληθεῖς τῶν λόγων. Probl. 5, 35, οἱ βραχεῖς τῶν περιπάτων. Eur. Suppl. 343, οἱ δυσμενεῖς βροτῶν. And frequently so with participles. See Krüger, Gr. Gr. § 47, 9. Bernhardy, W. S. p. 155.

[7] See Jelf, Gr. Gr. § 684.

[8] Dobree compares Alexis ap. Athen. ii. p. 63, F.

BL. No one: I am your witness in this; don't[1] ask her.

CHR. For as life is at present circumstanced for us men, who would not think it to be madness, or rather still a demoniacal possession? For many men who are wicked are rich, having accumulated them[2] unjustly; while many who are very good, are badly off, and suffer hunger, and live[3] with you [*to Poverty*] for the most part. I say, then,[4] that there is a way, proceeding upon which[5] a person might procure greater benefits for men, *namely*, if Plutus were ever to have the use of his eyes and put a stop to her.

Pov. Nay, O you two old dotards, partners in nonsense and folly, of all men the most easily persuaded not to be in your right senses, if this were to happen, which you desire, I deny that it would profit you. For if Plutus were to have the use of his eyes again and portion himself[6] out equally, no man would practise either art or science; and when both these have disappeared through you, who will be willing to be a smith, or to build ships, or to sew, or to make wheels, or to make shoes, or to make bricks, or to wash, or to tan hides, or *who will be willing* to break up the soil of the earth with ploughings and reap the fruits[7] of Ceres, if it be possible for you to live in idleness, neglecting all these?

CHR. You talk nonsense;[8] for our servants shall toil at all these things for us, as many as you have now enumerated.

Pov. Whence then will you have servants?

---

[1] Cf. Ran. 1012. For μηδὲν, see note on Ran. 434. "For the unusual cæsura, see Elmsley, Heracl. 649." *Dobree.*

[2] αὐτὰ, i. e. their *riches*, implied in the word πλουτοῦσι.—It is the Greek custom, where the omitted notion is a *general* one, that the allusion to it should be made in the *neuter* gender. Cf. Krüger, Gr. Gr. § 43, 3, obs. 11.

[3] μετὰ σοῦ σύνεισιν. "So Eubulus ap. Athen. viii. 340, D., μετὰ Καράβου σύνεισιν Eur. El. 943, μετὰ σκαίων ξυνών. Cf. Plato, Legg. i. p. 639, C. Theopompus ap. Athen. xii. p. 531, F. Plato, Symp. p. 195, B. Priscian, xvii. p. 1104." *Dobree.* Similarly Ran. 102, εἶτα διδάξας Πέρσας μετὰ τοῦτο. Cf. Nubes, 975. Aves, 811. Porson, Præf. Hec. p. 41.

[4] In other texts οὔκουν .... ἥντιν' ἰὼν, where τίς is understood.

[5] See note on Ran. 136.   [6] See Porson, Præf. Hec. lvi.

[7] "ἤδη τὸ ἔπος τοῦτο τῆς μέσης κωμῳδίας ὄζει." *Scholiast.* Boissonade thinks it is either a parody or an imitation of some tragic passage.

[8] See Krüger Gr. Gr. § 46, 5.

CHR. We will buy them for money, to be sure.

Pov. But first, who will be the seller, when he too has money?

CHR. Some one wishing to make gain, having come as a merchant[1] from Thessaly, from amongst very many kidnappers.[2]

Pov. But first of all, there will not even be any one, not even a kidnapper, according to the statement, I ween, which you mention. For who that is wealthy will be willing to do this[3] at the hazard of his own life? So that, having been compelled to plough, and dig, and toil at the other labours yourself, you will spend a much more painful life than the present one.

CHR. *May it fall* on your own head![4]

Pov. Moreover you will not be able to sleep either in a bed,—for there will be none,—or in carpets; for who will be willing to weave them when he has gold? Nor, when you lead home a bride, to anoint her with dropping unguents; nor to adorn her with sumptuous[5] garments, dyed, and variegated. And yet, what advantage will it be to you to be rich, when in want[6] of all these? But from me all these which you stand in need of are easily obtained; for I sit, compelling the artisan, like a mistress, through his want and his poverty, to seek whence he shall have subsistence.

CHR. Why, what good could you procure, except a swarm of blisters[7] from the bath, and of children beginning to be

---

[1] "Als Kaufmann aus Thessalien." *Droysen.* "Join ἔμπορος ἥκων, as in vs. 1179." *Dobree.*

[2] Hemsterhuis and Hare (Epist. Crit. p. 49) read παρ' ἀπίστων in place of παρὰ πλείστων. Dobree has adopted this in his edition of the *Plutus.* Eur. Phœn. 1416, πολλοὶ παρῆσαν, ἀλλ' ἄπιστοι Θετταλοί. "The Thessalians had the character of being sorcerers, deceivers, and slave-dealers." *Voss.* "In itself πλείστων is a good reading. Cf. Eur. Andr. 451. Aristoph. ap. Athen. iv. p. 173, D. ἔμπορος is used for *slave-dealer* by Eubulus ap. Athen. iii. p. 108, E." *Dobree.*

[3] See note on Lys. 134   [4] Cf. Pax, 1063. Ach 833.

[5] See note on vs. 268.

[6] The full form is τί πλέον ἔσται σοι πλουτεῖν ἀποροῦντα. Eccles. 1094, οὐδὲν ἔσται σοι πλέον. The construction is precisely that explained in the note on vs. 287, *supra.*

[7] φῴδων depends on κολοσυρτόν. "The bathing rooms were in winter the refuge of the indigent. When benumbed with frost they crept too near the furnace and so got blistered." *Voss.* Teles, Stob.

hungry, and of old women ? and [1] the quantity of lice, and gnats, and fleas, I don't even mention [2] to you, by reason of their multitude, which buzz [3] about my head and torment me, wakening me and saying, " You will suffer hunger ; come, get up."[4] Moreover to have a rag instead of a garment ; and instead of a bed, a mattress of rushes, full of bugs, which wakens [5] the sleepers ; and to have a rotten mat instead of a carpet ; and a good-sized stone against one's head instead of a pillow ; and to eat shoots of mallow instead of bread ; and leaves of withered radish instead of barley-cake ; and *to have* the head of a broken jar instead of a bench ; and the side of a cask, and that too [6] broken, instead of a kneading-trough. Do I not [7] demonstrate you to be the cause of many blessings to all men ?

Pov. You have not mentioned my way of life, but have attacked that of beggars.[8]

Chr. Therefore we say, I ween, that poverty is sister [9] of beggary.

v. p. 69, 22 (Poverty is speaking) ἢ οἰκήσεις οὐ παρέχω σοι, πρῶτον μὲν χειμῶνι τὰ βαλανεῖα, θέρους δὲ τὰ ἱερά.

[1] I greatly prefer φθειρῶν δ᾽, the reading of Porson, Dobree, and Kuster.

[2] Dobree compares Philetairus ap. Athen. xiii. p. 587, F. Herod. vii. 9.

[3] An allusion, perhaps, to Æsch. Ag. 893.

[4] Dobree compares Plutarch, T. ii. p. 1044.

[5] Eupolis ap. Athen. ix. p. 397, C., μή ποτε θρέψω παρὰ Φερσεφόνῃ τοιόνδε ταῶν, ὃς τοὺς εὕδοντας ἐγείρει. Aristoph. *Onerariæ*, Fragm. xv., σπυρὶς οὐ μικρὰ καὶ κωρυκὶς, ἢ καὶ τοὺς μάττοντας ἐγείρει.

" Der immer den Schlafenden wach hält." *Droysen.*

[6] See note on Eccles. 594. " A rare transposition. Diodorus Stobæi, lxx. p. 429, 53, τὴν ἐσομένην καὶ ταῦτα μέτοχον τοῦ βίου. Plato, Rep. i. p. 341, C., οὐδὲν ὢν καὶ ταῦτα. Julian, Cæs. p. 312, B., ἔχων καὶ ταῦτα σπουδαῖον κηδεστήν." *Dobree.* Vs. 259 has nothing whatever to do with the present formula. There καὶ means *even.*

[7] " ἄρα frequently by itself denotes *nonne.*" *Matthiä.* See Lys. 648. Krüger, Gr. Gr. § 69, 9. Porson, Præf. Hec. p. vii. (ed. Schäfer.) Monk, Alc. 351. Hermann, Vig. n. 294. Cf. Soph. Aj. 277. Thuc. i. 75.

[8] For this position of δὲ, Porson refers to Eccles. 625, 702.

[9] "See Ruhnken, Tim. Lex. p. 2. Theon. Smyrn. Mathemat. p. 7 Georg. Pisid. Vit. Vanitat. 106. Foot, *Commissar.* act ii. sc. 2, p. 28. Johnson, *Rambler,* lvii. Hipponax ap. Athen. iii. p. 78, C. Alcæus ap. Stob. xciv. p. 455 Æsch. Theb. 500. Agam. 503." *Porson.*

Pov. Aye, you who also *say* that Dionysius is like Thrasybulus. But my mode of life is not thus circumstanced, no, by
Jove, nor will it.[1] For a beggar's mode of life, which you
describe, is to live possessed of nothing ; but that of a poor
man to live sparingly, and attentive to his work ; and not to
have any superfluity, nor yet, however, to have a deficiency.

Chr. O Ceres ! how blessed is his life which[2] you have
set forth, if after sparing and toiling he shall leave behind him
not even wherewith to be buried.[3]

Pov. You are trying to scoff at and ridicule me, heedless
of being earnest, not knowing that I render men better both
in mind and body than Plutus[4] does. For with him[5] they
are gouty in their feet, and pot-bellied, and thick-legged, and
extravagantly fat ; but with me they are thin and slender, and
grievous to their foes.

Chr. For, no doubt,[6] you bring about the slenderness for
them by hunger.

Pov. Now therefore I will discourse to you respecting so-
briety, and will demonstrate that orderly behaviour dwells
with me, but that riotousness belongs to Plutus.

Chr. In sooth it is very orderly to steal and to dig through
walls.

Bl. Yes, by Jove ;[7] how is it not orderly, if he must escape
notice ?

Pov. Consider therefore the orators in the states, how,

---

[1] " Doch ist so nicht mein Leben bestellt, bei Zeus! nein, wird es
    auch nie sein." *Droysen.*
For this emphatic repetition of the negative, cf. vs. 712, *infra.*
Ran. 1043, 1308. Thesm. 718. Nub. 344, 1470. Theoc. iv. 29 ; v. 14 ; vi
22 ; vii. 39. Menander, *Colax*, Fragm. i. ed. Didot. Soph. Ajax, 970.
Demosth. p. 372, 13 ; 399, 24 ; 413, 16 ; 421, 17. Schneidewin, Hyperid. Orat. p. 42. Krüger, Gr. Gr. § 67, 11. obs. 3.
[2] Cf. vss. 289, 987. Lys. 748, 1022. Aves, 820. Pax, 840. Ach.
829. Vesp. 1377. Hom. Il. xiii. 612, 650. Krüger, Gr. Gr. § 57, 3,
obs. 7.
[3] Cf. Acharn. 691. Eccles. 592. Æsch. Theb. 737. Soph. Col. 790.
Eur. Phœn. 1461. Cicero, Rosc. Amer. ix.
[4] For this construction, see note on Eccles. 701, and cf. ibid.
vs. 810.
[5] See note on Eccles. 275.
[6] " Ja wohl." *Droysen.* See note on Ran. 224.
[7] This verse in Dindorf's edition is bracketed as spurious. Bentley had already pronounced it an unmeaning interpolation. See
Porson, Advers. p. 34.

when they are poor, they are just towards the people and the
state; but when they have become rich out of the public
purse, they immediately become unjust, and plot against the
commons, and make war upon the democracy.

CHR. Well, you don't speak falsely in any of these things,
although[1] you are exceedingly slanderous. But you shall suffer none the less—don't pride[2] yourself on this—because you
seek to convince us of this, that poverty is better than riches.

Pov. And you too are not yet able to refute me about this,
but talk nonsense and flap your wings.

CHR. Why, how is it that all shun you?

Pov. Because I make them better. But you may see it best
in[3] children; for they shun their fathers who are very well-dis-
posed towards them. So difficult a matter is it to distinguish
what is right.

CHR. You will say then[4] that Jupiter does not correctly distinguish what is best; for he too has wealth.[5]

BL. And despatches[6] her to us.

Pov. Nay, O you who are both of you purblind in your
minds with old-fashioned prejudices, Jupiter is certainly poor;
and I will now teach you this clearly. For if he was rich, how
would he, when celebrating the Olympic games himself, where
he assembles all the Greeks every fifth year, have pro·
claimed as conquerors the victorious athletes, having crowned
them with a chaplet of wild olive?[7] And yet he ought[8]
rather *to crown them* with gold, if he was rich?

CHR. By this therefore he certainly shows that he honours
riches. For through parsimony and a wish to spend none of

---

[1] See note on Eccles. 159, and note ᵇ on p. 716.
[2] The parenthetical sentence refers to the οὐ ψεύδει τούτων οὐδίν.
[3] See note on Ran. 762.   [4] See notes on Aves, 161, 1308.
[5] " For all his pelf he keeps to himself." *Wheelwright.*

　" Und der ja behalt sich den Reichthum doch."   *Droysen.*

[6] See Matthiä, Gr. Gr. § 471, 9. Fielding has mistranslated Bentley s Latin, and consequently misrepresented his view of the passage.

[7] The reading varies between κοτίνῳ and κοτίνου. Porson, Dobree,
and Dindorf read κοτινῴ, as if from an adjective κοτινοῦς. It occurs
again in vs. 592. " For adjectives in οῦς, see Blomf. ad Pers. 85.
Elmsley, Med. 1129." *Dobree.*

[8] See note on Thesm. 74. This is not an example of double protasis. For καίτοι, see note on Eccles. 159.

t, he crowns the victors with trifles and lets his wealth remain by him.[1]

Pov. You seek to fix upon him a much more disgraceful thing than poverty, if he, though rich, be so stingy and avaricious.

Chr. Well, may Jupiter utterly destroy you, having crowned you with a chaplet of wild olive!

Pov. To think of your daring[2] to contradict me, that all your blessings are not through poverty!

Chr. One may learn this from Hecate, whether to be rich or to suffer hunger is better. For she says that those who have property and are wealthy send a dinner every month, while the poor people snatch it away before[3] one has set it down. But go and be hanged,[4] and don't mutter any thing more whatever. For you shall not convince me, even if you should convince me.[5]

Pov. "O city of Argos,[6] you hear what he says!"

Chr. Call Pauson, your messmate.

Pov. What[7] shall I do, unhappy woman!

Chr. Go to the devil quickly from us!

Pov. But whither on earth shall I go?

Chr. To the pillory; you ought not to delay, but to make haste.

Pov. Assuredly you will have to send for me hither sometime.[8]

---

[1] "*Divitias sibi servat.*" *Brunck.* "ἐᾶν is used in the same sense by the Scholiast on Av. 1283." *Dobree.*

[2] See Krüger, Gr. Gr. § 55, 1, obs. 6, and note on Nub. 268.

[3] Cf. Ran. 166.

[4] "Nun hol' dich die Pest!" *Droysen.* Cf. vs. 610. Eur. Heracl. 285. Androm. 709, 715. Arist. Ach. 460. Plaut. Men. ii. 2, 21. Thom. Mag. p. 895. "See Taylor on Lycurg. p. 328." *Dobree.*

[5] "Convince a man against his will,
  He's of the same opinion still." *Gay.*
Strato ap. Athen. ix. p. 383, B.,

$$\text{τὸ δ' οὐκ ἂν ταχὺ}$$
$$\text{ἔπεισεν ἡ Πειθὼ μὰ τὴν Γῆν οἶδ' ὅτι.}$$

[6] From the *Telephus* of Euripides. The same line occurs again in Equit. 813.

[7] See note on Lys. 884.

[8] "*Aliquando.*" *Brunck.* "Dereinst.' *Droysen.* See Nub. 1236. Vesp. 1235. Pax 1087, 1187 For ἐνταυθί, see Elmsley, Acharn. 733.

Chr. Then you shall return ; but now go and be hanged! For it is better for me to be rich, and to leave you to wail loudly in your head.[1] [*Exit Poverty.*]

Bl. By Jove, then, I wish, when I am rich, to feast along with my children and my wife ; and going sleek from the bath, after I have bathed, to fart at the artisans and Poverty.

Chr. This cursed wretch is gone. But let you and me convey the god as soon as possible to the temple of Æsculapius to put him to bed in it.[2]

Bl. And let us not delay, lest again some one come and hinder us from doing something useful.[3]

Chr. Boy Cario, you must bring out the bed-clothes, and convey Plutus himself, as is customary, and the other things, as many as are ready prepared in the house. [*Exeunt Chremylus and Blepsidemus.*][4]

Cario (*returning from the temple*). O you old men, who very often at the festival of Theseus[5] have sopped up soup to very little bread, how prosperous you are, how happily you are circumstanced, and the rest of you, as many as have any claim to a good character !

Cho. But what news is there, O good sir, about[6] your

[1] " τὸ κεφαλὴν πρὸς τὸ κλάειν σύναπτε και μηδὲν ἔξω λάμβανε. ' *Scholiast.* Lys. 520, ἔφασκ' ὀτοτύξεσθαι μακρὰ τὴν κεφαλήν. Vesp. 584, κλάειν ἡμεῖς μακρὰ τὴν κεφαλὴν εἰπόντες τῇ διαθήκῃ. Lys. 1222, κωκύσεσθι τὰς τρίχας μακρά. Cf. note on vs. 734, *infra*

[2] " ἐγκαταθήσοντες." *Scholiast.* For the dual of the subject with the plural of the verb, see Matthiä, Gr. Gr. § 301, and cf. vss. 73, 417, 430, 464, 736. " *Ut illio incubet.*" *Brunck.* But ἐγκατακλίνω is a *transitive verb.*

[3] Cf. Eccles. 784. Lys. 20.

[4] There is here a long interval of time, during which Plutus is taken to the temple of Æsculapius and cured of his blindness. In the first edition, probably, the parabasis came in here : at all events a long choral ode must have intervened between vs. 626 and 627.

[5] This feast was held on the eighth day of every month in commemoration of that hero's return from Argolis on that nay of the month of July, on the sixteenth of which was held the Cynœcia, or commemoration of his uniting Attica in one town. the account of which is given by Thucydides, ii. 15.

[6] Soph. Trach. 1122, τῆς μητρὸς ἥκω τῆς ἐμῆς φράσων. Philoc. 439 ἀναξίου γάρ φωτὸς ἐξερήσομαι. Elect. 317. τοῦ κασιγνήτου τί φής; Hom. Od. Λ. 174, εἰπὲ δέ μοί πατρός τε καὶ υἱέος. In these constructions the genitive per se expresses what *belongs to*, or *concerns*, the persons mentioned. See Krgüer, Gr. Gr. § 47, 10, obs. 8. Her

friends? for you appear to have come as a messenger of some good news.

CA. My master is most prosperously circumstanced,—or rather Plutus himself; for instead of being blind, he has been[1] restored to sight, and has been made clear-sighted in the pupils of his eyes, having found Æsculapius a friendly physician.[2]

CHO. You tell me a matter for joy, you tell me a matter for shouting.

CA. 'Tis your lot to rejoice, whether you wish it or no.

CHO. I will loudly praise Æsculapius blest in his children, and[3] a great light to mortals. [*Enter wife of Chremylus.*]

WIFE. What in the world means the shout? Is some good news announced? for, longing for this, I have been sitting in the house this long while, waiting for this fellow.

CA. Quickly, quickly, bring wine, mistress, in order that you yourself also may drink,—and you are very fond[4] of doing it, for I bring you all blessings in a lump.

WIFE. Why, where are they?

CA. You will soon learn by what is said.

WIFE. Be quick and finish then some time or other what you are for saying.

CA. Hear then; for I will tell you the whole affair from the foot to the head.[5]

WIFE. Nay, not on my head, pray.[6]

CA. Not the blessings which have now taken place?

mann, Vig. Append. p. 703. Bernhardy, W. S. p. 150, 152. Modern grammarians have very justly rejected the very unphilosophical ellipse of a preposition.

[1] "From the *Phineus* of Sophocles." *Scholiast.* Cf. Æsch. Eum. 104, and Blomf. Gloss. P. V. 508. "See Aldi Hort. Adon. p. 97, b., and Loheck, Phryn. p. 34." *Dobree.*

[2] Eur. Danaid. Fragm. ix., τίνος θεῶν βροτῶν τε πρευμενοῦς τυχών.

[3] The position of the words in the original is very remarkable.

[4] Cf. Thesm. 733—738.

[5] Plaut. Epid. v. 1, 16, "Contempla, Epidice. Usque ab unguiculo ad capillum summum festivissima est." "Aristophanes here rallies the extravagant superstition of the Athenians, who were afraid of hearing even good news, when told in an ominous manner. By an apt collocation of the words, he has introduced the very phrase εἰς κεφαλήν σοι, which was used as an imprecation, which immediately frightens the old woman, and drives both Plutus and her curiosity out of her head, with the fear of the omen." *Fielding.*

[6] See Krüger, Gr. Gr. § 62, 3, obs. 12.

WIFE. Nay, rather, not the troubles.[1]

CA. As soon as we came to the god, conveying a man, at that time most miserable, but now blessed and fortunate, if there ever was one,[2] we first conveyed him to the sea, and then washed him.

WIFE. By Jupiter, then he was fortunate, an old man washed in the cold sea !

CA. Then we went to the temple of the god. And when our wafers and preparatory sacrifices were offered on the altar, and our cake in the flame of Vulcan,[3] we laid Plutus on a couch, as was proper, while each of us began putting his mattress in order.

WIFE. And were there any others also in need of the god ?

CA. Yes, there was one Neoclides,[4] who is indeed blind, but out-does[5] in stealing those who see : and many others having all sorts of diseases. But when the sacrist[6] of the god put out the lamps and ordered us to sleep, telling us if any one should hear a noise, he must be silent, we all laid down in an orderly manner. And I could not sleep · but a pot of porridge which was lying a little way off from the head of an old woman strongly affected me, towards which I desired exceedingly to creep. Then on looking up I see the priest snatching away[7] the cakes and dried figs from the sacred table. And after this he went round to all the altars round about, if any where a cake might be left ; and then he consecrated these—into a sack.[8] And I, supposing[9] there

---

[1] She puns on the word πράγματα. See vs. 649.

[2] "The Scholiast rightly observes that εἴπερ τις ἄλλος is more usual." *Dobree.* Nub. 356, εἴπερ τινὶ κἄλλῳ. See Krüger, Gr. Gr. § 69, 32, obs. 14.

[3] Eur. Iph. Aul. 1601, ἐπεὶ δ' ἅπαν κατηνθρακώθη θῦμ' ἐν Ἡφαίστου φλογί. Ion, 707, καλλίφλογα πέλανον ἐπὶ πυρὶ καθαγνίσας.

[4] Cf. vs. 716, 717. Eccles. 254, 398. According to the Scholiast, he had been guilty of appropriating the public money.

[5] Cf. Equit. 659. Aves, 363.

[6] "ὁ προπ. τ. θ. is *ædituus Æsculapii, ædituus ædis Æsculapii, ædituus ab Æsculapio :* for these formulæ are all found in ancient inscriptions." *Fischer.*

[7] This will remind the reader of the history of Bel and the Dragon.

[8] "Dann aber weiht er alles das——in den Sack hinein." *Droysen.*

[9] "Und Ich, in der Meinung, so zu thun, sei wer weiss wie fromm." *Droysen*

was great piety in the thing, got up towards the pot of porridge.

WIFE. O most daring[1] of men, were you not afraid of the god?

CA. Yes, by the gods, lest he might get to the pot before me, with his garlands on ; for his priest taught me that beforehand.[2] But the old woman, when she heard my noise, stretched forth[3] her hand ; and then I hissed and seized it with my teeth, as if I were an Æsculapian[4] snake. But she immediately drew back her hand again, and lay down, having wrapped herself up quietly, farting for fear more offensively than a weasel. And then I swallowed greedily the greater part of the porridge :[5] and then, when I was full, I rested.

WIFE. But did not the god come to you?

CA. Not yet. And after this now I did a very laughable thing indeed ; for as he was approaching, I farted very loudly ; for my belly[6] had been blown out.

WIFE. Doubtless he was immediately disgusted at you on account of this.

CA. No ; but a certain Iaso,[7] who was following along with him, blushed a little, and Panacea took hold of her nose and turned away her head ; for I fart no frankincense.

WIFE. But he himself?

[1] "Du verwegenster Mensch." *Droysen.*

[2] "Denn es hatte das der Priester zuvor mir klar gemacht."
Droysen
See vs. 676—681.

[3] "ἐξέτεινε." *Scholiast.* The reading of this line involves the disputed point, whether the Attics ever elide the ι of the dative singular. The affirmative is maintained by Porson, (Præf. Hec. p. 24,) Hermann, (Hec. 906, Doctr. Metr. p. 56,) and Monk (Alc. 1123); the negative by Elmsley (Heracl. 693, Soph. Rex, 1445) and Lobeck (Ajax, 801). See Gretton's Elmsleiana, p. 41. Krüger pronounces it "extremely doubtful." No example, I believe, has been found in ancient inscriptions. See Rose's "Greek Inscriptions," p. 67. The ι of the dative *plural*, on the other hand, is *never* elided in Attic Greek, though frequently in Epic. See Krüger, Gr. Gr. 2nd part, § 12, 2, obs. 3.

[4] See Liddell's Lex. in voc. παρώας.

[5] See Krüger, Gr. Gr. § 47, 28, obs. 9. Dorville, Char. p. 281.

[6] Hegiochus ap. Athen. ix. p. 408, B., ἔτνος κυάμινον διότι τὴν μὲν γαστέρα φυσᾷ.

[7] "Iaso and Panacea, daughters of Æsculapius ; here two female friends of the priests." *Voss.* See Aristoph. *Amphiaraus*, Fragm.]

CA. No, by Jove, he did not even take notice of it.

WIFE. Then you represent the deity to be boorish.

CA. No, by Jove, not I ; but a dung-eater.[1]

WIFE. Ha, you wretch !

CA. After this I immediately covered myself up for fear ; while he went round in a circuit inspecting all the maladies very regularly. Then a servant set before him a small stone mortar and a pestle and a small chest.

WIFE. Of stone ?[2]

CA. No, by Jove, certainly not, not[3] the little chest.

WIFE. But how did you see, the devil take[4] you ! who say you were wrapped up ?

CA. Through my little threadbare cloak ; for, by Jupiter,[5] it has[6] no few holes. First of all he began to pound up a plaster[7] for Neoclides, having thrown in three heads of Tenian[8] garlic. Then he beat them up in the mortar, mixing[9] along with them gum and squill ; and then he moistened it with Sphettian[10] vinegar, and spread it over, having turned his eyelids inside out, that he might be pained the more. And he crying out and bawling, jumped up and ran away, while the god laughed and said : " Sit there now,[11] plastered over, that I may stop[12] your excusing yourself on oath from the Assembly."[13]

WIFE. How very[14] patriotic and wise the god is !

[1] See Porson, Advers. p. 65. "For he has to see, examine, and taste potion, pill, urine—and worse." *Droysen.*

[2] The interest the good woman takes in the parts which are not at all essential to the story, is extremely characteristic of her."
Droysen.

[3] See note on vs. 551, *supra.*

[4] See note on Thesm. 879.

[5] "μά is to be referred to οὐκ, as Brunck rightly observes. See vs. 343, and Alexis ap. Athen. vi. p. 258, E." *Dobree.*

[6] For this use of the imperfect, cf. vs. 801, *infra.* Ran. 811. Pax. 141, and Bernhardy, W. S. p. 375.

[7] See Blomf. Gl. Prom. V. 488.

[8] Dobree proposes Τηνίας, referring to Elmsley, Quart. Rev. No. xiv. p. 419—460.

[9] See Mus. Crit. ii. p. 24.   [10] Cf. Athen. ii. sect. 76.

[11] See note on Thesm. 1001.   [12] See note on Lys. 1243.

[13] By giving him a valid excuse. Cf. 747.
" Dass du künftig schwörst,
Ich hinderte dich zu kommen in die Ekklesie." *Droysen.*

[14] See note on Aves, 924.

Ca. After this he sat down beside Plutus :[1] and first he handled his head, and then he took a clean napkin and wiped his eyclids all round : and Panacea covered his head and the whole of his face with a purple cloth. Then the god whistled ; then two snakes rushed forth from the temple, prodigious in size.[2]

Wife. O ye friendly gods !

Ca. And these two gently crept under[3] the purple cloth and began to lick his eyelids all round, as it appeared to me. And before you could have drank up ten half-pints of wine, mistress, Plutus was standing up having the use of his eyes : and I clapped my hands for joy, and began to wake my master. But the god immediately took himself[4] out of sight, and the snakes *took themselves* into the temple; while those who were lying in bed near him, you can't think how[5] they began embracing Plutus, and kept awake the whole night, until day dawned. But I praised the god very much, because he had quickly caused Plutus to see, while he made Neoclides more blind than *before*.

Wife. How much[6] power you possess, O king and master ! But [*to Cario*] tell me, where is Plutus ?

Ca. He is coming. But there was a prodigious[7] crowd about him. For all those who were formerly just, and had a scanty subsistence, were embracing him and shaking hands with him for joy ; but as many as were rich, and had much property, not having acquired their subsistence justly, were contracting their brows,[8] and at the same time looking an-

[1] See Liddell's Lex. in voc. Πλούτων.

[2] μέγεθος is the "Accusativus Respectûs." Cf. Aves, 1000, 1251, 1700. Pax, 229, 674, 675. Equit. 41, and see Krüger, Gr. Gr. § 46, 4. Lhardy ad Herod. ii. 19. Arnold, Greek Exercises, § 134. Bernhardy (W. S. p. 117) calls it "The Accusative for defining the quality."

[3] See note on vs. 504, *supra*.

[4] We might rather have expected the simple passive.

[5] See note on Ran. 54.

[6] For the construction, see Krüger, Gr. Gr. § 50, 11, obs. 1. Bernhardy, W. S. p. 325.

[7] See Krüger, Gr. Gr. § 51, 10, obs. 12, and compare note on Vys. 198.

[8] Aristænetus, i. 17, p. 44, μὴ σκυθρώπαζε καλή γε οὖσα, μηδὲ τὰς ὀφρῦς ἄναγε, εἰ γὰρ φοβερὰ γένοιο, ἧττον ἔση καλή. Cf. Antiphanes ap. Athen. vi. p. 226, E.

gry. But the others were following behind with garlands
on, laughing and shouting in triumph; and the shoe of the
old men was resounding[1] with their steps in good time.[2] But
come, do you all together with one accord dance, and leap,
and form a chorus; for no one will announce to you when you
go in that there is no meal in the bag.

WIFE. And I, by Hecate, wish to crown you for your good
news[3] with a string of cracknels,[4] who have announced such
tidings.

CA. Do not then delay any longer, for the men are now
near to the door

WIFE. Come then, let me go in and fetch some sweetmeats[5] to be showered as it were over his newly purchased
eyes. [*Exit wife of Chremylus.*]

CA. But I wish to go to meet them. [*Exit Cario.*]

PLU. (*entering, accompanied by Chremylus and a great
crowd of people*). And first I salute[6] the sun, and then the
illustrious soil[7] of the august Pallas, and the whole land of
Cecrops, which received me. I am ashamed of my misfortunes, because I associated with such men[8] without my knowing it, but shunned those who were worthy of my society,
knowing nothing, ob, unhappy me! How wrongly I acted
both in that case[9] and in this! But I will reverse them all
again, and henceforth show to all men that I unwillingly gave
myself up to the wicked.

CHR. (*to some by-stander*). Go to the devil! How troublesome a thing are the friends who appear immediately, when
one is prosperous! For they nudge me with their elbows, and

---

[1] Eur. Med. 1180, στέγη πυκνοῖσιν ἐκτύπει δρομήμασιν. The passive voice is rare; but compare Thesm. 995.

[2] Cf. Thesm. 985.   [3] For the construction, cf. Equit. 647.

[4] Lys. 646, ἔχουσ' ἰσχάδων ὁρμαθόν.

[5] See Liddell's Lex. in voc. κατάχυσμα. For the construction,
cf. Pax, 235.

[6] Dindorf remarks on the abruptness of this address. It would
seem to be a continuation of an address begun before he left the
temple, wherein he had been returning thanks to Æsculapius.

[7] Hemsterhuis compares Eur. Andr. 1086. Iph. T. 972. Æsch.
Choeph. 1035—1037. See Mus. Crit. ii. p. 117.

[8] οἴοις = ὅτι τοιούτοις. See Jelf, Gr. Gr. § 804, 9. Matthiä, §
480, obs. 3. Hermann, Vig. n. 194.

[9] ἐκεῖνα, his associating with the wicked; ταῦτα, his shunning the
good. Cf. note on Lys. 134.

bruise[1] my shins, each of them exhibiting[2] some good will. For who did not address me ? What a crowd of old men was there not around me in the market-place? [*Enter wife of Chremylus.*]

WIFE. O dearest of men ! Welcome, both you, and you ! Come now, for it is the custom let me take and pour[3] these sweetmeats over you.

PLU. By no means ; for on my first entry into the house, and .when I have recovered my eye-sight, it is in no wise becoming to carry out any thing, but rather to carry in.

WIFE. Then, pray, will you not accept my sweetmeats ?

PLU. Yes, in the house, by the fireside, as is the custom. Then also we may avoid the vulgarity of the thing ; for it is not becoming for the dramatic poet[4] to throw dried figs and sweetmeats to the spectators and then force them to laugh at this.

WIFE. You say very well ; for see ! there's Dexinicus[5] standing up, with the intention of snatching at the dried figs ! [*Exeunt Plutus, Chremylus, wife, and attendants.*]

CA. (*coming out of the house*).   How delightful it is, sirs, to fare prosperously ! especially if one has brought out nothing from home.[6]   For a heap[7] of blessings has rushed into[8] our house, without our committing any injustice.   Under these circumstances[9] wealth is a very delightful thing.   Our meal-

---

[1] "φλῶσι· συντρίβουσι, θλίβουσι, ξύουσι." *Scholiast.*

[2] See notes on Vesp. 554. Ran. 1075. Eur. Orest. 1694, χωρεῖτε νῦν ἕκαστος. Hom. Il. H. 175, ἐσημήναντο ἕκαστος. Cf. vs. 1196, *infra.*

[3] Cf. note on Lys. 864.

[4] διδασκάλῳ—προβαλόντα. Cf. note on vs. 287. Aristophanes has here forgotten what he had formerly done himself. See Acharn. 805—807. Pax, 963.

[5] "Dexinicus is otherwise unknown." *Droysen.* The reading, however, is very uncertain. The early editions mostly exhibit ὡς δὲ Ξένικος, of whom no more is known than of Dexinicus. For this use of the imperfect, see Bernhardy, W. S. p. 374.

[6] i. e. without any outlay. "ἐξενεγκόντα· δαπανήσαντα." *Scholiast.*

[7] Achilles Tatius, vi. c. 4, ἥκω σοι φέρων ἀγαθῶν σωρόν Synes. Epist. 94, ἀγαθῶν ἑσμός.

[8] Xenarchus ap. Athen. ii. p. 63, F., ἀλάστωρ τ' εἰσπέπαικε. Cf. Athen. i. p. 7, F. Soph. Rex, 1252.

[9] "Es ist so das Reichsein doch ein gar zu süsses Ding." *Droysen.* "There is a difficulty in οὕτω, which the editors have not understood. οὕτω is *nempe*, and refers to οὐδὲν ἠδικηκόσιν. *Cum nihil in-*

chest is full of wheaten flour, and our wine-jars of dark wine with a high perfume.[1] And all our vessels are full of silver and gold, so that I wonder. And our oil-jar is full of oil; and our flasks are full of unguents, and our garret of dried figs. And every vinegar-cruet, and platter, and pot has become of brass; and our rotten, fishy chargers you may see of silver. And our lantern has suddenly become of ivory. And we servants play at even and odd with golden staters; and we no longer wipe ourselves with stones,[2] but always with garlic, through luxury. And at present my master is sacrificing within a swine, and a goat, and a ram, with a chaplet on : but the smoke drove me out ; for I was not able to remain within ; for it stung my eye-lids. [*Enter a Just Man attended by his servant.*]

J. M. Follow with me,[3] my little boy, that we may go to the god. [*Enter Chremylus.*]

Chr. Ha ! who is this who approaches ?

J. M. A man, formerly wretched, but now prosperous.

Chr. It is evident that you are one of the good, as it appears.

J. M. Most certainly.

Chr. Then, what do you want ?

J. M. I have come to the god : for he is the author of great blessings to me. For having received a considerable property from my father, I used to assist those of my friends[4] who were in want, thinking it to be useful for life.[5]

justi feceris divitiis pollere res est jucunda." *Boissonade.* Cf. Aves, 656, 1217, 1503. Bentley, Brunck, Porson, and Dindorf consider the line to be spurious. Hemsterhuis proposed ὄντως in place of οὕτω. There are no *grammatical* reasons against joining οὕτω with ἡδύ, only that Cario has not *yet enumerated* the blessings.

[1] Pherecrates ap. Athen. vi. p. 269, B., πλήρεις κύλικας οἴνου μέλανος ἀνθοσμίου. Cf. Eccl. 1124. Ran. 1150.

[2] Cf. Pax, 1230. Macho ap. Athen. xiii. p. 578, E., and Athen. xiii. p. 584, C. Adag. 896,

τρεῖς εἰσὶν ἱκανοὶ πρωκτὸν ἐκμάξαι λίθοι,
ἂν ὦσι τραχεῖς· ἂν δὲ λεῖοι, τέσσαρες.

[3] For this construction Dobree refers to Plato, Menex. p. 235, B. Xenoph. Hellen. v. 2, 19. Lexicon Sangerm. ap. Bekk. Anecd. i. p. 368.

[4] Vs. 928, ὑμῶν ὁ βουλόμενος. Aves, 1312, ἐκείνων τοὺς προσιόντας. Eccles. 195, τῶν ῥητόρων ὁ τοῦτ' ἀναπείσας. Eurip. *Phryxis*, Fragm. xv., βροτῶν οἱ βλέποντες. See Bernhardy, W. S. p. 155.

[5] "Which course I judged to be of use in life." *Wheelwright.* Terence, Andr. I. i. 38, "Id arbitror apprime in vità esse utile."

CHR. Doubtless your money soon failed[1] you.

J. M. Just so.

CHR. Therefore after this you were wretched.

J. M. Just so. And I thought I should have as really firm friends, if ever I might want them, those whom I had before done kindness to when they were in want: but they began to avoid me, and pretended not[2] to see me any longer.

CHR. And also[3] laughed at you, I well know.

J. M. Just so. For the dearth[4] which was in my vessels ruined me.

CHR. But not now.

J. M. Wherefore with good reason I have come hither to the god, to offer up my vows.

CHR. But what has the threadbare cloak to do with the god,[5] which this servant is carrying in your retinue?[6] tell me.

J. M. This also I am coming to the god to dedicate.

CHR. Were you initiated,[7] then, in the Great Mysteries in it?

J. M. No; but I shivered in it for thirteen years.

CHR. But your shoes?

J. M. These also have weathered the storm along with me.

---

[1] See Porson, Hec. 1141.

[2] So Pax, 1051, μή νυν ὁρᾶν δοκῶμεν αὐτόν, *then let us pretend not to see him.* Cf. Equit. 1146. Ran. 564. Eur. Med. 66. Hippol. 465. Iph. T. 956. Rhes. 684. Æsch. Prom. V. 394. Herod. i. 10. Plato, Rep. viii. p. 555, E. Lucian, *Timon,* c. 5, οἱ δὲ πόρρωθεν ἰδόντες ἑτέραν ἐκτρέπονται, δυσάντητον καὶ ἀποτρόπαιον θέαμα ὄψεσθαι ὑπολαμβάνοντες, τὸν οὐ πρὸ πολλοῦ σωτῆρα καὶ εὐεργέτην αὐτῶν γεγενημένον. Eur. Med. 561, πένητα φεύγει πᾶς τις ἐκποδὼν φίλος.

[3] "καὶ is to be translated by *and also,* when it adds a clause in which the verb of the foregoing clause, or a synonymous one, occurs. Otherwise καὶ—δὲ corresponds to our *and also.* In these, καὶ means *also,* and δὲ means *and,* (in negation, οὐδὲ—δὲ,) and they *always* (except in Epic Greek) have an emphatic word *between* them opposed to a foregoing one." *Krüger.* See Porson, Orest. 614. For εὖ οἶδ᾽ ὅτι, see note on Lys. 154.

[4] " *Quum squalent exinanita vasa nihilque in iis superest, quod mensam luculenter instruat.*" *Hemsterhuis.* "Das verschimmelte Hausgeräth dekreditirte mich.'' *Voss.*

[5] " *Quid facit, quid pertinet ad deum Plutum?*" *Hemsterhuis.*

[6] See Bernhardy, W. S. p. 254.

[7] "It was the custom to dedicate the garment in which one had been initiated in the mysteries to some deity." *Droysen.* See Bernhardy, W. S. p. 190

CHR. Then were you bringing these also to dedicate them ?

J. M. Yes, by Jupiter.

CHR. You have come with very pretty[1] presents for the god. [*Enter an informer attended by his witness.*]

INF. Ah me, unhappy! How I am undone, miserable man, and thrice unhappy,[2] and four times, and five times, and twelve times, and ten thousand times! alas! alas! with so powerful[3] a fate have I been mingled.

CHR. O Apollo, averter of evil, and ye friendly gods! what in the world is the misfortune which the man has suffered?

INF. Why, have I not now suffered shocking things, who have lost every thing out of my house through this god, who shall be blind again, unless law-suits be wanting.

J. M. I imagine I pretty nearly see into the matter; for a man is approaching who is badly off; and he seems to be of the bad stamp.[4]

CHR. By Jupiter, then, he is rightly[5] ruined.

INF. Where, where is this fellow who singly promised he would immediately make us all rich, if he were to recover his sight again[6] as before? On the contrary, he has[7] ruined some much more.

CHR. And whom, pray, has he treated thus?

INF. Me here.

CHR. Were you of the number of the wicked ones and housebreakers?

INF. By Jove, there is certainly[8] no good in any of you, and it must be that you have[9] my money.

[1] See Krüger, Gr. Gr. § 69, 15, obs. 1.

[2] See Porson, Præf. Hec. p. 30. Cf. Ach. 1024. Eccles. 1098. Ran. 19. Pax, 1271. Thesm. 209, 875. Pollux, vi. 165.

[3] Properly an epithet of wine which will bear mixing with a great quantity of water. Soph. Antig. 1311, δειλαίᾳ δὲ συγκέκραμαι δύᾳ. Cf. Æsch. Cho. 744.

[4] Cf. vs. 957, *infra*. Ran. 726. Acharn. 517.

[5] Cf. Ach. 1050. Pax, 271, 285. Equit. 1180. Demosth. p. 141, 14. Plato, Symp. p. 174, E. Krüger, Gr. Gr. § 56, 8, obs. 2. Bernhardy, W. S. p. 476. Hermann, Vig. n. 229. Dorville, Char. p. 297.

[6] Cf. vs. 221, 113. Pax, 997, 1327. Soph. Rex, 132. Plato, Gorg. p. 489, D.

[7] See Krüger, Gr. Gr. § 56, 3, obs. 1. Bernhardy, W. S. p. 310. Donaldson, Complete Greek Grammar, § 390.

[8] "οὐ μὲν οὖν, *non utique, haudquaquam.*" *Fischer.* See Krüger, Gr. Gr. § 64, 5, obs. 4.

[9] See note on Thesm. 882.

Ca. O Ceres, how insolently the informer has come in ! It is evident that he is ravenously hungry.[1]

Inf. You cannot be too[2] quick in going speedily to the market-place ; for you must there be racked upon the wheel and declare your villanies.[3]

Ca. Then you'll suffer for it.

J. M. By Jupiter the Preserver, this god is of great value to all the Greeks, if he shall utterly destroy the informers the wretches,[4] in a wretched way.[5]

Inf. Ah me, miserable! Are you also laughing at me, who are an accomplice ? for whence have you got this garment ? But yesterday I saw you with a threadbare cloak on.

J. M. I care nothing for you : for see ! I wear this ring,[6] having purchased it from Eudemus[7] for a drachma.

Chr. But it is not possible *to wear one* against an in- former's[8] bite.

Inf. Is not this great insolence ? You mock me, but you have not stated what you are doing here. For you are here for no good.

Chr. Certainly not, by Jove, for your *good;* be well assured.

Inf. For, by Jove, you will dine at my cost.

[1] See Aulus Gellius, N. A. xvi. 3, 9.
[2] See note on Eccles. 118
[3] See note on Nub. 589.
[4] Aristophanes has been obliged to commit what looks very like a solecism, in order to bring κακοὺς κακῶς together. See note on Ran. 1388. For εἰ, see Elmsley, Acharn. 338.
[5] See note on Eccles. 730.
[6] See note on Lys. 1027. Antiphanes ap. Athen. iii. p. 123, B.,
ἐὰν δ' ἄρα στρέφῃ με περὶ τὴν γαστέο'. ὃ τὸν ὀμφαλὸν, παρὰ Φερτάτου δακτύλιός ἐστί μοι δραχμῆς.
[7] Eudemus was a manufacturer of these rings. For the genitive, see note on Thesm. 425.

[8] "Doch ist darin nichts gegen der Sykophanten Biss." *Droysen.*
" *Sed nullum reperias contra sycophantæ morsum.*" *Brunck.*

Dobree commends this translation of Brunck's, and cites Eur. Andr. 268. Med. 516. Diogenes Laert. vi. 51. Arist. Thesm. 530. Phi- lostr. Her. p. 14. See Bernhardy, W. S. p. 213. Dawes, M. C. p. 380. ed. Kidd, and for the objective genitive, see Pax, 133. Soph. Ajax, 2. Eur. Hippol. 716. Demosth. p. 41, 5. Xenoph. Anab iv 5, 13. Krüger, Gr. Gr. § 47, 7, obs. 5. The construction of Soph. Phil. 643, is quite different. See Schneidewin's note on the passage.

CHR. For the sake of truth[1] may you burst, together with your witness, filled with nothing.[2]

INF. Do you deny it ? There is a great quantity[3] of slices of salt-fish and roast meat within, you most abominable fellows. [*Sniffs.*] uhu, uhu, uhu, uhu, uhu, uhu.[4]

CHR. Do you smell any thing,[5] you poor wretch ?

J. M. The cold, perhaps ; since he has on[6] such a threadbare cloak.

INF. Is this bearable[7] then, O Jupiter and ye gods, that these should commit outrages upon me ? Ah me ! how grieved I am that, good and patriotic as I am, I fare badly.

CHR. You patriotic and good ?

INF. As never man was.

CHR. Well now, answer me when asked—

INF. What ?[8]

CHR. Are you a husbandman ?

INF. Do you suppose me to be so mad ?

CHR. Or a merchant ?[9]

INF. Yes, I pretend to be,[10] upon occasion.

CHR. Well then, did you learn any trade ?

INF. No, by Jove.

CHR. How then, or whence, did you live,[11] if you do nothing ?

INF. I am manager of all the affairs of the state and private affairs.

[1] See Liddell's Lex. in voc. ἀλήθεια. For ὡς δὴ in wishes, see Hom. Od. A. 217.

[2] "I remember Porson's translating it, ' *May you burst—but not with eating.*' διαῤῥαγῆναι is sometimes used as an hyperbole, as in Equit. 701. [Pax, 32.] Alexis ap. Athen. vi. p. 258, E. Phœnisides, ibid. x. p. 415, E. Anaxilas, ibid. x. p. 416, E." *Dobree.* "*May you and your witness burst your bellies—but not with meat.*" *Fielding.*

[3] See note on Thesm. 281. Xenoph. Cyrop. i. 1, 5, σφενδονητῶν πάμπολύ τι χρῆμα.

[4] These are expressed by the nasal organs in pairs, and a longer breath is given to the second of each, so as to make an iambus.

[5] "ὀσφραίνω τοῦδε καὶ τόδε. Εὔπολις Αἰξίν." *Priscian.*

[6] See Priscian, xviii. p. 1193, 15, ed. Putsch.

[7] Cf. Acharn. 618. Soph. Rex, 439, and see note on Thesm. 520.

[8] See Hermann, Vig. n. 25.

[9] See Krüger, Gr. Gr. § 69, 4, obs. 4. Liddell's Lex. in voc. ἀλλά, II. i.

[10] Cf. Eccles. 1027.

[11] Cf. Aves, 1434.

Chr. You? Wherefore?[1]

Inf. I please to do so.

Chr. How then, you house-breaker,[2] can you be good, if, when it in no wise concerns you,[3] you are then hated?

Inf. Why, does it not concern me,[4] you booby, to benefit my own city as far as I be able?

Chr. Then is to be a meddling busybody to benefit it?

Inf. Nay, rather, to aid the established[5] laws, and, if any one do wrong, not to permit it.

Chr. Does not the state, then, purposely appoint judges to preside?

Inf. But who is the accuser?

Chr. Any one who pleases.

Inf. Then I am he; so that the affairs of the state have devolved on me.

Chr. Then, by Jove, it has a sorry patron. But would you not prefer that,[6] to keep quiet and live idle?

Inf. Nay, you are describing the life of a sheep, if there shall appear no amusement in life.

Chr. And would you not learn better?

Inf. Not even if you were to give[7] me Plutus himself, and the silphium of Battus.[8]

Chr. Quickly lay down your cloak.

Ca. (*to the informer*). Ho you! he is speaking to you.

Chr. Next take off your shoes.

Ca. (*to the informer*). He says all this to you.

---

[1] See Liddell's Lex. in voc. μανθάνω. Krüger, Gr. Gr. § 56, 8, obs. 3. Bernhardy, W. S. p. 476. Herm. Vig. n. 194.

[2] Plaut. Pseud. iv. 2, 22, " Parietum perfossor."

[3] See note on Lys. 13, and for εἶτα, cf. note on Thesm. 885.

[4] Some MSS. and editions exhibit μοι—εὐεργετεῖν μ'. Dobree compares Soph. Rex, 823, [350.] Philoc. 369. Add Elect. 958. Eur. Med. 1236. For this construction, see Classical Museum, No. xxv. p. 243.

[5] Cf. Demosth. p. 720, 14. Xenoph. Mcm. iv. 4, 16

[6] See note on Thesm. 477.

[7] Cf. Nub. 108. Acharn. 966.

[8] Battus led out a colony from Thera, an island in the Ægean Sea, and founded the city of Cyrene in Africa, and was its first king. See Herod. iv. 154. Silphium formed a great branch of Grecian commerce with Cyrene. See Catull. vii. 4. The silphium of Battus was as proverbial as the gold mountains of the Persian king. For this position of the article, see note on Thesm. 1101.

INF. Well now, let any of you that pleases come hither against me.

CA. "Then I am he." [*Seizes the informer and strips him of his cloak and shoes.*]

INF. Ah me, miserable! I am stripped in[1] the day time.

CA. For you do not hesitate to get a livelihood by meddling with other people's business.

INF. (*to his witness*). Do you see what he is doing? I call you to witness this.[2] [*His witness runs off.*]

CHR. But the witness whom[3] you brought is running away.

INF. Ah me, I have been caught alone.

CA. Do you bawl now?

INF. Ah me, again and[4] again!

CA. Do you [*to the Just Man*] give me your threadbare cloak, that I may put it on this informer.

J. M. Certainly not; for it has been this long while consecrated to Plutus.

CA. Where then will it be better dedicated than around a knavish man and house-breaker? But Plutus it is fitting to adorn with grand dresses.

J. M. But what shall one make of the shoes? tell me.

CA. These also I will instantly nail fast to this man's forehead, as if to a wild[5] olive.

INF. I'll begone; for I perceive I am much weaker than you. But if I find a comrade, even of fig-tree wood,[6] I will to-day make this powerful god give me satisfaction, because he singly and alone is manifestly putting down the democracy, having neither prevailed upon the Senate of the citizens nor the Assembly.

J. M. Well now, since you are marching with my panoply on, run to the bath, and then stand there in the front and

[1] Cf. Demosth. p. 1125, ed. Reiske.
[2] See note on Ran. 528.
[3] See notes on Thesm. 502. Nub. 863.
[4] See Herm. Vig. n. 235.
[5] "They especially chose the strong-lived olive to hang up their consecrated gifts on, for it took no hurt, though it were stuck all over with nails." *Voss.* Cf. Virgil, Æn. xii. 768.
[6] i. e. a cudgel, but with a pun on his own profession (συκοφαντρία), as in Vesp. 145. Ach. 726, 826. The commentators, however, understand σύζυγος literally, and take σύκινος to mean *weak*.

warm[1] yourselt. For I also once held this post. [*Exit informer.*]

CHR. But the bath-man will take and drag him[2] out of doors by the testicles ; for when he has seen him he will perceive that he is of that[3] bad stamp. But let us two go in, that you may offer up your vows to the god.[4] [*Exeunt Chremylus and Just Man.*]

OLD WOMAN (*entering and bearing some cakes on a platter*). O dear old men, have we really come to the house[5] of this new god, or have we altogether missed the road ?

CHO. Nay, know that you have come to the very door,[6] my little girl ; for you ask seasonably.[7]

OLD WOM. Come then, let me summon[8] some one of those within. [*Enter Chremylus.*]

CHR. Certainly not ;[9] for I myself have come out. But you must tell me for what in particular you have come.

OLD WOM. O dearest sir, I have suffered dreadful and unjust things : for since what time this god began[10] to have the use of his eyes, he has made my life to be insupportable.[11]

CHR. What's the matter ? I suppose you also were an informeress[12] amongst women ?

OLD WOM. No, by Jupiter, not I.

CHR. Or did you not drink in your letter,[13] having obtained it by lot ?

---

[1] Alciphron, Ep. i. 23, δραμὼν ἐπὶ τὸ βαλανεῖον ἐθερόμην.

[2] Cf. Equit. 772. Aves, 442, and vs. 1053, *infra*. Prose writers use the *middle* form in this construction. See Bernhardy, W. S. p. 147. Krüger, Gr. Gr. § 47, 12, and compare note on Nub. 689.

[3] Compare vs. 862, *supra*. ἐκεῖνος in such constructions denotes *celebrity* or *notoriety*. Cf. Vesp. 236. Eurip. Troad. 1188. Isocr. de Pace, p. 172. Demosth. Coron. p. 301, 19. Krüger, Gr. Gr. § 51, 7, obs. 7. Bernhardy, W. S. p. 279.

[4] A rare construction. See Thom. M. p. 396. Bernhardy, W. S. p. 86.

[5] Cf. Soph. Elect. 1104. Rex, 934. And for this position of the demonstrative, see note on Aves, 813. [6] Cf. Ran. 436.

[7] An intentional ambiguity ; as ὡρικῶς also means *like a pretty girl, prettily*. The old woman had come upon the stage in a girlish dress, and tricked out like a coquette. [8] See note on Lys. 864

[9] "*There's no need of calling any one.*" Fielding. For ἐχρῆν see note on Thesm 74.   [10] Cf. vs. 114, 1173.

[11] See note on vs. 197, *supra*.   [12] See note on Eccles. 713.

[13] The passage will be intelligible enough on referring to Eccles 982—986. Cf. vs. 277, *supra*. See also Krüger, Gr. Gr. § 69, 4, obs. 4

OLD WOM. You are mocking me ; but I burn with love,[1] unhappy woman.

CHR. Will you not then quickly tell me what is your love?

OLD WOM. Hear then ! I had a dear youth, poor, indeed, but, for the rest,[2] good looking, and handsome, and good. For if I wanted anything, he used to perform everything for me decently and well, while I assisted him in all his wants in the same manner.

CHR. But what was it he especially wanted of you, on each occasion ?

OLD WOM. Not much ; for he was marvellously respectful to me. But he used to ask for[3] twenty drachmæ of silver for a mantle, and eight for shoes ; and he used to entreat me to purchase a tunic[4] for his sisters, and a little mantle for his mother ; and he used to beg for four medimni of wheat.

CHR. Certainly, by Apollo, this is not much which[5] you have mentioned ; but it is evident that he respected you.

OLD WOM. And these moreover he said he asked of me, not on account of lewdness,[6] but for affection, that while wearing my mantle, he might think on[7] me.

CHR. You describe a man most marvellously[8] in love with you.

[1] Cf. Macho ap. Athen. xiii. p. 577, E.

[2] "ἄλλως δὲ, *übrigens aber*, is often found. See Arist. Plut. 976. It ought very probably to be restored to Thesm. 290, where ἄλλως τ' is now read." *Hermann.*

[3] For this use of the particle ἄν, cf. vss. 1140, 1142, 1143, 1180. Pax, 627, 640, 643, 647, 1200. Eccles. 307. Aves, 506, 520, 1288. Ran. 911, 915, 946, 948, 950. Lys. 510—518. Harper's Powers of the Greek Tenses, p. 85, 86. Krüger, Gr. Gr. § 53, 10, obs. 3. Brunck, Soph. Phil. 290. Porson, Phœn. 412, ad Xenoph. Anab. i. 5, 2. Hermann, Vig. n. 286, 287. Dawes, M. C. p. 441. For εἰς, cf. vs. 1012. Herod. ii. 98. Lysias, p. 908, ed. Reiske. Elmsl. Med. p. 150.

[4] For this use of the singular, see Bernhardy, W. S. p. 60.

[5] See Krüger, Gr. Gr. § 57, 3, obs. 7. Cf. vs. 289, *supra*, and note on Lys. 597.

[6] "οὐχ ἕνεκα φησὶ, τοῦ ὑπηρετεῖν μου τῇ ἀσελγείᾳ." *Scholiast.* "He did not ask as the reward of his performances." *Fielding.*

[7] "Read μεμνῇτο from Suidas voc. μεμνῇτο." *Porson.* See Lys. 235, 253. Krüger, Gr. Gr. § 31, 9, obs. 5. "See Aldi Cornucopia f. 186, a. Brunck on Soph. Phil. 119. Elmsl. Rex, 49. Heracl. 283, and Addenda." *Dobree.* "Cf. Blomf. Callim. H. Apoll. vs. 10." *Dindorf.*

[8] "See Pors. Opusc. 221. Elmsl. Ach. 193. Heracl. 544, and Addenda." *Dobree.*

OLD. WOM. But the abominable fellow now no longer has the same mind, but has changed very much. For when I sent him this cheese-cake here and the other[1] sweetmeats which are upon the plate, and whispered[2] that I would come in the evening—

CHR. What did he do to you? tell me.

OLD WOM. He sent back to us besides this milk-cake here, on condition[3] that I never came thither any more; and besides, in addition to this, when[4] sending it off he said, " Once in olden time the Milesians[5] were brave."

CHR. It is evident that he was not very bad[6] in his character. So then,[7] being rich, he no longer takes pleasure in lentil-porridge: but formerly, through his poverty, he used to eat every thing as a relish.[8]

OLD WOM. And yet formerly, by the two goddesses,[9] he used always to come to my door every day.

CHR. For your burial?

[1] See note on Lys. 864.

[2] See Liddell's Lex. in voc. ὑπειπεῖν. "Rightly Budæus and Stephens '*quum prædixissem.*' Cf. Vesp. 55. Thuc. i. 65. Demosth. Cor. p. 245, 12. Aristocr. p. 639, 10." *Dobree.* "Und dabei ihm sagen liess." *Droysen.* See Bernhardy, W. S. p. 216, 264, and note on vs. 90, *supra.*

[3] See Krüger, Gr. Gr. § 65, 3, obs. 3, and § 55, 3, obs. 6.

[4] "The meaning in my opinion will be plainer if you refer ἀποπέμπων to ἄμητα. Some one, perhaps, may prefer to understand it in this way : *Et super hæc præterea dici jussit misso ad me nuncio.* This I do not condemn in toto, but think such a use of ἀποπέμπω very rare." *Hemsterhuis.*

[5] "This proverbial senarius is cited by Aristoteles ap. Athen. xii. p 523, F." *Dobree.* It occurs again in vs. 1075, *infra.* See also Vesp. 1060, and note on Lys. 108. ὅτι is often put before the very words of the speaker. In this case it is the Greek substitute for our inverted commas. See Krüger, Gr. Gr. § 65, 1, obs. 2.

[6] Hemsterhuis translates it, " *apparet moribus esse juvenem istum haud sane absurdis. Tum porro nihil est mirum, si divitiis auctus non amplius lenticula delectetur.*" Toup (Emendd. Suid. ii. p. 328) translates it, " *The young man was very obliging.*" This I do not understand. For τις, see note on Aves, 924.

[7] This can scarcely be the true reading. Kuster proposes ἐπεί γε, which does not appear to be an Aristophanic form. εἴπερ γε, the conjecture of Dobree, seems better.

[8] " ἅπαντα ἐπεσθίειν is *omnino omnia opsonia edere ad panem.*" *Beck.* For the construction, cf. vs. 1148. Nub. 860. Hermann, Vig. n. 219. Kön and Schäfer on Greg. Cor. p. 146.

[9] νὴ τὼ θεώ in the mouth of a woman always means Demeter and Cora.

OLD WOM. No, by Jupiter, but merely through a desire to hear my voice.

CHR. Nay, rather, for the sake of getting something.

OLD WOM. And, by Jove, if he perceived me afflicted, he used to call me coaxingly his little duck and little dove.

CHR. And then, perhaps, he used to ask[1] you *for money* for shoes.

OLD WOM. And when any one looked at me when riding in my carriage at the Great Mysteries, I was beaten on account of this the whole day; so very jealous was the young man.[2]

CHR. For he took pleasure, as it seems, in eating alone.

OLD WOM. And he said I had very beautiful[3] hands.

CHR. Aye, whenever they offered twenty drachmæ.[4]

OLD WOM. And he said I smelt[5] sweet in my skin—

CHR. Aye, like enough, by Jove, if you poured in Thasian[6] wine for him.

OLD WOM. And that I had a gentle and beautiful look.[7]

CHR. The man was no fool, but knew how to devour the substance of a lustful old woman.

OLD WOM. In this therefore, O dear sir, the god does not act rightly, who professes to succour whoever happen to be wronged.[8]

CHR. Why, what must he do?[9] speak, and it shall be done immediately.[10]

OLD WOM. It is just, by Jove, to compel him who has

[1] "See Lucian, Dial. Meretr. xiv. T. iii. p. 320, 97." *Porson.*
[2] Dobree compares Stobæus, x. p. 132, 22.
[3] See Arnold's Greek Exercises, § 19. Cf. vs. 1022, *infra.*
[4] Wherever the penult of this word is long Dindorf writes δαρχμὴ, as in this passage, and Vesp. 691, and Pax, 1201. Cf. Macho ap. Athen. xiii. p. 581, B. Plato, ibid. x. p. 442, A. Antiphanes, ibid. vii. p. 299, E. Philippides, ibid. vi. p. 230, C.,
[5] See note on Pax, 529. Dindorf reads ὄζειν με.
[6] Cf. Hermippus ap. Athen. i. p. 29, E. Ibid. cap. 51, 52.
[7] Cf. Philetærus ap. Athen. xiii. p. 559, A.
[8] Dobree compares Isocr. Paneg. p. 51. Demosth. pro Rhod. p. 113. Megalop. p. 121. For this use of ἀεί, see Krüger, Gr. Gr. § 50, 8, obs. 9; § 50, 10, obs. 5. Hermann, Præf. Suppl. p. ix. Blomf. Gloss. Prom. V. 973. Monk, Alc. 710. So τὸν στραταγὸν ἀεί, Inscript. Ætol. ap. Rose, "Greek Inscriptions," p. 35.
[9] For this singular construction, see vs. 438, *supra*, and Krüger's important remarks, Gr. Gr. § 54, 2, obs. 4. Cf. Hermann, Vig. n. 08.
[10] See Krüger, Gr. Gr. § 53, 9, obs. 3. Matth. Gr. Gr. § 498

been benefited by me to benefit me in turn ; cr he deserves to possess no blessing whatever.

CHR. Did he not then repay you every night?

OLD WOM. But he said he would never desert me while I lived.

CHR. Aye, rightly; but now[1] he thinks you no longer alive.

OLD WOM. For I am wasting away through grief, O dearest friend.

CHR. No, but you have rotted away, as it appears[2] to me.

OLD WOM. Indeed, then, you might draw me through a ring.[3]

CHR. Yes, if the ring were the hoop of a sieve.

OLD WOM. Well now, see! here's the youth approaching,[4] whom I have been accusing this long while; and he seems to be going to a revel.

CHR. He appears so: at least he is certainly coming with a chaplet and a torch.[5]   [*Enter a young man with a lighted torch in his hand and followed by a band of revellers.*]

YOU. I salute you.

OLD WOM. (*to Chremylus*). What says he?

YOU. My ancient sweetheart, by heaven, you have quickly become gray.

OLD WOM. Unhappy me, for the insult with which[6] I am insulted!

CHR. He seems to have seen you after a long time.

OLD WOM. Since[7] what time, O most audacious, who[8] was at my house yesterday?

---

[1] See note on Thesm. 646.

[2] Cf. vs. 390. Nub. 1271. Ran. 645. Eccles. 1127.

[3] Shakspeare, Henry IV. part i. act ii. sc. 4, " When I was about thy years, Hal, I was not an eagle's talon in the waist; I could have crept into any alderman's thumb-ring."

[4] For this use of καὶ μὴν ὅδε to announce the coming of a new character on the stage, cf. Equit. 691. Eccles. 1128. Lys. 77. Æsch. Theb. 368. Soph. Ajax, 1168. Antig. 526, 626, 1257. Quart. Rev. vol. ix. p. 354.

[5] Cf. Antiphanes ap. Athen. vi. p. 243, C., and Apollodorus, ibid vii. p. 281, A.

[6] See note on Aves, 143, and Krüger, Gr. Gr. § 47, 3, obs. 2. See also note on Thesm. 835.

[7] See Matthiä, Gr. Gr. § 377, C.

[8] For this use of the relative, cf. Ran. 487, 740. 1058. Pax, 865.

Chr. Then he is affected in a manner opposite to most people ; for, as it seems, he sees sharper when he's drunk.

Old Wom. No, but he is always saucy in his manners.[1]

You. (*holding the torch close to her face*). O Sea-Poseidon[2] and ye elderly gods, how many wrinkles[3] she has in her face !

Old Wom. Ah ! ah ! don't bring the torch near me !

Chr. Upon my word she says rightly ; for if only a single spark catch her, it will burn her like an old harvest-wreath.

You. Will you play with me for a[4] while ?

Old Wom. Where, wretch ?

You. Here, having taken some nuts.

Old Wom. What game ?

You. How many teeth[5] you have.

Chr. Come, I also will have a guess ; for she has three, perhaps, or four.

You. Pay up ! for she carries only one grinder.

Old. Wom. Most audacious of men, you don't appear to me to be in your right senses, who make a wash-pot of me[6] in the presence of so many men.

Nub. 1226. Vesp. 487, 518, 558. Aves, 150, (where the true reading is ὃς οὐκ,) and Bernhardy, W. S. p. 293, and p. 139.

[1] Another reading is τοῖς τρόποις. For this see Bernhardy, W. S. p. 118. Krüger, Gr. Gr. § 46, 4, obs. 1.

[2] Hipponax ap. Athen. xv. p. 698, C., μοῦσά μοι Εὐρυμεδοντιάδεα, τὴν ποντοχάρυβδιν ἔννεπε. "The young man swears by the old gods, and especially by Neptune, who was a veteran amongst the gods, and not a stripling, like Apollo and Bacchus." *Droysen.*

[3] Thuc. vii. 36, ᾧπερ τῆς τέχνης. Soph. Ajax, 314, ἐν τῷ πράγματος. Æsch. Theb. 803, ἢν λάβωσιν χθονός. Herod. vii. 170, οἳ τῶν ἀστῶν. Plato, Phædr. p. 270, A., πᾶσαι ὅσαι μεγάλαι τῶν τεχνῶν. See Bernhardy, W. S. p. 153.

[4] "*Aliquantisper.*" *Brunck.* διὰ χρόνου is used in the same sense in Vesp. 1252, 1476. Lys. 904. Similarly Pax, 56, δι' ἡμέρας. (Cf. Ran. 260. Pherecrates ap. Athen. xiii. p. 612, A.) Thuc. ii. 4, διὰ νυκτός. Pax, 396, διὰ παντὸς ἀεί. (Cf. Soph. Ajax, 704.) Arist. *Horæ*, Fragm. i., δι' ἐνιαυτοῦ. See Bernhardy, W. S. p. 235. More frequently, however, διὰ χρόνου means *after a long time, after a long interval;* as in vs. 1045, *supra.* Pax, 570, 710. Eur. Iph. A. 627, ed. Hartung. See Hermann, Vig. n. 377, B.

[5] As though he were going to play at odd or even. Plato, Euthyd. p. 194, C., οἶσθα Εὐθύδημον ὁπόσους ὀδόντας ἔχει, καὶ ὁ Εὐθύδημος ὁπόσους σύ. Cf. Lysias ap. Athen. xiii. p. 612, E. Aristot. Rhet. iii. p. 126, 15, ed. Sylburg.

[6] "Du mich zur Waschbank deiner schlechten Witze machst?"
Droysen

You. Upon my word you'd be the better for it,[1] if one were to wash you clean.

Chr. Certainly not, for now she is playing the cheat:[2] but if this white-lead[3] shall be washed off, you'll see the wrinkles in her face quite plain.

Old Wom. You don't appear[4] to me to be in your right senses, old man as you are.

You. Perhaps, indeed, he is tempting you, and is touching your breasts, fancying that he escapes my notice.

Old Wom. No, by Venus, not mine, you abominable fellow.

Chr. No, by Hecate, certainly not! for I should be mad. But, young man, I won't suffer you to hate this girl.

You. Nay, I love her beyond measure.

Chr. And yet she accuses you.

You. What does she accuse me of?

Chr. She says that you are an insolent person, and that you tell her, " Once in olden time the Milesians were brave."

You I will not quarrel with you about her.

Chr. Why so?

You. Out of respect for your age; for I would never have suffered another to do so; but now go in peace, having taken the girl along with you.

Chr. I know, I know your meaning; perhaps you no longer deign to be with her.

Old Wom. But who is there to permit him?[5]

Dobree refers to Bekk. Anecd. i. p. 58, 27. Toup, Suid. iii. p. 101—103.

[1] Cf. Nub. 1237.

[2] Ælian, V. H. 12, 1, γυναικῶν καπηλικῶς τῷ κάλλει χρωμένων.

[3] Cf. Athenæus, xii. p. 528, F.; xiii. p. 557, F.; p. 568, C. Shakspeare, Timon of Athens, act iv. sc. 3, " Paint till a horse may mire upon your face."

[4] See Krüger, Gr. Gr. § 67, 7, obs. 5. Elmsley, Med. vs. 487. Hermann, Opusc. iii. p. 200. To Hermann's examples add Soph. Colon. 1166. Trach. 586. Arist. Pax, 1051.

[5] " These words I think should be given to the old woman. She had been powerfully affected by the words οὐκέτ' εἶναι μετ' αὐτῆς, therefore she hastily replies 'fierine potest, ut quisquam permittat, et justum putet, ne quid rei amplius ipsi pro solita consuetudine mecum sit?' So strong does she think her claim upon the young man to be." *Hemsterhuis.* " *Quis autem est permissurus?*" Brunck. " *Who is he,*

You. I would not have to do[1] with one who has been embraced by thirteen[2] thousand years.

Chr. But yet, since you thought proper to drink the wine you must also drink[3] up the dregs.

You. But the dregs are altogether old and fusty.

Chr. Then a straining-cloth will cure all this.

You. Come, go within! for I wish to go and dedicate to the god these chaplets which I have on.

Old Wom. And I also wish to say something to him.

You. But I will not go in.

Chr. Be of good courage, don't be afraid! for she shan't ravish you.

You. Now you say very well: for I have been pitching her up long enough already.[4]

Old Wom. Go in, and I'll enter after you. [*Exeunt Old Woman and Young Man.*]

Chr. How forcibly, O King Jove, the old woman sticks to the youth like a limpet.[5] [*Exit Chremylus.*]

Enter Mercury, who knocks at the door, and then runs away, frightened at the noise he had made.

Cario (*from within*). Who's that knocking[6] at the door? [*Comes out and looks about.*] What's this?[7] It appears to be nobody. Then certainly the door shall suffer[8] for creaking without cause. [*Retires again.*]

who is so free to deliver me up?" *Fielding.* "Wer denn ist mein Vormund hier?" *Droysen.* Cf. Pax, 881. Equit. 143.

[1] Cf. Eccles. 890. Mœris, p. 131. Pollux, ii. 125; v. 92.

[2] Porson and Dobree would read ἀπὸ, i. e. 13,000 *years ago.* Which reading needs no refutation.

[3] Sappho, Fragm. 102 (ed. Bergk), ὁ δὲ κάγαθὸς αὐτίκα καὶ κάλος ἔσσεται. Compare also Eccles. 495. Plato, Euthyph. p. 13, A. Hom. Il. A. 81, 82. For this use of the plural of the verbal, see Acharn. 394. Nub. 727. Lys. 122, 411, 450. Krüger, Gr. Gr. § 44, 4, obs. 2. Kön, Greg. Cor. p. 130.

[4] Cf. Pax, 354.

[5] Cf. Vesp. 105. Athenæus, iii. p. 86, B.

[6] Mœris, p. 211, κόπτει τὴν θύραν ἔξωθεν, ψοφεῖ δὲ ὁ ἔνδοθεν, Ἀττικῶς· κροτεῖ δὲ Ἑλληνικῶς.

[7] See note on Vesp. 183.

[8] See Liddell's Lex. in voc. κλαυσιάω. It may, however, be rendered, "Surely then the door makes a noise and creaks without cause"

MER. (*running out of his hiding-place*). Cario! You, I say![1] stop!

CA. (*coming out again*). Hollo, you! Tell me, did you knock at the door so violently?

MER. No, by Jove; but I was a going to; and then you anticipated me by opening it. Come, run quickly and call out your master, then his wife and children, then his servants, then the dog, then yourself, then the sow.

CA. Tell me, what's the matter?

MER. Jupiter, you rascal, intends to mix you up in the same bowl and cast you all together into the Barathrum.

CA. The tongue[2] is given to the herald of these tidings. But on what account, pray, does he purpose to do this to us?

MER. Because you have done the most dreadful of all deeds. For since what time Plutus began to have the use of his eyes as before,[3] no one any longer offers to us gods either[4] frankincense, or laurel, or barley-cake, or victim, or any thing else.

CA. No, by Jupiter, nor will he offer them. For you took bad care of us aforetime.[5]

MER. And for the other gods I care less; but I am undone, and am ruined.

CA. You're wise.

MER. For formerly I used to enjoy all good things in the female innkeepers' shops as soon as it was morning, wine-cake, honey, dried figs, as many as 'tis fitting that Mercury

---

[1] See note on Aves, 406, and Quart. Rev. vol. ix. p. 360.

[2] "γίγνεται = ἀποδίδοται, *tibi cedit.*" *Dobree.* So ἐπιγίγνεται, Demosth. p. 947, 7. Many editions read τέμνεται, which has been adopted by Voss and Droysen in their translations. "The tongue of the victim used to be cut out as an offering to Mercury. Cario means that Mercury's own tongue should be cut out for his ill tidings." *Voss.* Cf. Pax, 1060. Aves, 1705. Athenæus, i. p. 16, B. Schol. on Apoll. R. i. 517.

[3] Cf. vs. 866, 968, 1173.

[4] See Krüger, Gr. Gr. § 67, 11, obs. 2, and cf. vss. 137, 138. Nub. 426. Aves, 979, 1134. Julian, Orat. vi. p. 195, B., οὐκ ὀβολὸν, οὐ δραχμὴν, οὐκ οἰκέτην ἔχων· ἀλλ' οὐδὲ μάζαν. Aristoph. *Thesmophoriazusæ Secundæ*, Fragm. ii. *Lemniæ*, Fragm. x.

[5] See Liddell's Lex. in voc. τότε, i.

should eat: but now I go to bed hungry with my legs lying up.[1]

Ca. Is it not then with justice, who sometimes[2] caused
their loss, although you enjoyed such good things.

Mer. Ah me, miserable! Ah me, for the cheese-cake[3]
that was baked on the fourth day!

Ca. "You[4] long for the absent, and call in vain."

Mer. Ah me for the ham which I used to devour!

Ca. Leap upon the bottle[5] there in the open air.[6]

Mer. And for the warm entrails which I used to devour!

Ca. A pain about your entrails seems to torture you.[7]

Mer. Ah me, for the cup that was mixed[8] half-and-half!

Ca. You cannot be too quick in drinking this[9] besides and
running away.

Mer. Would you assist your own friend in any way?

Ca. Yes; if you want any of those things in which[10] I am
able to assist you.

Mer. If you were to procure me a well-baked loaf and
give it me to eat, and a huge[11] piece of meat from the sacrifices
you are offering within.

[1] Toup (Emend. Suid. i. p. 27) translates this, "*But now I go to
bed hungry and lie in a garret.*" Elmsley (on Ach. 599) approves of
this translation of Toup's. "In my opinion the only correct view
is that of Hemsterhuis ad Hesych. voc. ἀναβάδην." *Dobree.*
[2] "Who allow them to be found out in their cheating." *Droysen.*
See note vs. 1046, *supra.*
[3] Cf. vs. 1128, 1132, and see note on Lys. 967. "The fourth day of
every month was a festival of Mercury." *Droysen.*
[4] "This was uttered to Hercules by a voice from heaven, as he
was vainly calling upon his Hylas." *Voss.*
[5] See Smith's Dictionary of Antiquities in voc. Ἀσκώλια. Virgil,
Geor. ii. 384. Here it is merely a paronomasia from the preceding
οἴμοι κωλῆς.
[6] The notion of *rest* in this class of constructions is somewhat
rare. See, however, Bernhardy, W. S. p. 264.
[7] Cf. Thesm. 484.
[8] See Athenæus, x. c. 36. Archippus, ibid. x. p. 426, B. Aristo-
phon, ibid. xi. p. 472, C. Strattis, ibid. xi. p. 473, C. Acharn. 354.
Equit. 1187.
[9] i. e. ταύτην τὴν πορδὴν, ἣν πέπορδα. For the construction, see
note on Eccles. 118.
[10] "ὧν = ἐκείνων ἅ, *si quo eges eorum in quibus.*" *Fischer.* See Pax.
559, 1279. Krüger, Gr. Gr. § 51, 10, obs. 1.
[11] Cf. Eur. Hippol. 1204. Kuster cites λόπας νεανικὴ from Athenæu

Ca. But there is no carrying out.[1]

Mer. And yet whenever you stole[2] any little vessel from your master, I always used[3] to cause you to be undetected.

Ca. On condition that you also shared yourself, you house-breaker. For a well-baked cake used to come to you.

Mer. And then you used to devour this yourself.

Ca. For you had not an equal share[4] of the blows with me, whenever I was caught in any knavery.

Mer. Don't bear malice,[5] if you have got possession of Phyle; but, by the gods, receive me as a fellow-inmate.

Ca. Then will you abandon the gods and stay here?

Mer. Yes; for your condition is much better.

Ca. How then? do you think desertion a fine thing?

Mer. Yes; " for his country is every *country*, wherever a man is well off."[6]

Ca. What use then would you be to us, if you were here?

Mer. Post me beside the door as turnkey.

Ca. As turnkey? but we have no need of turns.[7]

Mer. As merchant,[8] then.

Ca. But we are rich: what need then for us to maintain a huckstering Mercury?

Mer. Well, as deceiver, then.

Ca. As deceiver? By no means. For we have no need of deception now, but of simple manners.

Mer. As conductor, then.

---

[1] " *But they must not be conveyed out.*" *Fielding.* Thesm. 472, κούδεμι' ἐκφορὰ λόγου. Euphron ap. Athen. ix. p. 380, A., οὐκ ἦν ἐκφορὰ κρεῶν τότε.

[2] Cf. Thesm. 812. Vesp. 1201, and Mus. Crit. i. p. 522. See also note on Ran. 1228.   [3] See note on vs. 982, *supra.*

[4] See Bernhardy, W. S. p. 149.

[5] Referring to the amnesty passed by Thrasybulus after the occupation of Phyle. See Xenoph. Hell. ii. 4, 43. Andocides, Myst. p. 39, and p. 43.

[6] " A verse of Euripides,—at all events of some tragedian, as Hemsterhuis remarks." *Dobree.* Cicer. Tusc. v. 37, " Patria est, ubicunque est bene." Ovid, Fast. I. 493,

" Omne solum forti patria est, ut piscibus æquor."

For the construction, see Harper's Powers of the Greek Tenses, p. 124. Hermann, Vig. Append. p. 756.

[7] Cf. Eccles. 1026.   Cf. Ach. 816.

CA. But the god now has the use of his eyes; so we shall no longer want a conductor.

MER. Then I will be president of the games. And what further will you say? For this is most convenient for Plutus, to celebrate musical and gymnastic[1] contests.

CA. What a good thing it is to have many[2] surnames! for this fellow has found out a scant living for himself *by this means.* No wonder all the judges often seek eagerly to be inscribed in many letters.[3]

MER. Then shall I go in upon these terms?

CA. Aye, and go yourself to the well and wash[4] the puddings, that you may immediately be thought to be serviceable. [*Exeunt Mercury and Cario.*]

PRIEST OF JUPITER (*entering hastily*). Who can tell me for certain where Chremylus is? [*Enter Chremylus.*]

CHR. What is the matter, my good sir?

PRIEST. Why, what else but[5] bad? For since what time this Plutus began to have the use of his eyes, I perish with hunger. For I have nothing to eat; and that too, though I am the priest[6] of Jupiter the Preserver.

CHR. Oh! by the gods, what is the cause?

PRIEST. No one deigns to sacrifice any longer.

CHR. On what account?

PRIEST. Because they are all rich. And yet, at that time, when they had nothing, the one, a merchant, used[7] to come and sacrifice some victim for his safety; and some other one, because he had been acquitted on his trial; and some other one used to sacrifice with favourable omens, and invite me too, the priest. But now not even a single person sacrifices any thing at all, or enters *the temple,* except it be more than a myriad to ease themselves.

[1] Dobree cites Bekk. Anecd. i. p. iii. 18. Pollux, iii. 142. Plato, Menex. p. 249, B.; Legg. p. 658, A. Thuc. iii. 104.

[2] "Aristophanes laughs very prettily at the great number of names which the gods gave themselves, as if they took so many only to catch by the one what they could not catch by the other. Callimachus introduces Diana praying to Jupiter to suffer her to be always a virgin, and to give her several names." *Madame Dacier.*

[3] i. e. in many tickets. See Eccles. 683. [4] Cf. Equit. 160.

[5] Cf. Nub. 1495. Lysippus ap. Athen. iii. p. 124, D. Bernhardy, W. S. p. 352.

[6] Cf. Aves, 1516. [7] See note on vs. 982, *supra.*

Chr. Do you not then receive your lawful share of these ?[1]

Priest. Therefore I also am resolved[2] to bid farewell[3] to Jupiter the Preserver and stay here in this place.[4]

Chr. Be of good courage ! for it will be well,[5] if the god please. For[6] Jupiter the Preserver is present here, having come of his own accord.

Priest. Then you tell me all good news.

Chr. We will therefore immediately establish—but[7] stay here—Plutus where he was before established, always guarding the inner cell[8] of the goddess. But let some one give me out here[9] lighted torches, that you may hold them and go before the god.

Priest. Yes, by all means we must do this.

Chr. Call Plutus out, some of you.[10] [*Enter Old Woman.*]

Old Wom. But what am I to do?

Chr. Take the pots with which we are to establish[11] the god, and carry them on your head in a stately manner, for you came yourself with a party-coloured dress on.

Old Wom. But on what account I came ?

Chr. All shall be immediately done for you. For the young man shall come to you in the evening.

Old Wom. Well, by Jove, if[12] indeed you promise me that he shall come to me, I'll carry the pots. [*Takes up the pots and puts them on her head.*]

Chr. (*to the spectators*). Well now, these *pots* act very differently from the other pots. For in the other pots the

---

[1] "τῶν ἀφοδευμάτων." *Scholiast.* Cf. Thesm. 758.

[2] See Liddell's Lexicon in voc. δοκέω, ii. 2.

[3] See Hermann, Vig. n. 206. Bachmann's Anecdot. ii. 40, 19.

[4] "Cf. Vesp. 765, 766. Soph. Colon. 78. Eupolis ap. Stob. iv. p. 31. Solon, Fragm. xxviii. 11, ed. Gaisford." *Dobree.* Add Pax, 1269. Eur. Hippol. 112. Soph. Elect. 1456. Lobeck, Ajax, p. 206. Hermann, Vig. n. 206. Bachmann's Anecdot. i. p. 40.

[5] See Krüger, Gr. Gr. § 62, 2, obs. 3. Cf. vs. 347, *supra.*

[6] See note on Eccles. 984.

[7] "Wir wollen sogleich ihn weihen—wart' ein wenig nur—
     Den Reichthum, wo er ehedem geweihet stand." *Droysen.*
Chremylus says this to stop the priest, who was hurrying away to salute the deity.

[8] See Böckh, Publ. Ec. ii. 189, and compare note on Thesm. 1040.

[9] Cf. Ran. 871.

[10] Eur. Rhes. 687, παῖε, παῖε πᾶς τις. Cf. Pax, 301, 458, 510, 512, 555. Aves, 1186, 1190, 1196.

[11] Cf. Pax, 923.   [12] See note on Equit. 1350.

scum [1] is on the top ; but now the pots are on the top of this old woman.

Cho. Therefore 'tis fitting that we delay no longer, but go back to the rear; for we must follow after these, singing.[2] [*Exeunt omnes.*]

[1] He puns on the different significations of γραῦς, *an old woman,* and the *scum* of a pot. Cf. Bekk. Anecd. i. p. 88, 8.
[2] In the *Lysistrata* also he dismisses the Chorus singing.

THE END.

SUPPLEMENTARY EMENDATIONS.

ACHARN. 430. This ought to have been translated, "*I know a man, Telephus the Mysian.*" See Bernhardy, W. S. p. 51.

ACHARN. 951, πρὸς πάντα συκοφάντην. The correct construction is that mentioned in the note on the passage. See note on Thesm. 532.

EQUIT. 1080. This ought to have been translated, "*Hear the oracle which he ordered you to avoid, viz. Cyllene.*" Κυλλήνην is in apposition to ὃν χρησμόν. See Bernhardy, W. S. p. 55.

"EQUIT. 1376, ἃ στωμυλεῖται, *sie mögen schwatzen bei Gelegenheit.*" *Bernhardy.*

NUB. 178, διαβήτην λαβών. This ought to have been translated, "*Having taken it for a compass.*" See note on Plut. 314.

"NUB. 179, ἐκ τῆς παλαίστρας ϑοἰμάτιον, *das zu denkende Gewand in der vorausgesetzen Palästra.*" *Bernhardy.*

VESP. 585. The correct ordo is, εἰπόντες τῇ διαϑήκῃ μακρὰ κλάειν τὴν κεφαλὴν, and τὴν κεφαλὴν is the Accusativus Respectûs after κλάειν, as I have rightly shown in the note on Plut. 612. For the gross error in the text, I was indebted to Bothe's edition, whose worthless book it was my good fortune to be without during the other plays.

"VESP. 933, κλέπτον τὸ χρῆμα τἀνδρὸς, *der ganze Kerl ist Dieberei.*" *Bernhardy.*

AVES, '3 οὐκ τῶν ὀρνέων Φιλοκράτης. This ought to have

been translated, "*Philocrates of the poultry-market.*" See Bernhardy, W. S. p. 228, and note on Lys. 557.

Aves, 293. "Zweideutig Aristophanes Av. 293, ἐπὶ λόφων οἰκοῦσιν, *mit Büschen.*" *Bernhardy.*

Aves, 652. The view of the construction taken in the note is remarkably confirmed by the following passage: Xenoph. Cyrop. ii. 1, 5, τοὺς μέντοι ʽ́Ελληνας τοὺς ἐν τῇ ʼΑσίᾳ οἰκοῦντας οὐδέν πω σαφὲς λέγεται, εἰ ἕπονται. The accusative in both of these passages is an example of Accusativus de quo ; for which, see note on Plut. 33.

Aves, 1406. The translation given in the text is undoubtedly the only correct one. See Bernhardy, W. S. p. 332.

Lys. 391. The examples cited in the note are *nihil ad rem.* The position of the article shows that ὁ μὴ ὥρασι is *attributive* (= *the rascally Demostratus,*) and cannot be taken as an *imprecation.* See Bernhardy, W. S. p. 81, and p. 95.

Thesm. 394, τὰς οὐδὲν ὑγιές. See Bernhardy, W. S. p. 323.

Ran. 207, βατράχων κύκνων. This ought to have been translated, "*frog-swans,*" after the analogy of the constructions given in the note on Aves, 1154. Cf. Krüger, Gr. Gr. § 57, 1, obs. 1. So Aves, 1059, κάμηλον ἀμνὸν, *a camel-lamb.* Ibid. 169, ἄνθρωπος ὄρνις, *a man-bird.* See Bernhardy, W. S. p. 50.

Ran. 251. Mr. Mitchell's interpretation is the only correct one. See Bernhardy, W. S. p. 256.

LONDON:
PRINTED BY WILLIAM CLOWES AND SONS, LIMITED,
DUKE STREET, STAMFORD STREET, S.E., AND GREAT WINDMILL STREET, W.